The Incredible Adventures of

FREDDIE FIXIt

A Story of Magic, Mystery and Trickery

Come on a journey of magic and mystery as
Freddie Fixit makes unbelievable
discoveries in his beloved forest.
His life will never be the same again as
he battles to save his friends and family.

M.E.B.M Kirwin

Grosvenor House
Publishing Limited

The right of M.E.B.M Kirwin to be identified as the author of this
work has been asserted in accordance with Section 78
of the Copyright, Designs and Patents Act 1988

The book cover is copyright to M.E.B.M Kirwin

This book is published by
Grosvenor House Publishing Ltd
Link House
140 The Broadway, Tolworth, Surrey, KT6 7HT.
www.grosvenorhousepublishing.co.uk

A CIP record for this book
is available from the British Library

ISBN 978-1-80381-928-0

Dedication

To Michael, my constant companion, inspiration and support.
Without which the story of Freddie Fixit
would not have come to fruition.

Images from Perchance A.I. Image Generator

Introduction

Have you ever wondered if magic is real? Did great Wizards exist and perform unexplainable feats of magic, such as turning mice into horses or a pumpkin into a fabulous carriage or even making objects disappear?

Perhaps magic may not be real in our world, but on the planet Astoria, much like our very own Earth, but in a Galaxy too far away for us to see even through the most powerful telescope, magic is definitely real. It is on the world of Astoria that our story begins, where there are only two large continents, Trollia and Enchantica, and several large and small islands. A vast deep blue ocean separates both continents and the islands. An ocean where fish can fly over the water or dive and swim, but cannot walk on the land, often caught by monster sea birds that swoop down and scoop up the fish in mid air. Below the surface of these oceans lurk enormous creatures a kilometre in length that can leap out of the water and catch the sea birds in their huge jaws. These dangerous waters have kept the two continents apart for thousands of years.

The continent of Trollia had very few trees, bushes and plants. There were some mountains and hills along with scrublands that made Trollia very inhospitable. Scattered around the land were tribes of Trolls, who were large, heavy biped creatures not unlike the early Cavemen on our Earth, but taller and bulkier. The Trolls lived a very simple life, being of low intelligence, they were basically dim-witted, and often fought with each other, soon forgetting why they were fighting. Living mainly in caves and hollows because they were not clever enough to build any kind of shelter, like a simple hut. These things did not bother them because Trolls knew no better, being all brawn and no brain with sausage-like fingers and toes.

In contrast, the continent of Enchantica was a paradise of forests, rivers, lakes, hills and meadows. It was the perfect home for countless supernatural beings living happily side-by-side. There were mischievous Water Nymphs, perfect Pixies, grouchy Goblins, fun loving Fairies, playful Imps, grumpy Ogres, good Witches and wary Warlocks. The supernaturals built stunning dwellings, Water Nymphs constructed spectacular homes on floating islands in the great lakes, Ogres built lots of crude looking bridges over the rivers under which they made their homes. Fairies used magic to build incredible walkways in the trees, connecting elaborate dwellings in which they lived. The Great Wizards lived in a magnificent and palatial castle from where they ruled over the land of Enchantica keeping peace and harmony among the supernaturals for a thousand years.

Sadly, after the Great Troll Wars, the Trolls and almost all the supernatural beings were wiped out. Soon after, human creatures began to emerge all over the two continents and islands, eventually populating everywhere. No one knows exactly where humans came from, but they most probably travelled through a tear in the fabric of space from another world.

Our story begins on the continent of Enchantica in the small village of Elfington, surrounded by a large forest of ancient trees, in the hollow of a long extinct volcano that holds many secrets.

Freddie Fountain is a very special young boy who lives in Elfington village and makes a surprising discovery one day while exploring his favourite place, the forest, 'his forest' as he calls it.

Freddie is drawn into a world of long forgotten magic and mystery. His journey leads him into dangerous, mystical and magical adventures where his very life is at risk. Come on this journey and enjoy Freddie's adventures, be amazed at the things he uncovers, feel his happiness and feel his sadness, but most of all, share the wonder of everything he discovers.

Contents

Chapter 1   Freddie Fixit saves Wiggly Tiggly   1

When Freddie saves a curious forest being he receives a very magical reward.

Chapter 2   The Crystal Cavern   42

Freddie and Wiggly's discovery changes their lives forever.

Chapter 3   The Attack of the Mole Goblins   71

Freddie and Wiggly battle ferocious creatures to save the Elfin children.

Chapter 4   The Mystery of the Disappearing Screws   119

When gates and fences, doors and displays fall apart around the village, Freddie Fixit comes to the rescue.

Chapter 5   The Rise of the Morphlins   177

Can Freddie and the Elfins save their friends and families from a monstrous and powerful foe?

Chapter 6   Nightmares and the Dream Snatchers   250

Freddie is caught by a clever magical trap that puts all the Elfin and Sproggle children in danger.
Can Freddie and Wiggly save everyone again?

Chapter 7   The Emergence of Magic   332

When the snowman winks and Freddie's dreams come to life. He goes on a journey to find the truth about magic.

Chapter 8   The Attack of the Beastrolls   408

*Supernatural creatures escape when a natural disaster
unearths their ancient prison.*

*Together, Freddie and Merlin attempt to beat this most
powerful, ancient and mystical foe.*

Chapter 9   A Supernatural Awakens   486

*Freddie's magic awakens a supernatural being, which causes
mayhem.*

Chapter 10 Evil will not Prevail   548

*Billy Bates meets his father again, but it is not
a welcome reunion.*

CHAPTER ONE

Freddie Fixit saves Wiggly Tiggly

When Freddie saves a curious forest being
he receives a very magical reward.

Freddie Fountain often let his vivid imagination run away from him. Today he was the intrepid 'Freddie the Explorer' on the hunt for wild beasties in his beloved forest of tall, tall trees and big bushy bushes. He was dressed in khaki shorts and a khaki waistcoat his mother had made for him and a rimmed hat his father picked up from a car boot sale. Then of course, there was his trusty 'magic staff' with which he could save the world.

In reality, Freddie's magic staff was a gold sprayed broom handle with a wooden knob screwed on top, but it looked fantastic and completed Freddie's imaginary character, along with his ever present rucksack that went everywhere with him.

So far he had seen nothing unusual as he walked along the narrow dirt track, poking the bushes here and there with his trusty magic staff just like he had seen explorers do on television.

He soon came upon his most favourite spot in the whole forest and stopped to admire a very tall, very green, pine tree, its long drooping branches laden with big brown pinecones. What made this tree so unique was the rambling rose that grew up among the branches reaching almost to the top.

During the summer when the rambling rose was in flower, the fir tree looked like it was decorated with hundreds of fairy lights from the bright red rose flowers. In the autumn and winter the rosehips (these are the seedpods of the rose flower) were big, like really big and also bright red. When the fir tree branches were covered in frost or sprinkled with snow, the tree looked like a very beautiful Christmas tree, with red rosehips and light brown cones for ornaments. That was not all, for beneath the big fir tree grew a very large holly bush with bright green prickly leaves and bright red

1

berries. This holly bush grew all the way up to the lower branches of the fir tree making it look like the fir tree grew all the way down to the ground.

Freddie stood and stared. "If ever there was such a thing as magic, this has got to be it," he said out loud, to no one in particular, admiring the spectacle before him. Freddie called the fir tree his 'Special Christmas Tree'.

Freddie Fountain is a cute looking, extraordinary and popular 10 year old boy, born to do amazing and unbelievable things. Standing just short of 150 centimetres tall, his blond hair is kept neatly trimmed so everyone can see his beautiful, bright blue eyes. Freddie's teacher had once told his parents that their son had a 'happy disposition', unsure if that was good or bad, they looked it up in a dictionary and found it meant Freddie always seemed to be happy and smiling. He was full of energy most of the time and always needed to be doing things, he was very active and could not sit still for any length of time.

Freddie was always keen and happy to help villagers and friends whenever a problem occurred he was usually able to fix it and that is how he got his nickname, Freddie Fixit. He is the only child of parents Susan and Jacob Fountain and they live in a fairytale cottage with a beautiful thatched roof with a thatch squirrel sitting right on the top in the picturesque village of Elfington. An ornate wooden picket fence, painted in white, runs all around the front garden, with a rose covered arch over the white picket gate. Beds of multicoloured flowers stretched around the neatly trimmed lawn, it is a place Freddie's parents like to spend time together and Freddie sometimes helps them by pulling out weeds. He especially likes to mow the lawn, cutting it so that it has lovely straight stripes.

Freddie and his parents call their cottage 'Home at Last.' It may seem a strange name for a house, but whenever they go to work, shopping or school, the moment they walk through the front gate, they sigh and say, "So glad to be *home at last*."

The cottage is the very last house when leaving the village, or the very first house when coming into the village. There is only one road into and out of Elfington village because it is nestled in the centre of a massive, but long ago extinct volcano. The high cliff faces of stone and volcanic rock that surrounded the village were too high to be called hills and too small to be called mountains, so the villagers called them *mount-hills*. The village is surrounded by a magnificent ancient forest full of oak trees, walnut trees, sycamore trees, elm trees and chestnut trees with giant fir trees poking up above the canopy. This wonderful woodland reaches out from the village for almost a kilometre right up to the high walls of the mount-hills. From day to day nothing spectacular ever happens in the sleepy village of Elfington, it is a small community where everyone knows each other, it is a happy place with happy people.

* *

One warm sunny summer day, when the sky was blue and cloudless and the sun shone brightly making everything warm and cosy, Freddie decided to go exploring in *'his forest'* as he called it. Although he had lots of friends with whom he often played, he was at his happiest playing and exploring in his forest, by himself.

Freddie liked to march between the tall trees pretending to be a soldier, or a pirate or an explorer and even a wizard, his mother had made all kinds of outfits for him to wear. Freddie knew every tree and bush in the part of the forest around his home and never got lost, so his parents were happy to let him have his imaginary fun. His most favourite game was being an explorer, his father had called him a Pioneer.

"Dad, why would anyone put a pie in their ear?" (Pie in ear) Freddie queried.

Both parents burst into laughter, much to Freddie's confusion.

"Did I say something funny, Mum?" Freddie asked.

His mother explained a Pioneer was actually an explorer, not someone sticking pies in their ears. Of course Freddie and his parents had a long laugh at his misunderstanding.

So today Freddie set off as a Pioneer to explore the forest. He put on his rucksack and his mother had made him his favourite jam sandwiches, along with an apple, a chocolate bar and a small carton of orange juice. He wore khaki shorts and the waistcoat his mother had made for him and a brimmed hat his father had found for him at a car boot sale. Freddie put a compass and a pair of binoculars in his rucksack and carried the gold staff his father had made for him, so he looked like a cross between an explorer and a wizard.

Freddie set off with his watch on his wrist, waving to his mother and promising to be home by 4 o'clock. Through a gate at the bottom of their back garden he entered his forest. Once among the tall trees he took out his binoculars and looked to his left and to his right and then straight ahead along the narrow dirt trail. It was not a proper pathway like on the streets, but more a track that he had made during the many times he had walked through the trees and bushes.

Freddie continued his way along the track, poking the bushes with his staff and in a loud voice shouting, "Come out! Come out, wild beasties!"

He came to a sudden halt as the bush in front of him jiggled and made funny grunting noises. "A beastie," he whispered, to no one in particular. Freddie jabbed the bush and jumped back as a wild beast scurried onto the track, he gasped when it stopped and looked at him. Freddie took his binoculars and looked at the beastie more closely, it was huge and covered with long things like knitting needles. Freddie laughed, "Ha, ha, you look just like a stiff broom without a handle!" He put away his binoculars and crouched down to get a little closer and touched the beastie with his staff very gently. It suddenly curled into a spiky ball and Freddie fell back in surprise. "A clever trick, beastie!" he piped, getting up again giving the prickly ball another gentle prod with his staff. "Now what kind of beastie are you, prickly ball?" he said quietly to himself.

He lifted his rucksack off his shoulders and unzipped it to pull out his 'Book of Beasties'. It was a homemade book Freddie and his father had made one rainy day when he could not go outside to play. His father had a lot of magazines from which he and Freddie cut out pictures of beasties and glued them in a scrapbook. Then Freddie's father would explain to him all about the beasties and Freddie wrote it down next to the pictures. He opened his book and there on page three was the rolled up prickly beastie on the track in front of him. Actually Freddie already knew what it was, but as an intrepid explorer he had to make sure and mark his sighting down in his book.

"So Mr Hedgehog, are you going to stay there all day?" he asked his beastie.

"*Hedgehogs roll up when they feel threatened, their prickly spines stop them from being eaten by bigger beasties,*" Freddie read out aloud from his book, to no one in particular. "*Sometimes they roll up*

4

when crossing roads and get squashed by car and lorry wheels. Oh, that's terrible! The poor little things," he cried as he read from his book. "Well Mr Hedgehog, Freddie the Explorer will save you," he told the beastie and rolled the Hedgehog with his staff until it was safely under a bush.

Freddie marked his hedgehog sighting down in the book then put it back in his rucksack. With a twist and a turn he got his rucksack on his shoulders and skipped cheerfully along the track to do some more exploring.

"It's fun being an explorer," he said, to no one in particular, and stopped not far along the track when he spotted something on a tree trunk. "I wonder what that is?" he said to himself and lifted his binoculars to his eyes for a closer look. "Oh goodie, another beastie with a long bushy tail." Straight away Freddie took his rucksack down again and got his book out to identify this new beastie that could climb trees. He looked at it again through his binoculars, it was quite cute with reddish brown fur.

"Oh, oh!" It was looking straight at him. "What are you, Mr Bushy Tail?" he said, to no one in particular, as he turned the pages of his book. "Oh, I've found you, you're a squirrel!" he called out so loud the squirrel dashed up the tree until Freddie could no longer see it. "That's another tick for my book," he said. "I wonder if these beasties have their own notebooks for when they spot humans?" he chuckled.

He could just imagine a squirrel wearing glasses thumbing through his notebook thinking, *'What kind of beastie is that walking on two legs? Must be a monster!'*

Then Freddie suddenly stopped moving. "What's that?" he gasped, holding his hand to his ear to listen more carefully. He could hear birds singing, hedgehogs grunting and something else, something unusual in *his forest*, so he sat down on a patch of soft grass, cross-legged and listened.

"There it goes again!" he said, to no one in particular. It was a kind of crying. *'Maybe it is a bird of some sort needing help'*, he thought. Then he remembered his father had told him that foxes sometimes sound like they are crying, so he took off his rucksack and got out the book of beasties and looked up Mr Fox. Sure enough, he had written about the sound they make being mistaken for a child or baby crying.

"This needs Freddie the Explorer to investigate!" he said, to no one in particular. Jumping up, he began walking slowly, with giant steps, sniggering quietly to himself because he looked funny. He stopped and listened with his hand to his ear. "Over that way," he whispered, then set off again, trying not to step on twigs and stones. Another squirrel scurried up a nearby tree and made him jump. "Oh! Mr Squirrel you scared me," he called quietly up the tree where the squirrel had climbed. Suddenly something dropped from the tree as Freddie walked away and it made him jump again. "What's that?" he gasped, looking behind him and seeing two acorns laid on the track. "Are you throwing acorns at me now, Mr Squirrel? Naughty, naughty," he chuckled.

Slowly and quietly Freddie walked towards the sound and it began to get a little louder. "It really does sound like someone crying, I wonder why foxes do that?" he whispered to himself as he tiptoed in the direction of the sound. He stopped and lifted his binoculars to look towards the sound. "That's a funny looking fox," he whispered, to no one in particular. Freddie crept as quietly as he could, closer to the strange looking animal, letting his binoculars hang loose around his neck.

"When animals feel threatened or are trapped they can turn on you, so be careful!" Freddie was remembering what his father had told him and approached carefully and quietly. He stopped and looked through his binoculars again. "It almost looks like a tiny boy with a hat on!" he whispered, as he let his binoculars drop and moved a bit closer. Now he could see exactly what was making the crying noise, not a fox at all, not even an animal, but something even stranger. He was sure what he could see was a small boy in the distance, sitting on a log and crying, so he tiptoed closer and closer until he was almost standing in front of the unusual little boy.

The little boy did not notice Freddie at first, he was too busy rubbing his eyes and his right leg, between sobs and tears. When Freddie got quite close he realised this was no ordinary boy, he looked a bit smaller than Freddie to begin with. His face was thin with large round eyes and stubby nose, pointy chin and ears, straggly hair pushed out from under a floppy pointy hat. The boy's body was skinny too, his arms and legs spindly with funny knobbly elbows and knees.

'Maybe he doesn't eat his vegetables,' Freddie thought as he stared at the little boy still sobbing. In fact Freddie had never seen a boy like him before.

"Why are you crying, are you lost?" Freddie asked with a soft voice so not to scare him.

Before the funny little boy answered he jumped with surprise and turned to look at Freddie with his big teary eyes.

"Oh!.. No! No! No! No! You can't be seeing me, you can't!" he cried with tears running down his wrinkled cheeks, and then he covered his eyes with his bony fingers.

Freddie looked at the boy and was a bit confused. "But I *can* see you little boy, why shouldn't I see you?" he asked innocently.

"Elfins are not allowed to show themselves to Sproggles," the little boy answered with a squeaky voice, peeking through his fingers and sounding fearful.

Freddie giggled. "What are Elfins and Sproggles?" he chuckled.

But the little boy again repeated, "No! No! No! You can't see me!"

Freddie giggled again. "But here you are and here I am, Freddie the Explorer and I *do* see you and I know you can see me," he replied.

The funny little boy dropped his hands and looked directly at Freddie and replied. "Yes, yes. I know, but it's not allowed! - Not allowed!" He trembled and shook like he was afraid.

Freddie moved closer and knelt down so he could look at the little boy more closely. "My name is Freddie, what are you called?" he asked, holding out his hand like his parents had taught him to do when meeting new people.

The little boy flinched away and gasped, thinking Freddie was going to hit him.

"Oh, sorry! It's alright, I'm not going to hurt you, but what's your name?" Freddie tried to comfort his new friend.

The little boy sat back up and looked at Freddie's smiling face. "I am called Wiggly," he replied, ignoring Freddie's outstretched hand.

Freddie giggled. "Oh! Wiggly is a funny name."

The little boy seemed to relax a little hearing Freddie giggle.

"My parents gave me that name because I was always wiggling about when I was very little and never keeping still. My sister is called Giggly, that's because she ...."

Freddie finished Wiggly's sentence, "She giggles all the time?"

Wiggly giggled. "You're nice, not like I was told Sproggles were like at all."

Freddie laughed. "Is that what you call me, a Sproggle, then what are you?" he asked, still giggling.

"Well I'm an Elfin, that's what I am, an Elfin," Wiggly replied with a chuckle.

"So why are you crying, Wiggly?" Freddie asked more seriously.

Wiggly looked down and pointed at his leg.

Freddie had not noticed as he had been looking at Wiggly's face, but now he could see Wiggly's leg was caught in a horrible trap. Two half round metal bars hinged like a jaw had snapped closed on Wiggly's little leg, jagged metal triangles all along each edge closed together. Luckily a small stone was also stuck between the metal triangles stopping the trap from closing completely. If those nasty metal triangles did close they would have bitten Wiggly's leg right off.

"I can't get my leg out of this trap, I'm not strong enough to open it," he said, beginning to cry again.

Freddie looked at the trap, it looked a bit like the shape of his mother's home made pasties, it was very rusty though and must have been there for many years. He gasped realising he could have stepped in it himself or one of his friends and that would have been painful. "Maybe I'm strong enough to open it," Freddie suggested with a big friendly smile and a pat on Wiggly's shoulder. But try as he might he could not open the trap, there was nothing for Freddie to get hold of. Then he noticed a little lever at the bottom of the trap.

"I wonder what that does?" he said pointing to the lever.

Wiggly shook his head, he did not know either.

"I know, maybe I can prize it open with my magic staff," Freddie said.

Wiggly's face suddenly lit up. "You have magic?" he said excitedly.

Freddie giggled. "Not really, my magic staff is a broom handle spayed gold, it's only pretend magic," he explained.

Wiggly's smile disappeared, he thought for a moment Freddie might be a wizard.

But no matter how hard Freddie tried, he still could not open the trap, the brush handle was just too thick. "Oh, phooey!" he shouted, to no one in particular, making Wiggly jump and then wince.

8

Freddie banged his brush handle down hard and it clipped the little lever at the bottom of the trap. Suddenly the rusty old metal-jawed trap sprung open.

Wiggly quickly pulled his leg out. "Whoopee!" he cried out in his squeaky voice, "you did it Sproggle Freddie, you did it, whoopee!" Wiggly jumped off the log and began dancing around shouting, "Whoopee I'm free, whoopee!"

Freddie watched and giggled seeing his new friend so happy and skipping about.

Eventually Wiggly sat back on the log, puffing and blowing, he had tired himself out.

Freddie could not help chuckling at his new friend, he was so funny.

Wiggly stood up and only reached up to Freddie's shoulder. "Thank you so much Sproggle Freddie, you are very kind and I like you." Then he hopped about a bit more.

"You don't stay in one place very long do you?" Freddie laughed.

"No," Wiggly cried, "I'm a jiggly, Wiggly!" and laughed.

When Wiggly stopped for a moment, Freddie said to him, "This is a horrible nasty thing to leave lying around, it might kill a poor squirrel or rabbit if they got caught in it."

Wiggly stood still and looked at Freddie. "Sproggles put these traps all over the forest to catch little bunny rabbits. My people have found them all over and destroyed them but they missed this one though. That's why we think all Sproggles are killers, not nice like you Sproggle Freddie." he explained.

"Well I don't know who set these traps, Wiggly, or why they want to kill fluffy little rabbits, they are so cute and shy," Freddie replied.

Wiggly looked sad and explained, "Sproggle Freddie, other Sproggles eat rabbits after they have been caught and killed."

"Oh no! That's just horrible," Freddie cried out and made Wiggly jump again. "I understand why your people don't like Sproggles, poor little bunnies! Where do you live, Wiggly? I come to the forest a lot to play games, I pretend I'm an explorer like today, why have I never seen you or any of your people about before?"

Wiggly smiled. "Oh, we do live in the forest here, but we avoid all Sproggles, so we live underground, come on I'll show you, but you must promise never to reveal this to another Sproggle or we would be hunted and killed, just like the rabbits."

Freddie was shocked to hear that adults could or would do such a thing, but then they had set all those horrible traps. "You're too skinny for a Sproggle to eat you, Wiggly," Freddie said not quite understanding.

"Oh! I suppose I am. I don't know if Sproggles eat Elfins, but if they did they would wipe us out."

"You can trust me, Wiggly, I will never, ever, tell anyone your secret," Freddie reassured him.

"Follow me then," Wiggly giggled.

"Wait, what about the trap?" Freddie cried out.

"Oh yes! Let's close it and take it with us," Wiggly replied.

Freddie dropped a heavy stone into the trap, which jumped up as it snapped closed like a hungry crocodile. He pulled and pulled the closed trap until finally the spike holding it in the ground came out. It shot up so suddenly that Freddie fell backwards with a bump and just missed squashing Wiggly. "Oh, that was close! I nearly fell on top of you," cried Freddie. He scrambled back to his feet grabbing the horrible rusty metal trap.

"Let's go then," Wiggly called.

Freddie grabbed his staff and caught up with his new friend who took his hand.

They walked for a little while going deeper into the forest. Freddie recognised some of the trees that he had played around and climbed up, but not too high in case he fell down and hurt himself. Soon they came upon a very large and old oak tree.

"Funny, I don't remember seeing this tree here before, it's really huge," Freddie said. He let go of Wiggly's hand to stretch his arms out to see how wide the tree was and both it and Wiggly disappeared. "Oh! Where are you?" he cried.

Wiggly took hold of Freddie's hand again and like magic Freddie could see the big old oak tree and his new friend.

"What just happened, Wiggly?" Freddie asked looking very bewildered.

Wiggly giggled. "When you said you had a magic staff I thought you were a wizard. Elfins have magic, Freddie, and you can only see the big old oak tree because you were holding my hand. It has a magic enchantment on it so only Elfins can see it, you'll see, just watch."

Freddie was trying to understand, his friend just told him that magic was real.

Wiggly placed his free hand flat on the tree trunk and spoke some strange words, "Efum - Efum - Natum - Efum."

Freddie looked at his new friend curiously, wondering what he was doing. He stepped back, pulling Wiggly with him when the tree began making groaning and creaking noises. "Wiggly!" Freddie called in alarm, "The tree, it's going to fall, listen!"

Wiggly just smiled and said, "It's okay Freddie, you're safe with me, just watch."

Freddie gasped when a thin black line rose from the ground and up the tree trunk, almost as high as Freddie was tall, it curved round in an arch at the top, then moved back to the ground, just like someone drawing a line with a felt tip pen. "What's happening?" he whispered.

"Just watch," Wiggly replied excitedly.

The black line became a little thicker and began to look like a door. Freddie watched fascinated as a door began to open inward revealing a spiral staircase inside the big old oak tree.

"Come on," Wiggly chuckled seeing the surprise on Freddie's face, then pulling his new friend by his hand inside the tree trunk.

Freddie was speechless, not only had he never seen this huge tree before, but amazed it had a secret door, a magic door. Once inside the tree they began descending down the spiral staircase. After taking just a few steps down, Freddie noticed the door closing behind them. They were then left in semidarkness, lit only by green glowing moss-like plants. They had been going down and round until Freddie had to stop, he was out of breath and pulled Wiggly up sharply.

"Not far now," Wiggly said pulling on Freddie's hand again. When they reached the bottom there was another door and Wiggly repeated the same words again and the door creaked and groaned open until they were bathed in bright light just as if they were outside in the sunshine again.

Freddie had to shield his eyes with his free hand for a moment while they adjusted to the light.

"Come on," Wiggly urged excitedly, dragging his new friend, "I want you to meet my parents and sister."

Freddie moved his hand to look around and he got a real surprise. They seemed to be in a busy town, with houses and shops, but smaller than his house and the shops in his village. The sky was bright blue just like a cloudless sunny day, the air felt warm and smelled so fresh. The roads were not like those he was used to, but made up of small square blocks of stone neatly squeezed together. He noticed all the buildings did not have an upstairs, just a downstairs and remembered his mother telling him that this kind of house was called a bungalow.

When they emerged through the door at the bottom of the spiral staircase there were lots of people walking about and children playing, but when they saw Freddie they quickly ran inside, doors were closed with loud bangs and he could see faces in windows watching them.

"Nearly there," Wiggly called out as they were running along the cobbled road.

Freddie did not hear Wiggly because he was too preoccupied looking around at the strange world he had wandered into.

Wiggly finally stopped and Freddie bumped into him almost knocking him to the ground.

"Oops! Sorry, Wiggly, I wasn't paying attention. Have we arrived?" Freddie apologised a little breathlessly.

Wiggly chuckled, "You are a funny Sproggle. Yes, we're here, this is my house, do you like it?"

Freddie looked at the building set back from the road with a pretty garden with a white stick fence around. A stone path like the roads led from a little gate to a round-topped door, it reminded him of his own home except Wiggly's house looked a bit like a loaf of bread with a door and windows. It was painted a yellow colour with a green door and windows and Freddie thought it looked really charming. "It's really nice, Wiggly, my house has a fence like yours," he replied.

"Well down here we don't get wind or rain or snow, so we build our homes mostly of mud," Wiggly explained. "Come on, let's meet my parents." Once again he pulled on Freddie's hand and led him through the door, by turning a doorknob this time.

The doorway was only just high enough for Freddie to pass through without ducking his head.

"Mummly, Daddly, come meet my new friend!" Wiggly cried out as they entered the house.

They were standing in one big room, with chairs and a sofa at one end with a fireplace, a table in the middle with chairs around it and a kind of kitchen at the other end. There was a doorway opposite the front door that Freddie assumed must lead to bedrooms and a bathroom. Wiggly's parents and sister were sitting on chairs when he and Freddie burst in.

"Mummly, Daddly, Giggly, this is my new friend, Freddie, he saved my life!"

Wiggly's parents and sister suddenly jumped up and rushed towards the two friends and Freddie found himself being hugged by Wiggly's mother, father and sister.

When they pulled apart, Wiggly introduced everyone. "Freddie, this is Mummly, Mrs Tiggly and Daddly, Mr Tiggly and this is my sister Giggly."

Freddie thought all their names were very funny sounding and struggled not to giggle, because his parents had taught him such things were rude and unkind.

Mr Tiggly held out his hand and Freddie shook hands. "You're the first Sproggle to ever see our world, thank you for returning Wiggly to us safe and sound. Now please call me Daddly, everyone does."

Freddie was surprised and smiled at the kindly Mr Tiggly. "Thank you, Mr Tiggly. Err! I mean Daddly," he chuckled at his little mistake.

Mrs Tiggly smiled, agreed and said, "Yes, thank you for returning our naughty son and please call me Mummly."

Again Freddie was a bit bewildered by it all.

Giggly looked identical to Wiggly except she had a plait of hair on each side of her head. "Oooh, you're very handsome, Freddie, especially when you smile," she said, giggling.

Freddie felt a little embarrassed and blushed bright red.

"I see you found one of the Sproggles' nasty traps, I thought we had found all of those," Daddly observed seeing the metal monster across Freddie's rucksack.

Freddie reached round and handed the horrible rusty trap to Daddly, who took it away through the door opposite the front door and soon returned.

Mummly gave Freddie a big smile and said, "Come, sit down by the fire on a comfy chair and tell us all about how you met Wiggly."

Freddie took off his rucksack and placed it on the floor, then sat on the comfy sofa with Wiggly. Mummly and Daddly sat on comfy chairs opposite and Giggly sat on a big comfy cushion on the floor.

Wiggly held Freddie's hand while he explained everything to Mummly, Daddly and Giggly. How he had heard Wiggly crying when he was exploring in the forest and ran to help, somehow managing to open the trap and saved his new friend.

Wiggly's parents and sister clapped their hands and smiled and laughed when Freddie finished his tale.

"You must stay and have dinner with us, Freddie," Mummly said.

Wiggly and Giggly were nodding their heads and giggling.

Freddie was happy to stay for a while as his parents would not be worried about him until it got close to teatime.

"Can I ask a question?" Freddie was looking at Mummly and Daddly when he spoke.

"Of course, I expect you may have a lot of questions," Daddly replied.

"Well," Freddie began, "I play in the forest a lot, mostly by myself. I like to explore and see the wild animals, but I have never seen the big old oak tree that has the door to your world."

All the Tiggly's chuckled.

"Well," Daddly began, "many, many years ago Sproggles and Elfins lived side by side, Sproggles liked the open fields and Elfins liked the woodlands. Over time more and more Sproggles were born and they began cutting down the trees for more and more open land to farm. Very soon there was not enough woodland for Elfins and that was the beginning of the 'Great Sad Times.' We moved underground and a powerful Wizard created the big old oak tree and a doorway to our new world, then put a magical enchantment on it so Sproggles could never see it, they walk right through the place where the tree stands, that's why you have not seen it before."

Freddie thought about what he had been told and then asked, "Why could I see it this time?"

Wiggly laughed. "Have you forgotten that I said it's because I was holding your hand? Otherwise as I reached the big old oak tree it would look like I just disappeared."

"Oh yes! When I let go of your hand, you and the tree did just vanish." Freddie grinned, looking at Wiggly. Then turning back to Mummly and Daddly he asked, "If we are underground, why does the ceiling above your house look like a blue sky?"

14

Mummly was happy to answer that question. "It's what Sproggles call magic. The Great Wizard made our home down here to be like the land above ground, we don't know how it works exactly, but we have a night and day, just like you do."

Freddie thought about it and he kept thinking about magic. "Do you all have some magic too?" he asked.

Wiggly's sister Giggly sat up and replied, "Only one or two Elfins do, they are special and help keep the Wizard's magic working, but most of us don't have magic. But it is possible sometimes by Town Elders using Fairy Dust," she replied.

When Freddie heard the word 'wizard' it made him jump up with excitement. He loved stories about wizards and magic but never thought they were true, just fairy stories. "You have a Wizard?" he blurted out with excitement. "A real live Wizard?"

Wiggly laughed at Freddie's excitement and answered, "Elfin's did have a wizard, the greatest wizard that ever lived, but he vanished a long time ago. Sadly, none of us have ever seen him."

Freddie sat back down a little disappointed for he thought he might have had the chance to meet a real wizard, that would have been something very special. Then he had a sudden thought. "Oh! I have some food in my rucksack." He picked it up from the floor and unzipped it, pulling out the pack of sandwiches, juice and apple. "My Mum packed it for me when I left my house this morning," he said cheerfully.

"How lovely. Bring them to the table," Mummly said as she moved to the kitchen end of the room.

Within a few minutes the table was full of all kinds of nuts, berries, mushrooms and salad leaves. When they were all seated at the table, Wiggly asked Freddie what was wrapped in the shiny parcel.

"These are jam sandwiches, Wiggly, do you not have them here? They're very yummy." Freddie opened the aluminium foil wrapper. His mother had put two slices of bread together with jam in the middle and he had two of these sandwiches. He took a knife-like cutting tool from the table and cut each of his sandwiches in four, giving one piece to each of them to try.

The Tiggly's took the sandwich from Freddie and looked it over, sniffed it and turned it round in their hands before taking a bite.

Wiggly jumped up in his seat. "Oh wow! This is so yummylicious, Yum! - Yum! - Yum!"

Freddie chuckled at Wiggly's excitement.

Then Giggly jumped up and said exactly the same thing. "This tastes so, so, yummified!" she cried out and Freddie kept on laughing.

Mummly and Daddly looked at their children in surprise and then at Freddie before taking a bite.

Daddly's eyes opened wide and Mummly licked her lips. "This is very nice for a treat, Freddie, do you know how it's made?" Mummly asked.

Freddie stopped laughing at Wiggly and Giggly and looked at Mummly. "I have watched my Mum make bread, that's the two white sheets, and also jam, that's the red stuff inside. I remember Mum saying to make bread you need flour and yeast and for the jam you need fruit and sugar."

Wiggly piped up, "Oh, what's flour and yeast?"

Freddie thought for a minute with his finger on his lip, he remembered seeing a television programme about flour. "Well," he replied, "flour can be made from seeds like wheat and barley, they are grass like plants. The seeds are ground up between two stones until they become a very fine powder called flour. I think yeast is a kind of fungus like mushrooms, I can find out more for you from my Mum."

After their meal they all moved back to the seating area in front of the log fire and sat down on comfy seats. Wiggly sat with Freddie on the comfy sofa.

Daddly said he wanted to give Freddie something special as a reward for saving his son. "May I have a look at your rucksack?" he asked and Freddie handed it to him. Daddly stood up and walked over to the kitchen end of the house.

Freddie heard him speaking to some kind of small door that sprang open.

Daddly reached into the cupboard and brought out a large jar containing something that twinkled and sparkled like a hundred Christmas tree lights, then brought it over to the seating area. Daddly held up the jar and said to Freddie, "This is Fairy Dust, it's very rare and our most precious possession." He opened the jar and took out a small pinch and sprinkled it over Freddie's rucksack, whispering some strange words. "There," he said with satisfaction, "your rucksack is now magical and can give you almost anything you can picture in your mind. Try it, Freddie, it will only work for you, to anyone else it will be just like an ordinary rucksack."

Freddie looked amazed, hardly able to believe what Daddly had just told him. He looked at Daddly. "Is it really magic? Oh! This is so exciting," he replied as his trembling hands took his rucksack back from Daddly.

Wiggly and Giggly were also excited and stood up to watch what Freddie would do.

When Wiggly got really excited his legs would start to run on the spot very fast and that's what was happening as he watched his new friend.

Freddie looked at Wiggly and laughed, mystified by his friends behaviour. "What should I ask for?" Freddie said eagerly.

"Just unzip it and put your hand inside," Daddly explained, "and think of what you want and it will appear in your hand, as long as it's small enough to fit inside the rucksack, of course."

Freddie unzipped the top of his rucksack and put his hand inside, thought for a moment with his eyes closed so he could see in his mind clearly what he wanted and then pulled his hand out. A loaf of bread came out of the rucksack in his hand. He put it on the small table between the comfy chairs, then put his hand back inside and pulled out a jar of strawberry jam.

"Oh! This is truly magic, thank you so much, Daddly, I will be able to help lots of people with my magic rucksack now." Freddie chuckled with excitement, he dipped his hand into his rucksack again until on the table stood the loaf of bread, a jar of jam and some margarine spread.

Wiggly and Giggly looked at the food with hungry eyes. "Can we have bread and jam for tea, please Mummly?" they pleaded and Mummly smiled, nodded and said that they could.

Freddie spent the afternoon talking with Wiggly, Giggly, Mummly and Daddly, finding out much more about the Elfins and their world. In turn the Elfins asked about Freddie and the Sproggle world and listened enthusiastically. It had been a long time since Elfins had spied on the Sproggles, so everything that Freddie told them was new and interesting.

* *

When Wiggly escorted Freddie back through Elfin town, somehow word had spread about Freddie saving Wiggly and lots of Elfins stood outside buildings and clapped their hands. It made Freddie feel quite special and proud that he had been able to help Wiggly and meet all these lovely Elfins.

When they reached the top of the spiral staircase Freddie was out of breath and had to stop a moment, trying to recover. "How," puff, "many," puff, "steps?" puff, he asked.

Wiggly laughed and giggled. "It's only 145 steps," he replied.

Of course there was no longer a door to see until Wiggly placed his palm on the inside of the tree trunk and said the magic words again.

Freddie watched, enthralled as the magic door began to form like it had when they were on the outside, then it sprang open inwards and the two friends stepped outside.

"Will you come and see me again?" Wiggly asked holding on to Freddie's hand.

"Am I allowed to come see you?" Freddie asked.

"Oh, yes you can, but you must have your rucksack with you so you can see through the enchantment, then put your hand on the tree and say the words and the door will open for you. You must repeat it when you reach the bottom as well, just like I did. Do you remember the magic words Freddie?"

"I do because they sounded funny. They are - 'Efum - Efum - Natum - Efum', am I right?" Freddie replied with a big grin.

Wiggly nodded excitedly. "Yes that's right, now you must keep this a secret otherwise we would be in danger. If the Sproggles ever found out about us they would hunt us down because we are different to them, remember what Daddly said!"

Freddie smiled and hugged Wiggly. "I promise not to tell anyone and keep you all safe, because I like all my new friends."

Freddie waved goodbye and when he was a little way from the tree it just disappeared, he could see right through the space where it had been. He smiled to himself, now he knew that magic really did exist and he had a magic rucksack. He was so excited and realised he was a very lucky person and was so happy he sang his favourite song, *'All things Bright and Beautiful.'* He sang and marched along the pathway swinging his arms like a soldier. When he arrived back home his mother asked if he had a nice adventure and he told her all about his travels, leaving out the bit about the Elfins.

** **

Over the next few months Freddie became a regular visitor to Elfin Town. People would call out and welcome him back. *'They are such nice people,'* he thought to himself, *'it's a shame Sproggles couldn't be as nice as Elfins, especially Billy Bates, the class bully.'*

"Hello, Freddie, how are you today?" called Mrs Twinkly.

"I'm very well thank you, Mrs Twinkly, how are you? Oh, how is little Star? Is she better now?" he replied.

"Oh yes, she's much better now, thank you. She's even going to school again. Thank you for the medicine, it worked really well."

Freddie skipped along and when he reached the Tiggly's home, Wiggly and Giggly were always excited to see him, as were Mummly and Daddly.

On one visit he thought about a pizza and pulled one from his rucksack, everyone thought it was amazing and so simple to make. Mummly and Daddly had devised a way to make flour and Freddie had brought a cookery book for them and now Elfins were enjoying lots of different and interesting foods like berry crumble, sausage rolls and of course, fairy cakes.

Wiggly showed Freddie their school and introduced him to Miss Noall, the school's teacher, who was very interested in his stories about the way Sproggles lived on the surface. Unlike Freddie's school, the Elfin school allowed children to attend when they wanted and most of the Elfin children liked going to school where they learned all manner of things like weaving with long strips of dried grass, which mushrooms are safe to eat and how to read and write.

On one of his visits to the school Freddie announced excitedly, "Oh Miss Noall! I know my four times table, it has a tune that goes like this, lah lah, lal la-ah, one four is four, two fours are eight, three fours are twelve......." Very soon Miss Noall was singing and Wiggly joined in as did the other children.

"Oh, that's so much fun!" all the children called out. "Can we do it again please?"

So Freddie happily led the chorus of the four times table.

After that school visit, Wiggly took Freddie to a new shop that had opened using the new flour and recipes from Freddie's cookery book.

Freddie was so excited when he saw the sign above the shop, 'FREDDIES', he clapped his hands together. "My parents would be so proud if they knew about this," he chuckled.

"It must be our secret though," Wiggly cautioned.

The smell coming from 'FREDDIES' bakery was very yummy and they walked inside where people were being served lots of nice treats. Mr and Mrs Flowers were in charge of baking all the lovely things.

"Hello, Freddie," they called when they saw him and Wiggly, "come and try this new cake," they said, offering them both something that looked like an orange speckled cone.

"This is called a Madeleine," Mrs Flowers told them as Freddie and Wiggly took the small cake and tried a bite.

"Oh wow!" Wiggly cried, "this is super-dooper Mr and Mrs Flowers." He took a second bite and a third.

Freddie laughed at his friend and his eyes lit up when he tasted the cake himself, "Oh, yes, Wiggly is right, this is delicious!" He took off his rucksack and held it flat on the table, then thought about one of his favourite cakes. It was, of course, a jam tart and Freddie pulled out a plate with six strawberry jam tarts. "These are called jam tarts, I think they are easy to make, try one."

Mr and Mrs Flowers took one of Freddie's jam tarts.

Wiggly reached out and helped himself too. After he had taken a large bite, he jumped up and down again. "Super-dooper too!" he cried.

Mr Flowers looked closely at the tarts, studying around the edges of the pastry, then sniffed the underneath and said, "I think we can make these as well, thank you, Freddie."

"What's all the noise in here?" cried the Flowers' twins, Rose and Violet, as they ran inside the shop, home from school. "Oh! Hello again Freddie and Wiggly. Freddie taught us a new way of doing sums with a tune," they said together excitedly.

Everyone was eager to hear it so the twins began to sing the four times table and they all clapped their hands when the children finished.

"You have given us so much, Freddie, we're so happy you found Wiggly and brought him home when he was in trouble," Mrs Root said patting him on the back.

Freddie always felt such happiness being able to help the people of Elfin Town. He had always liked helping others, like his parents, friends and villagers, now he had even more friends to help. All too soon it was time for him to go home after all the excitement. He said his goodbyes to Mummly and Daddly, Giggly gave him a hug and told him to come again soon and he promised he would.

Wiggly climbed up the spiral staircase with his friend and opened the door in the big old oak tree and made Freddie promise to come and visit again soon.

Freddie was so full of joy he skipped his way through the forest until he reached his garden gate then ran to the back door. Inside the house his mother and father were pleased that Freddie seemed even happier these days.

On Monday morning Freddie was on his way to school with his magic rucksack on his back. Today his mother walked along side him, she was on her way to the shops and the school was on her route to the High Street.

"You're very jolly this morning son," his mother smiled and chuckled.

Freddie looked at his mother and returned her smile. "Mmm, it's my favourite lessons today Mum, Art this morning and Modelling in the afternoon," he answered.

They were approaching Mr Bootle's house with its clipped hedges all around his garden that were too tall for Freddie to peek over the top. Mr Bootle was a very clever person because he clipped the very top of his hedges into animal shapes. The first Freddie and his mother came across was a running rabbit, next a sitting rabbit, then a cat and a dog, all looking so neat and impressive.

They stopped and heard a voice of someone talking loudly.

Freddie looked at his mother, asking the question 'who is that?' by raising his eyebrows.

His mother chuckled. "I think that sounds like Mr Bootle," she said.

They heard him again, a bit louder this time. "Oh, you silly, silly thing, stop messing me about! Oh dear, not another one! Oh dear, oh dear."

When Freddie and his mother reached the space in the hedge where Mr Bootle's gate was, they noticed him with his hands on his head, looking at his gate, which was hanging at a funny angle.

"Mr Bootle, whatever has happened?" Freddie's mother asked with some concern.

"Oh! Hello Mrs Fountain, Freddie," he replied looking from his broken gate, to them. "The pesky screws fell out of the hinge on my gate into the long grass and I just cannot find them to repair it. I have only got this one and I need five in all, I guess I'll have to call the Handyman in to fix it."

Freddie looked and smiled at Mr Bootle. "I think I have something in my rucksack to help you, Mr Bootle," he announced. He took his rucksack off his shoulders and unzipped it, then looking at the screw in Mr Bootle's hand, rummaged around inside and pulled out four shiny metal screws the same size. "Will these help fix your gate, Mr Bootle?" Freddie asked with a big grin on his face, holding out his hand showing the four screws.

"Oh Freddie, they will be just the job! You are a handy helper to have around," Mr Bootle replied eagerly and took the shiny screws from Freddie, fixing his gate hinge in a jiffy. "Just a minute Freddie!" Mr Bootle cried, dashing off towards his front door. No sooner gone than he was walking back to Freddie and his mother. Mr Bootle gave Freddie a bar of chocolate. "Here's a little reward for being so helpful," he said with a big smile on his face. Then he spoke to Freddie's mother, "You must be very proud of your son, Mrs Fountain, I hear he helps a lot of people, you have taught him well."

"That's very kind of you, Mr Bootle, we are proud of Freddie, he's always willing to help where he can. Good job we were passing this morning," she replied.

They waved goodbye to Mr Bootle and carried on with their journey. On reaching the junction where Freddie turned left to his school and his mother turned right to the High Street and the shops, she wished him a nice day at school and they waved goodbye to each other.

Freddie hurried along to his school and met up with his best friend Jimmy, who was waiting at the schools gates for him.

Jimmy was excited to see his friend and hear how he had helped Mr Bootle fix his garden gate as they walked together into the playground.

While sitting on a bench waiting for the bell to ring, Andy joined them and helped Freddie eat the bar of chocolate he had been given as a reward for helping Mr Bootle. The school bell rang just as they swallowed the last pieces of chocolate and they joined the other children lining up for morning assembly, where they sang a happy song to get them all in a good mood for the day.

The Headmistress, Mrs Doohall, read out the day's notices and then explained that Miss Brushes was not able to come to school today as she was poorly and Mr Longfellow would take her morning class. It just so happened that Miss Brushes was Freddie's teacher so he and his friends were a little disappointed. After assembly Freddie's class lined up outside the Art room ready for their lesson.

Mr Longfellow arrived and he allowed them to enter the classroom and stand by their desks.

"Please sit down children," Mr Longfellow instructed them. He could see they all looked a little glum. "My name is Mr Longfellow," he told them, "but just for today you can all call me by my first name."

The children sat up and looked at each other in surprise, murmuring around. No teacher had ever let them be called by their first name, and they were all so intrigued they forgot about being glum.

Freddie raised his hand.

Mr Longfellow spoke to him. "Yes young man, what is your name?"

He smiled and told him it was Freddie.

"Well, Freddie, do you have a question for me?"

Everyone was looking at Freddie, their sadness long gone.

"Mr Longfellow, you said we could call you by your first name, could you tell us what it is please?" he asked.

Mr Longfellow smiled and looked around at his class who were completely engrossed so far.

"Of course children, my first name is......, here, I will write it on the chalk board for you, it's easy to pronounce." He turned to the green chalkboard and wrote three letters, S - I - R, then turned to look at his class again, still smiling.

Once again the whole class were looking at each other and mumbling, until Juliet called out, "Oh Sir, that's cheating!" and the rest of the class giggled.

"Just my little joke to brighten up those sad faces of yours. I know you're disappointed that Miss Brushes is away, she's feeling poorly, so I thought it would be nice if you each made a get well card for her."

The children liked that idea, looking happy and excited because Miss Brushes was popular, she was kind and funny and helpful.

Mr Longfellow brought out sheets of coloured card, coloured paper, scissors and glue, paint, glitter, coloured pencils, brushes and felt tip pens and lots of useful things, then let the children choose what they wanted. Some cut paper flowers and others cut out heart shapes, the art room was a hive of activity and Mr Longfellow walked around helping where it was needed.

Morning playtime came round so quickly. The whole class had been completely engrossed making their individual cards for Miss Brushes.

After playtime they were putting the finishing touches on their get-well cards, when Mr Longfellow called out, "Does anyone have a pencil eraser, I cannot find one anywhere?"

The boys and girls looked blankly at each other until Jimmy called out. "Please Sir, Freddie will have one Sir, he can always fixit."

Freddie walked to his teacher's desk with his rucksack and pulled out a lovely big pencil eraser.

"Oh! That's just the job, Freddie, thank you," Mr Longfellow said, giving Freddie a nod and a smile.

"We call him Freddie Fixit Sir!" Jimmy called out.

The class chuckled and clapped their hands and cheered.

Poor Freddie felt a bit embarrassed and his face turned bright red.

Mr Longfellow offered the pencil eraser back to him after he had rubbed out the pencil lines. Freddie smiled and told him, "Oh that's alright Sir, I have more of them in my rucksack, please keep that one for when you need it next."

Mr Longfellow thanked Freddie for his kindness and generosity. "I'll make sure I don't lose it, here look, I've put my first name on it."

Freddie looked and Mr Longfellow had printed *Property of SIR*. Freddie giggled and thought he was a lot of fun to have as a teacher.

Jimmy collected all the get-well cards and handed them to Mr Longfellow.

"I will deliver these lovely cards to Miss Brushes after school today," Mr Longfellow said. "I am sure she will be delighted with them all."

Some children at Freddie's school had hot meals at lunchtime served in the dining hall, they also had the option of bringing a packed lunch. Freddie always brought a packed lunch because his mother cooked a lovely meal at teatime for them to sit down and eat as a family. As it was a sunny day Freddie and his friends sat outside at a picnic table to eat their lunch, when one of their class friends hobbled his way past them.

"Hey! William, what's wrong?" Freddie called out.

William stopped next to Freddie with his right shoe in his hand. "My shoelace snapped and my shoe keeps falling off every time I try to walk," William replied.

"Freddie Fixit to the rescue!" shouted Jimmy and everyone chuckled, except William, who looked confused.

"Don't pay them any attention William, I might have something in my rucksack to help," Freddie said. He lifted it off the floor onto his knee, unzipped it and fished out a new black shoelace. "Here we are, let me thread it for you."

William gave his shoe to Freddie, who looped the lace through the holes like his father had shown him a long time ago. He handed it back to William who was all smiles now and Freddie shuffled along the bench seat so William could sit to put his shoe back on and tie the new lace.

"Thank you, Freddie, you really are Freddie Fixit."

That gave rise to them all giggling, including William, who was invited to eat his packed lunch with them.

* *

When school finished at 2.30 in the afternoon, Freddie's mother was waiting for him at the school gates, like lots of the mothers did, but usually for the younger children.

Freddie was walking with his friend, Jimmy, when they spotted Freddie's mother.

"Oooh hello, Mrs Fountain," Jimmy called out politely.

"Hello, Jimmy," Mrs Fountain smiled, "you both have dabs of paint on your chins. I thought you were supposed to use a brush not eat the paint, boys!"

"Ha, ha! You're very funny, Mrs Fountain," Jimmy laughed, trying to wipe the paint off with his thumb.

"Mu-um!" Freddie protested and laughed as well. "We've had a super time making get well cards for Miss Brushes who is poorly, and we built a fort out of lolly sticks in the afternoon. Best day ever," Freddie told his mother.

"That's right and we painted it green, Mrs Fountain, it looked really epic!" Jimmy added enthusiastically.

At home Freddie's mother asked him if there was anything special he would like for tea.

"Could we have a sponge cake and custard, please?" he replied.

His mother set to and got all the ingredients ready as Freddie watched. When she began mixing the flour, sugar, butter and eggs together, she exclaimed, "Oh dear, my favourite spoon!" The handle of the wooden spoon had broken in half and she was left holding one piece in each hand.

Freddie smiled. "I think I might have something to help with that," he said and dashed upstairs to get his rucksack. He rushed down the stairs with a thump, thump, thump, into the kitchen.

His mother laughed. "Oh! I thought it was that herd of elephants running down the stairs," she said.

Freddie looked at her mischievously. "Mu-um," he replied, "how would I fit elephants in my bedroom?"

They both laughed.

Freddie thought he had the best mother, she always smiled and made him laugh. He unzipped his rucksack put his hand inside and thought about glue. "Look Mum," he said, holding up a small cardboard box. "It's glue, look, 'Dinosaur Glue', sticks everything fast," he said reading the words on the box.

"Well I've never heard of Dinosaur Glue, but let's give it a try," his mother replied.

Freddie took the tube out, unscrewed the top and looked at the instructions. "It says put a small dab on each piece, hold them together and say Abracadabra!"

His mother laughed again. "Must be magic glue in that case."

Freddie applied a dab to each broken end of the spoon and put them back together. While he held them he and his mother said the magic word together.

"Abracadabra!"

Freddie took one hand away and the spoon stayed in one piece.

"Oh! Freddie, you are a clever boy, the spoon is mended. Where did you get that glue from?"

This was a bit tricky. Freddie had been taught to always tell the truth and he hated telling lies. "Oh! It has been in my rucksack for ages, I think maybe Mr Dimples gave it to me or was it Mrs Lionhart, I can't quite remember." He answered with his fingers crossed behind his back.

Freddie's mother was so pleased to have her spoon again and did not ask any more questions, then carried on mixing the sponge cake for their tea.

Freddie put the tube of Dinosaur glue in the kitchen oddments drawer thinking it would come in useful another time.

* *

Later that week Freddie and his friends were in the school playground talking together before the bell rang. His friend Melanie had slipped down and grazed her knee and it looked red and sore, but she was brave and did not cry.

Freddie looked and said, "I think I may have just the thing in my rucksack." He took it off his shoulders, unzipped it and pulled out a sticky plaster. "Let me put it on your wound, Melanie," he said and peeled off the tabs then gently applied it to Melanie's knee.

"Thank you, Freddie, you are a good friend," she said smiling again.

"Freddie Fixit to the rescue again!" Jimmy called and they all laughed.

Billy Bates, or Bully Bates, as the children called him, came over to see what all the commotion was about. "What's going on here?" he growled, but no one answered. He looked at everyone with a stern face and focused on Freddie. "Oh! It's you again, Freddie the Fool," then snatched his rucksack.

"Hey, give that back, it's mine not yours!" Freddie cried out bravely.

But Bully Bates pushed Freddie aside. "Let's see what good stuff you've got hidden in here then!" he growled and laughed. "You're always a goodie two shoes helping people." He unzipped the top and felt inside, then turned it upside down. "Hey! There's nothing in here. Why do you carry it around if it's completely empty?"

While Bully Bates looked confused Freddie grabbed his rucksack back, quickly thought of something and felt inside his rucksack. "You missed this, Billy Bates," he cried and pulled out a full water pistol and began squirting water all over Billy Bates' trousers.

"Ha! Ha! Ha! Billy Bates has wet his pants!" Freddie's friends laughed, pointing at the very obvious wet patch on the front of the bully's trousers.

A crowd soon gathered, all laughing at Billy's wet trousers and pointing at him.

Billy's face turned bright red and he ran off pushing people out of his way trying to hold the cold wet material off his skin. He ran out of the school gates and back home, fortunately he lived almost next door to the school.

His mother scolded him when he walked inside the house thinking he had wet himself. "A grown boy like you shouldn't wee himself, go upstairs and change your clothes, make sure you wash yourself so you don't smell, be quick, you're late for school already!" His mother did not give him a chance to explain, but he told her he was unwell and did not return to school for a few days.

After Bully Bates had run away everyone cheered Freddie shouting, "FREDDIE FIXIT to the rescue, FREDDIE FIXIT!"

It was Friday and everyone was usually really happy because tomorrow was the start of the weekend and they could play all day. During the morning playtime, William, one of Freddie's friends, looked glum.

"What's the matter, William?" Freddie asked him. "You look like you lost 50 pence and found a penny."

Jimmy giggled loudly when he heard what Freddie said.

Freddie smiled at Jimmy and explained. "Oh, that's what my Dad says to me when I look glum."

William looked at Freddie and replied, "Mummy gave me an apple to bring to school to have at lunchtime and I can't find it, I must have left it on the kitchen table."

Freddie put his hand on his friend's shoulder and comforted him. "That's alright, William, I've got an extra one in my rucksack, you can have that one if you like?" Freddie took his rucksack off his shoulders, unzipped it and slid his hand inside thinking about an apple and pulled out a big red shiny one. "Here you are, William," he said holding it out for him to take.

William's face lit up like a firework display with a huge smile. "Oh, that apple is so big and shiny, can I really have it?"

"Of course you can," Freddie replied putting it in William's hand.

"Oh, that's so kind of you," William thanked him, still smiling like a Cheshire cat.

"So much kinder than Bully Bates," Jimmy said looking at the other end of the playground where Billy Bates sat on his own, glaring at them.

Freddie's class had a History lesson with Miss Viking in the afternoon. It was another of his favourite subjects, actually he really liked all the lessons. He could not understand why some children did not like school very much as there were so many things to learn about the world and how it worked. Today Miss Viking was going to teach them about the Romans and she showed them slides of Roman soldiers and told stories of their conquests. Everyone was fascinated because Miss Viking was an excellent storyteller, she could do all the different voices and actions, bringing her stories to life. She would jump up in the air with a pretend sword to fight off the Romans' enemies, one time when she jumped up her foot twisted as she landed and broke the heel of her shoe right off.

"Oh dear! I got a bit excited there children, didn't I?" She picked up her shoe in one hand and the broken heel in the other, wondering what to do.

The whole class looked straight at Freddie.

He stood up and said, "Miss, I think I have something in my rucksack to help with that."

Everyone in his class cheered, except Billy Bates, who was glaring even more at Freddie when he unzipped his rucksack and fished out a tube of Dinosaur Glue.

"We have to put a small dab on each part then put them back together and say Abracadabra," he explained to Miss Viking, who could not help grinning at her little knight in shining armour.

Of course everyone laughed again when Freddie told his teacher how to use it.

"Is it magic glue then?" Miss Viking asked.

Freddie giggled and replied, "I don't know Miss, but it mended my Mum's wooden mixing spoon."

So Miss Viking placed a dab of Dinosaur Glue on each part of her shoe heel and put them together.

Then everyone chanted, "ABRACADABRA!" and laughed, all except Billy Bates, who sat with his arms crossed and a face like thunder.

When Miss Viking pulled on the mended heel it was stuck fast and she was amazed. "Freddie, this glue is wonderful, where did you get it from?"

Ah, this was awkward. Was he going to have to avoid telling the truth again?

Jimmy stood and called out, "Freddie has lots of stuff in his rucksack Miss, that's why we all call him Freddie Fixit, cause he fixes lots of things."

That saved Freddie's bacon, he hated not telling the truth, but he had to protect his secret at all costs, even if it meant telling a little lie.

"That's wonderful, Freddie, it looks like you're a popular little boy. Thank you for fixing my shoe, Freddie Fixit," she chuckled and Freddie blushed just as the school bell rang for the end of the day.

Everyone gathered around Freddie as they left the classroom, except Billy Bates, he decided he did not like Freddie Fixit Fountain at all. 'Why am I not popular like him? It's not fair,' Billy thought, 'not fair at all when Freddie has so many friends and I have none.'

When Freddie returned home from school, he ran upstairs like a herd of elephants and changed from his school uniform into his play clothes. As it was a warm sunny afternoon he was going to play in the garden. At the bottom of Freddie's garden was 'his forest' as he called it, or sometimes it was a jungle full of elephants and wild animals, he loved to play and explore in and around the trees and bushes. Today though, Freddie was still excited about the Romans from his history lesson and from his rucksack he pulled out a toy sword and small shield. In his imagination he was a Roman Centurion fighting off the enemies of the Roman Empire. He swung his sword in the air, then jabbed and poked at his pretend enemy. He was having great fun fighting off the barbarians that Miss Viking had told them about in the lesson, when he heard a loud hissing sound.

"Psssssst! Psssssst!"

Freddie stopped and listened, it sounded like steam whooshing or something, he looked around completely puzzled. "Who's there?" he called, dropping his sword and shield.

"Psssssst! Psssssst!" he heard again, then spotted something between the wooden slats of the fence at the end of the garden. He dashed over and laughed. "Wiggly, what are you doing here?"

"Shush!" Wiggly said holding his finger to his lips. "I sneaked out. We're not supposed to come this far, but I've got something important to show you." His legs were jumping up and down like he was running on the spot as he spoke, but he held onto the fence and his head stayed still.

Freddie grabbed his rucksack and opened the gate to meet his friend.

Wiggly took hold of Freddie's hand and led him away into the woods.

They had not gone very far when Wiggly stopped and said, "Look, Freddie, look!" he was pointing to their right hand side.

Freddie looked. "What am I looking at, Wiggly?" he asked, "I don't see anything."

Wiggly jumped up and down again excitedly. "Exactly, exactly! That's my point, I don't see anything either!"

Freddie looked at Wiggly and gave him a curious smile. "I don't get it, Wiggly?" he replied.

"No, but somebody got it, come and look closer," Wiggly said, dragging Freddie further off to the right.

"Oh my goodness!" Freddie cried. "Who could have done such a thing? This is terrible, it's not right, they are not allowed to do this, my Dad said so!" Freddie was so alarmed at what he was seeing, or not seeing more importantly, as they both looked down at three tree stumps.

Someone had cut down three very old trees almost to the ground and stolen them, there was no trace of any branches, just piles of leaves and twigs.

"Who did this, Wiggly, do you know?"

Wiggly scratched his head under his pointy hat. "We felt the ground shaking yesterday, but no one dared come up until things went quiet again and we discovered these trees had all gone. These trees were hundreds of years old, Freddie. It has started again, Sproggles are cutting down our trees again!" Wiggly was very upset and tears dripped from his eyes.

"I'll have to tell my Dad, see if we can discover who and why they are doing this. You go back home and stay safe, tell your parents that I am going to get my Dad to find out what he can, okay?"

Wiggly's tears dried up and he smiled, then gave his friend a big hug. "Thank you, Freddie, I knew you would help, bye now," he said as he waved, skipping back to the big old oak tree.

Freddie took off his rucksack and pulled out a ball of bright yellow string and tied it to one of the tree stumps. He unwound the string as he made his way back to his home, he wanted to make sure he could find the exact spot again.

As soon as his father returned home, Freddie was very excited and wanted to take him into the woods straight away. "Please Dad, something terrible is happening in the forest!" he pleaded.

His father could see Freddie was very upset about something and agreed to go with him.

Freddie had hold of his father's hand and was pulling him along. "Hold your horses there Freddie, we don't want to trip over and get hurt, let's take it a bit more steadily."

He knew his father was right and they slowed down and followed the path of the yellow string which Freddie had left.

When they reached the end of the string, Freddie's father saw the three tree stumps. He cried out, "Oh my gosh, Freddie! This is very serious because these woods are protected, they can never be cut down. Well done son," he praised, giving Freddie a gentle pat on his head. "I will call the council, we need to find out who is doing this quickly and stop them."

Freddie's father took out his mobile phone and photographed the tree stumps, then they returned home. Freddie was asking all kinds of questions about the forest and why they were protected and who would cut the trees down. His father was on the telephone straight away to the council members to report the missing trees.

Freddie was very keen to find out what was going on and was again full of questions as they enjoyed their teatime meal.

"It looks like we have tree poachers in our woodland. Apparently it has been happening all over the country because wood is now so expensive that criminals are cutting down and stealing ancient trees. The wood from these trees is highly prized and can make a lot of money when sold," Freddie's father explained.

"How can we stop them then, Dad? Freddie asked. "We have to stop any more of our trees from being stolen."

"I have arranged for several council members to take turns patrolling the forest during the night, the culprits will be back to take more trees if they think they have got away with the three they have already stolen. If we can catch them then we can prevent any more of our lovely trees from being cut down," Freddie's father explained to him.

"Oh, can I come, Dad, please?" Freddie pleaded.

"I'm sorry son, it's too dangerous, the criminals may have weapons," he replied.

Freddie and his mother looked worried. "Will you be alright, Dad? You won't get hurt will you? You must be careful!" Freddie was almost in tears, he loved his father so much and did not want him getting hurt.

Mr Fountain patted his son on the head lovingly. "Yes, Freddie, William's father and I are going on patrol tonight and we will be very careful, the police are on standby and we have walkie-talkies direct to them," his father explained.

Both Freddie and his mother were very pleased to hear that, they did not want him getting hurt or anything worse.

Freddie hardly slept that night, he kept waking up thinking he could hear a noise from the forest. When he looked out of his window he thought he could see a torchlight flashing here and there. "I hope Dad and William's dad are safe," he whispered, to no one in particular. Then returned to his bed, snuggled under the warm duvet and fell fast asleep.

When morning finally arrived Freddie was up and out of bed really early. He got washed and dressed then ran down the stairs like a herd of elephants. He needed to see his father and make sure he was not hurt. When he dashed into the kitchen he was relieved to see both his parents sitting at the table talking. Freddie ran to his father and wrapped his arms around him in a huge hug. "I'm so glad you're safe, Dad. I was dreaming about you last night, I woke up and looked out of my window and I'm sure I saw lights flashing in the forest!" Freddie gabbled after he let his father go.

Both his parents chuckled at Freddie, whom they loved very much and were so proud of. He seemed to be liked by everyone who knew him, it is something all parents want of their children.

"Come, sit down, Freddie," his mother urged.

It was only then that Freddie noticed something. "Dad, you have a cut on your face!" he said with concern.

"Oh yes, I was going to put a sticking plaster on it, but we seem to have run out of them," his father replied.

Freddie's face lit up. "Oh, Dad, I have just the thing in my rucksack." He had dropped it on the floor when he hugged his father, so he bent down to unzip it, then felt inside and imagined a box of sticking plasters. When he lifted his hand out he was holding a box of them. He soon found a big enough plaster, pulled off the tabs and stuck on his father's wound.

"That seems to be a magic rucksack, Freddie," his mother chuckled.

"Well done, Freddie, you really do fixit," his father laughed and hugged his son again.

"What happened in the woods, Dad?" Freddie asked before any more questions came up about his rucksack, which he zipped back up quickly.

His mother had no idea how right she was.

His father patted the chair next to him for Freddie to sit on. "I was just about to explain to your mother when you and that herd of elephants came down the stairs," his father said and laughed.

"Aww, Dad!" Freddie groaned, blushing.

"So I can tell you both at the same time now," his father added. "William's father and I went out at 10pm last night with our thick coats, torches and walkie-talkies and walked slowly around the forest. I had forgotten just how wonderful and old some of the trees are. We spotted a little den that had a sign declaring 'Freddie's Secret Base.'

Freddie's mother chuckled, "Not so secret now, Freddie," she said.

"Oh Mum," Freddie said shyly. "What happened next, Dad?" he asked.

"Well everything was quiet for a long time, we heard owl's hooting and some hedgehogs grunting, then we came upon the tree stumps that you and I saw, having circled around for a while. Sometime after midnight we thought we heard some voices and followed to investigate. As we got closer there was a glow of lights in the distance and we could hear machines running too. So we approached very quietly and hid among the bushes, that's how I got my face scratched."

Freddie was so excited. "What did you see, Dad, was it the thieves?"

His father laughed. "Calm down son and I'll tell you, but you're right, it was the thieves," he replied.

"Oh! Who was it, did you recognise them?" Freddie asked almost jiggling off his seat.

"Shush and I'll tell you," his father said and his mother laughed. "What we saw, was two men, they had a kind of trailer with a generator and chainsaws, and they were about to cut down a beautiful ancient walnut tree that must be well over a hundred years old. I text my friend at the police station, we couldn't use the walkie-talkies without being heard by the thieves. My friend text back saying the police were on their way and to leave my phone switched on so they could find our location. William's father had brought a rucksack with him filled with a lot of stuff and he pulled out a small box with a domed light on the top and gave me a police whistle. When he turned the box on, the dome on top started flashing like a blue police light and a siren sounded while I blew the whistle, we had to stop them from starting to cut that tree down."

Freddie was off his chair by now, standing by his father holding onto his arm he was so excited.

"What happened, Dad?"

"Let your father finish, Freddie!" his mother laughed.

His father continued. "The two men dropped everything and scarpered, they ran like frightened rabbits, leaving all the lights on and machines running. So William's father and I walked over to the area, fortunately we were in time and they had not started cutting into the tree. We turned off the machines but left the lights on so the police could locate us more easily, they arrived about fifteen minutes later. The police took all the equipment away with them to the Police Station."

"So did the thieves get away? That's a shame, they might try again," Freddie said answering his own question.

His father laughed. "Well not quite. They did run off, that's true, but William's father and I recognised both men."

Freddie was jumping up and down with excitement, like when he needed to go to the toilet. "Oh, who was it? Do I know them? Have they been arrested?"

"Hold your horses, son," his father chuckled.

"But I haven't got any horses, Dad," Freddie said with a screwed up face.

"It's just a saying, Freddie, it means wait and see," his mother laughed.

"Yes, son, they have now been arrested. The trees they stole a couple of nights ago were still on their property, cut up into smaller logs ready to sell. The men, yes you do know them, it was Billy Bates' father, Robin and his younger brother, Robby."

Freddie was shocked and then said, "Hang on, Dad, I didn't know Billy Bates had a younger brother?"

Both his parents laughed. "No, not Billy Bates brother, silly sausage, but the brother of Billy's father, Billy Bates' uncle. They had a lot of trees on their property between them and tried to tell the police that they were all trees blown down by the wind, but the police were having none of that, charged them with theft and kept them in the police cell for now. I expect they will be allowed to go free until the trial if someone can raise the £1000 bail money."

"I don't understand what that means, Dad, what is bail money?" Freddie asked looking a bit confused.

His father explained that when someone is arrested they might be allowed to go home until their trial, provided they've only committed a small crime, like stealing a bottle of milk. If it is a serious crime, like hurting someone or stealing something that is very valuable, then the magistrate may let the person go home to wait for their trial, if someone or they themselves can pay the bail money and guarantee they will turn up for their trial. If they fail to turn up for their trial the court keeps the bail money and instruct the police to arrest that person again.

"What happens if they do turn up for their trial then?" Freddie asked.

"In that case the bail money is returned."

"Wow! That all sounds very complicated, it's much easier to be good and kind. I don't understand why some people choose to be bad!" Freddie replied.

**

Billy Bates did not return to school the next day or any day ever again. Freddie heard the family had moved away and he felt a little bit guilty because he was not sorry he would not see Billy Bates again. No one had really liked him because he was always bullying and hurting other children, stealing things and being nasty to them as well.

When Saturday arrived, Freddie asked his parents if he could go play in the forest.

His mother and father said he should keep an eye out, but thought the forest was safe enough now the thieves had been caught.

Freddie put on his play clothes and rucksack, then hopped, skipped and jumped all the way to the big old oak tree. He placed his palm on the big old oak tree trunk and spoke the magic words, "Efum, Efum, Natum, Efum."

When the door appeared and opened he dashed inside making sure it closed behind him, then ran down the stairs excitedly. He was out of breath when he reached the bottom and had to rest for a moment before repeating the magic words again to open the door into Elfin Town. He ran along the road waving at everyone as he passed them by, not stopping until he reached the Tiggly's house. When Wiggly invited Freddie inside, he was puffing and panting trying to catch his breath for ages.

Giggly and Wiggly were highly amused and chuckled at their new friend.

When Freddie told the whole family the good news about the tree thieves being caught they cheered, celebrating the saving of their precious forest. The news spread around the town very quickly and Elfins gathered outside the Tiggly's house to congratulate Freddie. When he went outside they all clapped their hands and cheered, singing, 'For he's a jolly good Sproggle,' Freddie smiled and felt a little embarrassed, his face turning bright red.

The Town Elder approached Freddie and shook his hand. "Well done, Freddie, you're our hero, saving the trees is so important, they give us the air we breathe and the food we eat."

"That's very kind of you, Mr Bumble, and every one," Freddie replied, "but my father is the real hero. He and his friend patrolled the woods until they caught the thieves."

Mr Bumble presented Freddie with a beautiful round stone that looked like it had fairy dust trapped inside it. "Keep this as a reminder of our friendship, Freddie, it is a special Fairy stone," he said.

Freddie was so pleased to receive it, "Oh! It's so beautiful," he replied.

"When you look at it at night-time you will be able to see the Fairies as they used to be," added Mr Bumble.

After everyone had returned to their own homes, Freddie said to Wiggly, "I can see why Mr Bumble is called that, when he wears his black and yellow striped jumper he reminds me of a bumble bee!"

They had a little laugh then the Tiggly family took Freddie up above ground into the forest and to the trees that had been cut down.

Daddly brought out the jar of Fairy Dust from his bag and took the last pinch that was left inside and sprinkled a little on each of the tree stumps.

"This is the last of the Fairy Dust," Daddly said sadly. "Let's stand well back now everyone," he added.

Freddie looked confused. "What's happening?" he asked Wiggly.

"Oh Freddie, this is so exciting. Just watch, it's incredible. You'll see, it's unbelievable," Wiggly replied, his little legs running on the spot.

Suddenly the ground around them began to tremble, just a little bit to start with, then it really began to shake. Leaves lying on the ground jiggled up and down, as did small stones and bits of soil.

Mummly looked at them with a big grin on her face and said, "It's starting, children."

Like some magical miracle the three tree stumps began to twinkle and sparkle. The ground around them trembled and shook like an earthquake. The Fairy Dust began to swirl round and round like a 'Catherine Wheel firework,' rising up slowly. Then the three tree stumps began to grow taller, very slowly, as the Fairy Dust rose up into the air.

"Hey, the stumps, they're getting taller!" Freddie said excitedly.

Sure enough, the three stumps grew higher and higher, sprouting branches and leaves as they reached toward the blue sky. Everyone looked up and watched the leaves and flowers unfold and Freddie thought it the most beautiful thing he had ever seen. When everything finished, the three trees looked exactly like they had before they were cut down.

"Wow. Now that really is magical!" Freddie cried. "That Fairy Dust is powerful stuff."

Daddly looked at him and smiled, "You're right, Freddie, but that is the last of it in the whole town. There are no more Fairies, the Sproggles wiped them out many years ago," he explained.

Freddie felt ashamed of all the humans and what they had done. He just could not understand why people did bad things, it was so much more rewarding to do good things, people liked you and if you helped them, then one day they might help you in return. Best of all, when Freddie helped someone it made him feel so happy inside, it was the best feeling ever!

* *

Back at home Freddie asked his parents if there were such beings as Fairies.

"Now that's a strange question son," his father replied. "Fairies are not real, they are mythical beings like Unicorns and Elves," his father added.

Freddie knew some of this could not be true. "Did they never ever exist then, Dad?" he asked.

His father looked at his son and smiled. "I don't really know, Freddie, some parts of our history are not very clear, such as magic, wizards and witches. I suppose it is possible they may have existed a long, long time ago. The legend of the wizard Merlin and King Arthur is well known, but there is no real proof that either existed. Some people believe that Fairies and magic do exist. For me to see a tiny little seed grow into an enormous tree, well that's magic, it's truly wonderful. On the other hand, if things were not true, why would we know about them in the first place?"

Freddie furrowed his brow with what his father had told him. "How would we know about them if they were not true?" he said to himself quietly.

That night Freddie lay in his bed before going to sleep trying to make sense of everything he knew and what his father had said, *'How would we know about them if they were not true.'* He rubbed his chin and talked to his hands. "I know Fairies must have lived because Daddly said that the Fairy Dust was from Fairies. I know magic is true because I have a magic rucksack and I have seen how magic made the stolen trees re-grow. Therefore the stories about Wizard Merlin must be true too. Yes, of course, the Elfins talk of *the great wizard.* Could that have been Merlin?"

Freddie smiled to himself, it was beginning to make sense to him and he reached over to pick up the Fairy stone that Mr Bumble had presented to him. It glowed a very pale green. He looked at it closely, blinked his eyes and thought something moved inside. "W-what was that?" he whispered. The more he stared at the Fairy stone, the brighter it became and more things inside it began moving. He could not take his eyes off the glowing stone, it was like he was looking into another world. "Wow," he whispered, "this is like magic!" Freddie brought the Fairy stone closer to his eyes and stared, now he could definitely see things inside it, like tiny, tiny butterflies. "Oh gosh!" They're not butterflies at all," he gasped quietly. "They're tiny people with beautiful twinkling wings." Then Freddie remembered what Mr Bumble had said when he gave the Fairy stone to him. *'When you look at it at night-time you will be able to see the Fairies as they used to be.'* As he watched he began to realise that Fairy Dust was actually falling from the Fairies wings as they fluttered, making the ground underneath them twinkle and sparkle. "So that's where Fairy Dust comes from," he whispered to himself. Freddie yawned and lay back on his pillow, just managing to put the Fairy stone on his bedside cupboard before falling asleep.

Lovely dreams of beautiful glittering Fairies flying around the fields and woodlands doing magical things filled his slumber. In his sleep filled mind, Freddie could not understand why Sproggles would want to get rid of Fairies and magic. Why were they so afraid? Maybe he never would understand.

CHAPTER TWO

The Crystal Cavern

Freddie and Wiggly's discovery changes their lives forever.

On Sunday morning Freddie decided to go on an adventure in *his* jungle, so he put on his explorer's clothes and rucksack, of course. His mother packed his favourite, jam sandwiches, a chocolate bar and an orange drink to put in his rucksack.

Before he left the kitchen his mother reminded him, "Have you put your watch on, Freddie, and remember to be home before tea at five o'clock, okay?"

Freddie smiled and held up his arm showing his wristwatch, then gave her a hug and set off. He closed the kitchen door behind him and trotted off down the garden, through the gate and into 'his' wonderful forest. "I wonder if I will see any wild beasties today? Maybe a family of rabbits," he chuckled, to no none in particular, as he poked the bushes with his magic staff.

The sun was shining through the trees creating beams of light as if a tall giant was shining lots of torches from above. One of the sunbeams shone on an amazingly big bushy bush covered in pretty yellow flowers. As Freddie got closer he could smell the lovely perfume of the flowers, it was just like oranges being peeled.

"Oooh, this bush smells so lovely," he said, to no one in particular.

"You can eat my flowers!" a squeaky voice announced, which seemed to come from the bush.

Freddie jumped back in surprise. "What's this, a bush that can talk? Can you really talk Mr Bush? Can I really eat your flowers?" He moved closer to the bush, uncertain about it talking.

"You can eat my flowers, but not too many, they are very sweet!" the bush replied.

Freddie stared in disbelief. He was talking to a bush, or rather the bush was talking to him. He scratched his head under his wide brimmed hat and chuckled to himself.

"Are you a magic bush, Mr Bush?" he asked.

"Yes, but only for you, Freddie," the bush replied.

Freddie was startled and jumped back again. "H-how do you know my name, Mr Bush?" he stuttered.

"We all know you, Freddie, you are our hero," the squeaky voice replied.

Freddie could not believe his ears and got close enough to hold one of the flowers and sniff the lovely smell of oranges being peeled.

"Oh, that tickles, Freddie!" the bush giggled.

Freddie stepped back again and put his hands on his hips, looking intently and disbelievingly at the bush. Now he really was completely confused. Then he noticed the bush was shaking. "Oh! Mr Bush, are you frightened?" he asked.

The bush giggled some more.

"Wait a minute! Wait a minute!" Freddie cried out. "I know that voice. Wiggly, is that you playing games with me?"

The bush giggled and shook again, then Wiggly jumped out and made Freddie jump as well.

"Oh! Wiggly you tricked me and made me jump out of my skin. How did you know I was in the forest?"

Wiggly skipped up to Freddie and gave his friend a hug. "I was coming to find you when I heard you talking, but I couldn't see anyone with you, so I hid behind this bush to watch and make sure you were alone. When you walked up to it I couldn't resist a bit of fun," he said chuckling.

"That was so clever, Wiggly, I really thought it was a magic bush talking to me until your giggles gave you away," Freddie replied.

"Actually," Wiggly said smiling, "you can eat these flowers, but not too many as they will make you feel sick as they are so sweet. Have a taste," Wiggly said handing a flower to his friend.

"Oooh, that does taste nice, just like oranges," Freddie observed.

"What are oranges?" Wiggly asked.

Freddie lifted his rucksack down, unzipped it and felt inside while thinking about the fruit then pulled out a big juicy orange and gave it to Wiggly. "This is an orange, it's a fruit from a country where the weather is very hot. You peel the skin off and eat the juicy bits inside, try it."

Wiggly used his thin fingers with sharp nails to peel off the orange skin.

"Now put your thumb down the middle and open out the segments," Freddie told his friend.

"Oh! Ah! Oh!" Wiggly cried, as juice from the orange squirted everywhere, all over his face and straight in his right eye.

Freddie howled with laughter watching Wiggly jumping about and shouting. He pulled out a wet face cloth from his rucksack for Wiggly to wipe away the sticky juice. "Now peel off one segment and put it in your mouth, then suck out the juice and swallow the rest," Freddie instructed.

"Oh! This tastes toowabbyfabby!" Wiggly cried and gobbled another segment. He liked it so much he ate the whole orange. "Oh Freddie, that was delicious! You must let Mummly, Daddly and Giggly try some too." Wiggly laughed. "Oooh, my hands are all sticky and smell delicious!" He chuckled while wiping them with the wet face cloth.

"Does this bush have a name?" Freddie asked.

"We call it the 'buzzy bush,'" Wiggly replied.

"That's a funny name," Freddie said with a grin.

"It's because when the sun shines, the insects flock to the bush and drink the sweet nectar from the flowers and the bush buzzes, listen," Wiggly replied.

Freddie could hear the insects already and nodded with a smile. "Well 'buzzy bush' it is then," he replied. "How do you know it's safe to eat the flowers, they might make you unwell?" he asked.

Wiggly smiled, looking pleased with himself. "There are a lot of plants that are not good to eat, that's true, but we Elfin's discovered the safe ones many years ago. You must ask an adult about plants that are safe to eat before trying them though. Tell all your friends that too, otherwise they could become very unwell," Wiggly replied.

Freddie nodded in agreement then asked, "Oh, Wiggly, why did you come looking for me?"

"Oh, yes! I nearly forgot. Actually it's something very exciting." Wiggly's legs were running on the spot while telling Freddie. "I have something to show you, you'll be so amazed. Quickly, follow me!" Wiggly chuckled, taking Freddie's hand and pulling him towards the big old oak tree.

When the door opened into Elfin Town, lots of people were moving around and chatting to each other. As soon as they noticed Freddie and Wiggly, they called out to them.

"Hello Freddie! Hello Wiggly!" Shouted Mr Plum.

The boys both waved back to him. "Hello Mr Plum, where's Mrs Plum today?" Freddie asked.

Mr Plum smiled and replied, "Oh, she's at home looking after Victoria and Blue." Freddie already knew Victoria was Mr and Mrs Plum's daughter and Blue was their son.

Wiggly took Freddie towards his house and then walked past it.

"Oh! Aren't we going inside your house to say hello?" Freddie asked.

Wiggly laughed. "Oh no, this is much more interesting."

They travelled quite a distance, passing a lot of houses of all shapes and sizes, there was even one shaped like a boot.

"Who lives in this house?" Freddie asked curiously.

"That's Mr and Mrs Heel's home where Lacy and Stud live, you've met them already haven't you?" Wiggly answered.

Freddie nodded, he remembered Lacy, she really liked him and hung on his arm whenever they were together. Freddie sniggered, he thought it was cute and he did not mind her clinging to him, much better than the likes of Bully Bates. "We've never been this far away from the houses before," Freddie said to Wiggly. Looking back the way they had walked they could only see the town in the distance.

"Look!" Wiggly cried excitedly, stopping suddenly.

"Ooof!" Freddie cried as he bumped into Wiggly, turning round from looking at the town to see why Wiggly had stopped and what he was so excited about.

In front of them was the outside wall of the town. It looked smooth and shiny, but more importantly there was a big wooden door that was taller than Freddie's father.

"Where are we and where does this door lead to, Wiggly?" Freddie asked. He was a bit puzzled as to why there would be a door in a wall of stone. Next to the door was a bench seat made from a long flat rock and Wiggly pulled his friend down to sit with him.

"After those Sproggles cut down our trees the other day, the Elfin Council had a meeting and Daddly is one of the Council Elders. They decided to check out our emergency escape tunnel, as it had not been inspected for a very long time. Daddly said he could not recall the tunnel being checked and he's nearly a hundred years old. They thought there might even have been a cave-in and the tunnel could be blocked and that would be no use if we needed to escape in the future.

45

Freddie sat up and looked at Wiggly. "Did you just say that Daddly is nearly a hundred years old?"

Wiggly nodded, "Mmmm!"

"Wow," Freddie cried, "that's totally amazing, he doesn't look that old at all."

Wiggly laughed, "We Elfins can live to be three or four hundred years old or even older."

Freddie thought for a moment before replying. "That means Daddly is not really that old then!" He was amazed because he had not given the age thing a thought until now. "So how old are you, Wiggly?" he asked.

Wiggly laughed again. "Oh! I'm only nineteen years old. How old are you?"

Freddie looked Wiggly up and down and scratched his head under his hat, and answered, "I'll soon be 11 years old, in another month."

Wiggly stood up and looked at his friend. "Goodness me! Sproggles are big for your age then. When I was ten years old I was half your size."

They both had a good laugh about it all, it made no difference to either of them, age was just a number, it was the friendship that was important.

"So is this the door to your escape tunnel then, Wiggly?" Freddie finally asked.

That started Wiggly jiggling with excitement again. "Yes, yes it is! Come let me show you, it will be amazing." Wiggly put the palm of his hand on the door then spoke the magic words and the door swung open all by itself.

The tunnel was dimly lit with little star-like crystals in the walls and ceiling. The two friends walked inside holding each other's hand. It seemed quite dark in the tunnel compared to outside and when they were too far inside the tunnel to run back and escape, the door closed shut and then everything seemed very dark. They were hardly able to see each other's faces.

Freddie let go of Wiggly's hand for a moment and took off his rucksack and unzipped the top. He created an image in his mind of two torches and when he pulled out his hand, to his constant surprise, there were exactly the two torches he had been thinking about. When they switched them on the whole tunnel lit up.

"This magic is so amazing, Wiggly. I just have to think of something and it appears inside my rucksack, it's really cool!" Freddie's voice was full of excitement and wonder.

"I know what you mean, Freddie, even though magic is not uncommon for Elfins, it's still kind of incredible that things can change or appear, especially with Fairy Dust," Wiggly chuckled.

Freddie noticed the walls looked hard and glossy. "What is going on with the walls, Wiggly, they almost look wet?"

Wiggly moved to the wall on his side and put his hand on it. "Look, it's not wet. It's a special enchantment to prevent anyone, especially Sproggles, breaking into the tunnel. The Wizard made this tunnel, that's why the ceiling is so high," he replied.

Freddie looked at his watch and it was nearly 10 o'clock. "Come on, let's get going."

Wiggly nodded and took hold of Freddie's hand, then they began to walk at a steady pace, the bright light from their torches made the journey much easier.

"This tunnel seems to be sloping downwards a little bit, Wiggly, shouldn't it be going upwards?" Freddie asked his friend as they walked along.

"Yes, that is a bit curious, but this tunnel goes under your town right over to the woodlands on the other side," Wiggly replied.

They seemed to be walking in a straight line, but there appeared to be no end in sight.

When Freddie looked at his watch again he cried, "Crickey! We've been walking for over half an hour, Wiggly, let's have a rest."

They sat down on the stone floor and leaned against the wall, then Freddie took out the orange juice and chocolate bar and shared them with Wiggly.

"Oh, this is really nice. What do you call it?" Wiggly asked.

"It's chocolate, it says on the wrapper, **Creamy Milk Chocolate**," Freddie replied looking at the paper that had been wrapped around the chocolate bar. "But I don't know how they make it from milk," he added.

Having enjoyed the snack and drink, they carried on and finally reached the end of the tunnel and yet another door.

"Does this lead to the outside then, Wiggly?" Freddie asked.

"No, but you will see where it does lead in a minute, it's really exciting!" Wiggly replied, jiggling his feet and running on the spot in anticipation. "This is the exciting part!" He placed the palm of his hand on the door and spoke some magic words and it swung open into a bright area beyond. "Come on!" Wiggly called, pulling Freddie along and through the doorway.

Once inside they found themselves standing in a large circular room that had a high ceiling like the inside of an upside down bowl. There were five doors as tall as the doors in a Sproggle's house and as soon as they stepped into the room the door they had walked through closed behind them.

"Where are we?" Freddie asked, turning off his torch and looking around in wonder.

"Daddly said this is the safety chamber, only one door leads outside through another tunnel, three doors lead to booby trapped tunnels and the other to somewhere special only Elfins can go," he replied.

"How can you tell which door is which?" Freddie asked.

"Oh, that's easy. The three doors that are booby trapped have a skull and crossbones on them, just there." Wiggly pointed to the middle of the three booby-trapped doors.

"But I don't see anything on the doors, Wiggly," Freddie replied.

"That's because they're magic symbols only Elfins can see, it's an extra layer of safety, Daddly said."

Freddie looked confused, rubbed his forehead and asked, "So which door do we go through?"

"This one," Wiggly said excitedly. He put his palm on the door and said the magic words. "Natum, Renata, Nepo, Rood."

The door creaked open inwards to another brightly lit chamber.

"How did you know those words?" Freddie asked as Wiggly pulled him through into the next chamber.

Wiggly giggled. "It's written on the door, but ...."

".... Only Elfins can see them." Freddie finished Wiggly's sentence and chuckled.

This room was very different and Freddie stood looking in amazement, his eyes wide open, he certainly had not expected to see all this.

Wiggly was so excited, his little legs were running on the spot again. "Isn't this something?" Wiggly chuckled seeing his friend's expression.

This room was huge, also with a ceiling like the inside of an upside down bowl, but it was light blue like the Elfin Town sky, making it very bright, like daylight. There was a big fireplace with old blackened burnt out logs, dusty rugs on the dusty floor and various types of chairs, some soft and cosy, others hard and uninviting. There was a big round table in the middle of the room with books and scrolls all covered in a thick layer of grey dust. By each side of the fireplace stood pots and pans stacked together with all kinds of spoons, but everything was covered in a really thick layer of dust.

"What is this place, Wiggly? Everything is bigger than the furniture at my home and yours, no Elfin or Sproggle lived here. Was it a giant?"

Wiggly was again jiggling his legs and feet. "Oh! I thought you'd never ask, Freddie," he said. "THIS!" he said holding out his hands, "this is where the Great Wizard lived, it was his final home before he disappeared!"

Freddie's jaw dropped open. "Wow! If this is where the Great Wizard lived, then WOW! Wiggly, he must have been tall, a giant even," he replied.

"Daddly told me the Great Wizard created the escape tunnel and this home for himself, less than a year before he vanished. He said the Great Wizard could see the future and that we would need this escape tunnel one day Then the Great Wizard said his goodbyes to all the Elfins and left us. When the tunnel door closed the Great Wizard was never seen again."

Freddie looked quite excited now and said, "I asked my Dad if Wizards and Fairies were real and he told me that he didn't really know for sure."

Wiggly looked at his friend. "Yes, yes, Freddie! Well now at least you know that Fairies and Wizards are real, just like Elfins and Goblins."

"Huh! You mean Goblins are real too?" Freddie announced.

"Oh yes of course and by all accounts they were not very nice. Anyway, they haven't been seen for hundreds of years," Wiggly replied. "Anyway, the Wizard left Elfin Town a long, long time ago, maybe three hundred years ago or even more and I don't think anyone has been down this tunnel since then," Wiggly told his friend.

Freddie looked around and asked, "Where do those two doors lead?"

Wiggly chuckled, his legs running on the spot again and said, "One is the Great Wizard's bed chamber and wash room. The other, well come and see, help me pull this door open," Wiggly said.

They grabbed the big round metal ring handle, the heavy door opened slowly as they pulled and it took them both to fully open it.

"This is so hard without magic!" Freddie said.

Once the door was open they stood looking into another huge room with blue-sky ceiling.

"Oh my goodness, Wiggly, this is just, it's just, unbelievable! Do you think the Great Wizard created his magic in here?"

Wiggly was nodding his head and pulling Freddie along inside, this time the door stayed open, it not being magical.

The room had two levels, with the upper level being like a wide balcony going all around the walls. It was covered in bookcases full of books of all shapes and sizes. The ground floor was like a laboratory, with a long bench against the wall and another long bench in the middle of the room. On them were tripods, boxes and bags, spiral see-through tubes, long and short clear cylinders, jars and jugs of stuff. Cabinets with glass doors against the other wall were filled with jars and bottles, tubes and flasks, the whole room was an Aladdin's cave of scientific bits and pieces. Everything was, of course, covered in a thick layer of dust, not even a mouse or a fly had disturbed it with their footprints.

Wiggly and Freddie clambered up the dusty spiral staircase to the balcony floor, then stood and looked down at the Great Wizard's laboratory.

"Wow! You were right, Wiggly, this is really exciting. Just think, we are standing in the very place that the Great Wizard lived and worked before he disappeared. Do you think he's still alive?" Freddie turned to his friend, wide eyed at the thought the Great Wizard might still be living.

Wiggly looked a little sad. "I don't think so or why would he have abandoned his Elfins?" he replied.

"Oh, well that's true. Still, this is proof that he did exist, because none of the Elfins that are living now have ever seen him, have they?" Freddie said trying to be a bit cheerful.

"Yes, Freddie, you are right, but I think there may be one or two Elfin's old enough to remember the Great Wizard," Wiggly replied feeling a bit brighter.

They clambered up a spiral staircase, laughing and tripping on the narrow steps, until they were standing on the balcony.

"Wow! Look at all these books, Wiggly, there has to be hundreds of them, even more than in my school library," Freddie announced.

"What's a library?" Wiggly asked.

"It's a special place with shelves like these, filled with all kinds of books. There are story books and science books, encyclopaedias, picture books and so many things to sit and read."

Wiggly pulled a book from a shelf and blew the dust off in a big cloud that made them both cough and laugh. He opened the book and then asked Freddie, "What is all this scribble on the pages?"

Freddie had a look. "I have no idea, but it looks a bit like sums," he replied.

"You mean like the four times table and stuff?" Wiggly smiled thinking about the times table tune his friend had taught them.

Freddie nodded, but could not understand any of it. Then he took a short fat book from the shelf and just opened it rather than getting a cloud of dust again. "Oooh, this looks like a spell book!"

Wiggly moved over to him to look. "What does it say, Freddie?"

"I can only read a few words, they don't make a lot of sense, look, 'Evol Noitop - Ekat eno yriaf tsud hcnip,' the words don't make sense unless it's a magic language perhaps?" Freddie guessed.

"That is strange, isn't it? Let's split up and look at a few others shall we?" Wiggly suggested.

They walked in opposite directions then both reached out and began lifting books down and opened pages. Here and there they saw something that looked familiar but mostly they could not understand anything.

Then Freddie spotted a golden book on the shelf and when he tried to take it, the book would not budge. "That's strange, why would a book be stuck to a shelf?" he said to himself. He tried again, but it did not even move a little bit. He put his foot on the bookcase and pulled with both hands and it moved a tiny bit at the top, as if it was fixed down at the bottom. "Wiggly!" Freddie shouted and his friend dashed round to him.

"What's the matter?" he asked.

"Give me a hand to pull this book off the shelf, it seems to be stuck."

"There are lots more books to look at, why not leave it?" Wiggly replied.

"No I can't! I must see what this is, it could be very important, Wiggly, please help me!"

Wiggly put his foot on the bookcase like Freddie and they both pulled hard.

"Oh! It's moving, keep pulling," Freddie cried.

Suddenly the book pulled away at the top, it was hinged at the bottom front corner, and they both fell to the floor of the balcony.

"Are you alright, Wiggly?"

"Yes, Freddie, are you?"

Freddie nodded and then cried, "Oh look! Only the top part of the book has come away!"

Suddenly there was a strange, whirring, mechanical, grinding sound.

"What is it, Freddie?" Wiggly whispered a little bit alarmed.

They grabbed each other's hands and listened, looking around for the source of the noise.

"It sounds like gears turning," Freddie whispered back.

An unexpected loud crack echoed and made them jump and cling together. The bookcase seemed to move a little bit.

"It's going to fall on us, Freddie!" cried Wiggly.

But a section of the bookcase began to move backwards, not forwards. The two friends watched it warily.

"Oh!" they both cried as the bookcase creaked and groaned and slowly began to move sideways behind the other bookshelves.

"Look, look!" cried Wiggly with a mixture of fear and excitement.

"It's a secret tunnel!" Freddie cried and his face lit up with this discovery.

Wiggly was really excited. They stood up and he was already running on the spot again. "Oooh Freddie! Do you think this is how the Great Wizard vanished?" he asked.

Freddie rummaged in his rucksack and pulled out the two torches again.

"I wonder why this tunnel is not lit up like the other tunnel?" Wiggly asked.

"I guess it was never intended to be used again like the others. We were lucky to have discovered it, otherwise it may have remained a secret forever!" Freddie replied.

"Oh, yes! I think you must be right, Freddie. Do you think it's safe? Oh! Maybe it's booby trapped!" Wiggly replied, suddenly a little concerned.

They looked at each other and Freddie asked, "What kind of traps are in the other tunnels?"

Wiggly thought for a moment. "I think Daddly said that part of the floor is magical, it looks solid but it is really a very, very deep chasm that cannot be crossed over, so invaders would fall in. Oh, then another chasm opens behind them so that there is no way to escape by going backwards either!"

"Wow, that sounds terrible," Freddie cringed. "Those people would just starve to death, that's horrible!"

"Yes, that would be terrible, Freddie, but Daddly told me when they fall into the chasm, the magic transports them far away outside without any memory of being in the tunnels."

"Ah! That is clever, but I think we need to find a long stick to poke the ground just in case," Freddie said.

Wiggly chuckled, "Oh! No need, the magic can be seen by Elfins, so I can see the trap and have magic words to make them safe, I just remembered that."

They set off down the dark tunnel, the walls seemed to absorb the light from the torches so they could not see too far ahead.

"This tunnel is really tall, the Great Wizard must have been very tall too," Freddie observed as they walked slowly, hand in hand. "The tunnel is sloping downwards quite quickly, Wiggly, we're going down even deeper!"

Wiggly looked at Freddie, then the floor again. "Wait!" Wiggly cried. "I see it, I see the chasm edge to the booby trap!"

"I only see a solid floor, Wiggly," Freddie answered. "Can you remember the magic words?"

Wiggly thought hard, put the palm of his hand on the wall and said, *Uno Wollasu Ytefas!* He jumped up and down again. "It worked, it worked, Freddie, we can go on now!"

Freddie was not so certain and poked the floor with the pole they had found in the Great Wizard's laboratory.

"I'll go first," Wiggly volunteered and pulled Freddie behind him at arms length. Freddie knew he would not let his friend fall if the spell had not worked.

"Are we past the chasm yet, Wiggly?" Freddie asked.

Wiggly stopped and chuckled. "Oh yes, it's well behind us now," he replied and they walked on side by side travelling deeper and lower.

Freddie asked, "Do you have any idea in what direction we are heading?"

Wiggly stopped and closed his eyes, licked his finger and held it in the air.

"What are you doing?" Freddie laughed.

"We Elfins can sense direction, which is useful when tunnelling," he replied.

"Oh! That is clever, Sproggles need to use a compass, I have one in my rucksack," Freddie suddenly thought and took it from one of the pockets. "That's funny," Freddie declared, "the needle is spinning round and round!"

"Doesn't matter, Freddie," Wiggly laughed. "I think we are close to being under the mountain on the other side of your town."

"Oh Wiggly," Freddie giggled. "That's not a mountain, it's a very high hill, and the villagers call it a mount-hill."

They both laughed and it echoed eerily in the dark tunnel.

"Someone else is following us!" Wiggly announced, pulling them to a halt.

"That was our voices bouncing off the walls, Wiggly, it's called an echo," Freddie explained giggling. They continued, steadily walking onwards until they came to a dead end, the tunnel just seemed to stop, no doorway, no junction, nothing. "This is very strange," Freddie observed. "Why would the Great Wizard have a secret tunnel that was a dead end, it doesn't make any sense to me?"

"I don't understand either, Freddie, it's as if whoever built this tunnel just stopped making it and left. Why would they lay that trap we passed a while ago?" Wiggly puzzled, scratching his head. Then he walked up to the dead end and put his hand on it. "It feels solid enough," he said tapping the wall, "it sounds solid enough too!"

"Do you think the Great Wizard is playing tricks, like it's actually a door but in disguise to fool anyone who might just find this tunnel?" Freddie asked. "How about trying your magic words, it might open like the other doors," he suggested.

Wiggly placed his hand on the wall and spoke the magic words, but nothing happened.

"I guess we'll have to go back then," Freddie said disappointedly. He turned to walk away, but Wiggly did not move, he was thinking.

"Are you coming?" Freddie asked, turning to see if Wiggly was following. He saw Wiggly with his hand still on the wall and chanting, *"Snifles Yams Sap Ylefas."*

"What are you doing, Wiggly?" No sooner had he asked the question, that he got his answer.

The wall began to open, piece by piece, like taking pieces away from a jigsaw puzzle. Behind the opening a light was becoming increasingly brighter until the two friends could no longer look at it and had to turn their eyes away.

"How did you know?" Freddie asked while they stood with their backs to the intense light.

"I just remembered, long ago we had a different magic word for the big old oak tree door. It was the old password that opened the wall," Wiggly replied.

"Way to go, Wiggly! You are clever. Just when we thought this was the end, you saved our exploration, but that light coming from the doorway is far too bright."

They switched off their torches and put them in Freddie's rucksack. Then he thought about something to protect their eyes and magically pulled out two pairs of sunglasses.

Wiggly put on the sunglasses Freddie had given him and sniggered at Freddie when he put his sunglasses on.

"What's so funny?" Freddie asked.

"You look quite funny with those on, I can't see your eyes, just funny shaped black holes," Wiggly replied then grabbed his friends hand. "Come on, let's go explore." He was excited again and his little legs were running on the spot.

Ahead of them was another tunnel, but they could not see how long it was due to the bright light at the end of it. They walked slowly, hand in hand with Wiggly slightly ahead. Both friends were very excited and their eyes slowly adjusted to the light while wearing the sunglasses.

"These are very clever, what are they?" Wiggly asked.

Freddie chuckled. "They are called sunglasses. When the sun is very bright we wear them to stop our eyes hurting," he replied.

While Freddie was explaining, Wiggly had suddenly stopped and Freddie bumped into him again.

"Ooof!" Wiggly cried as they collided.

"Ooof!" Freddie cried, "why did you just st......." Freddie did not get a chance to finish his question because he was looking at the same thing as Wiggly.

The two friends, still holding hands, stood side-by-side, motionless, wide eyed and stunned.

Freddie had never seen anything like it ever, not on television, or even in a book.

Wiggly just stood staring with his mouth open, unable to speak.

"What do you think it is?" Freddie eventually asked in a low whisper.

Wiggly was shaking his head slowly, he had no idea.

"It's so big, it's enormous, as big as a sky scraper!" Freddie whispered.

Wiggly laughed and turned to his friend. "What's a sky scraper? You surely can't scrape the sky it's too high up?"

Freddie laughed loudly and his voice echoed. "Ha, ha, ha! - Ha, ha, ha! - Ha, ha, ha!" Then he said more quietly, "No, silly, a skyscraper is a very tall building with lots and lots of floors, maybe as many as 20 or even more."

Wiggly nodded again and returned his gaze.

"It's the biggest, the widest, the tallest I have ever seen," Freddie whispered.

"Look, look," whispered Wiggly. "Look at those glittering shiny crystals, they're everywhere. Oh look, there's more over there too." Some of them were almost as tall as him and lots more were smaller, the whole place was filled with crystals. "It's so pretty," Wiggly whispered.

They were both spellbound looking into the enormous cavern. It was so tall they could not see the ceiling, so long and deep they could not see the sides. A narrow winding pathway led downwards from the tunnel entrance where they were standing, snaking around the hundreds of sparkling red and blue, yellow and green crystals. A mixture of fear and excitement ran through their bodies and minds.

"You're shaking, Wiggly," Freddie whispered.

"I know. Can you feel it, like you are looking at something incredibly important?" Wiggly whispered back.

"Yes, yes, I do like, like, the King and Queen might just appear," Freddie replied and realised that he too was trembling. "My Mum has a ring on her finger with the same red glittering crystal in it, Dad told me it is her engagement ring and the crystal was a ruby. He said it was worth a lot of money, just think how much these would be worth?" Freddie whispered to Wiggly.

"What is money?" Wiggly whispered back.

"Sproggles go to work to earn money so they can use it to buy things they need, like food and clothes and homes. Sproggles without any money find it difficult to buy food and other things," Freddie tried to explain.

"I'm glad I'm an Elfin then. We all help each other, we don't need money like Sproggles," Wiggly replied in a low voice.

They emerged into the brightly lit cavern and began walking slowly along the twisting, winding path one careful step at a time. They were not looking at their feet because there was so much wonder to see in this cavern. They made their way downwards towards the bottom where they could see an enormous flat mirror, reflecting all the beautiful crystals, some of which seemed to be floating in mid air.

Wiggly stopped and looked horrified, suddenly realising what Freddie had said about the crystals. "You mean Sproggles value crystals like these?"

Freddie smiled innocently and replied. "Why yes, I think they would go mad to get hold of all these beautiful crystals."

Wiggly looked even more horrified. "WHAT! WHAT! WHAT! WHAT!" His voice echoed and the crystals jiggled and gave off a high-pitched ringing sound. He quickly put his hand on his mouth and looked at Freddie. "Please, Freddie," he whispered, "promise me the Sproggles will never know about these? Please."

Freddie could see the concern on Wiggly's face. "I won't tell if you don't," he whispered giving his friend a big smile.

"If the Sproggles ever knew about this place they would destroy everything, including all the Elfins!" Wiggly added and Freddie nodded his head showing he understood.

The pathway wound around rocky outcrops and clusters of crystals of all sizes, as well as single, tall crystals. Freddie led the way with Wiggly holding his hand.

"It feels like we are being watched," Wiggly whispered.

Freddie felt it too and stopped without warning and this time Wiggly bumped into him.

"Ooof!" Wiggly groaned. "Ooof! Ooof! Ooof! Ooof!" His voice echoed.

"Ha, ha!" Freddie laughed out aloud, "Ha! Ha! Ha! Ha! Ha!" he covered his mouth with his hand. "Listen!" he whispered.

Wiggly put his hand to his ear. "I can't hear anything," he replied in a soft voice.

"That's my point, it's total silence, not a dripping sound or scratching or anything," Freddie answered.

"Oh, so it is, I've never heard so much nothingness," Wiggly said, still listening.

"COME! COME! COME! COME!" A deep, rich, kindly voice echoed suddenly.

The two friends quickly squatted down, shaking with a sudden fear.

"Freddie, I'm scared," Wiggly whispered nervously hiding his head in his hands.

"COME! COME! COME! COME!" The deep voice repeated.

Freddie looked up and peeped around, but could not see anyone.

"COME! COME! COME! COME!"

"Who is it, Freddie?" Wiggly whispered as he also looked up.

"I can't see anyone or where the voice is coming from," Freddie whispered back as the two friends stood up again nervously.

"COME! COME! COME! COME!" The voice echoed around the huge cavern. The crystals jingled and made the ringing sound again, so it was impossible to tell where the voice was coming from.

"Let's go back, it could be something really bad, Freddie," Wiggly said, trembling.

Freddie pulled him into a hug. "Whoever it is, Wiggly, they must be friendly otherwise it would be telling us to go away, wouldn't it?" Freddie whispered.

Wiggly stopped shaking and looked at Freddie. "Yes. Yes, of course. I guess you are right, the voice is inviting us in. Oh, that makes me feel much better," Wiggly smiled.

"Let's carry on along this path. It seems to be getting narrower so walk behind me again, Wiggly, here take my hand." Freddie held out his hand and Wiggly held onto it.

The two friends continued walking slowly along the narrow path as it twisted and turned around huge boulders and between more clusters of crystals.

"This is like a pirate's treasure trove," Freddie said.

"COME! COME! COME! COME!"

This time Wiggly came to a halt, yanking Freddie backwards so quickly he nearly fell on top of his friend.

"It's okay, Wiggly, I think it's a friendly voice."

"What's a pirate?" Wiggly asked too loudly. "What's a pirate? pirate? pirate? pirate?" His voice echoed around the cavern again.

Some of the crystals jingled and wobbled.

"Ooops, I keep forgetting to whisper." Wiggly chuckled quietly.

Freddie was smiling too. "A pirate has a ship on the ocean and steals gold and jewels from other ships, then hides them in a big cave on a deserted island," he replied to Wiggly's question.

They were just over half way down when they stopped and the deep voice echoed again.

"COME! COME! COME! COME!" This time it was even louder and all the crystals jiggled and jingled.

The two friends covered their ears, as the sound was so loud and bounced around the cavern.

Freddie looked back along the pathway and could see the black hole of the tunnel where they entered the cavern. "The tunnel exit is still there, Wiggly. That's good, at least we can run back and escape if we need to," he whispered.

Wiggly looked back too and smiled.

When they continued on, the path began to get wider, allowing the two friends to walk side-by-side holding hands. Very soon they were almost upon the huge flat mirror at the bottom of the cavern, just a little further and they would be close to the edge of it. A huge boulder in front of them suddenly hid the flat mirror from their view and when they followed the path around it, both friends came to a sudden halt. In front of them was a wide band of twinkling, sparkling glittery stuff stretching all around the flat mirror, as if it was protecting it.

"What do you think this sparkling material is, Wiggly?" Freddie asked as they were standing at the edge of it.

"Well it looks just like Fairy Dust," Wiggly replied, mesmerized by the twinkling and sparkling, like millions of tiny coloured lights flashing on and off.

"Is it safe to walk on do you think?" Freddie asked.

Wiggly shrugged his shoulders, he did not know the answer.

Freddie reached out with his right leg and stepped lightly on the sparkling stuff. "It feels soft, like moss in the woods," he told Wiggly.

Then they both stepped onto it.

"Oooh, it makes my feet tingle and tickle. Oooh, ha," Wiggly giggled quietly.

"Look," Freddie gasped in a low voice.

"What? Where?" Wiggly replied looking around.

"The mirror," Freddie said.

Wiggly looked where Freddie was pointing.

"Oh my, that's not possible is it, Freddie?" Wiggly exclaimed in a whisper, shunting round behind his friend. The perfectly flat and smooth mirror that reflected all the beautiful crystals was changing shape, something seemed to be rising up from the middle of it.

"Wiggly, Wiggly," whispered Freddie, pulling Wiggly beside him. "Look," he said in a low voice and pointed. "Wiggly! It's not a mirror."

"But it looks like a mirror, Freddie, but I've never seen a mirror do that, what can it be?" Wiggly asked.

Freddie pulled them across the sparkling glitter to the edge of the mirror and dipped his finger in it. "Wiggly, it's a lake, a huge lake of water," he whispered excitedly.

Something that looked like a pointed funnel began to rise up from the lake. Then as more and more began to rise up Wiggly and Freddie realised it was not a funnel at all. The two friends stepped back into the middle of the glittering ring around the lake and watched, fascinated at something rising quickly from the water.

"Hey, that's a pointy hat like mine! MINE! MINE! MINE! MINE!" Wiggly covered his mouth and giggled. "Keep forgetting," he said looking at Freddie.

Of course, Freddie giggled too, the echo this time was not so scary and sounded quite funny.

"Wow," they said together.

Below the pointy hat appeared the bearded face of a very old man. The two friends tried to step back, but their feet were held fast and they could not move.

The feeling of being trapped frightened Wiggly and he called out, "Daddly! Daddly! Daddly! Daddly!" It made him start trembling because his echo this time sounded fearful.

"Don't be scared, Wiggly, I'm here with you," Freddie said trying to comfort his friend. He was trying to be brave because he too was just a little scared. "Look, Wiggly, look!" Freddie said pointing to the thing rising from the lake.

Wiggly looked up from his hands. "It's a man with a long beard and pointy hat," he said.

The thing rising from the lake seemed to be a statue, a massive statue of an old man with a long beard almost down to his feet, wearing a head-to-toe gown and holding a long knobbly tree branch with a claw at the top grasping a crystal.

"It's not a real person, Wiggly, it looks like a statue made of stone. We have them in towns and cities, they are made to remember people by," Freddie said, forgetting they were trapped and could not move. "It looks like pictures I've seen of Wizards and Magicians in books."

"Oh, yes!" Wiggly began to talk loudly then dropped his voice to a whisper. "Daddly told me that our Wizard was called Merlin!"

"MERLIN!" Freddie cried out. "MERLIN! MERLIN! MERLIN! MERLIN!" Freddie's voice echoed loudly throughout the great cavern.

"COME! COME! COME! COME!" The voice seemed to come from the statue this time and the boys stared at it in wonder.

"Hey, I'm floating, Freddie, hold me, I'll fall," Wiggly cried in a low voice.

But Freddie was also rising up in the air.

They held onto each other tightly.

"We're flying!" Wiggly gasped.

The boys rose up into the air above the lake and began to move over it towards the statue.

"I - I can't swim, Freddie. Is that statue thing going to eat us?" This time Wiggly's voice was loud enough to echo and Freddie's name bounced around the cavern.

"I'll save you, Wiggly, I'm a good swimmer, I have my silver lifesaver medal," Freddie replied, quite enjoying the sensation of flying.

They floated silently just above the surface of the lake, which was now so calm again it looked like a mirror once more. Freddie and Wiggly drifted towards the base of the big statue and then stopped.

"Oh wow, this statue is really tall!" Wiggly said in wonderment looking up at it.

"Look, Wiggly, there are some words chiselled in the base of the statue."

"What does it say, Freddie?" Wiggly asked, feeling a little less nervous and a bit more excited.

Freddie read the scrolling letters out aloud, but not too loud.

"When the land is again at peace, once more will Merlin walk among the trees."

"Oh!" Wiggly gasped.

They both started to rise into the air in front of the statue. They were so fascinated by the intricate detail they forgot to be scared. It was as if a real person had been sprayed with stone coloured paint.

Wiggly gasped again when they were level with the Great Wizard Merlin's face.

They could see every hair in his eyebrows and lashes, every wrinkle in minute detail. The two friends looked at the Wizard's face with their eyes wide open in amazement and a little bit of fear. They were holding onto each other tightly with both hands while they just hung in midair, having reached Merlin's head.

"Ooh!" Wiggly cried, his surprise echoing again when they saw the crystal in Merlin's staff begin to glow and give off a low ringing sound. "I don't like this, Freddie, I want to go home," Wiggly whispered as he trembled in Freddie's arms.

Freddie was not feeling that brave either but tried to be strong for Wiggly.

They were hanging high up above the lake and nothing seemed to be holding them up, no wires or cables or balloons, nothing. The Wizard's crystal suddenly shone brightly and began shooting out beams of crimson light that struck some of the floating crystals.

"What's happening, Freddie? I'm scared, I wish we hadn't come now, we're going to fall in the lake and drown."

Freddie hugged him closer. "It's alright, Wiggly, if we were in danger I think we'd know it by now. I have a good feeling about all this, stay calm and let's see what happens," he whispered back, only believing some of what he had said to his nervous friend. Freddie looked up at the Wizard's crystal, which was still shooting beams of crimson light at the other crystals. They reflected it to each other until there were hundreds of beams crisscrossing the cavern. Freddie thought it looked beautiful. "Look, Wiggly, see all the wonderful lights."

Wiggly pulled his head from Freddie's shoulder and looked up. "Oooh, that is beautiful," he whispered back.

All the while the Wizard's crystal was almost singing, the sound was high pitched but going up and down the musical scales just like a song. When it stopped the crystal just seemed to switch off and the pretty red beams of light disappeared too.

Freddie and Wiggly looked at each other in surprise and then they suddenly began moving slowly again, descending over the lake towards the band of twinkling lights around it. Behind them, the statue began sinking back into the lake and the deep voice echoed out to them.

"STAY! STAY! STAY! STAY! STAY!"

They reached the edge of the lake and landed in the same spot in which they had originally stood, but they could not move their feet again, they were trapped.

63

"Look!" Wiggly cried, forgetting about the echo as he pointed upwards.

Some of the crystals began falling slowly downwards as if being lowered on a rope. They hovered above the lake and began to glow and pulse, they hypnotised Freddie and Wiggly, who could not take their eyes off them. One of the crystals moved towards the edge of the lake close to them, then it shone so brightly that they had to turn away. When the light faded, they turned back to look.

Freddie cried out, **"WIGGLY!** WIGGLY! WIGGLY! WIGGLY!" his voice echoed around the cavern. He put his hand over his mouth and whispered, "What is that?"

A slim figure, half Freddie's height, floated in the air. On its back, fluttering slowly back and forth were sparkling butterfly-like wings that looked like skeleton leaves. The slim figure's face was the most beautiful Freddie had ever seen, pretty blue eyes above a tiny nose and ruby red lips, long hair flowed down over its shoulders as far as the waistline, twinkling silvery white. Red crystal shoes adorned the tiny feet and strips of silvery white glittering material formed a skirt looking like lots of flower petals, above which was a sparkling silky shirt. There was a jewelled crown on top of the flowing hair and in one hand was held a short wand that seemed to have a shining star on the end.

"What is it, Wiggly?" Freddie asked again as he stared open mouthed.

"Oh err, I think it's a Fairy. Yes, it's a Fairy," Wiggly finally managed and smiled.

"I thought they were all wiped out long ago?" Freddie replied.

"Me too, that's what Elfin's always believed," Wiggly whispered.

The Fairy moved closer and the boys tried to move back, but still could not move their feet. The Fairy stopped and Freddie just stared, she was just extraordinarily beautiful.

'Welcome Elfin. Welcome Sproggle.' The Fairy's voice was like a lullaby, soothing and calming and Freddie's face smiled, as did Wiggly's.

When they heard the Fairy's voice, the boys gasped again because she did not move her lips, her mouth continued smiling at them.

'You are the first in hundreds of years to discover Merlin's Crystal Cavern. How are you called?' she asked.

The two friends just stared helplessly for a moment while the Fairy's question worked through their numbed minds.

Wiggly waved his hand. "I'm Wiggly Tiggly and this is my best friend, Freddie," he stumbled over his words.

The Fairy spoke in their minds again. *'I am Sophia, Queen of Fairykind. You have just had the privilege to see Merlin and read his inscription.'*

The boys looked at each other, not quite understanding that what they had seen was the real Merlin, not a statue.

'That time is not yet upon us children,' the Fairy Queen began to explain. *'People of this world have yet to find peace among themselves, it may take many hundreds of years before Merlin and Fairykind can once again wander on the surface. This place is protected by the most powerful enchantment, no intruder, Sproggle or otherwise, can penetrate it. Herein are the last of Fairykind. All one thousand gathered together and of course, you saw Merlin with your own eyes.'*

Freddie felt a little more comfortable, the Fairy Queen was so kind looking and even Wiggly had stopped trembling.

"Please, your Majesty, we cannot move our feet, are we stuck here forever?" Freddie took a deep breath before saying his words, pretending to be brave.

The Fairy Queen waved her wand in a circle and the boys were able to move their legs again.

"Oh, thank you, your Majesty," Wiggly said in a quiet voice.

"Your Majesty, we don't see any of the Fairies you mentioned, or Merlin, just a statue of him," Freddie said.

The Queen of Fairies continued to smile and replied. *'Freddie, I sense you are a very special, kind and honest Sproggle. One day all Sproggles will be as you are. What you saw in the middle of the lake was not a statue, but the Great Wizard Merlin himself. He sleeps and waits. Look around you boys, at all these crystals, each one a Fairy, sleeping and held in a spell cast by Merlin. When he again wakes, then so shall all the Fairies.'*

Wiggly and Freddie looked around them, wide eyed again.

"Wow, all these crystals, each one a Fairy, that's so beautiful," Freddie gasped quietly.

Wiggly moved a little closer to the Queen of Fairies and asked, "Please, your Majesty, my people have run out of Fairy Dust and without it the magic that protects us will soon fade away and we may be discovered. Would it be possible to have some to take back?"

The Queen answered Wiggly in his mind. *'You are a good and loyal Elfin. It is not by chance you came across Merlin's Crystal Cavern, even though he slumbers, he watches over you. Unknowingly you have been summoned by the Great Wizard, he understands your plight and your mission to replenish the Fairy Dust for your people.'* She waved her wand again and the twinkling stuff they stood upon rose up in three little swirling whirlwinds and filled up three large jars that appeared out of thin air, like the one Daddly kept his Fairy Dust in. Once they were full, lids appeared and began to screw on the jars, which then floated towards Wiggly and Freddie. *'Give these to your parents, Wiggly. When you are a grown up with your own children you may again return to fill your jars.'*

The jars fitted in Freddie's rucksack one by one, seeming to vanish, he felt no extra weight and it made him smile. *'Magic is so incredible,'* he thought.

'Remember, Wiggly, only Elfins can use the Fairy Dust to create magic, it will not work for any other creature. Remember this new password for entry into this cavern, ADONAY BOTANAH,' the Queen replied.

"Yes your majesty, thank you so much, this will help all Elfins, thank you," Wiggly said.

'The doorway will once again close when you pass through it and will not open again for another fifty years, even with the new password. The enchantment will send any non-friendly visitor back to the surface with no memory of where they have been. Now it is time for you to return and for me to sleep once more. Goodbye and safe journey home Elfin Wiggly and Sproggle Freddie, until we meet again,' the Fairy Queen replied and suddenly became a bright light again as she waved her wand.

The two friends closed their eyes until the bright light faded and when they opened them again, the Fairy Queen was once more in crystal form and rising up towards the ceiling.

The boys turned and made their way back up along the path, holding each other's hand. So full of amazement they had no words to speak to each other until they reached the tunnel entrance into the cavern. They stood looking back into the vast cavern, just as they had when the doorway first opened, it still looked really awesome.

"Look, Wiggly, isn't this the most beautiful place you have ever seen?" Freddie said as they stared into the Crystal Cavern one last time.

"Yes, Freddie, it is and that's the first Fairy I have ever seen," Wiggly said, looking and smiling at his best Sproggle friend.

"I never thought I would ever see one," Freddie replied quietly.

"Did you see how huge the Wizard Merlin is?" Wiggly whispered.

"He's a giant, isn't he?" Freddie replied. "Come on best friend, let's get back and tell everyone of our adventure."

"Daddly is going to be so amazed we are bringing Fairy Dust home with us," Wiggly replied.

The two friends turned and walked away from the Crystal Cavern. They had to stop when the entrance closed behind them, making the tunnel go dark.

"Oh that's a bit scary," Wiggly declared. Even with his enhanced vision he could see nothing at all, which was strange for an Elfin as they could usually see something in near darkness.

Freddie unzipped his rucksack and pulled out the torches. *'Funny, the jars were not in there when I felt inside for these torches,'* he thought, trying to understand where things went. They took off their sunglasses which were no longer needed and they disappeared into Freddie's rucksack.

"Oh, hang on, Freddie!" Wiggly cried, pulling him to an unexpected stop. "I nearly forgot the booby trap, it must be close by now!"

"Oh Wiggly, I can see it, I can really see it!" Freddie called out in surprise.

Wiggly turned to look at Freddie. "How is that possible, only Elfins should be able to see it?" he answered with a question.

"Something has changed, Wiggly, remember the Fairy Queen said something about us being summoned and that I was a special Sproggle and that Merlin watches over us. Perhaps that has something to do with me seeing what you see," Freddie suggested.

"Yes! Yes!" Wiggly replied excitedly. "Of course, don't you see? It was no accident that I got my leg trapped, or you helped me and I showed you Elfin Town. Merlin had planned it all along somehow, even though he's frozen in time."

Freddie stood and looked at his friend, astounded. "Do you really think Merlin is so powerful?" he asked in a shocked voice.

"Yes, Freddie, just look what he has done. He created all the Elfins as his helpers, created our town and the escape tunnels and his home and that library!" Wiggly replied excitedly.

Again Freddie was overcome with awe, he began to understand why Sproggles must never know about magic or find this place. "Try saying the magic words, Freddie, can you remember them?" Wiggly suggested.

Freddie nodded, placed his hand on the wall and uttered the magic words. "It's working, Wiggly, the floor is solid again!" he declared excitedly.

Wiggly took his hand and pulled him along until they were well past the trap. "The Fairy Queen is right, Freddie, you are special," he grinned admiring his friend.

Finally, when they reached Merlin's library, Wiggly gasped, "Oh good! The bookshelf door is still open."

So the two boys walked through the bookcase doorway and into the bright light of the library. They switched off their torches for a little while and pushed the book trigger back into place. Gears whirred and clanked as the bookcase slid back across and forward until it looked like the rest of the shelving.

"Let's rest a while and have a drink, Wiggly, I'm feeling a bit tired," Freddie admitted.

Wiggly nodded.

They sat with their legs hanging down from the balcony while sharing a bottle of water Freddie had magically made appear from his rucksack.

"I still can't believe we've actually seen the most powerful Wizard of all time and the Fairy Queen!" Freddie exclaimed.

"It's exciting, isn't it? Since you found me and helped me, my life has been much more interesting, I never thought I would be, or even could be, friends with a Sproggle!" Wiggly confessed and chuckled.

Rested and refreshed, the two friends made their way through Merlin's living room and into the chamber.

Wiggly looked at Freddie and asked, "Can you see the words on the doors now, Freddie?"

Freddie looked at each of the doors in turn, they were blank for just a moment, then suddenly the words began to form as if someone was just writing them. "I - I do, Wiggly, I do! Wow, this is so exciting!" he replied.

"You have been given a very special gift Freddie, you're half Elfin now!" Wiggly chuckled.

With their torches back on and keen to get home, Wiggly pulled Freddie along at a running pace and they made it to the end of the escape tunnel in only twenty minutes. Poor Freddie was out of breath and needed a sit down on the rock that looked like a bench, situated outside the escape tunnel door. Both sat quietly until Freddie told his friend that he was ready. They skipped along the roadway until they reached the Tiggly's house and they were feeling so very happy.

Freddie and Wiggly were so excited when they rushed inside they could hardly tell Daddly, Mummly and Giggly about their adventure quickly enough.

"Whoah! Slow down boys, you're far too excited and we can't understand what you're saying. Now take a deep breath and start again," Daddly said trying to calm the two boys.

Both took a deep breath, then Wiggly started again. "The Fairy Queen said that it was no accident we found Merlin's Crystal Cavern, that we had been summoned there to refill the Fairy Dust for our people, and she said Freddie was a very special Sproggle," Wiggly gabbled.

Freddie's face was alight with excitement too. "And, and we saw Merlin, the Great Wizard himself! He's in the Crystal Cavern waiting!"

"What! You never did?" Giggly gasped. "Really, you saw the Great Wizard? Did he talk to you, what's he like, how tall is he ....?" Giggly was firing questions at Freddie and Wiggly until Mummly stopped her mid sentence.

"Giggly stop, take a breath before you faint!" Mummly cried, hardly able to contain her laughter.

Wiggly began to answer, still full of excitement. "The bottom of the cavern is covered in a huge lake......"

"We thought it was a great big mirror, the surface was so flat and shinny........" Freddie interrupted.

Then Wiggly interrupted Freddie. "Merlin rose up out of the lake, and he is so tall........"

69

"He's a statue, well it was him really because he is sleeping and waiting........" Freddie barged in.

"And, and......... we were flying in the air, across the lake and then........." Wiggly said, interrupted by Freddie.

"We floated right up to Merlin's face!" Freddie finished and gasped, flopping back on the comfy sofa that he and Wiggly had stood up from while telling their story.

Giggly was jumping up and down with her own excitement. "You were flying?"

"Oh! Daddly, I have the jars of Fairy Dust in my rucksack," Freddie suddenly remembered and unzipped the top then reached inside, pulling out three large jars of sparkling Fairy Dust, one at a time.

Daddly was so pleased with his son and good friend Freddie. "You two boys have saved all the Elfins for a very long time to come," he praised them.

"For fifty years at least!" Wiggly laughed.

* *

That night Freddie had the most wonderful dream that seemed so very real, all about the Fairies and Merlin finally waking up. He stood with Merlin and looked around the world and it was a beautiful place, so peaceful, every Sproggle helping and caring about each other. Fairies, Elfins and all creatures living in peace and harmony. When he woke in the morning he was a little sad thinking that he would never see the world in the distant future. But then he was happy that Merlin had allowed him to see what a wonderful place the world would finally become.

CHAPTER THREE

The Attack of the Mole Goblins

*Freddie and Wiggly battle ferocious creatures
to save the Elfin children.*

Today was the last Saturday in the month and Freddie was really excited, he had saved all his pocket money and now had enough to buy the plastic model kit of the famous Red Baron's Triplane. It was a very special model kit that when painted in Baron Richthofen's bright red colour would look spectacular among his collection. He loved gluing the parts together and then painting his models and would spend hours being very careful about every detail. He had lots of models, mostly aeroplanes, and for Christmas and birthdays the first thing on his list of presents were model kits.

His father had put screw eyes in the ceiling of Freddie's bedroom from which he hung his treasured, painted model aeroplanes. He had also made him some shelves to display his other models of Roman soldiers and the like, his favourite was a Loondoon Beefeater. After a visit to Loondoon to see the changing of the guard at Buckleham Palace and the Beefeaters at the Tower of Loondoon, his parents bought Freddie the Beefeater model kit to remind him of their visit.

The village of Elfington was a long way from any big towns, but it had a lot of local shops. Even though Freddie's home was at the edge of the village it did not take long to walk to the High Street. There was a greengrocer, a hardware shop, an optician, a chemist and a Post Office as well as a charity shop and a small supermarket. The most important one for Freddie was Mr Balsa's 'Model Shop.'

Although he was nearly eleven years old he still enjoyed taking walks with his parents and today he and his father walked together to the shops. They chatted and laughed with each other in the warmth of the summer sun and under the cloudless blue sky.

"Freddie, I have a joke for you. What do you call a bee trying to make up its mind?" his father said chuckling.

Freddie liked jokes and tried to think of an answer. "I don't know, Dad?" he replied.

"Well, you would call it a *Maybee*," his father chuckled.

"Oh, that's really clever, Dad, I must remember that. I have one for you. What do bees chew?" Freddie asked, chuckling while thinking about his answer.

"Oooh, that's a good one, Freddie, let me think. How about honey?" his father replied.

"Nope!" Freddie laughed, "they chew *Bumblegum!*"

Freddie's father laughed, "That's clever too, yes, Bumblegum, like bubblegum."

Wherever Freddie went he always carried his rucksack. "You never know when you might need something to help someone," he would say, to no one in particular.

Freddie and his father crossed the road to the opposite footpath and bumped into the mother of one of Freddie's school friends.

"Hello, Mrs Kuff," they said at the same time, which made them chuckle.

Mrs Kuff did not appear to hear them straight away, as she seemed to be struggling with something. "Fiddle faddle!" she mumbled. She stood up straight and jumped sideways when she saw Freddie and his father. "Oh goodness, you gave me a fright!" she gasped.

"Sorry, Mrs Kuff, we did say hello, but you were so busy you didn't hear us," Freddie's father apologised.

"It's not a nice thing to frighten people, it could make them quite poorly," Freddie's mother had told him long ago when he had jumped up from behind the sofa and made her drop the book she was reading.

"How are you both?" Mrs Kuff asked once she caught her breath and the smile returned to her face.

"We're fine, Mrs Kuff," Freddie's father replied. "Thank you for asking."

Freddie said excitedly, "We're off to the Model Shop to buy the famous Red Baron's Triplane model kit, I've saved all my pocket money."

Mrs Kuff looked at Freddie and chuckled, then said to his father, "Oh, Freddie is such a lovely boy, always smiling and happy. You and Mrs Fountain must be very proud of him."

Freddie felt embarrassed and hot as his face turned a bright red.

"He is that, and we are proud of him, he's a good boy most of the time." Mr Fountain replied patting Freddie on the head.

"Aw Da-ad!" Freddie protested with a giggle.

"What seems to be the problem, Mrs Kuff, you appear to be struggling with something?" Freddie's father asked.

"Oh! The handle on my favourite shopping bag has broken and that's even before I fill it with groceries," she replied.

Freddie's ears pricked up when he heard Mrs Kuff say that. "Oh, Mrs Kuff, I think I have something to help with that!" he cried, pulling his rucksack from his shoulders and unzipping it. He felt inside and created a picture in his mind, then pulled out a short length of thin rope a bit like washing line. "We can push each end through those big eyelets and tie a knot in them, that should fix it!" he chirped and gave her his biggest smile. Freddie gave the rope to his father who could tie a tight double knot at each end creating a replacement handle for the broken one.

"Oh, that's even better than the original handle, Freddie, it's so strong, I can't thank you both enough, it's so kind of you," Mrs Kuff praised them.

Freddie was turning bright red again, but he and his father were all smiles. *'It feels good when you help someone,'* Freddie thought to himself.

"I know my daughter Anne is in your class at school, Freddie, so I will send a little treat for you with her on Monday as a reward," Mrs Kuff said kindly.

Freddie liked Anne, she was kind like her mother and he had befriended her when Bully Bates began teasing her.

"What a silly name, Anne Kuff! Ha, ha, ha! Bet your dad's a policeman, 'cause they have anncuffs, don't they? Ha, ha!" He was relentless and made poor Anne cry every time he taunted her.

Freddie had taken Anne by the hand and shielded her behind him. In a brave, angry moment, shouted at Bully Bates. "Leave her alone, Billy, you're just a nasty, horrible person. Just go away!"

Billy Bates was so shocked that Freddie had stood up to him, he did walk away, but was already planning how to make Freddie look as silly as he had just made him look.

"That's very kind of you, Mrs Kuff," Freddie's father said on his behalf.

"One good turn deserves another, I always say and my daughter told me how brave Freddie had been to stop Billy Bates bullying her at school. She's so much happier now with lots of friends thanks to him."

Freddie's face turned a brighter red, Mrs Kuff's story had made him quite embarrassed.

"I wasn't aware of that," Freddie's father replied. "I'm pleased he and Anne are friends," he said patting his son on the shoulder. He was enormously proud of Freddie, who had turned out to be kind, thoughtful and helpful.

The three walked together until they reached the grocery shop where Mrs Kuff bade them goodbye. The Model Shop was a little further along the road and Freddie was keen to buy his model, but when they reached the shop.....

"Oh, Dad, the sign on the door says the shop is closed! I wonder if Mr Balsa is poorly?" Freddie asked looking at his father.

"There are lights on inside the shop, Freddie, so let's try the door just in case Mr Balsa has forgotten to change the sign to read OPEN." Freddie's father turned the door handle and pushed, to his surprise it opened quite easily and the little bell above the door rang out loud and clear, so they stepped inside.

Mr Balsa walked through a multicoloured curtain from a room behind the counter. "Mr Fountain and my favourite customer, Freddie, welcome," he announced as the door clicked shut behind them.

"We thought you were poorly, Mr Balsa, because your door sign says the shop is CLOSED," Freddie replied much more cheerfully.

"Ah yes, that's such a nuisance, when I went to change the sign from CLOSED to OPEN this morning, the little knob that moves the slider across dropped off and I cannot find it anywhere! I think it sprouted wings and flew away," Mr Balsa declared.

Freddie giggled at Mr Balsa's remark. "Can things really grow wings and fly away?" he asked.

This time it was his father and Mr Balsa's turn to laugh.

"It's just one of those things we say, Freddie, when we can't find something. In fact things seem to go missing all the time, take my glasses for example, I had them when I opened the shop but I'm blessed if I can find them now," Mr Balsa replied.

Freddie laughed, Mr Balsa was very funny the way he told you things, but what amused him most was Mr Balsa's glasses were up on the top of his head. Freddie was pointing but laughing too much to speak.

"Did I say something funny?" Mr Balsa asked innocently.

"Excuse Freddie, Mr Balsa, he knows where your glasses are, that's why he's laughing."

"Oh good," Mr Balsa replied, turning and swivelling his head round and back again so quickly that his glasses dropped right back into place from his head onto his nose. "Hey! That's a clever trick Freddie, how'd you do that?"

Freddie was still chuckling away and Mr Balsa's antics made him laugh even more.

"You must have slipped your glasses up on your head earlier, Mr Balsa, that's where we could see them when you thought you had lost them," Mr Fountain explained.

"Of course, I remember now! I was pricing some models and slipped them up when I heard the doorbell ring. Silly me, but thank you both," Mr Balsa replied.

Freddie settled down and smiled saying, "I think I might have something in my rucksack to help fix your door sign, Mr Balsa." He slipped his rucksack from his shoulders and unzipped the top. When he put his hand inside he pretended to be sorting through lots of things. "Now where is it?" he said quietly. "Oh, here it is!" he cried and pulled out a small bright red knob with a screw sticking out of it. "Will this do, Mr Balsa?" Freddie asked hopefully.

Mr Balsa looked at what was in Freddie's hand with amazement. "Well bless my soul!" he declared, "I do believe that might just fit the sign. It's a different colour, but that will make it easier to find if it drops off again." He walked around the counter and Freddie handed him the bright red knob, then Mr Balsa took it, tried it on the door sign and it fitted perfectly. He screwed it in place and slid the sign from CLOSED to showing OPEN.

"Oh, goody!" Freddie cried clapping his hands, "now the shop is properly open."

"It fits perfectly, Freddie. Well done, what a resourceful chap you are!" Mr Balsa replied. He walked back to the counter all smiles just like Freddie and his father.

"I've saved all my pocket money, Mr Balsa, for the Red Baron's Triplane model kit," Freddie announced, bringing out a small purse then tipping the contents onto the counter. Mr Balsa went to get the model from the shelf, then placed it on the counter. He picked up the coins and notes Freddie had emptied from his purse and counted it carefully.

"I'm afraid you're fifty pence short, Freddie," he said to a crest fallen little boy hoping to take home the model he had saved for.

Freddie opened his purse and checked there was no money left inside, then looked at Mr Balsa. "But that's how much it was when I came to buy my model last month, I remember it clearly," he said sadly.

Mr Balsa nodded his head. "You're right there, Freddie, but this is new stock that came from the manufacturer last week and they have increased the price, I'm sorry about that."

Poor Freddie, he dropped his head feeling quite disappointed. He had looked forward all month to having this model.

His father was just about to tell Freddie that he would make up the difference, when Mr Balsa said cheerfully, "I tell you what, Freddie, I will give you a discount of fifty pence as a reward for helping me fix my door sign, how about that!"

Freddie looked up at Mr Balsa and smiled like a Cheshire cat. "Really, Mr Balsa, you would do that for me?"

Mr Balsa was laughing to see Freddie so happy and was nodding his head to Freddie's question. "That's very kind of you, Mr Balsa, are you sure you won't be out of pocket with your kind gesture?" Freddie's father asked.

Mr Balsa was still chuckling as he handed the box to Freddie. "I think it would have cost me more than fifty pence to buy a new door sign, so I will put it against repairs and everyone is happy. What I find most heart warming is that Freddie offered his help without being asked and without expectation of reward, he is a very special young man. I only wish everyone had a kind and generous heart like your son, Mr Fountain, I'm sure he makes you very proud indeed."

Freddie put the model box in his rucksack carefully and they waved Mr Balsa goodbye. "See you next month," Freddie called back as they walked through the shop door with a sign that now declared the Model Shop was OPEN.

The next stop was the hardware and tool shop, Mr Fountain needed to replace a lost tool. This shop had always fascinated Freddie because there were so many interesting things to look at. Outside the hardware shop all kinds of pots and pans hung from hooks, along with buckets and bowls. There were brooms of all shapes and sizes displayed in a large metal dustbin, looking like a big firework going off. The shop window was full of wonderful tools, bottles and boxes of things that Freddie had no idea what they were or what they were used for.

Mr and Mrs Potts owned the shop, which was called 'Home Hardware and DIY' and it was Mrs Potts behind the counter when they arrived.

"Why hello, Freddie and Mr Fountain, how are you both?" She was a very jolly person, with rosy cheeks and bright red lipstick, always smiling and laughing.

Freddie excitedly told her how Mr Balsa had helped him buy the new Triplane model kit.

She chuckled away listening to his story, then asked, "What brings you both here today?"

Freddie's father explained. "I need to buy a new tape measure, I seem to have lost or mislaid mine. I've looked everywhere."

"It must have grown wings and flown away then, Dad!" Freddie chuckled.

Mrs Potts walked over to the tool section in the shop and brought back three different types and sizes of tape measure and put them on the counter.

"Ah! This is the one I usually have." Freddie's father pointed to the middle one.

"If I may make a suggestion, Mr Fountain," Mrs Potts replied. "If you choose one of the others you would always know if you found your old tape measure. If you buy the exact same style, you may have found your old one and never realise."

"Oooh, that's so clever of you, Mrs Potts!" Freddie chirped looking at his father. "Don't you think so, Dad?"

Mr Fountain did think it a wonderful idea and indeed chose a different tape measure to the one he could not find.

"I'll just write out your receipt, Mr Fountain," Mrs Potts said, hunting all over the counter. "I have a pen here somewhere."

"Probably in the same place as my lost tape measure," Mr Fountain chuckled.

Mrs Potts laughed at as his remark, still hunting for her pen. "It's amazing, I think they sprout legs and run away," she laughed.

When Freddie heard her say that he looked at his father, quizzically.

"It's another saying when we lose things, they don't actually grow legs," he said with a little laugh.

"Oh! Mrs Potts, I think I have something to help," Freddie said taking his rucksack off and feeling around his model box, then pulled out a blue ballpoint pen. "Here it is, Mrs Potts, you can use this."

Mrs Potts looked up from under the counter at Freddie holding out the pen and she looked like she could cry.

"Oh Freddie, you are a little angel, so helpful. My son William told us how you helped him with his broken shoelace at school, you're a very kind young man," she said and looked straight at his father. "You must be so proud of him, Mr Fountain?" she said.

"His mother and I are very proud of Freddie, Mrs Potts, he always seems ready to help everyone."

Of course Freddie's face turned bright red as he gave the pen to Mrs Potts, listening to what they were saying about him. In fact he really did not think he was special at all, he was just, Freddie.

"Ooh, Freddie, you look so cute with your little blushing cheeks!" she said with a chuckle, taking the pen and then wrote out the receipt. Then she held the pen out to return it to Freddie.

"You can keep that, Mrs Potts, it's a spare one. You should tie a piece of string on it so it can't run away though."

She laughed and then stopped to say, "You know that's not a bad idea, Freddie, I don't know why I never thought of doing that myself. Freddie Fixit to the rescue again, well done Freddie," she laughed out loud. Freddie and his father were about to leave when Mrs Potts said, "Here you are Freddie," as she handed him a roll of tape fixed to a card sleeve declaring 'Dinosaur Tape' on it. "Fair exchange is no robbery, I always say," Mrs Potts said.

"Oh! Thank you, Mrs Potts, I'm sure this will come in very useful. Look, Dad, it says it even works under water, how clever is that!"

"That's very kind of you Mrs Potts," Freddie's father thanked her and she was laughing again.

"One good turn deserves another, I always say," she replied.

They said their goodbyes and began to walk home.

"It seems I have a very helpful son indeed," Freddie's father chatted to him as they walked. "It was kind of you to protect Mrs Kuff's daughter at school and help William, he gets upset easily, not like his mother and father at all. I'm very proud of you son," he told Freddie, stopping to give him a hug. "Jump up, piggy back home!" he said and Freddie hopped on his father's back and they finished their journey telling funny stories and laughing.

* *

That afternoon Freddie opened the box of his model kit and took out all the contents. He placed the plastic moulded parts to one side on his desk, the glue and paints and paint brushes on the other side and smiled. He picked up the instructions that showed him which parts to glue together and in what order.

"Oooh, this will be lots of fun!" he said, to no one in particular. He looked up at his other models hanging from his bedroom ceiling to make sure there was a spare hook for the Red Baron's Triplane to be hung. For the next hour he separated all the parts and sanded off all the little extra bits of plastic where they had been joined together and also the edges that would be glued and made sure they fitted together perfectly. When he was satisfied everything was correct and numbered like the instructions, he put everything back in the box for safekeeping.

"I'll begin putting my model together tomorrow," he said, to no one in particular. It did occur to Freddie that he could just magic a model kit from his rucksack, but that idea was not without problems. Firstly, he would feel very guilty using the magic for selfish reasons. He was happy to use it to help others or occasionally pull out a plaything that he returned when finished with. Secondly, he would have to explain to his parents how he came to have an expensive model kit without going to buy it from the model shop. That alone might mean he would have to explain about his magic rucksack, but more importantly it might expose the Elfins to danger if anyone, even his mother and father, knew about them. Freddie valued his models all the more because he had saved up his pocket money to buy them, then gluing the model parts together, finally painting them, it made him feel very happy.

At half past two his friend Jimmy arrived. They had arranged on Friday to go play in the park that was just along the road from Freddie's house.

A knock on the door and cry of, "Is Freddie Fixit at home?" through the letterbox made Freddie's mother laugh as she opened the door and invited Jimmy inside.

"Here he comes," she said, "along with the herd of elephants!"

Jimmy looked at her and giggled.

"Jimmy!" Freddie cried, tripping on the bottom step and stumbling into his friend. "Oops! Sorry, Jimmy, are you okay?" Freddie apologised and Jimmy just laughed even more.

"Bet those elephants pushed you trying to get past!" he giggled and Freddie laughed as well. "Off you go you two, I have some cleaning to do while you go play," Freddie's mother urged, unable to keep from smiling at the two happy boys.

As they jogged along to the park, Freddie told his friend about his adventures during the morning and along the way they bumped into one of the older boys from their school.

"Hello, I know you two, don't I?" he said to them both.

"Oh yes, I've seen you about, you're Joanne's brother James, I think," Jimmy replied.

James smiled. "That's right. What are your names?"

"I'm Jimmy and this is my best friend, Freddie," Jimmy chirped.

"So where are you two off then?" James asked.

"To play in the park," Freddie replied.

"Be careful then, some teenagers were messing about on the playground equipment earlier. They're really too old and too big for the swings and the other things. They're just trouble, that's why I'm on my way home," James' warning was kindly meant. "Do you want me to come along with you to make sure it's safe?" James volunteered.

Jimmy looked at him and asked enthusiastically, "Oh, would you? That would be great, don't you think so, Freddie?"

Freddie felt a little safer knowing James would be with them and the three walked on through the tall stone pillars that had once held two huge and heavy metal gates. Freddie's father had explained to him a while ago they had been melted down during the war to make guns.

James walked with Freddie and Jimmy all the way to the playground area. He was very friendly and chatted to them both as if they had been friends for a long time.

The older teenagers were nowhere to be seen, but they had left a trail of rubbish and damage behind them. One of the swings was broken, the slide was smeared with mud and lumps of turf, the roundabout seemed undamaged, as was the climbing frame.

The three boys set about picking up all the litter that had been strewn about until the whole area was clean and the rubbish put in the litterbins. Then they set about cleaning the slide.

James removed the turf while Freddie fished into his rucksack and brought out a pack of wipes.

"Freddie Fixit to the rescue!" cried Jimmy, laughing his head off.

James looked at Freddie, quizzically.

Jimmy chuckled, "Freddie has a magic rucksack, whenever there's a problem he can usually fix it, so we call him Freddie Fixit."

Poor Freddie, he blushed bright red, he could not get used to being in the limelight.

"I see," James replied with a smile and friendly pat on Freddie's shoulder.

They managed to clean the slide back to its highly polished shine and Jimmy had to be the first to try it. He clambered up the metal steps and launched himself down the polished surface. "Oh, wow!" he cried as he gained so much speed he was propelled off the end of the slide and landed with a bump and "OW!" on the grass a metre or two away.

Freddie and James found Jimmy's flight incredibly funny and laughed together, much to Jimmy's dismay.

"We polished that too well I think," Jimmy said rubbing his behind as he walked back to his new friend and Freddie.

"What about that swing, have you anything in your rucksack to mend that broken seat?" James asked.

"Actually I do!" Freddie replied.

Jimmy started calling his friend, "Freddie Fixit!" again.

James chuckled. "That must get annoying?" he said.

"Not really, I know he means well, but I have Dinosaur Glue and Dinosaur tape that was given to me at the hardware store." He fished around in his rucksack and pulled them both out. "We can glue the wooden seat and wrap the tape around it to make it safe and strong."

That's exactly what they did.

"We have to say ABRACADABRA now," Freddie explained as they glued the two halves of the seat together.

James chuckled but entered into the spirit of things.

"ABRACADABRA!" they called out together and then wrapped the seat in Dinosaur tape to make it good and strong again. All three sat on the bench seat admiring their handiwork.

"Joanne says you play the guitar really well," Jimmy said to James.

"Well I don't know about that, but I do like to play my guitar. I suppose I'm quite good, but I broke my plectrum so I will have to wait until my parents go into town before I can replace it," James replied.

"What's a plectrum?" Freddie asked.

"Oh, it's a small triangular piece of bone or plastic with slightly curved sides and corners. I use it to run across the strings, it gives a different sound from using my fingers," James answered. Freddie smiled knowingly. "I've seen them on TV when bands are playing. What colour was yours, James?"

"It was sort of brown and orange swirls, but the colour isn't really important. Why do you ask?" he replied.

Freddie pulled his rucksack between his legs, unzipped it and felt around inside. "It's in here somewhere," he mumbled as James and Jimmy watched with interest. "Here it is!" he cried and pulled out a piece of brown plastic with orange swirls.

"I don't believe it, how on Astoria could you have one of those in your rucksack, Freddie?" James cried.

Jimmy almost fell off the bench he laughed so hard and loud. "Don't you know his name by now, it's Freddie Fixit!"

"Will this do then, James?" Freddie asked.

"Why yes, yes, but you must let me pay you for it," James insisted.

"Oh no, James, that's all right, it's just cluttering up my rucksack and I have no use for it. I just pick things up when I'm walking about thinking they may come in useful to someone. I didn't know what this was called until you spoke about your broken one," said Freddie kindly.

James took the plectrum that Freddie offered and was all smiles." You must come to my house tomorrow and I'll play you a tune or two," James invited.

"Oooh that will be fun. What time?" Jimmy asked.

"How about after breakfast?" James suggested.

Freddie and Jimmy were all smiles and nodded, agreeing to meet him then.

James left them to play, whistling a happy tune as he went, looking back and waving to his new friends.

Freddie and Jimmy headed for the swings and decided to see who could swing the highest.

Jimmy was away quickly and swinging back and forth.

Freddie got himself seated firmly and began to swing his legs to get moving.

They were very quickly swinging at the same rate, but Jimmy was determined to go faster and higher.

"Look at me!" he cried, almost horizontal.

"Slow down, Jimmy!" Freddie cried out as he slowed himself down to a stop.

Jimmy slowed down too, on seeing he had won. "Wow! That was fun," he chuckled.

"Too high for me," Freddie admitted.

They played on all the equipment for another hour before heading home.

Freddie told his parents about James and his invitation to hear him play the guitar at his house tomorrow.

Freddie woke quite early on Sunday morning and began gluing his model Triplane together before he went downstairs. By the time his mother called him for breakfast he was well on with completing it. "Just the top and bottom wings and supports to add now," he said, to no one in particular. Then he galloped down the stairs full of happiness at getting so far with his model kit and looking forward to visiting James.

"There's that herd of elephants again," his father chuckled as Freddie skipped into the kitchen. "Hey dad," Freddie smiled, "only one elephant today!" he chuckled.

"What are you up to today son?" his father asked as his son spooned milky flakes into his mouth.

Freddie swallowed his mouthful and replied, "Have you forgotten, Dad, James is going to play his guitar to me and Jimmy this morning?"

"Oh, err, of course not, son, just testing to see if you had forgotten!" his father replied with a wry grin on his face.

Freddie giggled, his father always said that when he forgot things. After he had helped his mother dry the breakfast bowls and cutlery, he dashed back upstairs with a clatter and stomp.

"Leave the elephants upstairs, Freddie!" his father called after him, still laughing at his son.

"Da-ad!" Freddie called back. "It's only me!"

His mother and father laughed between themselves at their son's antics.

Freddie called for his friend, Jimmy, and they skipped along to James' house. On their way they bumped into Mr and Mrs Bakewell who owned the cake shop, and were looking at their son Choco's trousers. Choco was also in Freddie and Jimmy's class at school so they stopped to say hello.

"Hello, Mr and Mrs Bakewell. Heya Choco," Freddie and Jimmy greeted together.

"Good morning Freddie and Jimmy, you're both up and about early," Mr Bakewell replied, "are you going somewhere important?"

"We're off to listen to Joanne's brother, James, play his guitar," Jimmy volunteered.

Choco's eyes lit up. "Oh! Do you think I could come?" he said enthusiastically and looking at his parents for approval.

"I think so, it would be nice for James to have a bigger audience," Freddie replied.

"Can I Mum?" Choco asked looking at his parents with his big round eyes.

"Not unless we can fix that trouser zip of yours. I'm sure I had a safety pin in here," his mother replied sorting around in her handbag.

Jimmy looked at Freddie and mouthed, "Freddie Fixit," smiling.

Freddie took his rucksack from his shoulders, unzipped the top and felt inside. "I think I have one in my rucksack, Mrs Bakewell," he said pulling his hand out and holding up the very thing.

"Freddie Fixit to the rescue!" called Jimmy, unable to help himself and laughing away.

"Well that is helpful, Freddie," Choco's mother said taking the safety pin from him and fastening her son's trouser zip that insisted on unzipping all by itself.

"There, that should hold it in place until you come home, son," she told him.

"Thank you, Freddie," Mr Bakewell said. "You're a very handy young man to have around. You must both come and have tea with us as a thank you," he said to Freddie and Jimmy, who readily agreed.

James got everyone seated on cushions on the floor in the living room, including his sister. Everyone sat quietly while James tuned his guitar strings.

"What are you doing, James, I don't recognise that tune?" Jimmy asked.

James chuckled. "This is not a tune, Jimmy, the strings change their sound in warm and cold rooms, so I first have to tune them so they sound harmonious," he explained.

Jimmy nodded, not that he really understood what James meant.

Finally James strummed the guitar and the sound was very pleasant. Then as requested he played Freddie's favourite, 'All things bright and beautiful,' and they all sang along to it. James was really very good with his guitar, he could strum across the strings with his plectrum or he could pluck the strings one at a time with his fingers and that sounded 'really cool!' according to Jimmy.

After a while James' mother brought them all fizzy drinks and biscuits, which they devoured while chatting about how good James was.

"This tune I've been practicing for a while now, it's a classical piece, quite difficult, so I hope you all like it," James explained, then strummed and plucked at the guitar as well as drumming the wooden body, much to the fascination of all the friends listening. Even James' parents came to listen and when he finished everyone was completely silent. James felt a little disappointed thinking they had not enjoyed it, but then everyone began clapping their hands and calling out how fantastic it had been, even his mother and father applauded and their faces glowed with pride.

Choco, Jimmy and Freddie thanked James as they were about to go home.

Freddie beamed James a big smile. "I've never heard anything so wonderful. Do you think I could ever play the guitar?" he asked.

"Show me your hands," James replied.

Freddie looked a little surprised, but held out his hands.

James held them in his hands. "You have nice long fingers, ideal for playing the guitar or piano, because they will reach around the neck of the guitar to hold the strings down to make the chords, or you could probably reach a whole octave on the piano."

Freddie did not really understand what James had said but smiled anyway.

"I can teach you if you really want to learn," James volunteered.

The surprise on Freddie's face was a picture. "Oh, really? Oh, yes! I'd really like that," he replied enthusiastically.

"Ask your parents if it's okay and you can let me know, then we can arrange for me to come over with my guitar for you to try out and see if you like it or not, okay?" James explained.

Choco suddenly cried out, "OOOOH! ARRRRH!" then began hopping around like a one legged duck.

"Choco love, whatever is the matter?" James's mother asked as she rushed to help him.

"It's my safety pin, it has come undone! Oooh! Ow! And it's, ouch, ouch, sticking in me, Oooh!" poor Choco cried tearfully.

"Try and stand still Choco and let me sort it out for you," James's mother said kindly.

He tried to stand still, without a lot of success, and was now turning a bright red as James's mother retrieved the open safety pin.

"Oooh! Thank you, that really hurt," he said and allowed her to fasten it back safely.

Jimmy and Freddie could not help sniggering into their hands, trying not to make things worse for their friend.

When Freddie got home and during their lunch, he described to his parents how wonderfully James had played for them and how he had offered to teach him to play the guitar.

Freddie's parents thought it was a great idea for him to learn to play a musical instrument.

"If James thinks you suit the guitar then we will consider buying one for you, Freddie," his father told a very surprised little boy.

After lunch Freddie finished putting the last pieces of his model plane together. The glue dried quickly and he was able to sand off any that had squeezed out from the joints. "There, you're ready for a coat of red paint now," he said, to no one in particular. Not wanting to rush finishing his model, he decided to read a book until it was time to visit the Bakewell's for tea.

* *

He called for Jimmy on the way and when they arrived Choco invited them inside and showed them the treats his mother had made. There were banana and chocolate spread sandwiches, which were Freddie's second favourite to jam sandwiches. Of course there was a huge choice of cakes and pastries, sausage rolls, pork pie and cocktail sausages on sticks, jam and lemon tarts, custard slices, fairy buns, butterfly muffins and scones.

The boys played a game of snakes and ladders while Mrs Bakewell finished preparing the party food for them. When they sat to the table all three boys had a really nice time and Choco's mother fussed around them encouraging them to eat lots.

Afterwards the three friends disappeared into Choco's bedroom and played Ludo, they had a lot of fun and were very competitive and by chance Choco managed to win the game.

"Choco," Jimmy asked while they played the game, "how come your mum and dad gave you the name Choco? I mean it's a nice name and all, but unusual, is it foreign?"

Choco blushed, turning bright red and replied shyly, "Well Mum is a chocolate fanatic, she uses it in all her cakes and things and there's always lots in the fridge."

"So your mum shortened the word Chocolate to Choco, hey that's so cool!" Freddie said excitedly.

"Mmmm, sort of. You know our family name is Bakewell, and my first name is Choco, well I don't tell everyone this so don't laugh and never tell anyone, but my middle name is Lait." Choco waited for a response.

Freddie and Jimmy were quiet, both furrowed their brows trying to work out what Choco was so concerned about.

"No, no really? So cool!" Jimmy finally piped up. "Your full name is Choco Lait Bakewell! So cool, Choco!"

Freddie was feeling a bit dim and repeated under his breath, "Choco Lait, Choco Lait. OH! Chocolate. Yeh! So Cool!"

"Your parents are so cool, my middle name is John," Jimmy replied.

"I don't have a middle name, I'm just Freddie Fixit..... Oops! I mean Fountain!" Freddie laughed, "Jimmy, you've got me at it now!"

The three laughed together and carried on with their game.

Later, Freddie and Jimmy thanked Choco and his parents for the very special tea and made their way home. It was only seven o'clock and still light, so they could walk home safely. Had it been dark then Freddie's father would have collected them. When Freddie dropped Jimmy off at his house he wandered along thinking about learning to play the guitar. James had made it look easy, but he had been playing for a very long time. When he was almost home he spotted something glinting in the forest behind his house.

"What could that be?" he said, to no one in particular. He walked down the side of his house towards the trees and the object, which seemed to be flashing on and off. When he reached the edge of the forest it looked darker inside than usual, but he could see quite clearly what it was that had attracted his attention. He looked around but no one seemed to be about, so he took a deep breath and walked slowly in the direction of the light.

When he reached the source of the flashing light he discovered it was a torch hanging on a length of string from a tree branch. It had looked like it was flashing as it twirled around in the breeze. "Who could have left that there, and why would they?" he said to himself. "Hello!" He called out placing his hands either side of his mouth like he had seen on television when people wanted their voice to sound over a long distance. "Anyone there?" he called but got no answer. Freddie pulled the torch down and ran home to show his father.

"Well I haven't seen that trick in years, Freddie," his father told him as his son let the torch dangle from the string.

"Why is it there? Who left it and what's it for, Dad?" he asked.

His father smiled and put his arm around his son. "It's a very old method of catching rabbits. Long ago, people used to be very poor, so they would catch rabbits for food. I'm surprised you didn't see any snares around."

Freddie looked puzzled and horrified at the same time. "How can you catch a rabbit with a torch, Dad, I don't understand?"

His father chuckled and looked at his curious son. "Well it caught you didn't it!" he replied smiling.

"Aw, Dad!" Freddie huffed.

His father explained further. "Rabbits are inquisitive too and will be attracted to the light and get caught in the snares below it."

Now Freddie only looked horrified. "Oh no, Dad! We must go save the poor rabbits, if Sprog... erm! I mean if people are going to eat them!" (Freddie almost gave himself away and said Sproggles!)

Father and son set off to the place where Freddie had found the torch hanging from a tree. They soon reached the spot and Freddie explained, "It was hanging from this branch, Dad," pointing to the low branch of a tree.

"Search around, son, and look for a wooden stake hammered into the ground with a loop of wire fixed to it," his father said as they shone their torches around the tree and under the bushes.

"Dad, Dad!" Freddie cried out loudly. "I've found one and a poor rabbit is trapped!" He was not far from the place the torch had been hanging.

Sure enough, a pretty, fluffy grey rabbit had its paw caught in the snare trap.

Freddie's father rushed to his son then reached down and picked the rabbit up, trap and all, pulling the wooden stake out at the same time. "Can you loosen the loop of wire from around its paw while I hold the rabbit safely."

Freddie's little fingers managed to slacken the wire and remove it from the rabbit's foot.

"Now massage the rabbit's foot around the wire mark," his father explained.

"Why am I doing this, Dad?" Freddie asked.

"We don't know how long this little rabbit has been struggling, so you're just massaging its paw to get the blood flowing otherwise it may not be able to walk." After a minute or so he placed the rabbit down on the ground and it looked up at Freddie and his father as much to say *'thank you'* then slowly moved away. It had a little bit of a limp, but was soon scampering along.

Freddie and his father found several more wire snare traps, fortunately without rabbits caught in them, so they pulled them up and took them to dispose of back at home.

Back inside the house Freddie and his mother and father sat together in the sitting room.

Freddie felt very sad. "Why do people kill rabbits and eat them, Dad?" he asked.

Freddie's father put his arm around his son as they sat on the sofa. "Many years ago people were very, very poor, so poor that they didn't even have enough money to buy food to feed themselves and their children....."

"...Oh Dad! That's terrible when we have so much," Freddie interrupted.

"Times were hard," his father continued, "work was not as plentiful or as well paid as it is these days, so money to buy things was not available. Men would lay snares to catch rabbits to feed their families. They would skin them and boil the meat with whatever vegetables they could find, usually just potatoes and that would feed them all for a few days. Back then there were so many rabbits that they were considered vermin."

Freddie looked puzzled. "What's a vermin, Dad?"

"It's another name for pests like rats, only rats are not so good to eat. Rabbits breed very quickly and soon overrun farmers' fields eating their crops. People would grow vegetables in their gardens only for a family of rabbits to get in and eat everything above ground. So you see rabbits were not seen as fluffy cute pets, but as thieves stealing food from their families. Even though people caught and ate lots of rabbits they still bred too quickly and they were everywhere destroying all the precious food in fields and gardens. The Government created a disease that only killed rabbits, called Mixomatosis, and it basically made them go blind so they died being unable to find food."

"I feel sorry for the rabbits, Dad, they were only trying to survive, but I understand how desperate people must have been," Freddie admitted.

"There is still some of the rabbit disease about so it's not safe to eat wild rabbits. Rabbit meat is still eaten, but they are farmed like pigs and chickens. Our woods are protected and no animals may be caught in them, it's a local bylaw."

Again Freddie looked puzzled. "What's a bylaw, Dad?" he asked.

His father smiled and hugged his inquisitive son. "Bylaws are rules that local townspeople place on woodlands, parks and so on to protect them and keep them as they are. So it may not be against the law to catch animals in all woodlands, but it is in our woodland."

"Do you think they will try again?" Freddie asked.

"Probably not. Once they return and see the torch and snares are missing they will know that they have been discovered. The trouble with these snares is they are designed to catch the rabbits by the neck and the more it pulls ...."

"Oh Dad!" Freddie interrupted. "The poor little rabbit would choke and die!"

"Yes, but these snares are also a danger to squirrels, foxes, badgers, hedgehogs and even a small deer," Freddie's father explained.

The next day and for the rest of the week, the interesting lessons at school distracted Freddie from his discovery of the snares and poor rabbits. He had lots of fun playing with his friends during the schools breaks now they could laugh and play without Bully Bates interfering.

On Wednesday after school, James visited Freddie for his first guitar lesson. James showed him how to hold the guitar and grip the neck and reach round with his fingers to press the strings down on the metal frets to create a chord. "You're doing very well, Freddie, your long fingers help you reach around the guitar neck to press the strings down. Would you like to learn your favourite song?" he asked.

Freddie's face beamed. "Could I? That would be so great," he replied enthusiastically.

"Okay, there are only six chords to learn and I've drawn them on this sheet for you. Now the first is C, so let me show you how to do it."

Freddie handed James the guitar and he showed Freddie where to place his fingers to make the right chord sound, then he played the first two lines and Freddie clapped his hands enthusiastically. "Your turn now," James said handing the guitar to him. "The first chord is C and strum twice, once for *'all'* and second for *'things'* okay?"

Freddie stretched his fingers across the strings and strummed.

"That's it, Freddie. Press down on the fret a little harder. Good, you've got it," James encouraged. "Now chord F for the words *'Bright and'*. Oh! Nearly, try it again. That's it you've got it. Okay now the A minor chord for the word *'Beautiful.'* Wow! Freddie, you're good. Now put them all together and sing the words, it helps with the tune," James explained.

After only ten minutes Freddie had just about mastered the first line of his favourite tune when his mother came in with drinks and snacks.

"Mrs Fountain," James said excitedly, "just listen to Freddie, he's really good at this."

Freddie's mother sat on the edge of the bed and Freddie began to strum the chords James had taught him and he sang the words too.

When he finished his mother clapped her hands excitedly. "Freddie, that was so clever, you seem to have taken to the guitar," she praised. "Thank you, James, it's very kind of you to spend time with Freddie."

James smiled. "It's my pleasure, Mrs Fountain, Freddie has the perfect hands for it and a natural ability to remember the chords, it usually takes a good hour to memorize just three chords so he has done really well. Actually this is my old guitar, so Freddie can borrow it to practice on. I think he will be able to play the whole song very soon," James added.

"You must thank James, Freddie," his mother said.

"Can I really borrow this guitar, James?" Freddie was so surprised.

James nodded with a big smile.

"Oh, thank you, James, it's very kind of you. I really like playing it," Freddie beamed.

"A word of warning," James replied. "The strings will make the tips of your fingers sore until the skin thickens like mine." James showed his fingers to Freddie. "So don't spend more than fifteen minutes a day practicing for now, okay?" James looked at Freddie who seemed to have slipped into his own little world.

"Freddie!" his mother called.

"Oh yes, Mum, sorry." Freddie held out his hand, "James, look!" Sure enough his finger tips looked red and sore already. "Thank you, James, thank you so much for lending me your guitar. If Mum and Dad do buy one for me would you come with us to choose the right one?"

James laughed. "See if you like it first, there's no rush. If your fingers get too sore you'll struggle to hold a pencil or paint brush, so don't overdo it, but I will be very happy to guide your choice of guitar when that time comes."

* *

Freddie practiced playing his guitar the rest of the week and even though his fingers hurt a little, he persevered until he could play the whole of his favourite tune. He could not wait to show his parents and after teatime on Friday he played and sang 'All things bright and beautiful' to them.

Freddie's mother and father gave him a round of applause, they were just amazed and delighted with their son's progress.

Saturday seemed to come around quickly and after breakfast Freddie returned to his bedroom for another five minutes on his guitar. He was sat on the bed concentrating on his finger positions on the guitar neck and humming the tune, when something on the ceiling caught his eye, a ring of light flashed on and off. "I wonder what that can be?" he said, to no one in particular, putting down his guitar. He watched the ring of light flash on and off for a minute or two before jumping off his bed to investigate the source. When he looked out of the window he could see a small dot of white light blinking on and off between the pickets of the wooden fence at the bottom of the garden.

"There's that herd of elephants again!" Freddie's father chuckled as his son scrambled down the stairs.

"It's only me, Dad, I left the elephants upstairs!" he called back laughing.

Freddie slipped on his shoes and rushed through the kitchen door, down the garden to the fence and the flashing light, but as soon as he approached, it stopped flashing. "Who's there?" Freddie called out cautiously, scanning the bushes behind the fence where the light had been.

The bush rustled and shook, so Freddie tiptoed closer. "Hello Mr Bush, how are you and why are you blinking like that?" he whispered.

The bush shook again and Freddie heard something that made him jump back in surprise.

"COME!" It was a deep voice that he had heard once before, belonging to Merlin. "COME!" the voice said again.

Freddie skipped through the gate and straight to the bush thinking Wiggly might be playing a trick on him again, but no one was hiding in the bush. He felt a sudden coldness like a cool wind blowing over him. "Mr Bush, what must I do?" He was worried, something must be wrong.

The bush spoke to him again. **"COME, the ELFINS need you!"**

Freddie froze and then remembered what the Fairy Queen had told them. *"Even though Merlin is resting he watches over you."* Freddie realised that Wiggly or the Elfins must in trouble, so he dashed back into the house and up the stairs like a herd of elephants. He changed into his explorers play clothes with hat and magic golden staff, and of course his rucksack, and then dashed back downstairs.

"I expect it must be getting a bit crowded in your bedroom with all those elephants up there, unless they came down with you this time!" his father chuckled and teased his son.

"Aww - Da-ad!" Freddie protested with a little laugh.

"Just off exploring, Dad, to see if there are any more snares about."

His mother was in the kitchen and quickly made him jam sandwiches with a drink and chocolate bar. "Be back by 4 o'clock, there's a good boy," she instructed as he skipped off out of the door and down the garden path into the forest.

When he reached the bottom of the spiral staircase inside the big old oak tree, he opened the door with the magic words and was surprised at what he could see, or rather what he could not see. "What's happening?" he said, to no one in particular.

Everywhere was deserted, doors were closed and windows shuttered, it looked like Elfin Town was a ghost town.

He walked slowly along the road looking all around. One time he thought he saw someone dart from one building to another in the shadows. "This is really spooky!" he whispered to himself.

There was not a sound, no voices, no machines, nothing.

When Freddie reached the Tiggly's home he knocked on the front door.

Daddly opened the door with a sad and worried look on his face. "Come inside, Freddie, we've been expecting you," Daddly invited.

Freddie stepped inside the warm room. He saw Mummly sat in a comfy chair and then Wiggly and Giggly ran up to him and gave him a hug.

"We're glad you're here, Freddie, we knew you'd come," Wiggly greeted.

"What's happened? Why is everywhere quiet and deserted?" Freddie asked feeling worried.

"Come and sit down and we will explain," Daddly said and guided them to the comfy seats.

"How did you know to come visit today?" Wiggly asked and Freddie explained to them all about the flashing light and talking bush and that he thought Wiggly was tricking him again. It brightened the mood and they had another laugh telling the story again of how Wiggly had tricked Freddie with the buzzing bush.

"Something terrible has happened," Daddly began when they had settled down. "Yesterday Elfin Town was attacked!"

Freddie looked horrified. "I don't understand, how could anyone attack? You are protected by a magic enchantment, aren't you?" he asked. Before anyone could answer he continued. "So that's why homes are shuttered and people are too scared to come out! Who was it and what did they want?" Freddie had a horrible feeling this was about the crystal cavern and the crystals. "Not the crystals!" he cried out.

"No!" Wiggly replied. "It was the Mole Goblins!"

Freddie looked puzzled, he had never heard of such a creature.

"They tunnelled under the town until they surfaced in the school and kidnapped all the children," Daddly explained.

Poor Wiggly and Giggly were already in tears and Mummly was unusually quiet.

"I don't understand, why have they taken the children?" Freddie was almost in tears himself now, he knew all the children, they loved him and he loved them all back.

Mummly answered with sadness in her voice. "Elfins are not fighters, Freddie. We are helpers and doers, not fighters, so we had no way to defend ourselves, even if there had been time."

"But why would they take your children?" Now Freddie cried and trembled at the thought of what they might do to them. "No! Oh no! Don't tell me they're going to eat them. No, no!" he cried, shivering at the very thought.

"We really don't know, Freddie. They left a ransom note, but it makes no sense!" Mummly replied in tears.

"Do you have it, could I see it perhaps?"

Daddly walked over to a cupboard, retrieved the note and handed it to Freddie.

Freddie opened the folded paper, turning it one way and another, then he too looked perplexed.

"These are not proper words, they make no sense. They look like some kind of spell," Freddie announced holding the note in front of him, still twisting and turning it, screwing his face trying to make any sense of it. He held it up against the light of the window to try and see the lettering more clearly.

Giggly suddenly jumped up and shouted, "That's it!" and grabbed the note from Freddie's fingers and took it straight to the window, holding it at right angles to the glass. There they could see the note reflected in the shiny glass, like a mirror.

Freddie, Mummly, Daddly and Wiggly moved to the window and in the reflection they read,

'YOU WILL BRING A JAR OF FAIRY DUST
IN EXCHANGE FOR YOUR CHILDREN
SOON OR WE WILL EAT THEM'

"Giggly, you're a genius," Freddie cried.

"Oh Dear! Oh Dear!" Daddly groaned. "They don't understand that Fairy Dust only works for Elfins, not Goblins. Even if we give them what they want, only an Elfin can use it to make magic, we're sunk!"

Freddie thought for a moment. "What if I magic a jar of Fairy Dust from my rucksack, would that work?" he asked hopefully.

They all shook their heads.

"Magic cannot make more magic, you could not magic a magic wand that performed real magic. If you tried all you would get is something that looks like Fairy Dust, but it would just be twinkling dust, not magical," Daddly replied, crushing Freddie's idea.

He thought for a moment and then asked, "What do these Mole Goblins look like?"

Daddly guided them all to sit down in the comfy chairs while he answered Freddie's question. "They are as tall as you, Freddie, but they don't need clothes as their bodies are covered in short silky black fur," he began.

"They have arms and legs like we do, but covered in silky black fur," Mummly continued. "Oh! and they have hands and feet with long claws that they can retract like a cat, they use them to excavate tunnels."

Giggly burst out with, "Their heads are pointed and they have no neck, but two large eyes, a short stubby nose and their mouth is filled with needle sharp teeth and they look very scary."

Freddie scrunched his face up. "Oooh, they do sound horrible. How did they manage to tunnel through the Wizard's enchantment on your walls and floors?" he asked.

"We also wondered about that. They have a heightened sense of smell, but even with their big eyes they cannot see well. They may have some way of detecting magic and found a weak spot in the floor that just happened to be under the school," Daddly replied.

"I can't understand why they didn't just take what they wanted while they were here?" Freddie asked.

"We're not sure either, possibly the light was too bright for them, if it had been night time and dark they may have hunted down the jars of Fairy Dust themselves, we would have no way to stop them," Daddly replied.

Mummly made them all a nice hot cup of dandelion tea.

Freddie sat thinking out aloud. "So they have a keen sense of smell and most probably don't like bright light. Mmmm! I have an idea."

Four pairs of eyes were focussed on Freddie, hopeful his idea might help them.

"I will go down the tunnel and save the children, but I will need someone to help me."

Wiggly jumped out of his seat and immediately volunteered. "I'll go with you, Freddie, they scare me, but I feel safe with you."

Wiggly's parents looked fearful until Daddly said, "We will be worried about you both doing this, but Wiggly, you are old enough to make your own decisions now. Please be careful and help Freddie bring our children home safely."

Wiggly smiled. "Thank you, Daddly and Mummly. I will be careful and we will bring the children home, won't we, Freddie?"

Freddie also smiled, he had no idea what he was getting them in to, but was gambling that he could take advantage of the Mole Goblin's weaknesses and use them against them. "Come outside with me, Wiggly, I need to teach you something," Freddie said taking his friend's hand to lead him through the front door. "Can you pick up some of those small pebbles, Wiggly?" Freddie asked as they walked round to the back of the house. When they stopped both of them had a handful of small stones. Freddie took off his rucksack, unzipped the top and thought about something, then pulled out two catapults.

Wiggly giggled. "What are they, do you put them over your eye when it hurts?"

Freddie laughed. "Not really, Wiggly," he chuckled. He had put his stones on the ground and picked one up while giving the other catapult to Wiggly. "Watch and I'll show you what these are for, they are called catapults," he said arranging some sticks in the ground a little distance away. He loaded his catapult with a stone, pulled back the elastic and let go. The stone whizzed through the air too fast to see but one of the sticks suddenly snapped in two.

"Oh, wow!" Wiggly cried out.

"Now Wiggly, put a pebble in the pouch, that's right. Now hold the catapult in one hand like I did and pull the pouch back, aim at the sticks and let go. That's it! You've got it!"

Wiggly's pebble flew through the air, hit the ground and bounced over the sticks. He almost fell backwards in the process. "Whoa! That's powerful!" he cried.

"Have another go, Wiggly. Aim a little higher, you've almost got it," Freddie encouraged.

This time Wiggly hit a stick and it snapped in half. "Whoopee!" he cried with excitement and his legs running on the spot again.

"That's perfect, Wiggly. Now stand still and have a few more goes so that you get used to loading, aiming and firing." Freddie chuckled at his friend's antics.

Wiggly was soon hitting the sticks every time and Freddie clapped his hands to show how pleased he was.

"Okay Wiggly, we are ready, it's time to save the children!"

Back inside the house Freddie pulled two powerful torches from his rucksack.

When he switched one on it was so bright Giggly had to shade her eyes. "Wow, those Mole Goblins won't like that," she said and applauded supportively.

Next, Freddie pulled out a box from his magic rucksack that looked like it contained pretty glass balls with a liquid inside them.

"What are those?" Wiggly asked.

"These are our surprise ammunition for the catapults, be careful not to break them," Freddie warned.

Wiggly frowned and shook his head questioningly.

"You'll see very soon," Freddie told him. Then he pulled out two nose clips. "These are what I use when I go swimming, you use them like this." Freddie opened one of the clips and put it on his nose and it closed his nostrils. "Id topth da wa'er gowin tup by doze," he said.

Giggly burst out laughing, followed by Wiggly, Mummly and Daddly.

"So funny, Freddie," Giggly cried.

Freddie took the clip off his nose. "I said, it stops the water from going up my nose!"

And they all laughed a bit more.

"We're ready then." Freddie announced.

"Be careful both of you, remember the Mole Goblins have very sharp claws," Wiggly's parents told them, and then everyone hugged.

Freddie left his rimmed hat and magic golden staff at the Tiggly's house.

Wiggly ran off to the sleeping area to change his clothes and came back wearing thick long trousers and a thick long sleeved jumper. "Just in case those Mole Goblins try to scratch or bite me," he explained.

Everyone set off down the deserted road heading toward the school. It seemed strange to Freddie not seeing any Elfin children about when they entered the school building. The teacher, Miss Noall, and one or two Elfin men were standing guard in the classroom looking very glum when Freddie and the Tiggly's arrived.

"Oh, Freddie! How wonderful to see you, do you think you can help?" Miss Noall asked.

"We have a plan!" Wiggly replied excitedly, but standing still this time.

"You do? How fantastic!" Miss Noall replied a little more cheerfully, as did the other Elfins.

"Where is the tunnel?" Freddie asked and then spotted a huge rock on a wooden board in the very middle of the classroom.

Miss Noall pointed to the rock. "We had to make sure no Mole Goblins crept into the town during the night," she said to the unasked question.

The three Elfin men carefully managed to move the rock off the board and uncover the tunnel entrance.

Freddie shone his torch into the tunnel and the intense light beam lit it up like sunlight. "It doesn't seem to be too deep," Freddie said inspecting the hole in the floor.

"Look!" Wiggly noticed, "it turns at the bottom towards the hills."

Freddie took off his rucksack and reached inside, pulling out a roll of something.

"Oooh, what's that?" Giggly asked with interest.

Freddie smiled knowingly and replied, "This is a rope ladder, it's something I've seen on television that was used to escape from a burning building." He smiled and fixed one end of it to the heavy rock and then rolled it out and down the tunnel entrance. The rope ladder was just long enough to reach the bottom of the tunnel.

"Oh! That's clever, Freddie, now we have an easy way to climb down instead of jumping," Wiggly said looking admiringly at his friend.

"Even better," Daddly added, "you have an easy way of getting back out of the tunnel too!"

Daddly, Mummly and Giggly hugged Wiggly, then Freddie.

"Good luck, bring our children home safely. Be careful boys, those Mole Goblins are fearsome creatures, watch out for their claws," Daddly warned.

Freddie reached inside his rucksack and brought out two more very powerful torches. "Take these torches, if any Mole Goblins appear, shine the light into their faces, that should scare them off," he explained handing over the torches. Then he began making his way down the rope ladder.

Wiggly followed once Freddie reached the bottom. "It looks a lot deeper from the bottom, Freddie," he said looking back up to Daddly who was waving them off.

"Torches on then, Wiggly, let's do this." Freddie had just set off when he stopped abruptly, causing his friend to bump into him yet again.

"Ooof! What's the matter?" Wiggly whispered rubbing his nose.

Freddie put his finger to his lips. "Shhhhh! Listen!"

With hands to their ears they could hear faint sounds.

"Must be a long way off," Freddie whispered, "but if we can hear them, then they can hear us so we must go very quietly, okay?" he added.

They began to walk slowly along the tunnel. It was very straight so they could see well ahead with their bright torchlight.

"Hey, this tunnel is almost under our house," Wiggly whispered as they continued along the smooth walled passageway. A bit further along, ten minutes or so later, he whispered again, "Now we are under the, what do you call them? Oh, yes, mount-hills." Then, after they had been walking for a good fifteen minutes more, Wiggly whispered, "We're under the open fields now."

Freddie already knew Elfins had a good sense of direction and it was helpful because he had no idea where they were. "Let's just rest a minute," Freddie suggested and they sat down. "Turn your torch off for now, save the battery," he said lifting off his rucksack and bringing out two cartons of juice and a chocolate bar each.

"You have nice tasty things in your world, Freddie," his friend whispered as he swallowed his last piece of chocolate and licking his lips.

They had just put the wrappers and cartons back into Freddie's rucksack when Freddie jumped to his feet. "Did you hear that?" he whispered.

Wiggly jumped up, switched on his torch and listened. An eerie wail screeched along the tunnel.

"That's a Mole Goblin calling, I'd know that sound anywhere," Wiggly replied quietly.

Freddie reached in his rucksack once more and pulled out four hook and loop straps. "Give me your left arm, Wiggly," he instructed, then strapped the torch to his friend's outstretched arm. "Now you can shine your torch and hold the catapult at the same time. Take these straps now and fasten my torch on my arm please."

Wiggly took the torch and straps and copied what Freddie had done with his torch.

"Thanks, Wiggly, now get your catapult loaded and hold it by the pouch, ready to fire. Aim at their body," Freddie explained urgently.

"Will it kill them?" Wiggly asked.

"No, you'll see what happens and it should give them a nasty fright. Let's proceed slowly and be ready to shine your torch right in their faces, okay?"

It was still a bit tricky holding the loaded catapult and pointing the torch.

They held the catapult ready with their torch on the same arm and lit the way, then moved forward at a snail's pace.

Freddie was in front because the tunnel had narrowed and was only wide enough for one person, then he stopped without warning and Wiggly collided with him yet again. "Ooof!" he gasped and chuckled. "Sorry, Wiggly, but look!" Freddie exclaimed.

"Oh! That's a big problem," Wiggly whispered in agreement.

"Is there any secret writing on the walls, Wiggly?"

He squeezed past Freddie and examined the walls, turned and shook his head. "Nope, both tunnels look identical and there are no markings anywhere."

"How do you think the Mole Goblins know which tunnel goes where?" Freddie asked.

Wiggly had an idea. "Switch off the torches and squint your eyes," he whispered.

With the torches off they squinted their eyes and looked around. It took a moment for their eyesight to adjust.

Then Wiggly gasped, "Look, the right hand tunnel seems to be slightly glowing red and the left tunnel glowing slightly green. Red means danger in the Elfin world," Wiggly whispered.

"It means the same to Sproggles, like stop, but green means go or okay," Freddie whispered back.

"Green it is then." Wiggly agreed.

They switched their torches back on, having relaxed the catapults that had been making both their arms ache. They came to another fork in the tunnels.

"The left one is greenish again," Wiggly said once they switched off their torches for a moment and were in the darkness again.

"Where do you think we are?" Freddie asked.

"We passed your house and the open fields and are heading in the direction of the disused quarry," Wiggly replied softly.

"My Dad took me to see the quarry a while ago, it's full of smelly water now they've stopped taking stone from it. Dad said it's very deep, cold and dangerous and never to play near it," Freddie whispered to Wiggly.

Wiggly was leading, he then came to a sudden stop, so of course, Freddie bumped into him. "Ooof, ow!" Wiggly cried, then covered his mouth with his hand, almost hitting his face with the torch strapped to his arm.

"Why did you stop, Wiggly? Oh, I see!" Freddie exclaimed quietly, looking at the solid wall in front of him that he was squashing Wiggly against. He stepped back and let Wiggly move from the wall. "A dead end! Why would they stop tunnelling?" Freddie asked, "and where did they go?"

"Oh look, Freddie, it's not a dead end but a tee junction!" Wiggly groaned as they pulled themselves apart.

They took the left tunnel after switching off their torches and squinting their eyes to see it was glowing green.

"We're heading for the Great Barrow," Wiggly whispered and stopped again, but this time Freddie was ready.

"I thought that the Great Barrow was an ancient burial tomb," Freddie said.

"I've heard of it but Elfins have no record of it being constructed so it must have been a very long time ago," Wiggly replied in a quiet voice. They walked on for another five minutes then Wiggly stopped again.

"What is it, Wiggly?"

Wiggly was looking into a big empty chamber with lots of wooden doors.

The two friends looked around, shinning their torches about and when they were confident there were no Mole Goblins about, they stepped in with their backs to the wall and looked around in amazement.

"Wow! I count 15 doors, Wiggly. What do we do now?" Freddie said feeling a little daunted.

Wiggly turned to his friend with a look of disappointment on his face. "I wonder why they have doors on these tunnels?" he said.

"Maybe these doors are their homes," suggested Freddie.

"They have something on each door, Freddie, look!"

Freddie shone his torch at one door after another. "I don't see anything, Wiggly. What do you see, does it give us any clues?"

Wiggly walked from door to door shaking his head until he arrived at door number nine, then he got a bit excited.

Freddie rushed to his friend's side. "What is it, Wiggly, what do you see?" he asked.

"I don't understand what's on the other doors, but this one has three bars on it, so maybe this is their jail where our children are being kept," he replied.

"Only one way to find out Wiggly, get your catapult ready," Freddie replied as they loaded their catapults and switched off their torches. Freddie pulled the ring of rope attached to the door, which creaked and groaned, opening into another short tunnel. He closed the door behind them and walked to the end of this tunnel, finding themselves in yet another big empty circular cavern. There were lots of doors, not solid as before, but made of straight wooden branches, just like prison doors might look. The cavern was dimly lit from above and just light enough for them to see without their torches. The silence was eerie and scary. So far the two friends had been lucky enough not to have bumped into any Mole Goblins, but that was about to change.

"Look!" Wiggly whispered as they stood in the shadows.

"What?" Freddie whispered quietly.

"Over there, I can just see someone behind the bars," Wiggly whispered back.

Freddie followed Wiggly's finger to the door at which he was pointing.

"Oh yes, look at the other doors, more figures. Let me shine a narrow torch light beam through each door and see what happens,"

Freddie replied. He released his catapult a moment while he adjusted the focus on his torch, then shone it on the dark wall opposite, a bright white dot of light appeared the size of a tennis ball.

"That's great, Freddie, I've got my catapult ready, so let's see if the children are in there and come to the doors or if it's Mole Goblins in there," Wiggly whispered.

Freddie flashed his torch at the first door and sure enough an Elfin girl came to the bars, then he shone into each cell in turn.

"So far they are all the children," Wiggly whispered, then he screamed out loud as a clawed hand suddenly appeared from nowhere and grabbed him, pulling him away from the wall. "HELP! HELP!" a terrified Wiggly screamed.

Freddie had been startled by his friend's cry and hesitated for a moment, before twisting the focus ring on his torch right up and shone it at the retreating black figure holding Wiggly. The Mole Goblin dropped his captive instantly and gave up a terrifying screech like a wounded eagle, then covered its eyes from the bright light.

Wiggly fell to the ground and quickly scrambled back to Freddie.

"Use your nose clip now, Wiggly," Freddie said while loading his catapult.

WHOOSH! ... SPLAT!

Freddie hit the Mole Goblin on its back and it screeched again, so loud that the sound hurt their ears.

"Bot's appenig?" *(What's Happening?)* Wiggly asked in a funny voice caused by his nose being pinched by the clip. He watched the Mole Goblin dance around, screeching and trying to shake off the projectile Freddie had fired. It turned and twisted, jumping up and down and then fell to its knees, suddenly falling down unconscious. "Bot is dat Fweddie?" *(What is that Freddie?)*

Freddie chuckled. "Bell dat verked bedder dan I'd doped Biggly. It'th a tink bomb. Da thmell ith tho howid dat de Bole Goblin'th acute thense ob thmell hath wendered it unconthiouth." *(Well that worked better than I'd hoped Wiggly. It's a stink bomb. The smell is so horrid that the Mole Goblin's acute sense of smell has rendered it unconscious)*

"Oh, bow! Fweddie you're tho clever do tink ob dat!" *(Oh, wow! Freddie you're so clever to think of that!)* Wiggly praised his friend.

Freddie smiled and replied. "Come let'th get de childwen and thcarper before ......!" *(Come let's get the children and scarper before....)*

But it was too late! Freddie did not get the chance to finish when one of the other doors opened and four big scary, ugly Mole Goblins rushed into the chamber coming to a sudden halt at their fallen friend. Four terrifying screeches echoed off the walls and ceiling almost deafening Freddie and Wiggly. The Mole Goblins were big, maybe two metres tall, their bodies covered in short black silky fur. They had short arms and legs, with long claws on hands and feet, only four toes and four fingers, no neck and two large eyes to see in the dark. A short stubby nose and mouth filled with needle sharp teeth that seemed to glint as if made of metal.

But before the other Mole Goblins had a chance to charge at the two friends, both had loaded their catapults with stink bombs and fired.

WHOOSH ... Splat! WHOOSH ... Splat!

They loaded again as the two that had been hit desperately tried to rid themselves of the stinking liquid from the bombs which had smashed, spilling their contents into their fur. They screeched and danced.

WHOOSH ... Splat! WHOOSH ... Splat!

The remaining Mole Goblins were hit and covered in the foul smelling liquid. All four leapt about making a terrible noise, then the first two fell to the ground unconscious, quickly followed by the second pair.

Wiggly was so curious to know what had rendered the Mole Goblins unconscious, that he took off his nose clip and sniffed. "Aw! That's really disgusting, what a stink!" he wailed and wretched, quickly replacing his nose clip.

"Quickly to de cellth Biggly, gib theseth nothe clipth do ower childwen before they collapth too!" Freddie ordered. *(Quickly to the cells Wiggly, give these nose clips to our children before they collapse too!)*

106

Although Wiggly was scared and he struggled to understand Freddie, he even managed a chuckle because of his friend's funny voice.

Freddie realised their nose clips were a problem and took his off briefly and repeated, "Quickly to the cells, Wiggly, give these nose clips to our children before they collapse too!"

They dashed to the doors, unfastened them and gave each of the children a clip for their nose as they were already pinching their noses with their fingers.

"Aw, what a thtink!" *(Aw, what a stink!)* one of the children called out making the other children giggle at the funny sounding voice.

When the children were all out in the chamber they jumped for joy and tried to hug Freddie and Wiggly.

Freddie took off his nose clip again and explained, "Quickly everyone, it's not safe here, follow Wiggly, we need to get you all safely back home. Keep those clips on your noses as well. Go! Go!"

The children were so excited that it took a moment for them to calm down and do as Freddie had told them. "Huway Viggly! Huway Fweddie! You thaved uth," they chanted. *(Hurray Wiggly! Hurray Freddie! You saved us)*

Then another took off his nose clip and cried, "Coo! What's that awful stink?"

Freddie laughed and took off his nose clip for a moment. "Put your nose clip back on!"

The children were so funny, but they calmed down and became quiet when Freddie shushed them. Wiggly shone his torch to the maximum beam brightness, then led the children through the short tunnel into the larger chamber.

Freddie followed behind making sure no one went astray. "Look for the green tunnel, Wiggly," Freddie called, taking his nose clip off as they both switched off their torches.

"BLOOK OUP!" *(Look out)* one of the children screamed as two Mole Goblins came at them from one of the red tunnels.

Wiggly quickly switched his torch back on, shining it directly at the Mole Goblin's eyes and they halted in their tracks, shrieking and covering their faces, then turning away from the beam of light.

Freddie turned on his torch and even the children shaded their eyes the light was so bright.

"Stink bomb them, Wiggly!" Freddie cried, in a funny voice that sounded like *'tink bum dem Biggly'* because of his nose clip.

Wiggly was ahead of Freddie's command. He loaded his catapult, aimed and fired,

WHOOSH! - SPLAT!

Hitting the back of one Mole Goblin, then he fired his catapult at the second one.

WHOOSH! - SPLAT!

A direct hit on both their backs. The Mole Goblins screeched and screamed, jumping around as if they were on fire.

The children all watched with fascination, ooohing and aarhing then clapping when the two Mole Goblins fell unconscious to the ground.

"Det's get going, lead on Biggly." *(Let's get going, lead on Wiggly)* Freddie's strange voice shouted, leaving the Mole Goblins behind them.

Wiggly had seen which tunnel to use, it being a different one that had brought them to the prison area. When they came to the fork, they switched off their torches again to look for the green tunnel.

"Bot's dat?" *(What's that)* Wiggly cried as they reached yet another small cavern with three tunnels. With the torches off he decided on the middle one. "Pollow be," *(follow me)* Wiggly cried. They switched their torches back on just as the children all screamed so loud it made Freddie and Wiggly's ears ring.

The cavern wall on both sides of them suddenly exploded, creating two new tunnels from which more Mole Goblins emerged.

"Quickly everyone," Freddie called taking his nose clip off for a moment and they made a dash for the middle tunnel. Just as Freddie was about to enter the tunnel behind the children, one of the Mole Goblins grabbed him by the shoulder. A sharp claw pierced his skin and made him bleed.

"Get off! Get off, you monster!" Freddie yelled out in pain.

Suddenly a bright light flooded the area and the Mole Goblins screeched their horrifying ear piercing wail.

Freddie pulled free when the Mole Goblin which had hold of him let go to cover its eyes. He pulled out two stink bombs and smashed them on the nearest Mole Goblin while Wiggly fired two more at the others. Freddie put his nose clip on quickly.

The Mole Goblins wailed and screamed, jumping around like crazy, clawing at their backs to rid themselves of the stinking liquid soaking into their fur and then they fell to the ground unconscious.

Freddie reached into his rucksack and pulled out a tennis ball sized stink bomb and smashed it in the tunnel as they all fled. He thought it would make everywhere stink ensuring they would not be followed.

"Are we going in the right direction, Wiggly? I have no sense of where we are," Freddie yelled, needing to remove his nose clip to speak.

Wiggly took off his nose clip and groaned at the smell then called back, still running at a pace, "Yes, Freddie, not too far now, nearly home!"

The children all cheered and laughed and puffed, it was hard for them to breathe with their nose clips in place as they tried to keep up with Wiggly.

Freddie was struggling, his shoulder was hurting and his tee shirt was ripped and soaked in blood. He panted as he tried to keep up with the children in front of him. He worried how he would explain all this to his mother and father, he would not be able to hide his wound and bloodied clothes. Freddie was afraid he might have to tell the truth and expose the Elfins to untold danger. At the very least his parents might forbid him to go into the forest ever again.

Wiggly stopped and everyone took the chance to breathe. "**LOOK OUT!**" Wiggly screamed as he looked back to check on everyone and saw the tunnel wall imploding right where a little girl was standing in front of Freddie.

A hairy-clawed hand grabbed her and dragged her screaming back into the tunnel that the Mole Goblin had just made.

"**GO! GO!**" Freddie screamed. "**I'll get Violet. NOW GO, PLEASE!**" he yelled.

Wiggly and the rest of the children ran as fast as they could, dashing down the last part of the tunnel until they reached the opening under the school.

Daddly and lots of other parents were waiting anxiously, having heard the screams coming from the tunnel.

Wiggly guided the children up the rope ladder and into the arms of their parents. The schoolroom was brightly lit to discourage any Mole Goblins coming out of the tunnel entrance. After Wiggly had climbed up and out of the tunnel he stood looking back, hoping to see Freddie with Violet.

"Wiggly, where's Freddie?" his father asked anxiously.

"Where's Violet? She's not here," her parents cried out.

Wiggly was so confused, his mind was in turmoil. His friend had gone after Violet and people were firing questions at him. He pulled off his nose clip, "I - I - I d-d -don't know, Daddly." He stumbled over his words as tears began to flow. "He's so brave, he went after Violet when a Mole Goblin broke through the tunnel and dragged her away," he sobbed.

Violet's mother cried out aloud and her husband tried to comfort her.

Wiggly looked down the tunnel hopefully, expecting to see his friend and Violet safe. When they did not appear Wiggly sucked in his tears and announced, **"I'm going back!"** Before Daddly could stop him, Wiggly had scampered down the rope ladder heading towards the tunnel where Violet had been taken. "Oh, that stink is awful!" he cried and put his nose clip back on.

* *

Meanwhile Freddie was following the Mole Goblin that had snatched Violet. "Boy, these Mole Goblins can move fast even with an Elfin in their claws," he mumbled to himself. He had his torch on full power and could see the two of them not too far ahead. When he heard Violet crying out, he was afraid she was hurt, so he stopped, loaded his catapult quickly and fired a stink bomb directly ahead. He missed his target but hit the wall making the Mole Goblin squeal and slow to a halt giving Freddie enough time to load his catapult again.

WHOOSH! ... SPLAT!

This time Freddie hit the Mole Goblin and it dropped Violet while it tried in vain to remove the stink bomb from its back. Scratching

110

behind it and wailing, leaping up and down until it finally collapsed unconscious on the ground, trapping Violet underneath it.

Freddie pointed his torch ahead and rushed to Violet's aid, pushing the heavy Mole Goblin off the little girl. "Are bou hurt Biolet?" *(Are you hurt Violet?)* Freddie asked concerned and panting.

"Do Fweddie." *(No Freddie)* she whimpered and then cried in alarm. "Fweddie you're bweeding!" *(Freddie you're bleeding)*

Freddie picked Violet up, holding her close to him. "Don't borry about dat Biolet, let'th get you to thafty and dome. Opay?" *(Don't worry about that Violet, let's get you to safety and home. Okay?)* he replied as he ran along the tunnel with Violet in his arms. He stopped suddenly and shivered. Directly in front of them was another Mole Goblin, but it was not shielding its eyes or turning away from the torch beam. The creature wailed and screeched so loud it made Freddie's ears feel like they would explode.

Violet cried out in pain, even with her hands covering her ears.

Then another screech came from behind him and Freddie realised they were trapped between two of the horrible creatures. For once his quick wits failed him and he stood frozen to the spot.

"Fweddie!" *(Freddie)* Violet cried shaking him.

'They're gonna eat me' was all that Freddie could think and it terrified him. He could not move a muscle.

* *

Wiggly had just turned into the new tunnel when he saw the back of a Mole Goblin that was facing into the beam from Freddie's torch.

"Fweddie!" *(Freddie)* he cried out bravely, but his whole body was trembling.

The Mole Goblin turned and Wiggly saw it was wearing something over its eyes.

"Fweddie!" *(Freddie)* Wiggly cried out again and the Mole Goblin looked like it was going to pounce on him.

Somewhere deep down, the love of his friend snapped Wiggly out of his fear. He loaded two stink bombs in his catapult and fired.

Both stink bombs hit their target. For a brief moment the Mole Goblin stood like a statue.

Fearful the creature had found a way to overcome the stink bomb smell, Wiggly fired another.

WHOOSH ... SPLAT!

The stink bomb hit the Mole Goblin right in the face. This time it screeched and wailed, jumped up and down so hard it crashed into the roof and walls before it collapsed unconscious.

"Fweddie!" *(Freddie)* Violet cried, still shaking him.

This time Freddie snapped out of his trance and saw the Mole Goblin ahead of them collapse to the ground and then spotted his best friend, Wiggly.

"Let'th get out of here Biolet," *(Let's get out of here Violet)* he said still clinging onto the little Elfin girl. He began to run, trampling over the fallen creature and heading towards his friend, Wiggly.

When they caught up with Wiggly, Freddie groaned, "Take Biolet and Wun Biggly!" *(Take Violet and run Wiggly)*

"But what ...." Freddie did not give Wiggly the chance to finish.

"Just wun! Biggly. Pleath!" *(Just run Wiggly. Please)* Freddie begged his friend.

So Wiggly took Violet in his arms and ran like Freddie had told him, back to the opening and safety. He helped Violet climb up the rope ladder and then scampered up it himself, pulling off his nose clip, waiting impatiently for his friend. "Freddie's hurt, Daddly, really badly, he's bleeding so much. A Mole Goblin stuck its claws into his shoulder. What if he collapses and doesn't get back? I have to go back."

This time Daddly held onto his son, having faith in Freddie that he would be all right.

When Freddie reached the junction of the two tunnels he fired several stink bombs down each tunnel hoping the smell would last for days down there. Although he was beginning to feel dizzy he managed to stagger further along, then reached into his rucksack taking out some motion sensor torches and set them down along the last stretch of the tunnel. "Dey'll ged a thhock if dey come thith far, de torcheth bill light up ben dey detect moobment and blind dem," *(They'll get a shock if they come this far, the torches will light up when they detect movement and blind them)* he said to himself. He remembered his father had fixed something like them on the ceiling outside his bedroom that lit up the landing at night when he wanted to use the bathroom.

"Freddie! Freddie!" Wiggly bellowed down the tunnel, desperately hoping to see his friend.

It seemed an age since Wiggly had pushed Violet up out of the tunnel entrance and scrambled up himself. He and everyone else waited anxiously, expecting and worrying about their brave Sproggle friend. A terrible stink was beginning to rise up out of the hole in the school floor making everyone back away, except Wiggly.

**

Freddie suddenly felt weak, his legs were like jelly and he tripped and fell flat on his face. Tears ran from his eyes as he began to think he would not make it, he lay exhausted and bleeding, all his fight had deserted him.

"Freddie!"

He heard the distant voice of Elfins calling his name, but his mind felt cloudy and fuzzy. Then he heard the multiple screeches of Mole Goblins way down the tunnels getting ever louder.

"Freddie!"

Again he heard his name being called and he pushed himself up on his tired, aching arms and then onto his knees. With his arms outstretched to the tunnel wall he hoisted his body up onto his feet.

'Freddie, you have done well, now stand up and get to safety.' It was the voice of Merlin in Freddie's mind encouraging him to carry on. He stood, wobbly, but standing on his feet, urged on by Mole Goblin screeches and the voices of his Elfin friends. He concentrated on the voices shouting his name and staggered toward the beam of light shining through the hole in the school floor.

"Freddie! Freddie!" The lone voice of Wiggly cried when his friend appeared at the bottom of the tunnel.

Freddie staggered and tried to climb up the rope ladder with his injured shoulder, which was still bleeding. He fell backwards, on to his back, feeling dizzy. He had no more energy left.

Wiggly could see Freddie was in trouble and scrambled down the rope ladder and grabbed his friend. "Let me help you, Freddie," he croaked, looking at Freddie's shirt, which was bright red all over. Wiggly stood behind Freddie and pushed him up the rope ladder until Daddly was able to take hold of Freddie's hands to pull him up.

Freddie cried out in pain as he was pulled out of the hole.

Wiggly burst into tears, he had never seen Sproggle blood and his invincible friend was screaming. He suddenly went quiet and fell limply on the floor.

When Freddie's head had finally appeared above the hole in the floor a huge cheer and applause sounded from all the Elfin parents holding their children he and Wiggly had saved.

Wiggly and Daddly helped Freddie out of the hole and into the schoolroom.

Parents and children parted the way for him as he collapsed onto the floor. He looked drained and exhausted, his shirt covered in bright red bloodstains and blood leaked from his shoulder onto the floor in an ever growing pool.

The Council Elder pulled up the rope ladder and then sprinkled a little Fairy Dust over the hole in the floor, it slowly closed up and disappeared as if it had never been there.

Wiggly and Daddly watched happy parents taking their children home, some got piggy back rides, others skipped along holding hands. All of them none the worse for their adventure, but chattering non-stop about how brave Freddie and Wiggly had been.

Freddie was barely breathing, he lifted his head slightly and tried to speak, then collapsed falling unconscious.

"Freddie!" Wiggly cried to his friend. "Daddly! Daddly! Help Freddie, please! He's been so brave, we must help him, please Daddly!" he implored.

Daddly and the Council Elder brought a stretcher and lifted the motionless Freddie gently on to it, he was still breathing but very weakly.

"Daddly, you must save Freddie, he saved us all, we need him, Daddly please!" Wiggly begged as tears streamed down his face while looking at his motionless friend.

Daddly looked at the Council Elder and shrugged their shoulders. "We don't know how to help him, Wiggly," Daddly replied.

"You must take him home to his parents, they will know what to do, please Daddly!" Wiggly continued to beg.

"Wiggly, if we do that, it will place every Elfin in danger, Freddie would not want that," the Council Elder replied.

"We have to do something, he's our hero, he saved our children, he saved me, you don't know what it was like down in the tunnels, it was so scary. Those Mole Goblins are huge and terrifying, Freddie fought them all off, we can't let him die. Look, he's hardly breathing. Oh, please, please! Do something, anything!" Wiggly fell to his knees beside his brave friend. "Freddie, I'm so sorry, you have to get well," he sobbed.

Even Daddly and the Council Elder had tears in their eyes, they just did not know what to do.

For the first time in a very, very long time in Elfin Town, the deep, kindly voice of Merlin echoed,

"BRING THE BOY."

Wiggly gasped and his tears stopped flowing and he looked at his father. "We can't get in the Crystal Cavern for another 50 years, Daddly. Where does Merlin want us to take Freddie?" Wiggly begged.

Daddly and the Council Elder knew exactly where Merlin wanted them to take Freddie.

"Go home to Mummly and your sister, Wiggly. Let us take care of Freddie. Now please, off you go, let us help him."

Wiggly thought to argue but changed his mind, he did not want to get in the way, he hung his head and obeyed his father, as all Elfins do.

Freddie was carried on the stretcher to a large round building in the absolute centre of Elfin Town. It was a long forgotten building, even though Elfins walked past it every day, they no longer noticed it. This was mainly due to the fact that it was Merlin's consulting room where Elfins could go and speak with the Wizard if they needed his help with any problems. Since he disappeared the building had been closed and locked, becoming almost invisible, yet in plain sight.

The Council Elder spoke the magic words and two doors slowly opened inwards. They carried Freddie on the stretcher into the round room, now empty apart from a large stone plinth in the centre on which Freddie was placed. Merlin's voice deep and kindly sounded again.

"LEAVE THE BOY."

Freddie was barely breathing now, he had lost so much blood that still dripped from his shoulder onto the stone plinth and then the dusty floor. The Council Elder and Daddly left the building and closed the doors behind them, then waited patiently outside, hoping that Merlin's presence was strong enough after all this time, to help their Sproggle friend and hero.

The roof of the building was like an upturned funnel, except without a spout, just a hole, and if Freddie had been awake he could have seen the bright blue-sky roof.

A few Elfin adults and children began to arrive and soon the whole town crowded silently around the building. Wiggly, Giggly and Mummly joined Daddly in his vigil, everyone was silent, but for the sound of their breathing.

"Look!" Violet cried out pointing to the sky, and a sea of faces all looked up at the same time.

Directly over the hole in the roof of Merlin's building appeared a beautiful blue crystal that slowly descended and slipped through the hole in the roof.

"It's a Fairy," cried Wiggly in a loud whisper. "It's a Fairy everyone, Freddie and I have seen one before, in the crystal cavern!"

The crystal descended through the hole in the roof and hovered above Freddie, then with a brilliant burst of light, transformed into the Fairy Queen. The bright light shone up through the hole in the roof like a brilliant torch beam and through all the cracks in the door, making those close by shade their eyes.

The Fairy Queen floated down and stood at Freddie's side, looking down on his slowly fading body. "Such a brave boy, Freddie," her voice soft and gentle. She waved her magic star wand in a figure of eight and special Fairy Dust filled the air, slowly settling on Freddie, covering him from head to toe. "Freddie, Merlin called upon you to help his beloved Elfins." Everyone waiting outside could hear the Fairy Queen's voice, they stood silently, eagerly hopeful Freddie would be well again. "You have been so brave in rescuing all the Elfin children. An act of total selflessness, you are a good person, Freddie, one day all Sproggles will be like you." The Fairy Queen waved her wand over Freddie's body and the bloodstains on his shirt began to disappear, his wound closed and healed like it had never existed, leaving no trace or scar. "Rise up, Freddie, you have much to do, Merlin grants you a charmed life, you will no longer succumb to injury or ill health for the whole of your special life."

Outside, every single Elfin held their breath, not daring to make even the smallest of sounds.

Inside the building the Fairy Queen rose up and transformed back into a beautiful crystal emitting an intense light that shone through the hole in the roof and the cracks in the doors. The crystal passed through the hole in the roof and up into the sky ceiling and every Elfin watched as it vanished into thin air.

Daddly looked at Wiggly as everyone breathed out the breath they had been holding. "Go wake your friend, Wiggly," Daddly said and opened the doors again.

Wiggly walked inside to see his friend still laying motionless on the stretcher. He knelt by Freddie's side and held his hand. "Freddie...... Freddie...... it's time to wake up now........ come back to us, to me, please Freddie," he whispered in Freddie's ear. Then he pulled back to look at the best friend he did not want to lose and who lay motionless, not even breathing. Wiggly looked out to his father waiting patiently at the doors, and shook his head as tears dripped rapidly from his eyes.

"Freddie!...... Please!...... Wake up!" Wiggly croaked in a low voice.

Suddenly Freddie sucked in a breath and slowly opened his eyes.

Wiggly wrapped his arms around him and hugged him tightly.

"Wiggly, I can't breathe," Freddie groaned.

Wiggly released him and eased back to let Freddie breathe and helped him sit up.

"What's happening, Wiggly?" Freddie asked when he saw the sea of faces looking at him through the two open doors.

The moment Freddie's voice pierced the deathly silence, a huge roar and cheer rang out from everyone outside.

Freddie suddenly felt embarrassed and blushed bright red.

Wiggly giggled. "You do look funny that colour, Freddie!" His friend looked at him and they both laughed.

Freddie suddenly remembered what had happened and looked at his tee shirt and then his shoulder that no longer hurt. "What has happened, Wiggly, was it all a dream?"

Everyone outside were still cheering and clapping.

Wiggly was so excited he stood up and his legs were running on the spot again. "No! No! It was real all right, you saved the children and fought off the Mole Goblins. You got badly hurt and Merlin sent the Fairy Queen to make you well again. Merlin has granted you a charmed life, you won't get sick or ever get injured again."

"Calm down, Wiggly! What are you saying, the Fairy Queen and Merlin saved me?"

"Yes! Yes!" Wiggly panted.

"Help me up, Wiggly," Freddie asked and together they walked out of Merlin's surgery and up onto the shoulders of the crowd who were still cheering them, calling Freddie and Wiggly their heroes. A title they had certainly earned. They carried them to the town square where a feast was quickly assembled for a celebratory party. The Council Elder presented Freddie and Wiggly with a medal of bravery and both boys had never been happier.

CHAPTER FOUR

The Mystery of the Disappearing Screws

When gates and fences, doors and displays fall apart
around the village, Freddie Fixit comes to the rescue.

Tomorrow will be Saturday and Freddie's check up at the dentist. Although he was not afraid of going, it was the subject of scary stories among his friends as they sat chatting on a bench in the school playground.

"Sometimes the dentist puts you to sleep and takes all your teeth out to sell to the Tooth Fairy," Jimmy taunted and rolled around laughing.

"Take no notice," Anne remarked, my Dad knows the dentist and I'll ask him to make sure he steals all of Jimmy's teeth when he goes for his check up next week!"

Jimmy stopped laughing. "Oh Anne! Please don't do that, if I haven't got any teeth, how can I chew toffees?"

Freddie chuckled. "Well you won't be able to chew them, Jimmy, but you can give them a nasty suck!" He and Anne laughed at his joke and even Jimmy had to join in.

There was only one dentist in Elfington Village, so Mr McCavity treated all the boys and girls eventually.

The bell rang for the end of afternoon playtime and it was back to model making for Freddie's class, they had been making papier-mâché heads for hand puppets. It was messy but loads of fun dipping strips of newspaper into a bowl of paste and laying them over the balloon that each of the children had inflated to form the basic hollow head shape.

"Remember class, you need four or five layers of paper strips crisscrossing all over your balloon so that the head is nice and strong," Miss Poppett explained.

BANG!

The sudden noise made everyone jump and a couple even screamed with fright.

Melanie burst into tears. "Miss, my balloon has burst!"

Miss Poppett walked over to Melanie and comforted her. "Never mind, Melanie," she chuckled, "you gave us all a bit of a fright, but let's find another balloon for you." Miss Poppett walked to her desk and opened the drawer where she kept all the spare balloons, but the drawer was empty. "Melanie, dear, I'm sorry but I seem to have run out of new balloons."

Poor Melanie began crying again.

Freddie had been engrossed in his own creation when Melanie's balloon bursting had made him jump. Some of his friends grinned when they saw him walk over to a tearful Melanie. "I think I have an extra one in my rucksack, Melanie," he said, unzipping his rucksack and reaching inside, pulling out a nice pink balloon in need of blowing up. "Here you are, Melanie, it's rosy pink just like your rosy pink cheeks."

"Freddie Fixit!.... Freddie Fixit!" some of the class called out, led by Jimmy, of course.

Miss Poppett looked up and smiled. "Well done, Freddie, you saved the day again!"

Freddie inflated the balloon to a size a little bigger than Melanie's fist and helped her put a few strips of newspaper on it so she could catch up with everyone.

* *

Jimmy and Freddie were walking home from school, chatting and laughing about their puppet making class.

"What puppet are you making, Jimmy?" Freddie asked curiously, he had been so busy with his own puppet he had no idea what any of his friends were making.

Jimmy stopped and smiled. "It's going to be a Pirate with a patch over his eye and a parrot on his shoulder," he replied excitedly. "What is yours going to be?"

Freddie was quite excited too. "Well, I was torn between a Roman Centurion or Merlin the Wizard," he replied. "But I decided to........."

Jimmy interrupted Freddie and chuckled, ".... It's a Wizard, isn't it?"

"Yes," Freddie laughed, "I thought it would be lots of fun and I might try to learn some magic tricks to make it even more mysterious."

Something glinted in the gutter and caught Jimmy's attention while Freddie was telling him about his Wizard puppet. He bent down and picked it up. "Look, Freddie, it's a shiny metal screw, like the ones my Dad uses to fix pieces of wood together."

Freddie looked at the shiny screw in Jimmy's fingers then cried, "Oh look, there's another one!" and he rushed past Jimmy to pick it up. "Give this one to your father as well, he might find them useful, "Freddie said.

Jimmy took the shiny screw from Freddie and slipped it, and the one he had found, into his pocket. "I wonder how they came to be just laying around, do you think someone dropped them from their toolbox perhaps?" Jimmy asked.

"Maybe someone left them there deliberately to watch who picked them up and arrest them for stealing," Freddie teased.

"Let's get out of here then in case they come after us," Jimmy replied as they ran off with Freddie chuckling having got his own back for Jimmy's scary dentist story.

Jimmy zipped through his gate and waved goodbye to his best friend.

Freddie skipped happily the rest of the way to his house and when he finally arrived home it was ten minutes before three o'clock. He was still excited about the puppet he was making at school and told his mother all about it.

"I'll have to give you a few sewing lessons then, so you can make a costume," his mother said smiling.

Freddie thought his mother was the best. "That will be super, Mum, I can sew stars and things on it and make a pointy hat. Oooh, and I will make a magic staff like mine with a crystal on the top of it."

His mother was getting a little carried away with her son's enthusiasm. "Perhaps your father can help you with that then, Freddie. Oh, while I remember, tea will be a little later today because your father is fixing a problem where he works and will be late getting home."

Freddie decided to go visit Wiggly as he had a couple of hours to fill before his father came home.

"Don't wander off too far and be home in time for tea at six thirty, okay?" Freddie's mother called to him as he vanished through the kitchen door.

Freddie waved to his mother watching him through the kitchen window and smiling while he dashed through the gate at the bottom of the garden and into his beloved forest. He had not gone far when something glinted in a beam of sunlight shining through the trees. "What is that?" he said, to no one in particular. He ran to the spot and to his surprise he found a shiny screw, just like the ones he and Jimmy had found earlier. "That's odd, that's very odd," he said out loud. "Anybody there?" he called and a squirrel chattered and scampered up the nearby tree. Freddie had a thought about a bird called a Magpie and lifted his rucksack from his shoulders and took out his homemade 'Book of Creatures'. "Ah! Here it is," he said to himself.

'Magpies are long tailed birds and are mainly black in colour. They are quite large, like a crow. Magpies have white bellies and white patches on the shoulders and wings. They have a habit of collecting shiny objects and filling their nest with them.'

"Oh! I wonder if a Magpie dropped this shiny screw?" Freddie said to himself as he put his book back in his rucksack, then picked up the screw and put it in a side pocket.

When he reached the big old oak tree, he looked around to make sure he was alone before speaking the magic words, forgetting being this close to the tree made him invisible. "Efum, Efum, Natum, Efum."

The shape of a door slowly appeared, much to Freddie's fascination, then it opened allowing him access to the spiral staircase. "Here goes," he said, taking a deep breath before doing his elephant impression round and round until he almost fell over at the bottom feeling quite dizzy. He took a moment to catch his breath and chuckled. "I must remember to take those steps a bit slower next time, but it would make a great slide, like a 'Helter Skelter.' Oh, but then you couldn't climb back up." He dismissed his idea and spoke the magic words again to open the door at the bottom of the spiral staircase, letting him into Elfin Town.

There were lots of Elfins around, everyone he met said hello. They welcomed him as one of their own, even though he looked completely different to them. In the distant past Sproggles had been very unfriendly to Elfins, which made him feel special to be so warmly accepted by them.

When he arrived at the Tiggly's home, Wiggly and Giggly were excited to see him. Mummly and Daddly were also happy to see him and they all sat in comfy chairs drinking dandelion tea for a while.

"We had a laugh in class today." Freddie began to tell his story.

Wiggly and Giggly sat up with interest.

"My teacher asked us to use the word 'fascinate' in a sentence and then we read out our answer to the rest of the class."

"Oh! I know what that means," Wiggly burst out.

"Sssh! Wiggly, Freddie is telling us the story," Giggly reprimanded. "Go on, Freddie, please," she said.

"Well, Jimmy read his sentence out first which made us all chuckle......"

"Oooh, what did he say?" Wiggly interrupted.

"Well," Freddie continued with a big grin on his face, "Jimmy read this out, *my friend got a new coat and it had ten buttons down the front, but my friend could only fasten eight.*" Freddie giggled again as soon as he finished.

But Wiggly looked at him with screwed up eyebrows.

Then Giggly burst into laughter, along with Mummly and Daddly.

"I don't get it, why are you all laughing?" Wiggly asked. "I was going to say something like that as well."

For a split second everyone fell silent, looking at Wiggly, then burst into laughter again. Poor Wiggly could not understand why they were laughing until Freddie quietly explained it was not 'fasten eight,' but 'fascinate.'

"Let's go to the park," Giggly suggested, trying to save her brother from further embarrassment.

Of course Wiggly thought it a good idea.

Freddie had not yet visited the Elfin Park so he was especially interested to see exactly what kind of park there could be underground.

They waved goodbye to Mummly and Daddly then made their way through the houses until they reached a huge open space covered in moss-like grass.

"What's that over there, Wiggly, it looks like a huge mirror?" Freddie asked.

"Oh, it's a small lake or a big pond, one or the other," Wiggly laughed.

"What do you do in this park, I don't see any swings, seesaws or a climbing frame?" Freddie said.

"What's a seesaw?" Giggly chuckled. "It sounds funny, like the noise a Donkey makes."

"No, no, Giggly, a Donkey brays, Heehaw, not seesaw!" Wiggly chuckled.

"Oooh, Wiggly is a smarty pants." Giggly teased her brother.

Freddie smiled and answered Giggly's question about a seesaw to change the subject. "Well a seesaw is a long plank of wood that is balanced in the middle on another piece of wood fixed to the ground, so when one end of the plank is on the ground the other end is in the air. Then one person sits at each end and the one on the ground end pushes up and the one in the air swings down to the ground and so on. Look, I'll show you." Freddie took his rucksack off and pulled out a ruler and a pencil eraser, then he placed the middle of the ruler on the eraser and pressed one end down, the other lifted into the air.

"That's too small to have fun on," Giggly giggled.

"Oh, this is just like a model, in my park at home we have a big version of this that children can sit on each end," Freddie replied.

"We like to play 'Tiggle-Taggle' sometimes," Wiggly said touching his sister and running away. "You're Taggled, Giggly," Wiggly shouted. "Run, Freddie, or Giggly will touch you and you'll be taggled and become the Tiggler.

Freddie was not fast enough and Giggly called out, "Taggled, you're the Tiggler!" and ran off.

Freddie realised how the game worked and he chased after them both, finally Taggling Wiggly. They played like this for a while until they were all out of breath and had to sit down.

"Do you play Frisbee or football?" Freddie asked, still panting from their game.

Both Wiggly and Giggly asked, "What's Frisbee?" at the same time and laughed as they panted, sounding like a bad case of hiccups.

Freddie reached into his rucksack and pulled out a bright yellow plastic disc. "This is a Frisbee guys, you throw it to one another and it floats on the air. It's good fun and when you get really good you can throw it at a special angle and it comes back to you," he announced.

"It sounds interesting, what do we need to do?" Wiggly asked.

Freddie got them to stand a good distance from each other in a triangle and he threw the Frisbee, spinning it at the same time. It sailed through the air and landed at Wiggly's feet.

"Oh, that was clever, Freddie!" Wiggly shouted as he picked up the Frisbee and tried to throw it. "OW!" he cried as it sailed a short way in the air and came back hitting him in the chest. "Not as easy as it looks!" he shouted while Giggly was beside herself laughing. He tried again and this time it spun behind him and floated back hitting his legs. "OW! OW!" he cried hopping about.

Freddie and Giggly were laughing so hard they had to sit down.

Fourth time lucky and this time Wiggly spun it as he threw, flying in Giggly's direction.

She jumped up and down trying to catch it as it sailed over her head, she turned and ran after it and now it was Wiggly's turn to have a laugh. Giggly had been watching despite laughing and picked up the bright yellow disc and launched it into the air. She got the hang of it straight away and it headed in Freddie's direction, sailing just above head height and he reached up and grabbed it in mid flight.

Wiggly and Giggly ran to him clapping their hands.

"That was really clever, Freddie!" Wiggly laughed, running up to his friend and patting him on the back.

"We like this game, Freddie, thank you for showing us." Giggly giggled and Freddie felt embarrassed and turned red in the face.

"You can keep this Frisbee," Freddie said. "Now that you know how to make it fly you can teach other children how to have fun with it," he chuckled. "Well at least Giggly seems to have mastered it. I'm sure a few more throws and you will too, Wiggly." Freddie tried to be kind to poor Wiggly, still rubbing the back of his legs.

They sat down and chatted while drinking the cartons of juice Freddie brought out from his rucksack.

Giggly piped up, "Look! There's something shining in the grass over there."

Freddie and Wiggly followed Giggly's hand to where she was pointing, but could not see anything.

Giggly jumped up and headed for the thing catching her eye. She bent down and picked up something small, then returned to her friend and brother.

"What is it, Giggly?" Wiggly asked as she sat down again.

125

"This!" she replied holding up a shiny screw.

Freddie looked at it in amazement.

"What is it?" Giggly asked.

"I know what it is," Freddie replied, "when I was walking to school with my friend Jimmy, we found two of them. They are screws made of metal for joining wood together. Then, when I was walking through the woods, I found another, look." He opened the side pocked of his rucksack and took out the shiny screw he had found.

"That's very mysterious," Wiggly said thoughtfully.

Giggly gave Freddie the screw she had in her hand and he put them both back in his rucksack side pocket.

"How do you mean, Wiggly?" Freddie asked as Wiggly rubbed his chin.

"Well it's a bit of a coincidence finding something like this laying around on your streets and in the woods. I guess someone could have dropped them up there, but not down here!" he replied.

Giggly looked confused. "I don't get it?" she said.

"Ah well, you see a Sproggle could have dropped the screws up there but not down here," Freddie explained.

"Oh, I see now," Giggly said jumping up, "because the only Sproggle to come down here is you." She clapped her hands with excitement having worked that out.

"But also it couldn't be an Elfin either because we are forbidden to leave the forest and no one has ever ventured into the Sproggle streets. I mean an Elfin would be immediately spotted walking about up there," Wiggly added.

All three rubbed their chins, a habit Freddie had picked up from his friend, while thinking about the problem.

"I wonder where these screws come from because Elfins don't use them, although they are interesting," Wiggly pondered. "Oooh, do you think someone has stolen them?" He jumped up with surprise at his own speculation.

Giggly looked at her brother and giggled.

"Well they look quite new to me, all lovely and shiny," Wiggly said and sat down again.

Freddie piped up, "Look at this both of you." He brought out his 'Book of Beasties' to show them. Freddie opened his book to the page about Magpie birds. "This bird is known for collecting shiny things, maybe one got down here by accident," Freddie suggested.

"We will have to keep an eye out for a Magpie then," Wiggly replied.

Giggly nodded and added, "It won't be hard, there are no birds or animals down here."

Freddie looked at Giggly wide eyed. "Hey! You're right, come to think about it I've never seen or heard a bird or animal in Elfin Town. Funny it never occurred to me before you said it." He looked at his watch, "Oh it's just after half past five. I have to go now, my Dad will be back from work soon and Mum will have tea ready," he explained.

"Okay Freddie," his friends said together and giggled, then they chased each other all the way to the spiral staircase door.

"What is that tall building?" Freddie asked as they reached the edge of the park.

"It's the steam house," Wiggly replied.

"A steam house, what does it do?" Freddie enquired.

"Daddly says the Wizard created it to supply lekytic and hot water. It also fills the lake over there," Wiggly replied, pointing back to the 'big pond'.

"What's lekytic?" Freddie asked, sniggering at the funny sounding word.

"Oh! I know what that is," Giggly jumped into the conversation, "when you flick a wall lever the magic candle comes on and it doesn't need a flame because the lekytic makes it shine."

"Oh, I see," Freddie replied, "Sproggles call that electric and your magic candles are called light bulbs. Do you think we could have a look inside?" he asked, his curiosity getting the better of him.

Wiggly looked at Freddie, not quite sure why he would want to look in the steam house. "We could ask Mr Ing," he replied, "he and his family live in the steam house and look after it all, come on!" He grabbed Freddie and Giggly's hands, dragging them towards the steam house. Wiggly knocked on the door and Freddie chuckled.

"What's funny?" Giggly asked.

"Listen!" Freddie replied. They all put their hands to their ears and Giggly laughed, followed by Wiggly, while Freddie was still chuckling.

"It's a funny sound," Giggly said listening to the 'Pfsssst! Pfsssst!' sound. "That's what you do in bed!" Giggly laughed at her brother.

"I do not!" he replied huffily. "It's you that Pfsssst's in bed," Wiggly added and Freddie doubled over with laughter.

"Come on guys, we all do it, my Dad does it really loud, sounds like a trumpet and makes me laugh every time," Freddie admitted when he could catch his breath from laughing.

Then the steam house door opened. "Hello, well bless my soul if it isn't Freddie, Wiggly and Giggly. What a nice surprise, come in, come in!" Mr Ing welcomed them. "Mrs Ing, kids, we have some important guests!" Mr Ing bellowed inside the house and after he closed the door there was a clambering of feet.

Freddie chuckled. *'My Dad would think that was two herds of elephants'* he thought to himself.

Excited voices, followed by the appearance of the Ing's two children, Chell Ing and Bill Ing, as they came scampering down the stairs, followed more quietly by Mr Ing's wife, Wynn Ing.

"Look everyone, it's Freddie and the two Tiggly children," Mr Ing announced, but Chell and Bill were already hugging all three and chattering away. Chell was the Ing's daughter and Bill was their son, both a bit younger than Wiggly.

"Mr Ing, Freddie was interested in the steam thingy."

Pfssst! Pfssst!

The three friends giggled again.

"Oh, you get used to that........." Mr Ing said as the sound caused more chuckles.

Pfssst! Pfssst!

"... we don't even hear it any more..."

Pfssst! Pfssst!

"Would you like to see the lekytic machine?" Mr Ing asked and Freddie's face lit up.

"Oh, could we please, Mr Ing?" Freddie was overjoyed.

Mrs Ing laughed. "Mr Ing will be excited to show you, we don't get many who want..."

Pfssst! Pfssst!

".....to look at the ugly thing," she said. "Back upstairs kids." Mrs Ing beckoned and the two children said goodbye with another little hug.

"You're my hero, Freddie," Chell whispered in his ear and he turned a little red in the face.

Mr Ing took them through an elaborately carved, round topped, wooden door in the little circular hall where they were standing, which was the only door other than the front door.

128

"Come this way children," he beckoned and closed the door behind them.

"WOW!......" all three gasped at the same time.

PFSSST! PFSSST!

The funny sound was much louder.

"Look, it's that pipe doing all the funny pfsssst, noises," Giggly declared, pointing at a shiny golden pipe that looked like a rolling pin.

"Ah yes," Mr Ing said. "That's the safety valve, when the pressure gets too high it ....

"PFSSST! PFSSST!

".......... that's it! The steam gets released," Mr Ing explained.

"Just like you in bed, Wiggly, when your pressure gets released." Giggly laughed.

Freddie chuckled, as did Mr Ing.

But Wiggly put on a cross and very red face.

"How does it work, Mr Ing?" Freddie asked to distract from Wiggly's embarrassment.

"Well it's complicated and I don't know exactly what everything does as this was the Wizard's invention, but basically what happens," Mr Ing began, "you see this pipe," he pointed to a shiny gold coloured pipe rising up from the floor and reaching all the way to the top of the machine. **PFSSST! PFSSST!**

"That pipe goes way, way, way, down into the ground until it reaches a source of boiling hot water. Then the hot water flows up to the top of the machine to make steam that spins a Nynamo that makes Lekytic so we can have flameless candles. Some of the hot water goes into the big tank over there and that supplies hot water to all the buildings in the town. That shiny pipe on top of it is the overflow, so when the tank gets full it sends the hot water into the lake where it cools down, in doing so it keeps the air temperature down here nice and warm all year round. The cool water is piped to all the buildings as well, for drinking water, cooking and washing, simple as that!"

Freddie gasped. "Wow! That's amazing, the Wizard Merlin was very clever all those years ago and it still works perfectly."

Mr Ing smiled proudly. "That's my job, to polish the pipes and oil the roundy, up and downy parts so it continues to work," he replied. "Now will you all stay for tea?"

Freddie looked at his watch again. "I'm sorry, Mr Ing, I have to get home, but another time though would be really nice," he apologised.

"That's perfectly fine, Freddie, you are always welcome in this house, you and Wiggly saved my little girl, Chell, from those Mole Goblins, we can never thank you enough." Mr Ing patted Freddie and Wiggly's shoulders proudly.

"I'd better be off then," Freddie replied. "I can find my own way now, Wiggly, so I'll see you all soon, okay?" Freddie left his friends to have tea with the Ings and he dashed off, getting home just in time.

* *

"Dad, can you bury a pipe deep down into the ground and get steam to make electric?" Freddie asked while they ate their lovely cooked tea of roast chicken, roast potatoes, peas and carrots that his mother had been busy preparing.

Freddie's father looked at him with surprise. "What makes you ask that, son?"

"Well I heard some people talking about it." *(This was not really telling a lie, he had heard Mr Ing).*

His father smiled, ever surprised at his son's curiosity. "Yes it is. It's something relatively new and it's called Geothermal Energy. In countries like Icyland they drill deep down into the ground and pump up boiling water heated by the volcanoes," his father explained.

"When you say it's new, how long is new?" Freddie asked, popping a piece of carrot into his mouth.

"I think the technology is about 50 years old, maybe less," his father replied.

"So it was not around 300 or 400 years ago then?" Freddie asked.

His father laughed. "Absolutely not son, electricity is barely a 100 years old, so no, 300 or 400 years ago lighting would have been with candles or oil lamps."

'The Wizard really was very clever indeed,' Freddie thought to himself and smiled.

* *

Freddie liked his dentist, Mr McCavity. He let Freddie call him Phil when it was only the two of them in the room.

"Open wide, Freddie, let's have a look at those *pearly whites*."

He made Freddie giggle when he referred to his teeth as pearly whites.

Mr McCavity poked and prodded with his pointy tool and mirror on long handles. "Close up for a minute, Freddie," he said, "now tell me how you brush your teeth."

Freddie beamed and explained, "Just like you showed me, Phil," he giggled again, not being used to calling adults by their first name. Not that Phil McCavity was that old at 25. "I brush down the gum onto my top teeth and up the gum onto my bottom teeth on the outside and inside and I think about the verse 'Twinkle Twinkle Little Star' while brushing before I rinse and wipe my mouth." Freddie beamed again, he had good teeth, perfectly aligned and shiny white.

"Well done, Freddie, your teeth and gums are perfectly healthy, no cavities so no need for me to be filling them."

Freddie laughed even though he had heard his dentist say this many times before.

"Rinse your mouth, Freddie, then you can go back to your mother," the dentist said smiling.

Freddie rinsed and jumped out the chair and back to the waiting room and his mother.

"All good, Mrs Fountain. Freddie's teeth are a credit to him, he's looking after them just right, well done, Freddie, see you in six months."

Freddie and his mother waved their goodbyes and began their walk home along the High Street, where met up with a puzzled looking Mrs Pilz.

"Hello Mrs Fountain and Freddie," Mrs Pilz greeted. "Would you look at that?" she said pointing to the shop door.

"What appears to be the trouble, Mrs Pilz?" Freddie's mother asked, unable to spot anything wrong.

Freddie was puzzled too, what could Mrs Pilz see that they could not?

"Oh, sorry, it's the door numbers, they look like number 19 but should be number 16. Somehow a screw has gone missing from the top of each number and they have turned upside down from 1 and 6, to a 1 and 9," she replied woefully.

Freddie's mind was whirring away. Could it be some of the screws he found were the ones missing from the Chemist door numbers? "Mrs Pilz, my friend and I found some screws on the footpath yesterday, on our way home from school," Freddie declared, taking his rucksack off to open the side pocket and pull out two screws. "Do you think these might be the screws that are missing?"

Mrs Pilz looked at the screws in Freddie's hand and smiled. "I think they might be, Freddie, let's see if they fit." She took the two shiny screws, turned the numbers the right way up and put them into the holes in the door. Mrs Pilz could only turn them a little bit with her fingers though.

Noticing that Mrs Pilz was struggling, Freddie announced, "I have something to help with that," and he unzipped the top of his rucksack, pretended to fumble around inside while he thought of the tool he needed, then pulled out a screwdriver.

"Well, Freddie, that is helpful," Mrs Pilz smiled, taking the screwdriver and fixing the screws into the door numbers good and tight. "Thank you, Freddie," she said as she handed the screwdriver back to him.

Freddie put it back in his rucksack, zipped it up and slung it back on his shoulder.

"Come inside, I have a little reward for you," Mrs Pilz invited and they all walked into the Chemist shop. "Here you are, Freddie, a little thank you for being so helpful." She handed him a lollipop wrapped in shiny silver paper.

"He's just been to the dentist, Mrs Pilz, not sure he should be eating a lolly pop," his mother explained.

"Ah, it's alright Mrs Fountain, this is a sugar free lollipop, so his teeth won't be in any danger of cavities," Mrs Pilz explained.

Freddie was not too sure he liked the sound of 'sugar free'. "Can I taste it Mum, please?" he asked and of course his mother could hardly refuse. He unwound the silver wrapping and popped the ball shaped lolly into his mouth and sucked. After a moment or two his eyes lit up and he pulled the lolly from his mouth. "Rhubarb and custard, Mum, it tastes of rhubarb and custard!" he exclaimed excitedly.

Mrs Pilz and Freddie's mother laughed together at Freddie's surprised delight.

"Let me have three of those lollies then, Mrs Pilz, they'll do as a treat over the next few weeks," Freddie's mother said and paid Mrs Pilz for them.

On their way home from the Chemist shop, Freddie stopped and picked up another shiny screw. "Look, Mum, there's another one. Where are they coming from and who's taking them?" Freddie said completely baffled.

His mother shrugged her shoulders. "I have no idea, Freddie," then she thought and said, "maybe someone is being mischievous and removing them from people's door numbers, like Mrs Pilz's door!"

Freddie nodded, maybe that was it, but a nagging thought about the screws found in Elfin Town did not quite fit that idea. When they reached their home Freddie rushed to open the gate for his mother and to his horror, instead of swinging open, it fell flat on the ground with a loud crash almost pulling him with it. "What's happened, Mum?" he cried.

His mother bent down to pick up the fallen gate and they both looked at it as if it was going to tell them what happened. "Looks like all the screws holding the hinges to the gate post have fallen out," his mother replied.

But Freddie was beginning to smell a rat, something or someone was taking shiny screws from people's property, but why, because they had very little value in one's and two's. Was it just coincidence that Giggly found some screws in Elfin Town, and how had he found one among the trees on his way to see Wiggly? He was puzzled and certain that he was missing something obvious, but what?

Freddie helped his father repair the garden gate with new shiny screws from his father's toolbox, which he kept in the garden shed.

"What's that you are doing to the screws, Dad, that's not a screwdriver?" Freddie asked as he watched his father doing something he had not seen before.

"This, Freddie, is an old carpentry trick. I'm removing part of the screw slot using this small, thin file. Now, when I've screwed it into the hinge and gate post, see if you can unscrew it?" His father explained and gave Freddie the screwdriver.

With the screwdriver in his hand he looked at his father and frowned. "That's easy, anyone can unscrew a screw with a screwdriver, that's what they're made for, isn't it?" he replied a little cockily.

"We'll soon see son, just have a go then," his father smiled knowingly.

Freddie placed the screwdriver blade into the screw slot, pushed a little and turned it anti-clockwise. "Oh! Oh!" he cried as the screwdriver slipped off the screw every time he tried to unscrew it.

His father was chuckling to himself. "Not so easy as you thought then, Freddie?"

"But I don't understand, Dad, why does the screwdriver keep slipping off the screw?"

His father explained. "Look at the slot on the screw. When you tighten the screw the screwdriver blade pushes against the side of the slot, but when you try to loosen the screw the blade slips up the slope where I filed away the edge and it slips out, so the screw can only be screwed in and not screwed out. No one is going to be stealing these screws again. You or Mum could have been really hurt when the gate fell down."

Freddie thought his father was a genius and gave him a big hug. "That's so clever, Dad, and so simple! I didn't think about getting hurt though."

Freddie's father frowned. "If this had been a door that you opened, if the screws in the hinges were stolen, the door would fall on top of you. You could be seriously hurt!"

Freddie realised his father was right, there was danger, if this was someone being mischievous then they were also putting people in danger too.

* *

On Sunday Freddie's Auntie and Uncle with twin cousins came to stay for a few days as it was half term holidays. Caleb and Drew were the same age as Freddie and he always liked it when they visited, because they would sleep in his bedroom, he used the camp bed and they slept in his big bed. His cousins were a lot of fun and most people could not tell them apart with them being identical twins. For some reason Freddie could always see who was Caleb and who was Drew and chuckled when his mother and father got the twins mixed up. The twins would often dress in the same clothes and giggle when people could not work out who was who.

They all had a picnic tea in the park on the afternoon they arrived and while the adults chatted to catch up with each other's news, the three boys enjoyed playing on the swings, seesaw and climbing frame.

"Look at me, Freddie!" Caleb cried as he hung upside down on the climbing frame.

"Whoa! Are you a monkey?" Freddie cried back at him, laughing.

They kicked a ball around for a while, then played throwing a Frisbee to each other.

Exhausted, they sat down to enjoy the picnic, with Freddie sitting between Caleb and Drew.

That night when the three boys went upstairs to bed they cleaned their teeth and dashed into Freddie's bedroom. Caleb took out a zip pouch from his sports bag.

"Oh, what's that for?" Freddie asked curiously.

Drew answered for his brother, "It's his insulin kit, 'cause Caleb is diabetic."

Freddie looked puzzled.

Caleb explained. "I became ill just after Christmas and the doctor said that I was diabetic. My body has stopped making insulin, which controls the sugar or glucose in my blood, so I have to put some in with this kit. I inject the insulin three or four times a day."

Freddie was fascinated, he had not heard about this disease. "What happens if you forget to do this, Caleb?" he asked.

Again Drew answered Freddie's question for his brother. "He might have a seizure or collapse into a coma."

"So do you carry your kit around with you always?" Freddie asked with interest, but also he felt it was important for him to know.

"Yes, I do. I always have it with me and Drew knows what to do if for any reason I can't do it."

"Can I see the kit and watch you do it please?" Freddie asked.

Caleb chuckled, "Of course, as long as you're not squeamish about syringe needles."

135

Freddie did not have much experience with injections and did not know if he was squeamish, but he did not think he would mind. It was something Freddie would not have to worry about for himself, since Merlin had granted him a charmed life and he would never be ill.

Caleb took out a small device and pricked his finger to squeeze out a drop of blood that he soaked on a tab sticking out of the device.

"That's a clever device, Freddie," Drew explained, "it measures how much sugar is in Caleb's blood and let's him know how much insulin to inject"

"Funny, I never realised that blood had sugar in it, I suppose it doesn't taste bitter, so it must be sweet, actually," Freddie chuckled.

"How is it, Caleb?" Drew asked.

"It's quite high, that means I have too much sugar in my blood, so I need to inject straight away," he replied.

Freddie watched with fascination. He had never seen anyone doing doctor's stuff on themselves before. He was captivated, it was like watching a medical programme on TV but in real life.

Caleb squirted the syringe in the air, a little jet of liquid shot out of the needle.

"Caleb is making sure there is no air in the syringe. If he injected any air into his muscle it could make him very poorly," Drew explained just before Freddie asked.

Caleb opened his pyjama jacket and pinched his soft belly into a bump.

Freddie cried out, "Oooh, that's... oooh!" when Caleb stabbed the needle into his belly.

Drew laughed, "Thought you weren't squeamish?"

Freddie scrunched his face. "I didn't know if I was, I guess I do now!" he chuckled.

When Caleb pulled the needle out of his belly Freddie groaned again. "Oh, it's gruesome!"

Both cousins laughed. "You get used to it," they said together.

Caleb put the cover back on the needle and removed it from the syringe, gave it a squeeze until it clicked and put it in a little box in his kit.

"It breaks the needle so it can't be accidentally or deliberately used again, if that happened it could have germs on it and cause an infection," Drew explained when Freddie looked at him.

"Oh!" Freddie replied. "You're very brave, Caleb, not sure I could do all that," he admitted.

"I couldn't at first, so Mum or Dad had to do it for me. Now it's okay, sometimes Drew does it for me just to keep him in practice. I don't really think about it now, I just do it."

Freddie admired Caleb's courage, even though he did not have much choice. He thought both his cousins were really brave.

They told each other scary ghost stories before settling down to sleep. Freddie quite liked sleeping on the camp bed, it was like being on holiday in a tent.

The next morning the three boys were up nice and early, had breakfast and were excited to be going to explore in the forest.

"Are there any monsters?" Drew asked and laughed.

"Oh, yes!" Freddie replied and Drew stopped laughing.

"WHAT! Really, there are monsters?" Drew cried.

Now Freddie was chuckling. "Oh yes, there's fluffy bunny rabbits and cute squirrels with bushy tails," he teased.

"Aw, you're pulling my leg, aren't you?" Drew said screwing his face up.

Caleb was laughing at his brother and Freddie.

"No, I never touched your leg, did I Caleb, besides, I couldn't reach it from this side of the table anyway," Freddie continued to tease.

"Okay you three, enough teasing for now," Freddie's mother laughed. "Caleb, have you got your insulin kit with you?"

"Yes auntie," he replied patting his pocket.

The three boys scrambled to put their shoes on, once Freddie pulled on his rucksack they scurried out of the kitchen, down the garden path and through the gate into the forest, laughing and giggling.

"It all looks the same to me, how do you know where are?" Drew asked. "Don't you ever get lost?"

Freddie smiled and nodded before replying, "Well I did a bit at first, but not now. There's a sort of a trail that the animals use so once you find it you know where you are. Just up here is the 'Buzzy Bush," he said pointing further up the track.

"Ha, ha! What's a 'Buzzy Bush' when it's at home?" Caleb asked sniggering.

"You'll see!" Freddie said racing ahead. "Here it is," he called, waiting for Caleb and Drew to catch up with him.

At that precise moment, a ray of sunshine hit the bush and it began buzzing.

"Hey, that's a talking bush!" cried Drew.

"Nah, it's a Buzz Stop! Get it? Buzz Stop!" Caleb laughed at his own joke.

"Oh, that's soooooo corny, Caleb," Freddie chuckled.

"What makes it buzz then, Freddie?" Drew asked.

Freddie shook the bush. "Look!" he replied as several bees flew up in the air then flew back to the bush. "The bees are after the nectar in the flowers."

"I see, that's why you call it the 'Buzzy Bush', because the bees are attracted to it. Cool!" Drew replied.

"The flowers are pretty and they smell nice too," Caleb observed with his nose hovering over a flower.

"Yes they are and you can also eat the flowers, here try one," replied Freddie plucking three flowers, one for each of them. "Make sure there's not a bee inside it before you put it in your mouth," he warned.

Caleb popped his in and Drew made a frantic buzzing sound that made his brother spit out his flower. "Arr! A bee, a bee!" he cried waving his hands around to shoo off the bee that was not even there.

Drew laughed. "Fooled you. It was me making the buzzing sound," he said to his twin brother, creasing himself up with laughter.

Caleb laughed as well, he could not be angry with his brother, it would be like being angry with himself.

"So can you eat any of the flowers in this forest?" Drew asked.

"No, absolutely not! Some plants are poisonous and you could die, others may make you really sick, so never eat flowers or berries unless an adult who knows it's safe tells you it's ok. This is a very important rule when you are in the forest or anywhere outdoors," Freddie replied very seriously.

"Okay Freddie, we understand," Drew and Caleb said at the same time, then laughed as they looked at each other.

"Hey! There's something glinting over there," Drew announced, pointing to something on the ground reflecting in a sunbeam. He rushed to see what it was. When Caleb and Freddie caught up with him, Drew was holding up a shiny metal screw.

"That's strange," Freddie gasped, "we've been finding them all over the place and on Saturday someone had stolen the screws from our front gate and it fell down!"

"Wow! That almost sounds funny, no one got hurt though did they?" Caleb asked.

"Fortunately it fell away from Mum when I opened the gate, it's quite heavy and rough so it would have given her a nasty cut or worse," Freddie explained.

Drew handed the screw to Freddie who put it in a side pocket of his rucksack.

"Hey, what's that sound?" Caleb said holding his hand to his ear. "It's a kind of squeaking, like a dog's toy?"

"This way," Drew called. Freddie and Caleb chased after him as he followed the direction of the sound. It got louder and louder and led them towards a small bush. "I suppose this is a squeaky bush!" Drew chuckled.

As all three stood looking at the noisy bush, a little animal crawled from under it.

"Aw, look, it's a little piggy-wiggy!" Drew cried as it snuggled up to his shoe. He picked it up and the piglet squealed and snuffled.

"It's so cute, you never said there were miniature pigs in the forest, Freddie," Caleb said as he tickled the piglet under its chin.

It was a surprise to Freddie as well, he had never seen any kind of pig in the woods before.

"Let me hold it, Drew, please," pleaded Caleb, his brother handed the piglet over to him. It wiggled and squealed, it did not seem to like Caleb as much as Drew.

Freddie had a bad feeling about this. "Might be best to put it down, Caleb, I don't know how it got here, but it was not on its own tiny trotters," he warned.

A nearby bush shook violently, then a very loud squeal and grunt came from it.

"Quickly, put it down, now! Put it down, quickly Caleb!" Freddie cried, but Caleb seemed to freeze on the spot. Freddie grabbed the piglet from his hands and put it down, pushing it away, but it did not seem to want to go.

From the nearby bush a big hairy snout appeared with long bottom tusks on each side of its jaw, two beady eyes looked fiercely at the three boys and the big animal squealed furiously and grunted, stamping its trotter *(foot)*.

"W-what is it?" Drew asked shakily.

"That's no pig," Freddie cried, "it's a wild boar! Quickly, run!"

The three boys began to run along the narrow track one behind the other with Freddie leading the way. Behind them, galloping trotters pounded the ground accompanied by loud squeals, the boar was giving chase.

"Quicker! Follow me!" Freddie cried out as they all puffed and panted, running as fast as their legs could carry them along the bumpy track. Freddie headed for the big old oak tree that only he could see and they ran around it and hid. Freddie held onto both of them, so they would basically disappear from sight, but to Caleb and Drew they seemed to be in plain sight of the boar.

The huge tusked beast suddenly stopped and looked this way and that, snorted and squealed, stamped the ground with its trotter.

"What's it doing?" Drew whispered, not realising that the boar could not see them.

"Poor eyesight, stay still and it will think we've gone," Freddie whispered back, making it up on the spot.

The boar turned around grunting and snorting and trotted back to its young piglet that had taken such a shine to Drew.

"Phew, that was close!" Drew gasped as they relaxed, trying to catch their breath.

Caleb looked at his brother and grabbed his arm. "I - I don't feel so good, Drew!" he gasped and fell into his arms.

"Caleb!" Drew cried, "Wake up! Wake up!" but Caleb just lay still, breathing very slowly.

"What's the matter, what happened?" Freddie asked with alarm in his voice.

"Don't know, don't know!" Drew tried to think, but he was scared as well. "Wait! It could be the running and he was frightened as well, it has changed his sugar levels. Quick, search his pockets for his kit, Freddie." Drew trembled. "Caleb, please Caleb, wake up!"

Freddie scrambled over Caleb and felt in all his pockets. "It's not here, Drew, it must have dropped out of his pocket while we were running away!"

Drew's face was white as a sheet and his forehead sweating, now he was trembling, frightened his brother might not make it back to the house. "He can't die, Freddie, he needs his insulin!" Drew said tearfully.

Freddie jumped up. "I'll run back along the track and find it, stay here and look after Caleb. Don't move, I know exactly where this place is, okay?" Freddie dashed off back in the direction they had come from, he looked everywhere, under bushes, leaves and twigs. "This is hopeless!" he cried out and then stopped dead in his tracks as a thought came into his mind. He knew exactly what was in Caleb's kit, so he pulled off his rucksack and unzipped the top. In his mind he could see everything in the kit and he slid his hand inside and pulled out an identical zipped case to his cousin's. He quickly opened it to make sure everything was correct. "It looks okay, it's the best chance," he said to himself and ran back like the wind to Caleb and Drew.

"Got it!" Freddie cried as he closed in on the place he had left his cousins. "Here!" he gasped as he handed the kit to Drew. Freddie bent over with his hands on his knees, puffing and panting as he watched Drew prick his brother's finger and squeeze out a drop of blood. Next he placed the blood on the tab sticking out of the sugar meter.

"Oh! That's not right," Drew cried.

Freddie looked but they did not mean anything to him.

"He needs his insulin straight away," Drew said almost tearful and his hands were shaking. "He can't die, Freddie, he mustn't die."

Freddie was trembling himself, but patted Drew on the shoulder as calmly as he could. "You know what to do, you can help, you'll do it right, Drew."

His cousin put the needle on the syringe and got it ready, like he had been shown, then pulled Caleb's shirt out of his trousers. "Can you pinch his belly like he did at your house, Freddie?"

Freddie took hold of Caleb's soft belly between both forefingers and thumbs and then Drew stabbed the needle in a different place to before. When Drew removed the needle he replaced the shield, snapped the needle and put it in the box, he did not notice that the box was empty.

Freddie released his cousin's belly and pulled his shirt back over.

"Have you any water in your rucksack, Freddie?" Drew asked.

Freddie pulled his rucksack off his shoulder and unzipped it, pulling out a small bottle of water and handed it to Drew. He unscrewed the top and moistened his brother's lips, then stroked his hair lovingly, talking to him slowly and calmly.

But Freddie could see Drew's hand trembling as he watched on, afraid his cousin Caleb might die. Nothing seemed to be happening and Freddie did not know how to help, so he packed up the insulin kit and put it in his pocket. "Should I go and fetch Auntie and Uncle?" he finally said and Drew nodded. "Stay here, don't move even if he wakes up, I know exactly where this place is, okay? Drew, okay?"

Drew looked up at Freddie with a sad, tearful face and nodded, then returned to look at his barely breathing brother.

Freddie scrambled to his feet, rucksack on his back and ran back along the track. "Too bad if that boar is still around," he thought as he dashed past bushes. Something caught his eye on the track ahead, he was not far from his garden but he stopped and picked it up. It was Caleb's kit that he had lost, so Freddie quickly exchanged the two and put the magic one back in his rucksack. He was so out of breath by the time he reached his garden gate and pushed through it. He could see his mother at the window and waved frantically to her. He burst into the kitchen, his face bright red and looking so scared. "Mum! Dad! Come quick," he panted and turned, hoping they would follow him. He looked back and his parents, Auntie and Uncle were in pursuit close behind him, wondering what Freddie was so upset about. When he reached the garden gate they had caught up and he stopped.

"Freddie, where are your cousins?" his father asked.

"Caleb's in trouble, he collapsed. Drew gave him insulin. Come quick, he won't wake up!" Freddie grabbed his father's hand and led him, his mother, Auntie and Uncle at a fast pace through the forest.

Freddie's father pulled them to a stop and asked his wife to go back and call an ambulance, before letting his son take the lead again.

Freddie did not take long to find his cousins, less than ten minutes running as fast as his legs could carry him. He was panting and gasping when he reached the big old oak tree. He could not see through it, but for his father, Auntie and Uncle, of course, it was not there at all, having a magical enchantment on it, and they ran straight through it to reach the twins. Freddie slowed down and crawled at a snail's pace around the tree to reach them.

Caleb was barely conscious, he lifted his head and looked around in a bit of a daze. "W-w-what h-a-a-ppened?" he croaked, his head bobbing from side to side as he tried to make sense of his situation.

Drew forced a smile as he held his brother. "You blacked out, Caleb, it must have been the running that did it."

Caleb looked a little bewildered.

Drew looked up at his father, mother and Uncle. "It was Freddie, he saved my brother after a big old boar chased us. We hid here, but Caleb just collapsed and we couldn't find his kit, so Freddie ran back along the path and found where Caleb had dropped it. He was really brave, that was a monster boar."

Freddie's Auntie wrapped her arms around her nephew and gave him a loving hug. "Thank you, Freddie, that was very brave of you," she whispered in his ear.

"Boy, am I glad your mother and I taught Drew how to inject his brother," Drew's father announced patting Freddie's back and then squatting down to hug both his sons. Drew's mother joined him.

Freddie's father put his arm around his son's shoulders. "Lucky you know these woods so well and could find this place again. Well done, son, you all make a pretty good team," he praised.

"Can you get up, Caleb?" his father asked.

With Drew's help Caleb managed to stand, but he was very unsteady on his legs.

"Jump up on my back, son," his father said and gave Caleb a piggyback all the way back to the house.

They walked in single file along the narrow track with Freddie leading the way and his father bringing up the rear.

Drew walked with Freddie and pulled out another shiny screw from his pocket. "This was under Caleb where he collapsed," he said to Freddie handing him the screw.

Freddie put it in his pocket and thought to himself, 'This was near the big old oak tree. The entrance to Elfin town, how strange.'

When they all reached the house the ambulance had just arrived and was waiting for them to return. Freddie's mother rushed to them all and Freddie explained what had happened while the paramedics took Caleb into the ambulance to check him over.

"What's your name, sonny?" The friendly paramedic called Jason asked.

Caleb looked at him, trying to focus. "It's Caleb," he replied.

"Good, now Caleb, let me and Rosy take a look at you, seems you passed out, is that right?"

Caleb nodded.

The paramedics gave Caleb a thorough examination, taking his blood pressure, checking his sugar levels, looking into his eyes and asking simple questions. When Jason cracked a little joke, Caleb giggled and seemed to be back to himself.

"Come on then, Caleb, let's get you back to the party!" Jason said leading him back into the house.

Caleb was feeling much better after a short nap and then they all enjoyed a lunchtime barbeque of hot dogs and burgers. While the adults sat in the garden chatting and counting their blessings, the three boys played kick-about with a football, laughing and calling out to each other.

Unbeknown to them, a pair of eyes had been watching them from the safety of a large bush at the bottom of the garden.

By mid-afternoon it was time for Caleb, Drew and their parents to return home.

Freddie helped Drew and Caleb to collect their belongings and pack them in their bags, then insisted on carrying Caleb's bags downstairs for him.

"I'm okay now, Freddie, thank you anyway," he had protested, but Freddie insisted and helped Drew put everything in the car.

"Hey Dad!" Drew called out. "Why's the number plate laid on the drive?"

Freddie looked and it struck him that someone had been busy, but everyone else walked round the car to have a look at the displaced number plate.

"This is very strange, it seems screws are going missing all over the village, the Chemist's door numbers, our gate and now this!" Freddie's father announced.

"We can't drive home without the number plate on the car, can we?" the twin's mother asked.

"I'm sure we can find some screws to fix the number plate back on the car," Freddie's mother replied.

"I think I have some odd screws in my rucksack Uncle, we've been finding them all over the place," Freddie said, taking off his rucksack and bringing out a few different screws, nuts and washers.

"Well done, Freddie," his Uncle praised. "I think a couple of those should do the job nicely," he said picking out a couple that looked suitable. He screwed them in with his fingers while the twins held the number plate in position. Freddie had already fished out a screwdriver from his magic rucksack. He handed it to his Uncle and Caleb sniggered.

"What you laughing at?" Drew asked.

"It's Freddie," Caleb chuckled, "his friends call him Freddie Fixit and you can see why, look how he's fixed this!"

Drew laughed and everyone chuckled hearing what Caleb had just said.

Freddie's Uncle passed the screwdriver back to Freddie and patted him on the head. "Thank you, Freddie, you're a little wonder. Is that rucksack of yours magic by any chance?" he said chuckling again.

"Oh! Yes Uncle, look." Freddie winked at the twins and put the screwdriver back into the top of his rucksack, zipped it up and said, "Abracadabra!" waving his hands over it, then unzipped it and turned it upside down. When nothing fell out of it the twins clapped their hands while the adults looked on amazed. "Abracadabra!" Freddie said again having zipped it up, then opened it again and fished out the screwdriver and chuckled, "Secret compartment!"

Even the adults clapped and laughed.

"What a neat trick, Freddie," Drew giggled, still clapping.

With the number plate screwed back on the car, Freddie and his parents waved goodbye to his Uncle, Auntie and cousins, then went back inside.

The pair of eyes that had been watching from afar disappeared into the forest.

* *

That night Freddie felt a little lonely. It had been so nice to have his two cousins stay, even for one night, and he sort of wished that he

145

had a brother like Caleb and Drew. He fell asleep dreaming about the screw thief and how they managed to steal the screws without being seen and how cheeky it had been to steal the number plate screws off his Uncle's car.

The next morning Freddie's father went back to work and his mother planned a visit to Grandma Fountain at the other end of the village. Freddie was keen to go as it had been a while since he had seen her. When they passed Jimmy's house there was a work van parked outside.

Jimmy spotted Freddie and came running out. "Hello, Mrs Fountain. Hey Freddie, guess what? When Mum opened the window this morning it fell out onto the path and smashed!"

"Oh, goodness, Jimmy!" Freddie's mother exclaimed. "Is your mother alright, not hurt I hope? We better say hello to her, Freddie."

Jimmy and Freddie ran into the house and Jimmy's mother met up with Freddie's mother.

"Brenda, Jimmy's just told me about your window falling out, are you hurt, did you get cut or anything?" Freddie's mother asked her close friend.

"Oh no, Susan, it was more shock than anything. The repair man told me all the screws had somehow gone missing from the hinges and that's why the window just fell out when I tried to open it."

Jimmy and Freddie dashed from the house and were standing next to their mothers.

Freddie looked at Jimmy's mother and said, "Jimmy and I have been finding the odd shiny screw on the footpath and I even found some in the forest," he said, pulling out two shiny screws from the pocket of his rucksack.

The repairman overheard and came over to have a look and remarked, "Well, bless my soul, if they don't look like two of the missing screws. Where did you find them, Freddie, boyoh?"

Freddie looked a little bewildered. "Well actually I found them in the forest, my cousin found one of them when we were quite a long way into the forest."

All three adults looked at each other with puzzled faces.

"That is very strange," the repair man began, "how did someone get the screws out without being seen, boyoh? And how did they end up in the forest, look you? This is very peculiar, boyoh! You know it's all I've been doing for two or three days now, just replacing missing screws, look you!"

Jimmy and Freddie looked at each other and giggled. Sam Bodgit, the repairman, spoke differently to them and Jimmy's mother explained that Sam was from Vales and he was Velsh, that was why he had an accent.

"Anyway all done now, your window has new glass and new screws, look you." Mr Bodgit said. "I gotta go see Mr and Mrs Ash next, they have a screw loose. Ooh, boyoh! I don't mean them personally, ha, ha!" His little unintentional funny remark made everyone laugh.

"You are funny, Mr Bodgit!" Freddie chuckled.

"Anyways, I mean it's their garden shed, boyoh! It's all wobbly, like. Mrs Ash just telephoned me, by all accounts Mr Ash is stuck inside being chased by spiders and the door won't open, ya-knows!" Sam explained.

The image of a wobbly shed with Mr Ash stuck inside with a loose screw and being chased by spiders kept everyone chuckling long after Sam had left.

Freddie and his mother stopped at the greengrocer's shop in the High Street on the way to Grandma's house. The shopkeeper was picking up apples, oranges and other fruit from the footpath, which had been on display on a wooden rack just outside the shop.

"What's happened?" Freddie's mother asked Mr Plum, who turned to see who was talking to him.

"Oh! Good morning, Mrs Fountain and Freddie, how are you both?" Mr Plum replied and before they could answer he carried on talking. "It's the most curious thing, I was stood outside here when an orange rolled off this display stand that I made a while back. So I picked it up and put it back. Next an apple did the same thing, it seemed to throw itself off the stand! I'm completely baffled, I can tell you. I actually watched one shiny screw after another unscrew themselves right out of the wood and then just disappear! Once a few screws had unscrewed themselves and vanished the rack fell apart and everything went everywhere!" Mr Plum looked in a state of shock recounting the event.

Freddie's mother gasped. "It seems screws are going missing everywhere. We just met Sam Bodgit, the handyman, and he is visiting homes just replacing screws!"

Freddie was deep in thought. *'If Mr Plum actually stood and watched shiny screws unscrewing themselves and then they vanished, it has to be something magical and the only place I know where there is magic is Elfin Town'*. He did not have all the pieces of the puzzle yet, but things were definitely pointing to Elfins.

* *

Grandma Fountain was pleased to see Freddie and his mother. "Come on in and sit down in the lounge, I'll put the kettle on," she chuckled, "and a nice glass of squash for you then, Freddie?"

Freddie nodded. "Yes please, Grandma, thank you," he replied with a big smile as she disappeared into the kitchen. His mind was still on Mr Plum's fruit display "How do you think screws can unscrew themselves, Mum?"

His mother looked at him and shook her head. "I have no idea, it seems impossible to me and if Mr Plum hadn't seen it with his own eyes, I wouldn't have believed it was possible. Maybe there is such a thing as magic after all."

When Freddie's Grandma returned they told her all that was going on and she chuckled away. "Some of my neighbours are complaining they've got loose screws too," she said, then put her hand over her mouth. "Not the neighbours, but gates and doors and things," she chuckled. "Got to be Imps, naughty Imps," she replied still chuckling.

"Grandma, what do you mean?" Freddie asked with a puzzled look on his face.

His Grandma sat down next to him and put her arm around her favourite Grandson, he always liked to cuddle into her when he visited. "When I was a little girl there were rumours that creatures lived in the forest," she said and laughed.

"Oh! What kind of creatures, Grandma? We saw a boar yesterday and it chased me and cousins Drew and Caleb?" Freddie interrupted.

"Oh! Not *those* kinds of creatures, but Elfins, Goblins, Imps and Fairies were all supposed to live in the forest, even a great wizard! None of us children would venture into the forest when I was little.

As I got older I began to think adults made up those stories to stop children going into the forest and getting lost."

Freddie's mother's ears pricked up and asked, "Those were just fairy tales though, Mum, weren't they? I mean Freddie plays in the forest all the time, he just about knows every tree and bush. You haven't mentioned you've seen any such creatures, have you, Freddie?" his mother asked.

"There's only me and a few rabbits and squirrels, oh, and hedgehogs and I did see a deer one time," he replied, not quite answering his mother's question as he did not want to tell lies to her.

"Why don't you go and play in the garden, Freddie, while your mother and I have a chinwag." Freddie laughed. "What's a chinwag, Grandma?"

His Grandma chuckled. "It does sound funny, doesn't it? It's just another word for having a chat," she replied.

Freddie liked playing in his Grandma's garden. She had a big swing made from tree trunks, a climbing frame with a rope net and a curving slide. He jumped up and ran into the kitchen and out the door into the garden. His smile was wiped off his face when he saw the swing, the seat was laid on the grass. "Not again!" he gasped. "Someone has stolen the screws." He took off his rucksack, unzipped the top and thought about the screws and a screwdriver, reached inside and pulled out what he needed. It was a bit fiddly trying to hold the seat, chain, screws and screwdriver all at the same time. "Whoops!" he said once or twice, to no one in particular, as a screw or the screwdriver dropped to the ground. "There," he said with a smile of satisfaction, putting the screwdriver back in his rucksack. "I do wonder where all the things go when I put them back in my rucksack, or where they come from. Magic is very curious stuff," he said quietly to himself.

When he sat on the swing it creaked and groaned as he made it fly high in the air. He loved the feeling of floating just for a second as he swung down, he felt as light as a feather and laughed loudly.

"Ooops!" He cried once or twice as his foot missed the next rung on the climbing frame rope net and he laughed again with his leg dangling through the net. Once he got to the top of the climbing frame he jumped on the slide and whizzed down crying, "Wheeeee!"

Freddie was quite happy playing by himself, but did enjoy having others to keep him company. While he climbed and slid down the slide, he thought about his cousins and Wiggly. The time seemed to rush by and he was surprised when his mother called him inside to have a lunchtime sandwich.

"Banana and chocolate spread just for you, Freddie," his Grandma chuckled.

Freddie liked his Grandma's sandwiches. She made all kinds, like cheese and jam, or peanut butter and jam, but his all time favourite was always just jam sandwiches.

"I mended the swing, Grandma, the screws had vanished, but I found some in my rucksack and fixed it," he told her proudly.

His Grandma chuckled. "Freddie Fixit eh, just like your Granddad, Freddie, he was handy just like you." She suddenly looked a little sad for a moment.

"You still miss him a lot, Mum," Freddie's mother said.

"I do dear, even though it has been more than two years since he passed away, I miss him every day. The house seems so lonely without him wandering around, ah well," she sighed.

Freddie did not really hear what his mother and Grandma had said, he had gone into his own thoughts about the missing screws. *'I know Grandma is right about Elfins and Goblins all those years ago and I know they still live underground out of sight. Could the screw thief be an Elfin or a Mole Goblin? But surely they would be seen. Maybe there are also Pixies, could they still be around? Maybe they were invisible or so small like flies, but then how could they get screws to unscrew and why, maybe they have magic to make the screws do that, but why, why would anyone take screws?'* His thoughts consumed him while his mother and Grandma chinwagged.

* *

That night Freddie's dreams were filled with an Elfin who had magic powers and could make screws unscrew themselves and then vanish. The next morning he woke up bright and early and skipped downstairs where his mother had breakfast ready for him.

"Mum, I'm going exploring in the forest to see if I can find any Elfins or Imps and other creatures," he told her.

"Well just be careful, I expect you would like some jam sandwiches to take with you," she chuckled.

Freddie galloped back upstairs to collect his rucksack and explorers hat, then galloped down again to pick up the packed lunch his mother had prepared.

"Now do be careful, Freddie, if you see that wild boar again run home as fast as you can, understand?"

Freddie nodded his head and smiled. "Yes, Mum, will do, don't worry." He had no intention of hanging around if he did come across that boar again. Once through the gate at the bottom of his garden he made his way through the forest, giving the bushes a gentle poke with his 'magic' golden staff as he went, just in case anything was lurking behind them. When he finally reached the big old oak tree he felt safe and uttered the magic words to reveal the doorway. "That's so cool," he whispered, to no one in particular, taking a moment to be in awe of magic. He ran down the spiral staircase at a fair rate of knots and felt quite dizzy when he reached the bottom. "Wow! So many steps," he gasped trying to catch his breath. Elfin Town was quiet when he walked through it to Wiggly's house, only one or two Elfins were out and about, who waved to him as he passed. Freddie felt so at home here, everyone was really nice to him and they were all lovely, no one said nasty things or argued or had fights, not like the world of Sproggles. When he reached his destination he knocked on door and Wiggly opened it.

"Hey, Freddie, come in, come in," he cried, delighted to see his friend.

Giggly rushed to meet him and gave him a really big hug, she was always pleased to see him.

"Let the poor boy get inside before you suffocate him," Mummly said as she saw Freddie through the doorway.

The whole family was at home, so Freddie explained everything he knew about the missing screws all over the village.

"Mr Plum the grocer, actually watched screws unscrewing themselves and then vanish into thin air!" he explained.

"Gosh, that's incredible. Actually, that's impossible isn't it, Daddly?" Wiggly asked.

But before Daddly answered Freddie asked another question.

"Is it possible for an Elfin to have magic to collect all those screws?"

Daddly looked concerned. "Well it certainly sounds like magic is being used, but I'm not sure how. If it were an Elfin they would need a jar of Fairy Dust, which could be seen by Sproggles, the Elfin would also be visible. It's a complete mystery. The thing is we don't use screws because they are too complicated to make, unlike Sproggles who have huge machines to make them."

Freddie already knew about that. Then something occurred to him. "Daddly, if Elfin's don't use screws, how do you fix things together?"

Daddly smiled and pointed to the big table. "Go have a look how the table is made, it will answer your question."

Freddie, Wiggly and Giggly got up and went to look at the big table. They looked at the top and then Wiggly lay on the floor to look underneath.

"Oh, Freddie, come down here and look," he suggested.

Freddie and Giggly laid either side of Wiggly and looked up.

"Oh wow, that's so clever, you don't need screws at all!" Freddie declared.

Wiggly was so excited. He had never thought about such things and he jumped up, "OW! OW!" he cried, bumping his head on the underside of the table.

Freddie could not stop his chuckle at Wiggly's misfortune and Giggly rolled around on the floor with laughter. Even Mummly had to giggle and Daddly gave a little snigger.

Wiggly was feeling a little giddy, rubbing his head.

Freddie helped him to stand up and patted his back sympathetically.

"Hope you didn't damage the table, Wiggly?" Mummly teased and laughed.

"Aw, Mummly, it hurt!" Wiggly confessed.

They all sat down in the sitting area and Daddly asked, "So do you have your answer children?"

Wiggly piped, "How come wood is so hard?"

Of course it made everyone chuckle a bit more.

Wiggly pulled a face and that made things worse, creating even more laughter.

When they settled down Freddie said, "It looks like round pieces of wood are pushed into holes that lock all the pieces of wood together."

Daddly clapped his hands and smiled. "That's right, we call it a peg and socket joint, we also use *sticky*."

That set Giggly off again and she was laughing, "*Sticky,* Daddly, what's *sticky?*"

All three children and Mummly looked at Daddly for an answer.

"Well *sticky* is made from tree sap and it's, well, sticky. It's put between the two pieces of wood before the peg is forced into the hole, then the joint never comes loose. Before we discovered *sticky,* we Elfins would suddenly find chairs fall apart or a table leg drop off!"

Wiggly laughed out aloud. "It would be quite a shock to suddenly find yourself sitting on the floor, or, or, or," he got excited, stood up and his legs were running on the spot again, "if the table leg dropped off all the food would slowly slide to the end and plop to the floor!" The way Wiggly said it made everyone laugh again.

Wiggly, you are very funny," Freddie chuckled.

"Would you like to see how furniture is made, Freddie?" Daddly asked.

"Oh! Could I? That would be very interesting," Freddie replied excitedly.

The whole Tiggly family and Freddie set off down the street heading for the lake in the park, or at least the other side of the lake. It was quite a long way around the lake and then they came upon a large building hidden in the shadows. The two large, gate-like doors at one end seemed to be the entrance and while they stood outside of them they could hear banging and buzzing sounds.

Daddly pushed open one of the large doors and they all walked inside in single file.

Their eyes were wide open looking at all the chairs, stools, tables and tools on display.

"Mr Burr! Mr Burr! Are you about?" Daddly called and an Elfin popped his head around a slatted wall directly in front of them.

"Daddly, Mummly, Wiggly and Giggly, how nice to see you, and you young man, must be Freddie?" the Elfin replied as the rest of him appeared from around the slatted wall.

"Everyone," Daddly announced, "this is one of my oldest friends, Mr Tim Burr. He makes all the things we need, like furniture and so on. Actually, Tim invented *sticky*"

"Lovely to meet you all, we don't get many visitors unless someone needs something making. And it's a pleasure to meet you at last, Freddie. I'm sorry we haven't had the chance to meet before now," Mr Burr replied.

"Freddie is on the trail of missing screws and it got us onto the subject of how furniture is made here without such things, so I have brought everyone here to see for themselves, if you don't mind giving us a tour?" Daddly explained.

Tim Burr beamed with delight and pride. "I'd be very happy to show you all, but be careful, it's very dusty in the workshop. Please come this way."

Everyone followed Mr Burr behind the slatted wall and into a huge room with lots of workbenches and tools and part made pieces of furniture.

"Teddy! Come welcome our visitors. Everyone, this is my son, Teddy Burr!" Tim Burr said proudly. "He's going to take over when I retire," he added.

Teddy Burr shook hands with everyone. Freddie remembered seeing Teddy at the party after he and Wiggly saved the children from the Mole Goblins.

"I didn't know you made such wonderful things, Teddy, but I suppose I didn't ask either," Freddie admitted.

"Well it was a bit exciting at the time, Freddie, and we only got the chance to have a quick chat as everyone wanted to talk to you. But welcome, come and see what we get up to over this side of the lake," Teddy invited.

Then Teddy and his father showed them lots of part made large and small comfy chairs, bed frames, cupboards, tables, even sweeping brushes. He demonstrated how they made holes with something that looked like a bow and arrow. A string was attached to each end of the bow and also wrapped around the arrow that had a metal tip, then a block with a small dint was placed on the other end of the arrow. When the bow was pulled back and forth it made the arrow spin and the metal end cut a hole.

"That's so clever!" cried Wiggly, completely fascinated, just like Freddie and Giggly were.

"Teddy, let them all have a go," Mr Burr told him.

Freddie had first attempt. "Wow! This is quite hard work, you must have big muscles?" he declared, red faced and puffing after he had made a just a shallow hole.

Teddy gave Freddie a big smile and chuckled.

Wiggly really got the hang of it when his turn came. "Oh yes, I like this, it's fun," he exclaimed.

"You're a natural, Wiggly, when you finish school come and work here!" Teddy announced.

Wiggly looked quite proud and was really interested in everything. "Do you really think I could do it?" he asked.

Mr Burr replied, "It would be wonderful to have another working here, a bit of younger company for Teddy as well, the job's yours if you want it!"

Wiggly looked at his mother and father who were nodding their approval.

"Thank you, thank you so much!" Wiggly replied with a huge smile on his face. "I would love to help make all these wonderful things with you. I accept!"

"That's wonderful, Wiggly, it'll be smashing to have the son of one of my oldest friends working with us. Now come over here and I'll show you how we make the pegs."

Everyone walked over to another bench that had a metal plate fitted with a hole in it the same size as the hole that they had just been making.

"This is good therapy," Mr Burr said, "we cut a short square of wood like this," he showed them a square section of wood as long as a fist with a little taper on one end, there were dozens of them on the bench. "Next we place the tapered end in the hole in the metal plate like this. Then we bash it through the hole with this *basher*." Mr Burr picked up a piece of wood as long as his arm, which was small and round at one end and thick and square at the other. He hit the square of wood through the hole with the *basher* and it popped out into a box under the bench. He picked up the result and showed them a perfectly round peg.

"That's just like magic!" Giggly said, completely fascinated.

"Who wants a go then?" Mr Burr laughed.

Wiggly was already running on the spot with excitement. They each tried to bash the square wood through the hole. Wiggly went first and picked up the heavy *basher* and lifted it above his head, then promptly lost control as it pulled him backwards. "Whoah!" he cried as Daddly saved him from tumbling onto the dusty floor.

Giggly was beside herself with laughter, actually everyone was chuckling.

Wiggly had another attempt, this time hitting the square wood in the hole just enough for it to stick up in the air. Then he used both hands to hold the *basher* and whacked the square wood four or five times until it disappeared. "Oh! That felt good, but it's very tiring," he declared.

Giggly could not even lift the *basher* and looked disappointed at first before descending into a fit of giggles.

Freddie said, "I think I have something to help with that!" and took his rucksack from his shoulders, reached inside and pulled out a shiny metal hammer with a wooden handle. "Try this Giggly, it's what my Dad calls *anammer*."

This time Giggly held the *anammer*, hit the square of wood only three times when it disappeared through the hole in the metal plate and she jumped up and down with excitement. "I did it, whoopee! I did it!" she cried much to everyone's amusement.

"Your turn, Freddie," Mr Burr said.

Freddie used the heavy *basher* and managed to make the round peg with five blows. He smiled with satisfaction, then looked at Mr Burr and said, "If this *anammer* is useful to you I'd like you to have it."

Mr Burr gave Freddie a huge smile. "That's very kind of you, Freddie, I think it will make this job much easier, even my daughter, Curly, might be able to make some pegs!"

Freddie was pleased he had been of help. "Mr Burr, could we see the *sticky* please?" Freddie asked.

Again Mr Burr was delighted. "Of course, he replied. Looking over to his son he called, "Teddy, show everyone how we make 'sticky' will you?"

"Come this way." Teddy beckoned them to the end of the workshop to a really big bench. "This pot has tree sap in it, it's from the Holly tree which doesn't go to sleep in the winter, so we can collect the sap when we need it," Teddy began to explain.

They all looked into the pot, one by one.

"It looks very watery," Wiggly observed, "does it really stick wood together like that?" he added.

Teddy smiled knowingly. "Quite right, it is watery and is no good like this, so we heat it up until it bubbles then add a bit of tree bark from an oak tree. Once it cools it looks like this." Teddy lifted a spoon from another pot and a thick liquid, like golden syrup, slowly dribbled from it back into the pot.

"Is it really sticky?" Wiggly asked.

Teddy chuckled, "Just put a tiny bit on the end of your finger, then touch that wood shaving over there."

Wiggly was excited again and everyone watched him touch the **sticky**, then the wood shaving, which immediately stuck to his finger. "Oh, it really is sticky!" he cried in surprise, shaking his hand like mad trying to get rid of the shaving. He flicked and shook up and down, side to side, while everyone was chuckling at his antics. "It's stuck, it's stuck!" he cried, still flicking here and there.

"Hold on!" Mr Burr called, coming to the rescue with a damp cloth, wiping Wiggly's finger and removing the wood shaving.

Giggly was howling with laughter again, her brother had looked so funny.

Mr Burr and Teddy took everyone upstairs to meet Mrs Burr and Curly and have a nice warm drink. They all sat around a big oval table with their cups of dandelion tea.

"Tell me about this mystery of yours, Freddie," Mr Burr asked.

Freddie explained to Mr and Mrs Burr, Curly and Teddy everything he knew so far.

"What! You mean a Sproggle watched a shiny screw unscrew itself from a wooden rack and then it just vanished into thin air?" Teddy Burr asked, not quite believing what he was hearing.

"That's right," Freddie, confirmed, "the screw turned round and round until it was almost out of the wood and then just disappeared."

"Well I never did in all my life!" exclaimed Mrs Burr. "That definitely sounds like magic, but whoever is responsible would have to be invisible and put a tiny bit of Fairy Dust on the screw and tell it to unscrew itself!" she added.

Everyone was silent, thinking about the mystery.

Then Daddly said, "Well we know who has jars of Fairy Dust, so apart from us with the Tiggly's jar, we can find out if any has gone missing. We know our jar is locked away and has not been out since Freddie and Wiggly brought them from Merlin's Cavern."

"It's definitely a starting point," said Teddy, "you might want to check yours though, just in case someone has crept in and borrowed it!"

"That will be our next three calls then, to check the jars of Fairy Dust," Daddly announced.

* *

At the Council leader's house, Mr Bumble unlocked his jar of Fairy Dust and explained, "Like you, Mr and Mrs Tiggly, this jar has been locked away since it was brought over here, we have not been in need of it." He opened the special cupboard with an enchanted lock and lifted out the jar of Fairy Dust, which sparkled and twinkled.

"It's still full to the top," Mummly observed.

Although this eliminated another jar of Fairy Dust, it was getting them no further on with solving their mystery. The next port of call was to the schoolteacher, who also lived at the school.

She invited everyone in and they sat in comfy chairs in her living room drinking strawberry tea. When the jar of Fairy Dust was brought out it was not full to the top, but this was the jar they had used to seal the hole in the floor through which the Mole Goblins had taken the children. It pretty much accounted for all the Fairy Dust in Elfin Town.

Freddie pondered over the problem in his mind. *'How is it possible to make magic without Fairy Dust?'* He looked around and then asked, "I know this may be a silly question too, but does such a thing as a magic wand exist, and if it does, could someone use it to steal screws and other stuff?

All eyes were suddenly on Freddie.

Freddie felt awkward and said out loud, "Mmmm! I knew it was a silly question!" then he began to blush.

"The Fairies all have star wands to make magic with and Merlin has his staff, so it's possible," the schoolteacher replied. "Well thought out, Freddie," she praised.

"One problem though, only a Fairy can use the star wand and of course, only Merlin can use his staff," explained Daddly.

They decided to walk across the park and head home from the school. They had learned lots, but were no closer to solving the mystery.

"Oh look," Giggly cried, "fallen stars!" Although it was still daylight, Giggly was pointing to something glinting in the moss grass and ran to the first one. She bent down and picked up yet another shiny metal screw. "Look!" she called to Freddie. "It's a shiny metal screw."

By this time the others had caught up to her, looking at the screw with puzzled expressions.

"This is definitely a clue," Freddie exclaimed excitedly, beginning to form an idea in his mind. "Let's see if that other glinting object is also a screw. Wiggly, could you go and pick it up please and stay where it is?"

Wiggly scampered away and picked up the shiny object, then, standing in the place where the screw was, he held it up. "It's another one, Freddie!" he called enthusiastically.

"Daddly, I have an idea," Freddie said. "Let's say the person doing this is an Elfin. Can you point out the direction of the door at the bottom of the spiral staircase?"

Daddly smiled knowingly. "It's in that direction," he said pointing beyond where Wiggly was standing.

"If I walk in that direction and stop a little way along, can you guide me left or right to be in line with the spiral staircase door?" Freddie asked and Daddly nodded he would. Freddie walked away from Daddly, Mummly and Giggly.

"What's he doing?" Giggly asked.

"Watch and see, Giggly," Daddly replied.

Freddie reached Wiggly and walked past him a fair way, then turned to look towards Daddly.

Daddly called out, "Bit to your left, Freddie. That's it, spot on!" Then Daddly walked all the way to Freddie and said, "I know what you are thinking now, Freddie. From here to Wiggly, and then from Wiggly to Giggly is a straight line, so the culprit must be walking in the direction from us towards Giggly!"

Freddie chuckled. "That's it exactly, Daddly. Now all we have to do is follow the straight line from here, passing Wiggly, then beyond Giggly and see where it leads."

They walked back and met with Wiggly, who did not understand.

When they reached Giggly, she had worked it out too. "Whoever is doing this must have dropped these screws while walking from the spiral staircase door to their house, so we just need to follow their footsteps," she explained.

"Yes, I see now!" Wiggly said, excited that he finally understood. "So let's go in a straight line then. You are clever, Freddie," he said with a big smile of admiration for his friend. Wiggly held onto Freddie's hand while they walked towards the town buildings.

"Looks like the culprit might live in one of those buildings," Daddly announced as they halted in their tracks, looking at the only three houses ahead of them.

"We know all the Elfins who live there, though," Mummly remarked. "The house on the right is where rugs are made by the Woollen family, in the middle is the shoe maker family and the other end house is where the Pages live, who make paper, then print and create all our books."

Everyone listened to Mummly carefully and wondered did the screw thief actually live in one of those three houses?

"Well it would not be the done thing to go accusing anyone without any evidence, they would be very upset and it's not the Elfin way," Daddly explained. "But I have an idea, let's all go home and I will explain."

When everyone was settled in comfy chairs in the sitting area of the Tiggly's home, Daddly explained his idea. "Freddie, can you reach into your rucksack and find a pair of plain glass spectacles?"

Freddie already had his rucksack on the floor and did just as Daddly had asked and out came a pair of spectacles with brown frames.

Daddly stood up and went to the Fairy Dust cupboard and unlocked it, lifting out the jar and taking it over to the sitting area.

"Oh, that's so pretty, all twinkling like that!" Giggly smiled.

"If you could hand me those spectacles, Freddie, I will sprinkle them with Fairy Dust."

Freddie passed over the spectacles as requested.

Daddly took them and then unscrewed the jar, took a tiny pinch of Fairy Dust and sprinkled it on the spectacles, muttering some words quietly, then handed them back to him. "Now, Freddie," Daddly said with a knowing smile, "these have a spell on them so that when you put them on you will be able to see anything that has magic in or on it."

Freddie was quite excited and put the spectacles on as soon as Daddly handed them to him.

"What do you see?" Wiggly cried excitedly.

"Whoah! That's incredible, so bright and pretty," Freddie announced beaming with a huge grin.

"Oooo, can I have a try?" Wiggly asked, holding out his hands hopefully.

Freddie took them off and handed them to his friend and Wiggly put them on, they were a bit big for his face so he had to hold them in place. "Wow, Daddly!" he shouted. "So pretty, the floor, look at the floor!"

Giggly looked at the floor. "It's just the same!" she said disappointedly, until Wiggly handed her the spectacles.

"Oooo," Giggly gasped, "it's so beautiful, like a million tiny stars!"

What they were seeing through the spectacles was everything touched by magic. Where it had been used, the whole object lit up like thousands of twinkling stars, just like the Fairy Dust. Giggly handed the spectacles to Mummly and then Daddly, so they could also enjoy the evidence.

"Any object that has been touched by magic, like the floor and the ground outside and even your rucksack, Freddie, will show up," Daddly explained.

Freddie looked through the spectacles again after Daddly passed them back to him. "Oh yes, my rucksack sparkles too, how wonderful," he replied still smiling.

"Everything will twinkle and sparkle like Fairy Dust if affected by magic, Freddie, so you should be able to discover who the culprit is when you go for a walk around your village," Daddly finished explaining.

"Daddly, that's such a clever plan!" Wiggly praised and everyone agreed that this should flush out the mysterious screw thief.

* *

Freddie returned home mid afternoon.

"You're home nice and early, Freddie, did you do anything interesting today?" his mother asked.

Freddie answered his mother with a question, trying to avoid telling her what he had actually been doing.

"Mum, do you think there is such a thing as magic?"

His mother put down the dishcloth and dried her hands, then sat down on the chair looking at her son. "Well I guess there are many things we see as magical," she replied.

"What sort of things, Mum?"

His mother thought for a moment. "Well, think about a small acorn. It falls to the ground and somehow detects soil and moisture, then it sends out a shoot that roots into the soil, eventually growing into a huge tree, many thousands of times bigger than the little acorn. Or a small seed that we plant in the ground, which grows into a very tall sunflower. For me that is just like magic, don't you think so?"

Freddie smiled and moved close to his mother and gave her a hug. "I guess so, Mum, I never thought about things like that, but now I do and you're right, it is like magic. Do you think God is a magician?"

His mother chuckled. "Your curiosity knows no bounds, but that's a good thing. For me, I would say yes, but other people will have different opinions, so we must never assume that only our ideas are the only truth, we need to respect what other people think too. My father used to tell me something when I got into an argument with anyone, his words of wisdom were these, *'Just because you disagree, doesn't mean you're right.'*"

Freddie looked a little puzzled.

"The thing is, Freddie, that I believe there is a God. There are lots of people who don't believe there is a God, so who do you think is right?"

Freddie looked even more puzzled. "Well you are of course, Mum," he replied.

His mother smiled and stroked his blond hair lovingly. "When you become older, you will see that people believe different things for different reasons and we should be able to accept it even if we disagree."

Freddie thought for a moment. "But shouldn't we tell people?"

"Well, we do in a way, it's called debating and discussing. Sometimes people change their minds, other times they change the minds of others, it's how the world works." His mother realised that this conversation was getting deeper than Freddie could probably understand, sometimes even she did not understand such things. "Tea won't be ready for a while, why don't you go play for a bit?"

"Okay Mum," he hugged her again. "I love you, Mum."

"I love you too, son," she told him and lovingly stroked his hair.

Freddie ran up the stairs like a herd of elephants and his mother chuckled to herself. He jumped on his bed and decided to read a book while waiting for his father to come home.

* *

The next morning the sunshine danced across Freddie's face through the gap in the curtains. He opened his eyes sleepily, roused from another dream about magical creatures wandering around in the world of Sproggles.

"Oooh," he cried, suddenly sitting up, "got to get up and go on patrol today, it's quite exciting," he said, to no one in particular.

During their breakfast Freddie asked his mother if she was going to the shops and when she told him she was, he asked if he could go with her. Of course, she was more than happy for him to go with her. "Mum, I'm going to be a secret agent in disguise today. Look, I've got these special spectacles so no one will recognise me, just like superman, Clark Kent!" Freddie was so excited.

His mother chuckled and smiled, wondering where all his imagination came from, but she was pleased he was such a happy, contented little boy. She found Freddie a beret style hat to help with his disguise. "You can be a Frensh secret agent if you wear this hat, Freddie," she said with a huge grin on her face, pleased to see him so happy.

Freddie was excited, he might be on the verge of uncovering the mystery of the stolen screws, but he was also a little nervous. *'What if it's Mr Bumble or one of the Baker children or even someone I don't know. Maybe there are other Elfins and magical people out there,'* he thought. "Come on, Mum, let's go, hurry!" he encouraged, pulling her along.

The very first shop on the High Street was the Florist, run by Mrs Bush, who was outside looking very puzzled.

"Whatever is the matter, Rose?" Freddie's mother asked, Rose Bush being one of her close friends.

"Oh! Morning Susan, and Freddie. Something very strange is going on. I think we have ghosts or something very weird. I put my flower rack out here just now and before I could fill it with flowers the side of it just fell off! Look! Somehow all the screws have completely disappeared!"

Freddie took a close look with his special spectacles, but he could not see anything magical.

Freddie's mother chuckled. "Don't mind Freddie, Rose, he's a Frensh secret agent today," she explained as he was so close to the rack he almost bumped his nose.

"I can fix that for you, Mrs Bush." Freddie smiled and fished four screws and a screwdriver from his magic rucksack.

"Well I must say you're a handy young man to have around, I can see why you got the nickname Freddie Fixit," she chuckled at her own humour. "I'll hold it together while you screw in those screws then, Freddie," Rose Bush added.

Freddie popped the screws into the holes and began turning the screwdriver, but he was not quite strong enough to screw them all the way in.

"Let me finish those off, Freddie," Mrs Bush said and he handed the screwdriver to her. "There, that's nice and strong again, thank you, Freddie, I think you've earned your nickname today!" Rose Bush thanked Freddie with a chuckle, and he turned bright red in the face. "Come with me," she said and he followed her inside the shop. He looked around in wonder at all the beautiful flowers and took a deep breath to enjoy the lovely scent in the air. "Let me give you a nice bunch of flowers that you can give to your mother, okay?"

Freddie liked that idea. He loved his mother a lot, she did so much for him and he liked to help her when he could and he knew she loved flowers. Freddie marched out of the shop holding a beautiful bouquet of multicoloured flowers.

"Look Mum, Mrs Bush gave me these flowers for helping her, but I'd like to give them to you," he said with a big cheerful smile on his face.

"Freddie, you are the best son any parent could ever wish for. Thank you, they really are lovely," she praised. Rose Bush was stood in the doorway and Freddie's mother mouthed the words, "Thank you" to her.

While his mother popped into the hairdresser to have her hair tidied, Freddie walked down to the newsagent to buy a comic with the money his mother had given to him. He walked past the butchers shop and Mr Lamb waved at him through the window and Freddie waved back with a big smile. The newsagent was two shops further along and Freddie could see a lot of people standing outside. Mr and Mrs Wordsworth, who owned the newsagent, had notices screwed to the wall advertising sweets or fizzy drinks and this is what people seemed to be looking at.

Freddie thought there must be some new ones attracting attention, but when he got there, they were all the same ones as usual. He liked the one showing the bottles of cola lined up like skittles in a bowling alley, but everyone was stood, just staring and that puzzled Freddie. *'Are they unwell,'* he thought, because they were making funny noises like gasps and oohs! So he decided to investigate, but he soon realised exactly what everyone was looking at so intently.

One of the brightly coloured enamel metal advertisements suddenly slid down the wall and fell flat on the footpath with a loud crash. Instinctively people stepped back out of the way, but remained gathered together.

"This is very curious," he whispered, to no one in particular. "What's happening, Mr Taylor?" he asked, recognising the man in front of him."

"Oh, hello Freddie, it's the most curious thing ever. You see the shiny screws holding the adverts to the wall? Well, they are just unscrewing themselves and vanishing into thin air!" he replied.

Freddie grabbed his special spectacles, put them on and looked at the next panel. He was so surprised at what he saw he stood rooted to the spot with his eyes wide open. One of the screws was unscrewing, but not by itself. Through his magic detecting spectacles Freddie saw exactly what was happening. A sparkling screwdriver was unscrewing the screws one by one, but that was not the best bit, for holding the screwdriver, was an Elfin. On his head was a pointy hat that also sparkled and twinkled like Fairy Dust. Freddie lifted his spectacles off his eyes and both the Elfin and screwdriver vanished. With the spectacles back on, he could clearly see the Elfin holding the screwdriver again.

"So that's how you are doing it!" Freddie whispered, then shouted out, **"Hey, you!"**

The Elfin froze and turned and looked straight at Freddie. When the Elfin recognised Freddie his face turned white and he squeaked, "Freddie!"

The Elfin knew Freddie could see him, but did not know how, so he stopped, turned and ran up the high street and into the safety of the forest.

The people around heard the squeaky voice call Freddie's name and thought one of them had shouted. They looked at each other a bit confused, shaking their heads as if to say, *"It wasn't me,"* then turned and began to walk away.

Freddie picked up the advertisement sign and leaned it against the wall. Mrs Wordsworth had just come outside to see what was going on.

"Hello Freddie, it has happened again hasn't it?"

Freddie looked up. "Has this fallen off before?" he asked.

"Oh yes, Freddie, twice already," she declared looking somewhat sad and puzzled at the same time.

Freddie smiled. "I've got some special screws in my rucksack, my Dad showed me how to make them unscrewable." He lifted his rucksack down and fumbled around inside, pulling out six screws with the back edge of the slot filed off, also a screwdriver. "I can put this back if you can hold it up for me, Mrs Wordsworth?" Freddie offered.

Between them they fixed the sign back in position on the wall and Freddie showed Mrs Wordsworth how it was impossible to unscrew the screws now.

"Freddie, you are so clever, just wait until Mr Wordsworth sees this!" She called her husband to come outside and take a look.

"Freddie! How nice to see you," Mr Wordsworth greeted him with a happy face.

"Look at this, Harry, Freddie has fixed the sign with magic screws!"

Freddie giggled, they were not really magic, but it was like his mother had said, magic appears differently to everyone.

"Look," Mrs Wordsworth added, "you just try and unscrew them, it is magic!"

Freddie handed Mr Wordsworth the screwdriver and try as he might he could not get the screws out. "Blimey, Freddie, you are a magician, this is amazing!" he praised and Freddie turned red in the face.

"It's a trick my Dad showed me, you just file off the back of the slot in the screw and the screwdriver just slips off when you try to unscrew it," he explained.

Mr Wordsworth was very impressed. Freddie reached into his rucksack and brought out a handful of special screws.

"Here you are, Mr Wordsworth, you can fix all the others so they can't be unscrewed."

"Thank you, Freddie," Mr Wordsworth said handing the screwdriver back to him. "I have one of these so I can do the replacements a bit later on, now come inside and choose a couple of comics as a reward."

Freddie was excited and went inside with Mr and Mrs Wordsworth. He chose a Superman and Batman comic and Mr and Mrs Wordsworth gave him a chocolate bar as well. Freddie ran back to the Hairdresser. He took a deep breath and suppressed his excitement, then sat down quietly to read his comics while his mother had her hair styled. On the way home he explained what had happened and gave the fifty pence piece back to his mother, but she said he could keep it and put it towards his next model kit for being honest about it.

After he and his mother had lunch together, Freddie asked if he could go play in the forest and his mother told him to put on his watch and be home by 5 o'clock.

* *

Freddie was bubbling with excitement about his discovery, but filled with nervousness, it was a big thing to accuse someone of stealing. Even though Freddie had not recognised the shiny screw thief, he hoped Daddly could help narrow down the possible suspects, yes, he definitely needed to speak with Daddly. With his play clothes on and rucksack over his shoulder, he ran into the forest through the gate at the bottom of his garden. He was so focussed on getting to the big old oak tree he completely forgot about the big wild boar. He was less than half way along the narrow track when he came to an abrupt halt. "Oh, no!" he cried out.

Blocking his way was the big boar with horrid looking tusks poking up from its bottom jaw. Freddie froze to the spot and the boar looked straight at him with its fearsome, beady eyes. The beastie snorted and grunted, bowed its head and pushed the soil up in the air with its snout.

'If you see that boar, run home as fast as you can.' Freddie remembered his mother's warning and he was just about to turn and run when the boar turned around and trotted behind the big bush next to it. Now Freddie was undecided what to do, he needed to get to Elfin Town, but that boar could hurt him quite seriously if it charged at him.

"What to do, what to do?" he whispered, to no one in particular, then he heard a squealing sound and the boar reappeared.

Freddie again could not move and expected it to charge at him, but it did not, instead it bobbed its head up and down, turned and trotted behind the bush. Freddie heard the squealing noise again. 'Is something hurt?' he wondered. The boar reappeared, bobbed its head, turned and trotted behind the bush.

"This is very odd behaviour, why does it not chase me like before?" he whispered to himself.

Once more the boar showed itself, repeated the head bobbing and disappeared behind the bush.

"You want me to follow you, that's it, isn't it?" Freddie said out aloud while he could hear some squealing going on. He realised he was shaking, he was afraid of this big boar, but he did not think it was clever enough to lead him into a trap. He moved slowly and silently towards the bush, nervously walked round to where the boar had disappeared. There it was and Freddie froze, he was really shaking now.

'Run home as fast as you can,' his mother's words ringing in his ears, 'run home.'

But the boar was sat down and just looked at Freddie, making a sad whimpering sound. Slowly Freddie walked on, getting closer to the boar and it bobbed its head and stayed where it was. He heard more squealing from under the bush and looked carefully. "Oh no," Freddie said softly. Now he understood why the boar had behaved as it did and not chased him, it was asking for his help.

The little piglet that he and his cousins had seen before was under the bush with its leg trapped in a rabbit snare. As it pulled and tugged and wriggled, it squealed and cried, but could not get free. The more it struggled the tighter the snare gripped its little trotter.

Freddie moved very slowly so as not to alarm the big boar and held the piglet's trotter, then loosened the snare to free it. Luckily the wire had not caused any damage, probably because the piglet was too small to pull very hard. He let the piglet go free and it trotted straight to the mother boar that squealed and huffed. Freddie pulled the snare out of the ground, he and his father must have missed this one when they removed all the other traps. He stood slowly and stayed quite still to let the boar and piglet trot off, but the boar had other ideas. She slowly approached Freddie until her head touched his leg. He was nervous she might butt or bite him, but instead she rubbed her snout gently up and down his leg.

"You're thanking me," he said softly and dared to reach down and stroke her head. "You're welcome," he said quietly, "go home safely."

The boar looked up at Freddie's face and he could swear she was smiling, then turned and trotted off with her piglet, raising her snout in the air and grunting as if saying, *"Thank you and goodbye."*

Freddie took a deep breath. "Oh boy, that was so scary for a while!" he gasped. "These snares are so cruel, I hope there are no more of them lying around." He put his rucksack down on the ground and opened it, sliding the snare inside then zipping it back up. "I wonder where the magic takes the things I put in there or take out? I guess that's why it's magic," he said, to no one in particular. His legs still felt a bit wobbly, so he walked slowly for the rest of his journey to the big old oak tree, where he sat against it for a little while. Then, feeling much better, he stood up and uttered the magic words and watched the door appear. He never got tired of seeing that happen. By the time he had walked down the spiral staircase and out of the door at the bottom, he was left puffing and blowing.

"Freddie!" he recognised that voice, it was the Town Elder.

"Are you alright, Freddie, you look very red in the face?" Mr Bumble asked kindly.

Freddie stopped to catch his breath and between gasps he explained about his run in with the boar.

"Oh dear! That's not good news. We rid the forest of wild boars many years ago, because they rip up the ground with their snouts searching for food and make everywhere look like bombs have exploded. Nothing grows and all the plants and bushes die off, because they eat all the tree and bush seeds so nothing gets replaced and the forest slowly dies."

Freddie had no idea of the damage they could do and wondered how they got back into the forest. "I'll have a word with my father, he is a trustee of the forest, he will know what to do," Freddie replied.

"Thank you, Freddie, we are so lucky to have your friendship."

They said goodbye to each other. Freddie had stopped puffing and blowing and ran the rest of the way to the Tiggly's home.

"Daddly, I saw the thief in the act of stealing shiny screws this morning," Freddie began as everyone sat in comfy chairs, eager to hear everything. "Like we suspected, it is an Elfin, but he was invisible. At first all I could see were the screws unscrewing themselves and it was really weird. When I put the magic spectacles on I saw him with a screwdriver unscrewing the screws, his pointy hat sparkled and twinkled like a jar of Fairy Dust. When I called out he stopped, turned to look at me and called out my name, so he knows me, but I didn't recognise him, Daddly!"

Wiggly and Giggly were so excited, especially Wiggly, who got up to stand next to Freddie with his little legs running on the spot.

Daddly smiled with satisfaction. "Well done, Freddie, it's a start. Now we know for sure the culprit is an Elfin, we have to narrow down our suspect. You say you didn't recognise the Elfin, but he recognised you. How tall do you think he was and maybe how old?"

Freddie tried to picture the Elfin in his mind. "Ah! Well, he was older than Wiggly and about your height, Daddly," he replied.

"That's good, that's very good!" Daddly said.

"How so, Daddly?" Wiggly asked.

Daddly smiled again. "Well, it means the Elfin is grown up and not school age, so we can rule out all school children and also we know the guilty party is male and not female," Daddly answered.

"Oh yes, I never thought of that, Daddly, you are a good detective!" Wiggly praised his father.

Mummly joined in the conversation, "If the culprit lives in one of the three houses where the trail of screws in the park led us to, then we can narrow down the search even more!"

"I don't understand, Mummly, we don't actually know who it is?" Giggly said looking quite puzzled.

"Not so, young'un. We know everyone who lives in those three homes and only one of them has an adult son ......" Daddly was interrupted.

Wiggly finished the conversation. "The Shoemaker."

Everyone looked at Wiggly following his outburst.

"That's right, Wiggly," Mummly agreed, "the Leatherhead's have a daughter Wiggly's age."

Wiggly burst into voice again. "Oooh, that's right, that would be Heeley and she's really clever at school."

Daddly and Mummly were nodding in agreement.

"The son is called Fred and he is grown up. He helps his parents in the shop, but he's very shy," Daddly concluded.

"If he's shy that could be why I haven't seen him, because I know just about everyone by now," Freddie added.

"Then I think we must pay the Shoemaker a visit," Daddly announced.

Freddie pulled his rucksack onto his back, then they all stood and made for the door.

Outside, Wiggly and Giggly both held Freddie's hand. They we so excited, nothing like this ever happens in Elfin Town. Elfins do not steal things, there is no need. If anyone needs something there is always someone who can make it. They do not have money, everyone does something to help in the community and they have all they need to live comfortably.

The whole family, including Freddie, marched across the park's moss grass towards the three houses. When they reached their destination, Daddly just opened the door, as it was a shop, and they all walked inside.

Mrs Leatherhead was stitching a pair of fluffy slippers. "Freddie and the Tigglys!" she called out in a loud voice, "how nice to see you all." She had a big smile on her face. She put the slippers to one side and stood up to greet everyone.

Daddly explained what was happening and that it narrowed down to Fred, so he might be the one they needed to speak with.

Mrs Leatherhead was a little shocked and replied, "Oh dear! That's not so good, I'm awfully sorry, Freddie."

Freddie smiled kindly. "It's not your fault, Mrs Leatherhead, we don't know for sure it is Fred. The Elfin I saw recognised me but I didn't recognise him."

Mrs Leatherhead still looked worried, this sort of thing never happens to Elfins. "Come to think of it I haven't seen Fred since early this morning. Actually, he has been out of the house quite a lot recently. That would fit with what's going on I suppose, I don't think he's at home now, but we can go upstairs and find out, follow me everyone." Mrs Leatherhead took them up some narrow winding stairs to one of four doors on the landing and she knocked on the second door. "Fred, lovey, are you there? Freddie and the Tiggly's have come to visit."

They all waited quietly expecting the door to open, but it did not.

"Mmmm, just as I thought, Fred's out again. I haven't been in his room for a long time, he keeps himself very private, but if he's not home we could have a little peek," she said turning the door handle. The door opened inwardly into the room and she gasped, "Goodness me!" at what she could see.

Everyone else squeezed through the doorway together and they gasped as well.

"Oh, so bright and shiny!" Giggly exclaimed shading her eyes.

"What is all this?" Mrs Leatherhead exclaimed.

The walls were covered in shiny metal screws, floor to ceiling, on every wall.

"It looks like Fred is the Elfin stealing shiny screws from the Sproggles," Daddly announced looking around.

"Well, this is a complete surprise!" Mrs Leatherhead gasped. "Fred has always been a shy, private boy, he doesn't really have any friends and rarely leaves the house. In fact the day Freddie and Wiggly saved all our children from those horrid Mole Goblins was the only time he came out with us all to celebrate and he seemed to disappear early that night. He was at home when we returned so we just assumed it was too much for him," Mrs Leatherhead explained and she was getting upset so Mummly comforted her.

Daddly whispered to Freddie to look around with the magic detecting spectacles.

Freddie took them out of his rucksack and put them on, then looked around the room. He gasped out loud.

"What is it, Freddie?" Daddly asked in surprise.

Freddie pointed and cried out, "In the corner, it's Fred, crouched in the corner like a frightened rabbit!"

"Where, I don't see him?" Mrs Leatherhead said.

"He's invisible, Mrs Leatherhead," Wiggly replied.

Freddie was still pointing and everyone was looking at the corner of the room. "His hat is sparkling and twinkling, it must be magic," Freddie said.

Fred looked up at them with tears dripping down his cheeks.

"Take your hat off, Fred, and come over to us," Daddly said in a kindly voice.

Fred reached up and took off his hat and he suddenly appeared.

"Oh! Goodness Fred, you gave me such a fright appearing like that," his mother exclaimed.

Fred stood slowly and walked with tiny steps towards Daddly with his head hung down.

"Now, Fred, look up at me and explain yourself," Daddly asked in a kindly voice again. Everyone waited silently for Fred's explanation.

"I'm sorry Mum, Mr Tiggly, I didn't mean to hurt anyone. I get nervous around other Elfins and on the celebration day when Freddie and Wiggly saved the children, I was excited to meet you Freddie. But everyone was pushing around to talk with you and I got nervous. I was about to go home when the Town Elder sprinkled Fairy Dust over the hole in the school floor and one little twinkle landed on my hat. Just then it was so busy and noisy and all I could think about was wishing I could disappear. I felt a strange tingle run up and down my body and my wish came true. It was as if I was there, but I wasn't there because it seemed like no one could see me. At first I was frightened, wondering if I would always be invisible, that even my Mum and Dad would never see me again and I got so scared I ran home and hid in my bed. In the morning I looked in the mirror and I was still invisible and I cried. I didn't want to be invisible any more."

Mrs Leatherhead wrapped her arms around her son to comfort him. "Go on son, tell us everything," she encouraged.

"My face felt horrible with sticky tears so I took my hat off to wash my face and when I looked in the mirror, there I was and I was so happy. I realised that it was my hat, when I put it on I vanished and anything I held in my hands vanished too!"

"Why did you start stealing shiny screws, Fred?" Freddie asked.

Fred looked nervous and was trembling. "A long time ago when I was walking in the forest I found three shiny screws, but I didn't know what they were or what they were for, but I found them fascinating. The shape wasn't like anything I had ever seen before and we had nothing like it in Elfin Town. I cherished them like they were precious jewels. I got to wonder where they came from and what they did. I know it was wrong, but with the magic hat making me invisible I thought I could explore the Sproggle village undetected. I was so amazed at all the things Sproggles have and I could see the shiny screws everywhere. I watched a man using a thingamajig to turn the shiny screws into wooden objects. Then when I found one of those thingamajigs under a bush, I had the idea to try and unscrew the screws. I tried one in a fence, the screw just turned and turned until it dropped out. When I picked it up it was so shiny I just had to have it. I really like them, as you can see. I got a bit out of control and over confident. I knew the Sproggles couldn't see me and I kind of felt like a wizard when Sproggles watched me doing it and made surprised noises." Fred hung his head again, feeling the shame of doing something that Elfins never do, taking things that do not belong to them, no matter how big or small.

Wiggly and Giggly felt sorry for him and patted him on the back, while everyone was quietly thinking.

"Fred," Daddly began and Fred looked up to face him. "First of all you must hand over your magic hat."

Fred held out his arm with the hat in his hand for Daddly to take.

"Thank you, Fred." Daddly rolled it up and put it in his pocket.

"Why are you not invisible, Daddly?" Giggly asked.

"I think it's because it was on Fred's head when it became magical, so that's where it needs to be placed to work," Daddly replied. He looked back at Fred. "Secondly, Fred, what you have done is wrong, Elfins do not take what is not theirs. However, luckily for you, no Sproggles or Elfins have been hurt, but you have caused a lot of chaos and suspicion. Sproggles do not know that magic actually exists, if they did it could cause a catastrophe. Again, luckily for you, Freddie has helped most of the Sproggles who lost screws and replaced them. You should thank him and be grateful."

Fred looked over at Freddie, who smiled warmly and held out his hand to Fred, who took it in his and shook it. "Freddie, I am so sorry for all the trouble I've caused for you and the other Sproggles. Thank you for putting things right, you are a very kind person."

Freddie patted Fred's back with his other hand. "I'm glad I could help and pleased we have solved the mystery," Freddie replied kindly.

Daddly began to explain, "Fred, I will speak to the Town Council. As no real harm has been done, I think they will forgive you as long as you promise to be good in the future."

Fred looked surprised. "Really?" he gasped.

"There is no point in trying to return the screws because Freddie has already replaced them, so I think the Council will allow you to keep them, they will be a constant reminder of what you have done," Daddly added.

Fred smiled. "Oh! Thank you, Mr Tiggly, I promise to be good from now on," he replied.

Mummly spoke to Fred. "I think it would be good for you to leave the house more and make friends. I suggest you help out at the school one day a week."

Fred looked surprised again. "Do you really think I could do that? It would be really nice to be helpful, like Freddie," he replied.

* *

Back at the Tiggly's house Daddly locked the magic hat and spectacles away with the Fairy Dust to make sure they did not get misused again. Once they were sitting in comfy chairs, with Wiggly and Giggly either side of Freddie on the comfy sofa, Freddie piped, "I'm beginning to understand why it would be bad for Sproggles to know about magic."

Wiggly squeezed his friend's hand. "How so, Freddie?" he asked.

"Well, we have seen how magic made one Elfin do bad things, and Elfins are used to knowing about magic and what it can do. Also, Sproggles are not like Elfins, you don't steal or tell untruths, or argue and fight with each other, so imagine what Sproggles would do if they knew magic existed. They would fight those who had magic to get it for themselves, Sproggles would get hurt and might even die, it would be terrible, they are just not ready to know," Freddie replied.

"They would probably want it for themselves to do bad things as well," Giggly added to the conversation.

"I'm afraid you are correct, Giggly, this is why Merlin is waiting. There will come a time, maybe a long way in the future, when Sproggles live in peace with each other, then they will be ready for Merlin to return," Daddly explained.

"Oooh, now I understand," Wiggly declared.

"Let's have a toast," Mummly said changing the mood.

"Oooo, I like toast, especially with strawberry jam," Freddie said as his mouth watered at the thought.

Daddly laughed. "Sorry, Freddie, not that kind of toast."

"Oh! Are there other kinds of toast then?" Freddie asked screwing up his face.

Mummly handed out glasses of Elderflower cordial. "This kind of toast is a good wish or congratulation kind of toast. We touch our glasses together gently and say a few words," Daddly explained.

They all stood up and put their glasses together like Daddly showed them.

Then Mummly said, "Here's to Freddie and all the Tiggly's on solving the mystery of the disappearing screws!"

"CHEERS!" they all called together.

The Town Council fully reprimanded Fred Leatherhead, to make him realise the gravity of his wrong doing. Apart from the fact that Elfins do not steal, he could have exposed them all to Sproggles.

To make amends he was to spend one day a week helping at the school and one day a month collecting items like dandelion leaves, tree sap, berries and seeds. Although it was a punishment, Daddly had explained to the Council that Fred was not a bad Elfin and needed some guidance and opportunities to meet people and make friends.

Over time, Fred became more confident and enjoyed being with the children, even developed a close friendship with the teacher, Miss Noall, who was a similar age.

CHAPTER FIVE

The Rise of the Morphlins

*Can Freddie and the Elfins save their friends and
families from a monstrous and powerful foe?*

Freddie was waiting at home for his friends Jimmy and William to
arrive. During school today his class had divided into groups
of three for a nature project and he was quite excited. Each group
had been given the same task, to collect leaves from three different
trees, to find a skeleton leaf, they also needed to find a scented
flower and make three tree bark rubbings. It was a long list of
things, including three types of seeds and three types of plant leaves.
Freddie and his friends had all rushed home to change into their play
clothes to then meet up at Freddie's house. William's mother dropped
him off just as Jimmy arrived at Freddie's front garden gate.

"Hello, Mrs Potts," Jimmy called out.

Mrs Potts opened the car door and stepped out to speak to
Jimmy. "Jimmy, how nice to see you," she replied in a jolly voice.
"I'm pleased William has teamed up with you and Freddie, I know
you will look after each other," she chuckled as if she had just been
told a funny joke.

"We'll take good care of each other, Mrs Potts," Jimmy answered,
helping William with his rucksack.

"Bye Mum, see you later." William waved to his mother as she
got back in the car and drove off, waving her hand out of the
window as she went.

Jimmy opened the gate and the two of them ran down the garden
path towards the house.

Freddie had spotted them arriving and was waiting for them at
the front door, along with his mother, who took all three boys inside
and closed the door.

"Have you all got your watches on?" Freddie's mother asked as
they gathered in the kitchen.

Each of them held their wrists in the air displaying their watches. They looked at each other, then at Freddie's mother, then giggled at seeing the funny sight of three arms waving about in the air.

"That's good boys, now be back here for tea at 6 o'clock, no later, otherwise I will have to send the elephants looking for you," Freddie's mother teased.

Jimmy and William looked at each other and then at Freddie and giggled.

"What elephants, Mrs Fountain?" Jimmy chuckled.

"Aww Mu-um!" Freddie protested.

"All the elephants Freddie keeps in his bedroom!" She smiled.

"Wow Freddie, do you really have elephants in your bedroom?" William asked in amazement.

Freddie was shaking his head and pulling a face. "No, it's Mum and Dad's little joke. When I come down the stairs they tell me I sound like a herd of elephants!"

Freddie's mother was laughing.

Poor Freddie was turning just a little red in the face.

Jimmy looked at Freddie's mother. "Oh! I wish you were my mum, Mrs Fountain, you're very funny."

She patted Jimmy on the head. "I'm sure your mothers love you both as much as I love Freddie," she replied.

"Aww Mu-um, embarrassing!" Freddie cringed, making everyone laugh and even he joined in.

"Okay boys, you can leave your bags here. I'll take them up to Freddie's room later, so off you go and have fun."

Freddie handed Jimmy the collecting box with paper envelopes for seeds and a pen to write on the envelopes. Then he pulled on his trusty rucksack and took the lead, opening the kitchen door to lead the way into the garden.

"Bye Mrs Fountain, thank you, see you later," Jimmy and William called and waved.

"What lovely boys," Freddie's mother said softly, to no one in particular.

The three boys marched along the garden path and before they even reached the gate William called out, "Hey! I can see some seeds."

Freddie stopped dead and Jimmy crashed into the back of him.

"Ooof!" Jimmy groaned. It was his own fault because he had turned to look at William and not noticed Freddie had stopped to do the same thing.

"What can you see, William?" Jimmy asked rubbing his head and looking puzzled.

"It's the roses, look, those red berries on them are called 'rose hips' and they are the seed pods of the rose," William explained.

"Oh, Mr Brains!" chuckled Jimmy. "That's great, do you think your mum will mind if we collect a few of them, Freddie?"

"Sure, no problem, Mum already told me we could have anything from the garden," Freddie replied. "William, as you spotted them you can have the honour of picking them, mind the thorns though."

William walked over the lawn to the flowerbed and carefully selected a bunch of four rose hips together and broke them off the rose bush neatly.

Jimmy opened the collecting box and gave William a paper envelope for the seeds and the pen to write the name on the envelope.

William wrote 'Rose Hips' on the envelope and slipped the seedpods inside, licked the sticky flap and stuck it down. "Here you are, Jimmy, our first find. Exciting isn't it?" William said cheerfully as he handed the envelope and pen back to Jimmy.

"Don't forget to tick the list, Jimmy," Freddie reminded his friend before Jimmy slipped the collecting box into Freddie's rucksack. "Okay gang, let's go to the 'buzzing bush', we can collect leaves and flowers, maybe even seeds!" Freddie said enthusiastically.

Before Jimmy and William could ask what a 'buzzing bush' was all about, Freddie was already ahead of them and out of the gate. They followed him and closed the gate, marching into the forest behind Freddie, who could not have been happier. He loved everything about the forest and now he had his two best friends along with him too.

"I've never heard of a 'buzzing bush' Freddie," William commented, flicking through his 'Wonder Book of Trees and Plants'.

"I don't think it's the real name, but you'll see why when we get there," Freddie replied.

They marched in single file along the narrow dirt path with Freddie in the front and Jimmy behind William.

"Hup, two, three, four! Hup, two, three, four!" Freddie called, pretending they were soldiers marching along the path. It was not long before they were standing in front of Freddie's 'buzzing bush.' It was quite wide and tall with leaves like a very small hand with five fingers. Just at that moment, the sun shone through the trees like a spotlight.

"Aww, that's really pretty!" Jimmy cried.

"Listen to it," Freddie urged and the friends put their hands to their ears.

"Hey! That's amazing. It really is buzzing!" William declared.

"It's all the bees drinking the sweet nectar from the flowers," Freddie explained.

"Oh yes, look! There's loads of them flying in and out of the flowers," Jimmy said excitedly. "Hope they don't sting us though," he added.

"You'll be fine, as long as you don't flap about or bother them," Freddie replied. "You can actually eat these flowers," he added, selecting a couple that had no bees on them, slowly pulling them off the bush. "Here, try one," he said, handing a flower to each of his friends.

William looked suspiciously at the pretty pink flower before putting it into his mouth.

Jimmy, however, shoved it straight into his mouth. "Hey, this really does taste sweet," he announced with surprise.

"It does taste lovely," William agreed.

"Can you find it in your book, William?" Jimmy asked.

William pulled his book from his pocket and thumbed through the pages. "Well, it's not exactly the same, but this looks a bit like it," William replied.

Jimmy and Freddie gathered around William to take a look.

"HAP-PO-FLO-RA bush," Jimmy read out with a struggle, "what a funny name," he chuckled.

"Let's collect leaves and flowers, see if there are any seeds too," William said.

"Be careful not to disturb the bees," Freddie warned.

Jimmy laughed. "You just said BEE careful not to disturb the BEES." When no one else laughed he sneered, "Well I thought it was funny anyway." He looked at the bush and carefully picked off three nice leaves.

William selected some flowers without bees in them and Freddie scouted about and managed to find some seed pods. They carefully labelled envelopes and placed everything in the collecting box.

"How did you know you could eat the flowers, Freddie? Because I think some flowers can make you very poorly, like 'deadly nightshade' for example," William asked.

"That's not a real plant, you just made that up," Jimmy laughed.

"No, it's a real plant, look," William protested and took his book out to show Jimmy and Freddie.

"Oh wow! It says here that the deadly nightshade plant is poisonous!" Jimmy announced with horror. "Hey! Freddie, how do you know the 'buzzing bush' isn't poisonous?"

Freddie smiled. "Well you're not feeling poorly, are you?"

Jimmy and William shook their heads.

"I was told by an expert *(Freddie was referring to Wiggly)*, otherwise I wouldn't eat the flowers. So you're right, Jimmy, we can't go around eating anything from the forest or even your gardens unless we know for sure it's safe."

Freddie took them around the trees and shrubs, then William suddenly cried, "Hey guys, there's something moving in that bush over there!"

The three friends stopped in their tracks and looked where William was pointing. Sure enough they saw the bush shaking.

'I wonder if Wiggly is playing tricks again', Freddie thought.

Then they heard a loud grunting sound.

"It's a wild animal!" William cried, scuttling to hide behind Jimmy, who had jumped behind Freddie.

Then, from behind the bush appeared a wild boar, not yet an adult, but quite big enough to make Jimmy and William nervous.

"Stay still," Freddie whispered, "or you'll frighten him." He already knew who this little fellow was, he could see the red ring around its trotter. Freddie bent down, held out his hand and called in a low friendly voice, "Hello boy, remember me?"

The boar snorted and looked Freddie up and down, then sauntered over to him and began rubbing his head on Freddie's outstretched hand.

"Good boy," Freddie said soothingly to the boar, while Jimmy and William were shaking behind him. Freddie stroked the boar's head. "Hello piglet, you do remember me, don't you? Good boy," his soft voice seemed to sooth the boar as it enjoyed being stroked. "Best run off home now young piglet," Freddie told the boar and it turned away and trotted off, grunting contentedly.

"Oh wow, Freddie, that was amazing! You can talk to the animals. Do they all know you?" William cried.

"I thought it was going to chase us!" Jimmy exclaimed.

"Me too!" William agreed.

"Wait 'till I tell everyone in the class back at school!" Jimmy declared rubbing his hands with excitement.

Freddie chuckled, looking at them both and remembering how scared he was when he saw the mother boar. "I saved that boar when it was a little piglet. Its huge scary mother led me to it, the poor thing had its trotter caught in a wire rabbit snare and was squealing away. Seems he remembered me too," he explained with a huge grin of satisfaction. "Come this way guys, there's a special tree I want to show you," Freddie said leading them off the dirt track a little ways.

"Oooo, that's Incredible!" William exclaimed as all three stood and stared.

"Never seen anything like this," Jimmy added wondrously.

"Did you do this, Freddie?" William asked, hardly able to take his eyes off it.

Freddie chuckled. "Magical, isn't it? I had no part in creating it, I just found it one day while I was exploring the forest. On that particular day it had been snowing and fluffy white snow was all over its branches."

Both Jimmy and William stared at the incredible sight.

"I call it my *Special Christmas Tree*," Freddie explained. "You can see the flowers and seed pods of the rose growing up through the tree, I think they look like tree decorations you have at Christmas."

William and Jimmy nodded their agreement, still smiling widely.

"We should tell everyone at school to come and look at it, I bet they will be amazed!" Jimmy suggested.

Freddie was not normally a selfish person, but he was a little bit protective about the forest, not only that, more people in the forest meant a greater risk the Elfins could be discovered. The thought of dozens of children trampling everywhere made him fearful. "Do you think we could keep this as our secret? If lots and lots of people come trampling through here they may ruin the forest," Freddie replied.

"Oh! That's a good point, you know what Peter Bull is like," Jimmy chuckled at the thought.

"Remember when we went camping that time and he tripped on the guide rope and flattened his tent?" William chuckled.

"Oh yes!" Freddie laughed. "He did the same thing twice more too. He certainly takes after his name!"

The three friends laughed together at Peter's clumsiness and agreed to keep the *Special Christmas Tree* their little secret.

They carried on collecting leaves and then made tree bark rubbings. Each of them chose a tree with wrinkly bark and placed a sheet of thin paper on it, then rubbed the side of a short piece of brown crayon over it. The patterns were really wonderful and William looked up each tree in his book so that they were able to name them on their rubbings.

Freddie could see the big old oak tree that allowed entrance to Elfin Town and wondered how the enchantment worked. "See that tree over there?" Freddie asked his friends, while pointing to the big old oak tree, "let's go look at it," he suggested.

He let Jimmy and William go ahead and to Freddie's utter amazement his friends walked right through the big old oak tree as if it was not even there, yet Freddie could see it quite clearly.

Jimmy turned to see that Freddie had not followed. "Why are you still standing over there?" he asked.

Freddie chuckled to himself because he could not see them behind the big old oak tree, to him it was solid, but his friends could see him through it. "Oh! I was just thinking it's getting close to 4 o'clock, shall we leave this now and go home?" Freddie cleverly diverted an awkward question, being unaccustomed to telling lies and much preferring to always be truthful, *'that way it's easy to remember things, liars need a very good memory,'* he recalled his father telling him when he was much younger.

William and Jimmy looked at their watches and agreed.

Freddie could not prevent a chuckle when they walked right through the big old oak tree again. They skipped and jogged through the woods along the dirt track in single file, chatting and laughing as they travelled.

When they reached the gate to Freddie's back garden, Jimmy cried out, "Oh look! The tent's up. It's big, isn't it?"

Mr Fountain had returned home early from work and erected the tent ready for the boys to camp out for the night. All three friends rushed to investigate.

"Wow, it's big inside too, lots of room!" William declared.

"That's good because my Mum says I'm a wriggler!" Jimmy replied sniggering.

"You won't be able to wriggle far in a sleeping bag, Jimmy," Freddie laughed.

"Best make sure we zip the flaps properly if Jimmy wriggles, otherwise he might end up outside!" William chuckled, and made Freddie and Jimmy laugh with him.

They rushed to the kitchen door and tumbled inside.

"Shoes off boys!" Freddie's mother announced. "You can go upstairs and clean up, tea will be ready soon," she added.

The three boys pushed and shoved each other, laughing as they clambered up the stairs.

"Goodness me!" Freddie's father smiled as he walked through to the kitchen. "That really does sound like a herd of elephants *and* buffalos too!"

The boys were so excited while eating the lovely tea of sausages, beans and chips Freddie's mother had prepared for them. They regaled Freddie's parents with their adventure about the boar and how brave Freddie had been.

Freddie explained, grinning, "It was the little piglet that I saved from the rabbit snare and it remembered me, Mum and Dad."

Freddie's parents were in awe of the three boy's energy and had laughed with them until their sides hurt. Once everyone had finished eating and laughing, Freddie's father told them to go upstairs and shower while he and his wife cleared up in the kitchen.

"Oh! I can help with the washing up," Jimmy volunteered. "I do it all the time at home."

William added excitedly, "Yes, me too, I'll help."

Freddie suggested that Jimmy washed the plates and cutlery, William dried them and he would put them away. "Go in the sitting room, Mum and Dad, have a rest, we can sort this out," Freddie urged and they did just that. When everything was washed, dried and put away and the kitchen was clean and tidy, the boys trooped upstairs to Freddie's bedroom.

Mr and Mrs Fountain laughed at the sound of them clomping up the stairs again.

"Not exactly twinkle toes, are they?" Mr Fountain chuckled.

It was quite early yet so the three friends decided to take turns to have a shower, clean their teeth, and change into their pyjamas, then play a game of Snakes and Ladders.

Freddie liked this game because he could never tell who was going to win and it looked like William until he threw a five on the dice and ended up on the number 99 square with a snake's head that took him all the way down to number 2.

William moaned until Freddie and Jimmy did exactly the same, all three ended up on square number 2. Only then did they all laugh and pack the game away and trundle downstairs.

"Watch out, the elephants are stampeding again!" cried Freddie's mother as the boys tumbled into the kitchen to find both of Freddie's parents laughing. "Now would you elephants, oh! I mean children," Freddie's mother began.

"Mu-um!" Freddie protested as he chuckled. "It's a joke," he said to William and Jimmy who were smiling. "When I charge up and down the stairs Mum and Dad say I sound like a herd of elephants!"

"Ha ha, my Mum reckons there's a stampede when we run up the stairs!" Jimmy revealed.

"Seems like all children wear lead boots when they use the stairs," Mr Fountain surmised. Meanwhile Mrs Fountain placed a cup of warm milk on the table for each of the boys, so they sat quietly and drank, leaving a milky smile on their faces.

"As it's only 8 o'clock, how would you boys like to watch a documentary with us before you disappear into the tent?" Mr Fountain suggested.

Freddie's two friends were happy to spend some time with his parents, they both thought they were a really special mum and dad.

When the documentary had finished, Freddie's mother explained, "Here's a key for the back door, in case any of you need the toilet. If one of you doesn't feel well during the night, get Freddie to come into the house and wake us up. Okay?"

"What's with your rucksack then, Freddie?" his father asked spotting it.

"Oh! I have a torch and other stuff in case we need them, Dad," he replied.

They all trooped off in single file with Freddie in front, through the kitchen, where they took off their slippers and slipped on their shoes, then out the door and across the lawn into the tent.

Freddie's parents had strung up some fairy lights around the tent and along the path to the house so they could easily find their way in the dark if they needed to.

Freddie's mother called out after them, "Goodnight boys, remember to get some sleep, don't stay up talking all night, okay?"

The boys all laughed and giggled as they opened the tent flaps and disappeared inside, leaving their shoes near the entrance and putting on their slippers, which they had carried with them from the house. Jimmy and William shuffled about inside while Freddie zipped up the tent flaps. Of course, they spent quite a while telling funny stories and jokes, making rude noises and laughing a lot.

When Freddie's father checked in on them at 10.30pm they were all fast asleep with big smiles on their faces.

The next day was Saturday and the boys woke early with the 'dawn chorus' of birds singing and chirping, just as the sun rose and it got light outside.

Freddie was first to lift his head just as his friends were stirring and cried out "Jimmy!" in his half asleep half awake state.

William jumped up with a fright. "What! What is it?" he cried in a panic.

"Freddie?" Jimmy answered, shuffling about. "Where's your head gone?" he cried out, and then giggled realising he must have wriggled a lot in the night as he had managed to slip right down in his sleeping bag.

"You gave me a fright," William groaned.

"Sorry William," Freddie confessed and giggled. "When I woke and turned to look at Jimmy I couldn't see his head."

They were all wide awake now and laughing together.

When Jimmy announced he needed the toilet, Freddie and William realised they also needed the bathroom.

"Let's go, but be quiet inside, Mum and Dad may still be asleep," Freddie explained.

They put on their shoes, carried their slippers, unzipped the tent, and tiptoed to the kitchen door, which Freddie unlocked.

"No elephants," Freddie whispered.

William had to stop himself from giggling as they put on their slippers and tiptoed up the stairs and into Freddie's bedroom.

"Best go barefoot to the bathroom so we don't make a noise, okay?" Freddie suggested, then looked at his friends. "You go first," he said to William.

"You can," William replied.

"Ooh! I gotta go, let me go first, quick, quick!" Jimmy moaned and dashed into the bathroom. He returned quickly with a big smile on his face.

"You next, William," Freddie said.

"You sure?" William replied but he was already making his way to the door. "I'll be quick!" William was back very quickly and then Freddie darted off to the bathroom.

"You've got funny toes," William said to Jimmy, causing Freddie to look when he returned.

"Mmmm, Mum says I have webbed toes," Jimmy replied.

"What! Like a duck?" Freddie giggled.

"No! It's just my three middle toes, look, the skin is almost up to the first knuckle, it makes them look webbed," Jimmy explained.

"That's why you swim so well," Freddie teased and William laughed, "you got built in flippers!" They all laughed so hard and loud they did not hear the door open.

"What are you all laughing at?" Freddie's mother asked.

"Oh, nothing much Mum, just Jimmy's flippers," Freddie replied.

The word 'flippers' seemed to start them laughing again.

"What a happy bunch you are," Freddie's mother smiled, "come down and have some breakfast when you have finished laughing at Jimmy's flippers."

"Your mum just said flippers!" William chuckled and the boys were off again, so Freddie's mother left them to it.

Once they had calmed down William declared, "This is so much fun, Freddie, I haven't laughed so much in a long time. I love all your models too, you're really clever."

"Well they're all kits so I just stick them together and paint them," Freddie replied modestly.

"I don't think I would have the patience," Jimmy declared, "look at the tiny little parts and your painting is so detailed. William's right, you're quite clever."

Freddie felt a blush starting and replied, "Let's go and get some breakfast, I'm starving!"

"Me too," Jimmy agreed.

"And me!" William chirped.

The herd of elephants scurried down the stairs, much to the amusement of Freddie's parents. "Tell me boys, how did the elephants get upstairs, we certainly heard them coming downstairs?" Freddie's father teased.

"Aw, Da-ad!" Freddie protested and laughed.

"You're very funny, Mr Fountain. You and Mrs Fountain make us laugh a lot," Jimmy chuckled. "Well it's nice to see you boys getting along with each other so happily, it makes being a mum and dad very rewarding," Freddie's father replied with a big smile.

"Who's for a bowl of porridge?" Freddie's mother asked and three eager hands shot up into the air.

After breakfast the boys spent the morning collecting the rest of their nature lesson items and the afternoon in Freddie's bedroom making a display ready to take to school on Monday. At just after 2pm Freddie ran downstairs for some drinks and when he walked into the kitchen he saw his mother and father.

"Hi Mum, Dad," he said cheerfully. "I've just come down for some drinks." Then he stopped in his tracks. "MUM! ... DAD!" He cried out so loud that Jimmy and William came tearing down the stairs into the kitchen.

"What's wrong, Freddie?" Jimmy asked as they rushed through the door to see Freddie just staring at his parents.

"LOOK! LOOK!" Freddie cried tearfully. "They're not moving, it's like they're frozen. MUM! DAD! Wake up!" Freddie sounded frightened as he walked up to his father. "Dad, what's wrong?"

Freddie's father was sat at the table looking down at a newspaper, but he was stiff and rigid, just like a statue. Freddie grabbed his father's arm and tried to shake him, but was unable to move him.

"Are they statues?" Jimmy whispered to William, but he was already crying and Jimmy wrapped his arm around him.

"Mum! Why don't you move? Say something, please!" Now Freddie was really scared and tears rolled down his face.

Jimmy and William were wrapped around each other and did not know what to do.

Freddie pushed and prodded his parents to no avail, they did not flinch and although he did not realise, his parents were still actually breathing but very, very slowly.

Not knowing what to do, the three boys huddled together just looking at Freddie's parents, sitting like statues. They were all tearful and Freddie was beginning to believe that some magic had turned his Mum and Dad into statues just like he had seen Merlin in the Crystal Cavern.

"Should we call an ambulance?" Jimmy whispered.

"But, they're statues, solid and hard, what can doctors do?" Freddie sobbed.

It had been barely five minutes since Freddie had discovered his parents in this condition and his friends had joined him, but it felt like hours to them.

"Hello boys, I didn't hear you come downstairs," Freddie's mother suddenly moved and spoke.

"MUM!" Freddie cried and rushed round to hug her.

"Oh! This is nice, what have I done to deserve this?" she asked.

"MR FOUNTAIN!" Jimmy cried, "You're moving again!" They were startled by him turning over a page of his newspaper, as if nothing had happened.

Jimmy and William rushed to Freddie's father and gave him a hug followed closely by Freddie.

"Hey! Hey! What's all this? Not that I'm complaining!" Freddie's father chuckled.

"Dad, Mum," Freddie turned to look at his mother.

"Have you boys been crying, your eyes are all red?" Freddie's mother asked before any of the boys could explain.

They just stared at the two adults, their eyes betraying their disbelief.

"What's the matter, boys? Why are you just staring at us?" Freddie's father asked.

All three boys were indeed staring from one to the other of Freddie's parents. Finally Freddie let go of his father, as did Jimmy and William, who still looked like they had seen a ghost.

"Mum! You scared us, you scared us so much!" Freddie croaked, choking back more tears.

His mother looked bewildered.

"How do you mean, Freddie?" his father asked.

The three boys moved to the table opposite Freddie's mother and looked at his father.

"When we came downstairs more than five minutes ago you both were stiff as statues," Freddie began explaining. "I, we thought you were, well, I mean, not alive anymore!" A tear dripped onto his cheek at the thought.

"It's true, Mr Fountain, you were not moving, I don't think you were even breathing, we didn't know what to do. We prodded and touched you but you never moved!" Jimmy explained.

Freddie's parents looked at each other, completely confused.

Freddie's father scratched his head. "It's funny I don't remember you boys coming down the stairs like a herd of elephants, or even sitting to the table," Mr Fountain admitted.

"Look at the time, love!" Mrs Fountain exclaimed.

"That's very strange, it's suddenly half past and I'm sure I just looked at the clock and it was coming up to a quarter past!" Freddie's father acknowledged.

"Mr Fountain, when Jimmy and I came downstairs we had heard Freddie shout out. Both of you were just like statues. You were stiff and didn't even move when Freddie called you. He even shouted to you, it was as if we weren't here, like you'd gone to sleep with your eyes open!" William further explained.

Mr Fountain shook his head and his wife looked quite worried and he could see everyone looked afraid. "I'm sure it's nothing to worry about boys, everything's alright now. If it happens again, then you must call 999 and get the paramedics to attend, they will know what to do. For now, let's just forget about it. Now what did you come downstairs for, Freddie?" his father asked trying to lighten the mood and stop the boys and his wife from worrying.

"Oh, err, I came down for some drinks," Freddie replied.

"Okay boys, you go finish your project and I'll bring you some drinks and snacks, okay?" his mother replied.

The boys walked slowly up the stairs, unable to get the vision of Freddie's mother and father sat like statues, out of their minds. They sauntered into Freddie's room and sat together on the bed.

"What I don't understand is what would turn your parents into statues for fifteen minutes and then be perfectly okay?" Jimmy stated.

"I don't know, Jimmy, they don't seem to be ill, I mean they are not coughing or got spots or anything, but something did turn them into statues, that's for sure," Freddie replied.

"Do you think they might have been playing a joke on us?" William asked screwing his face up.

"Your parents are very funny, Freddie, but they wouldn't do something like that, surely? I mean, you were crying and frightened and so were William and I. They never moved once, I don't think they looked like they were breathing, it can't have been a joke!" Jimmy replied looking at his friends.

Freddie thought about William's suggestion. There was no way his Mum and Dad would do that to him or his friends, it would have been so cruel. No, there had to be another explanation and he was certain magic was at the bottom of it. "You're right, Jimmy," Freddie replied, "my parents love me and are very kind and funny. To do something like that would not be kind. No, something's wrong, very wrong, but at least they seem to be okay now."

When they had settled down they started putting all their collected items on three display boards and Freddie's mother brought them drinks and snacks like she promised.

William watched her like a hawk, almost expecting her to freeze like a statue again, the whole situation had made him even more nervous than usual.

They were all eventually distracted with sticking their seeds and leaves on the display boards. Later that afternoon Mr Fountain drove Jimmy and William home, each with a part of their nature project ready for Monday at school. They sat in the back of the car and both were watching Mr Fountain to make sure he was really back to normal. As far as they could tell he was just the same as he always was, even making a joke that made them laugh.

"Hey, boys! Do you know what's small, green, round and hairy that goes up and down?" Mr Fountain asked, realising Jimmy and William were very quiet.

The two boys looked at each other somewhat puzzled. "No Mr Fountain, what is it?" Jimmy replied.

Mr Fountain chuckled, "Well it's a gooseberry in a lift," he answered, still chuckling.

Again the two boys looked at each other, then burst into laughter finally understanding the joke.

**

Freddie soon forgot what had happened, especially on Sunday when they visited his other Grandma in the neighbouring town.

"Shop!" Freddie's father called out as they let themselves into Grandma's front door. It was a sort of joke greeting he always did when they visited.

Freddie's Grandma came out of the kitchen wearing her apron and with a light dusting of flour on her face and arms.

"Hey Grandma, are you baking?" Freddie chuckled seeing the state she was in.

"Oooh, you're a clever one, Freddie Fountain, how can you tell?" she laughed.

They followed her into the kitchen where she was just about to put a sponge cake into the oven.

"Do you want to lick the bowl, Freddie?" His Grandma smiled, handing him the mixing bowl to eat the last few bits of cake mixture. Once the cake was in the oven she gave Freddie's father and mother a hug, then kissed Freddie on the cheek with a sloppy wet kiss.

"Oh, Grandma! That's really wet!" he protested, laughing.

Freddie's Grandma only chuckled and put a floury finger on his nose, chuckling some more when Freddie pulled a face. Then she announced, "I'll put the kettle on while you two go in the lounge, then you can tell me all your news."

Freddie handed the bowl back to his Grandma and she wiped his face with the dishcloth. "Thank you, Grandma. Can I ask you something?"

"Of course, Freddie, what's on your mind?"

"Is there an illness that makes people go stiff like statues?" he asked.

His Grandma thought for a moment and then replied, "Why yes, Freddie, it's something that happened a lot many years ago before doctors realised what it was. It can happen if you get a cut or a stab from the garden, like a sharp rose thorn, it's called Tetanus. It makes all the muscles seize up, but everyone gets an inoculation against it now so it's very rare. What makes you ask?"

"Oh, it was just something I saw and wondered what had happened?" he replied, trying to be as truthful as possible.

"Come on then, Freddie, give me a hand with the tea. Can you carry the cups? I expect your mum and dad are spitting feathers!" she laughed.

"Grandma, how can you spit feathers?" Freddie scrunched his face and chuckled. His Grandma was very funny and always made him laugh.

In the lounge Freddie kept looking at his mother and father and they noticed he was staring.

"Have I got something on my face, Freddie? his mother asked.

"No Mum, I was just waiting to see you spit feathers," he said.

His mother, father and Grandma laughed.

"What gave you that idea?" his father asked.

"Oh, Grandma said you were spitting feathers," he replied and they all laughed even more.

"It's just a way of saying someone is thirsty," his mother explained.

Then Freddie started laughing with them.

They were telling Freddie's Grandma all about their news.

"OH! My cake!" Freddie's Grandma suddenly cried, then jumped up and dashed off into the kitchen.

Freddie hopped up and followed her.

"Just caught it in time, Freddie, another few minutes and it would have made a good door stop!"

Freddie did not really understand what she meant but it sounded funny and it made him laugh again.

His Grandma tipped the sponge cake onto a cooling tray and then opened a drawer. "Oh, where is the thing? Something else that's sprouted legs and run off."

Freddie was laughing so much he had tears running down his cheeks.

"You can laugh, Freddie Fountain, but it's a very important piece of equipment," she chuckled.

"What is it, Grandma?"

"It's a little tea strainer that I use to sprinkle icing sugar on the top of the sponge," she replied.

Freddie still had his rucksack with him and rooted about in it, pulling out a wire tea strainer. He had seen his Grandma's before so he knew what it looked like.

193

"Here, Grandma, this looks like it," he announced waving it in the air.

"Oh good you found it. Well done, Freddie, you can have the first slice," she said, not asking where he found it.

All too soon it was time to return home, so Freddie gave his Grandma a big hug and kiss on the cheek.

"Love you, Grandma," he whispered.

"And I love you too, Freddie," she replied giving him an extra hug.

They jumped back in the car and waved through the windows as they set off back to Elfington Village. It was almost 4 o'clock when they got home so Freddie decided to explore their garden with the book he borrowed from William to find names for all the plants.

* *

On Monday morning Freddie was awake bright and early, excited about the nature day at school. His mother carried his display board as far as the school gates.

His father had made three boards, one for each of the boys to glue on their leaves, seeds, flowers and bark rubbings. Freddie and his mother had not walked far from their house when they came upon something strange, which frightened Freddie. Ahead of them they could see Archie and his mother, but they were just standing still, not moving.

"Mum! Mum!" Freddie cried. "It's happening again!" He grabbed his mother's hand and pulled her to a stop.

"Freddie, let go, please, I need to see what is happening, you'll be safe with me. Let's go on carefully, okay?" his mother reassured him.

He nodded a little reluctantly and they approached Archie and his mother, who were very rigid, just like statues.

"Barbara, dear, are you alright?" Freddie's mother called, perhaps a little too softly, but neither of them responded.

"ARCHIE!" Freddie yelled, making his own mother jump, but there was still no response from his friend. Freddie and his mother walked right in front of Archie and Barbara, looking directly at them at an arms length away.

"Barbara! Barbara! What's wrong?" Freddie's mother called loudly.

Archie and his mother did not seem to hear and certainly did not attempt to move in any way.

"Mum, I don't like this. Let's go, please!" Freddie implored.

But his mother was concerned and intrigued. "Is this what happened at home with your father and me?" his mother asked.

"It is, Mum, exactly, you were statues just like Archie and his mum. What's happening? This is scary, look at them!"

Mrs Fountain let go of Freddie's hand to touch Archie on the cheek and then his mother. "They're both still warm, but they don't seem to be breathing, Freddie, this is very strange indeed."

All of a sudden and without any warning, Archie spoke. "Hello, Freddie, Mrs Fountain."

It was so unexpected that Freddie jumped back and cried out, "Oh, flipping heck!"

Then Archie's mother spoke. "Oh, hello you two, is something wrong, you look a bit strange?"

Freddie's mother was startled and gasped out aloud, "Oh! My dear Barbara, you gave me such a fright!"

Of course, Archie's mother looked puzzled. "How so, what's happened?"

Freddie had recovered already and had his arms around his friend, Archie.

"When we reached you, Barbara, you were frozen like a statue, not even breathing, Archie too. There's something strange happening in the village. Freddie and his friends found me and Jacob frozen in the kitchen for 15 minutes on Saturday."

Archie was listening and looked a little strange.

Archie's mother screwed up her face trying to make sense of what Susan had just told her. Then she looked at her watch, "Goodness, it's five minutes to nine! We left home at half past eight and it never takes more than ten minutes to get to school. Somehow fifteen minutes have gone missing!" She made Archie and Freddie jump with her loud voice.

"Barbara, are you and Archie alright, you're not ill or anything?" Freddie's mother asked.

"We've been fine so far and I feel okay right now." Looking down at Archie, his mother asked, "Archie, do you feel unwell?"

Archie beamed a goofy smile, he had one adult front tooth and the other was only half grown. "I'm okay, Mum, let's go or we'll all be late for school!" he replied.

Archie and Freddie walked together with their mothers in front of them.

"Were we really like statues, Freddie?" Archie asked quietly.

Freddie nodded. "You were and it's very scary, Archie," he replied.

When they all reached the school gates just before nine o'clock, the boys took their displays from their mothers.

"Oooh, I like your display, Freddie," Archie said.

"I like yours too, Archie," Freddie replied and they soon forgot all about the incident as they walked to their classroom.

The two mothers decided to go and see the local police officer at the police station, which was also his home

Officer Cooper listened to the two mothers' experience and then admitted, "You are not the first people to tell me this, ladies. I have had two other reports exactly like yours. The strange thing is that none of you are unwell, before or after becoming statues and it seems to be fifteen minutes in every case. I have to admit I have never come across anything like ...." The police officer just froze part way through his sentence.

"Officer Cooper, are you alright?" Archie's mother cried, but he did not reply nor did he move.

"It's happening again. Do you think we are passing on some kind of disease, Barbara?" Susan asked.

Barbara shook her head and looked very concerned. "We can't do anything here, let's leave a brief note and go home," she suggested.

They made sure that officer Cooper could not fall off his chair, left a note stating the time he froze, so he could understand what had happened, and then they left. Both mothers were heading for the greengrocer's shop, they needed milk and bread, but when they reached the High Street they reeled back in shock. There were people randomly stood around on the footpath, standing like statues with others trying to talk to them and make sense of what was happening.

"This is bad, Barbara, we need to get help. Maybe there's some kind of chemical leak or something, maybe even aliens!"

"Who do we contact, Susan? We need to speak to the doctor's surgery, someone will know what to do."

Agreed on their course of action they headed off, passing other people in the High Street looking at their friends, who were frozen like statues. When the two mothers had almost reached the end of the High Street they turned to look back, alerted by shouts and cries of surprise, when the frozen people suddenly came back to life.

* *

At school everything was fine and all of Freddie's class presented their nature displays, which their teacher, Miss Poppit, had hung up all around the classroom.

"Well done everyone, you have all worked so hard and created a super job over the weekend. I'm very proud of you all, these are the best displays ever," Miss Poppit praised. "Unfortunately it's too early in the year for Conkers and Acorns, but there are so many wonderful things here already."

Freddie raised his hand.

"Yes Freddie." His teacher acknowledged.

"Miss Poppit, I think I have some conkers in my rucksack, would you like to see?"

"Freddie Fixit!" cried Jimmy and all the class chuckled.

Freddie reached into his rucksack and pulled out a handful of conkers and a sprig of two acorns in their cups. He took them up to his teacher.

"Well, Freddie, you are full of surprises. These are wonderful examples of the seeds from a Horse Chestnut Tree, and what tree do acorns grow on, class?"

Half the class raised their hands and the teacher chose Anne. "From the oak tree, Miss," she answered with a big smile.

"That's correct. Well you are all very knowledgeable and we should thank Freddie," Miss Poppit said.

The whole class gave Freddie a round of applause, with the odd call of 'Freddie Fixit' as he returned to his seat glowing like a red light bulb.

When Freddie returned home from school his mother explained what had happened after she and Archie's mother had dropped the boys off.

"Is it something in the air, Mum, like smoke that we can't see that's making people become statues?" he asked, but his mother really had no clue. Freddie changed into his play clothes and went into the forest, with a promise to be home before six o'clock. He made a beeline for the big old oak tree and disappeared inside, down the spiral staircase and straight to Wiggly's house. He ran like the wind so as not to get held up talking to anyone, knocking on the Tiggly's door, puffing and panting.

"Come inside, Freddie. Whatever is the matter?" Mummly asked when she answered the door.

Freddie walked inside and went to sit with the others in a comfy chair and slowly started to breathe normally.

"Something must be troubling you, Freddie, to be in such a hurry," Daddly said, while Wiggly and Giggly looked on expectantly.

Freddie nodded. "Daddly, something very strange is happening in my village. People are becoming like statues for fifteen minutes, then they are okay again as if nothing has happened!" he explained.

The Tiggly's looked from one to the other and shrugged their shoulders.

"Nothing like that has happened before as far as we know, Freddie," Mummly replied.

"Can someone who is using magic do that?" Freddie asked on the brink of tears and sounding a little scared.

"It's possible, but to what end, why would they do something like that?" Daddly replied.

Again everyone looked blankly at each other, puzzled as to why anyone would use magic for such a thing.

With everyone baffled, Mummly suggested they go talk with Grundly. "He's the oldest Elder in the town," she explained.

Freddie was surprised he had not heard about Grundly, nor met him, and was full of questions as they made their way to Grundly's home.

"How old is Grundly?" Freddie asked and Daddly stopped to think for a moment. "I do believe he is well over 300 years old, or is he 400 years old? Mmmm, he's been around for a very long time," Daddly replied.

"No way! I mean, wow! He has had a long life!" Freddie cried out aloud.

Everyone bundled through the door setting off for Grundly's home. They reached their destination, a house on the far side of Town, then Daddly knocked on the door. When Grundly answered, Freddie got an unexpected surprised. Grundly definitely looked very, very old, he stooped and it made him look a lot smaller than an adult Elfin and even his wrinkles had wrinkles. He had a long, white pointy beard that reminded Freddie of the Wizard Merlin.

The three children all looked at each other, not knowing what to expect, clearly Wiggly and Giggly had not seen Grundly either. He looked a bit frail and held a knobbly walking stick in his right hand for support, but when he smiled his eyes lit up like crystals, his face glowed and the corners of his mouth almost poked in his ears. He seemed to grow younger right before their very eyes.

"Welcome," he greeted them in a soft, kindly voice. "Mr and Mrs Tiggly, Wiggly, Giggly and Freddie, welcome, please come inside and sit down on comfy chairs."

Freddie was surprised that Grundly even knew who he was.

"Thank you, Grundly," Daddly replied and they all filed inside.

The house was much like the Tiggly's house. They walked in and sat down on comfy chairs around a log fire at the sitting area of the room.

When Grundly joined them he tapped his walking stick on the floor and a big winged comfy chair appeared, which he slowly lowered himself in to. He looked at each one of them in turn and finally at Freddie, a twinkle in his eye made Freddie feel like he was a good person and friend. "What brings you to visit an old Elfin this day, Mr Tiggly, family and Freddie?" he said, his voice kindly with a little wobble in it.

Daddly answered, "Freddie, would you like to explain what has been happening in the Sproggle Village, if you can?"

Freddie sat up and told Grundly all about the people suddenly turning to statues for fifteen minutes at a time. Grundly listened and smiled as Freddie talked.

Then Grundly replied, "I'm very pleased to meet you at last, Freddie. You are very precious to the Elfin people and I thank you for everything you have done for us. I'm afraid what is happening in your village is big trouble and I'm not sure that without Merlin we can fix it."

Freddie looked worried and scared. "Do you know what is causing all the trouble in the village, is it magic being used, Grundly?" Freddie asked.

"Indeed, I believe an ancient race of supernatural beings have somehow re-emerged. They are known as Morphlins. They are time thieves and they feed on time they steal from Sproggles and Elfins alike, gradually becoming fatter and taller. But the Morphlins can assume any shape, from an Elfin to a Sproggle, even animals. They are almost impossible to detect and even more difficult to stop."

The silence was deafening. No one spoke and Freddie suddenly exhaled, not realising he had been holding his breath, while Grundly explained about the Morphlins.

Wiggly spoke first. "Grundly, how do you know about these Morphlins?"

The old Elfin's beard rose at the corners as he smiled and again the wrinkles seemed to disappear and he looked younger again. "When I was your age, Wiggly, I was apprenticed to the great Wizard Merlin.

"But Merlin left us over 500 years ago!" Daddly exclaimed.

Freddie, Wiggly, Giggly and Mummly suddenly looked from Grundly to Daddly on hearing he was saying Grundly was ancient.

"This is true, Daddly, I have lived a very long life. 532 years ago Merlin visited me and told me it was time for him to take his leave and wait for the world above to be ready for magic. It was my duty to wait for the 'special one' to appear and school them in magic. I have waited so long and I fear it has been in vain." Grundly looked woeful, as if he had failed Merlin. Then he looked up at his visitors and smiled. "The great Wizard taught me how to harness the magic all around us." Grundly held out his hand, palm facing up, and suddenly a flame was dancing on it like that of a candle.

Freddie gasped, Wiggly and Giggly clapped their hands.

"I have not used magic much since he left to wait with Fairy Kind for the great change that is coming. Merlin used a time vortex to trap the Morphlins back then, but some must have been missed or somehow managed to escape the vortex."

"What's a time vortex?" Giggly asked curiously.

"It's the only way to stop the Morphlins and it takes a lot of powerful magic to create a swirling hole in the fabric of time. Like a whirlwind on its side, it sucks the Morphlins into it and imprisons them in time. They live the same moment in time over and over without end," Grundly answered.

"Oh! That sounds very cruel, Grundly," Freddie said.

"It's the best solution, Freddie. In the vortex they relive the same day over and over and have no memory of it, so it's the kindest form of prison. Unless they are stopped the world is in great peril and will come to an end," Grundly replied.

Everyone looked horrified.

"Oh dear, Grundly, if that is the only way, it looks like there is nothing to be done. Then are we all doomed?" Daddly said despairingly.

Freddie looked horrified. "Grundly, what will happen if we can't stop them?"

All eyes were on the one time Merlin's apprentice.

Grundly stared at them one by one with a grim look on his face. "Freddie, I'm sorry, but the Morphlins will eventually steal so much time from all your friends and family that they will lose their minds and become like living statues, unable to talk or move, or worse still, if they steal all your time you will be a pile of dust. They will no longer be the people they once were. The Morphlins will move onto the next community, that will be Elfin Town, then keep going until everywhere and everyone is destroyed. Sproggles may have powerful weapons now, but they cannot destroy the Morphlins."

Giggly began to cry. "Daddly, Mummly, I don't want to be a living statue or a pile of dust!"

Mummly hugged her daughter and comforted her while Freddie and Wiggly looked lost, with ominous expressions.

Daddly pleaded, "Dear Grundly, is there nothing we can do to prevent this disaster?"

Grundly looked at Daddly, then at Mummly holding her daughter, he saw the horror on Wiggly and Freddie's faces and sighed. Without saying anything more he struggled to stand with the aid of his knobbly cane and walked very slowly to the kitchen end of the long room with four pairs of eyes watching his every move. They watched Grundly place his cane down and begin to perform some strange ritual. Instantly, a bright aura, almost blinding, surrounded and engulfed the ancient Elfin.

Everyone gasped and Giggly jumped up at the spectacle, all with a look of awe on their faces. When the bright aura faded away, they could hardly believe their eyes.

"Grundly?" Daddly cried out as each of them stood, rubbed their eyes, unable to understand what they were looking at.

"Do not be alarmed, it is still Grundly standing before you!" his voice no longer frail, but deep, rich and powerful, replied to Daddly. Before them stood a powerful looking figure not unlike that of Merlin the Wizard. Grundly was no longer the feeble, ancient old man, but a tall and broad Elfin, wearing a long black cloak that made his slightly shorter white beard stand out. Atop his head a crooked and pointed hat and in his hand a knobbly staff with a crystal held in a claw at the top. Grundly approached, his walk no longer limping and needing a cane for support, but majestic like a King.

Freddie stood with his mouth wide open. Wiggly was rubbing his eyes raw. Giggly just stared in wonderment, while Daddly and Mummly smiled knowingly. Grundly had the face of a much younger man, gone all the wrinkles of the ancient Elfin apprentice.

"What have you done, Grundly?" Mummly asked, but had a shrewd idea.

"Please be seated everyone and I will explain." Grundly's voice was melodic, deep and soothing.

All eyes were on the new Grundly as they felt around with their hands to find their chairs and sit down.

As Grundly stood before them the air around them seemed electric, it crackled and popped and seemed to twinkle. He tapped his staff on the floor and everyone pulled back with a loud gasp of surprise as Grundly transformed into a Sproggle, tall, with short brown hair, young and handsome face, broad shoulders and looking very important, dressed in a blue pin striped suit but still holding his jewelled staff.

"Oh, so handsome!" Wiggly crooned and Freddie chuckled.

Grundly tapped his staff again and instantly became the Merlin looking Elfin again. "My time is near its end." Grundly sat down and began to explain. "Soon I will enter the Eternal Well, so I have summoned all my magic and condensed my remaining time into three days and three nights. We must find the Morphlins and trap them in a time vortex within three days and two nights. On the third night I must enter the Eternal Well. My magic will then be gone forever, we must not fail in this endeavour."

Everyone was silent, trying to take on board what Grundly was telling them.

"Grundly, sir, can we do this without Sproggles knowing about it? Otherwise it would risk exposing Elfins to the world?" Freddie was still thinking about his friends even with this new threat.

Wiggly looked at his friend admiringly, knowing he would never betray the Elfins.

"This is my plan, young Freddie. Wiggly will accompany us wearing the invisibility hat, you will wear the magic detecting spectacles and I will transform into the Sproggle you have already seen. Together we will walk among the Sproggles undetected while you look for the Morphlins, then we will follow them to their hideout and trap them."

Freddie was amazed that Grundly even knew about the invisibility hat and magic detecting spectacles, but it sounded like a good plan.

"What will I do, Grundly?" Wiggly asked nervously.

"You, young Elfin, will help me with my staff. I will need your youth and connection to magic to reverse the vortex otherwise it will continue to grow and suck in the whole world."

"But Grundly, isn't Wiggly too young, could I not be that help to you?" Daddly asked, concerned about his son.

"I'm afraid you would be of little help, Daddly. It is Wiggly and Freddie who possess Merlin's blessing, given when they were allowed to enter his crystal cavern. Only Wiggly and Freddie can touch my magic crystal staff without withering from its mighty power," Grundly replied.

Wiggly looked at Freddie nervously and took his hand.

"You can do this, Wiggly, you are so much stronger than you know." Freddie's voice became deep, as if Merlin was speaking through him. Freddie turned to Grundly and asked, "Grundly, sir, what would you have me do?"

"With the aid of the spectacles you will be able to see the Morphlins whether they are in Sproggle form or their own. You will also know that if there is a stranger in the village, they will most likely be Morphlins," Grundly explained.

"What do these Morphlins look like in their own form, Grundly?" Giggly asked.

Grundly tapped his staff and an image began to appear in the air in front of them.

Giggly screamed, Wiggly covered his eyes, Daddly and Mummly gasped loudly, but Freddie was wide eyed and held his breath.

Before them the image of a Morphlin appeared. The fat, white coloured, pear shaped head had a large single eye, the centre of it was like a slowly spinning spiral, very mesmerizing. Its mouth was filled with several rows of needle-like teeth that looked like they could bite off an arm or leg. Where its nose would be were a dozen or more finger length tendrils that wiggled and wriggled, testing the air. It had no hair, but all over the top of its head were long thin funnels that constantly moved up and down firing a ball of mist into the air. Its body looked like a stack of white tyres, all rippling up and down. It had fat podgy arms and hands with suction cups on the end of its three long fingers. It seemed to slither along the ground like a horrible fat slug and its body was covered in small, slimy scales like a reptile. Everyone was screwing up their faces in disgust.

"This is their true form, but the Morphlin can instantly change to any form, or make you think it's not there at all. Never look into its eye otherwise it will hypnotise you and you'll be lost, it will steal all your time. When that happens the victim falls to the ground as a pile of dust, that's all that is left when you have no time left to live. The suction cups on the end of its fingers are used to steal the time by attaching to the victim for only a few seconds. They are able to extend their arm to almost any length in order to reach their victims," Grundly explained.

Freddie exhaled with a gasp, not realising he had been holding his breath yet again. "Oh goodness, they look disgusting and scary. Where did they come from?" he asked.

"No one really knows, Freddie, but Merlin thought they may have landed on our world, Astoria as embryos inside a meteor from outer space, or stepped through a tear between universes," Grundly replied.

"They're aliens, wow, so there are things out in space!" Freddie gasped.

"What do you mean by 'between universes,' Grundly?" Wiggly asked.

Grundly smiled, his face beaming with kindness. "Merlin believed that our universe was one of countless others, like the pages in a book and if a page had a small tear in it you could see the next page through it. So it is with universes, very rarely a tear appears between two neighbouring universes and it is possible to step through that tear into the other universe, but they often close as quickly as they open. You would have to be incredibly lucky to be in the right place at the right time that the tear appeared," Grundly explained.

Wiggly was trying to understand what they had just been told.

"So did Merlin think that in the different universes lived different intelligent creatures?" Freddie asked.

"That's right. Also they could be more advanced than those of us in this universe. It might be that Morphlins can open these tears whenever they want and that's how they live, moving from one universe to another draining all those who live there before moving on to the next universe," Grundly explained.

Freddie and Wiggly looked horrified.

"We have to stop them, Grundly, we really have to stop them!" Freddie gasped.

Grundly tapped his staff and the horrible image of the Morphlin faded away. "Morphlins usually work in pairs, so there are a least two of them to find, but that's all it takes," Grundly began to explain to everyone. "When they have stolen enough time they divide themselves, then the two become four. When that four divide you have eight, so in no time at all there will be dozens of them. There is little we can do until first light tomorrow, they sleep in their hideout during dark hours feasting or dividing on the stolen time. Tomorrow, Wiggly and I will collect you from your home, Freddie. I will cast a spell on your parents that will make them think everything is normal, so they will not worry about you. Be ready at 8 am," Grundly impressed. He gathered them all together, then tapped his staff twice, and suddenly they were all standing outside the Tiggly's home, transported in a split second.

"Wow, that's neat!" Wiggly cried with a few agreeing nods from Giggly and Freddie.

Once inside the house Daddly went straight to his safe place and retrieved the magic detecting spectacles and the invisibility hat, giving them to Grundly, who smiled and said his goodbyes, then tapped his staff and vanished.

The Tigglys and Freddie were silent, they had no words for how they were feeling and when Wiggly started trembling Freddie wrapped his arms around his friend.

"It will be okay, Wiggly, I know we can do this. Grundly has faith in us and with his magic we can do this, we can save everyone we know and love." Freddie comforted his friend even though he felt just the same as Wiggly, he was determined that they would capture those horrible monsters.

Daddly and Mummly looked at each other and smiled, hopeful Grundly would be victorious.

Giggly hugged Mummly and looked up to her. "Is Wiggly going to be safe?" she asked.

Daddly stroked his daughter's head and reassured her, "Of course, Giggly, he has Freddie and Grundly to look out for him this time. Your brother and Freddie have been so brave already, so we just need to have faith."

Mummly looked at Freddie and said, "Freddie, you look a little pale, will you be alright to make your way home? Daddly will go with you through the forest if you would like. We don't want your parents to begin worrying about you."

Freddie let go of Wiggly. "Thank you, Mummly and Daddly, it's best I go alone, I can't let Elfins be discovered. I think I am okay now," he replied.

Mummly was still concerned about Freddie, he looked pale. The vision of those monsters had shaken them all and Freddie was no exception. "How about a nice cup of dandelion tea before you go, it will help settle your nerves," she suggested.

They sat in comfy chairs with Wiggly and Giggly either side of Freddie on a comfy sofa, while they sipped their tea in a strange silence.

Freddie did feel much better after Mummly's tea and the colour came back to his face. He said his goodbyes, with a special hug from Giggly, Daddly and Mummly.

Wiggly walked with his friend to the spiral staircase. "These Morphlins are scary, don't you think, Freddie?" he finally said, having walked all the way in silence.

"Yes, Wiggly, I do. I've never seen anything so strange and evil looking, even in my comics. Remember though that they won't be able to see you with the invisibility hat on and when you hold my hand they won't see me either. Grundly will look like a Sproggle, so we should be safe," Freddie replied.

"I wonder who the 'special one' who Grundly has been waiting for could be?" Wiggly said.

"Me too. Merlin gave Grundly a long life, it's a shame the 'special one' has not appeared," Freddie answered.

"Do you think this person is an Elfin or a Sproggle, Freddie?" Wiggly posed.

"Well only Elfins can use magic, so it must be an Elfin. I don't think Merlin would trust a Sproggle with powerful magic, do you?" Freddie replied.

"Mmmm, I guess you're right," Wiggly agreed. "I'm still nervous, I'm not sure I will sleep well tonight," Wiggly confessed with a sudden shudder.

When they reached the door to the spiral staircase, Freddie took his rucksack from his shoulders and reached inside. He pulled out a cute, fluffy stuffed bunny and gave it to Wiggly. "Keep this with you when you go to bed, hold it tight so you won't be alone, maybe you will sleep better."

Wiggly took the bunny and hugged it. "Oh, it's so soft and cuddly." He grabbed Freddie and gave him a hug, too. "Thank you, Freddie, I feel better already."

"I had best go," Freddie said when Wiggly released him, "it's getting close to teatime. I'll see you and Grundly tomorrow then." He gave Wiggly a quick hug then said the magic words to open the door. He waved goodbye to his best Elfin friend and disappeared, scampering up the spiral staircase. A little out of breath, he reached the top and spoke the magic words for the door to appear. When it opened he peeked outside just in case there was anyone about. He saw it was all clear and stepped outside, saying the magic words again quietly and watched the door close, then disappear. He looked around once more before stepping out of the enchanted area that made him invisible to Sproggles and was about to make a run for his house when he heard a noise and gasped out loud, quickly putting his hands over his mouth. It was his friend, Jimmy. *'What is Jimmy doing wandering around in the forest',* he thought.

It seemed his friend had clearly heard Freddie's gasp and looked straight at him, then scratched his head, turned and walked a bit further along.

"Of course! Jimmy can't see me because I'm still inside the enchantment of the big old oak tree," Freddie whispered, to no one in particular. He watched Jimmy vanish behind a big bush and then stepped out of the enchanted area and walked towards his friend.

"Oh, there you are, I've been looking all over for you for ages!" Jimmy chirped when he saw Freddie approaching him.

"I was just on my way home when I heard a noise and saw you turn behind this bush. What are you doing out here, Jimmy?"

Jimmy laughed, "Well I'm looking for you, obviously. Your mum said you were in the forest when I called at your house, so I came looking for you. Actually I'm completely lost so it's a good job you found me, Freddie Fixit," he giggled.

Freddie laughed with his friend. "If you come into the forest alone again bring a ball of string with you," he told him.

"What for?" Jimmy asked.

"Well, you tie the string where you start from and just reel it out as you go, then...."

".... You just follow it back!" Jimmy finished Freddie's sentence.

"Exactly. Now come on Jimmy banana brain, let's go home," Freddie replied laughing, forgetting about the Morphlins for just a little while.

* *

"Mum, can Jimmy stay for tea and sleep over tonight?" Freddie asked his mother and she was more than happy. She phoned Jimmy's parents who promised to bring over pyjamas, clean uniform underwear, socks and shoes and toiletry bag, so he had everything ready for school in the morning. Freddie and Jimmy tucked into fish fingers, chips and baked beans for tea and then sat and watched cartoons until Jimmy's mother brought over his things.

While Freddie and Jimmy's mothers had a nice chat, she told the boys, "Go get showered and ready for bed then, boys, I'll bring you some warm milk a bit later, okay?"

Freddie and Jimmy made a dash for the stairs and scrambled up, laughing.

"There go the elephants again," Freddie's mother laughed.

"I see you have them too," Jimmy's mother replied with a chuckle. "How does one little boy manage to sound like a dozen of them at times?"

Upstairs Freddie let Jimmy jump in the shower first while he cleaned his teeth. Then they swapped over and Jimmy cleaned his teeth and put on his pyjamas while Freddie showered.

Once Freddie was in his pyjamas they sprawled out on the bed and read comics. Freddie was glad to have Jimmy with him, it helped take his mind off his mission tomorrow. He wished he could have stayed with Wiggly, but he would not know how to do so without telling his parents lies and he hated thinking about ever doing that.

"Here you are, boys," Freddie's mother said to them when she brought up their warm milk, "when you've drunk this, lights off and time to sleep, okay?"

The two friends nodded and looked at each other and giggled, then made a beeline for the glasses of milk.

Freddie had inherited his parents' bed when they had a new one delivered. As it was a King size bed there was plenty of room for the two boys to share. After they turned off the lights, they played scary faces, shining a torch light under their chins and pulling weird expressions. They soon tired themselves out and despite everything that had happened in the village and in Elfin Town, Freddie did sleep, thanks to his friend, Jimmy, staying the night and keeping him company.

The two boys woke quite early, with Jimmy waking first and poking a wetted finger around Freddie's earlobe to wake him up.

Freddie sat up quickly and cried, "YUK!"

Jimmy giggled and Freddie did too, trying to stick his wet finger on Jimmy's earlobe.

By the time they had finished the bed was in a complete mess.

"Best tidy this, Jimmy, then we can get washed and see what's for breakfast."

It took no time at all to fluff the pillows, straighten the sheet and pull the duvet over, but Jimmy was in a playful mood and flicked the duvet over Freddie's head and they ended up rolling around on the bed making it untidy again.

"I need the bathroom," Jimmy announced crossing his legs. "Me too," Freddie agreed and they headed for the bathroom. Having emptied their bladders they washed their hands and faces. Jimmy managed to put a soapy finger around Freddie's earlobe, and before Freddie could get him back, he ran out of the bathroom giggling.

"YUK!" Freddie cried, wiping his ear dry as they changed from pyjamas to play clothes. "I don't think Mum and Dad are awake yet, so let's tiptoe downstairs and get some breakfast," Freddie whispered.

"What?" Jimmy asked, getting close enough to Freddie for him to stick a wet finger on Jimmy's earlobe. "Oh, yuk!" he chuckled.

They tiptoed down the stairs and into the kitchen and helped themselves to cereals, giggling between each spoonful.

"You eat like a monkey!" Jimmy chuckled.

"Eeek, Eeek!" Freddie imitated and they both laughed.

Freddie's parents opened the kitchen door and walked in to hear the boys giggling.

"Good morning boys, you sound happy. Did you sleep well?" Freddie's mother asked.

"Yes thank you, Mrs Fountain, Freddie's bed is sooo comfortable," Jimmy replied and made them all laugh.

Freddie's parents sat to the table with cups of tea. "Did you leave the elephants upstairs, boys? We didn't hear them come down as usual," Freddie's father asked with a big smile.

"Aw, Da-ad!" Freddie protested.

"I think they must still be up there, Mr Fountain. I'm sure I heard them trumping (he meant trumpeting)," Jimmy replied quite seriously, causing everyone to laugh again at his misuse of words.

They sat chatting for a while, then once the boys had finished their breakfast they dashed upstairs to change into their school uniform. At around 7.40am they tiptoed downstairs again and into the kitchen, taking Freddie's parents by surprise and making them jump. At 8am exactly there was a knock on the door and Freddie suddenly remembered what he had to do this day. His father walked to the kitchen door, unlocked and pulled it open.

"Wowee!" Jimmy cried excitedly on seeing who was at the door.

"What the.....!" Mr Fountain cried out aloud.

"Who is it?" Freddie's mother asked, leaving the table to join her husband at the door.

Grundly and Wiggly stood outside, much to Jimmy's excitement and Freddie's parents' surprise.

Before anyone could say anything more, Grundly tapped his magic staff and everyone froze to the spot, except Freddie. "You ready now, Freddie?" Grundly asked.

Freddie jumped down from the table, grabbed his rucksack and made for the door, easing around his mother and father.

"Come join us, Freddie, then I will cast my 'everything is normal' spell and they won't know you've even gone. Your mother will take Jimmy to school believing you are with them, so they won't know anything different," Grundly explained as he could see Freddie was concerned seeing his parents and Jimmy frozen like statues again.

Freddie hugged Wiggly while Grundly waved his staff, the crystal in the claw end glowed like sunshine making the kitchen glow all yellowy. Freddie watched his parents and Jimmy move about again and his father closed the door.

"That's really amazing, your magic is very powerful," Freddie said to Grundly.

"It is only a fraction of the power Merlin has, he can turn pigs into spiders, create thunder and lightening and make the ground rise up to make mountains!" Grundly replied much to the awe of Freddie and Wiggly. Grundly handed the invisibility hat to Wiggly and the magic detecting spectacles to Freddie, then tapped his staff to transform himself into a Sproggle. Although he still held his staff it was invisible to anyone else. Wiggly took off his pointy hat and Freddie giggled. "You look funny without your hat," he said.

Wiggly put it in his pocket and put on the invisibility hat and vanished into thin air.

Freddie put on the spectacles and could see Grundly's magic staff, and there was Wiggly again beneath the twinkling hat.

Wiggly held out his hand, which Freddie took in his, then he promptly vanished too. Because they were both invisible they could actually see each other, although Freddie did not quite know how that was possible.

"Now boys," Grundly began, "I can see you both clearly, but you will be invisible to everyone else. Don't let go of each other's hands though, otherwise, Freddie, you will suddenly appear out of thin air and might cause a commotion. Walk in front of me, that way no one will walk into you. Onward then, let's see if we can find these Morphlins!"

It was still early in the morning when they reached the High Street. The Newsagent shop always opened before the other shops for the early newspapers, so there were a few people roaming about. Grundly, Wiggly and Freddie headed straight for the Newsagent and stood well out of the way for a while just watching. As soon as the other shops began to open more and more people were walking up and down the High Street.

Grundly made his way to one of the bench seats, which were dotted around and the boys sat next to him, clinging tightly to each other's hands.

Wiggly whispered, "I've never been in your village before, Freddie, everything is so big and I've never seen so many Sproggles, it scares me a bit," he admitted.

Freddie smiled and replied very quietly, "I think they are all nice and kind, except for Billy Bates and his family, but they have moved away now. It was Billy Bates' father and uncle who cut down and stole the three trees in the forest."

Wiggly was just about to say something else when they all heard a horrible scream from outside the Greengrocer shop.

"Let's go investigate, boys, stay close together!" Grundly told them as he stood up and let the boys walk in front of him. When they reached the Greengrocer shop they saw a group of people, mostly ladies, stood together making quite a fuss.

"Mavis, Mavis! Wake Up!" one lady was calling.

Although the boys could not see clearly, Grundly was tall enough to look over the top of the people and saw one lady stood frozen in time.

"The Morphlins are around, boys," Grundly whispered down to them, "we have one victim already, more will follow, so keep a sharp eye out, Freddie!"

Freddie looked all around, but he could not detect anything unusual and nothing magical. A loud scream in front of the boys made Freddie jump and almost lose his grip of Wiggly's hand.

"Ahh! Something touched me! Something touched me!" the lady cried out.

People moved away quickly, leaving the frozen statue of Mavis in plain sight.

"Wiggly, remember Sproggles cannot see you!" Grundly reminded.

"Sorry Grundly, I couldn't see so I tried to move the lady and she screamed."

Freddie giggled with his hand over his mouth. "You are funny, Wiggly. That lady probably thought a big spider was crawling on her!"

Behind them was another commotion back at the Newsagent and they rushed there to see if the Morphlins were up to mischief. Sure enough, they saw two people, an elderly man and a young lady, stood like statues as other people gathered around them.

"I don't see them, Grundly, how are they doing this without me seeing them?" Freddie whispered.

"They can change their form instantly, but you should be able to see them, we are close and they can't be far away," Grundly whispered back.

More screams came from the Chemist shop area. Grundly, Freddie and Wiggly ran towards the commotion.

An elderly man was gently shaking an elderly woman by the shoulders. "Gladys, what's wrong, Gladys?" he kept repeating.

A younger woman, Freddie recognised her as the daughter of Gladys, was also frozen with her arm linked through her mother's.

"The Morphlins are around, Freddie," Grundly whispered when they were far enough away not to be heard.

Freddie was feeling frustrated. "I don't see them, Grundly, why can't I see them? This has just happened, they can't be out of sight already!"

"Do you recognise everyone, Freddie, are there any strangers because they could be the Morphlins?" Grundly asked.

"Do you know everyone here, Freddie?" Wiggly asked, repeating Grundly's question.

"I do, they are all people that live in the village. Wait! That man over there, he's not from the village," Freddie replied, pointing to a young man in uniform.

"It looks like the authorities have been called in boys, that's going to make things a bit easier to move around. I am clearly not a villager and if other non-villagers are about, I won't be so obvious," Grundly explained.

By noon they had been rushing from one end of the High Street to the other and had seen no trace of the Morphlins.

Grundly tapped his staff and they were instantly transported to his home. "We need refreshments before we carry on," he announced and tapped his staff again. On the table appeared a feast of all things Elfin and Sproggle. "Tuck in, boys. We have had no luck so far, these Morphlins are deceptive creatures," he told them.

Freddie and Wiggly stuffed themselves silly on all the treats on the table and Grundly chuckled at their enthusiasm.

"That was really special, Grundly, thank you," Freddie said politely."

"It was the best," Wiggly agreed.

"Are you ready for another attempt to find these repulsive creatures?" Grundly asked and the boys nodded, feeling certain they would be successful. Grundly tapped his staff and the remains of the feast vanished. He tapped his staff again and they were instantly transported to a quiet side road off the main High Street. "Hat and spectacles on then, boys, time for the hunt," Grundly said.

Wiggly put on the hat, Freddie the spectacles, then held Wiggly's hand. They both instantly became invisible. The High Street was a hive of activity for a small village.

"Is it usually this busy?" Grundly asked.

Freddie shook his head. "There are a lot of strangers here, some in uniform and quite a few youngish men, they're asking questions and writing on pads," Freddie replied.

"Hmmm!" Grundly responded. "Seems word has got out of the village, reporters are about.

The three of them set off towards a commotion near the Grocers shop. Three people were rigid like statues, two reporter types and a local lady. This was becoming a familiar sight and it seemed the local people were no longer shouting and screaming, but waiting in the knowledge that those frozen would be okay in a short while. They were oblivious to the danger that they were all in however.

Someone was taking photographs when a policeman came along and told everyone to, "Go about your business please!"

"Do you see anything, Freddie?" Grundly asked.

"I'm sorry, Grundly, I can't see any magic being used."

So it was for the rest of that day, until 2.30pm when school was almost at an end. They had rushed from one end of the High Street to the other, from one road to the park and back again, frustratingly always too late to see the Morphlins, just the Sproggle statues.

"Something has changed," Grundly observed. "Those last two Sproggles had more than fifteen minutes stolen, the Morphlins have moved on. When they go to the next stage they will be stealing an hour and after that they will start on the children. Once the Morphlins attack the children they may never recover because their time is worth less to Morphlins than an adult, so they will take many hours all at once. The children will be unable to distinguish reality and their minds will shut down and they will become living statues!" Grundly's words struck fear into Freddie and Wiggly.

"Grundly, we have to do something, we can't let things go that far!" Freddie appealed.

Meanwhile, the local police station had in fact called for reinforcements and the streets were being patrolled by a lot of police officers. With all of them and lots of reporters around, this, of course, was the best news for the Morphlins. There would be lots more victims and easier for them to move about by changing into a police officer. The authorities also sent a squad of soldiers in their camouflage uniforms and with so many strangers in the village the Morphlins could become a police officer or soldier, making detecting them almost impossible.

Grundly took Freddie and Wiggly into a quiet side road, made sure no one was about, tapped his staff and the next second they were back in Elfin Town and in Grundly's house.

Freddie let go of Wiggly's hand and he reappeared.

Wiggly removed the invisibility hat and he also reappeared.

Grundly tapped his staff and like magic he was old Grundly the Elfin again, he sat down looking very tired.

"Are you alright, Grundly?" Wiggly asked.

"I'm afraid I may not have as much time left as I planned. I feel my strength ebbing away like a leaking water barrel. We must complete our mission tomorrow, otherwise it will be too late and Elfins and Sproggles alike will be doomed," Grundly replied, drooping in his chair.

"What else can we do, Grundly? We just seem to be too late every time the Morphlins struck," Freddie asked almost in tears, fearing the worst for everyone.

Grundly sat up and tapped his finger on the side of his head, thinking. "Listen boys, I think the Morphlins are on to us, they've been playing with us, probably split up at opposite ends of the village and had us running around like headless chickens. Also I think that when they take on Sproggle form it masks their magic somehow, so we may have been looking straight at a Morphlin and never knew it," Grundly explained.

His words did nothing to cheer the two boys, who looked even sadder than before.

Freddie tried to think of something, some way of seeing the Morphlins. He jumped up with a bright look on his face. "I have an idea, Grundly. If the spectacles cannot see the difference between a Morphlin and a Sproggle, could you cast a spell on them to detect only real Sproggles? That way the one's who are not Sproggles must be Morphlins!"

Wiggly jumped up excitedly, clapping his hands and running on the spot.

Grundly looked at Freddie with a huge smile on his face. "Clever lad, clever lad, Freddie. That's what we shall do, well done, Freddie, we may yet succeed!" Grundly praised.

Wiggly grabbed his friend in a huge hug. "So clever, Freddie, what do your friends call you?" he teased.

"Freddie Fixit, Wiggly, as you well know!"

Wiggly giggled, "You might just have Freddie Fixed it then," and he hugged his friend again.

"I think we can do a little better, boys," Grundly announced, "if you can hand me those spectacles, Freddie." Grundly held out his hand as Freddie took off the spectacles and gave them to the old Elfin. Grundly stood up slowly and walked over to the table, the boys followed him as he put the spectacles on the middle of the table. "Trimodus Duplicos!" Grundly cried, touching the crystal of his staff on the spectacles. A ball of sparkling light covered them.

"Oooh," the two friends called out in wonder. When the sparkling light vanished, on the table were three pairs of spectacles.

"Oh, wow!" Wiggly cried out. "That's amazing!"

Freddie laughed and clapped his hands. "Oh, just like the magicians on the television."

Wiggly asked, "What's a telebision, Freddie?" Scratching his head and looking curiously at his friend.

Before Freddie could answer, Grundly broke in, "Now let's make these spectacles see Sproggles." Again Grundly touched them one at a time with his Crystal and cried, "Sproggles now detect alone!" Another ball of sparkling light covered the spectacles and then disappeared. "Wiggly, try on the spectacles and tell us what you see?" Grundly instructed.

Wiggly picked up a pair and put them on, they magically shrank a little to fit his head size, then he looked around. "Oh, I can see Freddie quite clearly," he announced. "Oh, that's so strange, when I turn to look at you, Grundly, you disappear, but I know you are there!" Wiggly said in amazement.

"Good, good, that means they are working perfectly," Grundly said with satisfaction. "Now, Wiggly, put your hat on the table please, Freddie can you take the other spectacles?" he instructed.

Wiggly obeyed, his eyes alight with joy guessing what Grundly was about to do.

"Trimodus Duplicos!" Grundly cried out, touching the hat with the crystal on his staff. The hat was covered with the ball of twinkling light.

Wiggly was so excited he was running on the spot again.

When the twinkling lights faded, on the table sat three hats.

"Tomorrow we shall each be invisible to Sproggles and Morphlins alike. I will adjust the spectacles so that we can see each other as well. We will split up and play the Morphlins at their own game and hunt them down!" Grundly cried with determination.

Freddie looked concerned. "Grundly, what will we do if we see one and the rest of us are somewhere else?"

"Oh, good question, Freddie, I never thought about that!"

Wiggly chuckled, 'Freddie Fixit' went through his mind.

"Okay you two, we need some way to communicate with each other or tag the Morphlin so it leaves a trail." Grundly tapped the side of his head while thinking.

The two friends watched in silence, wondering what they could do, when Grundly cried, "Got it!" making Freddie and Wiggly jump with surprise.

Grundly cleared the table and looked at the boys with a wry smile on his face. "You'll like this, boys," he said with a twinkle in his eye. He tapped the table with the crystal end of his staff and uttered, "Trimodus Caduceus Scintillateous!"

This time the twinkling light bubble was so bright Freddie and Wiggly had to shield their eyes. When they opened them again, on the table were three identical twirly sticks. The boys looked at them and then at Grundly, with a puzzled look on their faces.

"What are those for, Grundly?" Wiggly asked.

Grundly's whiskers lifted at the corners of his mouth as he beamed a smile. "Not four, only three," he chuckled.

"Huh!" Wiggly replied crinkling his face.

But Freddie laughed, "You said what are *'those four'* and there's only three!" he explained still laughing.

"Oh, yes! Very funny, Grundly," Wiggly giggled, "but what are they for?"

Grundly chuckled, "Just my little joke, boys. These, my friends, are Magic Wands!"

There was silence for a moment while the two boys digested what Grundly had said. Then they suddenly burst into life.

"Wow, oh wow!" Wiggly cried with such excitement his little legs were running on the spot.

"Are they really magic, Grundly, because I remember Daddly telling me he could not use magic to make magic?" Freddie asked with a germ of hopeful excitement in his mind.

"Quite so young Freddie, that is true of Fairy Dust, but my magic comes from Merlin himself who could harness Astoria's magic forces."

Freddie beamed the biggest ever smile and rubbed his hands together. He had always wanted a magic wand and to play at being a magician. "How do we use them, Grundly?" he asked.

"These are very special wands. By touching or even just pointing them at a Morphlin they will be coated with an invisible trail of dust, like Fairy Dust, that we will be able to see with our spectacles. The dust will fall off them and leave a trail that we can follow. Now that they are stealing more and more time for longer periods they will need to rest every hour or so. That means they will eventually lead us to their hideout!" Grundly proclaimed with pride.

The boys were even more excited, they would have a magic wand and it now looked like they would finally be able to catch the Morphlins.

"So tomorrow what we have to do," said Freddie, putting all the information together, "is find a Morphlin, cast magic dust on them with our wands and then follow them to their hideout."

Grundly nodded and smiled so wide his whiskers were tickling his ears.

Wiggly had calmed down but listened with his mouth open in awe of the Wizard's apprentice and his friend, Freddie.

Grundly added, "If one of us sees a Morphlin and uses their wand, they must hurry and find the other two of us."

"I know the village is not huge but how will we find each other, Grundly?" Freddie asked.

"Ah! I forgot to tell you, just ask your wand to find the others and it will take you to them," he replied. "Then we will follow the trail ready for the next step. Finding them is the easy part, creating the vortex is the difficulty, but I need enough life force to close it down once it traps the Morphlins. I can feel my power ebbing away more quickly than I would have liked, I only hope we can achieve this task successfully in time. If only Merlin were here this would be straight forward, for only he can tap into the limitless magic of Astoria and the very Universe itself." Grundly looked a little sad and Freddie also thought he sounded afraid that he might not be able to succeed with this vital mission.

All three were quiet, considering what had to be done tomorrow, when the room seemed to suddenly become brighter and brighter. Freddie and Wiggly looked up and around in surprised concern. This was very strange, even Grundly looked around a little mystified. The air seemed thick and pulsing.

Wiggly grabbed Freddie's hand, "What is it, Grundly, what's happening?" he trembled.

The bright light turned bluish, a deep, rich voice boomed around the room, seemingly coming from the walls and ceiling.

"I am watching over you, my children. You will succeed with your mission. I give to you all the magic you will need. Go save this wonderful world!"

From everywhere, twinkling, sparkling beams of light raced around the room, darting about, bouncing off the walls and ceiling, finally covering Grundly and the boys in twinkling light that seemed to soak into them and disappear.

Freddie and Wiggly's faces were wide eyed and mouths agape as they looked at each other and then at Grundly.

The Wizard's beard had shrunk considerably and he looked younger, his eyes seemed to glow and then dim again, his body seemed to straighten up like a much younger Elfin.

"Wh - wh - what happened, Grundly? Why do I feel all tingly inside?" Freddie asked.

"Me too, me too!" Wiggly agreed.

Grundly stood up and stretched, lifted his legs up and down and twisted his body. "We have just been blessed by the great Wizard Merlin. What you are feeling is his magic flowing through your body, as it is in mine, we are acting like batteries for magic. When the time comes and you both hold my magic staff, the magic stored in you will flow into the crystal and we can close the vortex," Grundly explained, even sounding younger.

"Oh, the feeling is fading now! I feel normal again," Wiggly chirped, looking at Freddie who was nodding in agreement that the same thing was happening to him.

"It's getting late boys." Grundly's voice sounded younger and stronger. "Wiggly, it's time for you to return home, Mummly and Daddly will be worried about you and want to know what you've been doing. Freddie, you need to be back home too. Your parents will believe you have been to school today, we will go out again tomorrow. I know you don't like saying things that are not true, but if your parents ask you if you had a nice day at school, you may have to say something that is not true. I'm sorry about that, if you can avoid it then please do. Wiggly and I will pick you up at 8.30am tomorrow. Now I will transport you to your homes. Freddie, Wiggly, you both ready?" Grundly asked.

Freddie and Wiggly both smiled and nodded.

Grundly tapped his staff twice and they both disappeared.

Wiggly suddenly appeared in the seating area of his house, much to Giggly and her parents' surprise. They all jumped when Wiggly spoke after he appeared from thin air.

"Hello everyone, I'm back."

Of course they were all eager to know how things had gone and Wiggly explained everything that had happened today and their disappointment and what they were planning tomorrow. "Oh, and Grundly was feeling that we might not succeed, when the room became bright and blue and we heard the great Wizard Merlin's voice. He was so calming and he gave us all some of his magic to help Grundly close the vortex. It's very exciting and scary at the same time. Did you know that the Sproggle village is huge? And it's full of Sproggles, they're everywhere!"

Daddly and Mummly laughed.

"They usually are up there, Wiggly," Mummly chuckled.

"Oh, yes, I suppose they would be," Wiggly giggled.

Freddie had appeared in his bedroom, where he quickly changed into his play clothes and ran downstairs into the kitchen where his mother was preparing their teatime meal. He ran to his mother and gave her a big hug. He wished he could tell her what had been happening to him today, he was bursting to tell someone, but he knew he had to keep it a secret.

"This is nice, to what do I owe this pleasure?" his mother asked.

"Oh, just being the best mum, Mum," Freddie replied, and that was the truth.

"Did you have a nice day then?" she asked.

"Yes Mum, it was very interesting today. Did you know that the village is full of police officers and the army? There seems to be lots of people turning to statues, like you and Dad did. Should we be worried?"

Freddie had cleverly answered truthfully and deflected his mother's curiosity about what he might have done that was so interesting.

"I'm sure the authorities will have the problem sorted out very soon. Maybe it's something in the air or in the water, we don't seem to be poorly after it happens. I'm sure it will all go away as quickly as it came, Freddie," his mother replied, stroking his hair.

"Can I go play in the garden?"

"Of course, darling son of mine, come back in for 5.30 and have your tea with us, okay?" his mother replied.

Freddie nodded and looked at his watch. He rushed off into the garden, pleased he had dodged telling any lies. His parents had taught him to be honest and truthful, so he would not be comfortable ever telling lies.

* *

At 8.30am the next morning, Freddie was ready and waiting when the knock at the kitchen door came. When his mother opened the door, to Freddie's surprise, Jimmy and his mother were standing outside.

"We thought Freddie might like to come with us this morning, Susan, if that's agreeable with you of course," Jimmy's mother suggested.

"Oh yes, that's lovely, thank you so much, I can get on with a few jobs. Off you go then Freddie, have a nice day, bye love!" His mother kissed Freddie on the forehead and sent him off with Jimmy and his mother.

Freddie did not know what to do, if he went with Jimmy he would miss Grundly and Wiggly and that would ruin all their plans. He followed them to the front garden gate and out onto the path. He was just about to make some excuse to go back to his house when Freddie heard a familiar tap, tap sound, and there in front of him were Grundly and Wiggly. Wiggly was giggling and even Grundly was smiling.

"Wow, that even convinced me, you both were so good!" Freddie chuckled.

"Quickly boys, put on your hats before anyone sees us," Grundly said and gave them each a hat. As soon as they all put them on they sparkled and twinkled.

"Oh, where are you?" Wiggly whispered.

Grundly tapped his staff.

"Ah, there you are, I thought you had vanished!" Wiggly said relieved.

"Well we have vanished as far as Sproggles and Morphlins are concerned. Now here are your spectacles and magic wands," Grundly replied.

"Wow! This is scary and exciting at the same time," Wiggly confessed.

"Just remember, you are invisible to everyone, so don't go touching Sproggles by accident otherwise they will think the village is haunted as well!" Grundly warned. "Are you boys ready then?"

Both Wiggly and Freddie replied together, "Ready!" Wands in hands, spectacles on their faces and feeling very positive about today, they had the blessing of Merlin, so they just had to succeed!

Grundly decided to divide the village into three parts, the High Street, the East side of the High Street and the West side of the High Street. "Wiggly, this is your first solo mission, are you ready?" Grundly asked.

Wiggly looked at Freddie apprehensively.

His friend put his arm around Wiggly's shoulder, "You can do this, Wiggly, just remember that no one can see you, and treat it like a game, okay?"

Freddie's encouragement was just what Wiggly needed. "Yes sir, Grundly, I can do this. Which area do you want me to patrol?"

"That's good to hear," Grundly smiled. "Well done, Freddie. Now Wiggly, I know I am asking a lot of you to go on patrol alone. Do you think you can take the East side?"

Wiggly beamed with confidence after his pep talk from Freddie and nodded his agreement.

"Now," Grundly began, "this applies to us all, do not confront a Morphlin if you see one. Work your way around to its back and use your wand to mark it. Then when you are far enough away from it and anyone else, ask your wand to find the rest of us, okay?" Grundly's voice was kind and understanding. He knew that Wiggly found the Sproggles and the Village overwhelming, but had confidence he could do what was needed. He was so much stronger than he realised and he would soon be tested to the limit. "Freddie, can you take the West side? I know you are familiar with this part of the village."

Freddie nodded to Grundly then gave Wiggly a comforting hug. "Remember they cannot see you," he whispered in Wiggly's ear.

With their spectacles on and wands in hand they set off and agreed to meet up at the park at 12 noon. Grundly had duplicated Freddie's watch so they all knew what time it was, if one of them spotted and tagged a Morphlin then they would meet up sooner than they planned.

At the top of the High Street, Wiggly turned east and walked away with a backward glance at his friends. Freddie turned west and waved to Wiggly and Grundly, who walked forward down the High Street.

Freddie liked this part of the Village and soon came across a soldier standing to attention and not moving. Thinking he was a victim of the time thief he walked right up to him and jabbed his finger in the soldier's arm.

"Huh, what! Who goes there?" the soldier cried out loudly.

It made Freddie jump out of his skin, just putting his hand over his mouth in time to muffle his own cry of surprise.

The soldier brought his rifle to chest level and looked around slowly enough for Freddie to move far enough away not to get poked by it. Unable to see anything, even though Freddie was now stifling a chuckle, the soldier dropped his rifle by his side and rubbed his chin, still looking around. "Must be my imagination, I swear something or someone touched me!" he mumbled under his breath, then stood back to attention.

Still holding his mouth trying not to giggle, Freddie realised that under different circumstances this could be a lot of fun. Then in his mind a voice said, '*A lot of trouble too!*' Now Freddie was looking around wondering who had said that, looking at the soldier intently, '*Was it him?*' he thought. Still looking around suspiciously, Freddie walked past the soldier.

Most of this side of the village was housing with only a few people about until he came across a Barbers Shop that he had not noticed before. It was set back, like it had once been a house, but had a big window and a spinning red and white spiral pole outside. Freddie looked through the window and saw a man sat in a chair waving his arms while the barber was trying to cut his hair, they were not statues so no Morphlins here, at least not yet.

Wiggly walked slowly along the first road looking left and right and behind him, still quite nervous being on his own above ground and in the village, wishing Freddie was with him. He came across a small park that had houses on three sides and a road running around it and he sat down on a bench seat for a breather. He noticed there were a couple of swings in the middle of the park. There were also lots of trees around, a bit like his forest, and it made him feel much calmer. There was no one else about, so no sign of any Morphlins, at least not yet.

"Attenn - shun! You there! ... Stand still or I will shoot!"

The loud voice made Wiggly jump so high he fell off the seat with a bump and gave a quiet yelp.

"Who's that? Show yourself!" demanded the voice.

A terrified Wiggly sat on the ground shaking, almost afraid to look around.

'*Remember no one can see you, Wiggly.*' Freddie's words calmed him and he looked up to see a soldier holding his rifle up at eye level and looking around for the sound he had heard.

"Come on Sam, you're just jumpy, calm down," the soldier said to himself, then put down his rifle and sat on the bench seat close to where Wiggly had been sitting.

Wiggly picked himself up, slowly and quietly, then stood at the end of the bench watching as the soldier fumbled in his pocket and pulled out a small box, flipped the lid and shook it. To his amazement, a round white tube slid out.

'*He must have magic,*' Wiggly thought.

Then the soldier took the white tube and put it between his lips.

'*What's he doing?*' Wiggly was thinking.

The soldier fumbled in his pocket again and brought out another smaller box that had a drawer, inside were long thin sticks with red blobs on the end.

Wiggly watched with fascination as the soldier slid a red headed stick on the box and it burst into flames. Wiggly squeezed his hand tightly over his mouth, watching the soldier set fire to the white tube between his lips, then there was lots of smoke and the soldier seemed to slump and gasp.

Wiggly rushed to help, thinking the soldier was on fire. He grabbed the white tube and threw it to the ground.

"What the.... who's there?" the soldier said and stood up quickly.

Wiggly stepped back and fell on his bottom, suppressing a yelp with both hands over his mouth.

The soldier stood transfixed, like a statue looking down at his cigarette on the ground. "Spooky, now I am seeing things, get a grip, Sam, move on, move on!" He hastily marched away, then ran as fast as he could, shouting, "Sarge! .... Sarge!"

Wiggly picked up the smouldering white tube and looked at it curiously. "Whatever is this?" he said to himself. "Why would that Sproggle put it in his mouth and set fire to it?" Wiggly rubbed his chin. "I think some Sproggles are quite potty." He looked around to make sure no one else was about before squashing the cigarette into the ground. The whole thing unnerved Wiggly and he too marched off looking around nervously. He walked on the footpath passing a privet hedge that he could just see over the top.

"OY!" a very loud voice shouted.

Wiggly was already nervous and the voice made him jump, then he almost fainted as a Sproggle's head suddenly popped up on the other side of the hedge.

"Get outta here!" the Sproggle cried. "Go on! Shoo! Shoo!"

Wiggly ducked down quickly, thinking the Sproggle was talking to him. 'Wait, he can't see me' he thought and stood up to look over the hedge to see what was going on. A man was shouting and waving his arms about at some birds in his garden, trying to scare them away. Wiggly giggled quietly with his hand over his mouth again, because the birds were taking no notice.

The man was flapping his arms and shouting when he suddenly froze with his arms in the air. Wiggly was still sniggering when he realised that the Sproggle was like a statue, 'Morphlins' he thought. Wiggly looked right over the hedge and could only see the one Sproggle. 'How is that possible?' he thought, then noticed a large animal running away and out of sight. 'Could that have been a Morphlin?' he thought. 'Wait, Grundly told us that Morphlins could take any shape.' Wiggly wandered around, now looking for the animal as well as Morphlins, but saw neither again. He looked at his watch, "Goodness, it's almost noon, I'd better get a move on," and he made a dash for the park.

Grundly had walked up and down the High Street, seeing there were more soldiers and police officers than Sproggles. He sat on a bench for a while, watching and listening for anything unusual, but there was nothing. He felt frustrated and what was worse, he could feel his strength ebbing away rapidly. Shortly before noon he tapped his staff and transported himself to the park to wait for Freddie and Wiggly.

Freddie had found the roads and houses pretty much deserted other than police officers and soldiers, and not many of them. He would not be prodding another soldier, that was for certain. At noon he made his way to the park to find Grundly sat on a bench, the park, too, was deserted.

"No sign of Wiggly yet?" he asked, although it was obvious he was not there.

Wiggly had got lost and it was fifteen minutes after noon when he finally arrived, pleased to see Grundly and Freddie sat on a bench waiting for him.

"Wiggly, thank goodness, we thought you had been discovered or worse and were just deciding to come look for you," Freddie cried and stood up to hug his friend.

"I got lost, so many roads that look the same to me," he replied and sat down with Grundly and Freddie.

"It looks very much like we spooked the Morphlins yesterday and they stayed in their hideout," Grundly suggested.

"I almost saw one, I think," Wiggly interrupted.

"How so?" Freddie asked.

"Well, this Sproggle was shouting at some birds and then became a statue. I didn't see any non-Sproggles about, only a big animal running away. Could it have been a Morphlin?"

"That's quite possible," Grundly explained. "They can take any form, which complicates things. I never thought it might be anything other than a Sproggle. On top of which, even with Merlin's magic, my time is running out fast. We really need to find them today or it may be too late!" Grundly was clearly afraid their mission might not succeed.

They sat quietly thinking for a while when Wiggly's stomach growled like a bear and he giggled.

"I guess we must all be hungry," Freddie said and smiled looking at his friend, then delved into his rucksack and pulled out jam sandwiches and orange juice to drink.

Wiggly looked around the park in wonder as they tucked into the welcome food. "This park is so big, Freddie. Ooh, I see some swings, what are all those other structures over there?"

Freddie pointed out a couple of seesaws, a climbing frame and a roundabout.

"Could we have a go on the seesaw, Grundly?" Wiggly asked.

"As long as the park is deserted I don't suppose it will hurt, but not too long boys, we have some searching to do," Grundly agreed.

Freddie let Wiggly sit on the seesaw first, then pulled his end down, whizzing Wiggly in the air. "Weeee!" Wiggly cried.

Then Freddie sat on the other end and jumped them both up and down.

"This is fun, we must have one in our park, Freddie," Wiggly suggested.

Grundly laughed at the boys, remembering that they were still just children and this was such a big thing to be asking of them. Had anyone come into the park they would have seen the seesaw bobbing up and down by itself, with the boys still being invisible, that might have caused a stir, but fortunately no one appeared.

When the boys returned, Wiggly was all excited. "That was so much fun," he announced.

"I think people are too frightened to come out," Freddie explained, "I only saw two people and a soldier, who I prodded, thinking he was a statue when he was just stood to attention. He jumped and I nearly gave myself away."

Wiggly chuckled. "Oh! I saw a soldier too. He set fire to his face with a round white stick and I grabbed it and threw it away. It spooked him and he ran off, Sproggles are very strange."

"That's called a cigarette, Wiggly, Freddie explained. It's a bad habit some Sproggles have. They light the cigarette and inhale the smoke, but it can cause them to become unwell."

"I found there were more police officers and soldiers than Sproggles in the High Street," Grundly offered.

"What will we do then?" Wiggly asked.

Freddie had an idea and suggested, "When school finishes lots of parents come to collect their children, so it might be where the Morphlins strike next if they have been laid low this morning."

Grundly sat up straight and looked at Freddie with a satisfied smile. "Good thinking, Freddie," he praised. "Then all three of us must be on guard outside the school, at that time. The Morphlins will need to feed so that is a good place for them to target. Right, now let's go and patrol our areas just in case we get lucky, then meet up at the school. What time does the school day finish, Freddie?" Grundly asked.

"It's 2.30pm so we have just over an hour. All the parents will gather around the school gates ten or fifteen minutes before the classes leave, so it would be a good idea to be at the school then," Freddie explained.

"How will I find the school?" Wiggly asked.

"I have an idea," Grundly announced. "Now hold your wands on my wand. 'Locatous Freddie,'" Grundly said and the wands sparkled for a moment. "When it's time, Wiggly and I can find you, Freddie, by asking our wands, 'Find Freddie', and the wands will transport us to your side wherever you are. So if you can be near the school at 2.20pm we will join you."

Wiggly looked excited, "Ooh! That's so cool," he chuckled.

"Okay boys, I will send you to your areas, keep an eye on your watches," Grundly said, then tapped his staff twice and the boys vanished, he tapped it again and he vanished, reappearing in the High Street, but he was invisible, of course.

All three searched their areas for what seemed like hours, without success. Wiggly saw only one Sproggle, as did Freddie, and the only Sproggles Grundly came across were soldiers and police officers. All the shops had closed because they had no customers, which did not make it any easier to find the Morphlins.

By 2.20pm Freddie was close to the school, far enough away to see all the parents and not bump into them.

Wiggly looked at his watch and waited until it read 2.20pm exactly. He was so excited with the next part he could hardly stand still. "Find Freddie," he said quietly to his wand. He felt a little rush of air and was instantly standing next to his friend. "Freddie," he whispered, making his friend jump and quickly gave him a hug.

Grundly suddenly appeared next to them and gave Wiggly a start. "Good, that worked very nicely. Did anyone spot a Morphlin?" Grundly asked.

The boys shook their heads. "Not even a Sproggle" they said together.

"Let's move a little closer then, boys," Grundly suggested just as they heard a commotion.

The three of them rushed around together to discover one of the waiting mothers had been attacked by a Morphlin and was standing like a statue. The other mothers were spooked and cowering back against the school railings looking scared and worried.

"Okay, Freddie, Wiggly," Grundly whispered out of earshot of the mothers who were deathly quiet, "let's split up, we must find these Morphlins."

Freddie went through the school gates, while Grundly and Wiggly patrolled both sides of the fence.

Despite there being one frozen mother among all the other parents, they were quietly buzzing in whispered discussion to each other.

Grundly and Wiggly looked at each Sproggle in turn and none disappeared, so none of them were the Morphlins.

"Where can they be? Where can they be?" Wiggly whispered to himself and a Sproggle turned to look in his direction.

"Did you hear something, Audrey?" she said and Wiggly covered his mouth with his hand.

Grundly heard a scream and tapped his staff to transport himself directly to the place where two Sproggles were looking at another who was standing like a statue, but everyone he looked at remained visible. 'Where are you?' he thought.

Freddie was walking along the footpath towards the main entrance of the school when the double doors swung open and he did a double take. 'Huh, what made those doors swing open on their own?' he thought. He realised something and took his glasses off. Now he could see that a mother and father were walking out. He looked through his glasses again and the two figures vanished. Freddie almost burst with excitement and surprise. Clamping his hand on his mouth just in time, 'It's them,' he thought, 'it's them' he told himself. Lifting his glasses up again, he stepped aside to let them pass. The female Morphlin was the closest to Freddie, who was invisible to her. As they passed by him he touched her with his wand. Fairy Dust, invisible to everyone else except Freddie, covered the Morphlin.

The Morphlin stopped in her tracks and looked directly at Freddie and he fell backwards with a bump, landing on his bottom. "Oooof!" he cried in surprise.

For a brief moment the Morphlin changed to its monstrous form and moved in Freddie's direction. Freddie lifted himself up on his hands and feet and scooted backwards, only to bump into Grundly and cried out again, "Oooof!" as the Morphlin homed in on his voice. Freddie closed his eyes, he knew they would find him and drain him of his time, even though he should have been invisible to them.

Wiggly appeared from the other direction and managed to touch the other Morphlin with his wand, it changed into its natural monstrous shape and looked directly at Wiggly. Both creatures stopped in their tracks, looking around at Freddie, Wiggly and Grundly, growling loudly in frustration.

Seeing they were in danger of being caught by the two Morphlins, Grundly tapped his staff and transported all three them to the safety of the playground, out of reach of the Morphlins.

There was a sudden loud sound of children's voices as they began to filter out of the school building.

The two Morphlins, back in Sproggle form, made a swift exit out of the school gates and down the road out of sight, leaving a magical, yet invisible trail behind them.

"Grundly and Wiggly, thank you," Freddie said, then hugged his friends. "I really thought they were about to grab me!"

Grundly was so pleased and thanked Freddie and Wiggly excitedly. "Well done boys, that was quite scary there for a moment, but you managed to tag them both, well done!" He was smiling so much the beard on the corners of his mouth was poking in his ears and Freddie giggled nervously. "Now, do you feel strong enough for the next stage, because that was the easy part?"

Freddie smiled, "We did get them good, didn't we?"

Wiggly giggled uneasily and asked, "Why did they change from Sproggle to Morphlin when I tagged them?"

Grundly thought for a moment, tapping the side of his head. "I think it was because they must have felt or sensed the Fairy Dust covering them and it broke their concentration to hold the Sproggle form for a brief moment. In their natural state they must be able to see magic, that's why they could see all of us. Fortunately, only we noticed their change, otherwise it would have caused a real panic," Grundly explained.

Suddenly they heard a lot of screams and cries from inside the school and they made a dash back through the main doors to investigate.

"Oh no!" Freddie cried out aloud. Fortunately there was so much noise from parents, no one heard him.

Wiggly gasped and grabbed Freddie's hand.

Grundly stared with a desperate and sorrowful expression, all three were horrified, unable to believe what they were seeing. One whole class and their teacher were all frozen like statues.

"That's what the Morphlins had been doing inside the school before we caught up with them," Grundly whispered.

Freddie was in tears. This was his class. His teacher. His friends, Jimmy, William, Anne and the rest who were solid, just like stone, it was horrible to look at. "Grundly, will they be alright? Tell me they won't be living statues. If only we had found those Morphlins sooner!" Freddie whispered tearfully.

Wiggly pulled his friend into a comforting hug and said, "I'm so sorry, Freddie, I know they are all your friends, so we must stop these creatures before they strike again."

Grundly looked at the boys and felt their pain. "Freddie," he said softly, patting him on the shoulder, "I hope they will all be alright, there are so many of them that the Morphlins may only have taken five or ten minutes of their time. If we can capture them soon enough the stolen time might be reversed, but I am only guessing. I hope they will be okay, I really do. My magic is ebbing away faster than I would like, boys. I know this is upsetting, but we must find those Morphlins and put an end to this nightmare," Grundly encouraged.

Freddie wiped away his tears and stood up straight, with Wiggly standing next to him like two boy soldiers. "Let's go and get them, then," he replied in a low voice.

The three would-be heroes made their way back through the main entrance doors of the school, through the gates and onto the footpath, where they saw the glittering trail of Fairy Dust which only they could see. It would not matter if the Morphlins realised they had been covered in Fairy Dust, they could not shake it, brush it, or even wash it off, they could not get rid of it in any way whatsoever. The three invisible friends followed the twinkling trail to the High Street, where two trails appeared from the one.

"Seems they split up here, maybe to confuse us if they realise we can follow them, but they will join up again somewhere along the way," Grundly sneered. "Let's follow the right hand trail boys, they will not get the better of us this time."

The Morphlins tried their best to confuse anyone trying to follow them. They were not invisible, so Sproggle police officers and soldiers could possibly just follow them out of curiosity, thinking they were strangers, not realising who they really were.

The trail took Grundly, Freddie and Wiggly through people's gardens, up one side of the road and down the other, round in circles. If anyone did see the Morphlins, the round about trail they were making would have looked suspicious. But they could keep changing Sproggle forms from ordinary Sproggles to a policemen or soldiers, even children and animals.

"They must know we're onto them," Freddie declared, looking at all the tracks crisscrossing, going this way and that.

"Look over here!" Wiggly called.

Freddie and Grundly rushed to his side to look at what he had found.

"Well done, Wiggly, the Morphlins hideout can't be far now. Just look at the prints, this Morphlin must have reverted to its natural shape, look at the difference," Grundly surmised.

"It's completely different, more like a side winding snake. I bet the monsters hoped changing to their creature shapes would throw us off their tracks," Freddie sneered.

Grundly took the lead with Freddie and Wiggly holding hands following behind. They wandered through a Sproggle garden where the Morphlin had trampled down flowers and crushed small bushes. Grundly stopped and tapped his staff and his magic restored the flowers and bushes. The trail took them to a fence at the bottom of a garden, which was just smashed to bits. After they walked through to the other side, Grundly restored the fence with his magic. The glittering Fairy Dust trail took them to the forest at the other side of the village.

"I don't know the forest on this side very well," Freddie admitted.

"That's alright, Freddie," Wiggly encouraged, "I know it well enough, so we won't get lost and we can always backtrack the Fairy Dust trail."

Grundly came to a halt and both the boys bumped into him. "Ooof!" they grunted. "Sorry boys, I forgot you were behind me, but look, there are two trails. That means both creatures are together again."

They followed the glittering trails quite deeply into the forest. It began to look a little scary to Freddie, being unfamiliar with it and he remembered the time Jimmy got lost and realised just how scared he must have felt. They were a long way from the village by this time and a large outcrop of rock came into view.

Wiggly ran ahead and then stopped, put a hand on his hip and scratched his head.

"What's wrong, Wiggly?" Freddie asked as he and Grundly quickly caught up to him.

"The tracks, they've vanished just here in front of the rock face," he replied in a confused sounding voice.

Grundly looked around and sure enough the trail just stopped. "That is strange," he puzzled. "The Fairy Dust should not have run out, yet the trail stops as if the creatures somehow jumped up in the air or grew wings and flew away."

Freddie looked at Grundly wide eyed, in disbelief, "Could they actually change their shape to a bird and fly away?"

"Or a dragon or flying horse?" Wiggly added.

"Well I don't really know, Freddie, but Wiggly thought he saw a large animal running away from a Sproggle that had been made a statue, so it's possible."

While Grundly was talking to Freddie they both suddenly heard a loud cry, "Ooof!"

When Freddie turned to look at Wiggly, he got a shock. "Wiggly, where are you?" he cried out because he could not see his friend anywhere. Freddie looked at Grundly, who shrugged his shoulders. "Wiggly?" Freddie called again.

"I'm here!" Wiggly cried, waving his arms and chuckling.

"Where? I can't see you," Freddie replied looking everywhere.

"Here!" laughed Wiggly, then he suddenly just appeared from the exact spot where the Fairy Dust trail had disappeared. Wiggly was bent over giggling. "Freddie, it's not real. The rock face is not real, it's an enchantment like the big old oak tree. I just felt a bit tired and leaned against the rock and fell to the ground with quite a bump!" Wiggly chuckled and walked into the rock face, disappearing again, then stepping back into the forest.

Freddie stood with his mouth open yet again. It was the strangest thing to see Wiggly walk through a wall and disappear.

"Well done, Wiggly! You've found their hideout," Grundly laughed and praised the little Elfin, then touched the rock face with the crystal claw end of his staff and chanted, "Evanesce! Evanesce!" and the concealed entrance was revealed, like a window blind being pulled up.

"What do we do now, Grundly?" Freddie asked.

Grundly looked very serious. "This is the most difficult part of our mission. Firstly, take off your hats and put them in Freddie's rucksack, your spectacles too."

All three lost their invisibility doing as Grundly had instructed.

"Why do we need to do that, Grundly?" Freddie asked.

"Our magic is more powerful when we are in our normal state of visibility and we will need every advantage we can get," he replied. "Now come, stand behind me, do not stand too close to the vortex otherwise it may draw you into it," Grundly warned.

Freddie grabbed hold of Wiggly's hand and they scuttled behind the impressive figure of the old Wizard's apprentice.

"That's perfect, boys. Now push your wands into the ground, crouch down and hold onto them tightly, the wand will anchor you to the ground, so don't let go," Grundly explained.

The two friends obeyed Grundly's instruction, their wands pushed easily into the ground and suddenly became impossible to pull out. They held onto their magic wands with one hand and each other with their other hand. "Ready," they called out.

Grundly began the incantation for the time vortex spell. He held his staff out with the crystal pointing to the cave entrance and made small circles with it. "Maestromous! Turbillonous! Timentious!" he chanted softly and a small spiral of blue crackling light began spinning around in front of the crystal. "MAEstromous! TURbillonous! TIMentious!" Grundly raised his voice a little louder and the spiral of crackly blue light grew larger. "MAESTRomous! TURBILLonous! TIMEntious!" Again Grundly chanted the words of the spell a little louder and the spiral of blue crackling light grew even bigger and there was a noticeable hum with the sound of the crackling. "MAESTROMOUS! TURBILLONOUS! TIMENTIOUS!" This time Grundly was shouting the spell over the noisy and ever growing spiral of crackling blue light. The air around the boys and Grundly became turbulent, dust and leaves began lifting from the forest floor, the very ground was trembling and the boys held more tightly to their magic wands and to each other. Grundly's hair and beard began to fly around and the boys could feel themselves being lifted and drawn towards the vortex.

"MAESTROMOUS! TURBILLONOUS! TIMENTIOUS!"

One last time Grundly bellowed his spell and the vortex grew so big it completely covered the rock face and the cave entrance.

The boys could feel its power pulling at them.

Grundly stood his ground, but his cloak, beard and hair were being drawn towards the massive, swirling, crackling time vortex.

Freddie and Wiggly looked at each other, gripping tightly yet being lifted off the ground.

"Hold tightly, Wiggly!" Freddie shouted at the top of his voice.

They watched the vortex create a spiralling funnel, which reached into the cave, probing deeper and deeper. Even though the vortex was noisy they heard the most terrifying shriek, like a thousand pigs squealing all at the same time.

The boys could hardly stand the noise, every instinct wanted them to cover their ears with their hands.

"HOLD FAST BOYS!" Grundly yelled.

The screams seemed to be getting closer and louder.

Then Freddie screamed, **"MORPHLINS!"** at the top of his voice.

He and Wiggly watched, horrified as the big ugly creatures seemed to be floating in the air, every part of them flaying around trying to grab a hold of something to stop them being extracted from their hideout. The vortex was too powerful for them to resist. Even as they tried to enlarge their bodies and wedge themselves in the cave, the vortex drew them in, sucking and pulling, distorting their body shape to something even more grotesque.

Freddie shuddered when it looked like the vortex would pull the Morphlins right through it and on top of them.

The pathetic creatures made one last attempt, growing several arms with claws trying to anchor them to the cave entrance. But their bodies were elongated and drawn into the time vortex and suddenly they completely vanished inside it, like fluff into a vacuum cleaner. The funnel extending into the cave entrance drew back and the vortex seemed to go much quieter, like some huge beast swallowing its prey, then sleeping while it digested its meal.

"Quickly boys, come, take hold of my crystal staff with me, we need to close the vortex and my magic is almost depleted," Grundly cried out.

Freddie and Wiggly struggled to stand down on the ground, then quickly let go of their magic wands and grabbed hold of Grundly, working their way around to grab the magical staff.

"That's right boys, don't let go, whatever happens, don't let go!" Grundly warned, then he began chanting his spell. "Terminatous!

Maestromous! Terminatous! Maestromous! Terminatous! Maestromous!" over and over.

Wiggly screamed, "FREDDIE! FREDDIE!" as a long thin arm with funnel-like fingers reached out of the vortex, waved around in the air, then locked onto Wiggly's head. He fell silent and rigid like a stone statue.

"**Terminatous! Maestromous!**" Grundly cried out at the top of his weary voice and the arm shot back into the vortex. "Hold on, Freddie!" Grundly croaked as his life force and magic began to fail him.

Freddie began chanting with Grundly, louder and louder, his arm began to sparkle and very quickly his whole body was engulfed in a sparkling aura. "What's happening, Grundly?" Freddie could only look at his friend, Wiggly, rigid like stone and he thought the Morphlin had taken all of Wiggly's time and he was gone, forever. "I can't do it, I can't do it!" Freddie cried out, with tears streaming down his face, terrified to let go of the magical staff.

The time vortex spun wildly, trying to pull them both into it. Their clothing and hair, even the skin on their arms, hands and face was being pulled towards the vortex.

"Again, Freddie," Grundly croaked as his legs began to fail him, but Freddie was terrified of the vortex and another Morphlin arm reaching out.

"**I can't do it, Grundly, look at Wiggly, he's gone and I can't do this without him!**" Freddie shouted, tears streaming down his face. He felt so tired and wanted to go home to the safety of his mother and father.

"**If we cannot close the vortex it will engulf the whole world!**" Grundly shouted.

'I am with you, Freddie. You will succeed.'

Merlin's voice flashed through Freddie's mind and seemed to spur him on. He grabbed Grundly with one hand and held onto the staff with his other, together they chanted.

"Terminatous! Maestromous! **Terminatous! Maestromous! Terminatous! Maestromous!**" Grundly faltered, suddenly sagged and dropped to his knees.

The vortex was at last just beginning to get smaller.

"Grundly, I can't do this on my own, I can't, I really can't," Freddie cried hoarsely, mourning his friend, Wiggly.

"Yes, you can!" a voice from behind called to him.

Freddie struggled to turn his head to look at who it was. "WIGGLY!" he cried and his friend took hold of the crystal staff with one hand and Freddie with the other, then they chanted together, all three of them.

"Terminatous! Maestromous!"

A powerful, sparkling aura enveloped all of them and passed down Grundly's magical staff, flooding the vortex with powerful, sparkling magic until it finally shrank to a tiny disc and disappeared.

Grundly fell sideways, sprawled out on the ground, his life force and magic completely and utterly consumed. His magic staff crumbled and turned to dust, as did the magic wands still wedged in the ground.

The sound of the utter quietness was deafening. The time vortex had been so loud, now it felt like Freddie and Wiggly had gone completely deaf. They held their hands to their ears and rubbed them, trying to get some feeling back.

Then Freddie saw Grundly lain flat out on the ground. "Grundly! Grundly!" he cried, bending down to shake the old apprentice to Merlin.

Grundly's hands and face were covered in deep, deep wrinkles and he looked ancient, something like an Egyptian Mummy he had once seen on the television.

"It's no use, Freddie," Wiggly said tugging on his shoulder. "Grundly's time has come, we must get him back to Elfin Town, quickly."

Even as they looked, Grundly seemed to be withering away, he was almost just skin and bone.

Tears streamed down Freddie's cheeks and dripped to the dusty ground beneath him. "Grundly, Grundly, please don't leave us, please!" he begged, but to no avail.

Grundly had given up every last bit of his magic and his life force to save his beloved Elfins.

"What do you mean, Wiggly?" Freddie sobbed. "Shouldn't we dig a grave here and bury him? Then all Elfins can come and say a prayer or something, when they want to remember him and what he did for everyone." Freddie felt so sad looking at his friend, Grundly.

"No, Freddie, Elfins do not bury our dead, but we have to get Grundly back to Elfin Town, it's really important," Wiggly explained.

The boys scouted around and quickly found two long branches, then Freddie magically created some rope from his rucksack for a makeshift stretcher.

Freddie gently held Grundly by the shoulders while Wiggly held onto Grundly's feet.

"When I count to three we will lift Grundly onto the stretcher, Wiggly, okay?" Freddie instructed.

An overwhelming feeling of sadness swept over the two friends and tears began to fall as they lifted Grundly onto the stretcher. He was so light now, they managed to pick him up with ease. They stood looking at Grundly, remembering when his beard would curl up when he smiled and the little jokes he played on them.

Freddie could still hear his friendly, calming voice.

Wiggly chuckled with his tears, remembering what Grundly had sacrificed.

"I didn't know Grundly for long, Wiggly, but he was important to me. Now he's gone, Sproggles will never know what he did to save them all, so we must make sure the Elfins never forget him, Wiggly, never," Freddie sniffed.

"We need to get a move on, Freddie, it's getting late and no one knows where we are!" Wiggly sniffed back his own tears.

Between them they lifted the stretcher with Wiggly leading the way, as he knew the quickest route through the forest. After what seemed a very long time they reached the big old oak tree.

"I'll go get help, Freddie, can you wait here with Grundly?" Wiggly asked and disappeared down the spiral staircase. A few minutes later he returned with two Town Elders and they took Grundly carefully down to the town.

"I've got to go home, Wiggly, Mum will be worried," Freddie explained, wiping tears from his face. They hugged once more.

"Come to Elfin Town after school tomorrow, Freddie, if you want to see something truly, truly wonderful," Wiggly told him and they said their goodbyes.

Freddie reached into his rucksack and pulled out a damp face cloth to wipe his teary, dirty face. Then he had a sudden thought, his class had been time stolen and might still be at school, so that is where he went first. Sure enough the police and army soldiers were all over the place, but Freddie knew how to sneak inside without being seen. He crept in through the toilet window and quietly joined his friends. He found sitting very still incredibly difficult, especially after all the excitement. He watched the clock reach 4 o'clock and suddenly everyone began to wake up at the same time.

"Freddie, why are we still at school, it's 4 o'clock, what's happened?" Jimmy asked looking very confused. Freddie shrugged his shoulders.

The teacher clapped her hands. "Children, it looks like we have been struck down by this mysterious illness. Does anyone feel unwell?" she asked.

They all looked at each other with puzzled faces and shrugged their shoulders.

"No Miss," Freddie called out, "everyone is alright." Only he knew what had really happened and he shivered at the thought that Grundly, Wiggly and he very nearly failed, then he felt sad again when he thought about Grundly.

"Hey, are you crying, Freddie?" Jimmy asked.

"I don't know, am I?" Freddie replied wiping his eyes. "Oh, that's strange," he added.

Their teacher responded and told them all to stand and file out row by row. "Your parents are waiting outside by the look of things. No school for any of you tomorrow, you must go see the doctor and get checked over to make sure that you are all well."

There was a loud cheer from all the children, an extra day off school was great even though they all really liked being at school.

"Goodbye children."

"Goodbye Miss," they called back and began to file out in an orderly fashion as if nothing had happened at all.

Freddie had the perfect cover story and he did not have to explain anything to his mother and father when he saw them waiting anxiously at the school gate. They hugged and kissed him and again tears began to drip down his cheeks.

"It's alright son, you're safe now," his mother reassured him, but only he knew that they were really safe and he longed to tell his parents, but he knew he could not.

"Hop up sunshine, you can be the jockey today," his father chuckled.

Freddie climbed up on his father's back and called, "Gee up, Neddy!" as his father gave him a piggyback all the way home. But Freddie was very quiet on the way, he felt overwhelmed by so many things that had happened in such a short time. He had never seen anyone die before and the image of Grundly collapsing and withering away haunted his thoughts.

Freddie's parents were worried about him, he was always a happy, loving little boy, but now he looked sad and withdrawn.

"You can tell us anything, Freddie, you know that don't you? If something is troubling you, don't bottle it up, let it out," his mother comforted him while she tucked him up in bed for the night.

Freddie tried to smile as he nodded his head, but it just would not come. After his mother closed his bedroom door and said goodnight, Freddie laid his head on the pillow and again the tears began to roll down his cheeks. He had seen things that young boys should never have to see, but worse than that he could not talk to his mother and father about any of it. He and Wiggly had just saved the whole world and they had lost Grundly in the process, he sobbed as he cried. He had become so attached to Grundly in just a short time and now he was gone, before his very eyes he saw Merlin's apprentice fall to his knees and collapse into a skin and bone corpse. He felt a deep sense of loss that just would not go away. He cried into his pillow and sobbed away until sleep eventually wrapped around an exhausted Freddie. But it was not a peaceful, happy sleep. Ghosts of evil Morphlin creatures trying to catch him made him wake and scream so loud his mother burst into his bedroom.

"What is it, what's troubling you, Freddie?" she asked.

"I see monsters in my sleep, so real Mum, they're so real!" he told her.

"They're just nightmares, Freddie, nothing to be afraid of, they're not real," she replied stroking his head.

He only wished that were true.

His mother sat and hugged her son, stroking his hair until he finally fell asleep again. Then she tucked him in and kissed his forehead. "Sleep tight, Freddie," she said and left him.

* *

Wiggly was similarly haunted by visions of the monsters in his dreams, they chased him relentlessly and finally reached out and touched him. In his nightmare he relived the minutes they stole from him. Watching his friend and Grundly struggling and chanting, but unable to move, unable to help as he was intended to do. He too cried out in the night, but he was much luckier than Freddie, when Mummly came to his bedside, he told her all about his nightmare and she comforted him and stroked his head until he fell asleep again.

Mummly knew exactly what Wiggly and Freddie had been through, she and Daddly would be there to support him, understand his anxiety and fears and help him through his troubles. She knew poor Freddie was not able to do that with his parents, he was very much all on his own while in the Sproggle world.

The next morning Freddie did not jump out of bed nice and early like he did every day.

Instead his mother came to him and woke him up. "Freddie, Freddie," she whispered gently, "time to get up, son."

He opened his eyes, but the sadness was still in his mind and heart, he looked at his mother's concerned face.

"What's troubling you, Freddie? You can tell me." She held him in her arms and comforted him as his silent tears ran down his face, he knew she would not understand. This was a journey he had to make alone. He got out of bed and went to the bathroom to wash his face, wash away the tears, but he could not wash away his sadness. He put on his school clothes and walked slowly down the stairs.

"What happened to the herd of elephants this morning?" his father joked, trying to cheer his son. The deep sadness that Freddie was feeling would not be cheered up.

His parents looked at each other not knowing what to do, all the time believing this event where the children became statues was to blame.

Freddie barely touched his breakfast and instead of going to school they went to see the doctor as his teacher had told the pupils to do.

"Hello Freddie, where's that lovely smile gone?" Doctor Snuggly asked.

Freddie looked up at him with his sad eyes, the tears glistening.

The doctor gave Freddie a thorough examination and a clean bill of health. "Freddie is alright physically, Mr and Mrs Fountain. We don't yet understand what caused the children and the adults, even the both of you, to have suffered this rigid form and then seem to be okay. The children seem to have suffered more, perhaps because they were affected for a longer time. My advice is to let Freddie be in his happy place, be that at home or with friends and let familiar things bring back his happy state of mind. Just support him and love him, hopefully this sadness will leave him very soon," the doctor explained.

When they all returned home, Freddie asked if he could go play in the forest.

His mother and father realised that it was where their son was the most happy and contented. *'Just let him be in his happy place,'* the doctor's words echoed through their minds.

Freddie did not change his clothes to be a pioneer or explorer, instead he took his rucksack, jam sandwiches, drink and chocolate bar and disappeared into the depths of his beloved forest. Of course he headed straight to the big old oak tree, but before he reached it a familiar grunting came from a nearby bush and he walked over to it. Out came the piglet boar, a little bigger in size now but still grateful to Freddie. The boar sidled up to him and rubbed against his leg.

For the first time since yesterday Freddie smiled. "Hello old friend, how are you?" he said rubbing the boar's head as it grunted with the pleasure of his touch. It trotted off and looked back with another familiar grunt as if to say "goodbye" and disappeared into the undergrowth. Freddie realised he felt just a little less sad.

"Kindness reaps its own reward," his grandma used to tell him, now he understood a little more what she meant.

When Freddie reached the big old oak tree, Wiggly was sitting down leaning against it. "Wiggly!" Freddie called and rushed to meet his friend.

Wiggly jumped to his feet just as Freddie reached him.

They hugged like they had not seen each other for weeks and weeks.

"How come you're sitting here?" Freddie asked.

"Waiting for you," Wiggly replied.

"But how did you know I was going to come here this morning?" Freddie asked.

"I knew you would, I don't know how, but I feel in some way connected with you. Maybe it was Grundly and his magic, I don't really know. But I know you feel sad and had nightmares," Wiggly admitted.

"How could you know that?" Freddie looked puzzled.

"I saw you in my dreams after I had my nightmares," Wiggly replied.

"I can't get what happened yesterday out of my mind, I've never seen anyone, well, you know, die before," Freddie said and felt sad again.

"Don't be sad, Freddie, something wonderful is about to happen, but be ready to expect a warm welcome when we go down to the town," Wiggly warned.

They scurried down the spiral staircase and when Wiggly said the magic words, the door opened at the bottom. Just about every Elfin in the town was waiting there to greet him and Freddie. They closed the door and just looked at the sea of happy Elfin faces.

Suddenly, two adults grabbed Freddie and Wiggly and lifted them on their shoulders.

"Hip, hip! Hoorah!" was cried out, "Hip, hip! Hoorah!" The Elfins cheered the two boys and a smile began to creep on Freddie's face.

"What's all this about, Wiggly?"

"You'll see," Wiggly replied, "just be patient."

The Elfins carried the two friends towards the park and Freddie spotted something he had not seen before, three large obelisks. The Elfins carrying the boys placed them down close to the obelisks then stood back in a semicircle. Freddie noticed that the obelisks were covered in large white sheets and wondered what was going on.

The Town Elder stepped forward and the boys turned to look at him with their backs to the obelisks. "Freddie and Wiggly," Mr Bumble began, "this Town and this world owe you a debt we can never, ever hope to repay. You saved every Elfin here and all the Sproggles in the entire world, you saved the planet." He moved towards the two friends and put his arms over their shoulders and turned them around to face the obelisks. "To commemorate the courage and bravery of you young boys, we unveil these likenesses."

He waved his hand, then two Elfins pulled away the sheets on the outer obelisks.

Freddie looked and gasped.

Wiggly looked on wide-eyed.

Stood up on stone pedestals were statues of them both and a plaque below stating,

'The world was saved by Freddie Fountain and Wiggly Tiggly. They found and fought the Morphlins'

All the gathered Elfins cheered and clapped their hands in appreciation of the danger the two friends had faced to save them all.

Freddie and Wiggly did not know what to say, they were so amazed and surprised at everyone's kindness and generosity.

The Elder spoke again. "We also celebrate the greatest Elfin of all time, Grundly, apprentice to the Wizard Merlin." The last obelisk was revealed, with a majestic looking Grundly holding his magical staff. Below his statue the plaque read,

'Grundly gave the last of his magic and life force to protect the world from the evil of the Morphlins'

Again the crowd cheered, both Freddie and Wiggly clapped their hands and smiled as tears rolled down their cheeks.

Suddenly Freddie felt that deep sadness sweep over him again.

The Town Elder made another announcement. "Now that Freddie is among us we will hold the NuElfin Ceremony at 2pm in the Cave of Eternity."

More applause and cheers from the crowd who were loud and happy. Then they all moved towards Freddie and Wiggly to shake their hands and pat them on the back before slowly dispersing.

Freddie's tears dried up and he realised he was smiling again, so many wonderful things were said to him and Wiggly and he felt uplifted and so happy being with the Elfins. "Wiggly, what is the NuElfin Ceremony and the Cave of Eternity?" he whispered.

"It's something so wonderful, Freddie, you'll be so full of joy and happiness when you experience it," Wiggly smiled, leaving Freddie's curiosity unfulfilled.

Wiggly's parents and Giggly stood with them looking at the statues after everyone left.

"You look so handsome, Freddie!" Giggly said looking admiringly at the statue and then at Freddie.

Freddie's attention was on the statue of Grundly and he felt that sadness again. Grundly had been so nice, thoughtful, generous and his friend, now he was gone and Freddie's heart hurt.

"Cheer up, Freddie," Daddly said putting his arm around his shoulder, "Grundly may have gone but it's not the end of his story."

Freddie looked up at Daddly. "What do you mean?"

Daddly smiled knowingly. "You will find all the answers at 2pm, for now let's go home and have a celebration lunch."

Freddie shared his packed lunch with Wiggly and family while Mummly had put together a lovely spread of nice things to eat and drink and they all ate too much. They had time for a quiet time in comfy chairs before the afternoon meeting that Freddie was so curious about. At ten minutes to two o'clock the Tiggly's and Freddie made their way to the Cave of Eternity where they met up with the rest of the town.

"Where's the cave, Wiggly? I only see a solid wall," he asked as they were ushered to the front where he saw Grundly's body laid out on a wooden plinth. When Freddie saw Grundly he began to feel sad again and tears rolled down from his eyes.

"Don't be sad, Freddie, something wonderful is about to happen," Wiggly comforted.

The Town Elder appeared and placed his hand on the wall in front of Grundly's body. The Elder recited the magic words, "Nepo Otsu Sith Rood," and the face of the wall began to disappear, leaving a wide cave entrance.

Four Elfins lifted and carried Grundly into the cave and everyone followed.

"This is it, Freddie, be prepared to be amazed," Wiggly beamed.

Deep inside the cave Freddie could see a strange blue light shimmering on the walls. The procession carrying the body of Grundly walked straight on, and then made a left turn. There it was, the source of the blue light, some kind of rectangular alter about the size of a grown Elfin, stood on a shiny floor. Above it a ribbon of blue light danced on its surface.

"What is this place, Daddly?" Freddie asked.

"This is the Cave of Eternity. It was created by Merlin so that his Elfins would never perish, as you will soon see."

Everyone gathered around the alter. Freddie, Wiggly and family were ushered to the front while two Elfins blew on instruments that looked like a trumpet bent at a right angle. The tune was slow and melodic and it made Freddie feel a little sleepy. "That's so relaxing," he said to Wiggly.

"Watch this next part closely, Freddie, you won't believe what you are seeing," his friend replied excitedly.

The blue light vanished and Grundly's body was placed on the alter, he looked so thin laid out on the smooth stone slab, then the fanfare began. The blue ribbon of light appeared again and danced on Grundly's body, getting brighter and brighter.

The Elfins began singing a beautiful song and Freddie felt his sadness drifting away. When they finished, the blue light became so bright everyone had to shield their eyes. Then there was another fanfare and the blue light vanished again and the music stopped.

Freddie thought he was hearing things when everything went quiet. '*That sounds like a baby crying,*' he thought to himself and got quite a shock when he opened his eyes.

The cave resounded with cheers and applause. Where Grundly's body had once lain, a wriggling baby Elfin could now be clearly seen. The town Elder approached the alter and picked up the baby Elfin.

Freddie smiled and felt a strange happiness flow through his whole body.

"Who lays claim to this infant?" the Elder asked, and a young couple who Freddie knew and had often chatted with came forward. They took the baby from the Town Elder, who asked, "What name shall this child be given?"

The two Elfin's looked at each other, then to Freddie and Wiggly. "We bestow the names Grundly Freddie Wiggly Lafferly upon this reborn in our Cave of Eternity," they spoke as one.

The crowd cheered and applauded again as the couple, with their baby, approached the two friends.

"Your names and your deeds this day will never be forgotten, Freddie and Wiggly. Grundly lives on here in this new born," Verity said to the boys and handed Freddie the baby.

"Ha ha, he's laughing," Freddie giggled, then the newborn gripped Freddie's finger and something very special happened. Closing his eyes for a moment, an image of Grundly appeared to Freddie.

'*Do not cry or mourn for me, Freddie, here I live on once more. Be happy again for you are much more special than you know.*' It was Grundly's voice talking to Freddie in his mind.

When the image faded Freddie opened his eyes and he smiled at baby Grundly Freddie Wiggly Lafferly. Freddie passed him back to his new mother who gave him to Wiggly, who chuckled and giggled until baby Grundly held onto his finger.

Then Wiggly closed his eyes and a vision of Grundly appeared in his mind. '*You are more special than you know, you have been blessed by Merlin and will do many important things in the future. Look after your precious friend, Freddie.*' The image vanished, Wiggly opened his eyes and gasped. Baby Grundly wriggled and chuckled and Wiggly handed him back to his parents.

The Town Elder led the townsfolk from the cave, which vanished behind them until it was again needed. There was a huge party for everyone in the town square, music was played and people were singing. The mood was very high spirited and happy.

Freddie got carried along with the merriment and was once more the happy boy again. When he got the chance, he asked Wiggly how this was possible.

"Merlin wanted to make sure his Elfins were still around when he returns. He knew it would be a long time in the future so he enchanted Elfins with a long life of hundreds of years. He also built in a failsafe. Even though Elfins have babies, it is not very often, so when an Elfin's life force leaves them they will be reborn as a baby. That way Elfins will never become extinct," Wiggly replied with a big grin.

"When baby Grundly held my finger I had a vision of old Grundly and he talked to me, told me not to be sad," Freddie explained.

"Me too, he told me to look after you," Wiggly laughed. "I think he got that the wrong way round!"

The boys laughed so hard they got hiccups and that made them laugh even more.

**

248

Freddie said his goodbyes to everyone. He really felt at home among the Elfins, they felt so much love for him and he loved them all too. Back in his forest he skipped along feeling really happy again. Two rabbits with three small baby bunnies hopped onto the path and stopped to look at him. He approached them slowly and bent down to look at them and they were not in a hurry to hop away.

"Hello Mr and Mrs Bunny, how lovely to see you and your little ones," he said in a quiet voice.

The baby rabbits hopped to him quite boldly and let him stroke them, then they hopped back to their parents.

"Bye, bye then my little friends," he said softly and the family began to hop away.

The bigger rabbit at the front stopped and looked back and Freddie could swear he heard a voice in his mind say, *'Goodbye and thank you Freddie.'*

By the time he got home he was so excited. He rushed into the kitchen through the back door, his parents were sat at the table looking worried. "Mum, Dad, I think the animals are talking to me, I just saw some baby rabbits and I'm certain I heard daddy rabbit say, 'goodbye Freddie.'"

Freddie's parents both stood up and rushed to him, giving him hugs and kisses.

"Looks like our happy son has come home to us!" Freddie's father said to a smiling wife and mother.

"I'm so relieved," Freddie's mother replied.

Even though Freddie had to keep the Elfins and other things secret, he chatted with his mother and father for a long time that night and when he finally went to bed he had sweet dreams and slept really well.

"Good night, Freddie," Wiggly said when he went to bed.

"Good night, Wiggly," Freddie said before he fell asleep.

CHAPTER SIX

Nightmares and the Dream Snatchers

*Freddie is caught by a clever magical trap that puts
all the Elfin and Sproggle children in danger.
Can Freddie and Wiggly save everyone again?*

Freddie woke up very early, even before his parents were awake and was very excited. He rushed into the bathroom and made himself comfortable, then washed his hands and face, then tiptoed downstairs. "No elephants this morning," he whispered, to no one in particular, quietly giggled. His first stop was to look at the calendar that hung on the wall near the kitchen door. There it was, a big red circle around today's date declaring, 'Freddie's Birthday.' He rubbed his hands together excitedly. "I wonder what presents I will get for my birthday?" he said to himself. His tummy growled and he suddenly felt a little hungry, so grabbed himself a cereal bowl and the box of 'Mega Monkey Nuts,' then poured them into his bowl. He tiptoed to the fridge and took the carton of milk to pour over his cereals and began scooping them up with a spoon.

His parents had arranged a party for him in the afternoon with a real magician and Freddie was very excited about that, of course he thought the Magician would be real, just like Merlin.

His mother sauntered into the kitchen with her dressing gown wrapped around her. "Goodness Freddie, you gave me a shock! You're up and about early," she said smiling at her son's milky lips.

Freddie looked at his mother with a puzzled expression. *'Has she forgotten what day it is?'* he thought to himself. "Aw, Mu-um!" he replied.

"Oh yes, it's Saturday, I thought for one moment you were up early for school," she teased.

Freddie looked down at his cereal bowl, looking glum, *'Mum has forgotten'*, he thought.

250

"Only teasing, Freddie. Happy birthday, son!" she chuckled and came to give her growing up fast son a hug. "I can't believe my little boy is 11 years old already, you've grown up so fast, Freddie," she told him. "Your father will be down in a minute, I think there might be a special delivery too."

Freddie did not know why he was so excited about this birthday, there was nothing that he really wanted, except a model kit maybe. Perhaps it was the thought of the party or the Magician or just seeing all his friends, he could not make up his mind.

When his father came down the stairs he was carrying a huge black bag filled with lots of things. "Happy birthday, son!" His father greeted Freddie with a very big smile on his face. "I think all this stuff has your name on it," he added.

Freddie's face lit up. "For me, all that? Wow, whoopee!" he cried and rushed to his father.

"Let me put this on the floor then you can have a rummage," his father said laughing at his son's excitement.

Once the huge bag was on the floor his parents gathered around him to watch him unwrap the presents. There was one very large, odd shaped object wrapped in paper with different aeroplanes printed all over it. Freddie lifted it out carefully. Once he pulled it all the way out of the black bag he got very excited indeed and looked back and forth to his mother and father. He looked at the gift label, 'Happy Birthday, Love from Mum and Dad'. Freddie realised what it was from the shape, so he unwrapped it carefully, his fingers were trembling as he peeled the tape off the paper. "I like this paper, I'll try not to tear it," his voice was trembling, just like his fingers.

His mother folded the paper as her son removed it from the present.

Then Freddie just stared at the maroon coloured fabric case in awe. His little fingers were shaking as he began to unzip it and lift the flap open. "Oooh, Mum and Dad this is really nice, thank you so much, I never expected I would get one of these." Freddie lifted it out of the case and placed it on the table, then hugged his mother and father who were so happy that their son liked the gift. Freddie sat back down and put his shiny new gift on his knee and strummed across the strings. "This sounds so lovely," and Freddie picked out some chords to play on his new guitar.

"This is the guitar James recommended for you so we're glad you're happy with it, son," his father said while Freddie quietly strummed with his fingers.

"Are you going to open your other presents, Freddie?" his mother asked, smiling at his happy face.

He laughed, "Oooo, yes, I forgot. This really is so nice, Mum and Dad, thank you, I just love my guitar," Freddie replied, sliding the musical instrument back into its case and zipping it up carefully. The next gift was from Grandma Fountain. "Coo! This is a big box," Freddie remarked as his shaking hands removed the wrapping paper. "Look, there are two model kits, a Vulcan Delta Wing and Concord. Aren't they great?" Freddie's cheeks ached with all his smiles and there were still more gifts to open. Music books for his guitar, a new tee shirt and shorts from his aunt and uncle, a variety of sweets from his friends and last of all was a small box. 'Happy Birthday Freddie. Best wishes from James', the card announced. When Freddie opened the box, inside was a velvet cushion and a shiny black plectrum with the words 'Freddie Fixit' engraved in gold letters. "Look Mum and Dad, it's perfect, isn't it? I'm so lucky."

He was lucky, but it was not by accident. Everyone in the village knew Freddie because one way or another he had helped most them in some way. It made him popular and loved by all his friends, family and villagers alike.

There was a knock on the back door and Freddie's father got up and walked to it. When he opened the door, no one was there. "That's strange," he said scratching his head, turning to Freddie's mother, "I did hear a knock, didn't I?"

Both Freddie and his mother nodded and walked to the door.

"Look, there's something on the path," Freddie said.

His father stepped outside to pick up the strange looking parcel. "There's a label, here you are Freddie, it's got your name on it," his father said.

They went back inside and Freddie put the parcel on the table.

"What's it wrapped in?" Freddie's mother asked.

"Seems to be wood of some sort, like thin tree bark," Freddie's father replied, feeling the wrapping.

"What does the label say? It looks like a leaf," his mother asked.

"It is a leaf, Mum, it says 'To Freddie from W and G and ET'. Wow! It must be from outer space if it's from ET!" Freddie giggled, although he knew exactly who this was from, his friends Wiggly and Giggly, ET was Elfin Town.

"Are you going to open it then, Freddie?" His mother seemed more excited than he was.

"Oh yes," he laughed, just admiring the wrapping that was tied with string of some kind. He carefully untied the bow and the wrapping fell away from the box inside. "Oh! There's writing on the box," Freddie said. "It reads, **'Place on the floor, press the button and stand back.'**"

All three of them were intrigued, so Freddie placed the box on the floor where there was space for them to stand around and he pressed the button. For a moment nothing happened and Freddie thought it was a trick, but then a tiny puff of twinkling dust flew up and settled on the box. Again nothing happened for a moment, then the box began to jiggle and wobble, so they stood a bit further back. The box jumped up off the floor, then opened like a flower in the sunshine, creating a beautiful wooden chair and Freddie knew exactly where it had been made.

"Isn't that the most wonderful chair? I've never seen anything like it," Freddie's mother declared with surprise.

His father was looking at it suspiciously, wondering how a box had transformed into a chair. "Well I've never seen anything like it either, look, there are no nails or screws or fixings of any kind. How does it stay together?" Freddie's father exclaimed.

"Give it a try, Freddie." His mother was keen to see him sit in the chair.

Freddie reversed into the chair and it seemed to hug him somehow. "Oooh this is so comfortable!" he remarked. "Have a try, Mum."

Freddie's mother went to sit on the chair and she suddenly and surprisingly ended up on the floor.

Freddie giggled, "Mum, how could you miss the chair?"

"Let me have a try," his father said helping his wife up, then he began backing into the chair and he ended up on the floor too.

Freddie howled with laughter, "Dad, you missed it as well."

Even his mother was chuckling.

His father stood up and looked at the chair and scratched his head and made a dive at it. Again he was on the floor, this time Freddie was in tears and so was his mother.

Freddie's father stood up and rubbed his bottom.

That only made Freddie laugh even more, so he sat on the chair to show them how to do it.

His parents had a few more attempts and ended up on the floor, eventually giving up.

"I guess this is meant only for you, Freddie. I don't understand how that is possible, some kind of trick!" his father admitted. "We had better take this and your other presents upstairs, it's clearly only going to let you sit on it," his father announced while Freddie and his mother were still giggling.

Freddie carried his special chair upstairs while his mother and father carried all his other presents, including his precious new guitar. "Dad, can I go play in the forest this morning?" It was not even nine o'clock yet but Freddie wanted to see Wiggly and the other Elfins, especially to thank them for his special gift.

Freddie's father looked at his wife.

"Of course you can, Freddie," his mother replied, "but be home by one o'clock so you can get ready for your party, everyone will be arriving at two o'clock. Your father and I will start getting everything ready while you're out playing. Have you got your watch on?"

Freddie showed her his wrist and smiled before charging up the stairs. He made a place in his bedroom for his various gifts first, then put on his explorers outfit. With the hat his father had found for him and rucksack on his back, he skipped back down the stairs, through the kitchen and out into the garden, heading for the gate and his beloved forest.

There had been a thunderstorm during the night and a huge clap of thunder had woken Freddie. He sat at his window watching the lightening flashes followed by the thunder. One lightening bolt seemed to have struck the heart of the forest, it was immediately followed by the loudest thunderclap, which made Freddie jump. "Goodness!" he gasped, instinctively holding his hand on his chest. "My heart is beating so fast," he gasped again.

He watched the storm move away quickly and was wondering if the lightening might have caused a fire, because that would be a disaster. When he could see no smoke or flames after half an hour looking through his binoculars, he went back to bed and slept soundly.

The next day as Freddie walked in the forest, the ground was wet, smelling of damp wood and leaves. Here and there were little puddles and Freddie spotted a hedgehog drinking from one of them.

"Hello, Mr Hedgehog, you must be thirsty," he said softly so as not to frighten it.

The pointy little face with a twitching nose looked at him and the hedgehog squeaked and grunted, *'Hello Freddie,'* he heard in his mind.

Freddie stopped in his tracks and exclaimed quietly, "No way! Did you just say 'hello Freddie?' No way!"

The hedgehog looked at Freddie again and squeaked, *'Yes Freddie,'* then waddled off under a bush and out of sight.

"I can't believe this, that's the second animal that I've heard speak to me. Is it my imagination? Something strange is going on!" he said, to no one in particular.

He suddenly had a thought about something Grundly had said to him. **"You're more special than you realise, Freddie!"** *'Did he mean I could communicate with animals?'* he thought. "No, that's not possible, is it?" He was talking to himself when he heard Wiggly's voice.

"Freddie! Freddie!"

A big smile appeared on Freddie's face when he saw his friend just ahead of him, he was so glad to see him that he forgot all about talking animals.

"I was just coming to see you, Wiggly," Freddie announced.

"Me too!" Wiggly replied laughing. "I mean coming to see you, not coming to see me!" he laughed again. Skipping towards his friend he rushed to Freddie and hugged him tightly. "Happy Birthday, Freddie," he chuckled, "did you like your present?"

Freddie laughed out loud as soon as Wiggly let go of him and when he told Wiggly how his mother and father had ended up on the floor trying to sit on it, they both laughed so loudly until their sides hurt.

When they calmed down Wiggly jumped up and asked, "Did you hear that thunder storm last night?"

Freddie nodded. "I did, it woke me up so I sat and watched it pass over the forest."

"It woke me too," Wiggly agreed. "It woke us all up. The ground was shaking and the lightening hit a tree, shall we go take a look?"

Wiggly was already excited and his legs were running on the spot.

Freddie laughed. "Calm down, Wiggly, do you know exactly where we need to go?" he asked as they began to half run, half walk, holding hands.

"Yes, it's a little way into the forest, past the old oak tree," Wiggly gasped as they broke into a slow trot.

It took them ten minutes or so to reach the spot. When they saw exactly where the lightening had struck they were shocked. There was a big fir tree looking like something had snapped it off about a metre from the ground. The stump was all jagged and the rest of the tree lay flat on the woodland floor. Luckily the fir tree had not collided with any other trees when it had fallen. The two friends walked up to the tree stump carefully.

"That looks so dangerous, it's all jagged and splintered!" Freddie exclaimed holding his friend back a bit.

Wiggly just stared at the damaged tree. "Wow, look at it, what a mess! The council will have to come and cut this up and take it away, then re-grow the tree from the stump," he explained.

"Oh yes, a sprinkle of Fairy Dust. It's amazing to watch, just like those other trees that Billy Bates' father chopped down," Freddie replied.

They walked around and along the felled tree, its branches all smashed to pieces where it had crashed to the ground.

"Look at that big black patch, Freddie, that must be where the lightening struck. It could have caused a big fire, I think we've been very lucky," Wiggly exclaimed.

"Why do you think the lightening struck this tree and not any of the others, Wiggly?" Freddie asked, not really expecting Wiggly to know.

His friend looked at Freddie and shrugged his shoulders. "I really don't know. This is the first time anything like this has happened that I know of, but look where the lightening bolt struck, there's a bit of a hole."

They both moved closer to the burned area and sure enough there was a blackened hole.

"I think there's something inside the tree. Look, Wiggly, it's a different colour in the middle of the hole."

Wiggly looked and they both stepped between the broken branches to get closer.

Freddie took off his rucksack and fished out a torch, then shone it where the hole was on the tree trunk. "Something's reflecting the torch light," Freddie announced excitedly and Wiggly could see it as well.

They got right up to the burned area and Freddie tried to reach into the hole. "I can't reach inside, my fingers are too thick. Do you think you can reach, Wiggly?"

Wiggly could get his thin, bony hand inside the round charred hole. "I can feel something smooth and round inside, like a metal tube or something," he said excitedly and pulled his hand out. "I can't pull it out though, the hole's not big enough."

Freddie fished around in his rucksack and brought out a small axe. "Let me make the hole a bit bigger, Wiggly, stand back please," Freddie said and began chopping away at the hole. It was soon big enough for him to see the metal object inside. "See if you can pull it out now, Wiggly!" Freddie said and they changed places. "Mind the jagged edges though," he warned.

Wiggly slipped his hand inside. "Oh! I've got it, I think," he declared and pulled out a long shiny metal tube.

"That must be why the lightening bolt struck this tree then," Freddie deduced. "Is that tube thing solid or hollow, Wiggly?"

They stepped back away from the tree branches and closer to the tree stump where there was more space. The boys sat down, leaning against the tree stump.

"It's definitely not solid, Freddie, listen," Wiggly shook the round metal object, "sounds like there's something inside it," he replied.

"Is there any way to open it, maybe from one end?"

Wiggly turned the tube one way then the other. "You have a look at it, Freddie, I can't see anything obvious," Wiggly said handing the intriguing object to his friend.

Freddie examined it carefully. "Look, Wiggly, these round bumps on each end, they must open it," Freddie explained and tried pressing them one at a time, and then together to no avail and got cross, giving it back to Wiggly.

Wiggly tried pressing and got even more cross. "Stupid thing, what's it doing stuck inside the tree anyway?" he cried and threw it down on the hard ground.

The tube bounced and one end jumped off, spilling out a scroll of parchment.

"Quick, Wiggly, grab it before it blows away!" Freddie cried.

Wiggly was already on his feet chasing the scroll, grabbing it, returning to his friend and sitting down close to him. He carefully unrolled the parchment. "Look, Freddie, it has symbols all over it."

Freddie looked on, "Ooh! It looks really old, all the edges are frayed," he replied.

They sat and stared at the parchment, turning it one way and another.

"It's very faint, can you understand any of it, Freddie?"

"I think so," he replied.

"What does it say?" Wiggly was so excited, it was like finding buried treasure. But who put it there?

"Let me get my magnifying glass, Wiggly." Freddie fumbled in a side pocket of his rucksack and pulled out a large round spyglass. "That's better, I think I can read this now, so here goes,

Be good. Be Kind. Unlock that in repose. Incubus now tethered. Be free to roam."

"It doesn't make any sense to me. What's an Incubus?" Freddie asked looking at Wiggly.

But before Wiggly could answer the parchment began to glow and Freddie threw it on the ground thinking it might burst into flames. The parchment stayed flat and all the faded words began to swirl around and around until they were a single large dot on the parchment.

"Wh-what's going on?" Wiggly cried as he and Freddie shuffled away from the parchment.

"I - I - I - don't kn...." Freddie did not have a chance to finish, because the big dot on the parchment began to rise into the air, like the paint from a spray can. It grew larger and larger, leaving the parchment completely blank. The black cloud took the form of a Sproggle and spoke, the voice sounded like someone shouting in a tunnel, echoing. **"Gratitude I give to you this day, my friend."**

Then it formed a misty cloud and disappeared up into the treetops.

The two friends looked at each other, more than a little worried.

"What have we done?" Wiggly cried. "What was that?"

Freddie grabbed the empty parchment and was shaking, fearing he had released something that should have remained locked away.

"I don't know, Wiggly, I really don't, but grab that metal tube and let's go ask Daddly!"

Wiggly picked up the metal tube and Freddie rolled the parchment and slid it inside, fitting the end cover back again. Then they ran like they were being chased by a ghost, through the trees, round the bushes, pushing branches out of their way until they reached the big old oak tree. Leaning against it for a moment to catch their breath, both boys were gasping and panting from their unexpected run through the forest. Wiggly uttered the magic words when he could breathe again and then they scampered down the spiral staircase.

Freddie, following behind Wiggly, lost his footing on the last few steps and tumbled down on top of him.

"Ouch! Oh crickey, Freddie!" Wiggly cried as Freddie pressed him against the door at the bottom of the stairs.

Freddie lifted himself off his friend and pulled Wiggly back up. "Sorry Wiggly, I tripped. Are you hurt? Let me see," he asked, putting his arm around his friend.

Wiggly felt himself all over. "Nope, I think I'm okay. Let's go." He said the magic words and the door opened for them. Luckily there were not many Elfins around so they had a clear path to Wiggly's house, where they rushed inside.

"Daddly! Daddly!" Wiggly yelled.

Daddly jumped up from his comfy chair, "What is it, Wiggly, what's wrong?"

Wiggly and Freddie ran to Daddly, both wrapping their arms around him.

"Come on boys, sit down, take a deep breath and explain what has happened," Daddly said leading them both to sit in comfy chairs by the fire.

The boys explained what they had done, telling part of the story in turns.

Daddly, Mummly and Giggly were looking from one boy to the other, like spectators at a tennis match. When Freddie and Wiggly finished they puffed and blew, still breathing heavily, but partly in fear of what they might have released.

Daddly looked at the metal tube. "This is a very strange metal, it remains highly polished even though it attracted the full force of a lightening bolt. This kind of metal is something that I have not actually seen before, however, I do know what you boys have found in the tube is a Spirit Failsafe. In the days of Merlin there were many dark forces that he battled and imprisoned in tubes with magical enchantment spells on them. But many of these spirits had craftily prepared failsafe spells to release them if and when Merlin caught them. Now tell me exactly what the words actually were, can you remember?" Daddly explained and asked.

Freddie nodded and repeated the words he had read out to Wiggly.

"The failsafe is designed to trick whoever finds it into releasing the spirit, just as it did with you both. The spirit that has been released is an Incubus," Daddly confirmed.

"But what exactly is an Incubus and what will it do, Daddly?" Wiggly asked.

Daddly rubbed his chin, doubtfully. "I cannot say, I am not familiar with this spirit," he replied. "Let's go to the school and see if there are any clues in the books," he suggested.

The whole family trooped to the school where the teacher was fascinated by their story and took the whole class along to help.

"Miss, what are we looking for again?" a young Elfin asked.

"I will write it on the board for everyone. Anything that mentions this word, INCUBUS," she said as she wrote it on the board.

Everyone went to the shelves and began taking random books and looking through them for the one word, INCUBUS.

Freddie looked at his watch, it was twelve noon, he would have to leave very soon. At a quarter to one o'clock lots of books had been looked through, but no reference to an INCUBUS had been found.

"I'm really sorry everyone, I have to leave now," Freddie announced.

They all waved him goodbye.

Freddie skipped through Elfin Town, up the spiral staircase and out into the woods. He dashed home and made it just in time for one o'clock.

"There you are, Freddie, go upstairs and have a wash and put on the clothes I have laid out on your bed," his mother told him.

Freddie's eyes were popping out of his head as he looked at all the party food his parents had prepared. "Wow, Mum! This looks amazing. You and Dad have really been busy," he said excitedly and then made for the stairs. Thump! Thump! Thump! Thump!

"It's those pesky elephants, they're back again!" Freddie's father announced with a chuckle, "Freddie's home I guess," he said to himself.

The moment Freddie had seen all the party food he completely forgot about the Incubus and dashed upstairs into the bathroom to wash his hands and face, then back into his bedroom to change his clothes. He picked up his new guitar and took it from the case, picked out a tune from one of the songbooks he had been given as presents and practiced the chords with the plectrum from his friend, James.

"Freddie! Grandma has arrived, come down and say hello," his father called and Freddie put down his guitar and galloped down the stairs.

"Happy birthday my very handsome grandson," his grandma beamed, swinging her arms around him and giving Freddie a big hug. "My word you've grown so big already," she said once they parted from each other.

"Grandma," Freddie was all smiles and a little red in the face, "thank you for the model kits, they are a perfect addition to my collection," he said giving her another hug.

Not too long after his grandmother had arrived, his uncle and two cousins came bouncing through the door into the sitting room.

"Freddie!" the boys called, sandwiching him between them and giggling. "Happy birthday!"

Freddie's friends started to arrive. Jimmy was first, quickly followed by William and Joanne, in fact everyone in his school class, because one way or another Freddie Fixit had helped them all and were his friends. Freddie's parents had invited James, too, and Freddie ran to him and gave him a hug, he held quite a special place in Freddie's heart.

"Happy birthday, Freddie. Did you like your guitar?" James asked.

"It's really nice, James, it sounds wonderful and thank you for the plectrum, that's really special," he replied.

"I'm glad you liked it, Freddie, you're doing so well now, you don't need me to teach you."

Freddie looked surprised. "But I like it when we play together, James, can we still practice together, please?" Freddie pleaded.

James laughed. "How can I refuse you, Freddie? Of course, if you want we can still practice together. Actually, I like it too, so I'm happy you want to continue."

The Fountain family's house was buzzing with children's laughter and gaiety. Freddie was so excited, the scroll and Incubus were far from his thoughts. Freddie's mother ushered everyone into the front room and got all the children seated on the floor ready for the Magician to appear.

* *

Meanwhile in Elfin Town, Wiggly and friends were still looking through all the schoolbooks, but eventually there were no more left to look through.

"I can't understand it!" Wiggly gasped in exasperation. "There is not one mention of an Incubus!"

Daddly gathered his children and wife together ready to leave. "Miss Noall, we are really very grateful to you and your class for all your help." Daddly thanked the teacher and all the children.

Miss Noall smiled and replied, "Oh, it's no trouble and I'm sure the children have enjoyed rooting through the books, it's a shame we didn't find what you needed. At least all the books are now neatly stored on the shelves for the first time in a long while."

Daddly and family made their way back home. Wiggly felt very concerned because they had no idea what they had released and what it could do. Whatever it was, he feared it would not be good. They were all a little disappointed as they walked through the front door and went to sit down in comfy chairs.

"I'll make us all a nice cup of dandelion tea," Mummly said trying to lighten the mood.

"I don't think there is any more we can do about this for now," Daddly said eventually. "I will ask around to see if anyone has books at home with a reference to the Incubus."

They sat quietly contemplating while sipping their tea, not really knowing what to say.

"Cheer up, Wiggly, there has to be an answer to this somewhere," Giggly said, hugging her brother trying to cheer him up just a little bit.

Tea break over, Daddly patted his son gently and smiled. "Come along, young Wiggly, guide us to the tree that was struck by a lightening bolt, then we can clear the area and restore the lovely tree." Daddly called on the Town Elders who brought saws, axes, large bags and fold-up wooden trolleys with them, then he collected his jar of Fairy Dust and they set off.

Wiggly guided the Elfins to the exact spot and everyone got to work, sawing, chopping, sweeping and bagging up pine needles.

The trolleys were unfolded and loaded with logs, then transported to the old oak tree where a chain gang of Elfins on the spiral staircase handed logs from one to another and carried them to a big pile away from the bottom door.

Back at the fallen tree site, Daddly sprinkled a small pinch of Fairy Dust on the jagged tree stump and everyone watched it slowly re-grow into the magnificent fir tree it had once been.

Wiggly watched with such excitement and for just a little while he stopped thinking about the Incubus.

The fallen tree trunk was quickly cut up and carted away, branches were cut into smaller lengths and bagged up. The pine needles were bagged and then sprinkled around the forest as a natural fertilizer. The Elfins swept the area clean and sprinkled a few pine needles about until it looked like nothing had ever happened. The forest was restored and now it would not attract any unwanted Sproggle attention.

Wiggly brought up the rear with Giggly and they swept the forest floor with a leafy branch to hide their tracks all the way back to the big old oak tree and home.

* *

At Freddie Fountain's house the children were all sitting on the floor busily chatting away to each other and giggling, when a small flash of light and puff of smoke caused instant silence in the room. When the smoke cleared, there stood the magician in a black suit and cape, top hat and magic wand in his white-gloved hand.

The audience clapped and cheered with excitement and anticipation.

"Greetings children, mums and dads, I am Alphonso the Great. Now! I wonder if anyone knows what you call a sleeping dinosaur?" he asked with a cheeky smile.

The children looked at each other and shrugged their shoulders.

"Okay, okay, you've twisted my arm, I'll tell you. A sleeping dinosaur is called a DINO-SNORE, get it, a Dino-snore."

Jimmy giggled loudly thinking it was very funny, then everyone laughed and clapped their hands.

"Now can I have Freddie the birthday boy come stand with me?" Alphonso the Great asked and Freddie jumped up excitedly, looking a little shy and red in the face, but he was smiling and the children gave him a round of applause.

"Now Freddie, I have a rubber pencil here," Alphonso the Great told him and held out an ordinary looking pencil in two of his fingers. He handed the pencil to Freddie. "Does it feel rubbery or bendy to you, Freddie?" the magician asked.

Freddie took the pencil, held it, squeezed it and tried to bend it, then shook his head. "No sir, it's hard like a normal pencil," he replied looking a little nervous.

"Oh!" exclaimed Alphonso the Great, "let me have a look, maybe I've given you the wrong pencil. Silly me!"

The audience all laughed at Alphonso saying 'silly me'.

The magician took the pencil from Freddie, who looked at Jimmy and shrugged his shoulders. Then Alphonso held the end of the pencil between his finger and thumb, wiggling it from side to side and sure enough the pencil seemed to flop about just as if it was made of bendy rubber.

The children and adults all clapped their hands and cheered with delight.

When the magician gave the pencil back to Freddie, he said, with a little smile on his face, "Here, try again, Freddie, it definitely seems to be bendy." He turned to his audience and said, "It did look bendy, didn't it children?"

The boys, girls and parents laughed and called out, completely enthralled by this clever Magician.

When Freddie took the pencil he could not make it bend like it was made of rubber, no matter how he tried.

The boys and girls all cheered and laughed and clapped their hands, even Freddie clapped and laughed after he returned the pencil.

"Oh, Freddie!" Alphonso the Great suddenly said and everyone went quiet, "I think you have something behind your ear!" he exclaimed and reached out to Freddie's left ear and pulled out a playing card, King of Hearts.

The children were fascinated and laughed excitedly at the magician's antics.

Alphonso the Great let Freddie sit down and called Jimmy to assist him. "Jimmy, do you know how oceans say hello to each other?" Alphonso the Great asked him.

Jimmy scratched his head and shook it, "No sir."

The magician chuckled and replied, "Well they WAVE of course!" and the children roared with laughter. "Okay, okay," he said, "now I'm going to perform a clever magic trick." He took off his top hat and put it upside down on the little table in front of him and asked Jimmy, "Have a look inside my hat, Jimmy, what do you see?"

Jimmy bent over the magician's top hat and looked inside, then back at the magician. "Nothing sir, I can't see anything inside your hat, it's completely empty," he replied.

"Excellent Jimmy. Now in my pocket here I have my magic wand," Alphonso the Great said and pulled out a long black stick with white ends. "When I tap the hat can you say the magic word, Abracadabra, Jimmy?"

Jimmy's face lit up and he had a big smile on his face. "Yes, sir!" he replied.

"Okay then, I will tap three times and then you say the magic word," the magician explained and tapped the hat.

Jimmy was so excited and said, quite loudly, "Abracadabra Jimmy!"

James and the adults laughed because Jimmy was only supposed to say Abracadabra.

"Sorry, Jimmy, you just need to say Abracadabra, okay Jimmy?"

Jimmy nodded and smiled as his face turned red.

The magician tapped the hat three times again.

Jimmy took a deep breath and cried out, "Abracadabra okay Jimmy!"

This time everyone burst into laughter, including the magician, but poor Jimmy looked mortified.

"Jimmy, we're getting a bit confused here, let me explain. When I tap the hat you say the word Abracadabra." The magician was nodding.

"Oh I see," Jimmy replied, feeling a little silly and turning even brighter red.

The magician tapped the hat three times and looked at Jimmy with a nod of his head.

"Abracadabra!" Jimmy cried out.

The audience were so quiet, but then erupted in applause when a cute little mouse crawled up from inside the top hat and sat on the rim.

"Thank you, Jimmy, you can go sit down now. Freddie, can you come up again, please?"

Jimmy was bright red in the face but smiling as he returned to sit down on the floor.

Freddie was also beaming as he came out to the front as Jimmy sat down again.

"Are you enjoying your birthday, Freddie?" the magician asked.

"Oh, yes sir, it's the best birthday ever," he said enthusiastically.

"Which present was the biggest surprise?" Alphonso the Great asked.

"Oh! That would be the super guitar that my parents gave me which James picked out, thank you James, Mum and Dad!" he called out.

The magician picked up the mouse and talked to it, then put it in his top pocket. "As a special treat, would you like to have a go with my magic wand, Freddie?" the magician asked.

Freddie's eyes lit up and he was so excited. "Oh, I would, sir, yes please," he replied.

"That's wonderful. When I give you the wand, just tap it on the hat three times and say the magic word, Abracadabra, okay?"

Freddie nodded excitedly with a big grin on his face and looked over at his parents.

Alphonso the Great handed his wand to Freddie who was all smiles with excitement. Even though he had his magic rucksack this was still very thrilling and, of course, he believed it was real magic.

Freddie reached out and took the wand. "Oh! Oh!" He cried out in surprise as the wand wilted like a dying flower.

"What's happened, Freddie?" The magician teased.

"I - I - I - don't know sir, it just bent over," Freddie replied wiggling the wand about.

All the children and adults were laughing and clapping thinking it was so funny to watch.

Poor Freddie was horrified thinking he had broken the magician's wand.

"Freddie Fixit!" Jimmy called out.

"Oh, I can fix it with some dinosaur glue sir," Freddie said quite worried.

"Let me have a little look at it, Freddie," Alphonso the Great said and took the wand from him. When Freddie let go of the wand it magically became stiff again in the magician's hand. "There, that's fixed it!" he said.

Once more the children clapped and cheered.

"Have another go, Freddie, it seems alright now, look," and the magician tapped the hat once.

Freddie reached out a little nervously and took hold of the wand, but as soon as the magician let go the wand drooped like it was made of rubber.

Everyone was laughing and cheering except poor Freddie, who looked completely mystified.

"Never mind, Freddie, I think, maybe, it only works for me," Alphonso the Great said kindly.

Freddie thought about that and how Grundly's staff only worked for him. He smiled and the magician let him sit down with his friends again.

Alphonso the Great entertained the children and adults for almost an hour, everyone was captivated with his magic tricks. "For my final piece of magic I have this small ball here." He showed everyone an apple sized, shiny white ball that he put on the small round table. "This, children, is my magic cape," he said twirling it off his shoulders to cover the ball with, which was on the small round table. "Now children, I want you to say the magic words for me, 'Izzy Fizzy Up and Bizzy', can you do that?" There were a lot of nods and calls of, "Yes."

"That's wonderful. I will count to three, then all of you say the magic words together." The magician took hold of the two corners of the cape nearest him, then looked at the children. "Ready? One, two, three!"

The children all called out, "IZZY, FIZZY UP AND BIZZY." Then the room fell silent until the ball under the cape began to rise. "Oooo," everyone called in amazement.

The ball lifted the cape up off the table and moved from side to side under it, then to everyone's surprise the ball appeared on the top edge of the cape and moved from side to side, then back under, doing all kinds of tricks, finally resting down on the table again. The magician took the cape away, twirled it around his shoulders and then held the ball in his hand as everyone erupted in cheers and applause. There was lots of laughter and Alphonso the Great thanked the children for being such a great audience.

"One last thing," Alphonso the Great said, "let's have three cheers for the birthday boy, Freddie. Hip! Hip!"

The children cried out, "Hurrah!"

"Hip! Hip!"

"Hurrah!"

"Hip! Hip!"

"Hurrah!" They clapped and laughed and Freddie was bright red in the face but laughing too.

Freddie's mother and father thanked Alphonso the Great and the children all cheered him too, then they were invited into the dining room for the party food. There was the expected rush while Freddie hung back to speak to Alphonso the Great. "Is this real magic, like the Wizard Merlin, Mr Alphonso?" he asked.

The magician smiled. "I can see you're a clever lad, look again at my wand."

Freddie took the wand from his hand, it immediately drooped. "Oh! It's happened again!" Freddie said disappointedly.

"Now hold it at the other end, Freddie."

When Freddie held the wand at the opposite end it was again solid. "Oh, it's a trick!" Freddie cried.

"Sssh!" the magician replied. "Let's keep that a secret between you and me," he smiled and winked.

Freddie went into the crowded dining room and everyone cheered for him to blow out the candles on his cake that Mrs Bakewell had baked and decorated in the shape of a guitar. After Freddie made his wish and blew out the candles in one puff, his mother cut the cake up into slices and put them on napkins to hand out to everyone.

Children drifted off with platefuls of party food and cake to find somewhere to sit down and enjoy it. For a short while only the chomping of food could be heard with the occasional laugh as someone dropped a pickled onion and rummaged around for it.

When everyone had finished eating and drinking fizzy lemonade and all the mess was cleared away, Freddie's parents ushered everyone into the front room again, then Freddie and James played some tunes on their guitars. They had been practicing together for a while and played Freddie's favourite song 'All Things Bright and Beautiful'. Then they played a couple more tunes before James played a solo piece that Freddie loved too. Everyone clapped their hands and cheered after the two boys finished playing.

Freddie's grandma was very impressed and gave them both a cuddle. "Thank you, James, for teaching Freddie. You both play so beautifully," she praised.

Then Freddie's uncle came and patted Freddie on the back, congratulating them both.

"Thank you, James, for everything," Freddie said a little later.

"I like teaching you, Freddie, you're a quick learner, you have a natural gift, you'll soon be better than me," James replied.

Freddie chuckled, he did not see that was possible, but he would like to be as good as James.

It was a happy time for everyone that afternoon.

"Best party ever!" Jimmy had told Mrs Fountain.

But little did they all know it could be the last party in the village for a very, very long time.

Freddie's Grandma was going to stay the night and when all the other party guests had gone home she asked Freddie if he would play his guitar for her. Although James was still teaching him and the pads on his fingers had not yet completely thickened, there was no stopping him. Freddie played a couple of tunes he had been practicing on his own and his grandma and parents clapped their hands in appreciation.

That night Freddie had very pleasant dreams and slept so well his mother had to wake him up in the morning. After breakfast they all went on a car trip to the seaside and Freddie was having so much fun he completely forgot about the tree struck by lightening, the scroll and the Incubus.

When they finally returned home after stopping at a hamburger restaurant, then dropping grandma off at her home, Freddie was completely exhausted, it had been a busy couple of days. His mother made them all a mug of warm cocoa then Freddie dragged himself upstairs, crawled in the shower, cleaned his teeth and slipped into bed, falling to sleep as soon as his head rested on the pillow.

At school the next morning before the lesson began, Jimmy was laid on his arms snoozing.

"Jimmy, Jimmy," Freddie whispered, nudging his friend to wake up.

"Uh! What! I'm up Mum!" he replied groggily.

Freddie giggled. "Jimmy, why are you so tired?" he whispered.

Jimmy looked at his friend. "Didn't sleep too well last night. I was having a lovely dream when it suddenly turned into a nightmare. It was so real, Freddie, a huge spider was crawling on my bed, with fangs snapping and all its eyes watching me. It was going to eat me, it was so real, I woke and cried out. Then every time I tried to sleep the spider came back. My Mum held me most of the night, but I couldn't stop the nightmares returning."

Freddie realised that poor Jimmy was actually very tired and at morning break time he slept with his head on the picnic table in the playground.

Day after day, more and more of the children in Freddie's class also had terrible nightmares, making them afraid to sleep and then they were too tired to stay awake in their lessons. By Friday only half the children turned up for school and those that did manage spent the day snoozing in short bursts, on their desks.

When Freddie looked at his friends they were very pale in the face and big dark bags appeared under their eyes. Jimmy was a bit more awake during the lunch break.

"Do you have the same nightmare over and over, night after night?" Freddie asked very concerned about his friend.

"Yes, this giant spider crawls up on my bed and I wake up crying and shaking and dare not go back to sleep," Jimmy replied.

William was nodding and explained, "In my nightmare Bully Bates is taunting me and hitting me, then I wake up afraid to go back to sleep. My Mum stays with me but as soon as I drop off the nightmare returns."

"I have nightmares too!" Joanne said. "I fall off a cliff and I'm screaming, but I never seem to land and then I wake up. My Mum takes me to sleep with her and Dad, but it's the same as William, as soon as I close my eyes the nightmare begins again."

"What about you, Anne?" Freddie asked.

"Oh, my dreams are filled with me running through the forest being chased by a ghostly black shape with bright shiny eyes, shouting that it wants to eat me. It's horrible, so horrible," she replied almost in tears.

"Freddie," Jimmy asked, "don't you have any nightmares then?"

Freddie shook his head. "No, I haven't had any bad dreams for a long time. That's very strange, I wonder why everyone in the class is having nightmares and not me?" he replied.

"Maybe it's because you're 11 while we are all still 10 years old," Anne suggested.

"That's true, Anne, but isn't Alex 11 as well and he didn't come to school today," Joanne offered.

"Joanne, how is your brother, James, is he having nightmares too?" Freddie asked.

"He's already 12 years old now and come to think of it he is having nightmares as well," she replied.

"Have any of your parents had nightmares?" William asked and everyone shook their heads. "So it seems it's just about everyone in the school, except Freddie," he concluded.

At home after school finished, Freddie sat on his special chair, the one only he could sit in, absently stroking his fingers across the strings of his guitar, deep in thought. "Is it just a coincidence that children are having nightmares after Wiggly and I released the Incubus Spirit?" he said quietly to himself. "We don't even know what an Incubus is, what it can do and why it had been imprisoned in the first place. I have to go see Wiggly tomorrow," he said, to no one in particular.

Freddie was up and about early on Saturday morning. He washed and dressed then tiptoed downstairs, careful not to sound like a herd of elephants, as his father would say. He opened the door into the kitchen slowly as it had a habit of squeaking and he did not want to disturb his parents who were having a well earned lie-in. Freddie jumped and cried out loudly when he saw someone standing by the table.

"Freddie, son!" his mother cried, jumping and turning to see him at the door.

"Aw, Mum! You scared me, I thought you were still in bed," he gasped, his heart still racing.

271

His mother laughed, "Well you nearly gave me a heart attack too, Freddie, creeping about like that!" she chuckled. "I suppose you've tied the elephants to your bed."

"Aww, Mum," He protested, then rushed to his mother and put his arms around her. "Sorry Mum, I was trying to be quiet, leaving the elephants in my bedroom this morning!" he declared and they both laughed.

"Go sit down and I'll make you some breakfast. Scrambled egg on toast do for you?"

Freddie beamed. "Yes please, Mum, I'd really like that. Can I help?" he replied.

"You can put the bread in the toaster, two slices for you and two for me," his mother answered.

They sat with orange juice and their scrambled egg on toast, chatting about what was happening at school.

"Everyone except me is having sleepless nights because of bad dreams, Mum," Freddie explained.

"I wonder if it's because our house is the last in the village?" his mother suggested.

"I never thought of that. My friend thought it might be because I was 11 already and they are mostly still 10, but James is having nightmares and he's 12," Freddie explained.

When they had finished their lovely breakfast, his mother hunted out the map of Elfington Village and opened it out on the table. They put little red sticky dots on the houses of Freddie's school friends.

"There, look Freddie, our house is here, look where all the red dots are," his mother said. "Just a minute," she stood up and reached into a cupboard and brought out some glass plates and placed one over the red dots. "There!" she said with satisfaction. "All the red dots fit inside the plate, but I'm really not sure what that means," his mother admitted.

Freddie's mother packed him his jam sandwiches, drink, apple and wafer bar, then he set off to explore his beloved forest in his explorers outfit.

"Be home by 4 o'clock. Have you got your watch on?" his mother asked.

Freddie showed her he was wearing his watch. He quickly lifted his rucksack onto his shoulders and marched through the kitchen door, down the garden path and through the gate and disappeared among the trees and bushes. Freddie was keen to see Wiggly and his family to tell them what was happening in his school. Skipping through the forest he made a circular route to the big old oak tree. That was just in case a forest visitor could follow an obvious track, right to the Elfin Town entrance. When he reached the big old oak tree he looked around, then stepped into the enchanted area around it and both he and the tree vanished to Sproggle eyes. He spoke the magic words, "Efum, Efum, Natum, Efum" and watched the door appear and open, then he hopped through it and almost tumbled down the spiral staircase he was in so much of a hurry. He could not help chuckling to himself as his footsteps sounded quite loud. "It really does sound like a herd of elephants," he laughed.

When he opened the door into Elfin Town he was surprised to see it so quiet, all the shops were closed and no one was around. "Is everyone having a lie-in this morning?" he said, to no one in particular.

The whole town had an eerie feel, like a ghost town and it made him feel uncomfortable. When he finally reached the Tiggly house he stood and shuddered before knocking on the door. A very sleepy looking Mummly answered and invited Freddie inside. Wiggly and Giggly were laid together on the comfy sofa with their eyes closed and Daddly was sat in his comfy chair with his eyes closed too.

"What's happening, Mummly, why's the town so quiet, why are Wiggly and Giggly sleepy and Daddly, too?" Freddie asked in a low voice, feeling nervous.

"It's the children, Freddie, they've had bad dreams all week, they're exhausted and so are Daddly and me," she replied.

"Oh, not the Elfins as well!" Freddie cried then held his hand over his mouth.

"What do you mean, Freddie?" Mummly asked and yawned.

"All the children in Elfington Village have been having nightmares too, except me," he explained.

"Freddie!" A happy voice cried as Wiggly stood up and sauntered over to him.

"Oh Freddie, it's good to see you, isn't it, Mummly?" Wiggly chirped, sleepily flinging his arms around his best friend. Wiggly took Freddie to the seating area, where they and Mummly settled down in comfy chairs.

273

"Did you find anything out about the Incubus?" Freddie asked hopefully.

For a moment there was silence, then Daddly and Giggly opened their sleepy eyes.

"Freddie, so glad you're here," Daddly said.

"Freddie was asking if we had discovered any information about the Incubus, Daddly," Mummly said.

"I'm sorry, Freddie, we have visited every home, opened every dusty box and book, looked in every hidey hole and asked everyone. The Incubus remains a mystery, no information has been unveiled by word of mouth or by pages in a book, I'm sorry." Daddly looked tired and defeated.

"That's too bad, Daddly. Do you think the Incubus is responsible for all the bad dreams?" Freddie asked.

Daddly rubbed his chin and replied, "I think it's too much of a coincidence that the Incubus is released then Sproggle and Elfin children begin having bad dreams."

"If that is the case," Freddie began, "it might explain why I have not had bad dreams. I remember the Spirit saying something like 'Gratitude to you this day my friend'. If the Incubus is doing this, somehow it has left me out as a thank you for its release."

Daddly sat up, like he had just received a shock. "That has to be it, Freddie, well thought out. Sadly it only leaves us back at square one," Daddly replied.

"Huh! What's that mean?" Giggly said, suddenly awake.

"Oh, you know, Giggly," Wiggly chuckled, "it's the board game, Chains and Dragons, where you fly up the board with a dragon or slide down a chain."

Freddie chuckled. "We have a game like that called 'Snakes and Ladders' where you climb up a ladder and slide down a snake. If you land on square 99 there is a snake's head and it slides you all the way back to square one."

Giggly screwed up her face and replied, "So you mean we know nothing more about the Incubus?"

"That's about the size of it," Daddly answered.

They sat quietly, looking at each other as if it would give them inspiration.

"I'll make a nice cup of dandelion tea, that might brighten us up a bit," Mummly announced.

Dandelion tea had become a firm favourite with Freddie and he looked forward to sharing a cup with his friends.

They all sat sipping their tea when Freddie had an idea. "What about my rucksack, could I think about the Incubus and pull out a book or scroll or something?"

Wiggly choked and spat some tea over Giggly who jumped and almost covered Mummly with the few drops of tea left in her cup.

"Daddly! Would that work?" Wiggly cried enthusiastically, suddenly feeling full of energy.

Again Daddly rubbed his chin and thought about the idea then replied, "I really don't know, but there's only one way to find out, over to you, Freddie."

All eyes were on Freddie, the little bit of hope had perked them all up and they watched him unzip the top of his rucksack and slide his hand inside. He closed his eyes and thought about the Incubus. "I've got something!" he cried pulling out his hand.

Wiggly sat back with his hands over his mouth, full of anticipation.

"It's another tube!" cried Giggly.

Freddie handed it to Daddly who opened the end and out dropped a scroll. He picked it up and unrolled it. "Oh, goodness!" he cried out, rolled it back up and pushed it back into the tube then handed it back to Freddie. "Put it back, Freddie, quickly," he cried.

Freddie grabbed the tube and dropped it back into his rucksack where it disappeared as quickly as it had appeared.

"That was close!" Daddly gasped.

"It was like the one we found, wasn't it, Daddly?" Freddie asked.

"Quite so, Freddie, it had the same words written on the scroll, had I read them out we would have another Incubus set free!"

There was a united sound of relief. "Oooh!"

"That is not going to help, unfortunately," Mummly declared, "let's see if we can think of anything else. I have some special acorn nibbles that might help."

They sat dipping their acorn nibbles in a fresh cup of dandelion tea, quietly in their thoughts.

Giggly yawned, her eyes heavy and Wiggly fidgeted his feet.

"Oh!" Freddie cried out making everyone sit up. Giggly jumped so hard she splashed her tea everywhere.

"Freddie, you scared me!" she scolded.

"Sorry, Giggly, are you alright, not burned or anything?" Freddie apologised.

"Sor-right, Freddie, my tea was almost cold anyway. Why'd you shout out?" she asked.

"Oh yes!" Freddie shouted again. This time Wiggly jumped, but his tea was already gone. "Oh, sorry, Wiggly, but I've just realised there's one place we haven't looked for information on the Incubus!"

Daddly, Mummly, Wiggly and Giggly sat up and looked at Freddie hopefully.

"Where might that be, Freddie?" Daddly asked.

Freddie beamed a huge smile and he suddenly felt very excited. "Why didn't we think about this before, it's so obvious!" he chuckled.

"What is? What's obvious?" Wiggly groaned.

"Merlin's library!" Freddie declared excitedly.

Now everyone sat bolt upright with smiles on their faces and with one voice the Tiggly family cried out, "YES!"

"Freddie, you're a genius. Why didn't we think of that? You're right, it's so very obvious that we missed it completely," Wiggly said.

"The only problem is there are so many books it would take weeks, maybe months to look through them all," Freddie said with dismay.

"Daddly, could we get all the men together," Mummly suggested. "Then they could go with Freddie ....,"

"And ME!" interrupted Wiggly.

"That way," Mummly continued, smiling at her son, "there would be many eyes on the books."

"Excellent idea, Mummly, I'll get right to it," Daddly replied and scooted out the front door, with renewed vitality.

"And why can't I come?" Giggly huffed, miserably.

"I think you would get bored very quickly and then you might slow things down if someone needs to bring you home," Mummly replied kindly.

"Okay, I guess you are right, it wasn't very interesting looking through the school library books," Giggly confessed.

In less than half an hour Daddly returned. "Come along then, I have lots of volunteers outside all ready to help," he declared.

As soon as Freddie walked outside, the crowd of Elfins cheered. "Well done, Freddie, you've come to the rescue again!"

"Freddie Fixit!" Wiggly cried, making the Elfins cheer again and Freddie blush bright red.

Freddie reached into his magical rucksack and brought out lots and lots of torches. Then Daddly led the squad towards the escape tunnel. When the door slammed shut behind the last Elfin to walk into the tunnel, it turned almost pitch black, then dozens of torches switched on and lit up the tunnel brightly. For almost everyone, except Wiggly and Freddie, this was their first visit to the escape tunnel. Only a few Elfins knew Merlin had a home and a laboratory at the end until the two friends had returned from their exploration and adventure into the Crystal Cavern.

Freddie looked at his watch, it was just after 10am, and he knew he would have to leave no later than 2.30pm in the afternoon to get home on time.

When they reached the anti-room the journey seemed to have been much quicker than the first time the boys were down here. But this time they had been chatting and even singing a song or two, so the time seemed to pass more quickly and more interestingly.

All the Elfins were wide eyed when they entered Merlin's home and laboratory. The air was filled with "Oohs" and "Arrrrs" and "Look at that!" One by one they climbed the staircase to the library on the gallery floor.

Daddly told everyone to spread out. "Please do not blow dust off the books or pat them, otherwise we will choke to death in clouds of dust."

There was a round of laughter, and then someone called out, "Daddly, how will we know if a book has already been looked through?"

"Good point, Gavin, any suggestions?" Daddly asked.

"How about turning the book so the spine faces inwards when we've read it?" someone else called out.

"Excellent suggestion," Daddly replied with a smile. "Let's do that everyone, if you find any reference to the Incubus, please bring that book to me, then we can examine those books in detail later once we have been through the whole library. Okay Elfins, let's get started!" Daddly called out.

Just like a Sproggle library, the only sound was of pages being slowly turned and books being closed gently. There was one Elfin or another coughing here and there as some dust inevitably escaped into the air. The whole process was slower than slow. Many of the books were faded and hard to read, others written in numbers like formula, or written in code or a strange language. But everyone was scanning page after page for one word, 'INCUBUS'.

At around noon, Freddie used his magic rucksack to produce bottles of water and took them round to everyone.

Most had brought a snack and they shared with those who had not.

Freddie shared his jam sandwiches and apple with Wiggly and Daddly, then he pulled out bars of chocolate as a treat for everyone.

There were lots of "Yum! Yum's!" around the gallery as the Elfins tried chocolate for the first time.

The mood was cheerful and while everyone stopped to drink and eat, some sang songs and made the break even better with happy tunes.

Freddie was keeping an eye on the time, it was already 1.30pm, another hour and he would, reluctantly, have to leave.

So far there had been no reference of the Incubus from any of the books already looked through, but the Elfins and Freddie had only looked at a small number of books because of the difficulties reading faded writing or dismissing unintelligible languages.

Freddie feared this would take days to get through them all.

"No luck so far," Wiggly said to Freddie, feeling disappointed.

"Maybe this was a bad idea after all," Freddie replied.

But Daddly was close by and encouraged them. "Come on boys, every book we look at is one less, nearly every book on the top two shelves has been turned back to front. Keep going, we will find what we need if we keep looking, I'm sure of it! Okay?"

Wiggly and Freddie nodded and smiled, Daddly's little pep talk cheered them up and they began to open and read through the books with renewed enthusiasm.

At 2.30pm Freddie called out, "Cheerio everyone, I'm sorry I have to leave now, otherwise my parents will send out a search party for me. See you all tomorrow."

There was a loud, "Goodbye Freddie!" from all the Elfins.

"You go too, Wiggly, you look tired and need some sleep," Daddly told his son.

Wiggly was tired, really tired and he did not need telling twice to go home.

The two boys waved goodbye and began the long journey down the dimly lit tunnel, arms round shoulders like the good friends they were. Freddie and Wiggly were both so tired they hardly spoke at all as they trudged their way back to Elfin Town.

Once they were out of the escape tunnel and back in the bright light of Elfin Town, Wiggly walked with Freddie to the spiral staircase door.

"Go home now, Wiggly, you look really tired. Try to get some sleep, think of all our happy adventures in your dreams to ward off those nasty nightmares, okay?" he told his friend. They gave each other a warm hug.

"Okay Freddie, see you tomorrow, hopefully we can find out something by then."

Freddie waved Wiggly off as he sauntered tiredly towards his home, then Freddie walked through the door and climbed the spiral staircase. At the top he spoke the magic words and the door opened in the big old oak tree. When he stepped outside he gulped in the fresh air and smiled. "Coo, that dust gets everywhere!" he said, to no one in particular, patting down his clothes to remove all the dust on them. He coughed until the dust cloud vanished then he made his way home.

That night he fell asleep thinking about all the Elfins who were helping to look through Merlin's library. *'Elfins are so friendly, kind and helpful. Merlin said that Sproggles will be like that one day too.'*

The next day, Sunday, Freddie slept until 9am. Unlike the day before, his parents were up and about way before him, in fact, his mother had to go to his bedroom to wake him up.

"Come on sleepy head, time to get up and have breakfast," she said shaking him gently.

"Aww, Mum, what time is it?" Freddie's voice groggy with him still halfway in dreamland.

"It's past nine o'clock son, you don't normally sleep in this late. Are you feeling unwell?" his mother asked with a little concern in her voice. She placed the back of her hand on his forehead. "You don't seem to have a temperature, Freddie, up you jump then," she said turning to leave him struggling to get out of his nice warm bed.

* *

After Freddie had left his Elfin friends in Merlin's library, they had been busy carrying on looking through the many books until teatime. Then they all returned to their homes to freshen up, the dust had seeped right through their clothes. Once nice and clean again they were able to hug their families and enjoy a meal. The chatter was all about Merlin's home, laboratory and shelves of books.

At seven o'clock they all met outside the escape tunnel door and made the journey back to Merlin's lair. They still had the torches Freddie had brought out of his rucksack and they chatted and sang until they reached the door to the anti-room.

Daddly divided the Elfins into two groups, with each group taking it in turns every three hours to look at the books or get some sleep. A few of the wives came along to help clean Merlin's living and sleeping rooms so those who were sleeping had somewhere dust-free to lay their heads. In this way the Elfins worked all through the night, opening and closing books, stirring up dust and coughing, reading, groaning, yawning, until every book had been examined.

From the whole library only two books made any reference to the Incubus.

Daddly and Wiggly were on the last shift, closing the very final book at quarter to four in the morning.

Daddly gathered everyone together. "Well done everyone, that was a mammoth task. Who would have thought that only two books among so many would have any reference to the Incubus. Let's pack up and go home to our loved ones and get some sleep."

The Elfins, although tired, clapped their hands, which was a mistake, as a cloud of dust rose into the air like a thick fog, making them all cough and flee the laboratory.

Once in the tunnel they sang songs to keep them awake until they reached their homes.

Daddly and Wiggly listened to their voices getting further and further away.

"Come on, Wiggly, let's get these books home so we can look at them with Freddie when he arrives," Daddly said, putting the two books with marked pages into his bag.

Then father and son made their way down the stairs from the gallery into the laboratory and then Merlin's sitting room. When they reached the door to the anti-chamber, Wiggly walked ahead and straight through the door, but when Daddly tried to walk through, he could not, coming to an abrupt halt, like an invisible door was ahead of him.

Wiggly walked back through the door. "What's the matter, Daddly?"

Daddly looked puzzled. "I have no idea, it's like an invisible wall, look." He tried to pass through the doorway again and just bumped into something that could not be seen.

Wiggly walked through the doorway again. "I can walk through, Daddly, this is strange," he said walking back through. "Let me hold the bag, Daddly, and you can try again."

Daddly handed the bag with the books to his son and ran at the doorway. To his surprise he passed straight through, tripping and stumbling to the floor.

Wiggly was so shocked he ran to Daddly to help him, but he bounced off some invisible barrier and ended up on the floor on his bottom. "Ooof! Ow!" he cried, more with shock than pain.

Daddly jumped up intent on helping his son, but held his hands in front of him to feel his way through the doorway.

Wiggly jumped up himself and before Daddly walked through the doorway he ran at it. This time he was ready but as he hit the invisible barrier, the force of stopping made him drop the bag and then he fell through on top of Daddly. Both fell to the floor again but Daddly broke Wiggly's fall this time.

"Wiggly, are you all right?" his father asked, picking him up from the floor.

"Uh! I think so. That was strange, I was pressing against some invisible barrier, but when I dropped the bag, it just vanished and I fell right through!" He giggled suddenly realising it was quite funny. "Ha, ha, ha!" he chuckled.

They both walked back through the doorway without a problem.

Daddly rubbed his chin and surmised, "It must be these books, they have an enchantment on them to remain in Merlin's library, watch," Daddly said. He threw the bag gently at the open doorway. It hit an invisible barrier and dropped straight down to the floor.

"Wow! Merlin was super cautious, Daddly, he obviously didn't want any books falling into the wrong hands and used for bad things," Wiggly figured out.

Daddly looked at Wiggly and scratched his chin again. "If the books cannot leave Merlin's home then we must copy down the parts about the Incubus, perhaps that way maybe we can take the information home," he explained.

Father and son returned to the laboratory looking for paper or parchment and writing tool, finding both without too much searching.

"Should we see if this parchment can be taken through the doorway before we copy anything?" Wiggly suggested.

"Good idea, son," his father replied.

They took the sheets of parchment and carried them through the doorway without any problems.

"Looks like our plan may work then, son. Let's get to it and copy what we need," Daddly said with a smile of satisfaction. "How about I write one line and we try again. It's no use writing everything only to discover we still can't take it out?" he suggested.

That done, Daddly held the parchment in front of him and safely walked through the doorway.

"Success! Well done, Daddly," Wiggly cried.

They sat at Merlin's table in his living room and took one book each to copy out the parts referring to the Incubus. They had a thin charcoal stick and carefully copied all the text from the books. It took them another hour, then Daddly returned the books to Merlin's library. He rolled the two parchments carefully, placing them in his bag. "Let's go, son, you look as exhausted as I feel, we still have a long trek back home."

This time they both walked through the bothersome doorway without any trouble, carrying on into the tunnel and the long walk back to their home.

* *

Giggly had bad dreams again that night while Daddly and Wiggly were busy in Merlin's library. Mummly had held her in her bed until she dropped off to sleep again, but every time she closed her eyes the bad dreams returned.

"Mummly, I keep falling into a deep pit with no bottom and I cry out but no one hears me," Giggly told Mummly, her voice teary and tired. She shook and trembled even though Mummly was holding her tightly, so neither of them really had any proper sleep.

It was almost 9 o'clock when father and son wearily walked through the front door.

Mummly heard them and left Giggly snoozing to go and greet them. "You look very tired, both of you. I'll make some dandelion tea, go and relax in the comfy chairs," she told them and they sauntered over to the seating area and flopped in the chairs.

By the time Mummly brought them the dandelion tea they had both fallen asleep, still wearing their coats and the bag with the parchments had dropped to the floor.

Mummly smiled. "Let's hope this will soon be all over, everyone is so exhausted," she said softly, waking Daddly and Wiggly to sip their tea before sending them off to bed.

* *

Freddie had slept really well, unlike all of his friends who were still experiencing terrible nightmares. Things in their dreams so horrible and fearful they would wake crying for their mums and dads, trembling and in need of a loving parents' hug until they settled down.

William was particularly badly affected, being a sensitive boy at the best of times, and his bad dreams made him so afraid he would not go back to sleep. As a result he moved around like a Zombie, bumping into things and other people, tripping over his own feet and landing flat on his face. One morning he missed the last step on the stairs and tumbled down, breaking his fall with his arm. He screamed and screamed with such horrible pain his mother came rushing to his side. "William, whatever is it, my little lamb?" she asked with concern in her voice.

"It's my arm, Mum, it hurts so bad," he said with tears rolling down his cheeks.

Fearing he may have broken a bone, his mother carried him out to their car whimpering, then sped off to the hospital in the nearby town. An X-Ray showed William had indeed broken a bone. "Your Radius bone just above the wrist has a fracture. This is like a break, but not right through the bone. This is one of the two long bones connecting your wrist to your elbow, the other bone is called the Ulna," the doctor explained. "We will need to stop it getting any worse by immobilizing your arm," the doctor added.

"You're not going to chop it off are you?" a frightened and tearful William cried as the tears streamed down his cheeks.

His mother hugged her son and told him softly, "No son, you get to keep your arm."

William looked at them and then sniffed at the doctor.

"I'm sorry, William, I didn't intend to scare you. I am going to wrap your arm in a special bandage that we wet first, then when it dries it sets nice and hard. This way it keeps your broken bones together so that they can mend themselves and that takes between 4 and 6 weeks, okay?"

William's tears dried up and he smiled weakly, "Okay," he croaked.

When they left the hospital William had a plaster cast on his left arm almost up to his elbow and wrapped around his wrist and thumb. He could move his fingers, but his arm was held firmly to give it a chance to heal.

"It still hurts, Mum, but not as much now, but I like the blue colour of this cast," he smiled and winced.

The doctor had to cut the sleeve from the cuff to the shoulder for his shirt to fit over his thick plaster cast. William was not very happy about that, but his mother told him he could have a new one when the cast came off.

* *

Freddie pulled on his rucksack, put on his hat and held his magic golden staff his father had made from a broom handle.

"What are you up to today, Freddie?" his father asked looking up from his Sunday newspaper. "Oh, a bit of exploring and I think I'll make a new secret hideout, Dad," he said, not quite telling a lie. He did want to make a new secret hideout, but he also wanted to check in on the Tigglys.

"Back by 4pm then, Freddie," his mother called to him as he skipped through the kitchen door, laden with chocolate spread sandwiches, an orange and a packet of crisps.

"Will do, Mum, bye now, bye Dad," Freddie called, feeling happy and quite excited. "I hope the Elfins have found out what this Incubus is and how to stop it," he said, to no one in particular as he opened the garden gate and charged into the forest. He looked down at the woodland floor and realised that he took the same route to the big old oak tree quite often and now there was a well-trodden track that could lead anyone straight to the Elfins. He found a branch with leaves still on it and began to brush the path, stirring up the soil, then pulling pebbles, twigs and leaves to cover it for most of the way to the Elfin entrance. "That's better, now it's not so obvious," he said to himself. "Oh, what's that?" he said out aloud, lifting his head up and putting his hand to his ear to listen.

'Freddie.' Was it a faint little voice calling his name or was it the breeze that just sounded like it? Freddie looked this way and that, up and down, everywhere. "Is someone there?" he called out.

'Freddie,' the little voice said again.

"Who? What?" Freddie said looking about again, then he noticed a fluffy brown rabbit twitching its nose, sat by his feet. Freddie crouched down and the rabbit did not run away. "Did you call my name, little rabbit?" He almost felt foolish asking a rabbit if it could speak.

'Freddie'.

This time he heard it clearly and it seemed to come from the fluffy brown rabbit, but it only twitched its nose and did not move its mouth, as there was something in it. Freddie reached out and stroked the rabbit's head and noticed its paw, which had a ring-like scar around it. "Oh hello, baby rabbit, look at you, you're all grown up," Freddie spoke softly so as not to frighten the rabbit that he recognised as the one he saved from the horrible snare.

The rabbit dropped what was in its mouth. 'Freddie need'.

He chuckled, this was silly, rabbits don't talk, yet he was certain this one was talking to him. He realised that he was hearing the words in his mind. He picked up the small ball of fluff and stroked his rabbit again and said, "Thank you, little one."

Then the rabbit hopped off under a bush and vanished.

Freddie was completely puzzled and shook his head as he stood up again. 'Talking animals, no way', he thought to himself, smiling. 'You are a very special boy', Merlin's words suddenly flashed through his mind again. "Did Merlin give me the ability to understand animals?" he said, to no one in particular. He put the ball of rabbit fur in a side pocket of his rucksack and made a final zigzag journey to the big old oak tree. He looked at his watch, it was past eleven already. "Wow, time flies when you get up late, it's nearly dinner time," he said to himself. On reaching the big old oak tree he looked around to make sure he was alone, then uttered the magic words. When the door opened he ran down the spiral staircase, still thinking about the little rabbit and chuckling to himself.

Once again Elfin Town was deserted and Freddie began to wonder if all the adults were still in Merlin's lair. He hurried along the empty, quiet road to the Tiggly's house, knocked on the door and waited, looking around and then knocked again and waited. Finally, he knocked a little louder and the door opened slowly, Mummly stood inside and invited him in.

"Oh Freddie, come on inside, I'm afraid Daddly and I were snoozing in the comfy chairs," she explained. "The children had bad dreams again last night, I hope we can sort this out soon," she told him, looking very weary herself.

"I do too," Freddie replied, taking off his rucksack and heading towards Daddly, still asleep in his chair.

"They worked through the night to get through all the books. Daddly and Wiggly have only been home since early this morning, as soon as Wiggly closed his eyes the bad dreams started. Daddly and I have slept with the children until an hour ago, snoozing in the comfy chairs. Go sit down, Freddie, I'll make a nice cup of dandelion tea to wake us up." Mummly soon brought two cups of hot tea and sat next to him.

"Did they finish the books and was there anything about the Incubus, Mummly?" Freddie asked in a quiet and nervous voice.

"Daddly briefly told me they had found only two books referring to the Incubus, but they had a spell on them and couldn't be taken from the library, that's all I know," she replied softly.

Freddie felt a little disappointed to hear this as he sipped his tea. Daddly was still fast asleep and he did not want to wake him. He was thinking that they would have to go back to Merlin's library to look at the books and find out what they could when he jumped, almost spilling his tea.

"FREDDIE!" Wiggly cried as he popped his head round the sleeping area door.

Freddie turned and saw his friend's smiling face.

"Sssssh! Daddly is sleeping, Wiggly, go wash and get dressed," Mummly ordered and Wiggly vanished with a cheeky giggle.

"Not any more!" a voice from the comfy chair announced

"Daddly, I'm sorry if we woke you," Mummly apologised.

"It's fine, Mummly," he replied. "Ah, Freddie, just the Sproggle I want to see," Daddly said when he noticed Freddie sitting quietly.

Freddie replied downheartedly, "Mummly said that you had worked hard all through the night reading the books, but you couldn't bring any of them out as they were enchanted. All we can do now is go back and read the information I suppose?"

Daddly sat up and took the cup of dandelion tea Mummly handed to him. "Thank you, Mummly, just what I need to wake me up. Now, Freddie," he said turning back to the sad looking boy, "it's not all doom and gloom, take a look in this bag." Daddly picked up the bag by his comfy chair and handed it over.

Freddie took the bag and pulled out the rolls of parchment. When he opened them a huge smile appeared on his sullen face. "Daddly, you're a genius, you've copied the bits about the Incubus from the books. That was quick thinking considering how tired you all must have been." he replied cheerfully.

"Well that may be, Wiggly and I were too tired to read what we wrote and just copied everything down about the Incubus. Some of it does not make sense, but it's exactly how it appeared in the books," Daddly confessed.

"Can you read it out aloud to us, Freddie?" Mummly asked, but before Freddie could answer, Wiggly and Giggly came bounding out of the sleeping area door.

"Yes, yes, read it out to us, Freddie!" they said together.

Freddie looked at the first sheet and was about to start reading when he stopped and closed his mouth.

"What's wrong, Freddie?" Wiggly asked.

Freddie looked at Wiggly. "Well you know what happened the last time I read out a scroll!"

Daddly gave Freddie a kindly smile. "As this is only a copy, Freddie, I think it will be safe enough, go ahead and read it out to us," he encouraged.

Freddie nodded his head and looked down at the parchment and began. "It says,

A dark Spirit has invaded our land that calls itself INCUBUS, the dream snatcher. All our children are having terrible night terrors.

287

The INCUBUS has the power to steal their happy dreams and feed on the fear they have from the night terrors it gives to them. The children have been subjected to this horror for ten and four nights and are collapsing with exhaustion. We fear they may not survive us unless we can rid our land of this evil spirit."

"So it would appear that the Incubus is responsible for the bad dreams of Elfins and Sproggles alike!" Daddly uttered.

Freddie looked at the second sheet and jumped up before sitting down again. "This looks like it's a spell to imprison the Incubus!"

"Oh read it out to us, Freddie, if you can," Wiggly said enthusiastically.

Freddie looked at the words and crinkled his nose, then said,

"Those touched by Merlin's hand, now gather thus items to scribe the holding spell.

There's a list here, but it makes no sense!" Freddie announced.

"Can you read the list out? Maybe it might mean something to one of us." Mummly encouraged.

"Okay, Mummly, here goes," Freddie answered, not very convinced.

"Leaf of Lion
 Root of Rot
  Seed of the Mighty
   Bark of the Dog
    Tuft of the Paw
     Petals of Gold
      Stem of Lips
       Eye of Tatty
        Amen of Croc

Combine to a paste.
Add Fungi without haste.
Tri days and plus to brew.
Nay thick lest it to chew.
Add seven drops from Merlin's Lake.
Write with quill the spell to make.

Constrain within this parchment thus,
Imprison now the INCUBUS

Lay down the parchment within the circle of seven candles lit and chant the spell just seven times. The spirit INCUBUS will be drawn to the parchment so. Once done, place the scroll within a sheath and hide it true from every thief."

Wiggly and Giggly looked totally confused, as if they had just listened to gobbledygook.

"It makes no sense, how can we do this. It's hopeless!" Wiggly said hanging his head.

"It does look like you are right, son," Daddly agreed.

"It seems very vague, but it is a list of ingredients," Mummly said trying to be positive and lift the mood as she pulled a face while thinking.

"Let's take one item at a time and try to make sense of it then," Giggly suggested. "What was the first one, Freddie?" she asked.

"Leaf of Lion," he replied.

"Well that's just doolally!" Wiggly sneered. "What kind of lion has leaves on it? They have fur, not leaves, it's bonkers!" he scoffed.

The room went quiet while the Tiggly's and Freddie rubbed their chins and scratched their heads.

Daddly shook his head from side to side.

Giggly had her head in her hands.

Wiggly was slumped in his comfy chair.

And Freddie had his eyes closed as if he had fallen asleep.

Trying to stay positive, Mummly announced, "Come on everyone, I'll makes us all another cup of dandelion tea, that'll perk us up."

Suddenly Giggly jumped to her feet and cried, "Mummly, Mummly, Mummly!"

Wiggly fell flat on the floor from his comfy chair with shock and surprise.

"What is it, Giggly, are you hurt child?" Mummly rushed to her daughter.

"No, No! Mummly, I've got it. I've got it!" She was almost screaming.

Freddie jumped out of his sleepy daydream thinking Giggly was on fire or something and Daddly looked completely perplexed.

"What have you got, Giggly?" Mummly asked concerned and grabbing her daughter.

"You just said it, Mummly, you just said it!" Giggly replied, almost too excited to explain.

"You're not making a lot of sense, Giggly," Daddly said finally, "sit down, take a breath and explain what it is that you have got," he added.

"But I am, don't you see? *Leaf of Lion*, it's the leaf of a dandeLION! That's what Lion has leaves, it's a dandelion!" Giggly was now shouting with excitement.

Wiggly pulled himself up from the floor, rubbed his bottom and cried out, "Hey, Giggly, you're so smart!" then gave her a big hug.

"Oh, well done, Giggly, how clever of you to work that out," Freddie cheered, jumping up and joining Wiggly to give her a warm hug.

"I will definitely go make us that cup of tea now," Mummly said walking to the kitchen area of the room.

The two boys released Giggly after she told them she could not breathe and they all sat down again in the comfy chairs with big smiles on their faces.

Mummly brought them all a steaming hot cup of dandelion tea, which they sipped while thinking to themselves.

"Let's see if we can work out what the other ingredients for this spell might be. Maybe they are right under our noses like the dandelion leaves," Daddly declared. "Freddie, can you tell us what the second item was again, please?"

"Root of Rot," Freddie replied looking at the parchment again.

"Oh, that's a hard one. Almost every plant has a root of some kind or other, so what's special here, what's a ROT?" Mummly replied.

Daddly rubbed his chin and wondered.

Freddie's face lit up and he suggested, "How about we think of any plant that has ROT in its name?"

Once again, chins were rubbed and heads scratched until Mummly spoke. "This may sound silly, but it keeps running around in my mind, how about a carrot? It has ROT in its name and is a root vegetable."

Suddenly everyone else sat up in their comfy chairs.

"Brilliant, Mummly!" Daddly cried. "That has to be it, I certainly cannot think of another plant with ROT in its name. Anyone else?"

The three children were smiling and shaking their heads.

"Let's settle on that then for the second ingredient, best write these down," Daddly suggested and Freddie pulled out a note pad and pencil from his magic rucksack to write down the ingredients as they worked them out.

"Freddie, what was the next ingredient?" Wiggly asked, feeling a bit more positive now they had worked out two of the puzzle ingredients.

"Seed of the Mighty," Freddie replied.

"Ooo, Ooo, I think I know that one!" Wiggly cried, almost falling off his chair in the process. "It must be the Mighty Oak tree, so it has to be an acorn!"

Wiggly got a round of applause. "Bravo, Wiggly!" the others cheered.

"Why did Merlin write the ingredients for the spell in a riddle, do you think?" Giggly asked.

Freddie and Wiggly both looked at her, then to Daddly.

"I guess it was to make it difficult for the wrong people to use his spells. What if this was a spell to turn people into frogs? In the wrong hands it could be disastrous. Just think, we were about to give up until Mummly encouraged us," Daddly replied. "What's next then, Freddie?" he added.

"Bark of Dog," he replied screwing up his face. "A bark is a sound, how can we collect that?" he questioned.

Heads and chins were being rubbed and scratched again.

"How can you have the bark of a dog?" Wiggly mumbled.

"Maybe we need to think outside the box here everyone?" Daddly suggested.

"What do you mean, Daddly?" Wiggly asked.

"Well we know this has to be a thing to add to the spell mix so it cannot be a sound. We instantly think bark is about an animal, but it isn't only a dog that has a bark, is it?"

"Don't seals make a barking sound?" Freddie asked.

"What's a seal?" Giggly asked.

"Oh, it's like a big fish that can live out of the water, I think it's called a mammal," Freddie replied.

Giggly only partly understood what Freddie had said. Before she could say anything more...

Wiggly sat up again, "Oooh, I know what else has a bark," he said with a big smirk on his face.

"What are you thinking, Wiggly?" Freddie asked.

"Oh, it's so obvious, Freddie, you'll laugh when I tell you," Wiggly teased.

"Come on! Come on!" Giggly said impatiently, forgetting about Seals.

Wiggly stood up and said, "It's a tree. It has a bark on the outside of it and that's a thing, isn't it?" Wiggly was so excited now his legs were running on the spot again.

"Well, well, Wiggly, who's a smarty-pants then?" Mummly teased and chuckled at her son's excitement, as she brought over more tea and some snacks.

"That's so clever, Wiggly, all we could think about was the dog part. So if we think about a tree, what kind of tree?" Freddie praised his friend.

"Oooooh, easy again!" Wiggly chuckled, his legs still running on the spot faster than ever.

"Sit down, Wiggly, before you wear a hole in the floor!" Daddly laughed.

"Come on, enlighten us then, oh wise one!" Mummly teased.

"Bark of Dog, tree bark is wood so the tree must be a Dogwood tree!" Wiggly's face lit up with a huge smile of excitement.

"Wiggly!" Freddie cried, equally excited and rushed to give his friend a hug.

Giggly, Mummly and Daddly all smiled and gave Wiggly a round of applause.

"I'm getting good at this, aren't I?" Wiggly chuckled once Freddie let go of him.

"Can you write it down, Freddie," Giggly said.

"This is going better than we first thought," Daddly said quite optimistically. "What was the next ingredient, Freddie, let's see if we can crack it?"

Freddie looked at the parchment and read out, "Tuft of Paw."

Lot's of frowns followed.

"Not so smug now, Wiggly!" Giggly teased her brother.

"Mmmm, let me think about this, tuft of paw," Wiggly mused.

"How is paw spelled, Freddie? Mummly asked.

"Its P-A-W," he replied.

"So that's like an animal paw, not someone who is not rich, but poor, P-O-O-R," Mummly explained.

"Or like something you pour out, like tea from a teapot," Giggly added.

It was Freddie who jumped up this time. "I got it, I got it!" he cried and rooted in his rucksack pulling out the ball of fur the little rabbit had given him.

"Oooh," both Wiggly and Giggly said together, "where'd you get that?"

Freddie chuckled. "This is going to sound crazy, but something called my name when I was on my way to the big old oak tree. The only thing around was the little rabbit which I had saved from the horrible Sproggle snare trap and it dropped this from its mouth and told me I would need it!"

Giggly laughed and Wiggly chuckled.

"Na, that's your imagination playing tricks on you!" Wiggly smiled disbelievingly.

"Wiggly, don't be so doubtful. This is not the first time Freddie has believed he can communicate with the animals. Remember, you and he have the great Wizard Merlin's blessing, so anything is possible," Mummly admonished.

Wiggly looked a little ashamed. "Sorry, Freddie, if you believe the rabbit spoke to you, then I believe you too," he apologised.

"Me too!" Giggly added.

"Thank you, to be honest I was beginning to think I *was* imagining things, but after the little bunny rabbit gave me this, I believe it myself," Freddie said.

Mummly agreed with him. "I think you are right, Freddie, on both things. Tuft of paw, a tuft of rabbit fur, I know Sproggles think a rabbits foot is supposed to be lucky."

"Huh, not so lucky for the rabbit though!" Daddly chuckled.

"Let's have a break," Mummly suggested, "let our brains cool down a bit, we can think about the next clue over a nice cup of dandelion tea."

Everyone nodded and relaxed in their comfy chairs taking a breather while Mummly got the refreshments ready.

Three children with small bladders rushed through the sleeping area door laughing and giggling, jostling about who was going to use the comfort station first.

When they came back and settled in the comfy chairs, Freddie reached into his rucksack and pulled out a packet of ginger nut biscuits. While they sipped their tea he passed the biscuits around.

"Oooh, these are nice," Giggly said munching away, "what are they called?" she said looking at the packet. "Gin-ger nut bis-c-u-its, what a funny name," she sniggered.

"If you dip them in your tea, they taste even better," Freddie replied.

Giggly tried and ate the biscuit. "Mmmm," she smiled.

Wiggly had a go, but left it in his tea too long so when he lifted it out, the biscuit bent and dropped into his cup with a plop. "Aww!" he grumbled.

But Giggly almost fell off her chair with laughter, even Mummly and Daddly could not help laughing.

"Not funny!" Wiggly moaned, then chuckled. "Yes, very funny!"

It was even funnier watching Wiggly trying to fish the soggy biscuit from his cup and he had everyone in hysterical laughter.

"Oooh hot, hot!" he cried, dipping his fingers into the hot tea. Finally, Mummly gave him a spoon and he smiled, scooping out the soggy bits and popping them into his mouth.

"Shall we look at the next item on the list then?" Mummly said. "Can you read it out again, Freddie, please?"

Freddie looked at the parchment. "Oh, it's Petals of Gold," he replied.

The room went quiet, cups put down and the empty biscuit packet put on the floor, chins were scratched and heads rubbed while they thought about this clue.

"Okay," Daddly said, "we seem to be working out these items quite well, so we might actually do this," he encouraged. "This next one must refer to a flower, as I can't think what else has petals!"

Mummly spoke next. "So what flower is gold, or maybe has gold in its name?" she said as an idea formed in her mind.

"It's a Marigold!" Mummly and Wiggly said together.

Wiggly clapped his hands and cheered.

"Oh well done both of you, so clever!" Daddly praised.

"Write it down, Freddie," Giggly said enthusiastically, "what's next?"

Freddie looked and read out, "Stem of Lips!"

"Hey look at the time," Mummly announced, "let's stop and have some lunch before we go any further. We can be thinking about stem of lips ready for later."

Freddie joined the Tiggly family at the table and fished out his chocolate spread sandwiches, orange and crisps, which he emptied into a dish. When he began peeling the orange, some juice squirted out.

"Oooh, my eye!" Wiggly cried and Giggly laughed, pointing at her brother with juice dripping down his face.

"That thing's dangerous!" Wiggly smirked, wiping off the sweet juice and tasting it. "Mmmm! that's lovely," he smiled, licking his lips.

Mummly and Daddly had to chuckle too.

"Good shot, Freddie!" Daddly said, still smiling.

Freddie divided the orange into its segments and put them into another dish. Everyone had some of the orange and also the chocolate spread sandwiches.

"Mmmm, this is precious!" Giggly yummed over the sandwich.

"I'll say, it's delicious!" Wiggly agreed.

Freddie reached into his magic rucksack and pulled out a large jar of chocolate spread and handed it to Mummly.

"That will make a nice treat, Freddie, thank you," Mummly praised.

"So what has lips?" Giggly said idly to herself. "Huh! We all have lips," she mused. "No one has just one lip, we all have two lips!" she said a little more loudly than she intended.

But Freddie's ears pricked up. "I think Giggly has done it again!" he said with excitement.

"How so?" Wiggly asked.

"Yeh, how so?" Giggly agreed with her brother.

Freddie beamed a smile. "Well, you just said we have two lips," he replied.

"And we do!" Giggly said, wrinkling her nose.

"Well try saying it quickly," Freddie laughed and Giggly looked puzzled.

"Go on!" Wiggly encouraged.

So Giggly huffed and began to say, "Two lips, two lips, two lips, twolips tulips. TULIPS!" she screamed, causing Wiggly's head to slip off his elbow and bang his chin on the table as he watched his sister. "OW!" he cried, then jumped up and repeated what Giggly had said. "You said tulips, tulips are flowers with Lips! Yeah!"

"Oh, well done, Freddie," Daddly praised.

"Hey, I said it!" Giggly complained.

"Of course, well done to you, Giggly!" Daddly encouraged and she sat up and smiled.

A little later they settled back into the comfy chairs at the sitting end of the room and looked a little sleepy, except Freddie.

"We've only two more to solve everyone, but we have a bigger problem," Freddie said.

"What are you thinking, Freddie?" Daddly asked.

"Well," he replied, "once we collect all the ingredients they have to be mixed with seven drops from Merlin's lake!"

Four sets of eyes looked at Freddie.

"We will have to go back to the crystal cavern and collect the water from the lake then," Wiggly pointed out.

"But that's the problem, Wiggly," Freddie replied.

"I don't see the problem," Wiggly yawned again.

"Don't you remember, when we left the crystal cavern we were told the wall would not open again for another fifty years?"

Wiggly was suddenly wide awake. "Oh crumbs! We're all sunk, Daddly, what can we do?" Wiggly looked very unhappy.

Daddly frowned and replied, "I really don't know, son, I suppose we can try it with our lake water, it might be the same as Merlin's," he suggested.

Mummly spoke up trying to remain positive. "Let's deal with that when we come to it, shall we? Now, what's the next item, Freddie? Let's stay positive everyone, we've come this far and I'm sure Merlin is watching over us."

Freddie looked around at the weak smiles and then read out the next item. "Eye of Tatty," he said slowly.

"This is strange, does it mean a real eye or is it the letter I?" Wiggly enquired.

"Well if we knew what a Tatty is, we would know which it is!" Giggly replied solemnly.

No one had a clue to this.

"Maybe I can ask my parents, they might know the answer?" Freddie suggested. "Amen of Croc, is the last one, any ideas?" he added.

The four Tiggly faces were completely blank.

"I hate to say this, but I think we are too tired to work these last two items out just now. Perhaps we should give it a rest, something might pop into our thoughts along the way," Daddly suggested.

"I've got to be home soon anyway, Daddly, so I'll scoot off and let you get some rest," Freddie announced.

Wiggly stood up lazily and hugged his friend, followed by Giggly.

"See you all soon, not sure when, in the meantime I'll try and work out the last two clues," Freddie said as he waved them all goodbye and slipped out of the front door, rucksack on his back. He was surprised how drained he felt and the quiet streets of Elfin Town did not help. He looked at his watch and it was just before three o'clock. Wearily, he climbed the spiral staircase and uttered the magic words then stepped into the forest, his forest. He sauntered along, kicking a stone here and there, when he spotted a squirrel clinging to a tree trunk. "Hello, Mr Squirrel," he said softly, but not knowing if it was a male or female. "I need some acorns from that tree, could you get some for me, please?" Freddie thought he heard the squirrel say *'okay'* as it scampered up the tree out of sight. "So much for the theory that I can talk with the animals," he whispered, to no one in particular. He was about to walk away when something hit the ground behind him. He turned and looked. "Wow!" he gasped.

Another hit the ground and another, until a dozen acorns lay on the track.

Freddie looked up and put his hands each side of his mouth and bellowed, "Thank you, Mr squirrel!" He picked up all the acorns and stuffed them into a side pocket of his rucksack, then he looked around, suddenly having a feeling that someone might be watching him. He ran off in a random pattern, just in case his feeling was right, making sure he could not easily be followed.

"You're nice and early, Freddie," his mother greeted her son as he charged through the kitchen door panting. "Have you been running?"

Freddie held his knees and nodded as he looked up at her.

"Why don't you go have a shower and put on some clean clothes before we have tea," she said.

Freddie welcomed the nice warm shower. *'I wonder if Wiggly had a shower or a bath, I must ask him when we next meet. I want to know where all the smoke from the chimneys goes to as well,* he thought to himself.

* *

Freddie and his mother walked to school most mornings even though he was now eleven years old. Freddie did not mind, he liked the company and most mornings he met up with Jimmy.

"I'm going to the shops so we can walk together," she would often say to him.

"Everywhere is very quiet, Freddie," his mother said, as it was unusual for the streets to be deserted at this time in the morning. There were no other parents taking their children to school or even at the school gates waving them off. When they reached the school there was a notice.

School Closed for 2 Days for Deep Cleaning

"I wonder if the authorities think the school has something to do with this bad dream epidemic?" Freddie's mother said to him.

Only Freddie knew differently to anyone else, it was all his fault and he felt sad.

"Hey, hey! Don't worry, Freddie, the school will open again on Wednesday, okay?"

He gave his mother a big smile and followed her to the High Street to help pick up a few things from their local shops.

The High Street was like a ghost town, completely deserted. It seemed all the parents had stayed home to look after their children who were becoming quite ill with the lack of sleep and from the horrible nightmares when they did manage to nod off.

Freddie and his mother called into the Greengrocer and bought what they needed to restock the food cupboards. On their way back to the house Freddie's mother caught one of her plastic carrier bags on something sharp and ripped it open, spilling the contents all over the footpath.

"Oh dear, that's a nuisance!" she gasped.

"It's okay, Mum, I've got some dinosaur tape in my rucksack, it's really strong."

Freddie's mother smiled and thought how lucky she was to have such a helpful son.

Freddie retrieved the dinosaur tape and began to wind it round the split carrier bag, then picked the shopping up from the footpath and put it back into the repaired bag. "There you are, Mum, all fixed," he beamed.

"What would I do without you, Freddie, you're such a clever boy," his mother praised her son, patted his head lovingly and made him blush bright red.

When they got home he helped his mother put the shopping away in the cupboards and then made her a cup of tea.

"It looks like you're going to be on your own for a couple of days, Freddie," his mother told him.

"That's okay, Mum, I have some models to make, practice my guitar and I'm still building my secret den in the forest, so I have lots to keep me busy," he replied.

"Well it's a nice sunny and warm day, why don't you go build your den while the weather is dry. You never know, tomorrow it could be raining," his mother suggested.

"Okay Mum, that's a great idea. Oh, you're not going to be lonely are you?" he asked.

His mother gave him a warm cuddle. "Such a caring son, Freddie, you know your father and I are very proud of you," she replied.

Freddie smiled and turned a little red in the face. "I know, Mum, and I'm proud of you and Dad, you're the best parents ever!" he told her.

"Off you go then, get changed while I go make you a packed lunch to keep you going. Home by four o'clock though, okay?"

"Okay Mum, thank you," Freddie replied and galloped up the stairs like a herd of elephants.

Freddie decided to change his route and skipped round this bush and that, going here, there and everywhere, almost getting himself lost. He stopped for a moment to catch his breath. "I'm not exactly sure where I am," he said, to no one in particular. "Let's see, oh! I know that giant fir tree with the giant pine cones, so I need to go this way," he said aloud pointing past the big tree.

'Freddie.'

"Huh!" he said looking around, "am I hearing things again?" he whispered to himself.

'Freddie,' the squeaky voice called again.

Freddie looked around and then looked down. "Whoa!" he cried, only just seeing a little hedgehog down by his feet. "Mr Hedgehog, I nearly trod on you, I'm so sorry, I wasn't expecting to see you there!" Freddie crouched down to look more closely. "Oh, what's this caught in your spines Mr Hedgehog?" Freddie got a bit closer.

The hedgehog's squeaky voice sounded again. 'Freddie need.' The hedgehog's pointy little snout and tiny eyes looked up at him and it snorted.

Freddie carefully picked out the pretty yellow and blue flowers. "I know these," he muttered.

'Freddie need,' the hedgehog's squeaky little voice repeated in his mind.

"Thank you, Mr Hedgehog, thank you," he called out as the hedgehog waddled away with a couple of grunts and snorts. He stood up and looked at the pretty flowers. "I do know these, what does Mum call them? Oh, bother, I just can't remember!" he cried out feeling cross with himself, but took his rucksack off his shoulders and placed the flowers carefully in a large side pocket. He had barely put his rucksack back on his shoulders when he heard a very familiar sound. "Piglet, where are you? I can hear you, come out, come out," he called quietly so as not to frighten the young boar. Sure enough his friend, the grown up Piglet, appeared from behind a large prickly bush. Freddie crouched down again and smiled. "Hello again, Piglet, what are you doing out here by yourself?" The young boar moved closer to Freddie and he stroked Piglet's head and back. Something dropped from the boar's mouth and hit the ground with a thump. Freddie thought it was a small rock the boar had mistaken for a tasty morsel to eat.

Piglet gave a little grunt, 'Freddie need,' sounded in Freddie's mind.

He was so surprised he fell back on his bottom. "You too, Piglet, you spoke to me." Freddie sat himself up again, still looking surprised, then scratched Piglet's ears. He liked it and squealed his pleasure.

'*Freddie need,*' Piglet's grunty voice said again.

Freddie looked more closely at the object that Piglet had brought. "It's not a rock," he chuckled, "it's a potato! Thank you, Piglet!" Freddie took his rucksack from his shoulders again and stowed the potato away in a side pocket, then he unzipped the top and thought about a big red apple. When he brought his hand out there was a lovely shiny apple in it. "Here, Piglet, have this as a reward. I don't know why I need the potato, but you seem to know that I do."

Piglet sniffed the apple in Freddie's hand and snaffled it up in its mouth with a chomp, chomp, chomp and he looked up at his friend Freddie. '*Good,*' the grunty voice said, then the young boar turned away and scuttled off at high speed.

Freddie stood up and scratched his head. "Who will believe this?" he said, to no one in particular. "That's four times at least animals have helped me. I don't even think Wiggly will believe me, I'm not even sure I believe me!" he chuckled. Looking around again he got his bearings and set off towards the big old oak tree and his friends. They would be surprised to see him today, as they know it's a school day for Sproggle children.

Elfin Town was still like a ghost town. Windows and shutters closed, the whole place was silent and eerie. Freddie did not hang around and ran like the wind until he reached Wiggly's house. The door opened, this time before Freddie had the chance to knock and Daddly stood in the doorway with a welcoming smile and friendly face.

"Freddie! This is a surprise, how are you here? Never mind, come on inside," Daddly chirped.

Freddie walked into the house, which was always warm and homely, while Daddly closed the door behind them.

"Come on, Freddie, come sit in a comfy chair," Daddly invited and then sat opposite him.

"My school is closed for two days, Daddly, they think this nightmare thing is something wrong with the school, so it's being deep cleaned, whatever that is," Freddie explained.

Daddly smiled. "I see, well it's good you're here, but I'm afraid Wiggly and Giggly are not very well, they have a fever and we don't really know what to do, Elfins just don't usually get ill."

Freddie looked very worried thinking about his school friends who were all becoming quite poorly. "My Mum gives me something when I have a temperature. I remember it sounds something like, 'Parrots eat'em all', but she warned me never to swallow any medicines unless a doctor or adult was there to give them to me. We could try it if you think it might help Wiggly and Giggly, Daddly."

Daddly looked a little hopeful. "Well Mummly and I are out of ideas, Freddie, and if it works for you it might work for Wiggly and Giggly," he replied.

They stood up and walked towards the sleeping area door opposite the front door.

Daddly opened the door and they stood in a small hallway with four doors. "This door is to Mummly's and my sleeping chamber," Daddly said pointing to the first door on the right. "The next door is the comfort chamber and on this side are Wiggly and Giggly's sleeping chambers." He pointed to the two doors on the left. He opened Wiggly's chamber door first and they walked into a large bright room with a bed and cupboard, a little desk and chair and a small chest of drawers and hanging rail full of clothes.

Freddie saw Wiggly laid in his bed and the sight shocked him. His best Elfin friend was as white as snow, all the colour had drained from his face, hands and arms. He rushed to Wiggly and knelt by his bed. "Oh Wiggly, I'm so sorry, this is all my fault, I'm sorry!" Freddie was on the verge of tears when his friend turned his head to look at him.

"F-r-e-d-d-i-e!" he croaked and took hold of Freddie's hand. Wiggly's eyes were big and sad, "Not your fault, Freddie, n-o-t," his voice was very weak.

"I'm sorry, Wiggly, really I am, if I hadn't read the words on that scroll none of this would have happened, I have to fix it somehow."

Daddly had popped out while they talked and returned with a cup of water.

"I have some medicine that might help you feel better, Wiggly." Freddie put his rucksack on the floor, unzipped it, when he put his hand inside he thought of the medicine his mother gave him. When he lifted his hand out he held a small yellow packet with a warning on it about only taking one tablet. Freddie gave the packet to Daddly, who read the instructions.

"Yes, Freddie, you're right. It is only one tablet for children," he said and took a single tablet and gave it to Wiggly, after Freddie had helped him sit up.

Wiggly gulped the water and washed the tablet down. "Thank you, Freddie," he forced a little smile and lay back down again.

"Get some rest, Wiggly," Freddie said as he and Daddly left to go see Giggly. She looked just the same and it frightened Freddie, he did not want to lose his two very dear friends.

Daddly lifted his daughter up and gave her the pill and water, which she gulped down.

"Freddie, you're here," her voice was just as weak sounding as her brother's.

"Get some rest, Giggly, hopefully this pill will help you feel better," Freddie replied, then let her lay down again. "We'll figure this out somehow."

Giggly closed her eyes and fell asleep.

"Let's leave them to sleep, Freddie," Daddly said and they returned to the seating area and sat in comfy chairs. "Did I hear you telling Giggly the animals are talking to you, Freddie?" Daddly began.

"Oh, err, well!" Freddie was a little embarrassed.

"It's okay, Freddie, I believe you. You have been blessed by the great Wizard Merlin and anything is possible," Daddly comforted.

"They don't say a lot, I mean so far it's been, 'Freddie' and 'Freddie need,' but I don't see them talking, I just hear them in my mind," he replied.

"Ah, what is it they think you need?" Daddly asked.

Freddie jumped up as he remembered something. "Oooh, that reminds me!" he said grabbing his rucksack and opening the side pockets. "On the way home I saw a squirrel on an oak tree and I asked him if he could get me some acorns and look!" Freddie took out the dozen or so acorns and put them on the little table in front of them.

"That's impressive, how did that happen?" Daddly asked.

"Well, I felt silly because after I had asked the squirrel if he could get me some acorns, he just scampered away up the tree. I was about to walk away when something dropped, it was an acorn, then another, until all these were on the ground."

"Amazing, you certainly do have a special connection with animals it would seem," Daddly chuckled.

"Oh, it gets even more strange. On the way over here a hedgehog told me 'Freddie need' and had these flowers in amongst its spines." Freddie took out the purple and yellow flowers and put them on the table.

Daddly looked at the flowers and said, "Those are crocus flowers, but well out of season. I wonder how the hedgehog found them and why he thought you needed them?"

"That's it! I could not remember what my Mum had told me they were, yes, yes, crocus! I really don't know, but I was about to walk away when a grown up piglet boar came up to me and dropped this at my feet, again saying 'Freddie need,' in my mind." Freddie pulled out the potato and put that on the table too.

"A potato," Daddly said, getting up to collect the copies he had made of Merlin's book. When he returned he read out the last two items to collect for the spell. "Eye of Tatty and Amen of Croc. This is amazing, I think Merlin is watching and guiding you, Freddie. Look, 'Eye of Tatty'. See this potato? There are little green shoots on it here and here," he pointed them out.

"Oh yes!" Freddie replied in wonder.

"Do you know what these shoots are called?" Daddly asked and Freddie shook his head. Daddly smiled knowingly. "They are referred to as the eyes of the potato and some Sproggles call potatoes Tatties!"

"Oh wow! Daddly, that's got to be it then, these are the Eye of Tatty, that's great!" Freddie was all excited.

"What's so great?" A voice behind them asked.

Daddly and Freddie turned their heads.

"Wiggly!" they said at the same time.

"Are you feeling better?" Daddly asked.

"I do, yes, I really do. I'm not hot and sticky now, my headaches have gone, I feel much better. That was a magic pill you gave me, Freddie." Wiggly flung his arms around his smiling friend, "Thank you."

"Yes! Thank you, Freddie," Daddly repeated just as Mummly came through the front door.

"Oh Wiggly, look at you, are you feeling better?" she called and rushed to hug him.

When they all let go of each other, Wiggly replied, "Yes, Mummly. Freddie gave me a magic pill, look, I'm really good again," he chuckled.

"How's Giggly?" Mummly asked.

"She's still sleeping, Mummly, but I think she'll be okay too," Wiggly replied.

Mummly hugged Freddie. "You've come to our rescue again, Freddie, I bless the day you came into our lives."

Poor Freddie turned bright red again. "Me too," he replied.

"Now, what have I missed?" Wiggly asked.

"I'll make us a nice cup of ....," Mummly laughed as three voices called out, "dandelion tea," and laughed with her.

Daddly explained about Freddie's items on the little table as they sipped their tea.

"You say a hedgehog gave you those crocus flowers and said 'Freddie need,'" Wiggly confirmed, then lifted his head when he had a sudden thought. "That's it! That's it!" he called out. "The last item is 'Amen of croc'. It's stAMEN of CROCus, don't you see?" Wiggly explained.

Silence followed for a moment while three pairs of eyes stared in wonder at a smiling Wiggly.

"Wiggly, you clever thing, how'd you work that out?" Freddie asked.

"I don't really know, it just popped into my head like magic," he answered.

"That means we know all the ingredients for the spell, now all we have to do is collect the rest," Mummly said cheerfully.

"What have I missed?" called Giggly, groggily, from the sleeping chamber door.

"Giggly!" Freddie cried. "How do you feel?" he said clambering over to her to give her a hug. Then Mummly came and hugged her as well.

Finally, Daddly and Wiggly came over and gave her a hug.

When they all sat back down in the comfy chairs Giggly chuckled. "How can anyone sleep with all this noise going on?" she yawned and giggled at the same time and it sounded like a hic-cup.

"We know what all the ingredients for the spell are now, Giggly, thanks to Freddie!" Wiggly told his sister, who giggled and yawned again making everyone laugh.

Freddie and the Tiggly family set about collecting all the items for the spell.

Daddly coordinated the search, leaving out those things already in their possession, thanks to Freddie and his animal friends. "The one thing we will not be able to acquire easily, if at all, is the water from Merlin's lake," Daddly said echoing Freddie's concerns of earlier. "I think that Merlin is helping us somehow, look at what happened with the Morphlin attack. Merlin helped us then, so I think if Freddie and Wiggly return to the secret tunnel and the Crystal cavern, Merlin will come to the rescue, I hope!" Daddly said crossing his fingers.

Freddie and Wiggly agreed, although Freddie was a little doubtful.

"You both have been blessed by Merlin's magic, you are special, you are a link between the Great Wizard and the present day. We have faith that he will come to our aid through you boys, if not, we may lose all our children and that would be a terrible tragedy," Mummly said trying to reassure everyone.

"Do you really think Merlin can help us with this last piece of the spell?" Wiggly whispered to his friend. Freddie smiled, put his hand on Wiggly's shoulder and nodded. "We have to believe it, Wiggly, we really do."

Once everything that could be collected was in the bag Mummly carried with her, they made their way back to Elfin Town.

"Everywhere is so quiet," Giggly whispered, "it's a bit scary," she added, then screamed and jumped when her brother cried, "BOO!"

"Wiggly, that was cruel," Mummly said with Giggly clinging onto her.

"Oh, I'm sorry, Giggly," Wiggly apologised.

Back at the house, after a cup of dandelion tea, Freddie and Wiggly set off to Merlin's cavern. When they reached the door to the escape tunnel, Wiggly spoke the magic words to open it. Once they were inside and the door had closed behind them, they lit their way with torches, which Freddie had again taken from his magic rucksack.

"I really hope Merlin is watching over us and will help us, Wiggly, if not it's like Mummly said, all Elfin and Sproggle children will become so ill they may not survive and when the Incubus spirit has exhausted the children it's bound to start on the adults. The whole world's fate is resting on our shoulders again. We brought this evil into the world, we must stop it one way or another." Freddie's words were sombre.

The journey along the tunnel seemed to take even longer than before, it did not help with Wiggly still feeling weak and tired. They made several short stops to rest and drink before they reached Merlin's living area.

"Fingers crossed," Freddie said, crossing his fingers on both hands.

Wiggly sniggered. "Why cross your fingers, Freddie, doesn't that make holding things difficult?"

Freddie looked at his friend, chuckling. "No, silly, it's a thing we Sproggles do to bring us good luck. We say 'Good Luck' and cross our fingers," he replied.

Wiggly still laughed as he pulled open the big door to the laboratory.

"Wow, looks like a stampede has been through here!" Freddie said, amazed at the chaos the room was in.

Wiggly raised a smile and replied, "Well there were a lot of Elfins in here not long ago, I expect they were too tired to tidy up after themselves. When this is all over, we must come back and restore everything otherwise Merlin will be disappointed when he returns."

Freddie agreed as they climbed the staircase to the balcony library.

"It looks funny seeing all the books the wrong way round, Freddie," Wiggly said as they looked for the book to open the secret door. They walked round the gallery until they found a single book still with the spine facing outwards.

"I bet someone must have struggled trying to lift this book from the shelf," Freddie giggled.

They reached up and both gripped the book, pulling as hard as they could.

"I feel too weak, Freddie," Wiggly announced.

"Just a little longer, Wiggly, I felt it begin to move," Freddie replied and with that the book hinged forward from the top and triggered the bookcase to open.

"I forgot how dark this tunnel is," Wiggly remarked, switching on his torch and shining it into the pitch-blackness.

They began walking, shining their torches around.

"Does this tunnel seem different?" Wiggly asked.

"It does, it seems longer, I'm sure we should have reached the end by now," Freddie replied.

"It also feels like we're walking down hill, it's a bit deceiving with only the torch light, but we are definitely walking downward," Wiggly said.

They continued walking for another ten minutes or so when Wiggly needed another rest and sip of water.

"I'm sure we should have reached the end of the tunnel by now and the floor is looking really steep, look at the angle we're sitting at," Freddie said.

Wiggly looked at Freddie and announced, "Hey, that's really strange. If you're sitting upright, then the floor is rising up from the direction we have come and sloping down in the direction we are going!"

"Huh!" Freddie chuckled, scrunching his face up.

"Aww, you know what I mean!" Wiggly laughed.

"Wait! Wasn't there a trap before, have you seen any sign of it, Wiggly?" Freddie suddenly remembered with some alarm.

"No. No, I haven't," Wiggly replied as they started off again.

"Coo! This is really steep now, best hold on to each other in case we trip, I'm sure we would roll downwards if we did!" Freddie said.

"Freddie, I think something is wrong!" Wiggly said, then stopped and pulled Freddie to him. "Remember, Merlin said the tunnel would not open again for 50 years!" Wiggly said quietly.

"But we need water from his lake, so maybe the time has changed somehow," Freddie replied.

"We could have fallen into a trap and be wandering around forever in the darkness," Wiggly said a little nervously.

Freddie felt that fear as well but also felt he had to stay strong. "Let's carry on for a while, we have to believe Merlin is looking out for us, don't we?"

They walked slowly, holding tightly on to each other because the tunnel was very steep now.

"Hey look, there's some steps ahead, but there were not any steps before," Wiggly cried. "What should we do, Freddie? It scares me."

Freddie felt scared too, all his instincts were telling him to turn back and run.

"C-O-M-E!.... COME!.... COME!.... COME!"

The deep, soft tones beckoned them.

"It's Merlin, Wiggly, he wants us to keep going." Freddie found his voice and was given courage by the sound of Merlin's voice. "Come on, Wiggly," he said optimistically, taking his friend's hand, "let's see where Merlin wants us to go."

The two friends followed the tunnel down the steps, which seemed to be turning one way then the other, until Freddie stopped.

"Look, Wiggly!" he said excitedly.

Ahead of them a bright blue light lit up the stairway and they no longer needed their torches, so they switched them off.

"C-O-M-E!.... COME!.... COME!.... COME!"

Again Merlin beckoned the two boys and they walked slowly down the steps until there were no more, just level ground.

"This light is so beautiful, Wiggly, it makes me feel calm and happy," Freddie observed.

"Me too," Wiggly agreed.

They walked onward until the blue light seemed to be coming from everywhere.

"Look! Look!" Wiggly cried excitedly.

In front of them the tunnel opened into a wider cave-like area with blue walls and ceiling. They walked into the blue cavern and looked around in complete awe, it was so beautiful.

Freddie suddenly cried, "No! This is impossible, I can't believe what I'm seeing!"

"What! What is it, Freddie, what do you see?" Wiggly began to feel nervous and a little uneasy.

"Look up, Wiggly. What do you see?" Freddie replied.

Wiggly looked up and squinted his eyes, then gasped, "No, Freddie, that's impossible! We're going to die!" he cried clinging to his friend.

Freddie pulled them over to the wall that curved overhead and down the other side, like being inside a huge bowl.

"What're you doing, Freddie? No don't! Freddie, don't touch that! Oooh!" Wiggly was almost hysterical, he closed his eyes and could not watch Freddie as he began touching the blue wall.

Freddie lifted his hand, clenched his fist with his index finger sticking out and touched the shimmering blue wall. "Wiggly, look!" he cried, shaking his friend who reluctantly opened his eyes.

"Freddie! Where's your hand gone?" Wiggly cried, looking at Freddie's arm touching the wall but his hand had disappeared.

"It's okay, Wiggly, we're safe, look." Freddie pulled his arm back and his hand appeared like magic and he waved it in front of Wiggly's eyes.

"Your hand, it was gone. Where did it go, Freddie, how is it back again?"

"Watch this time, Wiggly." Freddie reached out towards the blue shimmering wall and his fingers touched it, then began disappearing into it until his whole hand had vanished.

"Freddie, your hand. Where's your hand now?"

Freddie laughed. "Haven't you worked it out yet, Wiggly? This is not a wall at all, it's water, look," he pulled out his hand again.

"Huh! But it's not even wet, Freddie, how can it be water?"

"I don't know, Wiggly, try it for yourself."

Wiggly reached out his arm and slowly pushed his hand into the watery wall. "Oooh, it feels cold and wet, it is water. Wow! This is so magical, it's impossible," he cried. When he pulled his hand free it was not wet. "Oooh, this is quite spooky, don't you think? What's holding it up? Why doesn't it come crashing down on us?"

Freddie was too preoccupied to answer Wiggly but called out, "Wiggly, I think we are actually underneath Merlin's lake.

Wiggly turned to look at Freddie.

"Here, Wiggly, look up through the water, what can you see?" Freddie said excitedly.

Wiggly looked up through the water. "Freddie, that's amazing, is that Merlin's statue and what's twinkling above him?"

"You're right, Wiggly, that is Merlin in his statue form and it's the Fairy crystals that are twinkling," Freddie replied. "I think Merlin has created this for us to collect water from his lake, because we would not be able to go back into the Crystal cavern again and we have been going downwards for a long time, it has to be!" Freddie announced.

Wiggly hardly heard what Freddie said. The rippling blue light was mesmerizing him and he kept pushing his finger into the watery wall, completely fascinated. "Oooooh, Freddie, this is really powerful magic," he said still poking the wall and watching his hand vanish and then reappear completely dry.

Freddie took off his rucksack, unzipped the top and put his hand inside, pulling out a glass bottle.

Wiggly was in a world of his own, swishing his fingers in and out of the watery wall.

Freddie took the lid off the bottle and pushed it into the water of Merlin's lake and it filled almost instantly. Pulling it out again, he screwed the top on tightly. His rucksack had a special net pocket for bottles and he slid in the bottle full of Merlin's lake water to keep it safe, then slung his rucksack back on his shoulders.

"Come on, Wiggly, we have to go, I've got the water." He grabbed his friend's hand and gently pulled him away from the wall, back towards the tunnel they had entered through.

"So pretty!" Wiggly kept saying.

Freddie pulled him along, chuckling at his friend. The tunnel began to get dark and he switched on his torch.

Wiggly switched his torch on as well and they began walking up the steps when he suddenly asked, "What's that noise?"

Freddie knew exactly what it was. "Run, Wiggly! We have to run now! We must run for our lives, now, run, run!" he cried.

"What! What's happening?" Wiggly sounded confused hearing the alarm in Freddie's voice.

"It's the water, Wiggly, it's filling the tunnel. We must get to the top now, quickly!"

The boys ran up the steps puffing and blowing, but somehow finding a reserve of energy from the fear of drowning and their need to survive. When they finally reached the top of the steps they just had to stop and catch their breath, they puffed and panted, gasping and gulping lungs full of air. As they began to walk away, the water splashed and lapped over the top of the steps.

"Goodness, that was close, Freddie," Wiggly panted. "Why did Merlin do that?"

Freddie pulled his friend along up the sloping tunnel. "You said it yourself, Wiggly, it was powerful magic that held the lake back. When it was no longer needed, Merlin had to release his magic. Come on, let's go, we have what we need."

When the sloping floor began to level off they heard a slight noise behind them and turned to look. Shinning their torches they saw the tunnel close to a complete dead end.

"The tunnel has gone, Freddie, I guess we are safe now. Can we rest a minute?" The sudden effort of running was taking its toll on an already weary Wiggly.

They sat down and Freddie took off his rucksack and pulled out two cartons of orange juice. "Here, drink this while we rest. We were always safe, Wiggly, Merlin was making sure of that. I guess he was having a bit of fun with us, making the water come after us, but I don't think we were in any real danger," Freddie explained.

Wiggly smiled, then noticed the bottle of water, which glowed a pretty blue colour. "It's so beautiful, Freddie. When did you do that?"

Freddie laughed. "You were so fascinated dipping your fingers and hand in and out of the wall, you didn't see me take a bottle from my rucksack and fill it!"

Wiggly giggled. "Come on then, we have a long way to go yet," he groaned and yawned.

"Yep! A long, long way yet," agreed Freddie.

* *

By the time the two boys returned to the Tiggly's house poor Wiggly was completely exhausted and he flopped on a comfy chair and fell asleep straight away.

Freddie explained all that had happened to them and showed Daddly and Mummly the glowing bottle of water.

"Goodness, that was some adventure, Merlin's magic is still so powerful even though he's frozen in time," Daddly replied in utter amazement, looking at Freddie, then his son with admiration and pride.

Mummly gave Freddie a hug. "Now we have all the elements for the spell. We think you and Wiggly need to perform it together, but he's too tired just now," her voice was soft and caring. "I expect you must be weary too, Freddie."

He smiled at both Mummly and Daddly, they felt so much like a second set of parents to him. He felt very lucky to have all this in his life, even though he had to keep it secret. He looked at his watch. "Mummly, Daddly, I do have to go home before I am missed. Once the spell potion is made it has to be left for three or more days. Could you both get all the ingredients ground up and ready and I'll come back tomorrow so that Wiggly and I can mix things together?"

Mummly and Daddly nodded. "Everything will be ready for you when you return, Freddie." They hugged him close to them. "Thank you, Freddie, you know Wiggly and Giggly have been so much happier because of you, in fact the whole town is somehow brighter and more cheerful. We strongly believe you have been sent to us by Merlin's hand, to make us better, stronger, ready for his return," Daddly praised Freddie and gently stroked his head.

Freddie was smiling and feeling a little red in the face. When they parted he waved goodbye and raced through the deserted streets to the spiral staircase door.

* *

On Tuesday morning Freddie was up and about as usual, but felt a little sad.

"Why don't you go visit your friends? You must be missing them, that's probably why you're feeling sad?" his mother suggested.

Freddie knew why he felt sad was more to do with having to wait to fix the mess he had created. "All my friends are struggling to sleep and it's making them poorly," Freddie replied, but his mother was partly right, he was missing his friends, so he did as she suggested. He set off with the intention of visiting Jimmy, then thought about the magic spell potion and made a detour into the forest and to Wiggly's house.

"Ah Freddie, come in, come in," he was greeted by Mummly, who ushered him into the house and sat him in a comfy chair.

"Freddie!" a familiar voice called from the sleeping chamber door. An excited Wiggly ran to meet his friend and gave him a warm hug.

"You seem much brighter today, Wiggly," Freddie said when he could breathe again after Wiggly let him go.

"I can't sleep in bed without having nasty dreams, so Giggly and I have been snoozing in the comfy chairs and the bad dreams don't seem to come so quickly, so we have had a little bit of sleep," Wiggly replied.

"I can't stay too long, Wiggly, I'm supposed to be visiting my school friends, but I wanted to come and start the magic spell potion together with you, so shall we get started?" Freddie explained.

Wiggly smiled and jumped up. "Mummly and Daddly have got everything ready on the table," he replied, taking Freddie's wrist and pulling him towards it.

313

"Everything is here, Freddie," Mummly said waiting at the table. "If you want to read out the instructions, I can guide Wiggly to where each of them is, so he can put them in the bowl. Then you can both add the water from Merlin's lake and give it a stir," suggested Mummly.

"That's a good idea," Freddie agreed and picked up the parchments. He read out each ingredient and waited until Mummly pointed to the right one.

"How many dandelion leaves?" Wiggly asked.

"Well it just says *'leaf* 'so I guess it's just one leaf," Freddie replied.

Mummly handed Wiggly a single crushed up leaf.

"The spell says *'Seed'* not seeds of *'Mighty'*, so one acorn," Freddie announced.

Mummly handed Wiggly a single crushed acorn.

"The carrot is a bit more tricky, but the other parts are not big quantities so maybe the same amount as the acorn," Freddie said.

Wiggly placed the amount his mother handed to him into the bowl.

"Eye of Tatty', that must just be one eye and *'Petals of Gold'* must be all the petals of one marigold," Freddie suggested.

When everything was in the bowl, Mummly gave Freddie the pestle, which looked like a small baseball bat, so he could grind all the ingredients together. He got tired quickly, so Wiggly had a go, then Mummly, finally Daddly, who had just come home from collecting tree fungi that he added and then finished crushing until everything was blended into a thick paste.

"Now we have to leave this for three or more days before adding the water from Merlin's lake," Freddie said having read the instructions again. "I'll come back on Saturday and we can complete the potion and make the spell. I hope it works," he said.

"I'm sure it will, boys," Daddly encouraged. "Merlin has been guiding you so far, so have faith," he added.

Freddie said his goodbyes and headed off back into the forest and on to Jimmy's house, where he knocked on the door.

Jimmy's mother opened the door and gave Freddie a huge smile as she invited him inside. "Hello Freddie, well you're a sight for sore eyes," she said with a happy voice.

"Oh dear, have you got sore eyes?" Freddie asked looking at Jimmy's mother's eyes.

She laughed. "No Freddie, you're so cute, it means that I am really pleased to see you!"

Freddie laughed. "Oh, I thought you were poorly too."

"Jimmy is still in bed, come on up, I'll let him know you have come to see him," Jimmy's mother told Freddie.

They walked up the stairs slowly and Jimmy's mother opened her son's bedroom door. "Jimmy, Freddie has come to see you," she announced.

Freddie walked into his friend's bedroom to find him laid on the bed. Jimmy's face was as white as a ghost, dark patches under his eyes made him look like a Panda Bear. Freddie sat on the bed and held his friend's hand. "Are you still having nightmares, Jimmy?"

Jimmy forced a weak smile and nodded. "Every time I close my eyes the happy thoughts vanish and horrible monsters wake me up leaving me feeling frightened," he replied sadly. "What about you, Freddie, are you having nightmares too?"

Freddie shook his head. "Not so far. I don't understand why, really. The school has been closed for cleaning, they think pupils have caught a virus or something that's making everyone ill."

Jimmy's mother brought them some chocolate milk to drink. "Well, you look a lot brighter already, Jimmy," she said. "Freddie's visit is good medicine."

Freddie chuckled and even Jimmy did too. "I've got Snakes and Ladders with me, do you want to play?" Freddie asked cheerfully.

Jimmy nodded and they played for a while, drinking their chocolate milk and it cheered Jimmy up. He had been feeling sorry for himself before Freddie called to see him and when Freddie left he was feeling much happier.

Freddie spent the rest of the day visiting as many of his friends as he could.

He played the guitar for James and Joanne, it made them both feel much more cheerful and James looked at Freddie with pride.

As Freddie left after visiting each of his friends they were all feeling a lot happier and their mothers thanked him for cheering up their sons and daughters.

On his way home he passed the school and saw there was an even bigger sign on the gates so he ran over to read it.

School will be closed now for the rest of the week due to so many pupils being unwell and unable to attend

* *

The next morning was Wednesday and Freddie lazed in his bed thinking about everything. The sneaky way the Incubus Spirit had tricked him into releasing it. All of his friends being sick because of that, how really poorly they all looked, their faces so white and all having big black bags under their eyes. He knew nothing could be done to stop the Incubus until the spell ingredients had combined for at least three days. Yesterday had been only the first day and this was day two, he would just have to wait it out until at least Friday or Saturday.

For the next two days Freddie spent his mornings working on his model kits that his Grandma had given him for his birthday. In the afternoons he visited his friends trying to cheer them up, but it upset him to see them looking more and more poorly. None of them had slept properly for more than a week and they could not eat or drink very well because they were so tired.

Freddie went to visit William and when his mother answered the door she was in tears.

"They've taken him away, Freddie, I've lost my little boy!" she sobbed.

"I-I don't understand, what has happened to William?" Freddie was tearful as he asked the question, thinking that his friend had actually died.

"Oh Freddie, he looked so pale and thin with big black patches under his eyes, he couldn't sleep and he couldn't stay awake. The doctor came and put him on a drip to keep him hydrated but it didn't help, he just collapsed, Freddie, I lost my little boy!"

Freddie's eyes were streaming with tears, he could hardly breathe. *'This is my fault'*, he thought, *'I've killed my friend.'* "What have I done?" he said under his breath.

"They took him away last night, Freddie."

"Who took him?" Freddie croaked.

"The ambulance did, with its lights flashing, sirens, everything. They took him and the paramedics said William was so poorly I should be ready for bad news. I'm a mess, Freddie!" William's mother was a mess, her mascara had run with her tears in dark streaks down her cheeks.

Freddie suddenly realised what she had said, William was still alive. "You mean William's in hospital? Let's go and see him, can you drive us there? That's where he is, isn't it?" Freddie asked, desperately hoping that was what William's mother had meant.

William's mother nodded and looked at him. "You're a good boy, Freddie. Let's go then. Let's go," she replied. When they got in the car, William's mother drove like a racing driver, intent on getting to the hospital as quickly as possible. She had been so wrapped up in her own sorrow that she could not face visiting the hospital on her own, welcoming Freddie's suggestion.

Freddie closed his eyes all the way to their destination. The car was being driven so fast he was too terrified to look. When they reached the hospital, Freddie's legs were like jelly and he wobbled a bit as he got out of the car.

"Are you alright, Freddie? Sorry, I did drive a bit fast, didn't I?" William's mother apologised.

The hospital reception directed them to the children's ward and when they reached the double doors, William's mother was reluctant to go in. "What if he is even worse or gone altogether? I couldn't bear it, Freddie," she pleaded.

Freddie felt exactly the same, he did not think he could ever get over losing William, but something inside him urged him to go and see his friend. He took William's mother's hand and led her through the doors.

They passed bed after bed of sick children and did not see William. When they reached the end of the ward there were only two beds left, one was unoccupied, the other had a little girl sitting up reading.

That was the last straw for William's mother, and she burst into tears. "He's gone, hasn't he, Freddie?" she sobbed.

Freddie could not believe his friend had passed away, this was not right, it was all his fault for releasing that evil spirit. He felt down hearted and very sad, even if he could imprison this spirit he could not get his friend back, he hung his head in shame and blame.

"Freddie! Freddie!" A familiar voice called out loudly.

Freddie turned around and looked up, unable to believe his eyes. He pulled on William's mother's arm sharply. "Look!" he croaked.

"William!" his mother cried out through her tears as she and Freddie watched William bounding down the ward and into his mother's arms.

Freddie wrapped his arms around his friend as well and they group hugged for a moment.

When they separated, William's mother held her son at arms length by his shoulders and just looked at him with the biggest ever smile, the corners of her mouth almost put lipstick in her ears.

"William, you look better, how come?" Freddie asked.

Freddie and William's mother sat on the edge of the unoccupied bed, either side of William.

"Mum, I love you, and you Freddie," he said in his normal voice. "It seems I fell asleep in the ambulance, then they brought me here still asleep and I slept all through the night without any nightmares. I feel much better, I had just been to the bathroom when you came to see me." William gabbled his story and Freddie began to realise that William was out of the reach of the Incubus and that was why he had not had any bad dreams.

"There's something in the village causing this," Freddie said, explaining his thoughts to William and his mother. "We need to get all the children out of the village before anything nasty happens to them."

William and his mother were nodding in agreement.

"I think you're right, Freddie, leave it to me, I will get everyone to take their children out of the Village until we discover what's happening," William's mother answered.

William needed to stay in hospital for tests and monitoring for a day or two.

Freddie was happy to see William had already made some friends on the ward and would not be too lonely.

When Freddie and William's mother returned to Elfington Village she was on the telephone to all the children's parents explaining about her son's recovery and what all the parents needed to do and there was a mass exodus from the village. All the shops closed, mothers and fathers took their sick children away from the village, some to grandparents, others to family or even to hotels, anywhere away from Elfington Village so their children could get some sleep and get better again.

It took all Freddie's persuasion to prevent his parents packing him off to his Grandma's house in the city. It was not that he minded staying with his Grandma, he really liked to do that, but he had to be around at the end of the week to help with the spell to capture the Incubus.

** **

Thursday was a very long day for Freddie. The village was deserted, all his friends had left so he could not visit anyone. He really hoped Wiggly, Giggly and the other Elfin children were alright. He desperately wanted to go see them, but knew he would be too upset and if his parents saw that he had been crying, they might insist on him going to stay with his Grandma.

One good thing, Freddie's parents had lots of phone calls from the mothers and fathers of his friends. They told them their children had slept soundly during the night without nightmares and were feeling much better. They wanted to thank Freddie for knowing what to do when everyone else had no clue. All of them said the same thing, "Freddie Fixit to the rescue!"

Freddie's mother felt a deep sense of pride and joy, her little boy had once again helped people, never seeking anything for himself and always thinking of others.

But the Incubus was angry that all the children had moved out of the village and it decided to attack the remaining adults. In the village there were quite a few people who did not have children or they had grown up children who had left the village, there were others who were elderly. That night the Incubus visited every adult and snatched away their happy dreams, implanting terrifying nightmares. It spared Freddie's parents but attacked everyone else and by morning every remaining person in the village had been plagued with horrific nightmares. The Incubus fed on their fears and thirsted for more as it grew even stronger, not realising the Elfins were plotting against it.

** **

When Friday morning finally arrived, Freddie woke up quite early and crept downstairs to make his own breakfast. He settled for

'Dino Boulders' cereal and was thinking about his plans for the day when his mother walked into the kitchen.

"Oh Freddie, you're up nice and early. What did you do with the elephants, we didn't hear them come down the stairs?" she teased and chuckled.

"Aww Mu-um!" Freddie groaned.

"Only teasing, son," she chuckled.

By the time his father came down the stairs the phone had been ringing non-stop.

"Whatever's going on?" he asked.

"Seems a lot of villagers had nightmares last night," Freddie's mother explained.

"There's something attacking the village, maybe U.F.O's," his father replied.

"What's a U.F.O. Dad?" Freddie asked.

"It's an abbreviation for Unidentified Flying Objects, like flying saucers and aliens," his father answered.

"Do you really think there are creatures from outer space running around in the village, Dad?" Freddie asked.

His parents chuckled.

"No, son, that's all fantasy stuff, like magic and Merlin the wizard," his father replied.

Freddie's ears pricked up on hearing that because he knew for a fact that magic and the great Wizard Merlin were real. *So does that mean space aliens are real too?*' he thought to himself. "I think I will go hunting aliens in the forest then, Dad, it'll be a new adventure and maybe I can shoo them away!" Freddie announced, stampeding up the stairs.

"Funny, I didn't hear those elephants come down the stairs. Do you think they jumped out of his bedroom window and crept in the back door when we weren't looking?" Freddie's father said to his wife, both having a good laugh.

Freddie wore his explorers play clothes and rucksack on his back, complete with jam sandwiches, drink and apple as he marched through the forest. "I'm taking a wiggly, wiggly route," he said, to no one in particular, and then laughed at his unintentional joke. "I wonder if aliens really do exist and what they look like? Maybe they are like Sproggles. Hey, there could be some living in the village even. Or they might be like Elfins. Maybe Elfins are aliens? No, didn't Daddly tell me that Merlin created Elfins as his helpers, so they're definitely not aliens. But...." Freddie was talking out aloud and suddenly stopped in his tracks. "If Sproggles ever saw any of the Elfins, because they are so different to them, they might think they were aliens." He was suddenly aware he was talking out aloud and looked around to make sure he was alone, then continued in a loud whisper. "Oh wow, I guess Sproggles must never see Elfins in that case, if they did they might put them in a zoo like the animals, that would be terrible and so wrong. Sproggles must never find out about the Elfins that's for sure!" He made the decision and nodded his head. He suddenly began to feel sad remembering what had started the idea of aliens, the adults in his village were all having nightmares. By the time he reached the big old oak tree the reality of what was happening hit him like a slap in the face. "This is all my fault, I did this to everyone," he said quietly to himself. He opened the door in the big old oak tree and began descending into another world, one where he felt so at home. He was feeling bad at having put all his Elfin friends in danger and by the time he opened the door at the bottom, tears were rolling down his cheeks.

Elfin Town was still locked down and deserted, which did nothing to lighten his unhappy mood and guilty feelings.

Daddly opened the door, looking very tired with dark rings under his eyes

"Hello, Freddie, we're glad you're here, Wiggly has been asking for you."

Freddie walked inside and saw Mummly holding her two children on the comfy sofa and they all looked so poorly.

"What's going on?" Freddie asked softly once he sat down on a comfy chair.

Mummly gave Freddie a weak smile. "Welcome, Freddie, I'm afraid the bad dreams have been affecting adults *and* children for the last couple of days," she explained.

Freddie's tears began, he felt so guilty again as he looked upon his sickly second family. "I'm sorry, Mummly, this is probably all my fault again. All the Sproggle children were in danger of .. of .. well .. err .. never .. going back to school, so I got their mums and dads to take them out of the village and they all started to get better. But the Incubus has begun to attack all the adults in the village instead."

"Don't blame yourself, Freddie, you have such a big heart, you did the right thing," Daddly replied.

Wiggly opened his eyes and lifted his head off his mother's lap. "Freddie, you're here," he said weakly.

Freddie stepped over to his friend and gave him a hug and said, "I am, Wiggly, now we have to end this nightmare, do you feel strong enough to help me?"

Wiggly sat up and gave his friend a big smile. "I am now you're here, let's get rid of this Incubus Spirit together, for good," he replied.

"Everything is prepared for creating the spell, so now it's down to you both," Daddly announced.

Freddie took Wiggly's arm to support his friend as they walked to the table and sat side by side.

Seven candles had been placed around the parchment, a quill pen was by the side of the bowl filled with the spell ingredients.

Daddly lit the candles and explained, "Freddie, if you can put the seven drops of Merlin's lake water in the bowl, then you and Wiggly must stir it together, whatever magic you both possess is important for this part."

Freddie unzipped his rucksack and magically pulled out an eyedropper with a little rubber balloon on one end. He dipped the long glass tube of the eyedropper into the bottle of Merlin's lake water and squeezed the balloon end. The 'blub, blub, blub' noise made Wiggly chuckle weakly, as Freddie squeezed the air out of the eyedropper, then released the balloon. The bright blue water was sucked up into the glass tube of the eyedropper, then Freddie lifted it out.

"Oh, that's really neat," Wiggly croaked.

Freddie held the eyedropper over the middle of the bowl. "Let's count together," he said and gently squeezed the balloon on the eyedropper. A small drop of water formed on the end and dropped into the bowl. The blueness of the water made the contents suddenly begin to glow.

"One, two," as the second drop fell the bowl glowed even brighter.

"Three, four," two more drops and the contents began to fizz and bubble.

"Five, six," two more drops and the bowl came alive, rocking about on the table and bubbling like a pan of boiling water.

"Last one, seven!"

The contents of the bowl began to swirl round and round, then erupted into the air like an upside down funnel, sparkling like a firework, then settled back down into the bowl.

"Wow! That was dramatic," Freddie exclaimed.

"Now both of you hold this wooden spoon and stir the contents seven times," Daddly explained.

The boys took the spoon with Wiggly's hand under Freddie's, then began to stir.

".......... four, five, six, seven times. That's it boys, now pull the spoon out," Daddly instructed.

"Is that it?" Wiggly asked.

Suddenly, the contents began to fizz and hiss, then erupted into the air a second time. To begin with it was like a pretty firework going off again, then it suddenly changed.

"What's that?" Wiggly cried and pushed his chair back with a screech on the stone floor.

The erupting spell mixture turned from coloured sparkles to black and grey, then a face appeared. Its eyes looked fierce, staring at them all in turn as if it were alive.

"It has to be the Incubus! The spell is binding it to this place," Daddly exclaimed as the face continued to look at them one by one and then it roared, showing a huge mouth full of razor sharp teeth.

Freddie jumped back with surprise and fear.

Even Daddly moved back so quickly his chair went flying.

Wiggly lost his balance and fell to the floor, crying out as his bottom hit the hard stone.

There was a look of horror on Freddie and Wiggly's faces. Even Daddly stepped further away just in case the face of the Incubus could do something unexpected.

As suddenly as the face had appeared, it melted away and the spell mixture settled down, glowing effervescent blue.

The danger seemed to be over, chairs were picked up and they all sat back to the table.

"Oh, that's so pretty," Wiggly said, looking over into the bowl that seemed to light up the whole room in a bright blue glow, including Wiggly's face.

Daddly and Freddie joined Wiggly looking into the bowl. What remained was a dazzling blue liquid, even brighter than the water from Merlin's lake. The thick liquid looked so smooth, just like custard, it had no lumps or bits.

"Freddie, I think you had better write the spell, my hands are trembling too much," Wiggly suggested.

Daddly handed the quill pen to Freddie so that he could write out the spell. He, too, was nervous, he could feel trembles in every part of his body, including his hands. But he was responsible for releasing the Incubus and it was his duty to imprison it again. He slid over to where the parchment lay on the table surrounded by the seven candles.

Daddly poured some of the iridescent liquid into a small cup.

Freddie held the quill pen made from a Raven's black feather between his finger and thumb, then dipped it into the magic potion.

They all gasped as the liquid travelled along the feather making it sparkle like Fairy Dust, then the whole feather turned a silvery white colour.

Freddie tried to drop it, fearing his hand would turn the same, but it would not fall from his fingers, he was bound to the quill.

"Freddie, are you alright, does your hand hurt or anything?" Wiggly asked, concerned about the look on his friend's face.

Freddie had stood up when the feather began transforming, now he sat down again and his face looked calm. He smiled at Wiggly, "I'm fine now, Wiggly, I feel, I feel, well, magical. I'm sparkling inside, it's an amazing feeling. I think this is going to work, Wiggly. Can you read out the words, slowly please and I'll write them down?" Freddie did look tranquil, he no longer trembled. Suddenly in his mind a voice sounded, *'I am with you always, Freddie.'* It was a voice he recognised. "Merlin's just spoken to me in my mind, he says he's with me, always."

Wiggly and Daddly smiled and clapped their hands. They had a good feeling everything would be alright now Merlin had spoken to Freddie.

"Are you ready now, Freddie?" Wiggly asked and Freddie nodded.

"Constrain," Wiggly called out.

"How is it spelt, Wiggly?" Freddie asked, not wanting to make any mistakes.

"C - O - N - S - T - R - A - I - N," Wiggly said slowly, one letter at a time.

Freddie wrote the word in his best writing then looked at his friend. "Okay, Wiggly, what's next?" he said. Freddie was finding writing with the quill pen a bit tricky. He dipped it into the magic potion ready for the next word.

"WITHIN," Wiggly spoke slowly and clearly, "W - I....."

"That's okay, Wiggly, I can spell that one," Freddie chuckled as he wrote the word. "Okay, next word please."

Wiggly moved his finger along the words to make sure he did not miss one out or repeat them.

Daddly watched them both, smiling with pride at two very brave boys.

"THIS," Wiggly replied.

"Okay, next please, Wiggly."

Wiggly licked his lips and looked where his finger was pointing. "PARCHMENT," he said slowly.

"Can you spell that one please, Wiggly?"

"P - A - R - C - H - M - E - N - T," Wiggly replied, again slow and clear.

Freddie wrote down each letter as Wiggly called it out. "Phew! This is more difficult than I thought," he admitted.

"You're doing fine, Freddie, I can read your writing very clearly from here. You write very neatly, you'll have to give Wiggly a few lessons, his looks like spiders crawling all over!"

Freddie giggled.

Wiggly crinkled his nose, "Daddly, not fair!" he protested.

"Okay, I'm ready for the next word," Freddie said still smiling. "Let's just check we're right so far. I have, 'constrain within this parchment', is that right?"

Wiggly smiled and nodded. "Perfect, Freddie. Okay the next word is THUS." Wiggly was about to spell it when Freddie said, "Okay got it, next please."

Freddie dipped the quill again. Each time he did, a rainbow of colours travelled from nib to the end of feather.

"IMPRISON, spelled I - M - P - R - I - S - O - N," Wiggly said, anticipating his best friend would want that word spelled out.

Freddie wrote down the word, which he was not familiar with, then asked for the next word.

"NOW," Wiggly replied.

Freddie looked at Wiggly, "Yes, now please."

Wiggly giggled. "That's the next word, Freddie, NOW."

Freddie giggled as well. "Okay got that, what's next?"

Wiggly moved his finger along and replied, "THE."

"Got it, Wiggly, next one please," Freddie asked, dipping his quill pen and watching the rainbow of colours travel along the feather.

"This is the last word, Freddie, it's INCUBUS, shall I spell it?"

Freddie looked at his friend and nodded.

"Okay, Incubus in capital letters, spelled I - N -C - U - B - U - S."

Freddie dipped his quill pen once more and watched the rainbow colours ripple along the feather, then wrote the word. He fell back in the chair and gasped, "It's a bit scruffy, this quill pen seems to flick the magic ink."

"I can read it quite clearly, Freddie," Daddly reassured him.

"What do we do now, I've forgotten?" Freddie asked and Wiggly looked at the parchment Daddly had copied the spell onto.

"We have to put the parchment in the middle of seven burning candles and chant the spell seven times," Wiggly replied.

Daddly moved the bowl, cup and quill out of the way and put the parchment in the centre of the seven candles. "Down to you two boys now. Chant the spell, I will count and make sure it's not over or under. Watch my fingers, okay?"

The boys nodded and Wiggly reached out for his best friend's hand then Freddie held onto Wiggly's and smiled. *'I'm so lucky to have friends like these,'* he thought to himself. Both boys looked at the words on the parchment although they knew them off by heart now and began to chant the spell.

Daddly held up a finger for each time. On the fourth chant the letters began to jiggle on the parchment. On the fifth chant the letters began to move around on the parchment and formed a circle. On the sixth chant the letters began to spin, slowly at first, then faster and faster. On the last chant, as Daddly held up seven fingers, a sparkling bright blue funnel of spinning light appeared. Words of the chanted spell rose from the parchment and reached all the way up to the ceiling and passed through it. They all jumped off their chairs, ran outside and gasped at what they saw. Just above the roof of the house the spiralling funnel looked like a huge vortex, sucking like a giant vacuum cleaner, the words of the spell clearly visible as they slowly rotated around the vortex.

"Look!" Daddly cried pointing to the sky ceiling of Elfin Town, "I think it's the Incubus!"

"Yes! Yes!" Wiggly agreed, getting excited.

The vortex was making quite a loud swishing sound, through the sky the solid black shape of the Incubus was being drawn down into the centre of the spiralling funnel. Elfins began to come out of their homes and gather around the Tiggly's house. Freddie turned to look at them, their faces drawn and tired, ghostly white, yet they managed a smile as they witnessed the Incubus being pulled into the vortex.

"NOOOOO! .... NOOOOO!" it cried out in a deep, broken voice, as the powerful vortex seemed to be pulling it apart. The Incubus struggled against the magical force drawing it down. Its long claws tried to grip the sky roof of the town, huge gouges appeared and the Incubus screamed and cried out, its voice becoming so high pitched everyone had to hold their hands over their ears.

Daddly, Wiggly and Freddie looked on in horror as the evil spirit tried over and over to escape the powerful magic. Its arms extended over the top of the funnel trying to grasp the roof of the house and for a moment it looked like it might just pull itself out.

Wiggly stepped back in fear, no way was it going to touch him and he pulled Daddly and Freddie with him. "Stay back!" he cried.

'Now, Freddie, use your magic to finish off the Incubus,' Merlin's voice sounded so clearly in Freddie's mind and he stepped forward.

Wiggly grabbed his friend, but Freddie was too strong and moved closer to the struggling Incubus Spirit.

The whole town was now crowded around and gasped in fear.

Freddie bravely moved closer to the vortex and the Incubus. He held up both his arms and pointed his hands at the vortex. "Imprison now the Incubus," he cried, "IMPRISON NOW THE INCUBUS!" his voice echoed deep and powerful, again the crowd gasped.

Wiggly looked stunned, never had he heard Freddie's voice sound like that.

From Freddie's fingertips streams of sparkling Fairy Dust emitted, firing at the swirling vortex.

The Incubus shrieked and screamed as it became disembodied, sucked into the Fairy Dust sparkling vortex, now too powerful for it to resist.

Freddie stumbled but Daddly caught him and lifted him up, then they rushed back inside the house. Daddly sat an exhausted Freddie on a chair and they watched the vortex funnel grow smaller and smaller until it was just a circle of words spinning on the parchment. The words slowed down and finally reformed into the words of the spell and the silence was suddenly deafening.

"Freddie, Freddie, we did it! YOU did it!" Wiggly cried out.

From outside the house a huge cheer was heard as all the Elfins heard Wiggly's voice.

"How did you know what to do?" Wiggly asked, hugging his friend and full of joy.

They had caught the Incubus and they would all be safe again.

Mummly and Giggly had been standing at the table, mesmerized by the vortex and now Mummly could see Freddie looked pale and weak.

"Is it all over, Daddly?" Giggly asked, clinging to her father.

"I think so, Giggly," he replied.

"We're not safe yet," Wiggly announced, rolling the scroll up and sliding it inside the metal tube and screwing the cap back on.

"Freddie, love, how do you feel?" Mummly asked holding his shoulders to stop him sliding off the chair.

"Daddly, can you carry Freddie to the comfy sofa, I think he needs to lay down?" Mummly asked.

Daddly walked over to Freddie as soon as Mummly released him, picking up the limp little boy from the chair, taking him over to the comfy sofa.

"Is Freddie going to be alright, Daddly? I'm frightened, he looks so ghostly," Wiggly said, tears already forming in his eyes.

Freddie did look exactly as Wiggly had described, it was as if every bit of life had been drained from him.

"How did he know to do that, Daddly? Where did all that extra magic come from? I don't understand," Wiggly said tearfully.

Mummly lovingly stroked Freddie's brow, just as if he was her own son.

"I guess Merlin spoke to him again and told him what to do, Wiggly. He couldn't know any other way, that wasn't in the book or the spell," Daddly replied.

"He's not going to die, is he?" Wiggly's voice trembled.

Giggly began crying and put her arms around her brother.

Other Elfins were now trying to look inside and see Freddie for themselves, all very concerned about their friend and hero.

Outside the crowd was shouting, "Look! Look!" From the ceiling sky directly above the Tiggly's house where Freddie laid lifeless and pale, something pointed began to push through until a small crystal shape appeared, like those in the Crystal Cavern. It slowly descended and slipped through the Tiggly's roof as if it were not there and hung over Freddie's limp, pale body.

"Stand back!" Daddly told everyone. "I think Merlin is calling for Freddie."

A beam of pretty, sparkling blue light shone down from the crystal and bathed Freddie, getting brighter and brighter until everyone had to look away. When the light vanished, they turned around Freddie had vanished too.

"He's gone, where has he gone?" Wiggly cried.

Even Mummly and Daddly were shedding a tear until they heard a huge cheer from outside. The whole family rushed to the door and the entire town had made a pathway through the middle to where Freddie stood, looking bewildered. As he walked towards Daddly, Mummly, Wiggly and Giggly, the crowd cheered and patted his back.

"Freddie!" Wiggly screamed, rushing through the door, almost pushing his father out of the way. He grabbed his friend and hugged him tightly, still dripping tears.

"Whoah, Wiggly, what's all this?" Freddie asked as he was dragged back inside. "What happened, Daddly?" Freddie asked looking even more perplexed.

"We thought we had lost you," Wiggly gabbled. "A crystal beamed you away and then there you were outside," Wiggly garbled.

"I don't remember that. I was standing watching the vortex outside with you and then Merlin spoke to me. The next thing I knew was being outside in the middle of the whole town. Did we do it?" Freddie asked.

"You did, Freddie. Somehow you gave the vortex a boost of magic and the evil spirit is now locked up in the parchment," Daddly answered proudly.

"What do we do now?" Freddie asked.

Daddly walked to his special cupboard, which was magically locked and uttered some words, the door flew open and he took the jar of Fairy Dust from inside. "Come with me everyone. Freddie, bring the tube please," Daddly instructed and everyone, including the whole town, followed him round to the back of the house to the bottom of the garden. When they walked as far as they could, in front of them was the hard rock wall rising to the blue-sky ceiling.

"Hand me the tube please, Freddie," Daddly said. "Are we sure the parchment is safely inside?" Daddly asked.

Wiggly nodded, he had put it in the tube himself.

Daddly took a tiny pinch of Fairy Dust and sprinkled it on the tube and cast a spell.

> **"Seal this tube for evermore,
> the evil scroll no more to spore."**

The tube formed a sealed dome on each end that made it impossible to open again. Daddly took another small pinch of Fairy Dust and sprinkled the rock wall in front of him and cast another spell.

> **"Open wide a nice deep hole,
> in which to hide this dangerous scroll."**

The rock seemed to fizz, then a large, deep hole appeared in the middle. Daddly handed the tube to Freddie. "Now, Freddie, push the tube into the hole."

Freddie stepped forward and lifted the tube up to the hole and pushed it inside, then stepped back with a huge smile on his face. Was it really all over? He could hardly believe it.

Daddly sprinkled a little more Fairy Dust over the hole and chanted a closing spell.

> **"Forever close this hole for us,
> and make it like it never was."**

The rock fizzed again and the hole slowly closed and vanished.

Daddly turned to his family and gave them all a smile of relief. "The evil Incubus Spirit has put everyone through a great deal of pain. That is now at an end, it is locked away inside the rock in a tube that can never be opened again. The magic spell on it will ensure no Sproggle nor Elfin can ever get at the scroll and release the Incubus again."

Mummly clapped her hands with joy.

Wiggly, Giggly and Freddie group hugged and jumped up and down. Mummly walked over to Daddly and they hugged too.

The Elfins raised a huge cheer, thanking Freddie and Wiggly once again for saving them all, then they slowly returned to their own homes, happy life would soon get back to normal.

Back inside the house Mummly made everyone a nice cup of dandelion tea and they sat quietly in comfy chairs thinking about everything.

"I have learned a valuable lesson, Daddly and Mummly," Freddie began, breaking the silence. "If I ever find a scroll or magic spell book, I will never read it out aloud again without asking first." Wiggly nodded and said, "Me too. I never want to see or hear of another spirit like the Incubus ever again."

CHAPTER SEVEN

The Emergence of Magic

When the snowman winks and
Freddie's dreams come to life.
He goes on a journey to find the truth about Magic.

Sproggles and Elfins alike had been enjoying the peace and tranquillity of an uneventful year after the accidental release and then capture of the evil Incubus Spirit. Freddie's friendship with the Elfins had blossomed into a new high, both he and Wiggly were revered as heroes, having come to the rescue of all Elfins and Sproggles more than once.

Freddie felt completely at home in Elfin Town, he knew just about everyone and they knew and loved him and he felt the same towards them, too. The Tiggly family considered him as another son and his bond of friendship with Wiggly grew stronger than ever, each of them being able to sense when the other was troubled or unhappy.

Freddie and his school friends had all turned twelve years old and that meant they had to leave their beloved Elfington Village Junior School to attend the Comprehensive school in the nearby Evergrim Town.

Each morning Freddie and his friends would board a bus that took them to their new school where they were now the 'newbies,' feeling like small fish in a very, very big pond. The school was really big, with dozens of classrooms and hundreds of pupils. Freddie, William and Jimmy were lucky enough to be placed together in class 'Drake A'. All the other children from Elfington Village were dispersed into the remaining three classes for their school year, 'Drake B, C or D'.

A familiar face was also in class 'Drake A', that of Billy Bates. He had grown taller and slimmer, he looked very smart in his school uniform and with a short haircut he looked clean and tidy. He may have looked a different person, but he had revenge on his mind the moment he saw Freddie and his friends.

The very first lesson in their new school was mathematics with teacher, Miss Addemup. She instructed the class to take out their pencil and ruler ready to draw triangles. Sitting next to Freddie was Terrence, who had come from another village and did not yet know Freddie. He was quite a nervous boy, much like William, and he began to panic when he realised he had left his pencil and ruler at home.

Freddie noticed and said kindly, "Don't worry, Terrence, I have spare ones you can have." Then he unzipped his magic rucksack and pictured a pencil and ruler in his mind, pulling out one of each and handed them to Terrence.

"Thank you, Freddie, I'm so forgetful," Terrance said.

"Freddie Fixit!" whispered Jimmy, seated behind Terrence.

Terrance turned and asked, "What do you mean?"

Jimmy grinned. "Stick with us, Terrence, and you will soon find out," he replied.

Terrance was in trouble again in the Anglish lesson when his ballpoint pen ran out of ink part way through the lesson.

"Don't worry, Terrance, I have a spare one in my rucksack you can have," Freddie said calming Terrance and fishing out a shiny new ball point pen to give to him.

"I'm lucky you have a lot of spare things, Freddie, thank you so much!"

"Freddie Fixit again!" This time it was William who whispered as he was sitting behind Freddie and Terrence, next to Jimmy.

Terrance turned to look at William and then said to Freddie, "Is Fixit your surname, Freddie? Your friends keep saying Freddie Fixit"

Of course Jimmy and William heard Terrance and giggled very quietly and whispered to Terrance, "His name is Freddie Fountain, Terrance, but he always seems to be able to help everyone, he fixes things, so we all call him.........."

"...Freddie Fixit!" Terrance finished Jimmy's sentence and giggled, looking at his new friend who was blushing and smiling.

* *

The first week in the new school was strange and unfamiliar, so during break and lunch times the whole of old Elfington Village class friends converged together. As the days and weeks passed they were making new friends in their own classes and separating off into smaller groups. Just as Freddie, Jimmy and William had tended to spend their break times with their new friends, including Terrence, who Freddie had taken under his wing.

Billy Bates, however, had not made any new friends, he growled at anyone daring to talk to him, scaring them away. He did not want any distractions. "Freddie and friends, I'm gonna get you good, just you wait!" he mumbled under his breath as he spied on them every opportunity he got. He bided his time, sticking his foot out to trip up any of Freddie's friends whenever he got the chance. He would push into them and then profess, "Ooops! Sorry, I didn't see you there!" Little by little he was getting more and more bold as he realised they did nothing to stop him.

After half term break Billy grabbed Terrence, having followed him into the cloakroom. "You and that Freddie Fountain are such good friends all of a sudden!" Billy scowled, gripping Terrance's tie intent on hurting Freddie by hurting his friend.

"BATES, let him go!" The loud voice from behind startled Billy and he instantly let go of Terrance who fell to the floor. Billy turned expecting to see Freddie, but came face to face with James and a School Prefect.

"Run along, Terrance," James told him kindly, having picked him up and made sure he was unhurt, just a little shaken. James had been keeping an eye on Billy Bates, suspecting he was intent on making trouble, knowing him from their previous school. He had spotted Billy following Terrence and called one of the sixth form Prefects to help him prevent Terrence getting hurt.

"Bullying in this school will not be tolerated, Bates!" the Prefect berated. "Two days detention and think yourself lucky, if you had hurt that boy you would be facing suspension or even being expelled from the school completely!"

Billy Bates, like most bullies, was a coward and crumpled before the Prefect and James catching him red handed. After serving his detention, Billy laid low for a couple of weeks, watching, waiting, still intent on getting Freddie Fountain, some way, somehow, his jealousy fuelled his anger and resentment. He remembered the day Freddie had completely embarrassed and humiliated him squirting water on his trousers, causing him to run home and then getting punished by his mother for wetting himself. He watched Freddie and his friends, followed their routines and settled on the changing rooms on a day Freddie's class had outdoor games before lunch then would later all be in the showers.

Billy scared off all but the four friends larking about in the shower stalls, which were divided into individual stalls with a curtain across for a little privacy. The friends were oblivious to the fact that they were now all alone in the changing rooms. Freddie, William, Jimmy and Terrence were enjoying the warm jets of water, chatting and laughing in the plumes of steam.

Suddenly Jimmy screamed loudly, just like he was being murdered.

The other three friends suddenly fell silent and dashed from their shower stall to Jimmy's, who cowered shivering, his smile replaced with a look of fear, panic and surprise.

Billy Bates had filled a bucket with icy cold water and stood on a box in the next shower stall to Jimmy's, then tipped all the water over him. Billy could hardly contain himself, almost falling off the box he was laughing so much. "Ha, ha, ha, ha! Who looks stupid now?" he cried.

"What are you doing, Billy? That's cruel, not funny!" Freddie cried out as the four friends grabbed their towels and wrapped them around themselves.

Billy just sneered and laughed again. "Not so clever now are you, Freddie Fixit? Bet you can't Fix Jimmy, ha, ha!"

Freddie was really cross and stepped around to the shower stall to face his nemesis.

Jimmy was still in shock and shivered.

William and Terrance found a spare towel and wrapped their shivering friend as they moved out of the showers.

"Ha, ha, ha! You won't find your clothes either!" Billy laughed. "They're gone! Ha, ha, ha! You'll have to walk around like that! See how you like everyone laughing at **YOU** for a change! Freddie, oh so clever, Fixit!" Billy sneered and laughed so hard tears rolled down his cheeks. He clung to the curtail rail in case he fell off the box because he was laughing so much.

Jimmy shivered again, William and Terrance hugged their friend to warm him up and listened to Billy with horror at the prospect of leaving the changing rooms wearing only their towels.

Then something unexpected and totally incredible took place as the three of them watched on while Freddie confronted Billy Bates.

"**Get down and come here, Billy! NOW! NOW! NOW! NOW!**" Freddie's voice boomed and echoed, he was not asking, he was commanding. His voice was so very different, so deep and loud it echoed around the walls.

Billy appeared to stiffen as if afraid, his eyes glazed over and his body seemed to obey Freddie. In the most awkward fashion, Billy dropped the bucket he had been holding and like a robot, stepped off the box and moved towards Freddie. Billy was moving his lips but no words could be heard.

"**Go bring our clothes, Billy. DO IT NOW!**" Freddie demanded. Never had he been so angry, his face was bright red.

Jimmy, William and Terrance watched with their mouths wide open, not quite believing what they were hearing and seeing.

Billy walked like a wind-up toy out of the changing rooms to return with everyone's clothes.

"**Put them on the bench, Billy, and sit down!**" Freddie commanded and Billy obeyed.

"What's happening?" Terrence whispered.

"Don't really know," William replied.

"I've never heard Freddie get angry before, he's very scary. It looks like Freddie is really going to fix Billy now," Jimmy said with chattering teeth.

Freddie turned to his friends and in his normal, warm and friendly voice told them, "Grab your clothes guys and get dressed, but stay a while and just listen."

Billy sat like a waxwork figure, unmoving, except for his eyes, which were shifting rapidly from side to side.

The three friends got dressed quickly, never taking their eyes off Freddie and Billy.

Jimmy finally stopped shivering once he had his school uniform on again.

Then the three sat together on a bench opposite Billy. They had no idea what to expect and could not understand why Billy was acting like a statue.

Freddie, still in his towel, sat next to Billy. "**Look at me, Billy!**" he demanded in that voice again that boomed and echoed frighteningly.

Freddie's three friends shivered on hearing it.

Billy's head turned, his eyes still moving from side to side but sort of glazed as well.

"Look at his face, his eyes, what has Freddie done to him?" William whispered.

"This has to stop, Billy, we have done nothing to you, why are you being so cruel?" Freddie spoke so sternly, even his friends were shocked and sat up obediently. **"What's going on with you, Billy?"** Freddie demanded to know.

Billy's eyes unglazed and focused on Freddie, a tear welled up and ran down his cheek.

"He's crying, Billy's crying," Jimmy said very quietly.

Billy trembled and shook as if he was fighting himself.

"Tell me, Billy! Tell me NOW!" Freddie demanded in a voice that gave Billy Bates no choice but to answer.

"I-It's not f-fair," Billy quivered.

"What's not fair, Billy? What is it?" Freddie demanded in his loud, deep voice.

"Y-you, you, y-you're not f-fair. You have all these f-friends and I have n-none. N-no one likes me!" Billy suddenly began to pour out his feelings and his tears dripped.

Jimmy, William and Terrence looked on in amazement, it seemed to them that Freddie really was fixing Billy Bates.

"N-no one l-likes me. N-no one c-cares. M-my Dad is in p-prison. M-my Mum is never home, she d-doesn't c-care about me. N-no one cares about me, it's like I don't exist, it's not f-fair." Tears rolled down Billy's cheeks and he sobbed.

The three friends sat watching and actually began to feel sorry for Billy despite what he had just done to them. They gasped, not expecting to see what happened next.

Freddie put his arm around Billy's shoulder and pulled him close. "Then let me be your friend, Billy, let me care about you," he said in a warm friendly voice.

Billy stopped sobbing and straightened up and turned towards Freddie.

Jimmy thought Billy was about to punch Freddie and moved a bit closer to stop him, when Billy exclaimed, "R-really? Even after everything? After I've been horrible? You want to be my friend?" Billy's voice was a little shrill.

"I'd sooner be your friend than your enemy. Wouldn't you sooner be my friend than my enemy?" Freddie replied.

Jimmy, William and Terrence stood up and gathered behind Freddie and Billy.

"We would be your friends too," Jimmy said on behalf of the three of them.

Billy turned his head to look at each of them. "But I was just horrible and threw cold water over you and hid your clothes," Billy replied.

Jimmy laughed, "It was only water, Billy!" he answered.

"Now you can have four friends, Billy, isn't that better than no friends?" Freddie said, still with his arm around his shoulder.

All the years of hate and jealousy seemed to pour out of Billy's face and mind, his eyes sparkled and a big smile appeared. "Can I really, you're not fooling with me?" Billy cried happily.

Freddie shook his head and then left his three friends chatting with a transformed Billy Bates while he got himself dressed.

"Why didn't you tell us all this before, Billy?" Jimmy asked.

Billy looked at his three new friends. "I thought you all hated me," he replied.

William, feeling sorry for Billy, said, "It wasn't you we didn't like, Billy, it was all the horrible things you did. You didn't give us a chance to get to know you."

Billy hung his head. "I guess I never tried to be friends, I was so jealous, I never tried. Thank you for giving me a chance. I won't let you down, I promise."

By the time Freddie had dried off, dressed and returned, Billy and his new friends were smiling and laughing together. The sight of that scene made Freddie feel good inside. *'Better to have a friend than an enemy,'* he thought.

After Billy's transformation they all walked to the dining hall and had lunch together. They caused quite a commotion with all Freddie's other friends coming over to him one by one and forgiving Billy. Soon Billy Bates had made more friends than he ever thought possible and his face ached with something very new to him, he could not stop smiling. Finally he felt good about himself and with a huge beaming smile at Freddie he mouthed the words, *'Thank you, Freddie Fixit.'*

Billy Bates' life changed dramatically from that day. He joined the music club and wowed everyone with his skill on the keyboard. He was chosen to play in the under 13 football team and made even more friends, in fact he was never without someone by his side. Even the girls were amazed at his transformation and the one girl he had tormented, Anne Kuff, not only forgave him, but also became his dear friend.

"I don't know how you did it, Freddie," James remarked during music club a few weeks later, "but Billy is a completely different person. Look at him, he's laughing and joking, he's the centre of attention from being a bully to a really nice person." He looked at Freddie and wrapped his arm around his friend. "You're quite a special person, Freddie Fountain!"

* *

A carpet of snow had fallen overnight on Elfington Village and the forest around it, the ground was bright and white, twinkling here and there just like Fairy Dust. All the trees looked majestic with beautiful white coats of snow adorning all the branches.

When Freddie looked out of his window his eyes lit up. "Whoah! Look at all that snow, so beautiful, so magical!" he said, to no one in particular.

It was the weekend and that meant lots of free time to play with the magical white powder. He dashed to the bathroom and quickly washed, then back to his bedroom to get dressed. He stampeded down the stairs into the kitchen where his parents were laughing.

"I'm sure that herd of elephants is getting heavier!" his father chuckled as Freddie appeared.

"Aww! Da-ad! Not funny!" he complained with a big smile.

"Here we go, Freddie," his mother said placing a steaming bowl in front of him after he sat to the table. "I expect you'll be wanting to play in the snow, so I've made you porridge for breakfast to keep you warm."

Freddie looked at the bowl and grinned. "Oh! Thank you, Mum," he said looking from the bowl to his mother, "I really like porridge." 'Oh! Oh! There's no jam' he thought to himself.

"Here you are dear." His mother placed the jar of strawberry jam on the table with a spoon.

"Wow! That's just like magic, Mum, I was just thinking about jam!" he confessed.

* *

"Start with a big snowball in your hand, Freddie, then roll it in the snow to make it bigger. Why don't you make the head then give me a hand to roll the body," Freddie's father instructed as they began making a snowman.

Freddie soon had a good-sized ball suitable for the head, then he helped his father roll the ever-bigger ball for the body. "I'll help you put the head on, Dad, it's quite heavy." Freddie said excitedly and between them they placed the snowman's head on the big round body.

"Go see if your mother has a carrot for his nose, son."

Freddie dashed to the kitchen door and took the carrot his mother was waiting to give him.

"Now we need some eyes and mouth and buttons for his front," Freddie's father announced as they stood back and admired their handiwork.

"What can we use for them, Dad?"

"Well when I was a boy we used small pieces of coal, but now that we don't have open fires in our homes now, with central heating, there is no coal about," his father replied.

A tapping on the kitchen window made them both look and Freddie's mother was making a Tee sign with her hands.

"It's time for a cuppa, son," his father said smiling.

"I think I'll stay outside and hunt around to see if I can find something to decorate our snowman," Freddie explained.

His father agreed and left to go indoors.

Freddie decided to look in the forest for things to decorate their snowman. "I need some round stones, black ones would be best or red ones for buttons," he said, to no one in particular as he opened the garden gate and walked into his forest.

Although many of the trees had shed their leaves for the winter, they had also kept the forest floor mostly free of snow.

"Black stones, now where might you be?" Freddie said out aloud, crouching down and looking around and under some of the bushes that still had all their leaves. He was suddenly aware of something

340

large approaching him from behind, he turned to look and gasped. "Oh!" Freddie fell backwards, catching his fall by swinging his arms behind him. "You gave me such a fright!" he said as he came face to face with a beautiful deer.

It did not seem afraid of Freddie nor try to run away when he stood up again, quite the opposite, the deer moved even closer. It had no antlers and Freddie thought it might be young one or a female.

"Hello, I'm Freddie," he said quietly to the deer and it came close enough for him to stroke. "Wow! You're so beautiful, your fur is so soft to touch," he said softly.

'Freddie come,' Freddie did not see the deer speak with its mouth, but the words came into his mind. He did not feel afraid, in fact he was getting used to the fact that he could understand animals.

The deer turned and walked away and Freddie began to follow. He walked behind the deer for a minute or so before it stopped and began kicking the ground with its front hoof. 'Here, Freddie.'

The soft voice sounded in his mind again. When he looked down at the hollow the deer had made, he was surprised. "Oh, wow! Thank you so much," he said to the deer, which looked at him and seemed to smile, then turned and walked away slowly until it vanished among the trees. Freddie looked at the shallow hole and scratched his head. 'How did the deer know what I was looking for' he thought as he bent down to pick up the round black pebbles that were in the hollow. While he collected all the pebbles the voice of Merlin flashed through his mind reminding him he was special. For once Freddie did not have his rucksack with him so began filling his pockets with the shiny round pebbles.

Back in his garden he started placing the stones for the snowman's eyes and mouth, he decided on a smiling mouth, then pushed the pebbles in a line down the front for buttons.

His parents came out to have a look at the snowman.

"That looks really great!" his mother said with amazement.

"Where did you find those lovely black pebbles, Freddie?" his father asked.

When Freddie explained what had happened his mother gave him a hug.

"You are a very special son, even the animals are friends with you," she said proudly.

"It's quite rare to see a deer in these parts, the village and forest are surrounded by the mount-hills so they have no way to get into the forest other than by the road and that's quite dangerous for them. You are a lucky boy, Freddie. Now, don't stay out too long, come back indoors when you feel cold," his father said as his parents went back indoors.

Freddie thought his snowman needed hands and feet, so rolled a couple of small snowballs and stuck them either side of its body. Next he rolled two larger snowballs and stuck them to the bottom of the snowman for feet, he added more snow to shape them like big shoes. He stood back and looked at the snowman with a sense of pride and achievement, but he was beginning to feel cold and made his way back indoors.

Freddie spent the afternoon painting his latest model kit, a Chinook helicopter. It was fiddly, delicate work, but he had a steady hand and lots of practice and patience. The afternoon seemed to whiz by and before he realised what time it was, his mother was calling him to come down, as it was teatime.

That night it was a full moon and just before he climbed into bed he looked out of his bedroom window. The moonlight illuminated the whole of the back garden where his snowman stood proud and smiling. Freddie just gazed and admired him, thinking about the deer and the pebbles and he chuckled to himself. "Maybe tomorrow I can find you a hat, a scarf and a broom to hold in your hand," he said to his snowman. "I shall call you 'Snowy', yes, it's a great name." He yawned and walked over to his bed, climbed in and snuggled under his duvet. In his mind he created a picture of his snowman wearing a red baseball cap, a red and white striped scarf wrapped around his neck. Then he thought 'Snowy' needed a pipe and a Witches style broom in his hand. Filled with these images Freddie soon dropped off to sleep.

The next morning he tumbled down the stairs chuckling to himself, still thinking of his snowman all dressed up. "Hey Dad, I had a dream about 'Snowy'. Oh, that's what I'm calling our snowman, by the way. In my dream he had a red hat and red and white striped scarf. Oh, and a pipe and a broom held in his snowball hand!" Freddie was quite excited.

His father looked over at his wife, both had puzzled expressions on their faces.

"What's the matter?" Freddie said looking at them both. "Am I being silly again?"

"Have a look at 'Snowy,' Freddie," his father replied.

Freddie walked over to the kitchen window and looked into the garden at his snowman. "WOW! Dad, Mum, how did you know? I never had the chance to tell you until now! 'Snowy' looks great!" He clapped his hands with excitement.

When his parents said nothing Freddie turned to look at them. "What is it Mum, Dad, what's wrong?"

"Well, Freddie," his mother began to explain, "we thought you had put the hat, scarf, pipe and broom on your snowman, because your father and I didn't do it."

Freddie frowned, thought, then laughed, "You got me good, Mum. You're kidding me, right?" he replied.

"Your mother is right, Freddie," his father replied. "We really didn't do this and if you haven't then we have a mystery on our hands. What you described, red hat, striped scarf, pipe and broom, 'Snowy' is exactly like your dream," his father replied.

"I don't understand, Dad, how could 'Snowy' be like this if no one did it?" As Freddie spoke he had a sudden thought. *'I wonder if Wiggly did this for me during the night?'* "I think it must be one of my friends playing a trick on us, Dad," he concluded. While he stirred the jam around in his bowl of porridge he was thinking about 'Snowy'. *'How was it possible for me to see something in my dreams before it happened?'*

After breakfast they all went outside to look at 'Snowy' more closely.

"There's no name or anything on the scarf or hat," Freddie's father explained after examining them closely.

"This is a real pipe too," Freddie's mother said.

"I don't mind if it's real, Mum, it looks great," Freddie chirped.

"Look at 'Snowy's' shoes," Freddie's mother chuckled, pointing at the snowman's feet.

"You made a good job of those, Freddie," his father laughed as they took in all the details of their creation in snow.

Freddie knelt down at 'Snowy's' feet and patted bits of snow here and there to make the shoes look even more realistic. "They just need some kind of laces now," Freddie said as he stood up to admire his handy work.

"Be careful what you wish for, Freddie!" his mother chuckled, "your snowman might walk off in the night!"

Freddie thought his mother was funny and they all laughed at her whimsical remark.

His parents left him admiring 'Snowy' and then, as he began to walk away and follow them he gasped. "What? No!" he said out loud and stepped back to look at 'Snowy's' face again.

Hearing his gasp, Freddie's parents stopped and looked back at him. "What's got you all surprised?" his father called.

"UH!" Freddie gasped again as the snowman appeared to wink at him. He rubbed his eyes and ran after his parents. When he caught up with them he said, "I thought 'Snowy' winked at me!" This idea made his parents laugh.

"You're letting your imagination run away with you, son," his father replied.

"Yeh, impossible, right?" Freddie whispered to himself as his mother hugged him.

Back in the warmth of the kitchen they sat and enjoyed a cup of tea.

"Mum, what is tea made from?" he asked and his mother smiled.

"It's actually the leaves of a bush that only grows in hot countries like India and China. Young leaves are picked from the bushes and dried in the sun. Once they turn from green to black, they are crushed into tiny pieces we call tealeaves. When we pour boiling water on them they release the flavour of the leaves," she replied.

"Oh!" Freddie said in wonderment. "Can you make tea from other plants, like dandelion leaves?" he asked.

His father responded to Freddie's question. "Yes, Freddie, tea can be made from many different plants such a camomile or rose petals, but some plants are poisonous so it is important not to try plants unless they have been shown not to be harmful."

"As far as dandelion leaves are concerned," his mother continued, "it is possible, I know the leaves can be used in salads and the flowers are edible too."

Freddie nodded and smiled, he knew the answer really, but wondered if his parents knew about such things.

"May I go into the forest to inspect my secret dens, Mum? They may have all collapsed in the snow by now," Freddie asked and his parents nodded with a smile. He galloped upstairs to collect his rucksack, then downstairs again for some snacks his mother put out for him.

"Back before it gets dark, Freddie, we don't want you getting lost!" his father warned.

"Okay, Dad, I have my watch on and will be home before four o'clock. See ya!" he said having pulled on his boots and wrapped up warmly with scarf and gloves.

He skipped down the path then turned back to look at 'Snowy' and laughed. "Did he wink?" he said, to no one in particular. "Did you wink, 'Snowy'?" he asked his snowman and chuckled running off through the gate before he saw 'Snowy' wink again.

The forest floor had sprinklings of snow here and there and there were big blobs of snow under some trees where it had fallen from high branches. Being careful not to leave footprints, Freddie used a small branch to wipe them out as he made a beeline for the big old oak tree. Having spoken the magic words and opened the door, he scuttled down the spiral staircase, missed the last step and fell into the bottom door with a thump. "Oooh! Ow!" he cried, then giggled as he picked himself up and rubbed his head and nose. Once he spoke the magic words the door opened into Elfin Town. He looked around and everything was just the same, the Elfin's did not have winter and summer, it was warm like summer all year round.

At Wiggly's house Freddie sat around the fire in a comfy chair drinking hot dandelion tea Mummly had made for them all. "Daddly, can I ask you where all the smoke goes from your fires?"

Wiggly and Giggly looked at Freddie, then at Daddly, it was something they had just never thought about.

Daddly nodded his head and seemed to be searching his memory for the answer, finally replying, "That's a good question, Freddie, I know your parents love your enquiring mind and it makes us think about things we take for granted. But as far as I recall, the Great Wizard created special trees in the forest that have hollow centres. If you look carefully at our sky there are small holes dotted all over it, some of them carry smoke up through the centre of the trees and disperse it into the air. Some of the holes bring fresh air down into the town so that we can breathe."

"Wow!" Giggly cried, "that's so clever. How come we never knew about that, Daddly?"

Daddly was not certain. "It's not taught in the school any more and no one asks, I suppose."

Freddie thought about Daddly's answers and asked, "Why don't leaves and birds and other things fall down the hollow tree trunks?"

Mummly laughed, looking at her children who were wide eyed at Freddie's inquisitiveness.

Daddly smiled as well. "I don't know for sure, but I guess the Great Wizard put an enchantment on those trees to prevent anything like that happening."

Freddie was all smiles and nodding his head. "Thank you, Daddly, that's another mystery solved. Oh! I have something to tell you all," he suddenly announced. "My snowman suddenly had a hat, scarf and pipe overnight," Freddie declared to see how Wiggly would react, thinking it was him who put them on the snowman.

"Oh! Is it snowing?" Giggly piped excitedly.

"It has been and everywhere is covered in white except the forest, or most of it anyway," Freddie replied. "So you don't know anything about my snowman's hat and scarf then, Wiggly?" Freddie asked.

Wiggly looked at his friend and grinned. "Did you think I did it to play tricks? You did, didn't you?" Wiggly replied and laughed.

"Okay," admitted Freddie, "I did think that. So are you saying it wasn't you then?"

"S'right, not me, we didn't even know it was snowing, Freddie. Good prank though, bet your parents are trying to guess how they got there," Wiggly said.

"Magic!" Giggly announced excitedly, "got to be magic!"

Freddie looked at Giggly who was chuckling away, then at Wiggly who was nodding in agreement.

A knock on the door interrupted their chance to explore the idea further.

Daddly got up to answer. "Come on inside, Elder Spudlike," he greeted their guest. "Mummly, it's Tate!" Daddly called out as his friend walked inside the house.

Their visitor said his hellos and sat down with the children and Mummly while Daddly closed the door and joined them.

Mummly gave their friend a warm smile and announced, "I'll make us a nice cup of dandelion tea."

Town Elder Spudlike sat next to Freddie on the comfy sofa.

Freddie smiled and greeted him. "Hello, Elder Spudlike. How are your children, Fry and Crispin?" he asked politely.

Elder Spudlike returned Freddie's smile and replied, "They're doing fine, Freddie, now that horrible Incubus has been imprisoned and they can finally sleep peacefully. Thanks to you, Freddie, and the whole Tiggly family, of course."

Mummly brought over a tray of dandelion tea and handed a cup to everyone.

"What brings you to us this morning, Tate?" Daddly enquired.

"Well, I came to see if you could contact Freddie, but as luck would have it, he's already here," the Town Elder replied.

"Did you need help with something?" Freddie asked.

But the Town Elder did not get a chance to reply, a loud crack was heard and Daddly was suddenly thrown to the floor as the leg on his chair snapped.

"Ooof!" Daddly groaned when he hit the hard floor.

Wiggly jumped up immediately, "Daddly! Daddly! Are you alright?" he cried, helping his father back onto his feet.

Daddly looked quite bewildered and picked up the broken chair leg and stared at it. "Thank you, son, I'm fine, just a bit shocked that's all," he replied.

"What a shame, Daddly, that chair's not much good now," Mummly said, "best throw it away and replace it."

Freddie suddenly piped up, "Oh, I have something in my rucksack, a special glue, that will fix it!" Then he jumped up, grabbed his rucksack and got ready to unzip it. "It's called Dinosaur glue and it's really strong," he announced.

Giggly laughed. "Dinosaur glue, that's a funny name, Freddie!"

Daddly scratched his head and smiled, he somehow knew Freddie might come to the rescue. "I guess it won't hurt to give it a go, Freddie," he answered.

Freddie opened his rucksack and pulled out the Dinosaur glue, then he and Daddly turned the chair upside down. Freddie opened the tube of glue, applied some to each piece of the broken leg and pressed them together. "We have to say 'Abracadabra,' I nearly forgot that," he said and everyone, including the Town Elder, repeated the magical word.

"ABRACADABRA!"

Of course they all laughed thinking it quite fun.

"There, good as new!" Freddie announced with satisfaction, replacing the cap on the tube of glue and putting it back into his rucksack.

Wiggly grabbed the chair leg and tried to break it off again. "Oh! It really is stuck well, that's some strong glue, Freddie," he remarked.

Daddly also tried to loosen the chair leg and it held fast. "Well done, Freddie, I think it's just as strong, if not stronger than before," he praised.

"Freddie Fixit!" cried Giggly, giggling away as she watched Freddie's face turn bright red.

"Giggly, stop teasing poor Freddie," Mummly said.

Giggly said, still giggling, "Wiggly told me that's what the Sproggles call Freddie, because he helps to fix lots of things for everyone. Freddie Fixit!"

Daddly turned the chair the right way up and sat on it, shuffled about a bit and declared, "It definitely feels solid enough, Freddie, thank you again, you certainly live up to the name Sproggles call you!"

They all sat down again and then Mummly had a thought. "Tate, what did you need to speak to Freddie about?"

The Town Elder chuckled. "Oh yes! I almost forgot with all the excitement. It's the Orb of Destiny, it has suddenly become active," he replied.

"Well that's a big surprise," Daddly proclaimed, "it has been dormant for decades, or even hundreds of years!"

The Town Elder was nodding, as was Mummly.

"Yes, absolutely! Almost two centuries now, 198 years to be precise," Tate Spudlike replied.

Freddie was looking puzzled. "What exactly is the Orb of Destiny and how am I involved?" he asked.

Wiggly was straight in with the answer. "Oh, I know, Freddie, The Orb of Destiny is a very special artefact left to the Elfins by the great Wizard Merlin and it detects an emergence."

Freddie screwed up his face. "I don't understand, what's an emergence?"

The Town Elder elaborated. "Merlin foretold his Elfins that sometime in the future a special one would emerge and be able to command magic. As you know, we lost our apprentice, Grundly, during the attack of the Morphlins, now the Orb has detected a new magic emergence."

"Wow, that's really exciting," Freddie said as his face lit up with the thought he might get to meet a real live wizard. "But what if that person is not a good person and uses magic for bad reasons?" he asked with a worried look on his face.

"The Orb of Destiny let's us know by shining white for good magic and turns black for bad magic and would reject that person," the Town Elder replied.

"Oooh! What colour is the Orb shining?" Giggly asked enthusiastically and everyone was eager to know.

"It shone bright and white this morning when it summoned me," the Town Elder replied.

Freddie was smiling but with a slightly puzzled look on his face. "Why did you want to speak to me about this, is there something I can do to help find this special person for you?"

All eyes were on Tate Spudlike, looking for an answer. "Ah well, you see, Freddie, the Orb of Destiny is calling for the person by name, so we know who it is," the Town Elder replied with a big smile on his face.

"Who is it, Town Elder, who is it?" Wiggly asked jumping up, his legs running on the spot, hardly able to contain his excitement at this great event.

The Town Elder looked around and smiled. "Best sit down, Wiggly, I think you will be surprised."

"Oh, it's not Wiggly, is it?" Giggly grunted. "Tell me it's not my brother?"

The Town Elder chuckled. "No Giggly, it's not Wiggly," he said and looked at Wiggly, "I'm sorry."

Wiggly looked a little disappointed for a split second then asked excitedly, "Who is it then, Mr Spudlike?"

Tate Spudlike looked at Mummly and Daddly, then at Freddie, who was brimming with curiosity. He looked deeply into Freddie's eyes and said, "It's calling for you, Freddie, the Orb of Destiny is calling for you by your name!"

The sudden silence was very strange as everyone looked at each other, then at Freddie.

"**My name!**" Freddie blurted in utter surprise. "The Orb of Destiny is calling **my name?** How can that be? I'm not even an Elfin?" Freddie replied a little horrified.

The Town Elder put his hand on Freddie's shoulder. "The Orb of Destiny is never wrong, Freddie. Tell me, have you noticed anything strange happening to you or around you recently?"

"What about the snowman, Freddie?" Wiggly jumped up and cried out.

Freddie explained about his dream and the next morning the snowman had a hat, scarf and pipe.

"That's very interesting," the Town Elder replied, "very interesting indeed."

Freddie explained about the pebbles. "When I was in the forest looking for some black pebbles a deer spoke to me and asked me to follow, then it kicked the ground and uncovered a load of black pebbles."

"Aw, you never told us that!" Giggly sat up and said.

"That's also very interesting, Freddie, have you talked with other animals?" the Town Elder asked.

Freddie explained about the squirrel, piglet and hedgehog, turning more and more red in the face.

"That's amazing, Freddie," Mummly said.

Daddly, Wiggly, Giggly and Elder Spudlike were nodding their heads in agreement.

"But that's not magic, is it?" Freddie asked doubtfully.

"It could be the beginning, Freddie, I think that magic may be emerging in you. Perhaps Merlin has chosen you for a special purpose in this life. Will you come with us and place your hands on the Orb of Destiny and then we will know for sure? If you are chosen, the Orb of Destiny will guide you safely on your journey of emergence," the Town Elder replied.

Freddie was hot, red and flabbergasted. "Really? Do you really think Merlin has chosen me? Oh! It scares me, Elder Spudlike, surely I can't be the right person, I'm only a kid, I'm only twelve years old and I'm not even an Elfin. Why me and not Wiggly?" Freddie became tearful.

Wiggly dashed to his friend and hugged him. "Freddie, you're the one, it's always been you. Just think about it, you're the only one who can walk among Sproggles and Elfins alike, calling both your friends, you really are worthy." Wiggly expressed his heart-felt feelings to his best and closest friend in the world.

Freddie looked at Wiggly and raised a smile. "Do you really think so?" he asked and Wiggly nodded enthusiastically.

Daddly spoke up. "Freddie, this is a miracle. Ever since you came into our lives you have saved us so many times, you really are worthy. If you think about the train of events, it was no accident you met Wiggly, I think Merlin created that situation to bring you into our lives. When the Mole Goblins attacked, we did not know what to do and it was you, with Wiggly's help, who returned our children to us. I really think you are the 'Special One' that Merlin predicted."

Mummly and Giggly were nodding their heads, agreeing.

Town Elder Spudlike patted Freddie on the shoulder. "You are much older than your years, Freddie, and you are coming of age. The things that have been happening to you are not of your own making, they are signs that your emergence is beginning. Merlin has blessed you more than once and has chosen you for something very special."

Freddie looked at the Town Elder. "But I can't control these things, they just seem to happen. What if something bad happens?" Freddie's voice trembled.

"When you have held the Orb of Destiny, things will be a lot clearer for you. Have faith, Freddie, that Merlin has chosen well in you!"

"Let's go, Freddie!" Wiggly said eagerly, taking his friend's hand to pull him to his feet. A slightly less than eager Freddie stood up and let Wiggly pull him towards the front door. "Don't be scared, Freddie, you know Merlin is watching over us, don't you?" Wiggly said so cheerfully that Freddie wanted to please everyone and stopped pulling back.

Once outside the house Town Elder Spudlike led the way, chatting with Daddly while Freddie, Wiggly, Mummly and Giggly followed behind. He took them all towards the park and then veered off towards the tower that Freddie had seen many times, but had never visited. When they reached the tower, Freddie looked puzzled.

"There seems to be no door or any way to get inside," he whispered to Wiggly.

"Well it's a magic door like the big old oak tree," Wiggly replied and they watched as Elder Spudlike placed his hand on the stone wall and chanted, "Efas Egassap Otni Eht Rewot!"

Stone blocks began to vanish one by one until an opening the size of a door appeared.

"I'm not sure I'll ever get used to things like this," Freddie said looking at the new doorway then to his friend, Wiggly.

"Magic is cool!" Wiggly replied with a big smile.

They entered the tower which was surprisingly dark inside except for light emanating from the football sized Orb of Destiny glowing white, perched on a pedestal in the middle of the room. Once they were all inside, the doorway began rebuilding, brick by brick, until they stood in the darkness illuminated only by the eerie glow of the Orb.

Freddie was looking around, up and down, but he could not tell how wide or tall the tower was inside, it being so dark.

"So that Freddie understands his importance at this time, I would like us all to place our hands on the Orb of Destiny in turn before Freddie. Daddly, would you be first?" Elder Spudlike asked.

Daddly stepped forward and held either side of the Orb of Destiny. Immediately it dimmed, the tower became very dark until Daddly stepped back, then the Orb glowed brighter again.

Mummly followed next and the same thing happened, the Orb of Destiny dimmed and she stepped back.

When Wiggly held the Orb of Destiny it dimmed, as it did with Giggly and both of them stepped back.

Town Elder Spudlike stepped up to the Orb and when he held it in both his hands it dimmed for him as it had for all those before him, so he stepped away from it.

"Now you have seen how the Orb of Destiny reacts to us, Freddie. It is your turn to step forward and place your hands upon it," Elder Spudlike announced.

Freddie was nervous and his hands were trembling.

"Whatever happens, Freddie, don't take your hands off the Orb of Destiny, nothing bad will happen to you," Mummly said reassuring him with a pat on the back.

Freddie smiled as a thank you and stepped forward, lifting his hands up and placing them either side of the Orb.

At first it remained the same brightness, nothing changed and he was kind of disappointed. He looked behind for guidance from his friends and was about to let go and return to them, but suddenly the Orb began to get brighter and brighter, Freddie turned his head to look at it. It was so bright the Orb lit up the whole of the tower and Freddie could now see the size and shape of it. The tower was big and circular and very, very tall, he half chuckled as he thought it looked bigger inside than outside.

A narrow beam of light emitted from the top of the Orb and hit the ceiling.

Freddie gasped and instinctively tried to pull away from the Orb, but his hands seemed to be glued to it. He watched the beam shine up high, then it travelled down all the walls, brightly illuminating them. He gasped again, he could feel his fingers tingling. *'Whatever happens do not let go of the Orb.'* Mummly's words came into his mind but he could not let go even if he tried.

Somehow pictures began to appear on the walls, moving round and changing slowly, showing Freddie helping Wiggly out of that horrible trap when they first met, then he and Wiggly in Merlin's Crystal Cavern.

Everyone was mesmerized, trying to see every detail as a new image appeared and others vanished. It was as if someone had been filming Freddie's life. It showed him and Wiggly saving the children from the Mole Goblins. There were images of Freddie helping Sproggles, then more and more of his adventures appeared. The final image, which moved around the walls, was of Freddie talking to Billy Bates and the beginning of his friendship, showing how Billy changed from being a bully to a popular boy at school. The walls remained bright, but then Merlin's voice, deep and loving, was heard and seemed to be coming from everywhere.

"Freddie, you have shown great compassion and fortitude. A selfless desire to help others, without seeking reward. You have magic within your grasp, yet you use it only to help others, you have not let it lead you down the path of selfishness and greed. Your emergence has begun, but your journey is not yet complete."

Something began to materialise in the beam of light issuing from the top of the Orb, a beautiful golden ring. Merlin's voice echoed around the tower again.

"Freddie, you must find the three stones that belong in this ring. The first stone holds the magic of this world, the 'Earthstone.' The second holds the magic of the universe, the 'Sunstone.' And the third holds the magic of the ocean, the 'Moonstone'. Return to this place and set the stones where they belong in this ring, then your apprenticeship of magic will commence."

The walls of the room began to darken again leaving the ring floating in the beam of light shining from the top of the Orb of Destiny.

The Orb then released Freddie's hands and he took a deep breath he had not realised he was holding. He suddenly felt weak and his legs buckled under him.

"Freddie!" Wiggly cried out as his friend collapsed to the floor.

Daddly had been the closest. He moved quickly and managed to catch Freddie in his arms before his head hit the hard stone floor.

When Freddie slowly opened his eyes, five more pairs of eyes were looking down on him.

"Freddie," Wiggly said softly, "you had us worried."

Freddie smiled weakly. "Sorry, my legs just gave way. Is everyone else okay?"

"There you go young man," Elder Spudlike said, "thinking of others when you're the one who's unwell and collapsed!"

"There's no wonder Merlin chose you, Freddie," Mummly said in a soft, loving voice.

Freddie sat up. "Oh yes! I forgot about that," he replied.

"Can you stand up now?" Daddly asked.

Freddie nodded and Daddly helped him up onto his feet. "Thank you, Daddly," Freddie replied and scratched his head, looking at the ring floating in the beam of light above the Orb. "What do we do now?"

"I think we need to consult our oldest resident and Oracle about the three stones," Town Elder Spudlike replied.

Everyone looked at him and nodded, except Freddie. "I thought I had met everyone in the Town. Who is the Oracle?" he asked.

"You'll meet him soon enough, Freddie, but for now I think we should leave the tower," Elder Spudlike replied, placing his hand on the stone wall and uttering the magic words.

Freddie watched, still a little in awe, as the stones peeled away to provide their exit.

One by one they left the darkened tower for the bright light outside.

Freddie looked back at the ring as the stones slowly closed the opening until the wall looked solid again.

"I think maybe this has been enough for you today, Freddie," Daddly said kindly.

Freddie was nodding his head in agreement. "I do have a lot to think about, let alone what happens if we find those stones and place them in the ring," he replied.

"I think it would be best for you to go home now and rest, Freddie. By the next time you visit we may have some answers as to the whereabouts of the three stones," Elder Spudlike suggested.

Wiggly hooked his arm through Freddie's and smiled. "I'll go with you to the forest, Freddie." He and Freddie separated from Daddly, Mummly, Giggly and the Town Elder to make their way to the door for the spiral staircase. "I'd like to see your snowman, 'Snowy', Freddie," Wiggly said as they stepped out of the big old oak tree.

"'Snowy' is really big and he looks happy too." Freddie chuckled, taking his friend's hand to lead him through the forest to his back garden.

When they reached the gate Freddie went on ahead to make sure his parents were not in the kitchen. As luck would have it they were nowhere to be seen. He waved to Wiggly, who crept around the edge of the garden until he was in front of 'Snowy'.

Freddie moved over to Wiggly and said, "He's good, isn't he?"

Wiggly's legs were already running on the spot with his excitement. "Oh, he's the best I've ever seen," he replied, "actually, he's the only one I've ever seen!" he giggled.

"Freddie, is that you?" It was Freddie's mother.

"Quick, Wiggly, run, otherwise you'll be discovered," Freddie whispered to his friend. "Yes, Mum, just looking at 'Snowy', I'm coming inside now," he called.

Wiggly skipped over the garden fence and waved goodbye.

Showing maturity well beyond his years, Freddie managed to keep a cool head when he walked inside the house.

"What have you been up to, Freddie?" his mother asked casually while she was washing up a few cups in the sink.

"Nothing much, Mum, just wandering around the trees and bushes, they look so magical all sprinkled with snow."

His mother turned to look at her son. "You're growing up so fast, Freddie, you'll be off to university before we know it!" she said with a sad sort of smile.

Freddie laughed. "You want to get rid of me already, Mrs Fountain?" he chuckled.

His mother leapt from the sink with soapy hands and wrapped them around her son.

"Aww, M-u-m, you made me all wet, I've got bubbles in my ears!"

They laughed together, it was one of those memorable moments that they would both look back on in years to come.

* *

In the middle of the night Freddie woke with a start. He had been dreaming about Merlin, the Orb of Destiny, the pictures of his life, the ring and the three stones. He was hot and sweaty and all his previous composure seemed to have melted away.

"How can I be Merlin's apprentice? Why me? I'm just an ordinary twelve year old boy like all my friends," he whispered in the darkness as he sat up in bed trembling.

A little beam of moonlight shone through a small gap in the curtains, it seemed to dance and weave patterns on the carpet.

Freddie watched it with fascination, forgetting his concerns, mesmerized by the dancing light. "Funny," he said to himself, "it almost looks like letters are being written. There's an M and an E and R and an L. Oh gosh, it's spelling 'Merlin.' Now a W and an A and T, that's a C and an H an E and S." Freddie jumped out of bed and stood looking at the letters shining on the carpet. "It's the Wizard, **'Merlin Watches,'** that's what it spelled out!"

The moonbeam vanished and Freddie sat back on the edge of the bed for a moment a little bewildered before he climbed back under the duvet. "Am I dreaming that I'm dreaming?" he whispered to himself as his eyes closed and he fell into a deep and dreamless sleep.

Bright sunshine illuminated Freddie's bedroom announcing a new day. He woke feeling wide awake and alert, then jumped out of bed and opened his curtains to let the sunshine flood into his room even more.

"Wow, look at that!" he said, to no one in particular. "It's been snowing again during the night."

A thick carpet of snow had fallen to such an extent that the last two days of the school term had been cancelled due to the roads being impassable for buses and cars. This suited Freddie perfectly.

He washed, dressed and dashed downstairs, where his mother had porridge ready for him.

"That'll put hairs on your chest!" Freddie's father chuckled.

Freddie looked a bit puzzled and pulled his tee shirt up to look at his chest. "What use are hairs on my chest, Dad?" he queried.

His parents looked at each other and laughed, much to Freddie's wonder.

"It's just a saying, son, it sort of means it will make a man of you, because men have hairs on their chests," his father replied.

"Oh I see," Freddie said, still not sure what it all meant. "Can I go exploring in the forest today as there is no school?"

"Of course you can, son," his father replied.

"I'll prepare some sandwiches for you, remember to be home before dark," his mother said.

"Yes, Mum, thank you, Dad. I'll go clean my teeth and get ready then." Freddie replied and charged up the stairs.

Boots, duffle coat, scarf, hat and gloves, Freddie was ready and with his favourite packed lunch he returned to his beloved forest. His parents advised him to come home if he started to feel cold. His mother had made him put on a nice thick jumper under his duffle coat, gloves, and thick socks inside his Wellington boots. With all that extra clothing he was sure he would be plenty warm enough.

"It's always much warmer around the trees, Mum," he assured her.

"Don't you feel lonely or bored by yourself out there, son?" his father asked.

"Oh no, Dad, there's so many interesting things and the animals come and talk to me." He fell quiet, that had slipped out, now he was worried.

"You'll have to become a Vet then, son, you'll be in high demand," his mother chuckled, brushing off his remarks as kid's talk.

When Freddie stepped into the garden the snow nearly went over the top of his boots.

"Wow, this is amazing!" he cried, to no one in particular.

The whole garden looked like a twinkling white sheet, but something looked odd, very odd indeed. There were no other footprints from animals or even birds, except from 'Snowy' to the gate and from the gate back to 'Snowy'.

"That's really odd, where's 'Snowy's' face and buttons?" Freddie said out aloud. "His face must be covered with the new snow that fell last night," he said answering his own question and stepped one foot at a time towards his snowman.

'Snowy' did have a little layer of snow on him, but the carrot nose was missing as were his eyes, mouth and pipe, and his broom was on the opposite side.

Freddie was baffled. He looked at the footprints leading to the gate and back again. "Someone must have crept in the garden and taken 'Snowy's' face, but how strange is that?" he said, to no one in particular. Then he realised that the scarf was on back to front and he scratched his head through his hat. "There's something fishy going on here," he whispered to himself.

Freddie walked around his snowman, heading for the gate, when a sound from behind made him turn around. "Oh, no, that's not possible!" he cried out. "How can that be?" he gasped in surprise. "Who? How? What is going on?"

Freddie had found 'Snowy's' lost carrot nose and black pebble eyes and mouth, pipe and buttons. Somehow the impossible had happened during the night. 'Snowy' was now facing the garden gate, not the house. He had somehow turned around.

Freddie stood and stared, now he could see 'Snowy's' carrot nose and eyes and buttons and his pebble mouth, only instead of a happy turned up mouth it was turned down looking sad, not happy.

"That's why the broom seemed to be on the other side, only it was actually still on the same side," Freddie exclaimed, feeling rather puzzled. He walked back to his snowman and was about to give him his smile back, but said to him, "Don't look sad, 'Snowy,' look happy like me," and he beamed at his snowman, then gasped again and fell backwards into the snow almost disappearing in it as it was so deep. Freddie sat up and blinked. "Am I doing this, is this my magic emerging?" he whispered to himself in shock.

He stood up and brushed himself down then looked again at 'Snowy,' whose sad mouth now had a smile, all by itself. Freddie stood and looked at his snowman carefully, then the footprints to the gate. "Did you walk into the forest during the night?" he asked, then fell back in the snow a second time. "I think I'm going crazy," he said to himself as he stood up and brushed off the snow, "you winked at me, I know you did!" Freddie said to his snowman.

* *

Wiggly and Giggly were in hysterics when Freddie told them about 'Snowy' the snowman.

"You're so funny, Freddie, I wish I had been there to see all that!" Giggly laughed.

Freddie had to laugh with them, it was funny when he thought about it. The thing was his Elfin friends believed him, who else would? Certainly not any of his school friends.

Mummly had made a hot cup of dandelion tea for everyone while they discussed what to do. They had not expected to see Freddie for a couple of days, as he would normally be at school.

"I think our first visit should be to Jay Kay, the keeper of the ancient scrolls," Daddly suggested.

Freddie chuckled, Wiggly smiled and Giggly giggled.

"Take care not to offend Mr Kay when you meet him, he is now our oldest and dearest Elfin," Daddly advised.

"Yes, Daddly," the three friends replied together.

Freddie thought for a minute then asked, "When we were looking for information about the Incubus.........."

Giggly screamed at the mention of the Incubus and Wiggly almost fell off the comfy sofa.

"Sorry, Giggly," Freddie apologised. "What I was going to ask was.........." Again Freddie was interrupted.

"Did we look in the ancient scrolls?" Wiggly said.

Freddie smiled and nodded, then they all looked at Daddly.

"Indeed, I spoke with Jay Kay and he spent a few days searching his memory about the, you-know-what, but he had to admit he had no recollection of such a spirit," Daddly explained.

That satisfied Freddie's curiosity.

Mummly changed the subject quickly, seeing her children looking a little pale from the mention of the Incubus. "Freddie, we felt so proud of you, seeing all the things you have done. When we were in the tower we saw you help your Sproggle friends, especially the boy Billy Bates," she praised as they finished their tea.

"Now that we have seen how you help everyone in your village too, it makes perfect sense for Merlin to choose you, Freddie," Daddly added.

Freddie felt a little embarrassed and blushed. "Thank you, Mummly and Daddly, I only hope I can be the person Merlin thinks I am."

"Wasn't it Billy Bates who cut down the trees, Freddie? Giggly asked.

"It was his father and uncle," Freddie replied, "they are both being punished in prison, so Billy just lives with his mother now."

"Why did you make friends with him, Freddie, because he had been really horrible to you and your friends?" Wiggly asked.

Freddie told them the whole episode in the school showers, how he somehow commanded Billy, who then burst out with the way his life was. "He was lonely and that was something me and my school friends could fix."

Mummly and Daddly had been listening with interest and smiled with pride, just as if Freddie was their own son.

"This is another indication of how special you are, Freddie, and so humble with it. What you did by turning your enemy into a friend requires something extraordinary. No doubt your parents were especially proud of you that day," Mummly stated.

"Mmm, they were, but I think anyone could have done what I did," Freddie replied modestly.

Giggly jumped up and took Freddie's hand, pulling him to his feet, where she hugged him tightly and whispered in his ear. "Not anyone, Freddie, only you have this gift and we love you a lot!"

Freddie's face turned bright red.

Giggly released him from her bear hug and giggled. "Aw, you look so cute when you're embarrassed!"

* *

Once they had finished their tea, no one wanted to be left behind, so the whole family set off. They strolled through the town to Jay Kay's home. When they reached their destination and knocked on the door, a very elderly Elfin stood in the open doorway.

Freddie and Wiggly gasped out aloud and stood rigid for a moment.

"Grundly?" Freddie wheezed in surprise. "Grundly!" he said again with excitement.

The elderly Elfin smiled so wide his beard tickled his ears. "Freddie and Wiggly, Jay Kay at your service."

"B-but y-you........." was all Freddie managed.

Jay Kay explained. "I'm sorry boys, I know how fond you were of Grundly and I understand your confusion. Grundly was my brother, my older, much older brother. I guess I do resemble him quite a lot."

"But you even sound like Grundly, Mr Kay," Freddie said while Wiggly was still standing like a statue and staring.

Jay Kay smiled again and Giggly chuckled, seeing his whiskers reach his ears. "Mmmm, we were very much alike, Freddie, but I'm sure you did not come to see me just to look at me. Come in everyone. Oh, where are my manners, welcome Mummly, Daddly, Giggly and Wiggly and not forgetting you, Freddie. Come in please, come in."

They all followed Jay Kay through the door and Daddly closed it behind them.

Jay Kay turned and asked, "Who would like a glass of Elderberry cordial?" looking at the three children with that big grin on his face which still made Giggly chuckle.

"Ooh, yes please, Mr Kay!" all three answered together, then chuckled at each other.

Everyone sat down on comfy chairs while their host walked to the kitchen end and prepared the cordial and tea. Jay Kay arrived at the seating end of the room with a tray of drinks and handed them out. While they sipped their cordial and tea, Daddly explained what had happened the day before, much to Jay Kay's delight.

Jay Kay looked at Freddie, his eyes sparkled and his face lit up. "I'm not at all surprised Merlin has chosen you, Freddie. Despite the fact that this is the first time we have met, you'll be surprised to know that I know all about you. I can think of no one better suited or qualified to be the great Wizard's apprentice," he said kindly.

"Thank you, Mr Kay, I am quite overwhelmed." It was a little difficult to talk to Jay Kay and not see his hero and friend, Grundly.

Wiggly was having the same problem and try as he might he could not see Jay Kay as any other than Grundly.

Freddie noticed Wiggly and gave him a quick look before turning his gaze back to Jay Kay. "Last night I woke and watched a moonbeam spell out 'Merlin Watches' on my carpet, I guess the great Wizard really is looking out for me," Freddie explained.

Jay Kay was nodding. "Merlin has never really left his Elfins, Freddie. Even though we did not know what had happened until you and young Wiggly discovered the crystal cavern, we feel his presence all around us. Grundly waited all his life for the 'chosen one' and although he met you, Freddie, I'd like to think he knew who you were. Now tell me, what it is you have come to see me about?"

Freddie was not quite sure how to begin and looked towards Daddly.

"If I may, Jay?" Daddly began, "Freddie is, as he said, somewhat overwhelmed, but as you now know, he has been challenged to find the three stones for the magical ring in the tower. That is our mission today, as you are the keeper of the ancient scrolls, we hoped you could help."

The smile fell from Jay Kay's face and he looked a little sombre. "So, Freddie, you need to know how to find these stones, but I'm afraid I cannot help you," he explained.

"Oh!" Freddie said quite disappointedly.

Daddly looked at Mummly, Giggly looked at Wiggly and Freddie looked from Jay Kay down to the floor.

Jay Kay realised that he had not chosen his words very well. "You'll have to excuse this old Elfin," he said. "I don't get many visitors these days and rarely speak with anyone, so I could have explained myself a little better. Do not despair, Freddie. Come, come all of you, come, follow me," he said, standing and walking towards two doors. He opened the right hand door and walked through into the darkness and they all followed.

"Ooof!" Giggly gasped as she bumped into her brother.

"There are no windows in this room," Jay Kay explained and flicked on a switch to turn on a magic candle hanging from the ceiling.

"Oh wow!" Wiggly gasped, at a sight so unexpected it pulled him out of his trance-like state of mind.

Freddie and the Tiggly's looked around the room in utter amazement.

"What are all these, Mr Kay?" Freddie asked politely.

"This, Freddie, is the complete history of Elfin kind, dating way back to when Merlin first created us hundreds of years ago," Jay Kay replied.

"Wow, there are so many!" Wiggly cried.

All four walls, except for the doorway, were covered floor to ceiling in small square boxes each containing a dozen or more rolled up scrolls.

"Somewhere in here is the answer that you seek. I know it is here, I am old now, but when I was younger I read every scroll. It took me three years to complete, but I can no longer remember where specific information is stored now. I'm sorry," Jay Kay apologised.

"THREE YEARS!" Giggly cried out.

"Even with five of us looking through them it would take many months," Daddly explained.

"This seems almost impossible," Mummly gasped.

"Jay, do you think Freddie has enough magic now to direct him to a scroll which has the answers we seek?" Daddly asked as the idea came to him.

Jay Kay rubbed his bearded, pointy chin. "Tell me, Freddie, has anything been happening to you that might possibly be magical?"

Freddie smiled and Giggly Giggled as Freddie explained a few events that seemed to have no explanation.

"Excellent, Freddie, it seems your magic is indeed emerging fast. Just a moment," Jay Kay replied and left the scroll room. He returned with a short claw-ended staff with a dull red crystal held in the claw. "Take this, Freddie. Daddly, could you bring a chair for Freddie to sit upon, please?" he asked.

Daddly stepped back into the dining area and brought through a chair for Freddie as Jay Kay had asked.

"Now, Freddie, please place the bottom of the staff in the indentation on the floor."

Freddie looked down at his feet and spotted the place and did as he had been asked.

"Can you hold the magic staff in both your hands near the crystal?" Jay Kay asked.

Freddie arranged himself accordingly.

"Good, good! Now everyone form a circle around Freddie, then turn your back to him. Yes, yes, that's good," Jay Kay said. "Freddie, I want you to close your eyes and think only of Merlin's golden ring floating in the beam of light in the tower and do not open your eyes until I tell you, okay?"

Freddie nodded and replied, "Yes sir, Mr Kay."

"We need to give Freddie absolute silence everyone, so that he is not distracted. Okay?" Jay Kay asked, not waiting for anyone to reply. "Okay, Freddie, it's time now," he said.

Freddie closed his eyes and created a picture in his mind of the golden ring floating in the beam of light. The image was so clear in his mind he felt he could reach out and touch it. The crystal on the top of the staff in his hands began to glow, becoming a bright ruby red colour.

Wiggly saw the red glow all around them, turned to look and gasped out aloud.

Freddie opened his eyes and lost his concentration. "What is it? What's wrong?" he asked.

"Sorry! Sorry!" Wiggly apologised, "I was just surprised by the red glow and thought something was wrong."

"It's alright, Wiggly," Jay Kay said kindly. "Let's try again and it's important we all try to remain calm and quiet. Freddie, you are doing very well indeed, let's give it another go."

Freddie closed his eyes again, bringing the image back into his mind and the clawed crystal glowed ruby red again. For a little while nothing more happened and Giggly, who was getting restless, was about to turn and have a look herself when a single beam of red light emitted from the crystal. It hit the scrolls here, there and everywhere, like it was trying to escape.

Wiggly put his hand over his mouth in case he said something as the red beam slowed and then seemed to be searching for something, moving slowly from one scroll to the next.

Five pairs of eyes watched hypnotically as the beam wandered around the walls.

When it stopped, Wiggly held his mouth tightly, he was getting excited and had a hard job controlling his legs, which wanted to jog on the spot.

The red beam finally stopped on a single scroll on the wall opposite the door, four rows from the top and seven rows from the right. As the red beam shone on the single scroll it began to slide out from its box until it was halfway out. Then the crystal suddenly went dark and the beam of red light vanished too.

"You can open your eyes now, Freddie," Jay Kay told him.

"You did it, Freddie!" Wiggly was running on the spot with his excitement.

"I did? Really?" Freddie replied with surprise.

Daddly reached up and took the scroll down.

"A beam of light searched all the scrolls and picked one out," Giggly said excitedly.

"Take it into the dining area, Daddly," Jay Kay suggested.

They all walked out of the scroll room into the light of the house and made their way to the dining table.

Freddie brought the chair he had been sitting on and Jay Kay took the crystal claw staff from him and gave him a friendly pat on the back. "Well done, Freddie, the magic is already strong in you," he said.

At the dining table everyone watched with keen interest as Jay Kay carefully unrolled the ancient scroll made of cloth rather than paper.

"Look!" Mummly announced. "The title there is EMERGENCE."

They could all see it now and were trying to read the words, but they seemed to be in a strange language.

"Daddly, can you read out the script for us?" Jay Kay asked.

Daddly turned the scroll to face him and looked puzzled. "I'm afraid it makes no sense to me. Mummly, can you read it?" he asked.

Mummly looked at it and shook her head. Jay Kay turned it to him and again he was unable to read it. "That's very strange, I definitely read all these scrolls when I was younger," he said.

"Maybe that's it," Mummly suggested, "perhaps it can only be read by a young Elfin. Wiggly, see if you can read it?"

With Freddie sat next to him, Wiggly turned the scroll towards them. "No I can't," he replied sadly.

"I think I can read it," Freddie said a little surprised.

"That must be it, this is Freddie's quest, this scroll reveals itself only to him," Jay Kay replied. "Do you think you can read it aloud to us, Freddie?" he asked and Freddie nodded.

Search thy stones in vain
Lest by the chosen soul
Make pace from Kingdom's door
Thy rising sun ye guide
Gait as flies the crow
Advance till ye nay more can go
Seek out thy palm that fits
Spake out aloud ya title reversed
Thy Earthstone shall be exposed
And shall guide ye onward
Fay thy stones ye seek

As Freddie spoke the words they reformed into the language they could all read.

"Why are these things always in riddles?" Freddie asked a little exasperated.

"Well, Freddie," Jay Kay replied, "you have to remember this was written maybe 400 years ago or longer. Back then people spoke differently, they were not well educated and it is written to confuse everyone except the chosen one."

Freddie listened and nodded. "I see, I never thought about it like that. I suppose these stones are quite powerful."

"They are, Freddie, but only to the chosen one," Jay Kay answered. "For me, Daddly, Mummly, Wiggly and Giggly they would just be pretty stones. But that might not stop others trying to find them and make them work, even though they would fail," he added.

Mummly looked at the scroll. "I'm sure we can make this more understandable."

Jay Kay nodded. "Mummly, would you mind writing down what we agree are the meanings of each line. I'll get paper, quill and ink."

Mummly smiled and nodded, then took the writing materials when Jay Kay handed them to her.

"Let's take it line by line then," Daddly suggested. "Can you read it out again, Freddie, just in case we see it differently," he added.

Freddie smiled and nodded. "Search thy stones in vain lest by the chosen soul," he read out.

"Oh that's fairly obvious," Giggly said. "It is saying that only the chosen one can find the stones, nobody else would be able to find them."

"I think you're correct there, Giggly," Jay Kay agreed and she sat up and grinned.

"Have you got that, Mummly?" Daddly asked and she nodded. "Freddie, read out the next, please."

"It's a bit vague but reads 'Make pace from Kingdom's door'. Any ideas anyone?"

"I think 'pace' means to walk or run, which you do like pacing out your steps," Wiggly volunteered.

"That's good logic, Wiggly," Jay Kay agreed.

"But where is Kingdom's door?" asked Freddie.

"This is tricky," Jay Kay replied, "perhaps we need to think what things were like hundreds of years ago. If Merlin wrote this, where would his kingdom be?"

"Wouldn't the whole forest be his kingdom back then?" Wiggly asked.

"Yes it would, what's more, Elfins and Sproggles lived together above ground when Merlin was around," Jay Kay established.

Daddly sat up with a sudden thought. "Merlin was writing this for the future, not for that time in history."

"In that case, wouldn't Merlin be living in his quarters at the end of the escape tunnel?" Freddie suggested.

"Oh that's true!" Giggly piped up.

"So could the kingdom be this kingdom as it is hundreds of years in the future from when Merlin wrote the riddle?" Freddie deduced with a smile.

"If you're right, Freddie, then the kingdom's door........," began Jay Kay.

"The big old oak tree!" everyone said together then laughed.

"Okay I've got that now," Mummly announced, "what's next, Freddie?"

"Thy rising sun ye guide," he replied.

"Well what does that tell us?" Daddly asked.

Mummly replied. "Well I think we can all agree that the sun rises in the East, so I reckon that's the direction to walk from the big old oak tree."

There were smiles on everyone's faces as they agreed with Mummly while she wrote it down.

Freddie read out the next line, "Gait as thy crow flies."

This evoked quite a long silence with brows furrowed and fingers rubbed on heads and chins.

"This does not make a lot of sense. Gates are what you have on a fence to let you in and out of a garden, isn't it?" Freddie said. "Oh! Hold on though, it's not spelled G-A-T-E but G-A-I-T, what is that?"

"I've never heard the word before, I have no idea what it could mean," Wiggly replied.

"I have an idea," Freddie announced, reaching into his rucksack and pulling out a dictionary.

"Oooh, what's that?" Giggly asked.

"It's called a dictionary and it explains what words mean and how to use them," Freddie replied.

"Oooh, goodie, that's clever!" Wiggly chuckled.

Freddie flicked through the dictionary pages to words beginning with G and quickly found the word he was looking for. "Here it is, 'GAIT'. A particular way of moving on foot, such as running or walking," he looked up at everyone and smiled.

"Well done, Freddie, I guess it means to walk in this case then," Jay Kay said with delight.

"Keep that book on the table, Freddie, it might still be useful here, but the school could use it too!" Daddly suggested.

"So instead of GAIT we can use the word WALK as flies the crow, but that doesn't make any sense either because crows don't walk," Mummly replied.

"I think I understand the meaning," Wiggly offered. "Crows and birds in general fly in straight lines, so this must mean to walk in a straight line eastwards."

Once again there was a silent pause as everyone looked at Wiggly.

"Am I not correct?" he said beginning to doubt himself.

"I think you are perfectly correct, well done, Wiggly!" Jay Kay commended.

"This is going quite well, do you have that bit, Mummly?" Daddly said and she nodded. "Let's take a look at the next line then, Freddie," he asked.

"Advance till ye nay more can go," he replied.

"Does it mean keep walking till you drop dead?" Giggly said with a serious expression.

"What would be the point of that, Giggly, dead people can't find things, now can they?" Wiggly replied.

368

"Oh good, I was worried for while," she answered back.

"I think you're on the right track though, Giggly," Freddie began. "If you walk in a straight line, eventually something will be in the way, like, err, a mountain or a huge lake or even the sea!"

"So are we saying walk until something is in the path that stops any further progress?" Mummly suggested and it was nods all round.

"Look at the next line, this is much more difficult," Freddie said. "Seek out thy palm that fits."

Daddly proposed, "Maybe whatever stops you going onward is a forest of palm trees?"

Giggly and Wiggly chuckled. "I don't think there are any palm trees in the forest, Daddly, certainly not a whole forest of them!"

"Ah yes! I think that was a silly guess, but what else could it mean?"

"Freddie, have a look in your book, see if it might give us a clue," Mummly suggested.

Freddie picked up the dictionary and flicked through the pages until he reached words beginning with P and found PALM. "It reads, 'a palm is a tree that grows in hot countries. Also the inside part of your hand from your wrist to the base of your fingers.'"

"Of course, of course," Daddly called out enthusiastically, "it has to be the palm of your hand!"

"But what does it mean, find the palm that fits?" Freddie asked.

Daddly patted him on the shoulder. "I guess that part may become clearer once you reach the end of the journey."

"Okay, I have that in some form. What's next?" Mummly asked.

"Spake out aloud ya title reversed."

"I think that means your name, say it backwards, you'll have to practice that, Freddie," Daddly said and smiled.

"This is good, I think this will reveal the location of the Earthstone. We won't know any more until that time, somehow it will lead you to the other stones," Jay Kay concluded. He made more drinks and everyone sat on comfy chairs for a while, mostly discussing about Freddie and Wiggly's adventures.

Jay Kay said his goodbyes as they all left. "Freddie, good luck, we have faith in you, you are more special than you realise. Come see me again, I don't get out much these days. You too Mummly, Daddly, Wiggly and Giggly, you're always welcome. Bye now."

* *

"I'll make a nice cup of dandelion tea," Mummly said once they all returned home.

Daddly, Wiggly, Giggly and Freddie made for the comfy chairs and relaxed into them.

"That was quite exciting!" Giggly chirped.

"Especially when you used magic, Freddie," Wiggly added, swinging his arm around his friend as they sat on the comfy sofa.

Mummly brought over a tray of cups and set them down on the small table then handed them out. "How are you feeling, Freddie, this must be quite a lot for you to deal with?" she asked in a concerned, kindly voice.

Freddie looked at her as he took the cup of dandelion tea. "I'm not really sure, Mummly, it doesn't feel real, it's like I'm in a dream. I know magic is real and I guess I may be the only Sproggle in the whole world who does. But to think I have been chosen to use magic, to become Merlin's apprentice, well that's a bit scary. I'm only young and it's a big responsibility, I don't know if I can handle it. What if I hurt people unintentionally?" Freddie looked a little sad.

Wiggly whispered in his ear, "I believe in you, Freddie."

Freddie gave Wiggly a smile.

Daddly said, "Freddie, you have been chosen for everything that you are, kind, helpful, honest, truthful and reliable. You carry a rucksack that could give you fame and fortune, anything you could ever want and yet you only use it to help others. You are a very special person indeed and I can think of no one better qualified for the responsibility of using magic."

Freddie looked at Daddly and smiled coyly, then began to turn red in the face. "Thank you, Daddly, it's very kind of you to say such nice things. And I want to thank all of you for being my friends. I really don't feel special in any way, but I do get a good feeling when I help people, it just makes me happy," Freddie replied.

"Do you want to try and find the Earthstone today?" Wiggly asked.

"Well it's time for lunch now," Mummly interrupted, "so it will need to wait until this afternoon."

"I guess the sooner the better," Freddie replied to Wiggly. "Let's have something to eat first," he added.

The Tiggly family now included Freddie as an adopted son and they all sat around the big table in the middle of the house where Freddie shared out his jam sandwiches.

Mummly had made bread rolls to which she had added a few extra ingredients.

"These taste amazing, Mummly," Freddie said after his first bite of one of Mummly's rolls.

"Thank you, Freddie, it's thanks to you for introducing us to yeast, and we grind up all kinds of seeds to make flour," Mummly answered with a kindly smile.

Having had their fill of food they moved back to the comfy chairs to discuss their next move.

"I think I'll stay home, it's a bit chilly above ground for me," Mummly announced and Giggly agreed, she preferred the warmth of home to the icy cold of the forest.

Daddly and Wiggly decided to accompany Freddie on his search for the Earthstone.

"How will we know the exact direction of East, though?" Wiggly asked. "Even if we are off by just a little bit we could end up walking all around the world!"

Freddie and Giggly laughed at the thought of doing that.

"I have just the thing," Freddie replied and opened one of the pockets on his rucksack. He pulled out a round and shiny fat disc.

"Oh! What's that?" Giggly asked looking intrigued.

Freddie smiled and showed her and Wiggly the silvery disc resting in the palm of his hand. "It's called a compass," he handed it to his friend, "open it up, Wiggly," he said.

Wiggly took the compass and fumbled with it, finally pressing the tiny button on the side that made a lid pop up.

"Oooh, that's pretty!" Giggly said. "What does it do?"

"Look at it, around the edge are letters, N,E,S,W they stand for........"

".... North, East, South and West," Wiggly interrupted.

"That's right," Freddie chuckled and smiled at his friend, who surprised him so often. "The arrow is magnetic and always points to the north. Turn the compass, Wiggly, and watch the arrow."

"That's like magic, it just points the same way to the front door," Wiggly replied.

"So how do you use it?" Giggly asked.

"Well it's simple really, we hold it level and let the arrow settle down, then we turn the compass until the arrow head is exactly over the N for north," Freddie replied. "Then we know which direction is East, or West or South."

"That's really clever, but what makes it do that?" Wiggly replied.

Freddie unzipped his rucksack, imagined some things, pulled out a bar magnet and some iron filings. "Daddly, could I have a sheet of paper please?" he asked, and when everything was ready he asked Wiggly and Giggly to hold the paper at each end, then he sprinkled the iron fillings all over it.

"What are you doing, Freddie?" Giggly asked curiously.

"This is an experiment I did at school to explain how our planet is like a magnet. This bar magnet in my hand represents our world of Astoria, it has a north pole at one end and a south pole at the other. Now watch what happens when I bring it up to the underside of the paper." Immediately all the iron filings began to move and form arches when he did so.

"Oooh, that's pretty, just like magic!" Giggly said.

Freddie pointed to both ends where the magnet lay underneath. "This is the North Pole and this is the South Pole, just like our world, Astoria. What we can see here are invisible magnetic waves, but the iron filings make them visible on the paper," Freddie explained. "That's why the arrow on the compass points north, but we can trick it, watch." Freddie held the compass above the paper and slowly lowered it until the arrow swung round and pointed to one end of the magnet. "Now we know which end of the magnet is north," he said.

"Because the compass always points to the north!" Giggly announced with a big smile.

"I'll leave the magnet and filings for you to play with, Giggly," Freddie said much to her excitement. "I've got something else," he said fishing in his rucksack and pulling something out.

"What is it?" Giggly asked.

"This is a magnet game called 'Hairy Humphrey.' As you can see, it's a thin, sealed box with a clear window on top and a magnetic wand. On the inside bottom of the box is a picture of a Sproggle face and lots of loose iron filings. Remember when I held the magnet under the paper and the iron fillings moved? This game is similar, by holding the magnetic wand on the window over the iron fillings they will jump up like magic and stick to the underneath of the window, then you can drag them over the face. When you lift the magnetic wand off the window, the iron fillings will drop onto the face, so you can give Humphrey a super hair do, beard, moustache and eyebrows to change his looks and expression."

"Oh, thank you, Freddie," she replied, receiving the game from him with excitement.

"Why don't we have a compass, Daddly?" Wiggly asked.

"Well a compass would be useful, but Elfin's have something like that built into our brains, so we don't get lost in the forest," Daddly replied.

"Ooo, that's right, when Wiggly and I were in the Mole Goblin's tunnels he always knew where we were!" Freddie announced.

Wiggly nodded.

"Well between us and your compass we should be successful in finding the Earthstone," Daddly concluded.

All three were well wrapped up, Freddie had fished out of his rucksack scarves and gloves for Wiggly and Daddly, something they did not have in Elfin Town. They received a few odd looks on their way to the spiral staircase.

Freddie smiled and called out, "We're off hunting in the snow!"

When you are wearing lots of layers of clothes it's much more difficult to climb the spiral staircase, as Wiggly, Daddly and Freddie discovered. Once they emerged into the forest and stood outside the big old oak tree, it was much colder and the layers of clothes were needed to keep warm.

"I think east is this way," Daddly said pointing towards a big fir tree covered in snow, "check with your compass, Freddie, we need to be very exact," he added

Freddie flipped open the compass and when he looked at it, discovered Daddly was just about spot on. "It's just a little bit to the left so we should just miss that big fir tree," Freddie replied.

The forest floor was covered in a sprinkling of snow barely a centimetre deep, lots of snow was draped on tree branches and they looked quite magical. They left three sets of footprints leading from the big old oak tree in the snow as they set off, so Wiggly took a leafy branch and swished it around to rub them out.

Freddie checked the direction from time to time, but Daddly was more or less spot on as he led them forward. "Oooh, look!" Wiggly cried, pointing out other tracks in the snow.

"Those looks like deer tracks, that's interesting because we don't see many deer in the forest," Daddly answered.

"This is my favourite tree," Freddie announced as they approached his special Christmas tree.

"Oh, it's so beautiful, Freddie, with all the rosehips and cones and snow," Wiggly gasped, even though he had seen it many times before.

They stood and admired the tree for a little while before checking their direction and moving onwards. They barely walked another ten paces when Daddly stopped.

Wiggly was looking down at the deer tracks and bumped into Daddly. "Oomph!" he grunted and apologised, much to Freddie's amusement.

"Do you see it, boys?" Daddly whispered, pointing ahead of them.

"Wow," Wiggly said softly, "it's the first one I've ever seen!"

"I think that must be the same deer that helped me find the black pebbles for my snowman," Freddie said. "Let me see if I can approach it again," he added and walked ahead.

Daddly expected the deer to run off as soon as it spotted Freddie approaching, but it did not.

"Hello, Mrs Deer," Freddie said as he reached the deer and stroked its neck.

'Freddie come' he heard the deer's voice in his mind.

"I'm on a mission, it's very important, Mrs Deer," he replied.

But the deer repeated, 'Freddie come.'

Freddie beckoned the others, who joined him. "Mrs Deer wants us to follow," he explained as the deer began to move, so they followed.

"We're still going east," Daddly reassured them.

"Maybe Merlin has sent this deer to guide us then," Wiggly suggested.

Daddly thought it would not be long before they reached the edge of the forest as they continued to follow the deer easterly.

Freddie stopped to check his compass, then ran to catch up.

"How do you think the deer knows what we are doing and the direction?" Wiggly asked.

"The forest animals are much smarter than we think," Daddly replied as they approached a clearing, just beyond the edge of the forest trees.

There, in front of them was a rocky outcrop that was taller than Freddie and several metres wide.

The deer stopped and said, *'Freddie here,'* in Freddie's mind.

"Thank you, Mrs Deer," Freddie replied, much to Wiggly's bewilderment. "We're here, Mrs Deer just told me," Freddie explained as the deer wandered off back into the forest.

They approached the rocky outcrop.

"I've never seen this before," Wiggly said rubbing his chin. "Nor have I ever seen this kind of stone before in the forest, there's something strange about it!" he observed.

"What do you mean?" Freddie asked.

"Well look, Freddie, there's no snow on the stone and the ground around it is bone dry," Daddly answered.

"Oh yes, so it is. That's odd since it's not shaded by any trees," Freddie replied. When he stepped onto the clear area around the stone he listened and said, "Hear that?"

"It's a low hum, like loads of bees or something," Wiggly replied.

"Look at this, boys," Daddly called and they jogged over to him to see what he was looking at.

"Oh, that's not good, that's definitely not good at all!" Freddie announced as he saw what Daddly was looking at.

"There's so many, Freddie, must be hundreds of them, how will you choose?" Wiggly exclaimed in surprise.

"I have no idea, Wiggly, we're obviously at the right place, but Merlin is not making it easy. I guess this is to prevent the wrong person trying to find the Earthstone," Freddie replied.

What Daddly had been pointing to were hundreds of handprints pushed into the rock. There were small ones, big ones, Elfin ones, and even animal ones everywhere. Some were so high Freddie could not even reach them. He tried his hand in a few and they were too big, or too small, or the wrong shape. "This could take all day if I have to try every one and those up there I can't even reach!" Freddie announced with dismay.

Daddly thought for a moment. "I have an idea, Freddie. Let's try using what magic is within you, like we did to find the scroll."

"Oooh, that's a good idea, Daddly!" Wiggly said excitedly.

"If you close your eyes again and think of your hand, Wiggly and I will watch out for anything to indicate which hand print matches yours," Daddly explained.

"Good idea, Daddly, okay let's do that then," Freddie agreed.

They walked round to the opposite side of the outcrop, then Daddly and Wiggly called, "Ready, Freddie!" Wiggly sniggered at the rhyming words.

Freddie closed his eyes and tried to visualise his hand, it was not as easy as he thought it would be, but slowly a clear image of his hand formed in his mind.

"Got it!" Wiggly shouted with glee. "Come see, quickly, Freddie!"

Freddie and Daddly scooted round to Wiggly on the other side of the stone outcrop and sure enough one hand print, shoulder height, was glowing as if a light bulb was behind it.

"Oh, Freddie! Can you do it, can you say your name backwards?" Wiggly asked.

"It's tricky but I will try," Freddie replied.

"Try your hand in the indentation then, Freddie," Daddly said.

Freddie reached over, placing his fingertips then his palm into the hand indentation. "It's a perfect fit!" he called out looking at Daddly and Wiggly.

"How is this possible?" Wiggly asked and scratched his head.

"It has to be Merlin, Wiggly, he must have known Freddie would be here all those years ago!" Daddly explained. "Now, Freddie, it's time to chant your name backwards," he prompted.

Freddie looked from Daddly back to his hand sitting perfectly in the indentation. "Here goes," he said crossing his fingers on his other hand. "Eidderf!" he called slowly. "Eidderf! Eidderf!" he called a third time. He looked back at Wiggly and Daddly and shrugged his shoulders. All of a sudden the rock began to vibrate a little, then it shook and trembled.

"Move back boys," Daddly called, fearful the rock outcrop was about to explode.

All three moved away quickly. The rock outcrop continued to shake and as they watched from the edge of the snow a crack began to appear in it. Wiggly moved closer to Freddie and grabbed his hand as the crack in the rock outcrop, widened from top to bottom. The crack became wider and wider as the whole rock trembled and shook until, unexpectedly, it split open in two halves.

They all gasped in surprise.

The two parts tumbled to the ground with a massive crash that shook the ground. Birds fluttered into the air and snow fell from tree branches.

"Look! Look!" Wiggly cried excitedly.

Where the stone outcrop had proudly stood was a small ruby coloured, pyramid shaped crystal, glowing and floating in the air, slowly spinning as if held on an invisible thread.

"I'll get it!" cried Wiggly eagerly as he dashed closer, climbing on one half of the rock and reached for the ruby stone. "Oh!" he cried when his hand passed right through it as if the stone were made of smoke. He tried again and again, swishing his hand at the crystal. "I can't grab it, I can see it, but I can't get it!" he cried out disappointedly, climbing back down again.

"Let me have a go, Wiggly," Daddly said with a chuckle, reaching over the gap and finding he could no more grab the stone than his son. "That is most strange," Daddly remarked, "maybe it's meant only for you to touch and hold, Freddie, give it a go," Daddly suggested.

Freddie was not convinced. How could Merlin know he would be here and not an Elfin? This was such an impossible situation for him to get his head around. He walked towards the gap in the rock halves and reached between them to take the ruby crystal. To his surprise and mystification the stone felt solid and he wrapped his fingers around it and brought it back to show Wiggly and Daddly. They moved closer to Freddie and when he opened his hand there was the ruby crystal sitting on his palm, but when each of them tried to touch it their fingers passed through it.

"I guess this is meant for you alone, Freddie, and no one else, seeing as neither I nor Wiggly can touch the Earthstone," Daddly concluded.

"It's very weird," Wiggly chuckled. "I can see the crystal looks solid yet my fingers cannot touch it, that's definitely very weird!"

Freddie chuckled with Wiggly. "It doesn't seem possible and how could Merlin know I would be born hundreds of years in the future, then meet Wiggly and find a second family among the Elfins? I guess magic is completely different to normal life. I wonder what my Sproggle friends would make of it all?" he replied. Freddie unzipped his rucksack and dropped the Earthstone inside, it would be safe there, no one but he could find it in there no matter how hard they tried. He looked at his watch. "Oh, it's almost three o'clock, I had better head off home," he said.

"Let's head back to the big old oak tree together then," Daddly replied and they set off.

As they walked back towards the forest they did not see the two halves of the rock outcrop slowly close up again and look as if it had never split in half. All the hand imprints slowly disappeared until the surface was completely smooth and snow gradually covered the ground around it and on the top, until the rock blended in almost invisibly. Magic was indeed, very different to ordinary life.

Along the way the three chatted about Merlin and how he was still able to watch over them even though Freddie and Wiggly had seen for themselves he appeared to be a statue.

"I often wonder where things go when I put them back inside my rucksack," Freddie said, then told Daddly and Wiggly about the time Billy Bates had snatched his rucksack and turned it upside down only to find it was empty. Then when Freddie snatched it back, took out a water pistol and soaked Billy's trousers.

Wiggly had to stop walking he was laughing so much.

Even Daddly laughed loudly too.

"Freddie, you are so funny, but Billy Bates deserved all he got back then," Wiggly gasped.

When they reached the big old oak tree, Daddly and Wiggly disappeared through the magic door and Freddie headed for home. He grabbed a fallen twiggy branch and dragged it behind him, wiping out his footprints in the sprinkling of snow, a trick he remembered from a program on TV. The last thing he wanted was for anyone to follow his footsteps to the big old oak tree and find they just disappeared, because only he and the Elfins could see the tree. It could cause lots of problems, so much the better to avoid them with this simple trick.

** **

Freddie went to bed that night thinking about everything, how Merlin had watched over him and the Elfins. How magic could even exist, why Merlin had chosen him. "I'm just an ordinary kid," he whispered to himself.

'No, Freddie, you are very extraordinary, very special, remember this,' Merlin's voice sounded in his mind.

Freddie sat up in his bed and looked around, once again he was told he was special. "I don't feel special, Merlin, really I don't," he whispered.

'Soon you will, Freddie, just be patient.' Merlin's voice again sounded in his mind.

Suddenly feeling sleepy, Freddie lay back in his bed and snuggled into his pillow. "Good night, Wiggly, good night, Merlin, thank you for everything," he whispered and yawned, then quickly fell into a dream filled sleep. He saw himself in his dream state with Daddly and Wiggly, walking through the forest, he was in the lead holding the glowing ruby crystal in front of him. He saw a jumble of images, a cave, a spiral staircase, booby traps and Wiggly crying out.

Freddie woke suddenly and sat up in his bed, his forehead damp with sweat. "What was Wiggly trying to warn me about?" he whispered to himself. He looked at his clock, it was early morning, not quite one am, so he lay back and fell asleep with the same dream images repeating themselves.

During the night even more snow had fallen and the wind had blown it into deep drifts around the doors of Freddie's home. When he looked out of his bedroom window he noticed something was different outside, it was 'Snowy'. Somehow he had turned around and was now facing the house. Even more surprising was the expression on the snowman's face, his mouth no longer smiled, but now it turned downwards again, making him look sad.

Freddie chuckled. "How do you do that, 'Snowy'?" he whispered and wondered if his parents had noticed anything unusual about their snowman. He clomped down the stairs and into the kitchen. "Elephants on the loose!" he cried as he walked through the door.

His parents were sat at the table and laughed out loud having their little joke turned on them today.

"Looks like just the one today then, I guess they don't like the snow much," his father chuckled.

"Good morning, Freddie," his mother called, "porridge on its way," she added.

Freddie looked pleased and sat to the table next to his father. "Dad, do elephants really not like the snow then?" he asked seriously.

His father loved Freddie's inquisitive nature. "As far as I know, Freddie, elephants are found in Africasia and Indianasia. Both countries are very hot all year round, being close to the equator. I doubt it snows there, except maybe on mountain tops," his father replied.

Freddie looked at his father, thinking how smart he was.

"What's an equator, Dad?" Freddie asked.

"Ah, good question son, wait a minute." His father left the kitchen and returned with the world globe on a stand from the sitting room. "This is the best way to explain things," he replied. "You know Astoria orbits the sun, right?"

Freddie nodded.

"And you know our world, Astoria, spins around?"

Freddie nodded and replied, "That's why we have day and night, Dad, right?"

His father smiled and nodded. "Okay, look at this globe. Do you see all these lines going around it from the middle up and down?"

Freddie scrunched up his face. "Are those lines actually on the planet like that then, Dad?" he asked.

"No, these are imaginary lines only drawn on maps and globes to help us locate places on the planet. There's a lot more to this, son, than I can properly explain. There is a brilliant program on TV, which completely explains everything with lots of images, I'll hunt it out and we can watch it together," his father explained.

"That will be great, Dad," Freddie replied enthusiastically.

"It doesn't look like any of us will be going anywhere far today, the snow is half way up the doors. I'm not even sure we can even get outside!" Freddie's mother explained.

Mr Fountain's employer rang right on cue and told him to stay at home today, as the roads were impassable and dangerous.

Having an unexpected free day, they all went into the sitting room after breakfast and Freddie's father found the program he had mentioned, so they sat and watched it together. Learning about the planet's orbit and how the seasons occurred and most importantly why countries close to the equator were always hot and sunny.

Freddie had really enjoyed and appreciated the morning spent with his parents watching the documentary from which they had all learned a lot. After lunch, around one o'clock, the sun was shining and melting away the snow turning it slushy everywhere. The drifts around the kitchen and front doors disappeared making it possible to leave the house if Freddie and his parents wanted to.

Freddie's mother persuaded her husband to help her clean out the kitchen cupboards and they invited Freddie to help, but he was keen to go exploring in the forest.

"Be careful, Freddie, watch out for snow bombs and be home by four o'clock, okay?" his mother told him.

Freddie wrinkled his face. "What are snow bombs, Mum?" he chuckled.

"When I was your age I liked the forest too, but in the winter when it snowed, the snow would pile up on the tree branches. If you were not careful they could suddenly drop clumps of snow right on your head!" his mother explained.

"Oh," Freddie cringed, "That could be dangerous, like a huge snowball dropping from a great height. Wow! Thank you, Mum, I never thought about that. I'll be careful and be home before 4 o'clock," Freddie said, knowing his mother would worry about him. He donned his winter coat, scarf, gloves, boots and rucksack, of course, then headed out for the forest and Elfin Town.

* *

Inside Wiggly's home Freddie retrieved the Earthstone from his rucksack.

"Oh, that's so pretty," Giggly said excitedly on seeing the stone, attempting to touch it in Freddie's hand. "Oh, how weird!" she exclaimed when her fingers passed through the Earthstone. "How are you holding the stone, Freddie?" she asked.

"I don't know really. Daddly thinks it is for me and me alone," he replied.

"Well that makes a lot of sense," Mummly explained. "Clearly these stones will enable some powerful magic, if they fell into the wrong hands, someone could cause a lot of trouble."

"I guess you are right, Mummly," Daddly agreed.

"How are we to find the other stones?" Wiggly asked.

"The clue says the Earthstone will help to find them, if you remember," Daddly pointed out.

"But how?" Freddie asked.

"Well it's obvious," Giggly giggled a little smugly, "just ask it, it's magic after all!"

Four pairs of eyes looked at Giggly in wonder.

"What?" she laughed.

"Okay!" replied Freddie with a big smile on his face, looking from Giggly to the Earthstone, "let's give it a try." He concentrated on the Earthstone and said to it, "Find the Moonstone!"

Nothing happened, much as he had expected, it might be magic, but it was still a stone, it had no ears to listen with.

"Seems that didn't w.........." Wiggly stopped speaking suddenly as the Earthstone began to glow, just as if there was a light inside it.

"Oooh, that's even more beautiful!" Giggly cried.

Although they were calling it an Earthstone it was really more like a crystal.

"Oh! OH!" Freddie cried. "It's pulling me!" His hand holding the gemstone stretched out in front of him pointing to the door.

"Quick, Wiggly, coat on, we need to follow and help Freddie," Daddly cried. "Mummly and Giggly stay home please, we don't know what lies ahead!"

Freddie could not hold back any longer, the Earthstone was dragging him. Luckily he still had on his coat and boots. He let go of the Earthstone and it just stopped, floating in the air above his hand, shining brightly.

"We're ready, Freddie, let's go," Daddly said opening the door.

Freddie took the Earthstone back in his hand and it immediately began pulling him once more.

They moved quickly, not quite running, but not a walking pace either, along the main road and off towards the park. It took them across the moss grass to the opposite side of the lake and to the outer wall of the Town.

The Earthstone stopped pulling Freddie. "Oh! What now?" he said looking at Wiggly and Daddly.

"Why not ask it, Freddie?" Wiggly replied.

"Oh, of course!" he chuckled. "Earthstone, what do I do now?" he asked, concentrating on the crystal. Something spectacular began to happen, a horizontal beam of red light shining from the Earthstone hit the wall in front of them and began moving up and down. Then a second beam hit the wall, this time moving vertically, left to right and back again. The red beams began to move faster and faster.

"Oh, makes my eyes go all squiffy!" Wiggly cried shaking his head.

All of a sudden the two lines stopped and where they crossed a handprint recess appeared and the beams vanished.

Without needing to be told, Freddie tried placing his hand into the recess, it was yet another perfect fit. "Eidderf, Eidderf, Eidderf," he chanted his name backward, Freddie found it easier to say this time.

The ground rumbled and trembled and a crack appeared at the base of the wall, slowly rising to the sky ceiling.

"Look at that!" Wiggly cried.

As they watched, the crack widened more and more until it was wide enough to walk through, but inside was pitch black.

Freddie took off his rucksack and put the Earthstone inside, then pulled out three torches, handing one to Daddly and another to Wiggly. Once his rucksack was back on his shoulders they were ready to explore. "Wait!" Freddie cried. "Last night I had a dream, many times over and Wiggly was crying out my name. There may be dangers in here, booby traps that I cannot see like in the escape tunnel, but Elfins can see them," Freddie explained.

"Well in that case, Freddie, I will lead. You follow me and Wiggly can follow behind, that way we can protect you," Daddly replied.

The darkness seemed to swallow the bright beams of the torches, they could only see a little way ahead. The tunnel turned to the left, then to the right, then stopped at a seemingly dead end.

"That's weird, why a dead end? It makes no sense!" Daddly said. "Let's look all over the walls, use your eyes and hands to see if there are any triggers or hand prints," he suggested.

They shone their torches at the wall in front of them and felt the smooth surface with their fingers.

"Freddie!" Wiggly shouted.

Freddie and Daddly rushed over to him.

"What is it, Wiggly?" Freddie asked.

"This is very weird, look," Wiggly replied. "I can shine my torch all over and everything looks smooth and blank, but I can feel a pointy hollow here," he said with his hand on the wall.

Freddie reached over and slid his fingers along to where Wiggly's hand was on the wall. "Yes, I can feel it too. Clever, Wiggly, and it feels like the same shape as the Earthstone! Hang on, I'll get it out of my rucksack," he replied excitedly.

With the ruby red glowing Earthstone in his hand, Freddie pressed it into the pointy indentation on the wall. The ground began to rumble again.

"Look out!" Wiggly cried again as the floor began to disappear.

Freddie shone his torch at the hole and it revealed a stone spiral staircase. "This is like my dream!" Freddie explained.

"Same routine then boys, me first, then Freddie with Wiggly bringing up the rear," Daddly told them.

Slowly, they descended the narrow stone steps round and round making them all feel a little dizzy.

"I see a light down there, just a little further now boys," Daddly announced.

They stepped into a massive cave with huge stalactites hanging down from the ceiling and enormous stalagmites rising up from the ground. Some of them were tall and wide, others just short and thin.

"Oh, wow!" Wiggly exclaimed as he looked around.

"It's so incredible," Freddie said in wonder in a low voice.

"Those things hanging down are called Stalactites and are hundreds, if not thousands of years old," Daddly explained, "and the ones growing up from the ground are called Stalagmites," he added.

Wiggly and Freddie looked around in complete awe.

"The Stalagmites are created by lime dissolved in water dripping from the ceiling. Each drop leaves a little bit of lime behind, eventually the top and bottom will join together," Daddly further explained.

"Oooh! Just like Merlin's Cavern," Freddie said in a low voice.

"That's something to be careful about, any loud noise could cause the stalactites to come crashing down from the ceiling," Daddly warned.

"Where's the light coming from?" Wiggly whispered.

"Over there somewhere," Freddie replied quietly, pointing beyond some big Stalagmites.

All three walked towards the light source, the ground crunching under foot like they were walking on shells. They rounded a tall, fat stalagmite and stopped and stared, completely lost for words.

"Oh, sooo beautiful," Wiggly eventually whispered.

"Boys, I have never seen anything like this before, it is beyond words to describe what we are looking at," Daddly said softly.

"What do you think they are?" Freddie asked quietly.

"It's a bit like the Fairy Dust around Merlin's Lake," Wiggly answered.

"But these are huge in comparison to the size of Fairy Dust," Freddie replied.

"Let's get a bit closer boys, don't touch anything, we have no idea what might happen," Daddly whispered.

Wiggly took his father's hand and also Freddie's as they approached the magnificent sight.

Ahead of them was an enormous silvery mirror-like lake, surrounded by a ring of something that glittered like Fairy Dust, at least three metres wide. It was very much like Merlin's lake but bigger, much bigger. Whatever they were, rainbows of light danced above them and they were so beautiful, like a million rainbows shining up, even then it failed to express the real beauty. The cavern seemed to go on forever, disappearing into the blackness far away.

Wiggly stopped suddenly, pulling Daddly and Freddie to a halt. "Look, look," he whispered loudly. "They moved, those things around the lake, they're moving," he said excitedly.

"Wow, the lake is massive, just like Merlin's only bigger, much BIGGER!" "BIGGER! BIGGER! BIGGER! BIGGER!" Freddie forgot and called out really loudly in his excitement, only for his words to echo and the ground tremble.

Behind them a huge Stalactite crashed down from the ceiling and smashed into hundreds of pieces, which flew everywhere and made a loud crash that echoed around the cavern. A few other Stalactites wobbled and the three of them took cover behind the big Stalagmite close to them. They ducked down and covered their heads as plumes of white dust and debris flew past and over them.

When they looked up again, Wiggly could not help chuckling. "You have a white back," he said quietly to Daddly and Freddie.

"That was close, boys, we must remember to keep our voices down, okay?" Daddly whispered.

Wiggly and Freddie nodded their agreement with their hands over their mouths.

"Let's get a bit closer to that lake and Fairy Dust stuff," Daddly suggested.

Ahead of them, stretching all around the lake was a wide area of what now appeared to be lightly coloured crystals the size of tennis balls, which had looked just like Fairy Dust from a distance. But now they were emitting that beautiful coloured rainbow of lights. There were blues and pinks, yellows, oranges, greens and red ones that lit up the whole cavern around them. But they did seem to be moving about as Wiggly had pointed out. It was not much, but they seemed to jiggle among themselves as if they were alive.

When they reached the edge, Daddly crouched down to look more closely. "Boys, it's not the crystals moving but what's underneath them," he whispered.

But Freddie held back, he felt very unsure.

"It's okay, Freddie, come take a look," Daddly encouraged.

So Freddie moved a little closer.

"Oh, what's happening?" Wiggly whispered quite alarmed.

As Freddie approached, the crystals began to part.

"It's like they are making a pathway for you to the lake, Freddie." Daddly declared quietly.

Strange as it was, Freddie felt compelled to walk closer to the crystals and as he stood at the edge of them, they had parted to form a pathway directly to the lake.

"Look, look," Wiggly whispered excitedly again, slapping his hand over his mouth and pointing to the lake with his other hand. "Something is making ripples in the middle of the lake."

All three stood and watched as a large, long, yellow crystal emerged up out of the water and floated shoulder height above the surface.

"That must be the Moonstone," Daddly suggested.

Freddie looked bewildered. "How do we get to it, Daddly?"

Wiggly scratched his chin and said, "Well it looks far too big for the ring?" Feeling brave, he stepped on the path so he could take a closer look, but the crystals quickly closed the path off and drove him back. Whatever was making the crystals move rose under Wiggly's feet and forced him back towards Daddly, who caught him before he crashed to the ground.

"Wiggly, are you okay?" Freddie asked, feeling worried about his friend.

"Oh, err, yes, thanks to Daddly. That was a bit of a shock, it lifted me and pushed me, Freddie," Wiggly replied in a surprised, quiet voice.

"It very much looks like this is as far as we go with you, Freddie, this next part is for you alone," Daddly whispered, putting his hand on Freddie's shoulder in friendly encouragement.

As soon as Wiggly was standing away from the edge of the crystals they opened up the pathway again.

"I don't like this very much," Freddie announced. "What am I supposed to do if the crystals allow me to reach the shore of the lake? There's no boat for me to cross the lake to reach the Moonstone.

"My guess is that you will be fine, Freddie. You know Merlin is watching over you and he's testing you all the time. Just be brave like Wiggly and I know you are. Let Merlin be your guide and courage," Daddly said looking on the bright side.

Freddie took a deep breath and looked at Daddly and Wiggly.

They both nodded and smiled, Wiggly gave his friend the 'thumbs up' sign.

Freddie stepped onto the path the crystals had exposed, then stepped back immediately. "Ah!" he cried covering his mouth, forgetting about making a loud noise. "It's soft and spongy, I think I might sink," he whispered.

"Have faith, Freddie, have faith," Daddly encouraged again.

"You can do it, Freddie, if anyone can it's definitely you!" Wiggly said softly with a big smile on his face.

Freddie tried again, his foot sank a little but the surface held his weight, so he stepped on with his other foot and the same happened. Holding his arms out to balance himself on the wobbly ground, he walked a few more paces, then suddenly he could not lift his legs, his feet were stuck. "I'm trapped," he called looking round at his friends.

Daddly and Wiggly moved towards him, but the crystals closed around Freddie, stopping them getting close enough to pull him free.

Freddie was scared and he trembled.

"We're definitely not invited, Freddie," Daddly called quietly. "You can do this, you are braver than you think."

"Oh!" Wiggly suddenly called out as he watched his friend start moving.

"This is weird," Freddie called. He was moving along, but he was not walking, the ground or whatever it was, carried him along like he was on a conveyer belt until he reached the edge of the lake. The crystals had closed behind him making sure no uninvited were able to cross. "What now?" he turned to Daddly and Wiggly, shrugging his shoulders.

"Try asking the Moonstone, Freddie," Wiggly suggested.

He had forgotten he could ask the crystals what to do, so he turned to face the Moonstone, "Moonstone, what do I do now?" he said as loudly as he dare.

The Moonstone flashed brightly as if it was talking. *'Approach,'* sounded in Freddie's mind. He looked around wondering where the voice had come from. "Did you hear that?" he asked Daddly and Wiggly.

But they were shaking their heads, "We didn't hear anything, Freddie," they replied together.

"It told me to approach, but it's water, I will surely sink!" Freddie explained in a loud whisper.

"Have faith, Freddie," Daddly called supportively.

'Approach,' the voice sounded once again and the crystals rose up and began pushing Freddie into the water from behind.

He took a deep breath and stepped in the water and closed his eyes, he knew he was going to sink, any second his body would fall into the water and .... "Oh," he gasped quietly, opening his eyes, his foot seemed to rest on top of the water as if something was holding him up. Once more he took a deep breath, ready to bring his other foot into the water, when in his mind the Fairy Queen spoke to him. *'You have a charmed life, no harm or accident can befall you.'*

Feeling stronger, "Here goes," he whispered, to no none in particular. His next step was the same, his foot invisibly held up in the water. He felt encouraged, braver and took two more steps, now he was away from the shore, alone in the water.

"Look, Daddly, Freddie's walking on water, that's a miracle isn't it, who can walk on water?" Wiggly was excited, he had never seen anything like it before.

Daddly chuckled. "We know what magic Fairy Dust can do, Wiggly, but magic is so much more powerful than we ever imagined."

Freddie took one step at a time, holding his arms out to keep his balance, although he had no need, for he was walking on something solid beneath his feet, or so it seemed. The Moonstone was a long way from the shore in the middle of the lake and Freddie got closer with every careful step. Two more steps and he would be close enough to take it in his hand, he blew out a breath he had not realised he was holding. One, two steps and now he could reach the Moonstone. He raised his hand and placed it under the large crystal, which began instantly shrinking until it was the same size as the Earthstone, then dropped into his hand.

"Oh, cripes," Freddie said under his breath and his whole body trembled. Looking around and realising he was standing in the middle of this vast silvery lake, without a boat or even water wings and he suddenly felt afraid. His fear caused him to sink a little into the water making him even more afraid and he sank again up to his knees.

"**Moonstone, save me!**" he cried out aloud, his voice echoed around the cavern causing the walls and ground to rumble.

Stalactites fell and shattered on the ground making loud crashing sounds that set others off until a few minutes later, after the clouds of dust-like fog blew around the cavern, things settled down again.

"Freddie's in trouble, Daddly, we have to do something!" Wiggly said pulling on his father's arm.

Daddly stepped forward onto the crystal rim and his foot sank down to his knee.

"Daddly!" Wiggly cried and grabbed his father to pull him out, but he was not strong enough.

Daddly's leg began sinking even more.

When Freddie heard Wiggly cry out, he saw Daddly was in trouble. He commanded the Moonstone to take him to the shore. Suddenly Freddie was on top of the water again and travelling at speed towards the shoreline. As he reached the crystal rim it opened a pathway and Freddie took Daddly's hand.

"Moonstone, lift us up and out of this mud!" he commanded in a voice Wiggly hardly recognised, it was like an adult's voice. Freddie and Daddly rose in the air until Daddly was out of the muddy stuff and they floated back onto solid ground.

"Thank you, Freddie, I could not free myself nor was Wiggly able to pull me out, everything is certainly designed so that only the chosen one can progress," Daddly said.

Freddie looked pleased with himself and opened his hand. "I have it, the Moonstone, look how beautiful it is," he chirped quietly.

"Oh, it's so beautiful," Wiggly replied, mesmerized by the yellow glow from the Moonstone. "Freddie," he said pulling his gaze from it, "you looked incredible walking on water, who knew that was possible?"

"It was my courage that allowed it. When I suddenly felt afraid, that's when I began to sink, but I commanded the Moonstone and it helped," Freddie said. He offered it to Wiggly and Daddly, but neither could hold it, their fingers passing right through it.

"One more to go, Freddie," Daddly encouraged and they all smiled.

Freddie looked at his watch and said, "I have to get home, it's getting late and Mum will be worried." With that thought in mind, he put the Moonstone in his rucksack and they began their journey back.

All three felt even dizzier climbing up the spiral staircase and when they got to the top, Freddie retrieved the Earthstone from the wall and slipped it into his rucksack.

Wiggly walked his friend to the big old oak tree spiral staircase and bade him farewell at the forest door.

Freddie grabbed a twiggy branch to erase his footprints as he made his way homeward, with his mind full of the adventure and his heart still beating fast, knowing he had to have courage and believe that Merlin was watching over him.

* *

That night, Freddie's sleep was once again filled with a recurring dream. This time he was caught in a circle of flames with no way out and he was getting hotter and hotter, he could see Wiggly jumping up and down calling his name. Twice during the night he woke up with a start, hot and sweating. "Is Merlin trying to tell me something?" he whispered to himself in the darkness. He crept into the bathroom and cooled his face with a damp face cloth and looked at his tired eyes in the mirror. When he had cooled down he returned to his bed and drifted back to sleep to dream about the circle of fire all over again.

"Huh! Wiggly! Stop!" Freddie cried out, his body shaking and arms waving about.

"Freddie, Freddie," a familiar voice called to him in the distance, "Freddie!"

He opened one eye and almost jumped out of his skin, he sat bolt upright staring at his mother.

"Goodness, Freddie, did I give you a scare? I'm sorry son," his mother apologised, giving him a cuddle. When she released him and checked that he was wide awake she asked, "What's a wiggly, Freddie?"

He looked at his mother in horror. "W-what do you mean, Mum?" he replied nervously.

"Well, as I was shaking you to wake you up, that's what you said, wiggly stop," she answered.

Freddie did not want to tell lies to his mother and he was wide-awake now, feeling a little guilty. "Mum, I've been having funny dreams for a few nights, I guess it must be something to do with them." He was telling the truth, but holding a few important details back.

"I thought so, I think I heard you go into the bathroom during the night, but I wasn't sure if I was dreaming myself," his mother laughed. "Come on then lazy bones, get washed and dressed, I have porridge ready for breakfast," she added.

When Freddie burst into the kitchen he was full of energy and wide-awake ready for the promised porridge.

391

"Goodness, you're full of beans this morning, Freddie," his father remarked as his son plonked himself on the chair next to him.

"Not beans, Dad, I want to be full of porridge!" he replied and chuckled.

"Very good, son, you're on the ball alright!" his father grinned. "The roads are clear now so I shall be away to work this morning. Don't forget it's Christmas Eve tomorrow and we are visiting your Grandma, okay son?" his father reminded him.

Freddie had been so wrapped up in his search for Merlin's gemstones he had completely forgotten that it was nearly Christmas.

"Would you like to help me wrap a few presents this morning, Freddie?" his mother asked.

Freddie's eyes lit up, he loved wrapping presents. "Oooh, yes please, Mum, I do like doing that!" he replied enthusiastically.

He and his mother spent the morning together doing just that, listening to Christmas Carols and singing along with them. Freddie realised that he missed all the normal things that he did with his family and that his secret life was slowly becoming so important he wondered if his life would ever be just normal again. Part way through wrapping the presents they ran out of sticky tape.

"Oh, that's annoying, I had better pop to the shop and buy another roll," Freddie's mother said, rather annoyed with herself for not having enough.

"No need, Mum, I think I have some in my rucksack," Freddie chirped and dashed upstairs, pulling out a large roll of sticky tape from his magic rucksack, then galloping downstairs again.

When he handed it to his mother she chuckled. "I'm sure that rucksack of yours is magical, you always seem to have just what is needed," she laughed jokingly.

"It is, Mum. All I have to do is say 'Abracadabra' and things appear like magic!" Freddie giggled.

His mother looked at him a little bewildered then burst into laughter. "You almost had me believing you then, Freddie, naughty boy, pulling your mother's leg!" she replied and Freddie laughed along with her.

He had told her the truth apart from the 'Abracadabra' part, but now he knew for sure that people would find it hard to believe about all the things he got up to in Elfin Town and his friends, Wiggly, Giggly, Mummly and Daddly.

Later on he played some Christmas Carols on his guitar. He and his mother sang along together, it was one of those magical moments he would always cherish.

After lunch and with a couple of mince pies in his rucksack, Freddie headed out into his beloved forest, he still had a mission to complete. On his way through the garden he was pleased to see his snowman still standing with hat, scarf and pipe. He chuckled, "'Snowy,' what do you get up to during the night?"

'Snowy' was facing the forest again and had a very big smile on his face.

'Fun'

"Huh!" Freddie said in surprise when the word *'fun'* was spoken in his mind. He looked at 'Snowy' and giggled. "So you have fun, I can't imagine what sort of fun a snowman can have," he said to 'Snowy'. "Huh, did you just wink again? Gosh, I think I'm going bonkers now!" he chirped and ran off through the gate.

He made lots of tracks in the snow to confuse anyone who might try to follow him on his way to the big old oak tree. "I'm on my way, Wiggly!" he called out as he ran round and round giggling. He was in good spirits today. He had spent a lovely morning with his mother, 'Snowy' had spoken to him and winked, what else could make his day better?

When he met up with Wiggly and his family they sat and chatted for a while then set out on their search for the final gemstone.

Freddie let the Earthstone guide them and it took them back into the forest, still covered with snow on the ground and in the trees, but not enough to hinder them. "Look out, Wiggly!" Freddie cried as a whole load of icy snow tumbled down from the branches of a fir tree and crashed to the ground where Wiggly had stopped to catch his breath.

"Oh! Flippiddydo!" Wiggly cried out. "That was close, thank you, Freddie!" he gasped and hugged his best friend.

"My Mum calls those 'snow bombs', now I understand what she meant!" Freddie explained.

"Looks like the snow is beginning to melt, so we need to watch out for more 'snow bombs' like that," Daddly warned.

The Earthstone took them on a long journey through the forest and around the village until they came to a familiar spot.

"It's *that* cave!" Freddie cried out in surprise.

"Cave? What cave?" Wiggly questioned.

"You know, Wiggly, it's the cave that the Morphlins used as their hideout!" Freddie replied.

Wiggly suddenly turned very pale with a look of horror on his face and he shook and trembled, "Oooh! You're right, Freddie, I don't like this at all, it gives me the creeps!"

"It's okay, Wiggly, you two and Grundly vanquished those Morphlins, they're not coming back any time soon," Daddly comforted his son with a fatherly hug.

"I guess so," Wiggly said feeling much better, "but we never actually went inside did we, is that where the Earthstone is taking us?"

"Yes, it seems to be pulling me that way," Freddie replied.

Once again the three hunters stepped into the darkness, illuminated by torches Freddie had pulled from his magical rucksack.

"It's creepy, I can't help thinking there might be a Morphlin still lurking in here," Wiggly whispered.

"I'm sure they or it would have shown itself by now if that was the case, Wiggly," Daddly assured his son and Freddie.

"It goes back a lot further than I expected," Freddie commented after they had been walking slowly for at least ten minutes and could no longer see any light from the entrance behind them.

"Oh, this is unexpected!" Daddly exclaimed. "SPECTED! SPECTED! SPECTED!" his voice echoed around as they walked into a huge domed chamber. "Look how smooth the walls are, this can't be a natural cavern. It looks like it has been carved out and polished, but to what end, I have no clue?" Daddly observed.

Even the floor was smooth, flat and highly polished.

"What do you think we need to do next?" Freddie said aloud. "NEXT! NEXT! NEXT!" his voice echoed around the walls and he put his hand over his mouth.

"It's like we are in an upturned bowl," Wiggly whispered. "It's still creepy, do you think the Morphlins did this?"

Daddly and Freddie shrugged their shoulders.

"Why don't we walk around the walls with our hands like before and see if there is a clue, or hand imprint," Daddly suggested.

Shining their torches and sliding their free hands on the smooth wall, they slowly worked their way around until they had covered every part as far as they could reach from the ground up.

"Why would the Earthstone bring us here if there's nothing else to see and no sign of the Sunstone?" Freddie asked Daddly and Wiggly.

All three were silent and more than a little disappointed.

"We must be missing something, Merlin is testing you, Freddie, I'm sure of it," Daddly remarked.

"Hey, Freddie, why don't you ask the Earthstone? It worked before," Wiggly piped quietly.

"I just didn't think of it, Wiggly," Freddie replied shaking his head. He held the Earthstone in the palm of his hand. "Show me what to do next Earthstone."

The gemstone glowed brightly and floated off Freddie's hand. They watched as it moved silently through the air, circling round and round above them, then floating down towards the centre of the floor. Freddie shone his torch on the floor and there was a crystal shaped depression that the Earthstone settled into and became dim again.

"No wonder we couldn't find anything!" Wiggly chuckled quietly. "We never thought about the floor, did we?"

Suddenly the Earthstone began to glow brightly, illuminating the whole chamber.

"Wow, the dome is perfectly smooth everywhere!" Freddie said in awe as they looked around.

"Hey! Where's the entrance gone?" Wiggly cried with alarm. "We're sealed in, we will suffocate!" he cried running to the wall where the opening had been, patting it with his hand. "We're trapped, there's no way out!" he cried.

Daddly rushed to his son and hugged and comforted him. "Have a little faith ...." he did not get the chance to finish before they all began to feel strange.

"Oooh! Err! My stomach!" Wiggly mumbled.

"I feel lighter somehow!" Freddie said moving to Daddly and Wiggly and finding he was wobbly on his feet.

"I think somehow we are moving downwards, that's why we feel lighter and wobbly," Daddly said.

"Oh, like being in a lift in one of the big stores in the city." Freddie suggested.

"What's a lift?" Wiggly asked.

"Err, it's like a box that people stand inside, then it is hauled up so they can get off on different floor levels. Instead of a spiral staircase you could have a lift to take you up and down." Freddie tried to explain, but Wiggly was screwing up his face unable to visualise what Freddie was describing.

Then the strange sensations stopped as suddenly as they had started and the opening appeared again. Wiggly had been leaning on the wall when the entrance appeared again and he fell down onto the ground pulling Daddly with him, who was still hugging his son.

"Oh!" Freddie cried out, "this is like my dream last night."

Wiggly and Daddly scrambled to their feet and then were transfixed at what Freddie was looking at through the opening. They did not need their torches and switched them off.

"I've never seen anything like this before," Daddly exclaimed for a second time.

"I - I, d - don't like it, Daddly, you always taught us it was dangerous!" Wiggly stuttered, grabbing onto his father again.

Freddie shook his head. "I suppose the Sunstone will be right at home down here," he observed.

The chamber opened up into yet another vast cavern, the ceiling was supported by dozens of smooth, round stone pillars.

"These are not natural, the pillars have been made by someone, it looks like the whole place was constructed centuries or even thousands of years ago," Daddly said looking at the amazing sight ahead of them.

There were dozens of large, perfectly round holes in the perfectly smooth floor, through which blue coloured flames leapt up to the ceiling and seemed to light it up in an eerie blue colour.

"Have you noticed the air is cool, not hot like you'd expect with all these flames," Freddie said.

"That is strange, but these flames are different somehow," Daddly agreed. "But if we are to find the Sunstone we need to go and explore," he added.

"I'm afraid I know where it is, Daddly, but in my dream there was a large ring of fire and the Sunstone was floating in the middle of it. That's what we need to look for I guess," Freddie replied.

They set off from the chamber into the eerie blue cavern with Wiggly holding tightly to Daddly and Freddie. As they approached the blue flames and walked between them, there was no heat coming from them.

"What kind of fire is not hot?" Wiggly asked as they slowly navigated between the stone pillars and blue flames.

"Over there boys, I think that's the circle of flames you described, Freddie." Daddly was pointing to a huge wall of blue flames issuing up from the smooth floor.

When Freddie saw what Daddly was pointing at he froze to the spot and turned very pale.

Wiggly was yanked to a halt, as was Daddly, and they could see the look of horror on Freddie's face.

"What are you thinking, Freddie?" Daddly asked.

Freddie turned from looking at the wall of flames to look at Daddly. "In my dream, the Sunstone is in the middle of those flames. How am I going to be able to get it without getting badly burned?" he croaked. His eyes were glazing as tears began to form at the thought of getting near all that fire, how would he explain to his parents if he ended in hospital all burned, or worse, what if he did not survive. All these thoughts were going through his mind and terrifying him.

"Let's get closer, Freddie, and at least check if the Sunstone is actually in there. Then we can walk around and see if there is a safe way to get inside, there might be an area with no flames. All this is designed to scare off anyone who should not be here. You are the chosen one, Freddie, you have the right to be here, okay?" Daddly suggested, trying to calm Freddie with another hug from him and Wiggly.

Freddie was far from convinced. *'I'm only a child, why is Merlin testing me like this?'* he thought to himself.

Then out of the blue Wiggly piped up, "Freddie's only a child, why is Merlin testing him like this?"

Freddie jumped and looked at his friend. "Wiggly! Those are the exact words I just thought to myself! Did I say them aloud instead?"

Wiggly looked at Freddie and smiled. "No you didn't, they just came into my head!"

"Clearly you two are sharing some kind of mind link and it might be important, but let's get closer to this wall of flames and check things out," Daddly suggested.

Two dozen more strides and they were quite close to the flames, which suddenly began to roar loudly and grow in size as they approached.

"Step back, boys," Daddly said and the flames became eerily silent again.

"How come they don't normally make a sound, Daddly?" Wiggly asked.

"I really have no idea, son, this is something I've neither seen nor heard of before, flames like these should be making a tremendous sound, it's a mystery," Daddly replied. "Stay here a moment," he said and approached the flames. Immediately they roared and blazed, almost deafening them all. He reached out and offered his finger into the blue flames. He pulled his hand back quickly and cried, "Ouch!" sticking his finger into his mouth. "That burns!" he mumbled, pulling back to the boys as the flames turned silent again.

This did nothing to encourage Freddie, who was on the verge of turning back without the Sunstone and forget about being Merlin's apprentice.

"Look, look!" Wiggly cried suddenly, so excited his legs were running on the spot again. "It's the Sunstone, I can see it, Freddie, look!"

Daddly and Freddie looked where Wiggly was pointing.

Freddie wiped his eyes, things were a bit blurry.

"Indeed, Wiggly, I can see the Sunstone too!" Daddly said with a big smile on his face.

Freddie squinted his eyes trying to focus, he sniffed and concentrated, and then in an instant there it was, the Sunstone. The moment he saw it, the Sunstone seemed to react and began to glow bright yellow until it really looked like the sun.

"Whoa! That's incredible, what did you do, Freddie?" Wiggly asked, mesmerized by the wonderful glowing gemstone.

"It's the Sunstone, Freddie, it knows you are here, that's why it's glowing like this, it's communicating with you, I think you should ask it what to do," Daddly suggested.

Freddie was trying to control his fear, but it was in danger of overwhelming him.

Daddly stood behind him with his hands on Freddie's shoulders. "Take a deep breath, Freddie," he said softly.

Freddie inhaled and puffed out his chest.

"Now exhale slowly," Daddly said.

Freddie let out all the air in his lungs slowly.

"Now ask the Sunstone what you must do," Daddly said in a soft, kindly voice.

Freddie took another breath then spoke. "Sunstone, tell me what I must do?" His voice had a tremble of fear in it.

'Approach,' sounded in Freddie's mind.

"But I can't, I will be burned alive!" he protested.

'Approach!' repeated in his mind so loudly it made him freeze solid.

"You have to, Freddie, I heard the Sunstone too, you must do as it says," Wiggly said shaking his friend gently.

"Have faith, Freddie, remember you have a charmed life, Merlin gave you freedom from illness and harm. Try your finger like I did first, I think you will be fine," Daddly encouraged.

Freddie approached the wall of blue flames and it remained silent. He looked back at Daddly and Wiggly who were giving him the thumbs up. He lifted his hand and closed his eyes. His body shook and trembled, he had never been so afraid in his young life as he was right now at this moment in time. He raised his finger and pushed it forward.

"That's it, Freddie, your hand is in the flames!" shouted Wiggly.

Freddie opened his eyes and cried out, pulling his hand from the flames and looking at it. "It's alright, I'm not burned. How is that possible?" he mumbled to himself. He turned to Daddly and Wiggly and held his hand up to show them he was all right, then rushed back to them. "Look! My hand, is not burned like yours, Daddly, I don't understand, how can this be?"

Daddly hugged Freddie tightly. "It's like I said, Freddie, you have a charmed life, and Merlin is looking after you even now. The Sunstone is meant only for you to reach and hold, everyone else, like me and Wiggly or any Elfin or Sproggle, would suffer terrible burns with these flames. Only you can pass through them unharmed. I know you don't think you are special, but Merlin thinks you are and so do we. We have always thought so right from the first time we met you," Daddly encouraged and Wiggly was nodding and dancing with excitement. "Go get the Sunstone, Freddie, it's there waiting for you alone to collect," Daddly added.

Freddie stopped trembling and thanked Daddly and his friend Wiggly for their support. He took another deep breath and approached the wall of blue flames again. This time he did not stop, he walked into them and through them as if they were not even there. "Hee, hee, they tickle!" Freddie chuckled to himself as he walked among the dancing fire until he reached the Sunstone floating brightly right in the middle. He held out his hand. "Come to me," he commanded and the Sunstone dimmed, then shrank in size and floated down into the palm of his hand. "Oh, you are so beautiful!" he announced as it settled in his hand, then he turned around and walked back through the wall of blue flames, giggling until he emerged through the other side. When he reached Daddly and Wiggly he had a big smile on his face.

"Well done, Freddie," Wiggly cried.

Freddie opened his hand to show Daddly and Wiggly the crystal.

"Oh, that's the prettiest of them all, it's incredible," Wiggly exclaimed as he looked at the rainbow of changing colours of the Sunstone.

Freddie took off his rucksack and placed the Sunstone safely inside the magic zipped part.

Daddly led the way as they made their way back through the stone columns and flames.

"Is this the way we came, it looks different?" Wiggly whispered to Freddie as they walked together, arm in arm.

Daddly stopped and scratched his head. "I'm sure this is the way we came," he mumbled to himself.

"Are we lost, Daddly?" Wiggly asked.

"It would appear so," his father admitted. "I was certain we came this way," he added.

"Look!" Freddie said pointing around them.

"How come we didn't notice that before?" Wiggly asked.

"Well I don't think it happened on the way in," Freddie replied.

"Hmmm," Daddly grumbled, "it looks like this is another way to stop the Sunstone from leaving with the wrong person. Merlin is a very clever wizard."

"But if the pillars and flames keep changing around, how can we find our way out?" Wiggly asked.

They were faced with the stone columns and blue flames slowly changing positions to confuse anyone trying to find their way out.

"Do you think the Sunstone can find the way, Freddie?" Daddly asked.

Freddie retrieved the Sunstone from his rucksack and held it out in the palm of his hand, "Sunstone show us the way home," he commanded. Immediately the Sunstone lit up and began pulling Freddie back the way they had walked, then right at a stone pillar. Daddly and Wiggly followed closely behind at a pace as Freddie was almost running, then they realised that the Sunstone was weaving between pillars and flames before they moved. They turned round another pillar and much to their relief, the entrance to the big chamber was in front of them.

"Quickly, before things move around and we lose the entrance again," Daddly urged and they all made a dash for it.

Once inside the chamber, Freddie returned the Sunstone to his rucksack and fished out their torches.

"Oooh, that was quick," Wiggly gasped, as they clambered into the dark chamber. "I don't think we would have ever found this again."

Freddie shone his torch around and saw the Earthstone was still in the recess on the floor. "Earthstone, take us home please," he commanded, and the entrance closed off again.

"Oooh, that feels strange, like I'm being squashed!" Wiggly laughed.

"I feel heavy all of a sudden too!" Freddie chuckled.

When the sensation stopped, Freddie walked to the Earthstone and when he lifted it from the recess the entrance opened up again. He placed the Earthstone in his rucksack and zipped it up again before they made their way out through the dark tunnel.

"Fresh air!" Freddie piped up, sucking in and filling his lungs when they emerged into the daylight and his beloved forest.

With no time to lose, they hurried through the forest to the big old oak tree, down the spiral staircase, then ran across the park towards the tower.

Freddie retrieved the three gemstones from his rucksack while Daddly spoke the magic words to open the doorway.

Inside the round tower they looked at the beam of light emitting from the Orb, in which the ring seemed to be floating.

Daddly suggested, "I think you will need to reach into the beam and take the ring from it, Freddie."

Holding the gemstones in one hand, Freddie stretched over the Orb of Destiny with his free hand, letting his fingers wrap around the golden ring, watched eagerly by Wiggly and Daddly. "Should I put the stones in it now, Daddly?" he asked uncertainly.

"Well they all look far too big to fit in the ring, Freddie, but try putting the Earthstone on the ring and see what happens," Daddly proposed.

Freddie held the ring in one hand and placed the Earthstone on it, which at first covered the ring completely. "This is silly it's just too ...," Freddie stopped mid sentence as the Earthstone began to glow and pulse with bright light, suddenly shrinking and dropping into one triangle of the ring.

"Wowee, that was dramatic!" Wiggly chuckled. "Try the next one, Freddie, this is exciting," he added with his little legs already running on the spot.

Freddie placed the Moonstone on the golden ring and it began to glow.

Wiggly was completely mesmerized. "The colours are so beautiful, Freddie."

The Moonstone flashed brilliantly with rainbow colours projecting all over the dark walls of the stone tower, even Daddly was captivated. The colours pulled back into the Moonstone as it began to shrink and drop into the second triangle on the ring.

"One more to go, Freddie," Daddly encouraged.

Freddie looked at him, then Wiggly, who was beaming and running on the spot with excitement and smiled back at him. He placed the final crystal, the Sunstone, on the ring and it began to glow brightly, projecting beams of light just like sunbeams, lighting up the dark tower as if it was bright daytime.

"Whoah!" Wiggly gasped peeping through his fingers. "That's so bright and beautiful!"

As the Sunstone shrank in size it turned dim and dropped into the last triangle of the ring. Suddenly each of the stones lit up and threw beams of light right up to the ceiling of the round tower, like a film projector.

"Oh, look! Look!" Wiggly cried pointing to the walls.

Images of the Wizard Merlin appeared on the walls and standing next to him was Freddie. Then Freddie's image seemed to grow and change into a handsome young man.

"That's you, Freddie, as you will become," Daddly called to a stunned little boy.

"Hey, Freddie, you look so strong and handsome!" Wiggly cried, so amazed he stopped running on the spot.

The images faded as the stones dimmed to a tiny glow, then the three stones merged together and became one multicoloured, beautiful crystal gem.

"Oh, that's incredible! I've never seen anything so pretty!" Wiggly gasped as he admired the golden ring Freddie held in his fingers.

Just as Freddie was wondering what he should do next, a swirl of mist began to race around inside the tower, spinning, twirling tendrils wrapped around Daddly and his son.

Wiggly cried out, "Freddie!" and then they were gone, vanished.

The doorway closed up instantly and Freddie was enveloped in the noisy swirling whirlwind of white mist. It made him feel dizzy and faint, he could hardly see his hand and the ring held in his fingers.

"Stop," he called out weakly, not even able to raise his voice above the noise of the misty ribbons. "Stop! Please stop!" his cry feeble and fearful.

'PUT THE RING ON,' the voice of Merlin filled his mind, 'PUT THE RING ON.' The words and swirling mist seemed to rob Freddie of any capacity to think or move. 'PUT THE RING ON,' Merlin's voice demanded in Freddie's tormented mind.

Freddie mustered every ounce of strength in him to bring his hands together, the ribbons of mist wrapped around his arm pulling them back.

'PUT THE RING ON,' Merlin's voice commanded, relentlessly.

"Grrrrr!" Freddie growled and gritted his teeth, tears rolled down his cheeks. "I can't do it!" he yelled.

'PUT THE RING ON.' The swirling tendrils of mist flew around him faster and faster, filling him with fear, making him wobble on his feet. He could hardly distinguish up from down any more. He was so afraid he might not see his family again, or Wiggly and Giggly or the Elfins, he slumped and fell to sit on his heels. 'PUT THE RING ON,' Merlin's voice was insistent.

Freddie looked upward and cried out, "No! No! **No!**" and pulled his arms away from the tendrils of mist and slid the ring on his middle finger.

Power and strength suddenly filled his body and mind like he had never before felt. A blue aura formed around him and his body lifted up until he was standing up again. Feeling strong and powerful he cried, **"STOP!"** his voice so loud it bounced around the tower getting louder and louder. The building shook and the ground trembled. The mist vanished and he was suddenly alone in the darkness of the round tower, even the orb had gone dark.

Freddie gasped and took a deep breath. "Merlin!" he called, as tears still rolled down his cheeks. He pulled his rucksack off his shoulders and reached inside for a torch, but before he could switch it on something unexpected happened. The orb began to glow green, giving the tower an eerie glow, then *'He'* appeared.

"Merlin!" Freddie wiped his eyes. "Merlin, is that really you?" he croaked, his throat a little sore.

Before him an image of the Great Wizard appeared, but he was like a stained glass window, Freddie could see through him. "But ...I ...thought ...you ...were ...were...," Freddie stumbled over his words.

'You have done well, Freddie Fountain.' The voice in Freddie's mind was deep, kind and loving, it seemed to wrap him in a warm blanket. *'You have displayed courage and bravery well beyond your years. The ring you now wear cannot be seen or touched by any mortal, Elfin or Sproggle. It will teach you all you need to know about controlling the powerful magic that now dwells within you. Whatever you need to know, ask the ring. To use your magic for now, just touch the ring and your thoughts will be obeyed. When you are proficient with magic it will obey your thoughts alone. Use your gift wisely and not for self-gain. That is all, Freddie, we will meet again in the future.'*

Before Freddie could ask a hundred questions he had in his head, Merlin's image vanished and the doorway seemed to open before him in the tower wall. He walked towards the opening and for a split second it seemed solid, he pushed and finally passed through to the outside.

Daddly and Wiggly stood rooted to the ground, both had their mouths open in disbelief.

Freddie looked at his friends standing like statues and a cold shiver shot through his body, *'Morphlins are back'*, ran through his mind.

Suddenly, Wiggly rushed to hug his stunned friend, then pulled away and looked at him.

"Freddie, you're glowing, you have a pale blue aura. What happened, how did you do that? We heard you screaming, are you alright?" Wiggly gabbled.

Daddly walked up to them both and placed his hands on either side of Freddie's face and looked him in the eyes, even his eyes seemed to glow as if lit from behind. "Freddie," he said softly.

"Daddly," Freddie replied and sobbed, tears flowed in a stream and Daddly placed Freddie's head on his shoulder.

"Let it all out, Freddie, you've been through a lot, you've been so brave, so very brave," Daddly said supportively.

Wiggly stretched his arms around his father and his best friend while Freddie bawled and sobbed, his tears flowed fast, wetting Daddly's coat.

Daddly stroked Freddie's hair soothingly. "You're safe now, Freddie, the worst is over, everything will be fine now."

Freddie lifted his head and looked at Daddly. "Will it?" he sniffed. "Will it really?" Then Freddie looked at Wiggly. "What did you mean, Wiggly, when you said how did I do that, what exactly did I do?"

"B-but you, you walked through the tower wall, the door didn't open, you just passed through the wall like it was smoke!" Wiggly replied a little astonished.

"That's right, Freddie, it's why we stood like statues. At first you looked like a ghost with your blue aura, walking straight through the solid stone wall," Daddly further explained.

Freddie looked from Wiggly to Daddly then back at the tower, sure enough, there was no doorway open. "Wow!" he exclaimed. "No wonder you both looked so surprised!"

"Come on, let's get you back home and a nice cup of Mummly's dandelion tea," Daddly said softly.

Freddie gave a little chuckle and then a longer giggle.

Wiggly looked at him and giggled too.

"What's so funny?" Daddly asked.

Freddie laughed and laughed and both Daddly and Wiggly could not help laughing with him.

**

"There you go, Freddie, such a brave young man," Mummly said handing him a cup of hot dandelion tea.

"Hey, Freddie, what happened to the ring with the three gemstones in it?" Wiggly asked.

Freddie looked surprised. "Well it's here," he replied sticking out his hand and pointing to the ring. "Look, it's on my middle finger, glowing prettily, all the stones merged into one beautiful crystal."

They all looked and Giggly exclaimed, "Huh, I don't see anything but your finger!"

"But it's here, look!" Freddie stated and he took Wiggly's hand and placed his finger on the ring, but it passed through it and ended up pressing on Freddie's finger.

Wiggly looked confused. "Doesn't look like anyone else can see or touch your new Merlin ring, Freddie."

"What exactly happened when we were thrown out of the tower?" Daddly asked.

Freddie explained everything.

Mummly wrapped her arms around him. "You poor thing, you must have been terrified. I think Merlin was a bit mean to you, Freddie," she said trying to comfort him.

"So that's it then, that's why we can't see the ring, it's invisible to everyone except you, Freddie," Daddly summarized.

"It won't come off either," Freddie said trying to slide it off his finger.

"The important thing is that you have come to no real harm even though a great deal has been asked of you. Pay attention to Merlin's words about how to use your magic, Freddie, take it slowly and build up your confidence," Mummly advised.

"I will, Mummly, thank you. Thank you all. I'm not sure why I deserve your friendship, but I'm so glad to have it," Freddie replied.

"I think the shoe is on the other foot, Freddie," Daddly remarked. "We don't know why we deserve YOUR friendship, but we're jolly pleased we do!"

A group hug followed and a lot of laughter. Before Freddie returned home he said, "It's Christmas in two days, I want to give each of you a gift." He placed his finger on the Merlin ring and closed his eyes. Giggly suddenly cried out and found a beautiful Teddy Bear in her arms. Wiggly gasped when on his lap a shiny wooden guitar appeared. Mummly chuckled finding she was wearing a lovely winter coat. Daddly gasped when on his lap appeared three thick volumes of an Encyclopaedia. Freddie opened his eyes and four of his favourite Elfins were all smiles.

"Thank you, Freddie," they said in one voice.

"Seems you have an idea about how to use your magic and the ring, Freddie," Daddly said.

Freddie chuckled and then looked at Wiggly. "I can teach you to play the guitar, Wiggly," he said.

"Oooh, can you play a tune for us now, Freddie, please?" Wiggly begged.

Freddie laughed and took Wiggly's guitar and played his favourite tune, 'All Things Bright and Beautiful,' singing as he played.

The Tiggly's joined in the chorus and applauded when he finished.

"I'd best get home before my Mum comes looking for me," Freddie said still smiling.

CHAPTER EIGHT

The Attack of the Beastrolls

*Supernatural creatures escape when a
natural disaster unearths their ancient prison.*

*Together, Freddie and Merlin attempt to beat
this most powerful, ancient and mystical foe.*

"I've looked everywhere for my knitting needle, I have one of them here," Freddie's Grandma exclaimed, "but the other one has grown legs and run away!"

Freddie chuckled with the memory of a certain pen in a certain shop having done exactly the same thing.

"You can laugh, young Freddie Fountain," his Grandma said wagging her finger at him, "you try knitting with only one needle!" She laughed and her false teeth clattered in her mouth and that made Freddie laugh even more.

"Grandma, you're so funny. What does your knitting needle look like?" he chuckled.

"Freddie Fountain have you not got eyes," his Grandma laughed, "it looks just like this one," she said waving her only knitting needle in the air, but as she did, all her knitting slid off the end of her needle and onto the floor.

Even Freddie's parents had to laugh.

Poor Grandma cried, "Oh, fiddle faddle! Look what I've done now!"

Freddie placed his finger on the Merlin ring and made the lost knitting needle appear under the pile of partly knitted scarf that had fallen on the floor.

Freddie's Grandma bent down to pick up her lost knitting and promptly jabbed her leg with the one needle she held in her hand. "Oh fiddle-faddle!" she cried and Freddie and his parents howled at his Grandma's antics. "Ow! Ow! Ow!" she protested, dropping the needle in her hand to fall onto the floor with her pile of knitting.

"Oh, Mum! You'll have to be more careful, you'll be having your eye out with that needle," Freddie's mother chuckled.

Freddie's Grandma looked up at her audience and laughed. Clickety clack, clickety clack, her false teeth made such a noise, causing even more howls of laughter. She finally bent down and picked up her remaining knitting needle and the pile of knitting only to exclaim, "Well bless my soul, how did that get there?" on seeing the missing knitting needle laid on the floor.

Meanwhile, Freddie used his magic to thread his Grandma's knitting back on the needle. She picked up the lost needle and looked at her knitting, which had previously slipped off the other needle and fallen to the floor, it was now back on her knitting needle.

"Oh, jumping willacars!" she cried on seeing it. Mystified, she scratched her head and promptly tangled the needle in her hair. "The flipping knitting's got a life of its own, how'd it get back on there?"

Freddie, his mother and father were laughing so much their sides hurt.

"Grandma, you're even funnier than Mr Beanie on television!" Freddie said, panting after so much laughing.

His Grandma looked at him and winked, she loved to make people happy, especially her favourite grandson.

* *

Christmas day had been a really special time. Freddie's Grandma had come to stay for a few days and she lifted the burden Freddie had been feeling.

Being Merlin's apprentice had begun to sink in and he felt afraid of the power he had been gifted and he had no idea if he was responsible enough to use it wisely.

When his Grandma arrived on Christmas Eve he was so pleased to see her, he forgot about magic for a short time.

Earlier, his mother had been intending to bake mince pies while Freddie and his father sat in the kitchen chatting and watching.

"What are you looking for, love?" Mr Fountain asked his wife, noticing she was scrabbling about in the cupboards.

"I know I had a large jar of mincemeat in the cupboard, but can I find it? I guess it will have to be jam tarts instead, not very Christmassy," she replied disappointedly.

Freddie placed his finger on the Merlin ring and made a jar of mincemeat magically appear in the cupboard.

"Let me have a look dear," Freddie's father said, standing up and walking to the wall cupboards.

"It's no use, I've already looked," his wife replied.

Freddie's father opened one cupboard and found nothing, but in the second cupboard, "Oh! Looky here," he chuckled, holding up the jar of mincemeat that Freddie had magically put in there.

"Well, I just don't believe it, how could I have missed that?" Freddie's mother exclaimed. "Opticians for me next week!" she chuckled.

Freddie smiled to himself, he liked helping people, it made him feel good and now he had the means to do even more, but he also realised there could be serious consequences. What if putting the jar of mincemeat in the cupboard had made his mother go out of her mind knowing she had already searched all the cupboards? Yes, he would have to be very careful otherwise he could do more harm than good.

Then the Merlin ring spoke to him in his mind. *'Always be careful not to expose your magic.'*

Freddie's smile disappeared momentarily, this was indeed a heavy responsibility.

On Christmas Day morning, Freddie woke quite excited. It was early, only just after 6am, his parents and Grandma were still asleep. He was far too awake and excited to even think about going back to sleep, so he jumped out of bed and picked up a book from his desk. He had discovered it by accident while looking for information about Merlin in the school Library. 'Magic Tricks and how to Perform Them', was the title of the book.

'This might help me disguise my real magic,' he had thought at the time and took it out on loan over the school holidays. The introduction in the book announced, 'Magic is the ancient art of prestidigitation, where the hand is faster than the eye.' Freddie thought back to the Magician his parents had hired for his birthday party and the first trick was the drooping magic wand. "Well I know how that's done," he whispered, to no one in particular, looking at the diagrams showing the exact way it is performed. He was so engrossed in the book that when his mother opened his bedroom door at 8am she made him jump.

"Oh, Mum, you gave me a fright!" he cried.

She chuckled and told him to go wash and dress, then come down for breakfast.

Like a flash of lightening, he dashed into the bathroom and splashed his face before speeding back and pulling on his jogging bottoms and Christmas tee shirt with Santa climbing down a chimney printed on the front.

When he galloped downstairs his parents were already laughing and his Grandma looked at him and said, "Where are all the others, Freddie?"

He looked at his Grandma, rather puzzled. "Others Grandma, what others?" he said screwing up his face.

"Yes!" she said with a smirk on her face. "With all that noise you made coming down the stairs I thought there must have been several of you up there!" she chuckled.

Freddie stood with his hands on his hips and looked first at his mother, then his father and finally at his Grandma. "Aww, Grandma!" he complained. "Did my Dad put you up to this?"

"Up to what, my favourite Grandson?" she replied innocently.

His mother and father burst out laughing.

"You did, didn't you?" he accused, wagging his finger.

His father shook his head and said, "I'm afraid your reputation precedes you son."

Freddie had to laugh and his Grandma gave him a warm hug.

"Only kidding, favourite Grandson," she whispered in his ear and he chuckled.

Freddie sat down at the table, ready for their festive breakfast of two mince pies and a cup of tea. They had celebrated this way for as long as he could bite into a mince pie and he liked it because it made Christmas even more special. Only then was he allowed to open his presents, which were piled under the big artificial Christmas tree in the sitting room.

Freddie sat down on the floor, close enough to the tree to reach one parcel at a time and began to unwrap them, carefully removing the colourful paper from each present. "Oh, Grandma!" he cried out in disbelief. "Grandma, this is so amazing!" He jumped up and wrapped his arms around her and kissed her cheek. "Thank you, Grandma, it really is just what I wanted."

411

His Grandma chuckled and her false teeth rattled and clattered. "You're my favourite grandson, I'm allowed to spoil you now and again," she replied.

"He's your only Grandson, Mum," Freddie's mother called, and laughed watching them both.

Freddie sat down again and carefully unboxed his Grandma's gift, a shiny new laptop computer. Most of his friends already had one or they had a family shared one. Freddie's father had a company laptop that contained sensitive information so he was not permitted to use it, now he had one of his very own. Next he opened a really large parcel, the label declared, 'To Freddie with love from Mum and Dad'. Freddie turned to his parents with a mystified look on his face. "How did you know?" he asked.

"It was a last minute present, Freddie, I spotted the book you brought home and Mr Balsa in the Model Shop managed to get hold of it for me," his mother explained. "Is it going to help you?" she asked.

Freddie looked at the box, which declared, '**Everything for the Young Magician**'. He nodded, "It looks great, Mum, thank you both, it even has a cape and a pointy hat!" He opened the box and his eyes lit up, there was the droopy wand and he laughed.

"What's so funny, Freddie?" his Grandma asked.

"Look!" he replied, carefully lifting the wand at the end that made it rigid. "This is a magic, magic wand. Here Grandma, can you hold it for me a moment?" He held the wand out for his Grandma to take and when he let go it drooped like a wilting flower.

His Grandma looked surprised and then started laughing, 'clickety clack' went her false teeth, which made everyone laugh.

Freddie took back the wand and "Hey Presto!" it was rigid again, that little trick gained a round of applause from three happy spectators. When he had opened all his presents, he was delighted with the numerous sweets, chocolate, books, comics, model kits and clothes. Then he neatly folded all the wrapping paper and tidied things up.

"There's one more present for you," Freddie's father said handing him a small, lightweight box wrapped in a silver foil paper covered in white snowmen.

Freddie opened it carefully and once more his face lit up. "Dad, Mum, this is so amazing, some of my friends already have their own." He stood up and gave his parents a warm hug. "Thank you, I love you," he said, then went to hug his Grandma. "Thank you, Grandma, I love you too."

His Grandma shed a happy tear. "Freddie, I love you too. You are such a special boy, you're growing up so fast," she replied.

Freddie sat down again. "I have the best Mum and Dad," he said looking at his parents, "and the very best Grandma. Thank you all for these wonderful presents," he said gleefully. He took the last gift he had opened, a small box, and slid open the lid and there, snuggled in a foam wrapper, was his very own mobile phone.

"Here's the SIM card for it, son," his father said handing over a small plastic box, "this will allow you unlimited texts and 200 hours of calls every month. No data for the time being, but you can log onto the home WiFi if you need to, but use it responsibly, remember it's not a toy and keep it safe."

Freddie gave his father a knowing smile. "Yes, Dad, I understand. James told me he had almost got scammed into revealing personal things about himself, which could have hurt him and his family, so I will be very careful," he answered.

When they had tidied everywhere, Freddie took his presents to his bedroom. After he put his new phone and computer on charge he galloped downstairs for the big Christmas dinner. There was turkey of course, roast potatoes, sprouts, carrots and 'pigs in blankets,' he liked those more than the turkey.

After enjoying Christmas pudding, everyone settled down in the sitting room, Freddie played Christmas Carols on his guitar and they all enjoyed a singsong. Soon after the merriment, Freddie's Grandma fell asleep in the chair, her false teeth rattling quietly and his parents relaxed, reading.

Freddie shot upstairs to his bedroom to set up his laptop, following the start up instructions. He was no stranger to computers, his school had a whole suite of them that every pupil was taught how to use sensibly and safely. The Frensh lessons were also taken using laptops, almost self teaching the pupils, it was the modern way of life and his school taught them about internet safety and made them aware of those who would try and trick them into giving details about themselves, their parents and where they lived.

The rest of his afternoon was spent talking to, or emailing those friends who had mobile phones or email addresses. He wanted to let them know his new email address, 'freddiefixit@bmail.com' and his new mobile phone number. By the end of Boxing Day a few of his friends had returned mobile calls, emails or both, one of who had been Billy Bates. He had emailed Freddie from his mother's computer tablet, having set up an email address for himself a while back.

Billy's email read, *My Christmas was a bit of a wash out. My Dad's still in prison, my Mom doesn't seem to care about me and sleeps a lot in the chair. No presents this year, same as most years really. Hope you had fun, looking forward to going back to school and seeing everyone again.*

Freddie felt really sorry for Billy, since they had become friends Billy had been fun to be around. He showed his mother Billy's email.

"Poor boy, it's a shame he spent Christmas like that, it should be a time of family togetherness," Freddie's mother said, and then had a sudden thought. "Would you like to invite him for a sleepover, it might cheer him up?"

Freddie looked at his mother and smiled, she was always so kind and he had not even thought about that.

"Your father could pick him up while he's off work," his mother added.

When Freddie asked his father if he would mind picking Billy up, "More than happy to do that now that you and Billy are friends, we're proud of what you did for him, son," his father replied.

When Freddie emailed Billy and invited him to a sleep over, Billy did not need asking twice.

The following day Freddie and his father went to collect Billy in the car, they chatted incessantly in the back seats while Freddie's father drove them home.

Freddie's mother gave Billy a really warm welcome. "You've changed a lot, Billy," she said giving him a hug, much to Billy's surprise. "Look how handsome you are!" she added once she let go of him.

"Aww, thank you, Mrs Fountain, you're too kind," he replied shyly.

"Grandma, this is my friend Billy from school," Freddie introduced.

Grandma gave him a hug too and Billy chuckled. "Lovely to meet you, Billy, my daughter is right, you're going to break a lot of hearts with that handsome face," she said with a chuckle, her false teeth rattled in her mouth and Billy looked at Freddie who was already laughing.

Poor Billy, he was not used to all this attention and fell very quiet and very red in the face.

"Just call me Grandma, Billy, everyone does, okay?"

Billy smiled. "Thank you, err, Grandma," he replied a little hesitantly. "I've never met any of my grandparents," he replied.

"You poor boy," Freddie's Grandma replied and gave him another hug.

"Mum, let the poor boy breathe!" Freddie's mother laughed.

Billy soon got over his shyness and fitted in well with Freddie's parents and Grandma. Freddie and Billy played a few board games after teatime, then watched a film before they clambered upstairs to bed.

Freddie had inherited his parents big bed when they replaced it with a King size bed, so he and Billy shared the bed after washing and cleaning their teeth. They chatted excitedly for a while before drifting off to sleep.

But during the night Billy cried out, "No! Please! Don't! I'll be good! I will, Dad! Please don't!"

Freddie woke up with Billy shouting and thrashing about in the bed having a bad dream. He was so loud, Freddie's mother came rushing in to see what all the commotion was about.

When she turned on the light, Billy woke from his dream and looked terrified, his forehead bathed in sweat.

Freddie looked on sleepily while his mother held Billy in her arms and comforted him. "It's not real, Billy, just a bad dream, you're safe here with us, with Freddie."

Billy looked at Freddie and then Mrs Fountain and began to blush, feeling embarrassed. "I'm sorry, really sorry, it's ...."

"No need to explain, Billy, but if you want to talk about it in the morning, we will listen, we won't judge you," she said softly still holding Billy.

"I wish my Mom was just like you, Mrs Fountain, Freddie is so lucky," Billy replied almost in tears.

"It's over now, Billy, slide down and go back to sleep. Remember Freddie is close by, you're not on your own, okay?"

Freddie took Billy's hand. "I'll look after you, Billy, it's what friends do," he smiled and squeezed his friend's hand.

"Thank you, Freddie, I'm glad we're friends, I'm sorry I was horrible before."

When Freddie's mother left and switched off the light, Freddie stroked his friend's head. "I'll help you get rid of those bad dreams, Billy. Wake me if you need to talk, I don't mind, really."

Billy looked at Freddie and smiled. "I understand now why everyone likes you, Freddie, you're the nicest person I have ever met."

They did not talk any more and soon fell back to sleep.

The next morning Billy felt embarrassed and a little foolish. "I'm sorry about last night, Mrs Fountain," he apologised over breakfast.

"It's quite alright, Billy, we all have bad dreams from time to time which we soon forget about when morning comes," she replied.

"My Dad used to get very drunk and come home and drag me out of bed and hit me with his belt. Sometimes my Mom would try to stop him, but he would turn on her, too. I don't look forward to him coming home, Mrs Fountain. My bad dreams are always about him, but my Mom never comes in the night like you did last night," he explained sadly.

"We understand, Billy, that can't be nice for you, but I don't think your father will be home for a very long time. You may even have finished school, you'll certainly be older, taller and stronger. I don't think he will dare repeat his bad behaviour, even if he does return home," Freddie's father explained.

"Oh, I never thought of that. I will be older and not a little boy any more for him to bully. Thank you, Mr Fountain, you and Mrs Fountain are the best and Freddie too!" Billy said with a big smile wiping away his sadness.

For the next two days Billy enjoyed the love and friendship of Grandma and the Fountain family. He rarely stopped smiling and laughing. He became a firm favourite of Grandma, she called him her 'adopted grandson.' Billy was so happy he almost burst into tears and Freddie, rather than feeling jealous, was so happy to see his friend feel the love from his family that he had enjoyed all his life.

Freddie gave Billy a guitar lesson on Thursday morning. Just like Freddie, Billy found he had a natural gift for the musical instrument and was quickly strumming the three chords that Freddie had taught him.

In the afternoon everyone got excited playing the word game, 'Wordabble.'

Freddie excused himself from the second game after Grandma had won the first. In the quiet and privacy of his bedroom, he contacted the Merlin ring. "How can I help Billy get over his nightmares and his loneliness?"

The ring answered in his mind, 'There are two things you can do. First, give Billy something that is treasured by you. Tell him to hold it close to his chest and let it remind him of your friendship whenever he feels alone. Secondly, when he sleeps tonight, hold your ring hand on his forehead and wish away his fear of his father, your magic will do the rest.'

Pleased with his answer he rejoined his friend and family to discover Grandma had won again.

Freddie's mother left for a while to go on an errand while the rest tried to win against Grandma.

Unbeknown to Billy, Mrs Fountain had gone to see his mother and they had a great meeting. Mrs Bates appeared to be a very nice person and she felt sad when Freddie's mother told her of Billy's nightmare, but also how happy he had been to be 'adopted' by Grandma. "He is a lovely boy and has a lot to give, but he is growing up fast. If you miss your chance to be part of his life, you may never find the love and joy he can give you. It's up to you now, he's your son and he still loves you, show him you love him too and you will also enjoy the Billy who's laughed and chatted at my house."

That night before they went to sleep, Freddie took the opportunity to give Billy his favourite stuffed toy, his 'Yoda' from the Star Wars films. It had gone everywhere with him when he was younger and was very precious to him.

"Billy, I want to have 'Yoda', he's my favourite. Whenever you feel sad or alone, hold him to your chest and think of me and our friendship, of the happy times with Mum, Dad and Grandma and it will take away your sadness."

Billy was stunned, he was stuck for words for a moment and then replied, "Freddie, you have given me so much already just being my friend, are you sure you can part with your favourite to give to me?"

Freddie smiled and placed 'Yoda' in Billy's hands, "He's yours now, Billy, take good care of him and he will take good care of you."

Billy slept with Yoda in his arms that night and when Freddie was certain his friend was fast asleep he performed his magic, taking away Billy's fear of his father. Billy slept peacefully all through the night for the first time in a very long time. He woke up feeling so fresh and alive as if a great burden had been lifted from him. "I think 'Yoda' worked, Freddie, I slept without a single nightmare," he said as his face lit up with a big smile.

The two friends decided to play games on Freddie's laptop and Billy attempted to sit on Freddie's special chair, of course he landed on the floor with a bump.

"Ooof!" he cried, scratching his head and looking bewildered. "How did I miss the chair?" Freddie had been looking the other way. When he turned round and saw Billy on the floor, he chuckled, but before he could explain, Billy was up and making another attempt. This time he was holding onto the chair arms and lowering himself down, but before his bottom made contact with the seat, he was down on the floor again.

Freddie could not help laughing and Billy looked at him with a perplexed expression. "It only let's me sit on it, Billy, I think it's some sort of magic!" Freddie explained, helping his friend up and showing him how only he could sit on the chair.

Billy scratched his head and said in a puzzled voice, "I've never seen anything like it, Freddie, where did it come from?"

This was a tricky question for Freddie. "There was no one's name on the gift wrapping except mine, so we don't know for sure. We found out that only I could sit on it when Mum and Dad tried and they ended up on the floor just like you." It was the best he could do without telling a whole series of untruths that might test his memory sometime in the future.

"It's like magic, Freddie," Billy replied, looking in wonder at the chair and Freddie sitting on it. "Oh! I have a magic set here, want to see it?" Freddie asked.

It distracted Billy who was quite eager to see what Freddie could do and he howled with laughter when Freddie handed him the drooping magic wand. "That's the funniest thing I've ever seen, here have it back." Of course when Freddie took it back the wand was rigid again.

"That's magic, Freddie, how's it work?" Billy asked still chuckling, so Freddie showed his friend, just this once, how it worked. "Aww, that's really clever! So is all magic just tricks and presdi ..... watsit?" he asked, laughing again, being unable to pronounce the word, prestidigitation.

After lunch 'Snakes and Ladders' came out and caused a great deal of laughter. One by one they landed on a snake's head and twizzled down the board, or landed at the bottom of a ladder and whizzed up the board.

Somewhere around three o'clock the doorbell rang and Mrs Fountain jumped up to answer. When she returned she had a visitor follow her into the room.

"Mom!" Billy jumped up and cried out in surprise.

"Hello, Billy," she replied with a warm smile.

"Mrs Bates, let me introduce everyone," Freddie's mother said. "This is my husband, Jacob," she said, pointing to Freddie's father. "In the chair over there is Grandma and lastly............" she did not get a chance to finish her introductions.

Mrs Bates interrupted, "....... You must be Freddie, I'm so glad to finally meet you. Thank you for looking out for Billy, he needed a good friend and I'm pleased he found one. You are all he talks about, so I did wonder if you were some sort of magician!"

Billy and Freddie giggled, thinking about the drooping wand and Freddie blushed bright red.

Grandma invited Billy's mother to take off her coat and join in the fun and for the first time Billy could remember his mother laughed non-stop as they all played Snakes and Ladders.

Billy could not help looking at his mother wondering who this person was, so different to the mother he had left at home. She accepted the invitation to stay for tea and after a little while, she and Billy returned home.

"Thank you for this afternoon," Mrs Bates began while Billy packed up all his things. "I see why Freddie is a happy boy and I will try to be the same for my son, after all, he and I are all the family we have."

"Billy is welcome here any time. He and Freddie have become such good friends, so he can have a weekend sleep over whenever he wants. Please don't be a stranger either, Mrs Bates, our home is here anytime you need a chat or support," Freddie's mother replied.

"Thanks, and please call me Carol," Billy's mother replied.

The whole family waved to Billy and his mother as their car drove away slowly with Billy waving furiously out of the window with 'Yoda' in his hand.

That night Freddie felt a sense of loneliness. He had enjoyed having Billy staying with him, he was like the brother he always wanted and they had become more than just friends, he felt Billy was part of his family now.

The Merlin ring spoke to Freddie in his mind and showed him how to use his magic, what it could do, and more importantly, when not to use it. It taught him one thing at a time to master and the first lesson that night was moving objects with his mind.

'This is the skill of levitation. Sproggle scientists call it telekinesis. Now place your finger on the ring and command your bed to rise off the floor.'

Freddie did as instructed by the ring and whispered the words, "Bed rise up from the floor." The bed trembled a little then began to rise slowly, just as he had commanded.

'Now command the bed to stop and hold its position,' the Merlin ring instructed.

Freddie again whispered the words quietly, "Bed stop rising and hold that position."

The bed did as commanded and stopped in mid air 30cm off the carpeted floor.

'Now command the bed to return slowly and quietly,' the ring instructed.

Freddie whispered, "Bed return to the floor slowly."

To his amazement and delight his bed slowly descended to the floor and settled back on the carpet with hardly a sound.

'Well done, Freddie, remember you must anticipate any problems before you make commands. For example, had you just commanded

your bed to return, it would have dropped like a stone and made a lot of noise. This may be useful in the future, but you know both ways now. Practice this with smaller objects, using only your thoughts rather than words, for five minutes then you can go to bed and sleep.'

Freddie sat at his desk and began making commands. *'Pencil, rise just above the desk and come to my hand,'* this command he only formed in his mind. He watched with fascination as his pencil lifted up just a little way off his desk then travelled through the air until it rested in his open hand. "Wow, this is so cool!" he said quietly, to no one in particular. He put the pencil down and held out his hand, then commanded the book on wizardry on his bookshelf to come to him. He forgot to make his command specific and the book shot out from the bookshelf and headed straight for him at speed. He just managed to duck and the book whizzed past his head and finished up on the floor. "Ooops!" he chuckled and commanded the book to rise off the carpet slowly and sit in his hand. The book lifted up and gently sailed through the air and rested in his open hand. "Whew! This can be quite tricky," he whispered to himself with relief.

Freddie was feeling tired, more tired than usual. "I guess using magic is not without consequences, that's why I feel extra tired," he whispered. He stood up and walked over to his bed and sat on the edge. "One last attempt before I go to sleep," he yawned and commanded his chair to rise in the air and it did. Then he commanded it to rotate and it started to spin fast. "Oh! I meant only once, must be specific," he reminded himself, but watched his chair spinning in the air for a moment before commanding it to stop and return. The chair stopped spinning then dropped like a rock to the floor with a clatter. Freddie panicked for a moment thinking his mother might rush into his bedroom asking what had happened. He held his breath and waited, but this time no one came and he called it a night and crawled sleepily into his bed, falling fast asleep as soon as hit head rested on the pillow.

Saturday morning and it was time for Grandma to return home. She and Freddie hugged. "Love you, Grandma and thank you for making Billy feel welcome," he said.

She kissed his forehead. "He's had a rough time, your kindness has given him hope, Freddie. You are a very special boy and I'm so proud of you," his Grandma whispered in his ear. Freddie blushed and she pinched his cheeks. "You're so cute when you get embarrassed," she chuckled.

Freddie's father took Grandma home in the car, while Freddie helped his mother tidy the house, then they sat and ate mince pies.

Freddie began to think about Wiggly and his family, it had been a long while since his last visit before Christmas day.

"You look a little lost, Freddie," his mother said, "are you missing Billy?"

"Sort of, Mum, Grandma said my kindness had given him hope. Did I really do that, Mum? I don't feel like I did anything special."

Freddie's mother pulled him close to her on the sofa. "You have a big heart, son, you care about others and you affect them in good ways, they become better people. This is who you are, Freddie, and I hope you never change." His mother made him blush. "Grandma is right though, you are cute when you get embarrassed," she chuckled. "Why don't you give Jimmy or one of your other friends a ring and have a chat, that will surely cheer you up."

Freddie smiled. "That's a good idea, Mum, thanks, I can try my new mobile phone." He ran upstairs where he had left it on his desk, then jumped on his bed and commanded the phone to come to him slowly. The phone lifted and sailed through the air and settled in his hand. "I'm beginning to get the hang of this levitation," he said, to no one in particular. He found Jimmy's number in the memory and dialled.

"Hello, Freddie, Happy Christmas, can't talk long, a special uncle has come to visit and we're having a family get together, see you on Monday for school, bye." Poor Freddie, he had not managed to speak before his friend hung up.

The Merlin ring spoke to Freddie. *Something is amiss, Freddie, there is a disturbance in the balance of magic.*

Freddie wanted to ask the ring what it meant but his mother called him downstairs for lunch, his father had returned and they sat chatting over turkey and cranberry sauce sandwiches.

In the afternoon Freddie decided to visit Wiggly and wrapped up with coat, scarf, gloves and boots. He put some of his chocolate bars in his rucksack and promised to be home before it got dark, which would be around 4 o'clock. The snow had mostly gone and only a small ball remained of 'Snowy'. The carrot had disappeared, *'probably rabbits,'* he thought. The hat, scarf and brush lay on the grass but there was no sign of the shiny black pebbles he had used for 'Snowy's' mouth and buttons. "I wonder where they went?" he said, to no one in particular as he looked around on the grass. He felt a lot happier when he was in the forest. Freddie walked slowly, taking everything in and looking around, the sky was cloudless and blue and the sun shone down on the forest floor.

The Merlin ring spoke to Freddie. *'Don't go to the big old oak tree, someone is nearby.'*

Freddie stopped in his tracks and listened, he could make out the sound of faint voices and walked towards them. As he got closer the voices became louder and he hid behind a big evergreen bush to discover who was about in his forest. He could just see a man, a woman and a small child, a little girl, and she was making most of the noise, laughing and squealing when she got excited. Freddie did not recognise any of them. *'They must be visiting one of the families in the village and come out for a walk,'* he thought to himself.

At that precise moment the little girl screamed and the adults were making shooing noises.

Freddie giggled, it was piglet, he was fully grown now and looked a little scary.

The family did not hang around and ran off as fast as their legs could carry them.

The next thing Freddie realised was a snout prodding his leg. "Piglet!" he said, delighted to see him. "You've grown into a handsome boar," he added.

Piglet grunted and let Freddie stroke his head. *'Chase them,'* he heard in his mind from piglet.

"You certainly did," Freddie replied and giggled, "but you must never hurt Sproggles, piglet."

The boar looked up at Freddie and gave a nod of his head, as if showing he understood.

Freddie took off his rucksack and pulled out a shiny red apple and offered it to Piglet. "Happy Christmas, Piglet," he chuckled.

Piglet snaffled the apple and chomped away.

'Nice, Freddie,' he heard in his mind and he laughed out loud and stroked Piglet's head.

Piglet looked at Freddie and seemed to smile, then he grunted and trotted away into the forest.

"What a coincidence that piglet came along just at the right time," Freddie said, to no one in particular, scratching his head. "Wiggly. I was going to see Wiggly," he said out loud, his head scratching had jogged his memory. He backtracked to the big old oak tree and listened for any Sproggles out for a walk. He was thinking about opening the door when it began to open without him saying the magic words. "Oh! How did that happen?" he whispered.

The Merlin ring gave Freddie an answer. *'Magic obeys you now, Freddie, just by thought alone you can open enchanted doors.'*

He clambered down the spiral staircase and thought about the door at the bottom, then it too opened to his will.

All the Tiggly family were pleased to see Freddie, especially Wiggly and Giggly. He regaled them with his stories of Christmas, about Billy and they howled with laughter when he told them what had happened when Billy tried to sit on his special chair. Freddie was keen to tell them all about the things the Merlin ring had been teaching him.

"Can you show us what you have learned?" Wiggly asked excitedly.

"I guess I can use some extra practise," Freddie replied and levitated Giggly's comfy chair, with her in it, just off the ground and moved it around the room, then back again slowly, sitting back on the floor. Giggly was in hysterics laughing and giggling. Wiggly clapped his hands, while Mummly and Daddly watched with interest and a little concerned for Giggly's safety.

"Oh, that's so cool," Wiggly chirped after he stopped laughing.

"I nearly forgot, I brought something for you and Giggly," Freddie said and fished the bars of chocolate from his rucksack. "They are very morish and sickly if you eat too much all at once," he warned.

Wiggly and Giggly couldn't wait to try the chocolate and snapped off a small piece each. "Oh! Mmmm! Yummy!" they both mumbled as the chocolate melted in their mouths.

Elfins did not celebrate Christmas like Sproggles, because it is their religious celebration. Elfins had only been around since Merlin created them, so it did not have the same meaning for them.

They did celebrate Merlinmas with a festival every year on the date the Wizard left, never to return. That would be in a few months' time and Wiggly wanted to play his guitar at the festival.

Once they had all caught up with each other's news while drinking Mummly's hot dandelion tea, Freddie and Wiggly went into the garden for some guitar practice.

Wiggly had just about driven Giggly and his parent's crazy strumming the instrument chaotically.

Freddie opened his rucksack and pulled out a 'Begin to Play the Guitar' book, it showed lots of chord finger positions and a nice range of songs. "Let's concentrate on this song, 'Row, Row, Row Your Boat,' it only needs you to learn three chords. Freddie showed Wiggly where to place his fingers. "This is chord G, okay, and this is chord E, just one more, chord D." Freddie strummed his fingers across the strings for each chord.

"You make the guitar sound so lovely, Freddie," Wiggly said admiringly.

"Once you have practiced you can get everyone singing along. I'll play it for you so that you know the tune, then I'll teach you how to play it," he explained as they sat on a couple of large flat stones.

Wiggly applauded with great admiration. When Freddie finished singing the verse, he thought his friend was the greatest.

Freddie handed the guitar and plectrum to Wiggly and he practised the three chords. Freddie was impressed how quickly his friend grasped holding the strings tight against the metal frets to make the correct sound.

Unlike Freddie's soft fleshy fingertips, Wiggly's were much harder, almost wooden, pressing the strings down did not hurt him like they had when Freddie first learned to play. Within an hour Wiggly was confidently playing the tune without needing to look at the book.

"Let's go surprise your family, Wiggly," Freddie suggested. Of course, they had been able to hear a faint wailing noise while they were inside the house. When Wiggly played the song to them, they were spell bound.

"Wiggly, that was marvellous. Freddie, you are a good teacher," Mummly said proudly.

"Wiggly has a real gift, Mummly and I love his singing voice," Freddie replied.

"Now it gets a little more interesting because you can all help to sing.

Giggly, if you will sing with Wiggly, then I will bring Mummly and Daddly in on the third line, but we all sing the first line, it's called a roll, okay?"

Wiggly played and Giggly sang along, then Freddie, Mummly and Daddly came in on the third line. Freddie rolled his hands for Wiggly to keep going as they all did until Giggly could not help laughing and broke the chain.

"Oooo, that was so much fun!" Mummly exclaimed.

"You all have lovely singing voices too," Freddie complimented them.

Unbeknown to anyone, Freddie had recorded them on his mobile phone. "I have a surprise for you," he said and played their choral song back to them all.

"Wow, that's fantastic!" Giggly cried.

"We did sound good, didn't we?" Wiggly added with pride.

"Well done everyone," Daddly praised. "Wiggly, you have a lot to thank Freddie for, we never knew you had such a sweet voice!"

"I really think you and Giggly should do a duet at the festival, Wiggly," Freddie suggested.

Wiggly and his sister looked at each other with big smiles on their faces, nodding their agreement of Freddie's idea.

A knock on the door broke their jolly mood and Daddly got up to answer it.

"Ah, Town Elder Spudlike, good to see you, come inside please," Daddly said smiling, always pleased to see his old friend. "It's Tate, Mummly," Daddly called out inviting him inside.

The Town Elder walked into the living area and addressed everyone. "Sorry to disturb you, but the Orb is requesting your presence, Freddie. I have to say the singing sounded excellent, I do hope you will do something for the Merlinmas Festival."

Wiggly was keen to explain what they had just decided and Town Elder Spudlike was pleased.

Freddie left with the Town Elder and they chatted on the way to the Round Tower. When they arrived the doorway just opened without the Town Elder saying the magic words.

"Goodness, that's never happened before!" the Town Elder exclaimed.

426

"The Merlin ring has been teaching me how to use magic, so I just willed the doorway open," Freddie replied.

"Well, Freddie, you do seem to be progressing well with your apprenticeship," the Town Elder replied as they walked inside the Round Tower.

The Orb was glowing and the Merlin ring told Freddie to place his hand on the Orb of Destiny. Once he had done so, he could hear the deep, soft voice of Merlin in his mind.

'Freddie, you are falling behind with your training. Soon you will need all your wits about you to defeat the most cunning of adversaries. They have already begun their influence on the Sproggle world. If they reach my Elfins they have only you as their defence, they cannot endure the will of the Beastrolls. Go now and become stronger, that you may face this foe with all the magic obeying your will.'

Freddie felt sick to his stomach, he did not like the sound of what was coming at all, his legs felt weak and as they walked out of the Round Tower the doorway closed behind them. Freddie suddenly dropped to his knees.

"Freddie, what is it, are you alright, can you stand?" The Town Elder said sounding very concerned and helping Freddie to his feet. "You look so pale, Freddie, what has happened?"

Freddie stood with the Town Elder's help and looked at him with a frightened expression. "There is danger, terrible danger, Sproggles are in danger and Elfins too. Merlin has just warned me the Beastrolls are coming!" he replied with alarm in his voice.

"Freddie, I don't understand, what are Beastrolls?" the Town Elder asked.

"I don't know," Freddie replied, "but Merlin says Elfins cannot endure the will of the Beastrolls, they are powerful and evil. I was hoping you might know what they are, Merlin did not explain much else."

The Merlin ring spoke to Freddie. *'Freddie, you must go to Wiggly, now!'*

Freddie made ready to run, "I have to go Town Elder!" he apologised.

'Do not run, imagiport yourself!' the Merlin ring instructed.

"What is that?" Freddie asked out loud.

"What is what?" the Town Elder asked.

"Sorry Town Elder, the Merlin ring is talking to me in my mind, please excuse me."

The Merlin ring answered Freddie. *'Just imagine where you want to be, by Wiggly's side, touch the Merlin ring and you will be transported instantly.'*

Freddie had no idea what he was doing. "I don't get it!" he said out loud.

And the Town Elder looked and said, "Huh!"

Freddie did as the Merlin ring had told him, he thought about being with Wiggly, by his side, and placed his finger on the Merlin ring. The next thing he knew was hearing a scream and he was standing next to Wiggly.

It had been Giggly who had screamed when Freddie just appeared out of thin air.

Wiggly had fainted and lay on the floor with Daddly and Mummly looking over him, perplexed.

"What's the matter with Wiggly?" Freddie asked.

"Freddie, you gave us quite a fright!" Daddly explained.

"Oh! I'm so sorry, really sorry, the Merlin ring told me I had to come to Wiggly and my magic has instantly travelled me from the Round Tower to here. It told me to come to Wiggly quickly," he explained.

"Wow, that's so cool, with your magic you can travel anywhere in an instant!" Giggly gasped.

"The Merlin ring called it 'Imagiport," Freddie replied looking back at his friend.

"Wiggly just said he felt strange and collapsed, we just managed to catch him before he hit the hard floor," Mummly explained.

Freddie lifted his rucksack off and fished inside bringing out a small bottle from which he removed the top and waved it under Wiggly's nose.

"What's that?" Giggly asked.

"It's called smelling salts, for when people faint," Freddie replied.

Wiggly moaned and moved a little, then his eyes flickered.

"Wiggly, Wiggly, are you okay?" Freddie said in a soft voice.

"Oow! What happened?" Wiggly groaned as he let Freddie help him up from the floor and sit him on the comfy sofa, then sat next to him.

Freddie put away the smelling salts and wrapped his arm around his friend. "Can you remember what made you faint?" Freddie asked.

Wiggly screwed up his face and thought, then a look of terror appeared on his face.

"What is it, Wiggly?" Mummly asked.

"Monsters, I saw monsters in my head, terrible monsters!" Wiggly replied and burst into tears.

Freddie held onto him tightly, comforting him.

Wiggly slowly began to settle down and his expression changed.

Mummly asked Freddie, "Why were you summoned to the Orb, can you tell us?"

Freddie looked down, then up at his friends, his expression worried and sad. "Merlin has warned me the Beastrolls are coming. All Elfins are in danger and only I can help. They are already in my world and I don't know what to do!" Freddie was close to tears as fear gripped him again.

Daddly was beginning to put together the two events, Freddie's summons and Wiggly's fainting. "I think Wiggly has had a vision of these Beastrolls. They are so scary it caused him to faint."

"Can you remember what you saw, Wiggly?" Freddie asked a little concerned it might cause his friend to faint again.

Wiggly screwed up his face in thought, then looked at them wide eyed. "I can't, it has gone, it has completely gone!" he replied.

"That's like a dream, they seem to vanish as you wake up," Daddly said.

"It must have been a day dream then!" Giggly piped.

"Perhaps, somehow these Beastrolls are giving off vibrations that Wiggly picked up for some reason, maybe because you have been blessed by Merlin," Freddie suggested, still hugging his friend.

"Did Merlin say what these Beastrolls are or what they look like? Maybe that might jog my memory," Wiggly asked quietly.

Freddie shook his head. "No, only they were coming, but I'd rather you didn't remember them, Wiggly, it could make you ill again. Mummly, keep these smelling salts, just in case it happens again," Freddie said.

Mummly took the small bottle from Freddie and put it away in the draw on the big table.

"I was hoping you might know about the Beastrolls, the Town Elder didn't know either," Freddie added.

"Sounds like they are a new threat, Freddie, but then if Merlin knows of them they must have appeared in the past," Daddly explained. "I don't recall any mention of them among Elfins, but we will investigate. Maybe when you next visit we might be of more help," he encouraged.

Freddie was worried, the Morphlins had proved to be powerful enemies, now if these Beastrolls were only as powerful as Morphlins they would be in trouble, but he feared they were even more powerful and that thought scared him, really scared him.

* *

Freddie's mind was preoccupied all through their family meal at teatime.

His father was making eye and face symbols to his wife while Freddie fed his mouth with food in silence. "What's on your mind, son?" his father asked him when they finished eating.

"You're unusually quiet," his mother added.

Freddie looked at them both and smiled weakly, wishing he could tell them everything, maybe they could help him, but he knew that could end up wiping out the Elfins. "I'm not sure, I have a terrible feeling that something bad is going to happen and it's making me feel sad," he replied, not realising he had been so obviously troubled. It was also the absolute truth, Freddie never liked telling lies, especially to his parents.

"You know, Freddie, I think we all have that feeling from time to time and it generally results in nothing major," his father comforted, giving his son a big hug.

After helping with the washing up they gathered in the sitting room to watch the news.

"Hey, Dad! That's our village on the TV!" Freddie announced, suddenly becoming completely interested in the news.

"So it is! What's going on I wonder?" his father replied turning up the sound a little louder.

An aerial view of the village from a helicopter slowly ascended to show how Elfington Village sat in the bottom of a crater surrounded by high hills, almost mountains, with only one road in and out.

It showed the vast forest of trees surrounding the village houses and other buildings.

"That's our house!" Freddie cried out as the view from the helicopter scanned the whole village. "Look, there's the park!" he added.

Then the view from the helicopter showed it flying over the forest and hills to the other side.

"Look at that!" Freddie's father cried, pulling himself to the edge of his seat to get closer to the TV for a better view.

"That's huge, Dad! How come we never heard or felt anything when it happened?" Freddie asked imitating his father's viewing position.

"During the night a massive landslide of unknown scale in this country happened just outside the idyllic village of Elfington," the TV commentator explained.

"Look, Dad! What's that?" Freddie exclaimed as the aerial view turned to look at the landslide face on.

The massive landslide had flattened a huge area of trees on the other side of the mount-hills.

"Oh, my goodness, Jacob, it looks like the entrance to a Cathedral!" Freddie's mother gasped.

With the aerial view now looking full on at the exposed opening, it showed a stone arch held up by two columns on each side and it was huge.

"The experts are telling us that this gateway is very ancient, probably pre-dating humanity," the commentator explained. **"Specialist investigation teams are about to enter what could be an ancient burial chamber. Oh! Here we go, we have live visuals from one of the head cams."**

The cavern was so dark inside, it seemed to swallow the torchlight.

Freddie and his parents were glued to the screen.

Freddie felt a cold shiver run down his spine and he trembled.

"It looks like they are setting up some massive search lights to illuminate the chamber." The commentator continued, **"Here we go, I'm told they will be switched on in 4, 3, 2, 1. OH! MY! GOODNESS!"**

Then there was silence as the head cam scanned the vast chamber. It was deep, disappearing off to the right and left almost as if the whole hillside was hollow.

"What are those?" Freddie asked feeling very uncomfortable and not expecting an answer.

But in his mind the Merlin ring replied, *'Those are the Beastroll's prison pods, Freddie.'*

Freddie gasped and his parents looked at him. "They're prison pods, Dad, this is what I've been feeling is wrong, something terrible is about to happen!" Freddie cried as tears rolled down his cheeks.

His mother pulled him into a hug. "Calm down, son, it looks like these things are thousands of years old. Nothing can survive that long, right?" she comforted.

The explorers approached the first of hundreds of egg-like pods that were three times the height of an adult and four or five times as wide.

"These look like hibernation or incubation pods or even prison cells for all we know right now, we are being told," the commentator said. "Well, whatever was inside these must have been giants, they are huge!" he added.

The explorers walked down the double row of pods and the screen split in half showing two head cam pictures simultaneously.

The TV commentator explained what they were viewing. "Well to me it looks like all these pods are empty. Oh! Hang on, I'm getting more information, the word is that these things could be giant reptile eggs, maybe from the pre-human age. Oh! Wait! Wait! Professor DeGraff has found some kind of mechanism. Would you look at that, am I seeing right? Those are symbols and seem to glow somehow, this cannot be pre-human, surely?" The commentator was getting quite excited. "Oh, no! There's talk of aliens now and that maybe all this predates all life on this planet. Well folks, this gets more and more interesting."

Freddie's mother, pfuffed. "Oh, surely saying these are aliens is a bit far fetched!"

"Well I hope it's not, otherwise the village will be swamped with sightseers and military and goodness knows what!" Freddie's father announced.

"Look, they're moving along the other side, I can see some pods that are not open! Oh! What are they doing?" Freddie cried, now kneeling directly in front of the TV.

"Surely they're not trying to open one of them, are they?" Freddie's mother scowled in disbelief. "They have no idea what they are dealing with, this should be done in a laboratory, surely."

Freddie's father was nodding and added, "You're right, Susan, what if they are booby trapped and explode!"

"They have discovered some pods which appear unopened as you can see folks. Professor DeGraff is fiddling with the mechanism below it. I just heard he is trying to open it, apparently the black box affair below each of the pods is a control unit of some kind," the commentator continued excitedly.

Freddie, his mother and father watched transfixed as the professor brushed away aeons of dust and debris from the box.

"They shouldn't be doing that, Dad!" Freddie cried.

"Look at that!" the commentator cried excitedly. **"Oh wow! This is historic. Are we seeing alien life that existed on Astoria before mankind? I can hear the team discussing what to do. They think the symbols look a little like very ancient symbols, I can't say they look familiar in any way to me."**

"Hey! What are you doing?" They heard the professor's voice cry out as someone fiddled with the only thing that looked like a button on the block.

There was a sudden echoing crack that made everyone in the cavern jump back.

It was so loud through the television that Freddie toppled backwards, pulling his parents with him.

"Dad, I'm afraid something bad is about to happen, just like I thought!" Freddie gasped after they had sat back up.

The head camera pointed to the ceiling for a moment, then back down to the pod. A kind of mechanical whirring noise could be heard, followed by a high pitch screeching that made everyone jump again.

"OH, MY GOODNESS! The pod is actually opening. This is incredible!" The commentator was screaming by now.

"LOOK! LOOK! There's something inside the pod!" he cried.

"OH MY LORD! It's huge. It's some kind of giant. It must be two or three metres tall!" the commentator cried excitedly. **"Could this be first contact of an alien species from outer space?"** he yelled.

The pod opened about half a metre then stopped. Inside the occupant could clearly be seen, it was not a dinosaur, nor a reptile exactly, it was sort of humanoid with two arms and legs. The upper body was covered in shiny scales like a rainbow salmon. The head was round like a football and it had two eyes and a kind of mouth, the head was covered in scales too.

"Oh, something has just lit up on that panel, look at that! I'm seeing the ancient symbols moving about like a liquid. WAIT! LOOK! They're forming what look like letters. Is that a B? It looks similar. Now that could be an E. Oooh, that's got to be a W, an A. It's an R next and another E! Lord in Heaven, it's a warning!" The commentator was almost hysterical. "Wait, there's more, another B and an E, the next one is a snake, could it be an S? There's more appearing now and that's definitely a T. Oh, my, goodness folks! That spells out BEWARE BEAST. Is that even possible? Wait, there's even more appearing, an R, an O and an L and another L. Well folks, wherever these originated, they either had a sense of humour or were really warning anyone finding these. I reckon that says Beware Beasts Roll!" The commentator was frantic reading out what he thought the words said.

Freddie fell backwards and trembled. "Oh! No! No!" he cried out, his face full of horror. "That's not Beware Beasts Roll, it's the name of the creature, a BEASTROLL! Beware of the Beastroll," he cried out.

Freddie parents looked at his terrified face and were about to say something when the commentator began talking again.

"The professor is shouting something! Oh, it's not Beasts Roll, but BEASTROLL, Beware Beastroll. I don't know what a Beastroll is supposed to be but if that's this creatures name it's as scary as its name! But why should anyone beware, are we in danger?"

Freddie's parents looked from the television back to a trembling Freddie. His mother sat beside him and put her arms around him.

"How did you know, Freddie?" his father asked, looking both worried and bewildered.

"I just knew, Dad, something in my mind was telling me." He knew that the Beastrolls were dangerous and it scared him. "We're in danger, Dad, I can feel it. Terrible danger!"

'Do *not be afraid, Freddie, your magic is a powerful weapon against the Beastrolls,'* the Merlin ring said in his mind and calmed him.

"Freddie," his father called, helping his son back on his feet. "You look scared and are very pale," his father said.

"Oh, Dad," Freddie replied, sitting back on the chair with his father's help. "That thing just surprised me, that's all. Did you see it? It was huge and horrible," he gasped.

The Beastroll was a good two, maybe three metres tall and wore a kind of kilt made from strips of a leathery looking material. Its body, arms and legs were fat and podgy, like a thin man who had been inflated. Two short tusks pointing up from bottom jaw and a fat nose, it was covered in rainbow coloured scales making it look scary indeed.

All of a sudden cracking noises echoed around the cavern, cracks began to appear on the monster's body and the Beastroll began to crumble. A moment later all that remained was a pile of grey dust. The transmission went dark.

"Oh! We seem to have lost contact with the team, back to the studio while we try to get the visuals back," the commentator announced.

"Do you think they are aliens, Dad? What if some have escaped?" Freddie asked.

His father looked at his son. "Seems your feeling of something happening was right all along, Freddie. I really don't know what to make of it, we haven't seen anything like this before, but they must have come from somewhere at sometime and they're so big they can't hide anywhere that's for sure. I didn't see any evidence of weapons so they can't be very advanced or dangerous. Probably somewhere as life was evolving, this is a branch that did not survive," his father replied.

Freddie felt uneasy, the ring had told him the Beastrolls were in that cavern. The empty pods meant some had survived and left, but what did they want and why were the Elfins in great danger? He had questions that needed answers, otherwise how was he going to help not knowing what he faced. Freddie stood up, "I'm going to my room, Mum, I think I'll practice some magic tricks before I go to bed, to take my mind off those horrible monsters. I hope they don't give me bad dreams."

"Would you like me to bring you some hot milk shortly?" his mother asked.

"That would be nice, Mum. Night Dad, night Mum," Freddie replied a little subdued.

"Good night, Freddie, don't stay up too late, last day tomorrow before school starts," his father said warmly.

In the privacy of his bedroom, Freddie sat on his bed and asked the Merlin ring, "What are these Beastrolls, why are they so dangerous?"

'Unknown, Freddie, you must find the ancient scroll of the Troll wars. It is hidden in a secret vault in the Round Tower. Seek it to find your answers, but there is a huge disturbance in the magic, this could be the Beastrolls. Now your next lesson is creating a weapon!'

Freddie sat bolt upright on his bed at the mention of a weapon. "Must I use weapons?" he asked.

'These are defensive weapons, Freddie. First is the 'illumiflare', a ball of blinding light. What is the brightest light you can think of, Freddie?'

Freddie thought for a moment. "It's the sun, it's so bright I can't look at it without sunglasses," he replied.

'Good, when you place your finger on the ring, think of the sun being held in your hand.'

Freddie placed his finger on the Merlin ring and realised both his hands were occupied. "I can't do it, both my hands are in use," he said.

'Freddie, you can do this now without touching the ring, your magic is very strong. Hold your ring hand out palm up and think of the sun sitting on it,' the Merlin ring replied in his mind.

Freddie held out his hand palm up and concentrated on an image of the sun. Suddenly the most intense ball of light appeared in the palm of his hand. For a split second he needed sunglasses and they appeared over his eyes, then he propelled the ball of light and it hit the wall and vanished.

'Well done, Freddie, your magic gets stronger every time you use it, do you feel it?'

Freddie could feel a tingling sensation rising up in his body. "Yes I do," he replied.

'Now create a long length of thick rope in your ring hand,' the Merlin ring told him.

Freddie visualised a thick mooring rope he had seen on a ship moored in a dock sometime ago and it appeared draped over his hand. It was so heavy it fell to the floor.

'Now turn the rope into a giant snake and command it to wrap around your chair.'

"What? Oh," Freddie knew the ring would not repeat the lesson, but it was a shock, he did not like snakes, but he imagined a big python and suddenly the rope was a huge snake. Freddie trembled. The snake rose up and looked at him, its jaws open. 'Wrap around the chair!' he commanded in his mind and the snake instantly obeyed, twirling around his chair and crushing it to pieces.

'Now, Freddie, make the snake disappear.'

Freddie was trembling because the snake was so big. 'Snake vanish,' he thought in his mind and just as quickly as the python had appeared, it disappeared.

"My chair, how will I explain that to my parents and Wiggly, it's my special chair!" he sighed.

'Use your magic, Freddie,' the Merlin ring told him.

Freddie looked at all the splintered wood and thought magic could not help with that, but he would give it a try. 'Chair restore,' he thought in his mind and he watched all the pieces slowly lift into the air and begin to reassemble. In a few moments the chair was whole again and slowly settled down onto the carpet where it had previously been standing.

"Oh, this is so amazing!" he gasped, just as a knock on his door before it opened and made Freddie jump.

"Who were you talking to, Freddie?" his mother asked as she brought him a mug of hot sweet milk.

Luckily he had his magic set out and replied truthfully. "Just practicing my magic, watch this, Mum," he picked up a small white ball and a large black cloth, placed the ball on the carpet and covered it with the cloth while he sat with his legs either side. "Abracadabra, let the ball rise and fall." His magic obeyed and the ball rose up in the middle of the cloth, lifting it all up off the floor up to Freddie's shoulder height. In his mind he commanded the ball and cloth to return to the floor and it slowly descended and lay on the carpet as it had been previously placed.

"Oh, Freddie! That's so clever, you've learned that trick so quickly. How is it done?" she asked.

It was a question he had not anticipated. "Oh, err, well, it's a secret, Mum, we magicians can't reveal them, you know!"

His mother laughed and put the milk on his desk. "Don't stay up too late now, you need your sleep," she replied still chuckling, then kissed his forehead, bade him goodnight and left, closing the door behind her.

Freddie drank his milk while the thought went through his mind, *'Your magic gets stronger the more you use it'*. He tidied his magic set away before going to brush his teeth. When he returned he decided to practice just a little more and commanded his duvet to fold back. He giggled as he watched the duvet peel back enough for him to slide into the bed comfortably. He imagined the clothes he wanted to wear for the next day and his wardrobe door and drawers opened and closed while underwear and socks, tee shirt and jeans floated through the air and neatly stacked on his chair, then promptly slipped on the floor. He giggled, forgetting the chair would only allow him to sit on it and levitated his clothes onto the desk. He yawned and thought himself into his bed and giggled as he floated in the air, then turned at an angle and slipped under the duvet. He couldn't stop giggling until he suddenly felt guilty using magic for himself.

He lay on his pillow and fell asleep quite quickly, but that night the Merlin ring gave him no peace. It continued teaching Freddie how to use his magic, showing him how to command stones and rocks, big and small, to fly through the air towards a given target. It taught him how to create a deafening sound funnel and electrical hoops to immobilize any enemy. By thought alone Freddie could animate tree branches to sway and thrash, sweeping any adversary out of the way. As his magic grew he would be able to make objects, small and large, become invisible, like trees and bushes. He would eventually be so powerful he could even move almost anything from one place to another.

Freddie woke with a fearful gasping, sweating and panting. "Too much! Too much!" he gasped.

'Freddie, you must be ready,' the Merlin ring spoke to him calmly with a warning. *'The Beastrolls are the greatest threat you may ever face. The survival of the Elfins is in your hands. You must master your magic,'* the Merlin ring encouraged.

"Show me then!" Freddie spoke in a low voice and the Merlin ring created an image like a big TV screen and showed him how to create dust storms and whirlwinds, how to command thunder storms and lighting bolts. The power that his magic had and the things he could do terrified him. "What if I make a mistake or do something wrong?" he whispered.

The Merlin ring replied, *'Merlin has chosen well in you, Freddie, he knows your heart and mind, you are the right person to have the power of magic, you have always had it within you. Do not fear that you may be weak, for Merlin walks with you by your side. You can call on him and his strength whenever you may need to, you are not alone, Freddie, remember that. Go back to sleep now, rest and be refreshed for tomorrow, you must seek out the hidden scrolls.'*

The next morning Freddie woke up feeling bright and energetic, somehow he felt alive and on top of the world.

"Wow, you look like it's Christmas Day all over again, Freddie," his mother chuckled when he came down to breakfast.

Freddie and his parents chatted about the landslide and what they had seen on the TV the night before. After finishing they moved to the sitting room and switched on the TV, tuning into the news expecting to see further updates on the landslide and the revealed chamber.

"It's very odd," Freddie's father remarked, "there's no mention of it on any of the channels, nor in these newspapers!" He had expected the revelation to be headlines, but as he looked through the recently delivered Sunday newspapers there was not even a mention.

"What do you think it means, Dad?" Freddie asked even though he knew more than he could tell his parents.

"Well, it looks like the Government has put a ban on this story, possibly to stop thousands of curious people flooding into the area and preventing a proper investigation of the site."

"Can they really do that kind if thing, Dad?" Freddie asked.

His father scratched his head. "As this was all over the news last night, only the Government could demand the newspapers and television stations not to report on it, even then I'm surprised."

Freddie's mother was looking concerned. "Do you think we are in danger? I mean, if by any chance only one of those giant beastie things managed to live and escape, it could rampage through the village."

Freddie's mood changed, he knew there was danger but he could not explain without revealing how he knew. *'No one would believe me anyway,'* he thought.

The Merlin Ring spoke to Freddie, *'There is danger, there is a great disturbance in the magic. The Beastrolls are close, you must be careful.'*

"What's the matter, son, you look pale all of a sudden?" Freddie's mother asked feeling his forehead. "You don't seem to have a temperature."

"I'm okay, Mum, I just had a vision of those monsters, they're so scary." Freddie was as truthful as he could be.

"Why don't you call James and arrange some guitar practice to take your mind off things. You children shouldn't be worrying about this stuff, let the adults take care of things, okay son?" his mother suggested.

Freddie thought that was a good idea, he and James could have another rehearsal before school started again tomorrow.

While his parents scanned the newspapers, Freddie took out his mobile phone and thumbed through the directory until he found James' number and pressed dial. "Hi James, it's Freddie. Shall we get together for a rehearsal?"

James was quiet for a moment.

"Hello, James, are you still there?"

"Oh, sorry, Freddie, it's chaos here, a long lost uncle has turned up and everyone is fussing around him. I gotta go, he needs me to do stuff, see ya tomorrow, bye." James had sounded different somehow.

Freddie dismissed it as family excitement. He could well imagine how exciting it would be if a long lost uncle turned up. He scrolled his directory again and dialled William's number. "Hi William," he was hoping he could have a chat to a couple of his friends.

"Hi, Freddie, how's things?" William sounded chirpy, but before Freddie could answer William spoke again. "Gotta go, Freddie, a long lost auntie has turned up out of the blue and she needs me to do stuff, see ya tomorrow, bye!" and he was gone.

"Now that is strange," Freddie said quietly to himself, "Jimmy, James and William all having visits from long lost relatives." Then he said, a little disappointedly, "Mum, everyone seems to be busy with unexpected visits from relatives, so I might go play in the forest for a little while."

His father heard and replied, "I don't think that is a good idea, son, not while there's all this uncertainty about that landslide."

Freddie looked even more disappointed. "Okay, Dad, I'll go make a start on one of my Christmas model kits then, I guess you are right." He scampered up the stairs into his bedroom and took out one of his model kits. He laid all the parts out on his desk, but his mind was very distracted.

'Freddie, the flow of magic is in turmoil, the Beastrolls have begun their attack!' The Merlin ring spoke in his mind.

His heart beat faster and his face turned pale, fear made him tremble and shiver. He did not know what to do, but doing nothing was not an option. "I've got to do something," he said, to no one in particular and made up his mind. He took off his slippers and put trainers on, hooked his rucksack over his shoulder and imagined himself by the big old oak tree. Everything went black for a split second, then he was standing in the forest by the big old oak tree. He felt safe for a while knowing his father would sit reading the newspapers all morning and his mother would be busy in the kitchen baking and cooking, something she loved doing. Freddie looked around to make sure he was alone, when a deer walked up to him. He was surprised because no one or any animal should be able to see him so close to the enchantment that made the tree invisible.

The deer nudged him and Freddie gasped. "You can see me, deer?" he said.

'See you,' he heard in his mind, *'danger – no use door.'* Again the deer spoke to him in his mind, the deer was warning him, then it trotted off.

"What danger?" he whispered under his breath, shook his head and imagiported himself to Wiggly's front door. Again everything went black for a millisecond and he was standing outside Wiggly's front door.

The door swung open before he had time to knock.

"Freddie!" Wiggly cried with joy, "I knew it was you, you came by magic, didn't you?"

Freddie smiled and nodded.

"I knew it! Come on inside."

Freddie walked into the house and got a warm reception from Mummly, Daddly and Giggly. "How did you know I used my magic, Wiggly?" he asked his friend.

Wiggly stroked his chin. "I get a feeling in my chest, it happens a lot after tea time," he replied.

"That's when the Merlin ring is teaching me how to use my magic. Mmmm, that's very interesting, somehow we have a kind of magical bond," Freddie concluded. He explained to everyone about the landslide and what the Merlin ring had told him. "The Beastrolls are already here and they came from that cavern. I saw one before it crumbled to dust and they are huge ugly creatures as tall as your house."

The Tiggly family looked at Freddie, not quite understanding what he was telling them.

"Why are these creatures a danger? We are safe down here protected by a magical enchantment, are we not?" Mummly asked before anyone else could.

Freddie looked pale again, just the thought of the creatures made him fearful. "The Merlin ring said there's a great disturbance in magic. I think these Beastrolls are unaffected by magic, maybe they absorb it or their bodies act like a shield, I don't really know other than all Elfins are in danger and I have to protect you."

Daddly now looked a little pale. "I've never heard of these monsters, Freddie, they must have been around a very long time ago."

"Oh, that's why I was coming," Freddie replied. "The Merlin ring told me there's a secret vault in the Round Tower with information about the Beastrolls, but I sneaked out of the house so I don't have a lot of time," he explained.

"Then that's where we must go and quickly," Daddly said and everyone left at a pace to the Round Tower.

The doorway opened as Freddie approached.

Wiggly looked at his friend. "Did you do that?" he asked.

Freddie nodded his head. "Somehow the Tower senses me and opens the doorway."

"Oh, cool!" Wiggly replied.

Everyone stepped inside the dark tower, lit only by the dim glow of the Orb of Destiny as it floated above the column in the centre of the tower.

"Ring, how do I find the vault?" Freddie asked out aloud.

In his mind the ring replied, '*You must place your hands on the Orb of Destiny and chant the number 5, five times.*'

"I know what to do everyone, stand close to me." Freddie placed his hands on the orb and began to chant, "5, 5, 5, 5, 5."

The ground trembled and Giggly screamed a little fearfully, then the central column began to rise from the ground and Freddie let go of the orb as it too rose up with the column. The whole building was shaking, dust and small stones dropped from above and then the Tiggly's were swept out of the tower through the doorway by a strange and powerful invisible hand.

As the column rose, a large portion of the floor rose with it until a large vault emerged. The trembling ceased and everything became still and silent again.

Mummly, Daddly, Wiggly and Giggly were able to walk back inside the tower.

"Did Merlin put this here? Why would he do that? Why would he keep it a secret?" Wiggly asked.

"It is possible the information on the scrolls was better not to be known about, or Merlin needed to be certain they were kept safe if they were again needed," Daddly suggested.

"But how do you get inside, there are no obvious doors?" Giggly exclaimed, having walked around the vault.

"Ring, what must I do now?" Freddie asked.

'Place your ring hand on the vault,' the Merlin Ring replied in his mind.

"Stand back everyone," Freddie warned and placed his ring hand on the vault. It trembled gently and a section in the middle under the column holding the Orb lifted high enough to reveal two scrolls. Freddie reached inside and removed them carefully. As soon as his hand was clear of the vault it trembled again, the door closed and it began to descend into the stone floor until it had completely disappeared.

"Let's take these back to your house, Daddly," Freddie said and they rushed back.

Once inside, Daddly set the scrolls on the big table.

"I wonder why there are two scrolls?" Giggly asked as Freddie broke a wax seal on one of them and unrolled it.

"Huh!" he and Wiggly exclaimed.

"It's some strange language," Freddie added.

Mummly said to Daddly, "That looks like very early Elfin writing, Daddly."

"May I take a look, Freddie?" Daddly asked.

Freddie was only too happy to hand it over to Daddly.

"Yes, I think I can read this, it's been a while since I last saw this writing, so here goes," he said to four eager pairs of ears.

"Herein lies the Legend of the Beastrolls," Daddly began reading slowly.

Giggly clapped her hands with excitement and Wiggly leaned closer.

"In the distant past, many moons ago when in this land lived only supernatural beings, five Great Wizards watched over and protected the Elves and Imps, Pixies and Nymphs, Sprites and Fairies, every creature, great and small. The harmony endured a thousand or more years, but in that time in a far off land other creatures looked on this land with desire and hunger. Trollia was populated by the Troll Tribes, creatures of low intellect, who warred among themselves until the rise of the Beastrolls.

From where they came is unknown, possibly another dimension, but these creatures were smart, feeding on the life force and souls of the Troll Tribes. But the Beastrolls' hunger could not be satisfied by the lowly intellect Trolls and sought the powerful energy that radiated from this land.

Using anti-magic the Beastrolls were able to enslave all the Troll Tribes and wage war on our peaceful land. They traversed the ocean in huge vessels and ravaged this land, overwhelming all the supernaturals. The Beastrolls gorged their appetite on the fallen supernaturals souls' life force.

The Troll wars lasted a hundred years and the Beastrolls became so strong the Wizards alone could not defend this land."

"Oh, that's terrible, those nasty Trolls killed so many," cried Giggly.
"Go on, Daddly," Mummly encouraged.

"This land became a huge graveyard on which the Trolls danced their victory. The Wizards, united in their grief and anger, with the last of the Sorcerers, Warlocks and Witches, combined their magic and summoned a mighty storm over every part of this land.

Arrows of burning fire reigned down from the heavens for seven days and seven nights and vanquished every single Troll that walked the land.

The smart Beastrolls, however, hid away in a deep cavern while the Troll Tribes perished without any cover."

Daddly rolled the scroll up again having read all that was written. "Do you think some Beastrolls survived in that cavern exposed by the landslide, Freddie?" Daddly asked.

"Everything has gone quiet on the news and newspapers so I think some must have. Can you read the second scroll, Daddly, please," Freddie replied.

Daddly broke the seal on the second scroll and unrolled it.

"What does it say, Daddly?" Wiggly asked impatiently.

"This is slightly different for some reason, maybe written by a different hand, now let me see. Oh, yes! It reads right to left, that's why it seemed different," Daddly replied scratching his head a little until he figured it out. "The title of the scroll is,

A Powerful Wizard Foretold."

Daddly began and everyone looked at Freddie for a moment.

"What?" Freddie asked.

"The Wizards, even with their united and powerful magic, could not vanquish the Beastrolls, who's anti-magic and ability to enslave began to affect even the Wizards. So they created a vast chamber with enchanted pods, the like of which had never been seen before, that could imprison all the Beastrolls. Using their combined magic, the Wizards disappeared the Beastrolls and cast them into the pods that would imprison them for eternity.

The toll on the Wizards of using so much magic was great. Being immortal, the Wizards survived and regained their strength, but without their kindred supernaturals their life was empty and meaningless. They tasked Merlin to look after the land and bestowed on him all their magic. It was now for him to watch over the land until a new generation evolved to populate it and give it purpose once more."

There was total silence for a moment.

"Is that everything, Daddly?" Wiggly asked.

"No, there is more, this will surprise you all," Daddly replied.

"Before the Wizards gave up their magic they looked into the future and foretold of one who would come, when magic would be reborn.

The coming of a young and powerful Wizard will be born where the lay-lines intersect, on the fifth minute of the fifth hour of the fifth day of the fifth month, who will finally be able to dispatch the Beastrolls forever.

Beware, the Beastrolls are unaffected by simple magic. They are able to body shift and take on any form. They are irresistible to all who see them, no matter the form they adopt. Once seen, they enslave and slowly feed on the life force of every being until only a dry husk remains."

Again, silence fell on all five as they tried to digest what Daddly had just read out.

"Freddie, what is the fifth month on the Sproggle calendar?" Wiggly asked.

Freddie looked a little pale. "It's, let me see, January, February, March, April, May," he said counting on his fingers. "It's May," he replied.

Wiggly looked at his friend and said, "Isn't your birthday in May?"

Freddie nodded, still looking pale. "It's the 5th of May," he gasped. "Oh crickey! That prophesy, you don't think it's me, do you?" he cried. "I don't know what hour I was born, but I can ask my Mum, she's good at remembering that sort of stuff. But what are Lay-lines?"

Daddly smiled and answered. "Lay-lines are mystical, imaginary straight lines between supernatural hot spots and where they cross each other makes a very powerful magical place, like Stonlyhenge."

"How do you know where these Lay-lines are if they are imaginary?" Freddie asked.

Mummly answered. "There are maps. Actually, we have one here somewhere."

"I know where it is!" Wiggly cried, darting from the table to the sleeping area door. "Got it!" he shouted, waving another scroll about in the air as he emerged through the door. He was so excited he tripped on his own feet and sent the scroll flying through the air, to land on the table.

In a flash, Freddie moved so quickly he was a blur and reached Wiggly before he hit the hard stone floor. "Got you!" he gasped.

"Wow, thank you, Freddie," Wiggly wheezed.

"Freddie! How did you move so quickly?" Giggly shouted.

Freddie looked at Giggly, Daddly and Mummly. "I don't know, I just wanted to save Wiggly, I guess it's my magic."

"Thank you, Freddie, I think you saved Wiggly from having a nasty bump on his head or even worse," Mummly praised.

Freddie blushed and helped his friend back to the table.

"Quickly, roll the map out," Giggly said excitedly.

The scroll showed a map of their land with lots of dotted lines crisscrossing all over in different colours.

Daddly picked out Stonlyhenge. "See how these lines intersect at the standing stones," he said.

"Where is Elfington Village on this map?" Freddie asked.

"Just here," Daddly said sliding his finger up and across to where five coloured lines intersected. "There's the forest circling around the village and this is the road leading into the village. Actually the lines cross over just outside the centre of the village," Daddly explained.

Freddie gasped. "I think that is where my house is, right under where they all cross each other."

"It is your house, Freddie, I know it well, just on the edge of the village, that's exactly where all the lines cross," Wiggly stated.

"Were you born at home, Freddie?" Mummly asked.

"I don't know, Mummly," he replied, "does it make a difference?"

"Oh, yes! A great deal of difference. The number of things the prophecy tells seems to match everything about you, Freddie. You were born on the fifth day of the fifth month, your home is exactly on the intersection of five lay-lines, so if you were born at home on the fifth minute of the fifth hour, everything written thousands of years ago is all about you. You will become the most powerful Wizard in all history," Mummly announced.

Wiggly and Giggly gasped. Daddly was nodding and Freddie looked as white as a sheet and terrified.

"There's one more thing on the scroll," Daddly said, "it tells the name of this Wizard, well it's an ancient symbol, look." Daddly brought the second of the scrolls on top of the map and pointed to the symbol.

"What does that mean, it's not a name is it?" Giggly asked.

"I'm not completely sure but I do have something that might tell us more," Daddly said and stood up, walked over to the bookshelf in the sitting area and returned with a very old looking book of sorts. "This shows all the symbols that were used in ancient times, let's see if we can find it in here," Daddly smiled.

But Freddie was still feeling strange, he was afraid this powerful Wizard might be him.

Daddly turned page after page slowly and they all scanned each one.

More than half way through, Wiggly cried, "There! That's it!"

All eyes were glued on the page and Freddie almost fainted when he saw what the symbol meant.

"Seems to point to you again, Freddie, as the symbol is translated as the double letter FF," Daddly said.

"Yes! Yes!" Wiggly cried. "FF for Freddie Fixit, it has to be you, Freddie!" Wiggly laughed.

"Freddie isn't called Fixit, that's just a nickname. What's your family name, Freddie?" Giggly asked.

Freddie felt strange and his knees felt like jelly.

Wiggly grabbed him and sat him down on a chair.

Freddie could hardly speak and croaked, "It's Fountain, my family name is Fountain."

"Freddie Fountain, FF, it has to be you, Freddie!" Giggly said, excitedly.

Freddie was shaking. "But I'm just an ordinary boy, this can't be true, I'm only a kid, I'm twelve years old, how can this be?" He was almost in tears when a voice suddenly filled the air seeming to come from everywhere at once.

"FREDDIE"

Freddie stood up quickly. "That's my Mum, I have to go!" he cried and grabbed his rucksack. "Mum must have gone into my bedroom, what can I do?" Freddie said out aloud to a shocked audience.

The Merlin ring spoke to him in his mind. *'Imagiport into the bathroom, Freddie.'*

"Bye everyone and thanks." Freddie waved then he imagined he was in the bathroom in his home. In the blink of an eye he vanished from the Tiggly's home. Everything went black for a microsecond and he was standing in the bathroom in his home.

"Wow, I'm never going to get used to Freddie coming and going like that!" Wiggly exclaimed.

"Freddie does not realise just how powerful he already is. Look how quickly he can disappear and appear. His magic is very strong indeed and if he is to defeat these Beastrolls he will have to have magic even more powerful than that of all the Wizards long ago," Daddly said.

When Freddie appeared in the bathroom, which was just across the hall from his bedroom, fortunately the bathroom door was closed. He was glad that no one else was in there when he appeared out of thin air, he could never blame that on his magic kit. He slipped off his shoes and left his rucksack, then flushed the toilet and walked out of the bathroom wiping his damp hands on his shirt.

"Oh, there you are, Freddie," his mother announced as he stepped into the hallway to see her stood at his open bedroom door.

"Hi, Mum," he said trying to be as normal as possible.

"Come down for lunch, son, it's past 12 o'clock."

"Sorry, Mum, I lost track of time. What's for lunch?" It took all of his nerve to stay calm, because inside he was scared of the thought that he was this most powerful wizard that ever lived.

"Are you alright, son, you look a little pale?" his mother asked looking at his face.

Freddie was far from alright. "I just felt a bit queasy, I'll be fine," he replied as truthfully as he safely could.

While they ate their sandwiches Freddie was keen to know about his birth. "Mum, was I born in hospital?"

His mother laughed. "Now what made you think about that I wonder? But no, Freddie, you were not in hospital, my waters broke," she saw the confused look on her son's face. "Ah well, you know we mothers carry our babies in our tummies, right?"

Freddie nodded, still looking puzzled as to how this answered his question.

"Well the baby grows in a sack filled with a kind of water."

Freddie look shocked. "In water, how do they breathe?" he declared.

His mother chuckled. "Well they don't breathe, son. They are connected to their mother by an umbilical cord and it supplies oxygenated blood to the growing baby, it only breathes once it is born. When a mothers' waters break, it is a signal that her baby is ready to be born. When my waters broke, you were very keen to see the outside world and barely half an hour later you popped out. Your father helped me deliver you on the bathroom floor."

Freddie's mouth was wide open in shock and surprise. "How come you didn't go to hospital?" he asked.

"There just wasn't time, Freddie," his father explained. "Your mother's waters broke in bed and she woke me to get her to the hospital. I ran downstairs and phoned the hospital, but when I got back to your mother she was on the bathroom floor ready to give birth. If we had tried to get to hospital you might have been born in the car. The Midwife came mid morning and checked you and your mother were okay. She said it was the quickest delivery she had ever come across."

"So was I born in the middle of the night then, if your waters broke in bed?" Freddie asked, hoping that it was not the prophecy time.

"Well sort of, it was just after 5 o'clock in the morning, the sun had not yet risen so it was dark outside," his father explained.

Freddie gasped with his hand to his mouth. "5 o'clock," he croaked. "Wow! How much after 5 o'clock was I born, Dad?"

His father laughed. "Oh, I remember it well son, I held you in my arms at exactly 5 minutes past 5 am and you smiled at me."

Freddie suddenly felt strange, like he was going to be sick. "I feel sick, again, Mum!" he said and dashed upstairs and into the bathroom. His head was swimming with so much information. "It's true then, it's really true, all those years ago the Wizards predicted that I would be born, everything fits, it is me, but I'm not ready," he whispered to himself and he panicked, then stuck his head in the toilet pan. For a few minutes he emptied his stomach and his mother was there stroking his back.

"It's alright, Freddie, these things can be a bit difficult to hear," she said comforting him.

Freddie felt a little better and washed his face then followed his mother back downstairs. She gave him some milk to drink to settle his stomach.

"Dad, has there been anything on the TV about the landslide chamber?" he asked.

"Nothing at all, it's all very strange if you ask me," his father replied. "You feeling a bit better now, son?"

"Yes thank you, Dad, I never realised babies could be born at home, I thought they were all born in hospital," Freddie explained trying to cover his tracks.

Freddie returned to his bedroom once they had cleared the lunch things away.

"We're going out for a walk, Freddie, want to come along?" his mother and father asked as they popped their heads around his bedroom door.

"Oh, no thanks, I still feel strange and I want to check I'm up to date with everything for school tomorrow. You two can hold hands and talk about me," he giggled.

His parents left with a smile and made their way to the park, where they often met up with like-minded friends and spent time chatting.

Freddie lay on his back on the bed and suddenly felt so alone, something very new to him, he had lots of friends and everyone loved him. "I'm only twelve years old, I'm a kid, this is too much for me, I can't do it by myself," he said out aloud. A tear dripped from his eye and then another and another until they flowed relentlessly, his heart raced and his breath sobbed. He curled his knees to his chest and wrapped his arms around them. He felt lost and abandoned, given a gift he did not ask for and now there were Beastrolls on the loose that he was destined to defeat when all the great Wizards had failed. Freddie wallowed in his sorrow and mourned the happy childhood that seemed to be rapidly vanishing. He wondered why it had to be him, why now, why here in this quiet little village?

"FREDDIE!" a deep, loving voice called to him from every wall in his bedroom.

He sucked in a sob, wiped his arm across his eyes, sat up and looked around.

"FREDDIE!" The voice was warm, loving and powerful.

"Who is it?" he sniffed.

"You know who I am, Freddie, cast your eyes upon me."

He wiped his blurry eyes, blinked, then gasped, "Merlin!"

Standing in the middle of his bedroom was the tall figure of the Wizard, his pointy hat bending over as it touched the ceiling.

"You are not alone, Freddie, you have never been alone. You have been in my vision and under my guidance your whole life."

Freddie sat up and dangled his legs over the side of his bed. "I-I saw you, Merlin, you were a statue in the crystal cavern, h-how are you here?" he asked, no longer tearful or sniffing back his sorrow. He felt warm, calm and confident in the great Wizard's presence.

"I am many things, Freddie. I am here because your magic is so strong it draws my essence to you. In your times of need I will appear to you, but only for your eyes. It is not yet time for the world to discover magic is real," his voice, deep, calming and loving.

"You will really come when I need you?" Freddie asked, seeking Merlin's confirmation, while feeling stronger all the time.

"Yes, Freddie, now you wear my ring, in your times of need I will be with you at your asking," Merlin answered.

"I don't understand, Merlin, how can you be a statue and still be here with me?" Freddie asked crinkling his eyebrows.

"Tell me, Freddie, can you move from one place to another in an instant?" Merlin answered Freddie's question with another question.

"Yes. I can," Freddie replied.

"Do you understand how you can do that?" Merlin asked again.

Freddie looked at Merlin and replied, "Well I only know it is by magic, but I don't know how it works."

Merlin smiled. "This is the reality of magic, Freddie. The very ground, the air and the ocean all give up a powerful force that only a chosen few can absorb and control. This is what magic is. With this control the chosen can perform things that are impossible for ordinary beings like your parents and nearly all my Elfins."

Freddie now understood the very thing he was afraid of. "You mean I control the magic, it does not control me?"

Merlin laughed which made the room shake. "It flows through you, Freddie, like water through a tap, you have complete control to turn it on or off, just like a tap. It cannot control you, or change who you are, it cannot make you do bad or selfish things. You have been born pure of heart and mind, wherever you are you will be loved as you are already. Look how my Elfins adore you, they will do anything you ask of them. Look how your village boys, girls, men and women treat you as someone special, Freddie Fixit!"

Freddie jumped in surprise. "You know! You know that's what they call me, how can you know?" Freddie was blushing now.

"Did I not say I have watched over you your whole life? It helps pass the time while I wait for the world you will prepare," Merlin replied and laughed again. "I must leave you now, your parents are returning. Be confident that this house is now impenetrable to all supernatural beings, so you can be certain that your parents and anyone else under this roof will always be safe. Finally, some twenty Beastrolls escaped their prison and they hide in plain sight. Together you and I are powerful enough to vanquish them for all eternity, but be on your guard for they will deceive even you, Freddie! We will meet again, many times in the future. When the time comes you will know what to do, have faith and be strong, Freddie." Merlin vanished just before his bedroom door swung open and his mother announced they were home.

Merlin's visit had given Freddie a lot to think about and had driven away his thoughts and feelings of loneliness. Now he knew for sure that Merlin watched over him he felt much happier, also now he knew that he controlled the magic, he felt secure and safe. Knowing better what magic was, Freddie finally understood why it chose him as its master. He shivered at the thought of twenty Beastrolls, that number of enemies was a worry, but Merlin had said 'WE' would vanquish them, so now he felt a little more confident about beating them.

At a little after three o'clock Freddie checked on his parents. His father was watching football on the TV and his mother was engrossed in the newspaper crossword, he was safe for a couple of hours before they came looking for him. He was getting used to appearing and disappearing at will, the slight dizziness he first experienced no longer troubled him. He went back to his bedroom and put on a pair of trainers, then imagiported himself outside Wiggly's front door. He had a lot to tell his friends.

Again the door swung open and Wiggly stood smiling. "I knew it was you, Freddie, I could feel it," he chirped as his friend followed him inside the house.

When everyone was gathered in the sitting area and in comfy chairs, Freddie told them about Merlin's visit.

"We always knew you were special, Freddie," Daddly said patting his shoulder, "we are glad that Merlin chose you, now we really can all understand why it was not an Elfin," he added.

Wiggly and Mummly were nodding and smiling.

But Giggly looked puzzled. "I don't get it, Daddly, why did you say that?"

Daddly moved to his daughter and gave her a cuddle. "You are very smart, Giggly, but sometimes you miss the obvious. I say that because the scroll and Merlin said Elfins have no defence against the Beastrolls, even with magic we would be at their mercy."

"Oh, I see!" Giggly replied and giggled.

Freddie did not stay long, but advised them not to go above ground while the Beastrolls were on the loose.

Daddly said he would speak to the Town Council about sealing the doorway on the big old oak tree and the spiral staircase door as a precaution, just in case.

As soon as Freddie imagiported away, Daddly called an emergency meeting of the Town Council. "Freddie has told us that there are twenty Beastrolls that escaped the prison cavern. The scrolls tell us that Beastrolls and Elfins are mortal enemies so we must protect our town. We have no defence against them, if they get among us they will drain the life force of every adult and child, without mercy and leave us as dust."

The Council agreed to seal both doorways to the Town. The Council members carried a jar of Fairy Dust up the spiral staircase and added an impenetrable enchantment, then did the same on the bottom door. When it was safe again they would undo the enchantments.

"To no creature shall this doorway be revealed," Daddly chanted and sprinkled the door at the bottom of the spiral staircase with Fairy Dust.

The whole area sparkled and glittered and the door faded away leaving an impenetrable stone wall. With no way into Elfin Town, the Beastrolls would pose no threat, now they could not invade the mind of any Elfin to make them leave the sanctuary or invite them into Elfin Town, as there was now no way in or out of Elfin Town, except by the escape tunnel and that was protected by magic, no one would ever get into Elfin Town by that route.

* *

After they enjoyed a hearty home cooked roast chicken tea with jam roly-poly and custard for pudding, Freddie and his parents retired to the sitting room to catch up on the news. To their surprise there was an extended bulletin on the landslide cavern.

"When the cavern was entered yesterday," the announcer reported, "something caused a total equipment failure. The scientists tell us that the only known force that could do that would be a massive EMF wave, that's an Electromotive Force. However, we are back now and the scientists have been busy testing what they have found. Of the 200 pods only twenty are empty. Now, don't get alarmed viewers, it appears these pods and their occupants are thousands of years old. We saw one of them opened and the ugly monster inside turned to dust. It is speculated that the 20 or so empty pods were never occupied. The scientists strongly believe no life form could exist for that length of time and still remain alive. We are advised there is no need to worry about these giants roaming the countryside. It is widely believed that these creatures were a failed part of evolution. The mystery is the technology of the pods that appears to be superior to our own current technology. Could some advanced civilization have separated this line of evolution and put it in a form of hibernation or incarceration? I'm sure lots of theories will emerge in the next few weeks. For now, I leave you with the image of the occupant before it turned to dust."

On the screen appeared a giant, ape-like figure, that if you squinted your eyes had almost a human face. It had virtually no neck but had massive arms and legs, three fingers and a thumb, each with a long claw. It had a protruding bottom jaw with sharp teeth and a short tusk at each corner of its mouth. Instead of human feet it had elephant-like feet with three flat toes. Its skin was covered with scales like a fish and around its waist hung a kilt of what appeared to be leather strips bound on a chain. Tufts of blue hair stuck out along its forearms. It looked like a thing of nightmares, a real monster!

"Goodness, that's scary!" Freddie's mother announced on seeing the image again.

"Just as I thought, it was a failed branch of evolution," his father said smiling knowingly.

"You couldn't miss one of those if it escaped, that's for sure!" Freddie's mother added.

Freddie was quiet and his face pale, for he knew the empty pods had contained real live Beastrolls. *'How am I supposed to defeat one of those, let alone twenty of them?'* he thought to himself.

'Be strong, your magic is more powerful than you realise, we will succeed,' Merlin spoke in Freddie's mind.

"I'm going to have an early night," Freddie announced to his parents.

"Are you feeling okay, son?" his mother asked, "you look a little pale."

"That monster will probably give me bad dreams. Why do they do that when young children might see it and be frightened?" he replied. "I'm fine, Mum, I need my sleep, it's school tomorrow, remember," he added.

Freddie did sleep that night, but his dreams were peppered with images of Beastrolls attacking the people in the village and his magic not able to stop them. He woke several times, sitting bolt upright, sweating and trying to calm himself. "You can do this, we can do this, they are no match for us," he whispered to himself until he settled and returned to sleep.

** **

The excitement of going back to school and meeting all his friends again took away the tiredness that Freddie felt from a night of restless sleep. He was up and about, washed and dressed in his school uniform and ready to climb on the bus when it stopped outside his front gate. He clambered on board feeling so excited to finally see his friends and classmates, but when he looked around

456

the bus and saw it was barely half full, his disappointment was huge.

He could not see Jimmy or William, they would normally be waving at him, nor Anne, Marti, Carol or James. In his mind he recalled James and Jimmy saying something like, 'Can't talk long, got a long lost auntie turned up,' could it be connected or just a coincidence? He sat down in the seat where Jimmy would normally have sat with him, puzzled and feeling anything but excited now.

The morning was a bit of a blur for Freddie, he was distracted thinking about his friends, and he had been the only one from his village to turn up for school that day. They had all told him they would see him at school, yet none had turned up. His mind was in a whirl trying to join all the dots together.

"Can this be a coincidence?" he said out aloud at lunchtime while on his own. "So many things seem wrong, the landslide, the Beastrolls, Merlin, mysterious aunties and uncles appearing and then all the village children not turning up for school."

"Freddie!" a familiar and welcome voice bellowed across the playground. "What's this, Freddie Fountain sitting on his own? What's happened?" Billy began sarcastically, but as soon as he noticed Freddie's face, he became more serious. "What is it, Freddie?" He flung his arm around his friend.

Freddie smiled for Billy. "It's good to see you, Billy. How's things at home?" he asked trying to distract himself.

"You won't believe it when I tell you, my Mom has been really great. Did you know that your mum came to my house while I was staying with you and had a long chat with my Mom?"

Freddie sat up from his crouched position. "She did? When was that? She never said anything to me?" Freddie replied with amazement.

"It was Friday morning. When your mum went out, it was to see my Mom. I don't know what she said, but my Mom has been like a real Mom since. Not up to your mum's standard but a hundred percent better and I sleep with Yoda. Don't tell anyone, they'll think I'm a bit of a softy. And guess what? No more nightmares since I slept over at your house." Billy was brighter and happier than Freddie had ever seen him. "Looks like a Fountain Family Fixit situation!" Billy laughed.

Freddie slung his arm around Billy's shoulders. "I'm so glad to see you happy, Billy, you deserve to be happy," he told his friend.

"Thanks, Freddie, but what about you, why so glum?"

"There's something going on and I don't like it, Billy. You'll have seen about that landslide on the TV with those creatures from thousands of years ago. When I spoke to Jimmy and William they said they'd see me for school, but they were not on the bus, none of the village kids were on the bus. I'm worried there's something really wrong, Billy!" Freddie explained.

"Oh, that is weird, Freddie. I saw those creatures on the TV this morning. The experts are calling them, oooh, now what was it? Oh! Oh! I got it, Beast, no, that's not it, it's something Beast. OH! Got it, Beastrolls!" Billy said with a big grin on his face.

Freddie gasped. "I saw that too," he croaked.

"Beastrolls, never heard of such a thing, but ugly creatures, those tusks and claws, yuk!" Billy replied.

"If only they knew some had escaped," Freddie mumbled to himself.

"Huh? Billy said, not quite hearing.

"Did they say any more about this Beastroll name?" Freddie said a little louder.

Billy was very animated and buoyant. "Oh, yeh! Apparently those egg thingies are sat on a stone block with letters and things. One of the scientists worked it out and he said it reads, 'Beware the Beastrolls', funny name that, don't you think?"

"I do, Billy, it's a very weird name," Freddie replied feeling a little sickly.

"They reckon they are thousands of years old. Mom reckons they are space aliens, as they don't look a lot like humans. Although, big Bertha in the second year is a pretty close match!" Billy laughed out loud and Freddie got caught up in his funny joke and it pulled him out of his sad mood.

The afternoon lessons passed with Freddie paying little attention. At the end of the school day he sat alone on the bus again on the homeward journey. Instead of going straight home, he phoned his mum while on the bus. "I'm going to see Jimmy, Mum, he skipped school today, I need to see if he is poorly."

"Alright, Freddie," his mother replied. "It is strange that none of the village children turned up for school though. Don't be too late home, tea will be at 5.30, okay?"

Freddie jumped off the bus, marched straight to Jimmy's house and knocked on the door. When no one answered, he rang the bell, but still no one came, so he shouted through the letterbox. "Jimmy, it's me, Freddie! Are you there, Jimmy?" Still the door was unanswered.

"That's strange, no one home, where can they all be?" he said, to no one in particular. Freddie pushed open the letterbox and peeped through it. "Oh, what's that?" he cried, "looks like feet and legs. Gosh! It is, someone's collapsed!"

Freddie placed his hand on the door lock and it clicked as he used his magic and willed it to unlock, then he pushed open the door. Now he could definitely see a pair of legs. He dashed to the doorway from where they were protruding.

"Jimmy, Jimmy! What's wrong?" Freddie cried seeing his friend laid flat on his back on the floor, his face white, lips blue and he was barely breathing. Freddie bent down and touched his friend's face. "Jimmy, you're so cold, what's happened?" He shook Jimmy's shoulders, but his friend did not respond, his eyes remained closed and tears filled Freddie's eyes.

'BEWARE *the Beastroll is nearby, Freddie!'* in his mind the Merlin ring warned him.

Freddie looked up and around, then saw the head of Jimmy's mother on the floor sticking out of the kitchen doorway. He jumped up and ran to her, but when he bent down to touch her face he found she was in the same state as Jimmy, icy cold, white face, blue lips and she did not seem to be breathing at all.

Freddie felt sick, he trembled with fear because Jimmy and his mother looked like they were dying or worse. He got up and walked to the sitting room. When he looked through the door he saw Jimmy's father on the floor with an old woman bending over him.

"**Who are you?**" Freddie demanded in a deep voice.

The old woman looked up and gave Freddie an evil smile. "Well, well! Look what we have here. A boy with magic! Oooo, you will taste sooo **DELICIOUS!**" she chuckled with a rasping voice.

"**WHAT!**" Freddie cried with a thunderous voice that rattled the whole house.

"What are you? LEAVE HIM ALONE!" Freddie's voice thunderously loud and so commanding, creating a blast of powerful wind that pushed the old woman back against the wall. Far from being afraid, Freddie was angry and a magical blue aura glowed around him.

The old woman suddenly looked fuzzy and a kind of fog appeared around her.

Then Freddie bellowed louder than he had ever roared before, the house rattled and shook as if it were about to fall to the ground.

"LEAVE HIM ALONE!"

The old woman vanished in the whirl of smoke and when it cleared, there stood a giant monster. It was the very hideous creature Freddie had seen on TV from the landslide cavern. Its ugly head bent over against the ceiling, its fat body covered in hypnotically shimmering scales. Globs of yellow saliva dripped from its tusked jaw and its eyes glowed menacingly.

Right in front of Freddie was the very beast that he had feared. He took a sharp breath and trembled as his eyes finally witnessed the horrible creature that slaughtered all the supernaturals thousands of years ago, a BEASTROLL!

'Freddie,' the Merlin ring spoke to him in his mind. 'Remember this monster cannot hurt you, fight back against your instinct to be afraid. Now throw energy rings around the Beastroll to immobilize it.'

Freddie did not hesitate, somehow he suddenly felt strong and confident, just like Merlin had told him, 'When the time comes you will know what to do.'

He pictured the rings of energy around the monster and several rings magically appeared, wrapping around the Beastroll as they crackled and popped, imprisoning and immobilizing the hideous fiend.

The Beastroll looked shocked and struggled to get free. "What are you, Boy?" it growled loud and deep, like a huge bear, its voice making the windows rattle.

But Freddie ignored the captured beast while the Merlin ring spoke to him again.

'Go to your friend and do as instructed.'

Freddie rushed to Jimmy and knelt down by his friend.

'Place your hands on each side of his head,' the Merlin ring explained.

Freddie put one hand on each of Jimmy's cold cheeks.

'Now call on your magic to restore Jimmy's life force,' the Merlin ring instructed.

Freddie closed his eyes and pictured his friend laughing and joking around, lively and funny, loving and caring. When he opened his eyes they glowed the brightest blue that shone down on his friend's face. The blue aura around Freddie spread out and engulfed the stricken body of his best Sproggle friend.

The Beastroll roared like a hundred lions and the very fabric of the house shook and rattled, cracks appeared in the ceiling. The more the Beastroll struggled to get free the tighter and louder the energy rings squeezed making it roar even more. It was angry and a wisp of sparkling white vapour pulled out from the monster that roared and wriggled again. Then tendrils of sparkling vapour pulled from every part of the Beastroll and snaked their way out of the room, searching, twisting and turning into the hallway, pulled into the blue light pouring from Freddie's eyes. The light seemed to sew and fuse the sparkling white tendrils into every part of Jimmy's body and face until he glowed even brighter with a blue aura. The young boy's body began to move, Jimmy's chest rose as he took a long breath and slowly the blue aura pulled into his body.

The Beastroll fell silent and frozen, but the anger in its face was plain to see and it plotted its escape and revenge on this young wizard.

Jimmy took a big breath and slowly opened his eyes, looking up at his friend. The colour returned to his face and his lips turned cherry red, then as his eyes messaged his brain he croaked so weakly he could hardly be heard, "F-r-e-d-d-i-e."

Freddie eased his arms under Jimmy's neck and knees, then lifted him up as if he were as light as a feather and carried him into his bedroom. He laid his friend on the bed and smiled. "Rest now, Jimmy," he said, taking his hands away then stroking Jimmy's hair. "Sleep and recover my very special friend," Freddie's voice soft and commanding.

Jimmy closed his eyes just as a smile appeared on his face again and Freddie knew his friend would be all right.

Freddie rushed to Jimmy's mother and performed the same magical ritual until she too regained life, then he imagiported her into her bedroom and safely on the bed.

The Beastroll roared and screamed like it was being unravelled each time the tendrils were pulled from its body. The house shook and groaned as windows shattered and broke, walls and ceilings cracked causing holes to appear.

Freddie created an energy dome over Jimmy and his mother to protect them, then walked back into the sitting room.

The Beastroll roared again, **"What are you?"** The floor quaked and floorboards ripped up through the carpet, furniture tumbled up against the crumbling walls.

But Freddie totally ignored the captive beast and moved straight to Jimmy's father and placed his hands on his cheeks as he had with Jimmy. When Freddie's eyes emitted the blue beam that covered the lifeless body of Jimmy's father, the Beastroll roared and roared, struggling to get free. Only when Jimmy's father took a breath and had been imagiported to the bedroom with his wife under the safety of the energy dome did Freddie look at the monster.

"What are you, sorcerer?" The Beastroll roared furiously. No longer did its ugly head crush up to the ceiling, it seemed to have shrunk a little.

Freddie stood and looked at the monster, which was still trapped in the magical energy rings. "I AM YOUR DEMISE!" Freddie bellowed with a deep, loud voice that made the building tremble again.

"You should never have left your prison, now you will be vanquished for all eternity!" he roared.

The Beastroll cowered and pulled back its head, then it seemed to laugh. "You cannot defeat us with your puny magic, when we take all the life force in this village we will be unbeatable. Then we will release our brethren and take this world for our own."

"SILENCE!" Freddie roared and the monster's ugly mouth snapped shut and was sewn together with crackling magic thread.

The Beastroll morphed back to the quaint old Aunt, believing it could escape the energy rings but they shrank to hold the woman tightly. Like the monster it had been, her mouth was still wired together.

Freddie approached the Beastroll and stood right in front of it. It tried to back away but the energy rings held the old woman in place.

"**You cannot hurt me!**" Freddie said with a commanding voice and his eyes glowed blue once more. "**We are not afraid of you and your kind, but you will fear us, for we are your downfall!**" The words were not Freddie's but those of Merlin. Freddie raised his finger and the beast's mouth was freed.

"**We shall see!**" the old woman said and somehow absorbed the energy rings into her body then clapped her hands. "**We are anti-magic, Wizard, your tricks cannot harm us. These puny humans cannot resist our will, we are too strong, Wizard. Watch and fear us!**"

Jimmy, his father and mother suddenly appeared at the door.

"Stay back!" Freddie cried, creating a miniature whirlwind that threw the old lady into the bookcase. He watched it tip and empty its contents on top of her, then the heavy bookcase fell on top of her as well.

Jimmy's mother screamed and it gave Freddie a fright.

"What have you done?" Jimmy's father cried.

Despite being buried under the bookcase, the Beastroll had Jimmy and his parents under a powerful mind control once again.

Freddie had not anticipated this turn of events and it shook his confidence, he suddenly felt alone and fearful.

Dazed, the old woman raised her head and cried out, "Monster! Monster!"

Freddie shivered and felt confused, he was helping his friend, Jimmy, and his family, but they were turning against him.

"Get out of this house, Freddie!" Jimmy's mother cried. "Get out! Get out! You monster! You are no longer welcome here. Leave us alone, now get out!"

They were completely unaware that Freddie had just saved their lives and even his friend, Jimmy, helped to push him out of the front door and slam it shut.

Freddie stood staring at the closed door, he had lost his focus when his best friend pushed him out of the house. He trembled and cried out, "No! No! This is not right, this is not how it should be. That monster will take their life force again after all my effort!" Freddie fell to his knees, he was in pain, his heart hurt as it beat so fast, his mind screamed in agony, he suddenly felt weak and futile. His whole body trembled as the fear took hold of him. The Beastroll had managed to get into his head. Freddie did not know what to do, he could feel the Beastroll sending powerful mental commands trying to get him to submit to it. His confidence had failed him and fear flooded his mind and body. He suddenly thought, *'Merlin said he would come when I needed him,'* in a brief moment of clarity, Freddie looked skyward, held out his arms and cried, **"MERLIN!"** He bellowed so loudly it echoed in the clouds that rapidly gathered, thundering and flashing above him. He stood up and began walking in the middle of the road. **"M E R L I N!"** he roared and the very road beneath his feet rippled and trembled. Darkness fell over the village, the sun's light obliterated by black thunder clouds, which descended and surrounded the lone figure of 12 year old Freddie. **"M E R L I N!"** he yelled out once more.

"I hear you, Freddie." Merlin's voice rebounded in the clouds engulfing Freddie and he felt the Wizard's power surge through him. The dark clouds released bolts of lightening that struck Freddie from every angle making him glow brighter and brighter. He stood, holding his arms up embracing the power surging through him, a power that would have scorched any other creature. His heart beat rapidly, his eyes glowed and projected bright blue beams of energy, piercing through the dark clouds around him. He suddenly felt strong, energised, renewed as the magic of Merlin flowed through him, never had he felt so powerful. His body felt stronger, he no longer felt helpless and unready, he shrugged off the influence of the Beastroll's mind control. Instinctively he knew what had to be done and how he had to do it.

The swirling, flashing, thundering clouds vanished like smoke from a camp fire as Freddie held up his arms in the bright sunshine. He stood no longer a twelve year old boy, but as a young man, a twenty year old version, full of confidence. The ultimate power of magic now dwelled within him making the air around him crackle. His school uniform transformed to a blue and gold embroidered full length cape and gown. Atop his head a cone shaped wizard's hat and in his hand a claw-ended staff holding a bright blue crystal.

"We have arrived!"

Freddie's cry echoed through the air, piercing every home and every monster Beastroll.

In the blink of an eye he imagiported to his home, instantly appearing in the sitting room where his parents gasped in complete surprise.

"Who are you?" Freddie's father cried grabbing his wife to keep her safe.

Freddie looked upon his parents with so much love for them. "It's me, Dad," he replied, his voice deeper, calmer and commanding. "I am the person your son will become, but I cannot explain to you just now because the village and everyone here is in danger. When this is over I will explain to you then. **Go upstairs, go to bed and sleep. I will wake you soon and tell you everything.**"

Freddie's parents said no more and like obedient children they stood up and walked upstairs to their bedroom and lay, fully dressed, on their bed in each other's arms and fell into a magical slumber that only Freddie could wake them from.

Freddie imagiported himself to his parent's bedroom and saw they were sound asleep, he pointed his crystal staff at them and surrounded them in an impenetrable blue aura. Now that he knew his parents were safe, he imagiported to Elfin Town, directly into Wiggly's home.

The Tiggly's were not so surprised.

"Freddie, is that you?" Wiggly asked, a little uncertain.

"Yes, Wiggly, my very special friend. Merlin has bonded his spirit with me to enable the vanquishing of the Beastrolls."

Wiggly ran to his friend and gave him a hug. "You're so big now!" he exclaimed.

"Yes, this is the 20 year old version of me as I will be," Freddie replied. He created a vision of the Beastroll in the air and Giggly screamed. "It's okay, Giggly, this version of the monster cannot hurt you. They steal the life force of humans, I mean Sproggles, and it gives them great power to absorb magic, that's why Wizards of old could not vanquish them, only entrap them. But magic has gained strength while they lay trapped over thousands of years. There are twenty of them loose in my village and powering up to regenerate the many that are imprisoned in the pods. I know how to stop them, but you all must stay down here, if they see you they will swallow you whole and you will be gone forever. Now, I must return above ground and complete my task, wish me luck."

Each member of the Tiggly family hugged their friend and saviour before he imagiported away to save his village and the unsuspecting world.

Freddie judged that it would take the Beastrolls several hours to return to full strength after his attack. Jimmy's family were mindless, obedient captives waiting to be harvested, as were nineteen other families in the village where a Beastroll had taken over.

The Beastrolls were gaining strength rapidly even as Freddie returned to his village, feeding on the life force of their human victims. Men, women and children, were helpless and unable to resist the powerful influence of the monsters in their homes, willingly giving up that which was most precious to them. Once the Beastrolls had harvested all they needed they planned to return to their cavern of imprisonment and use the life giving power they would contain, giving their fallen brethren new life. They may just be a pile of dust in the pods, but with the power of human life force greater than any magic know to them, a great unstoppable army would rise. The human race had no defence against these invaders who had traversed from another darker dimension to feed on the life forms of this world. No weapon that humans possessed could harm these monsters who could send out a telepathic message far and wide, compelling men and women to disarm and come to them. The Beastrolls would turn humanity into mindless slaves on which to feed, just like humans farmed cattle, sheep and pigs for food. Soon the Beastrolls would farm humans for the same purpose.

Freddie imagiported to the centre of his village, in the knowledge that his own family and the Elfins were safe. He raised his staff and drove it down into the ground and the clawed crystal glowed bright red, lighting up the sky like a beautiful sunset. Using his mind to join with the elemental forces, he commanded, '*I call upon Mother Nature, the ocean and the universe to charge me with your magical power.*'

The ground all over the planet began to tremble, every blade of grass, every tree and flower released their magic into the air creating a green and yellow hue in the sky. The vast ocean, lakes and rivers fizzed and bubbled as if they were boiling and filled the sky with blue and violet colours. The universe channelled its magical power from every star and planet towards Freddie's world and turned the sky purple and orange. Men, women and children looked up in wonder at the sky, as it became one immense rainbow of colours swirling and twirling. Never had the world seen such a phenomenon, some thought it the return of their God, others feared it was the end of the world.

Freddie raised his staff into the air and it projected a beam of bright blue energy, which began to spin like a vortex and pull in the elemental magical power, drawing it all down into his staff and finally leaving the skies a wonderful blue. The power surged through his staff and into Freddie, charging him up like an enormous battery. No foe could defeat him now that he had become the most powerful Wizard in the universe. Now he had an endless supply of magic he could call upon to defeat and vanquish any monster that would threaten his world. Freddie fizzed and crackled with a bright blue aura and he looked undefeatable, he would put fear into the hearts and minds of any foes, including the Beastrolls.

Freddie held up his staff and cried out,

"I AM HE!"

Dark clouds formed again, thunder clapped and a mass of lightening bolts struck Freddie's staff and the crystal glowed, firing beams of bright blue energy in every direction like a disco glitter ball. Freddie's body crackled with the mighty power from the magic of the universe concentrated in him and when he lowered his staff the thunder and lightening ceased and the clouds vanished allowing the sun to shine down on the stricken village.

Freddie struck his staff once more and cried,

"BEASTROLLS, THERE IS NO ESCAPE!"

A powerful beam of pure energy fired into the sky from the crystal, exploding in the air like a thousand fireworks. Bright stars slowly fell to the ground pulling down an invisible and impenetrable energy dome over the whole village, imprisoning all within it.

"None shall leave. None shall enter!"

Freddie's deep commanding voice echoed throughout the village.

The Beastrolls heard and laughed, thinking, *'What can this puny magician do to us, we are invincible. Did we not steal the souls and life force of all supernaturals eons ago? This puny wizard is no match for us.'*

Freddie imagiported to William's home where he found his friend and family laid side by side in their sitting room.

The giant Beastroll, so tall it had to bend over in the room, did not see Freddie arrive. White tendrils of life force rose from William and his family, being absorbed into the monster's body. Suddenly the creature became aware of Freddie's magical presence and lifted its head to look at him. Evil red, glowing eyes looked upon Freddie and the Beastroll opened its ugly tusked mouth and laughed. **"Puny human, I will take your magic, you will not escape again!"**

Freddie tapped his staff on the floor and a crackling energy cage appeared and wrapped tightly around the Beastroll, engulfing and squeezing the surprised monster. It looked at Freddie and roared with such power that the building rattled and shook, every window cracked and shattered, cracks appeared in walls.

"RELEASE ME, PUNY HUMAN! You are too late! We are too strong!" A beam of red energy emitted from the monsters eyes, but Freddie's aura glowed brightly and absorbed it, making him even stronger. The Beastroll was shocked and fired another and another that only made Freddie stronger. His aura glowed and crackled with magical power and he smiled.

"WHAT ARE YOU?"

The monster roared with anger so violently that doors flew off their hinges and sailed across the room, slates on the roof tumbled to the ground, clattering and smashing to pieces.

"I am your executioner and protector of all living things on this world!" Freddie answered calmly, his voice deep, mellow and commanding. He pointed the crystal on his staff towards the Beastroll and it emitted a high-pitched whistle that quickly took the solid form of a hundred silver arrows. They hit every part of the monster, pinning it to the wall and it screamed and screamed. Walls shook, cracked and partly tumbled down, chunks of the ceiling fell and floorboards sprang up, ripping through the carpeted floor.

Freddie tapped his staff and energy as invisible as the wind pushed everything back into place. He smiled, these monsters had no idea what they were up against.

The Beastroll suddenly froze and went quiet as the energy cage around its ugly body tightened. When white tendrils of life force were squeezed from it, destined to return to those from whom they were stolen, the monster screamed again.

"NO!" the Beastroll roared. "**NOT POSSIBLE! WHO ARE YOU, BOY?**"

Again the building trembled, cracked and began to collapse around them.

Freddie tapped his staff and powerful magical energy restored the house as it had once been.

The Beastroll began shrinking a little as the energy cage squeezed all the stolen life force from it until it was its normal size, pushing up against the ceiling, still roaring.

"**SILENCE!**" Freddie cried and the Beastroll's mouth just vanished, no more could it complain and scream.

The life force tendrils returned to the bodies of William and his family. When they opened their eyes they were no longer under the influence of the Beastroll.

But the monster, unable to shout its orders, used a strong telepathic command ...... *"Kill him! Kill him! Kill The Wizard!"*

Freddie cast a shield around William and his family so they were unaffected by the monster's telepathic command. They slowly got to their feet and looked at the imposing figure of Wizard Freddie.

"W-who are you?" William asked timidly.

"You know me, William, look at my face," Freddie replied.

"Freddie? Is it really you?" William rushed to his friend but Freddie's aura repelled him, pushing him back to his family.

Freddie spoke in a deep but soft, commanding voice. "Go now, all of you to your beds, sleep a dreamless sleep. You will remember not this day when I wake you next."

Free from the Beastroll's control, everyone turned and obeyed Freddie. As William and his family left, Freddie wiped their memories so they would never have to fear the Beastrolls. For if they did remember, the world of magic and monsters would be revealed and this was not yet that time.

Freddie imagiported his captive to the centre of the village as dusk descended and the street lights came on.

"I cannot be here, free me!" the monster pleaded telepathically as it lay on the road, bound like a shark in a fishing net. *"Release me or my brethren will annihilate you, Wizard. Release me and you will be spared."*

Freddie only smiled contemptuously. "Your telepathic commands do not work on me, Beastroll. There is no release for you and your kind. You do not belong in this world and you will have company soon enough." Freddie moved on and imagiported to the home of James. His friend was laid on his bed, pale and lifeless, his lips blue and barely breathing and it saddened Freddie. He placed his hand on James' forehead. "I know you can hear me, James, I will save you and your family." Then he walked through the house and discovered James' sister was in the same state. He moved on to their parents' bedroom where he saw the Beastroll towering over James' mother and father drawing in their life force. **"STAND AWAY!"** Freddie bellowed his warning.

So startled was the monster that it stepped back against the wall then stared arrogantly at Freddie. **"PUNY HUMAN, your magic in this world is pitiful!"** It jeered loudly and roared with laughter, shaking the fabric of the house, cracks appeared, the ceiling splintered and parts of it fell.

Freddie tapped his staff and shot an energy cage around the shocked monster.

"RELEASE ME!" the Beastroll roared. Windows blew out, bricks crumbled and the house lurched and shook as if to fall down.

Freddie tapped his staff and restored the house as it had once been. He said no more and fired the solid white arrows, pinning the Beastroll to the wall. He commanded the crackling energy cage engulfing the Beastroll and it began squeezing. The stolen life force tendrils flowed from its ugly body, feeding them back into the lifeless figures of James and his family. The Beastroll struggled to free itself and roared again until Freddie disappeared its mouth.

One by one James and his family walked into the lounge where Freddie was waiting for them. James rubbed his eyes, hardly believing what he was seeing. "Am I dreaming? Who are you?" he asked.

His parents and sister joined him, huddled together, staring at their unexpected visitor.

"You know me, James, look at my face," Freddie replied.

"Freddie? Is that you, but how is this possible, you're only a boy, how are you a man?" James stumbled over his words, still unable to comprehend.

"James, you and your family have been attacked by monsters, you almost died. I came to save you, but I cannot allow you to remember, for that would alert the world to the existence of magic and it is not yet that time," Freddie explained, then telepathically commanded them, *'Go now to your beds and sleep, when I wake you, you will have no memory of this day.'*

The Beastroll had shrunk a little and before he imagiported it to join the other in the centre of the village, he said telepathically, "You should never have invaded this world. You and your kind will cease to exist and trouble no more worlds."

The two monsters now bound in crackling energy cages lay helplessly in the centre of the village. Both Beastrolls roared so loudly telepathically that the remaining Beastrolls marched out of their victim's homes to be greeted by a waiting Wizard.

"Release them or die, puny human!" one of the monsters demanded, not giving Freddie the option to reply, instead firing a red energy beam at him.

"FOOL!" Freddie cried as his aura absorbed the energy, empowering him even more.

The entire eighteen Beastrolls fired their energy beams together, hitting Freddie's aura, which began to glow brighter and brighter, until Freddie disappeared in a huge red cloud.

The Beastrolls roared with laughter having successfully vanquished the troublesome wizard. Two of the creatures moved towards the two Beastrolls trapped in the energy cages. The moment they attempted to free them they were instantly repelled, to their utter surprise, crashing into the other Beastrolls, who fell to the ground like downed skittles.

The red cloud that swirled and engulfed Freddie was quickly absorbed by his powerful aura and he stood proudly before the fallen Beastrolls. **"You cannot harm me!"** he roared. He pointed the crystal on his staff towards the three Beastrolls that had got to their feet and were charging at him, and encased them in an energy cage.

The remaining Beastrolls jumped up and sent out a powerful telepathic command to all the villagers they had yet to harvest.

Men, women and children appeared from houses, around corners and from the streets, all converging on Freddie. The villagers chanted, "MONSTER! MONSTER! MONSTER!" over and over. In their hands were rolling pins, cricket bats and the like, all intent on attacking Freddie.

Freddie was distracted from the Beastrolls for a moment, as was their intent, but he was unphased. Freddie sent an even more powerful telepathic message to the villagers, easily overriding the one from the Beastrolls. *'Return to your homes, my friends. Go to your beds and sleep until I wake you.'* The villagers turned around and silently made their way back to their homes where they lay on their beds and slept, waiting for Freddie to wake them.

The Beastrolls were stunned and one called out with a mighty roar that vibrated the very air, **"WHO ARE YOU?"**

Freddie turned to look at the menacing group of Beastrolls and smirked, sending them a telepathic message in answer to their question. *'We are your end.'*

The Beastrolls roared with anger and frustration, unable to understand how one puny human could thwart their conquest. Their eyes glowed bright red and they morphed to double their size, they were five metre giants compared to Freddie's adult stature. They stamped their feet and the ground shook, buildings began to collapse, the roads opened up like an earthquake had struck and trees around the village were uprooted and tumbled. They charged at Freddie like a herd of stampeding elephants.

Freddie was not afraid, he drew on the mighty magic of the ground beneath his feet, the ocean and the universe. He tapped his staff and with a single thought stopped the Beastrolls in their tracks, lifting them high off the ground two metres in the air. He tapped his staff again and the crystal fired a thick rope of crackling energy that wrapped them, like winding a ball of string, forming a massive, floating, crackling energy cage, binding the monsters so tightly together they could not even wriggle.

The Beastrolls roared and bellowed, firing red beams of energy from their eyes in every direction, but it made no difference, they were trapped and could not escape.

Freddie tapped his staff once again and the energy cage around the Beastrolls began to squeeze and crush the captives. Still they roared and howled as the cage crushed them all tightly together until they were back to their normal size. The immense sound echoed as it bounced off the wall of the energy dome over the village.

"There is no escape for you, you do not belong in this world!" Freddie cried. With one more tap of his crystal staff the solid sound waves struck the Beastrolls in every part of their ugly bodies, then the energy cages began squeezing, crushing them even more. Hundreds of life force tendrils flew out from the Beastrolls' bodies, like white snakes flurrying away as they sought out those from whom they had been stolen. Freddie watched with satisfaction, these and any other creatures that sought to invade his world had no chance of success.

When all the life forces had been returned, Freddie cast a spell over the whole village to go to bed in a dreamless sleep and wiped their memories of the whole day.

The Beastrolls roared and screamed as their physical size diminished until each of them was back to their normal, but still large, size. The energy cages that imprisoned them crackled and popped, tightening around them so that none of the monsters could even move, preventing them from individually transforming into smaller creatures and escaping through the cage gaps. The last cage descended and settled on the road alongside the other two cages. In a desperate and final attempt to gain their freedom, the fifteen Beastrolls bundled together and began to do something even more amazing and unexpected.

Freddie watched in wonder as one by one they morphed and merged with each other until only one gigantic Beastroll, fifteen metres tall and five metres wide, remained. It stretched the energy cage that bound it until it fractured and weakened, finally falling away, freeing the huge monster Beastroll. It looked down on Freddie and laughed, the air vibrated like the gust of a mega storm and blasted Freddie, making his cloak and hat trail in the wind, but he stood firm. The mega Beastroll looked truly gruesome with huge metre long tusks protruding from its lower jaw that dribbled globs of yellow slime. The scaly legs were like tree trunks and massive arms with clawed fingers looked like they could cut right through a concrete wall. The monster took one step and its great weight pushed a deep hoof print into the tarmac road.

"NOW, WIZARD, RUN FOR YOUR LIFE!"

The deep, roaring voice boomed so loud in the energy dome covering the village, house roofs were stripped away, windows and doors flew through the air. Fences and gates uprooted and sailed in the air like they were caught in a whirlwind, crashing and smashing against the energy dome over the village. Forest trees fell like lines of dominoes and lifted into the air, crashing against the dome. The ground shook so hard and so deep, every part of Elfin Town shuddered and Elfins cried out believing their world was about to come to an end. The monster Beastroll made a swipe at Freddie with its enormous clawed hand and it fired red beams of energy from its eyes.

The clawed hand struck Freddie and passed through him as if he were smoke. The beam of energy made Freddie's aura glow even brighter and he shook his head, *'They just don't get it do they?'* he thought. He looked up at the monster and smiled, he was not afraid. *'The bigger they are the harder they fall.'*

He levitated himself up in the air to look at the huge, ugly face, *'Do you believe that you can defeat us? We are the most powerful Wizards of all time. Compared to us you are puny. But it is too late for you now.'* Freddie's powerful telepathic message echoed in the monster's brain and made it shake and hold its head.

The infuriated giant monster Beastroll growled again and fired a red energy beam at Freddie, but he was a small target and it missed him, hitting the school instead, exploding the building and turning it to ashes.

A thick rope of pure crackling energy flew from the crystal on Freddie's staff and wrapped around the Beastroll dozens of times like a massive boa constrictor snake. It trapped the Beastroll's arms to its fat body and bound its legs tightly together.

The surprised monster desperately tried to free itself, shooting powerful, red energy beams from its eyes. This time when they struck Freddie's aura, instead of turning him to ashes they bounced off him and back at the monster. The giant Beastroll did not vaporize, but its own beams hit it with so much force, it threw it off balance. Unable to stop itself, the Beastroll tumbled backward and struck the asphalt road so hard it was half buried.

Every Elfin ran to the park area, terrified, watching their homes shake and crumble, with many of them falling to the ground. No building was spared from damage as the giant Beastroll tumbled to the ground causing earthquake-like tremors in Elfin Town. Daddly was hopeful Freddie could defeat the Beastrolls and restore their lovely homes when it was all over. But for now they were all homeless and huddled together, terrified the monsters might be too powerful even for Freddie, just as they had been too powerful for Merlin so long ago.

Above ground in Elfington village, the three Beastrolls still captive in one of the other energy cages roared like they could feel the pain of their companions. Red energy beams shot out from their eyes in anger, reaching up to the energy dome and turning it bright red, but they could not destroy it or break free.

Freddie tapped his staff and tightened their cage until they could barely breathe. He tapped his staff once more and the energy dome over the village crackled and popped, then began to get smaller and smaller. Finally it wrapped around the giant monster, the three smaller Beastrolls and the two single ones, pulling them together like a shoal of fish in a net.

"Your time here is at an end. There is no place for you in this world, there never was. You should have remained in your own dark dimension. Now it is time for this to end for all eternity!" Freddie cried out in his deep, commanding voice.

The Beastrolls struggled and groaned, but were held tight. **"Who are you?"** the giant Beastroll screeched, but Freddie ignored the monster.

It had been a busy night for Freddie, but now as daylight began to emerge, he imagiported every Elfin from Elfin Town to be by his side.

"Freddie!" Wiggly cried. "You're safe!"

"Yes, Wiggly, and soon the world will be safe also."

"They are certainly fearsome, Freddie," Daddly said.

"Especially that big one," Giggly added standing behind Daddly.

"How did that big one happen?" Mummly asked.

Freddie smiled. "They foolishly thought by merging together they could defeat me, but look at them now and see who is defeated?" he replied.

The sun was just peeping above the hilltops and the Beastrolls screamed for mercy, promising to return to their place of origin. The powerful blast of their screams blew most of the Elfins over. But, it was too late for the Beastrolls and they could not be trusted, even if Freddie released them.

The Elfins scrambled to their feet, a little shocked and afraid that the Beastrolls were still so powerful, even imprisoned as they were.

"Witness now, my friends, how powerful the sun magic is," Freddie said to his Elfin friends. He waved his staff and tapped it to the ground and the sun's rays made the crystal shine like the sun itself. Freddie pointed the crystal at the Beastrolls and they began to rise up into the air slowly, as if they were as light as a feather.

Once more the Beastrolls roared and screamed. In a final bid of defiance, they fired red beams of energy in every direction, hitting and blasting more buildings. The Elfins were in direct line of one beam from the giant Beastroll, but Freddie created a shield in its path that reflected it back and caused the monster to scream in pain. Freddie vanished the eyes and mouths of the remaining Beastrolls, no more would they harm his friends.

The Elfins watched in awe and silence as the powerful magic of the sun's beams powered Freddie's crystal staff.

When the Beastrolls were high in the air and illuminated by the rising sun, Freddie cried out with the dual voice of himself and Merlin, **"Behold the fate of those who would attempt to conquer this beautiful world."** From his crystal staff a spinning vortex of sparkling energy fired towards the captured monsters, engulfing and swallowing them. It contracted and squeezed until it exploded into multicoloured rainbows and stars, like a million fireworks going off all together.

The Elfins applauded and cheered in amazement.

As the dusty remains of the monsters began to fall back to the ground, Freddie waved his staff and cried,

"A great whirlwind we call upon.
Rise up, confine and take away,
the Beastroll dust this very day."

Once more from Freddie's crystal staff, spun out a swirling whirlwind that scooped up the descending remains of the vanquished Beastrolls to scatter them to every corner of Astoria so they could never again reform.

Freddie rotated his staff once and a second whirlwind spun out and the Elfins gasped at his mighty magic. He sent the whirlwind over the forest, over the hills and into the landslide cavern where the dusty remains of the Beastroll army lay waiting to be transformed.

Inside the cavern the whirlwind grew bigger and stronger, ripping out the pods and plinths, pillars and arches and most importantly, the dust of the Beastrolls. Pulling everything into its core, it whisked them off over the great ocean to an active volcano that shot fire into the air. The whirlwind descended into the core of the volcano, which incinerated everything so that never again could the Beastrolls endanger Sproggles and Elfins.

The landslide cavern remained a mystery to one and all, except Freddie, Merlin and the Elfins. Later the newspapers and TV stations reported that a freak whirlwind destroyed everything in the landslide cavern and nothing remained.

The Elfins cheered and applauded with such happiness because the Beastrolls had been vanquished and they chanted their hero's name. "Freddie! Freddie! Freddie!"

Wiggly and Giggly hugged their friend tightly and Wiggly cried, "Freddie Fixit!"

Freddie laughed out loud. "My dear friends, you alone have seen the power of magic and now you will understand why the world of Sproggles is not yet ready to know of its existence. Sproggles are not yet advanced enough to use it with the kindness for which it exists, but that time will come, it is a time that Merlin patiently awaits, as do I."

Every Elfin cheered again and came to lay their hands on Freddie, the greatest ever Wizard in all history and give their personal thanks for his bravery and friendship.

"Freddie, most of Elfin Town has been destroyed, we have nowhere to return to, can your magic help us?" Daddly appealed.

"Fear not, Daddly, when you return everything will be as it always was, I have already restored your homes, so now it is time for you to return. There is much to be done here in this village, ready yourselves, my dear friends." Freddie tapped his staff and imagiported the Elfins back to their homes in Elfin Town, he also restored the big old oak tree door and the spiral staircase door.

When Freddie surveyed his own village he saw the destruction the Beastrolls had caused, roof tiles and roofs blown away, gates and fences destroyed, windows smashed. The road destroyed and buildings on the verge of collapsing and other buildings completely destroyed, it looked like a war zone. Trees in his beloved forest fallen and uprooted, the beautiful gardens destroyed. He held his staff up high and called out a magical spell to restore the village as it was before the destruction.

"Homes and gardens and all the trees,
appear as before, that no one sees,
the destruction the Beastrolls have caused this day."

The road where the monster Beastroll had crashed down lifted and reformed itself. Roof tiles whizzed through the air, back from where they had fallen. Glass reformed and sailed back into window frames. Gates and fences pulled back together and stood in their original places. Every damaged building, be it a house, garage, shop or shed, instantly repaired as if nothing had ever happened. The gardens became beautiful again, full of flowers and the fallen forest stood again, tall and mighty as it had before. The school fantastically rose up from the rubble and became whole again. All these things happened instantaneously, just like time itself was in reverse and Elfington village looked like nothing had ever happened.

Freddie's next task was to wake the people of the village. He tapped his staff on the ground and a hundred beams of crimson light spun out to touch and envelope every dwelling in the village,

"Every man, woman and child,
wake now and live your lives.
Nothing shall you ever recall,
of this terrible time for one and all!"

The beams of energy faded and the crystal dulled again.

The villagers all opened their eyes exactly at the same time, feeling dazed. They looked around, slightly vague in their minds, but they saw everything was as it should be and were not concerned.

Jimmy raced downstairs, feeling so hungry he grabbed the box of cereals, sticking his hand inside and eating the 'Sugar Pops' straight from the box.

"Jimmy!" his mother scolded, "eat them like a civilized human being, put them in a bowl with milk. How old are you?"

Jimmy jumped, almost throwing the contents of the box in the air, then did as his mother had told him.

"Jimmy!" his mother cried again, "use a spoon, for goodness sake, don't tip the bowl straight in your mouth!"

Jimmy put the bowl down and started scooping with his spoon.

His mother chuckled seeing him with milk and pops stuck to his face.

"Aw, Mu-um. Spoilsport!" he replied.

James picked up his guitar and played the song he and Freddie were to play together at the school concert and his sister clapped her hands enthusiastically.

William put on his school uniform. It just had to be neat and perfect, then he fixed his tie, undoing the knot and re-tying it until it was perfect.

Everything in Elfington Village was as it should be, the residents would never know they had been victims of the world's most horrible monsters. They would never know how young Freddie Fountain had merged with Merlin and fearlessly fought the Beastrolls and won.

Freddie imagiported away before anyone had a chance to see him. He stood at the foot of his parent's bed, looking at them still fully dressed, holding hands and fast asleep. He smiled. "I'm back,

Mum and Dad, time for you to wake up," he spoke in a gentle but commanding voice.

His mother and father opened their eyes and looked at the tall handsome young man dressed in cape and gown adorned with a pointy hat.

"W-who are you?" his mother asked again.

"It's me, Mum, your son, Freddie, or at least your future son as I will be in a few years time. I have a lot to tell you, please get up and come downstairs." Freddie imagiported to their sitting room, removed his hat and sat waiting for his parents.

"What the devil?" Freddie's father exclaimed to his wife when Freddie just vanished. "Was that real or did we just imagine it? Why are we laid on the bed fully dressed, too?"

"I think it was real enough dear, so let's do as he asked," his wife replied.

Freddie was sitting in one of the armchairs when his parents walked hand in hand into the sitting room. He indicated for his parents to sit on the sofa opposite him.

They did so, mesmerized by this handsome young man who looked so much like their son, only older.

"I said I would explain everything to you, Mum and Dad, but what I am about to tell you and show you, I cannot allow you to remember, it is too dangerous for any human to know the truth," Freddie began.

"You say you are our son from the future, but where is our son from this time?" his father asked.

"I am both, Dad, and will be your 12 year old son again soon. Let me show you what happened to our village and you will understand." He pointed his staff at their television and showed the whole event, from seeing Jimmy's family being harvested by the Beastroll to crying out for Merlin's help. It showed their twelve year old son become the most powerful Wizard history will ever know.

Freddie's parents watched in horror, his mother screamed as they witnessed the devastation the monster Beastrolls created. They clapped when Freddie ensnared the monsters in a magical energy net and raised them into the sunbeams where they were finally vanquished. His parents cried tears of joy and pride, then stood up, trembling while moving to give their son a hug.

"We always knew you were special, son, but never imagined you would save the world," his father said proudly as tears rolled down his cheeks.

"We're so proud of you, Freddie, we love you so very much," his mother added with a few little sobs.

"There's a lot more I want to show you both," Freddie announced and stood up, "take my hands and I will show you why I love the forest so much."

They took hold of their son's hands and he imagiported them directly into the Tiggly's house.

"Freddie!" Wiggly and Giggly cried rushing to him and hugging him.

Mummly and Daddly hurried to greet him also.

"Mum, Dad, these people are the Tiggly family, they are Elfins and live deep under the forest. This cute, jiggling girl is Giggly."

Freddie's parents were a little in shock, but said hello to Giggly.

"I've always wanted to meet you both, Freddie talks about you a lot," Giggly chirped.

Freddie's mother and father laughed a little nervously.

"This is my very best friend, Wiggly," Freddie said introducing him.

"I'm so pleased to meet you, Mr and Mrs Fountain. Freddie told us how you tried sitting on the enchanted chair we gave him as a present," Wiggly said and again they all chuckled.

Freddie walked over to Mummly and Daddly. "These are Wiggly and Giggly's parents, Mummly and Daddly, they are like a second Mum and Dad to me, I love them all dearly."

Freddie's parents held out their hands to shake Mummly and Daddly's hands.

"Hello," Daddly said, "we've been expecting you, there is so much you need to know."

Mr Fountain spoke for the first time. "Hello everyone, as you already know I am Freddie's father, please call me Jacob, and this is Freddie's mother, Susan. We have seen what Freddie just did in the village and being here is also quite extraordinary."

"Come sit down in comfy chairs," Daddly invited and Freddie tapped his staff and created more chairs, much to his parent's amazement.

When they were all seated in a circle Daddly began to explain. "This is obviously quite a shock for you both, so let me give you a bit of background so you will understand everything."

Mummly stood and said, "I'll make a nice pot of dandelion tea."

Freddie smiled. "Allow me, Mummly." He tapped his staff and a low round table appeared in the middle of them all on which was a tray with cups and saucers and a big pot of steaming tea. "Will you be mother, Mummly?" Freddie asked.

Mummly chuckled, poured the tea and passed cups around to everyone.

Freddie's parents were astounded and looked on in disbelief.

"Oh, we're used to it now, Mr and Mrs Fountain, Freddie is our friend and hero," Wiggly volunteered.

"Forgive me if this sounds a little condescending to begin with," Daddly began explaining, "but you can plainly see we are not human like you. We are Elfins, as Freddie said earlier. We were created by the great Wizard Merlin as his helpers and we live here, underground below the forest in Elfin Town."

"You mean all the stories about Merlin the Wizard are true?" Freddie's mother asked hesitantly.

Freddie replied to his mother's question. "Merlin most certainly did exist and does exist, he is in stasis waiting for the time humans live in peace. King Arthur is not true, but Fairies are and other supernatural beings, but most were wiped out by the Beastrolls a millennia ago in the Great Troll Wars."

Freddie's parents nodded their heads hearing his words and finding it hard to take in.

"Sorry, Daddly, please continue." Freddie apologised for interrupting.

Freddie's mother took a sip of the dandelion tea. "Oh my, this is delicious, Mummly, I'd love your recipe for it!" she declared.

Freddie's father smiled at his wife's exclamation and nodded his agreement, it was very tasty.

"Please, Daddly, continue if you would," Freddie's father implored.

Daddly explained how Freddie had saved their son from a horrible trap set by Sproggles."

"Sproggles?" Freddie's mother interrupted again.

"Ah, apologies," Daddly explained, "this is the term used to describe your race, the humans who came to Astoria long after the supernaturals." He told them about Freddie's reward, a magic rucksack.

"Now I understand why you always had the right thing at the right time, Freddie," his mother laughed.

As Daddly revealed all of Freddie and Wiggly's adventures right up to dealing with the Beastrolls, he smiled so much his jaw ached.

"Now you see why Freddie is not only our friend but our hero," Giggly volunteered.

"And we love him, everyone in Elfin Town loves him too," Wiggly added.

There was a moment of silence while Freddie's parents absorbed everything they had heard.

Then, his mother turned to Freddie. "You kept all this secret, all this time, son? I understand why, but it must have been so difficult for you. You were living two lives, one with us Sproggles and the other down here with these wonderful Elfins. We've always been proud of you, Freddie. I know you said we couldn't keep all these memories, but could you not let us hold them and know who you really are? More importantly, we can support you now we understand everything."

Freddie looked at Daddly and Mummly and they nodded their approval.

"I've wanted to tell you both for so long. I never told you a lie, I was always truthful, but I felt so alone in our world and so complete here with my friends who know the real me. Daddly trusts you not to reveal the Elfins to the Sproggle world, so we can do it on one condition, that you agree for me to wipe away your memories of everything you have heard today and knowledge about the Elfins and supernatural beings, if ever you let it slip out, and that must include Grandma. Agreed?"

Both his parents nodded and smiled. "We think that is fair, son," his father replied.

"Then it's agreed, you can keep your memories," Freddie said with great joy in his heart.

The Tiggly family and Freddie toured the town and introduced Mr and Mrs Fountain to everyone.

"They all adore you, Freddie, you're so lucky to have their love and devotion," Freddie's father commented.

"Freddie has really earned every bit of our loyalty and love, just as he is loved by many among your friends and family," Mummly replied.

"That's so true, Freddie gives his love and help unconditionally without expectation of thanks or reward. All the village know and love him and we could not be happier," Freddie's mother said.

"We should have a celebration party," Council Elder Spudlike announced and everyone headed for the park.

"Look, Jacob," Freddie's mother cried as she spotted the statue of Freddie and Wiggly, unable to stop her tears of joy.

They stood and admired the statues for a while.

"These wonderful people really do admire and love you, Freddie, and you too, Wiggly. For a race that cannot defend themselves, you have been so very brave, no wonder Mummly and Daddly love you both so much," Freddie's mother announced.

Town Councillor Spudlike said a few words of praise and thanks to Freddie, then let him create a wonderful feast of delights to eat and drink with a single tap of his staff.

"I never realised that magic existed in reality, nor how powerful it could be," Freddie's father said to Daddly.

"In the wrong hands magic could destroy this wonderful planet and leave it a barren wasteland, that's why it had to be gifted to Freddie, who is pure of heart and without malice. He is the caretaker of magic and has been gifted eternal life as its keeper. When he reaches his twentieth birthday he will age no more, as you see him now is how he will forever be, awaiting Merlin's awakening." Daddly explained.

Freddie's parents had not realised just how important Freddie was now and would be in the future, and they could not have been more proud.

Freddie created swings, seesaws, roundabouts and climbing frames for all the children to play on, they laughed and giggled while they played and all the adults watched with big smiles on their faces.

Everyone wanted to talk to both of Freddie's parents and regaled them with their own stories of how Freddie had helped them. His parents loved to hear all the tales and continued to be amazed at their son's adventures and love for the Elfins. They could see why, the Elfin's were without the darkness that humankind harboured and Freddie's parents quickly became very fond of them too.

When everyone had eaten and drunk their fill, Freddie announced it was time for him to return. They all gathered together, Wiggly and Giggly held Freddie's parents' hands.

Freddie walked into the middle of the park and called out, "Merlin, my work here is done. It is time for me to return." He tapped his staff and a whirlwind engulfed him, his parents gasped.

"He will be fine," Daddly assured them.

Energy bolts leapt in and out and thunder echoed. His parents still looked concerned, but Wiggly and Giggly gave their hands a little squeeze. Suddenly the wind and clouds surrounding Freddie vanished as quickly at they had appeared and there before them all stood the twelve year old Freddie in his school uniform, just as he had been before his transformation.

Freddie ran towards his mother and father, who wrapped their arms around him.

"Three cheers for Freddie Fixit, the greatest Wizard of all time!" Wiggly cried.

Every Elfin and Freddie's parents proudly cried out their hoorays for their friend and hero.

CHAPTER NINE

A Supernatural Awakens

*Freddie's magic awakens a supernatural being,
which causes mayhem.*

During the Great Troll Wars, a very, very long time ago, the five Great Wizards only defeated the Trolls by combining their magic. As with all wars the number of lives lost was tragic, with every Troll annihilated, except the cunning Beastrolls.

Every supernatural, the Sprites, Imps, Ogres, Goblins, Witches and Warlocks and all the others, were wiped out, or so it was believed.

Only by the five Great Wizards joining forces did they manage to entomb the Beastrolls for eternity, after which, they could see no future without the supernaturals around. The Great Wizards bestowed their magic to Merlin, so he could bring about peace in the world. Merlin had saved some of the Fairies by hibernating them in beautiful crystals hidden away from the wars. Unbeknown to Merlin, a handful of other supernaturals had fled the wars and hid themselves far away.

The last surviving Water Nymph, a Prince called Nix, had fled to the small island now known as Fireland and sheltered in the warm volcanic waters. But Nix soon became lonely, never before had he been without friends and companions to socialise with and play tricks on and he became deeply unhappy. He finally realised that there was nothing left for him in this world. He did not know the Trolls had been defeated or that Merlin was the only Great Wizard remaining. Although he was an eternal being he had no wish to spend his life alone, so he travelled up into the mountain and found a deep and remote glacial cavern where he placed himself into hibernation, hoping one day things might be different. Over hundreds of years the cavern closed up with ice and snow completely encapsulating Nix. The Prince of the Water Nymphs was lost to the world.

**

Freddie and his friends were now in their third year at secondary school. Since defeating the Beastrolls, he and everyone he knew had enjoyed a normal, fairly uneventful and peaceful life. The Merlin ring continued to prepare Freddie in the use of magic and two years after his merger with Merlin, his magic was strong, so strong in fact, he was creating magic ripples, like a stone dropped in a pond, only his magic ripples travelled all around the planet. Sproggles could not see or feel it, but any supernaturals would be able to hear and feel Freddie's magic. Elfins were comforted by the long lost, but familiar magical ripple that they had known during the time when Merlin was among them, it made them feel safe.

Freddie's magic reached out and touched the mountain and glacier of Fireland. It was on his 14th birthday when he blew out the candles on his cake and made a wish, his magic sent out a massive and powerful ripple that woke Nix from his long sleep.

Nix's eyes opened and his body warmed, slowly melting the ice that encased him until he was free to move again. More and more ice melted until melt water flowed down the mountain to the lake and on to the ocean. Now the Prince of Water Nymphs was able to float and swim his way down to the great lake where he had once lived in hiding from the Beastrolls. Out of water, nymphs looked like young boys and girls. They all had curly blond hair, big bright blue eyes and shiny white teeth. The only difference to regular boys and girls was the fact their bodies were covered in iridescent scales like a rainbow salmon. In the water their legs transformed into a fish-like tail and they became Mermen and Mermaids and could swim faster than any water creature. Nix was particularly noticeable from other nymphs as his hair was the colour of gold, his face was more round than oval, he had rosy cheeks and looked very cute. This was far from the truth, cute he might look, but wherever water nymphs were about, mischief and trouble followed.

Nix swam down into the lake in the lowlands of Fireland where he again enjoyed the freedom to swim and frolic. He spent a few days feeding and exercising his muscles to regain his strength, constantly feeling the attraction of Freddie's magic. He had been hibernating for so long he could not quite remember what it was he was feeling, except something was calling to him. It was several days later while he was leisurely floating on his back in the water, looking up at the sun-filled blue sky, blowing fountains of water from his mouth and giggling when it splashed back down over his face. "Huh!" he cried, when he heard a sound that he had not heard for hundreds of years, voices!

Water nymphs have very keen senses of smell, taste and hearing, like many of the sea creatures, sharks for example, that can smell blood in the water from as far as fifty miles away.

The voices Nix could hear were quite a long way off, so he began swimming closer, eager to see if it was the Great Wizards or other supernaturals that had survived. Hiding among some floating vegetation, just in case it was Trolls or Ogres, he never liked Ogres, they were big and dumb. He chuckled to himself remembering he had tricked an Ogre into licking its big toe, having convinced it his toe tasted just like honey. He giggled again, he could see the huge beast rolling around on the ground trying, unsuccessfully, to get his big toe in his mouth. The Ogre only stopped when his mother came and beat his behind with a tree branch. "Ahh! Those were the days, so much fun, so many tricks to play," Nix giggled.

He approached the area where the voices seemed to come from and saw two figures on the shore. "Huh!" he said quietly to himself, "what are they? Not Fairies, they're too big, not Ogres, they're too small, nor Trolls." He sighed in relief knowing they were not Trolls. "So what kind of creatures are you I wonder?"

On the shore of the lake, two young Sproggle boys were sitting on small canvas stools, holding fishing rods with their lines in the water.

"Hinrik," Uggi chuckled. "Who told you that fish like bread?"

"Well it was my brother, actually. He said fish love it!" Hinrik replied sticking his tongue out.

"We'll see," Uggi laughed sticking his tongue out. "Let's see if the fish prefer your bread to my juicy maggots!"

Hinrik screwed his face up like a wrinkled prune and reeled in his fishing line, catching the hook and sticking a rolled up pellet of bread on it before casting it out into the lake.

Nix was fascinated, he had never seen creatures like these before, they were out of the water and did not have scales on their bodies, so they were clearly not water nymphs. Nix and his kind did have magic, for most of them it was quite weak, they could turn themselves invisible and levitate a few things. But Nix, being a Prince, had stronger magic and oddly enough he could feel it getting stronger as the days passed. He had the ability to shape shift and create small things at will, but his secret weapon was his eyes, anyone looking directly into his eyes would become hypnotised and obey his will, except the Wizards, of course. He was very curious, these were the first creatures he had seen since waking from his long sleep. Making himself invisible and morphing his fish tail into legs, he walked out of the lake and shook himself like a wet dog. Dried off, Nix walked towards the two Sproggles who were busy watching the lake and laughing. Nix got very close to them and liked the happy feeling he got from their laughter. He made himself visible, morphing his rainbow scales to pink skin like the boys he could see. "Hello," he said, imitating their language.

The two boys jumped and fell off their stools, almost losing grip of their fishing rods. The sudden appearance of Nix had startled them.

"W - who are you?" Uggi stuttered.

"I'm Nix," he replied, smiling cheerfully.

W - where are your clothes?" Hinrik asked.

Although Nix could change his shape, he could not magic any clothes. He had no use for clothes as he was normally covered in beautiful rainbow scales, so why would he cover them up? Also swimming would be a problem wearing clothes. Nix looked at himself and then at the boys and realised they were different.

"Oh, err, I can't remember where I left them when I went swimming," Nix said, not telling them the whole truth.

"Hinrik, you could give him your spare clothes," Uggi suggested and Hinrik jumped up and grabbed his rucksack. After unzipping it he handed Nix a pair of shorts and a tee shirt.

"You can borrow these, Nix," Uggi said.

"You're very kind," he replied, taking the clothes and feeling a bit self-conscious with both boys staring at his body. "What are you both?" he asked, furrowing his bushy golden eyebrows.

"I'm Uggi and this is my friend, Hinrik," Uggi replied.

The boys began to chuckle watching Nix put the clothes on. He was not used to them and had both legs in one leg of the shorts, promptly falling over.

Hinrik rushed to catch him and helped him put them on properly, then the same with the tee shirt.

"What is a Hinrik? Are you magical?" Nix asked hopefully.

"Huh!" Hinrik said. "Oh, no! Ha ha, Hinrik is my name, it's what I am called.

"So is Hinrik an Uggi?" Nix asked, a little confused.

Uggi sniggered, he thought Nix was really funny.

"No Nix, my name is Hinrik and this is my friend, his name is Uggi."

"Oh!" Nix said finally understanding. "What are you then?" he asked again.

Hinrik and Uggi looked at each other and shrugged their shoulders.

"What do you mean, Nix?" Uggi asked.

"Mmmm," Nix thought out aloud. "Well you have no wings so you're not Fairies, you're too small for Ogres and too big for Imps and you're definitely not Trolls. So are you small wizards?"

"You're very funny, Nix. We are just children, like you," Hinrik replied.

Nix smiled. "Children. Children. Mmmm," he said trying out this new word to him.

"We're fishing," Uggi explained, "he's using bread for bait and I'm using these." Uggi opened a small plastic box and inside were hundreds of writhing maggots. "Look!"

"Oh, may I try?" Nix said and Uggi nodded, so he reached into the box and picked out a few maggots and put them straight into his mouth. "Mmmm, delicious! The fish will definitely like those," he said seriously.

The moment Nix put the maggots in his mouth the boys cried out, "Oh, yuk, horrible!"

"Why do you catch fish?" Nix asked, eyeing up the box of squirming maggots.

"To eat them, of course," Hinrik replied.

"Oh, I get it! You feed the fish maggots and then eat the fish with maggots inside them, like a kind of stuffing," Nix said.

The two boys were beginning to think Nix was a bit strange. They were thinking he seemed to be saying that he had never seen anyone eating fish before.

"Why are you here then, Nix?" Uggi asked.

"Well, I was asleep for a long time and came down to the lake for a swim," he replied. He sensed the boys were getting uneasy and decided it was time to leave. "Do you like my eyes?" he asked casually and both boys looked directly into Nix's big blue eyes.

In an instant they both fell under his hypnotic magic and he told them to forget they had ever seen him. Then he took off the tee shirt and shorts, folded them and returned them to Hinrik's rucksack. Nix made himself invisible and as soon as he did the boys looked at each other.

"Oh! I've forgotten what I was saying," Uggi chuckled as they sat down again and reeled in their fishing lines to fix more bait on the hooks.

**

Freddie and nine of his school friends had been summoned to the headmasters study.

"What are we being accused of?" William asked nervously. "The headmaster only calls students to his study if they've done something wrong!" he added.

"I've been good, I haven't been in any fights or arguments in two years," Billy Bates remarked bashfully.

"We must have done something wrong for the headmaster to summon us to his study. It must be something really bad," Jimmy declared.

Freddie pulled everyone to a halt. "Look everyone, we have nothing to worry about, we are top in all our subjects and we are model students. Let's just wait and see, okay?" Freddie was confident he was right on all counts, as he knocked on the headmaster's door.

"Come in!" The deep, authoritive voice of the headmaster rattled the door against its frame.

Freddie turned the brass handle and opened the door, then the six boys and four girls marched in silently standing in a row in front of the Headmaster's desk.

"Relax boys and girls, you are not in any trouble, at least not today, not with me," the headmaster began.

All ten students let go a breath they had not realised they were holding in.

"You ten scholars represent a new era in this school. Your academic achievement is outstanding."

The students relaxed the muscles in their bodies, again they had not realised how tense they had become.

"You have attained top marks in all your studies. I offer each one of you my sincere congratulations, you are a credit to yourselves, the school and your parents."

They looked at each other with big smiles of relief on their faces.

"The school is creating a new class for the ten of you in order for you to achieve your potential. In this room, standing before me, I believe there is a future Prime Minister, a future company CEO, scientist or professor, people at the top of their field. People to lead and run this fine country of ours. At the end of this academic year you will sit your 'O' Level CE examinations (Certificate of Excellence), two years ahead of the mainstream. The following year you will sit your 'A' Level CE examinations, three years ahead of the mainstream. You will then be offered a place at Boxford or Canebridge University and graduate as professors at the age of 19, you will be among the youngest professionals in the world. I have spoken with all your parents and they have agreed to support you in this exclusive programme. The Government is financing you through to university graduation and guarantee you a career at the highest level. You will be the vanguards of a new era in leadership. Now it only requires each one of you to agree. It will be intense, but I believe you are all more than capable of this challenge. It's a big decision and you probably want to discuss it with your parents, so come see me at the end of school tomorrow and give me your answer." The headmaster was full of smiles and that was a rarity in itself.

"I'm in sir!" Freddie called out, not needing any time to think it through, it was exactly what he needed to stretch him.

"Me too, sir," Billy agreed. If his mother had agreed to it then that was good enough for him.

"I'm in too, sir," Jimmy announced. Wherever Freddie was he wanted to be on the same team.

There was a cascade of "Me too sir" that followed until everyone had agreed.

"Oh, that's excellent!" The headmaster was positively beaming and looked almost human. "Your new classroom awaits you then, a day early. Mr Chase will collect you in a moment, he will be your pastoral advisor during the rest of your journey through this school. Freddie, I am appointing you as spokesperson. If any of you have issues, talk with Freddie, if he needs support then Mr Chase or myself will always be available."

"Thank you, sir," echoed in unison from the ten students as they followed Mr Chase to their new seat of learning.

* *

Uggi and Hinrik, the two children he had met, intrigued Nix. He had no idea what 'Children' were, but he knew what they were not. "They are definitely not Ogres, Nymphs, Imps, Fairies or even Trolls," he mumbled to himself. He wondered if perhaps they were not supernatural beings like him and if so just how many 'Children' were there in this new era. Nix decided it was time to find out why magic had summoned him from his hibernation and when day turned to night, he walked out of the lake in his nymph form, covered in iridescent scales from head to foot. In the distance he could see a bright glow in the sky and wondered if other supernaturals had gathered around a huge bonfire like the old days. Oh, how he longed for those days, life for him was just perfect, he hated the Trolls for taking all that away from him.

Nix made his way towards the light and suddenly found himself on a hard flat surface without grass or moss. He reached down to touch it. "This is very odd," he said to himself. His eyes had adjusted to the darkness now and he looked at what was under his feet. "This is very strange indeed," he said out aloud reaching down to touch the surface. "Never have I seen or felt the like of this, it feels smooth and cold to my touch and it has lots of glowing eyes all down the middle. Who could have made this and what use could it be?" Nix was puzzled and all those eyes looking at him made him a bit nervous.

Little did he realise he was walking on an asphalt road, which had 'cat's eyes' down the middle and it would lead him to a small coastal town. He walked along the road although it felt very strange under his feet, avoiding the eyes glaring at him, until he declared, "Goblins and Ogres! Whatever is all that?"

Ahead of him was the town with brightly lit buildings making the glow in the sky.

"That's no bonfire!" he puzzled scratching his head. 'Children' must be very clever to make such things, whatever they are."

BARP! - BARP! - BARP! - BARP!

The loud noise and bright lights behind Nix made him instinctively jump sideways into the grassy verge as a speeding car whizzed by blowing its horn loudly.

He hid in the grass trembling and remembered when two large Ogres had once chased him through the woods, because he had dared to cross their bridge. Mind you, he had tied two flat stones to his feet and stomped very loudly crossing the bridge. "Hee, hee," he chuckled briefly. At that time he had shucked off the stones, scrambled up a tree and for good measure he turned himself invisible. But in past times some Ogres could see him even when he was invisible, so he had held his breath, watching as the Ogres puffed and grunted swinging spiky clubs. Only when it was safe had he jumped down from the tree and run to safety. He remembered he had been so amused at the time he laughed so hard his whole body shook and trembled, just like he was now, but this time it was with fear. It took a good few minutes for Nix to summon up enough courage to lift his head above the long grass to see if it was safe to come out.

"Goodness me! That must be a new kind of monster, like a Troll only bigger and faster. Oh, those poor 'Children', it's going straight for them, they will be in danger!" Nix was talking to himself out aloud trying to work out what to do. "The 'Children' were kind to me earlier on, I must try and help them."

Nix had it in his mind that 'Children' were the new creatures living in the land where he and other supernaturals had once lived, and saw men, women and children as one creature called a 'Children'.

Nix summoned up all his bravery, turned himself invisible and ran in the same direction as the monster. It had run so fast past him he had not been able to see it clearly. He remembered there were bright illuminations on it, white on its head and red on its behind. "It must have magic sunbeams so that it can see what it is hunting. That's very clever," Nix worked out for himself. He stopped and stared at the structures in front of him. "This has to be a nest of monsters and they have captured sunbeams everywhere. I can see some monsters, and 'Children' creatures seem to be trying to escape them," he muttered to himself.

What Nix was actually looking at were cars and vans parked outside dwellings and shops with people walking from one side of the road to the other, or getting in and out of vehicles. This made him think 'Children' creatures were trying to avoid the monsters *(cars and vans)* by running from one side of the road to the other.

"Wow, so many 'Children' creatures of all different shapes and sizes," he marvelled. (He did not realise that the tall children were actually adults).

"That tall one is holding the hand of a small one who seems reluctant. Oh, no! Is he going to feed the small one to the monster?"

Nix was watching a man put a child into a car then walk away, so it looked to him like the tall 'Children' creature was feeding the small 'Children' creature to the monster.

Nix was trembling again, but remained invisible and crept into the town. Using his magic he produced a large and very sharp dagger and crept up to the monsters. They seemed like giants to him, big and strangely coloured, *'They're not moving, they must be sleeping,'* he thought to himself. He crept up to a bright red one and touched its body and gasped. *'It feels so hard and cold, it must have very thick scales to protect it,'* he thought. Nix scratched his head and looked at his dagger. *'This will be no use,'* he thought, then spotted the softer looking, strange round feet and stabbed one of them good and hard. When he pulled the knife out he heard a loud hissing sound. He had never heard such a sound, which frightened him and he ran away. From a distance he watched the tall 'Children' creature that had been eaten by the monster spit the 'Children' creature out again after being stabbed in the foot by Nix's dagger. He laughed to himself, "At least I've saved one of the 'Children' creatures, so now I know how to save them all." He crept back to the town and stabbed the soft feet of the monsters, when they did not give chase, he got brave and stabbed all four feet on every monster. He smiled to himself as he watched 'Children' creatures that had been eaten, being spat out and walk free.

* *

'Freddie, there is a disturbance in the magic. A supernatural has awoken.' It was the Merlin ring warning him in his mind.

But Freddie was not afraid this time. His magic was powerful, even more powerful than when he battled the Beastrolls. "Can you detect what the danger is?" Freddie asked the Merlin ring.

'It is only a faint disturbance, Freddie, it is very distant or very weak or both,' the Merlin ring answered.

Freddie had been studying in his bedroom when the Merlin ring gave him the warning. As it was the weekend and his parents were at home, he jogged down the stairs.

"Sounds like the elephants are thirsty!" Freddie's father smiled. It never ceased to amuse him and at least he knew when his son was about.

Freddie looked round the door of the sitting room and walked in when he saw his parents. His father had been reading the newspaper and his mother sewing buttons on something or other.

"Mum, Dad, the Merlin ring is warning me of a disturbance in the magic. My magic has become so strong now that it has awoken a supernatural creature. I don't know if it poses a threat as yet, but I'm putting an enchantment over the whole village, including our home, to make sure everyone is safe. You have all been through enough, I can't risk anyone getting hurt, especially both of you," he explained.

"Will it be strong enough? Are you strong enough, Freddie? You're still only 14 years old," his mother asked. In her eyes Freddie was still her little boy and always would be, even though he was the most powerful being on the planet. She and his father still worried about him.

"No need to worry, Mum, nothing can affect my enchantment, it's stronger than the magic I used to keep the Beastrolls from leaving the village. No supernatural creature will be able to pass through it, but you and all the villagers will be able to come and go as you do normally," Freddie assured them.

"I need to warn the Elfins too, so I'll go pay them a visit now. Would you both like to come along?" Freddie asked.

Freddie's parents were always happy to visit Elfin Town, they were well known among the Elfins by now and especially the Tiggly family. Freddie took the hands of his mother and father in his and imagiported them all to Elfin Town, right outside the Tiggly's front door. Freddie knocked and Giggly opened the door.

"Freddie!" Giggly squealed, always delighted to see him. "Mr and Mrs Fountain, too. Come in, please," she invited their visitors.

The three Sproggles walked inside the cosy home and they immediately spotted Mummly.

"Hello, Mummly. How are you?" Freddie's mother asked.

"Susan, Jacob, and Freddie, how lovely. Giggly and I were just talking about you, Freddie. Come, sit in a comfy chair while I make some dandelion tea," Mummly replied with a big smile. She loved Freddie's visits, treating him like her own son, and she was always pleased to see his parents, they were such nice people.

Giggly was hanging onto Freddie's arm, she had taken a real shine to him and dragged him to the sofa so she could sit close to him. Freddie was flattered by Giggly's attention and they both knew it could only ever be a friendship. By the time they were all sitting comfortably Mummly arrived with a tray of mugs filled with dandelion tea.

"Why were you talking about me, Mummly, and where's Wiggly and Daddly?" Freddie asked sipping his tea.

Giggly snuggled up to Freddie, holding onto his arm and resting her head on his shoulder while her face was lit up with smiles.

"Ah well, it's because of Daddly and Wiggly we were talking about you, Freddie. They have gone to Merlin's library to look for a bone-mending spell. One of the school children seems to have broken her leg," Mummly explained.

"Oh, that's really terrible," Freddie's mother gasped. "Could your magic help her, Freddie?"

"Yes, Mum, of course. I wonder why Wiggly didn't call for me?" Freddie replied.

"Actually, I think they both wanted an excuse to visit Merlin's library," Mummly chuckled. "Boys and their toys."

"I can take you to Lucy's house, Freddie," Giggly offered. "She's the one with the broken leg."

"Okay, let's do that then, Giggly. Mum, Dad, will you be okay for a while?" Freddie asked.

His parents nodded and smiled.

"Yes son, we'll be fine, we have lot's to catch up with Mummly," his mother replied.

Okay, Giggly, let's go," Freddie said pulling his rucksack over his shoulder. He was going to imagiport them both, but Giggly was dragging him out the door before he had time to tell her. He let Giggly take him, hand in hand to Lucy's house, which was not very far away anyway.

"Freddie! Giggly!" Lucy's mother cried in surprise when she opened the front door.

"Hello, Mrs Tinker," Freddie and Giggly greeted together, making Giggly, giggle.

"Come on in," Mrs Tinker invited and showed them to the seating area where they all sat down on comfy chairs.

"I've come to help with Lucy's broken leg," Freddie explained.

Mrs Tinker was so happy to hear Freddie could mend her daughter's broken leg. "She's in her room laid on the bed, it's not easy for her to get about," Mrs Tinker explained. "Come with me," she said.

Freddie and Giggly followed Mrs Tinker through the sleeping area door and then through the first door on the left.

"Oh, Freddie!" Lucy cried on seeing him behind her mother.

Giggly popped her head from behind Freddie. "Hello, Lucy," she called.

"Oooh, Giggly, you've come too, that's really nice," Lucy said with a warm smile.

"Freddie's come to see if he can mend your leg, Lucy," her mother explained.

Giggly was already sitting on the bed with Lucy, who was her best friend.

"Really? You can do that, Freddie? Oh! It would be so nice to be able to walk around again. Mum and Dad have to carry me everywhere," Lucy replied excitedly.

Freddie walked over to Lucy. It was obvious which leg was broken as it was wrapped in lots of bandages.

"There will be a very bright light in a moment," Freddie said, "so can everyone please close your eyes and put your hands over them as well." When he was satisfied they were all doing as he had asked, he placed his right hand just above Lucy's broken leg and invoked his magic. Sure enough an intensely bright light glowed between his hand and Lucy's leg, lighting up the room.

"That feels so nice and warm," Lucy confessed.

Thirty seconds later Freddie told them it was safe to open their eyes as he had finished.

Giggly looked at Freddie and gave him a wide smile, then Lucy did too and she was already unwinding the bandages.

"It doesn't hurt anymore!" Lucy gabbled as she hurriedly unwrapped her bandages, pulling off the last bit to expose her leg.

"Look, Mum, my leg, it's perfect again!" she cried excitedly and a little tearfully.

"Oh thank you, Freddie, you're so kind. We're truly blessed that you came into our lives, who would have thought Elfins and Sproggles could be friends?" Mrs Tinker said.

"Try and stand," Freddie suggested and Lucy swung her legs off the bed and lifted herself up on both legs.

"That's amazing, Freddie, my leg feels the same as before I broke it and I have no pain any more. Thank you so much," Lucy said. Then she and Giggly picked some books to read together and settled on the bed.

"Come through and I'll make some tea," Mrs Tinker said.

"That's very kind of you, Mrs Tinker, but I need to go rescue Daddly and Wiggly from Merlin's library," Freddie replied and walked with Mrs Tinker back into the living area of the house. "It looks like Giggly is happy to keep Lucy company for a while, so I'll just go get Daddly and Wiggly," Freddie said and vanished as he imagiported himself to Merlin's library.

"Freddie, what a nice surprise!" Daddly called when he saw Freddie suddenly appear right in front of him.

Wiggly was up on the balcony when he heard Daddly mention Freddie's name. "Freddie!" he cried leaning over the balcony rail, losing his balance and tipping over the top, tumbling down towards the stone floor.

Freddie held out his hand and levitated Wiggly, making him fly around the room before lowering him down beside Daddly.

Wiggly ran to Freddie and hugged him tightly. "Oooh, thank you, Freddie. That was close, but I enjoyed the fly around!" he exclaimed.

"Hello, Wiggly. You need to be more careful, good job I was here," Freddie chuckled. He explained to Daddly and Wiggly that he had mended Lucy's leg and had come to take them home.

"Just as well," Daddly replied, "we have not found a spell to help so far."

"I can help with that," Freddie said and snapped his finger and thumb with a click. A book flew off the shelving and sailed down to the long bench in front of them. It opened by itself to a page where the letters moved around until they read, *'Spell to mend broken bones.'*

Wiggly laughed. "You're just showing off now, Freddie!"

"I'll copy it down, just in case we ever need it again," Daddly said smiling and thinking they should have called Freddie in the first place.

* *

Nix was feeling pretty pleased with himself believing he had saved all those 'Children' creatures, however it was not in his nature to be so kind and helpful. Water nymphs are mischievous and full of tricks, which got them into all kinds of trouble, consequently they were not the most popular of the supernaturals. Without realising what he had actually done, Nix had indeed caused a great deal of trouble in the town.

Satisfied he had saved these new creatures called 'Children', Nix ran towards the shore and walked into the sea where he morphed into a Merman and swam away from the town. He could feel a very powerful magical force pulling him and it was especially strong in the ocean.

'It has to be a Wizard, calling us all back to home,' Nix thought to himself while chasing through a school of small fish, making them dart and weave like they would from a shark or a whale. He was enjoying himself so much darting in and out of the panicking fish that he failed to notice three enormous and hungry Hunter whales approaching, attracted by the fish.

'Oh! I hope Merlin doesn't remember all the bother I caused before the Trolls invaded?' Nix was thinking when a Hunter whale was suddenly in front of him with its jaws open, scooping up the fish. A Water Nymph like Nix is small enough to be gobbled up by the giant whale, fortunately Nix is the fastest creature in the water and he pushed upward and out of the water six metres into the air. "Wheeee!" he cried and then, morphing his merman tail for legs, dived back into the ocean, ploughing through the fish and landed on the back of the whale that had almost swallowed him. He created suction cups on his legs and was able to cling to the whale as it tried to dislodge him.

Hunter whales are known for their intelligence and ability to work together, so another of the Pod was already swimming really fast towards Nix, intent on knocking him off the whale he was riding. But he was far too clever and shot up through the water, made a summersault in the air then dived back into the ocean and ended up on the attacking whale's back. Nix was having more fun than he had enjoyed in a long, long time, teasing the ocean monsters.

The three Hunter whales moved side by side with Nix in the middle and trapped his legs, then began to dive down deeper and deeper. The whales planned to drown their pest if they could not shift him any other way and Nix needed to breathe air, he did not have gills like a fish. These whales had not seen a water nymph before and did not know that Nix was the master of the water.

But he could do something no sea creature expected. *'STOP! Go back to the surface!'* He sent a powerful telepathic command to the Hunter whales, which they had to obey.

Instantly the whales made a swift change of direction towards the surface.

Nix would have been all right in the depths, water nymphs can hold their breath for almost an hour normally. *'Release me and go away!'* he commanded.

The Hunter whales parted, allowing Nix to escape, then they swam away just as they had been commanded.

Nix, being a Prince, was the ruler of all creatures that swam in the ocean, rivers and streams. When he gave a command, fish and mammals, no matter how small or how gigantic, could not escape obeying his every wish.

How he loved the smell, the vastness and calm of the ocean waters. He morphed his legs to his merman tail, then covered a great distance swimming really fast until he felt exhausted. Then he floated on the surface and swished his tail slowly while he caught his breath. He soon travelled across the ocean and headed for the shore where he shot out of the water and morphed from Merman to nymph boy with legs and landed on the deserted beach. He lay on the sand with the tide lapping over his legs, giggling to himself as the surf tickled his feet. It had been a very long time since he had teased the sea creatures and how he enjoyed it. He sat up, catching his breath and looked at the moon reflecting on the water. It was dark by now, but the light of the bright full moon sparkled on his iridescent scales as he began to stand up. Nix had excellent night vision, having larger than average eyes and he was enjoying looking at the ocean and beach when he heard an unfamiliar sound. He quickly crouched down and looked around in the direction of the noise and saw beams of sunlight and heard a strange growling noise.

"One of those monsters is on the prowl by the look and sound of it. Time for Nix to scarper!" he said out aloud and headed for the water. He morphed into his Merman form and swam away from the beach, leaping in and out of the water just like a dolphin. In this form Nix was completely at home in the ocean and he could swim so fast no other creature could catch him. Nix could again feel the pulling force of magic and it was stronger than ever. It had been such a long time since he had seen Merlin, the other Wizards and mixed with other supernaturals, the thought of which made him even more excited. He swam through the water like a torpedo fired from a submarine, whizzing past sharks and whales so fast they hardly had a chance to see him. He followed the direction of the magic while trying to think up a believable excuse for his past bad behaviour with Merlin when they at last met again. He was hopeful Merlin would forgive him, after all, he was a Prince.

* *

"How did you find your Germun oral lesson, Freddie?" Billy asked.

"Es war ganz einfach," Freddie replied smiling.

"Huh?" Billy said screwing his face up, because Germun was not a language he was studying.

"He said, 'It was quite easy,' Billy," William answered for Freddie as he was studying Germun with him.

"Das stimmt," Freddie chuckled.

"Freddie said, 'That's true'," William interpreted with a giggle.

"Okay, okay, smarty pants. Tout simplement parce que je ne prends que le francais!" Billy replied in Frensh, looking pleased. *(Simple because I only take Frensh.)*

Freddie laughed. "I'm sorry, Billy, I know you only study Frensh, I was only pulling your leg, not showing off," he apologised.

"How do you do it, Freddie, it seems so easy to ...." Billy did not get a chance to finish what he was saying, nor did Freddie manage to reply, because the fire alarm sounded all over the school, followed by an urgent speaker announcement from the Headmaster.

"This is not a drill. Please go to your designated safety zones.
Do not run. Stay calm. This is not a drill.
I repeat, this is not a drill!"

Suddenly, two boys barged past Freddie, Billy and William, knocking William to the floor.

Freddie instantly grabbed his friend and helped him to his feet. "Are you alright, William?" he asked looking William up and down for any signs of injury or blood.

"I-I think so, Freddie," William replied a little shaken.

"Did you see who those boys were, Billy?" Freddie asked.

"Sorry, I was distracted when William got knocked down," Billy answered.

"Let's get to the safety zone then," Freddie suggested and all three walked calmly out of the school building onto the playing fields.

To their shock and horror, they could see smoke billowing out from the area of the school offices. All the students lined up in their classes while teachers checked the registers to make sure all were accounted for.

With his enhanced hearing, Freddie could hear two voices calling for help. He recognised them as Mrs Blakely and Mrs Maundy, two of the school secretaries. Freddie called to his teacher, "Sir, I can hear people trapped in the building!" There was urgency in his voice.

But his teacher was calm. "The fire brigade will be here soon, Freddie, leave it to them. Stay put! Understand?" his teacher said with an authoritive tone.

Freddie nodded but feared it would be too late, so he sat down on the grass.

"Are you alright, Freddie?" Jimmy asked.

"A bit tired, let me sit a while," he replied. He closed his eyes and summoned his avatar in the form of a fireman.

"There we go, the fire brigade are here," Freddie's teacher exclaimed, seeing a fireman dash into the school.

Freddie could see what his avatar was seeing and headed straight for the administration offices. When his avatar reached that part of the school, Freddie could see that the only exit was a blazing inferno with raging flames consuming walls and ceilings. He heard one of the women, not screaming now, but crying. Freddie's avatar walked through the flames into the offices. The air was thick with smoke, but he could just see both secretaries. One was laid down and looked unconscious and the other was not far from the same. Freddie used his magic to blow the outside wall away and then grabbed the unconscious secretary and took her to safety. Next he picked up the second secretary and lifted her to safety well away from the burning building, both were now unconscious. Freddie used his magic to clear their lungs of smoke, repair the damage to their lungs and get them both breathing and conscious.

Mrs Maundy came round and looked at the fireman. "Thank you," she said, "you saved our lives. How did you get us out?"

"Luckily the wall blew out, Mrs Maundy, so I could carry you and Mrs Blakely out to safety. I have to go now, but you will be okay, the ambulance will be here soon. Go to hospital and get checked out," Freddie's avatar said and walked away.

When Mrs Maundy looked again he was gone.

Freddie opened his eyes and smiled then stood up with his friends.

"Miss! Miss! Are you all right? What happened?" Three sixth form boys and girls were checking the perimeter and spotted the two secretaries laid on the grass.

"We got lucky, one of the firemen came into the burning offices and pulled us out. He saved us both, he was so very brave!" Mrs Maundy explained.

"That's very strange, who was he, Mrs Maundy, because the fire brigade have not arrived yet, they are held up in a traffic accident!" Joseph, the Head Boy explained.

"How is that possible? We were trapped inside the building with no way out and the fireman walked through the flames. He said the wall had blown out so he was able to carry us out here to safety."

The sixth form students looked puzzled. Who was this hero? "Mrs Maundy, did you manage to see his face or would you recognise him again?" Julia, the Head Girl asked.

"To be honest I didn't take that much notice. Mrs Blakely here was unconscious and I was close to being overcome with the smoke. The strange thing is he knew my name and also Mrs Blakely's."

It was a mystery never to be solved and much talked about among the staff and students alike. Only Freddie knew the real truth, but he could not let anyone know.

The following day the local news channel and newspapers were full of ghost stories about a phantom fireman who saved the two secretaries from the burning school building.

"I guess that was you, Freddie?" his father asked over breakfast.

"You never said anything when you came home," his mother said.

"I didn't want you both worrying," Freddie replied.

"So did you go into the building yourself?" his father asked, knowing his son is immortal.

Freddie smiled and summoned his fireman avatar.

His parents jumped with surprise when the figure just appeared in the kitchen with them.

"I didn't, but he did," Freddie chuckled.

"Pleased to meet you, Mr and Mrs Fountain," Freddie's avatar said before he disappeared again.

"What was that, Freddie?" his mother asked, still quite shocked.

"It's a version of me that I can create, called an avatar. I see what it sees, it's like I'm actually there, wherever it is. That's how I saved the secretaries, they would have died if I hadn't done something because the fire brigade were caught up in an accident and would have arrived too late."

"Well, at least *we* know it was you, son," his father said placing his arm around Freddie's shoulder. "Your magic is becoming more powerful every day. It must be difficult for you not to use it all the time to help people."

"I do have to control it, sometimes a stray thought produces a magic effect, that could be a problem, but so far, I am able to hold it all in." Freddie replied.

"Your father and I want you to know how proud we are of you, son. You help so many and take nothing for yourself. Merlin chose the right person to bestow this gift upon," his mother praised.

Freddie galloped up the stairs.

"There go those elephants again!" his father chuckled.

In his bedroom Freddie took his text books from his faithful rucksack ready to study maths, a subject he really enjoyed, especially trigonometry.

His Merlin ring spoke to him in his mind. *'The disturbance is closer, Freddie, it's moving at great speed in your direction.'*

Freddie was sat at his desk in the special chair that only he could sit in. He rested his chin on his hands with elbows on the desk, closed his eyes and reached out with his mind. It was just like he was flying, high enough to miss the treetops. He let his magic go on the hunt, homing in on the creature he had awoken. Freddie sped overland until he reached the seashore, then travelled along the coastline in a northerly direction. Unable to identify where he stopped and hovered, he asked the Merlin ring, "Where is this place?"

'This is the Amberland coastline close to the Scotchland border. The supernatural is coming from the ocean and is close,' the Merlin ring answered.

Freddie watched, and then saw something like a large fish swimming just below the surface of the ocean, about to reach the beach. It shot out of the water and he could hardly believe his eyes. The creature was half human and half fish, a Merman. He remembered stories of Mermaids but never thought they were real. By the time the Merman landed on the beach it had two legs and was covered in beautifully shimmering scales like a rainbow salmon. It was a young boy who stood on the beach.

"What is this creature?" Freddie asked the Merlin ring.

'The creature is a water nymph. You should be wary, Freddie, they are mischievous, destructive and cause trouble wherever they are. This one is called Nix and was the Prince of Water Nymphs before the Troll Wars. He upset all the other supernaturals, especially Merlin before he disappeared,' the Merlin ring answered.

Freddie watched, fascinated, he had never seen the like of Nix before. He realised that the Prince of Water Nymphs must be hundreds of years old yet he looked like a ten year old boy. Nix suddenly vanished, one second he was visible, the next he was not.

"Where is Nix now?" Freddie asked his Merlin ring.

'Water nymphs are able to body morph from biped to merman or mermaid. They have magic that's not normally very strong, but Nix,

being a 'Royal,' has stronger magic. They can also turn themselves invisible,' the Merlin ring replied.

Freddie opened his eyes, back in his bedroom and was thoughtful. "So Nix is a Prince of Water Nymphs who is invisible and troublesome. I will have to keep my wits about me. At least he doesn't know who I am, but I know all about him now," Freddie said, to no one in particular.

* *

As Nix followed the source of the magic, he swam through the ocean at an incredible speed and when he reached the shallow water near the coast he shot out of the water up into the air.

"Wheeee!" he cried as he floated through the air. By the time he landed on the sandy beach he had morphed from merman to a water nymph boy. He had no idea that Freddie had been watching him, as yet he had no idea that Freddie was the source of the magic pulling him in like a fish on a fishing line. "Now let's find Merlin," Nix said to himself, deciding it must be Merlin calling him. Standing on the beach he turned himself completely invisible.

Water nymphs cannot fly but they can travel fast overland, although not as fast as they can travel in water. Now Nix began a slow walk to start with, over the grassy banks of the surrounding countryside, enjoying the feel of soft grass beneath his feet.

"I wonder if there are 'Children' creatures in this land where once there were only supernatural beings," he said as the daisies and dandelion flowers tickled his feet.

It was not long before he came upon something very strange.

Nix whispered to himself, "This has to be a nest, look at all those monsters huddling together, maybe they are breeding. Wow, they are big ones too, and they have only two feet. I can see some 'Children' creatures as well."

Nix watched and gasped when he saw a mouth open and eat a big 'Children' and a small 'Children' creature. He decided he had to do something and while he was invisible they would never know what hit them. He ran into the nest of monsters and produced his special dagger, then began stabbing the monster's feet, like he had before. But they hardly hissed at him, so he stabbed out their big shiny eyes and ripped the hard shell of their bodies, then ran off before any of them could catch him. From a branch high up in a tree some distance away, he looked on the nest and saw the monsters spitting out all sizes of 'Children' creatures.

Nix had actually come across a small caravan park and had ripped the caravans to shreds, stabbing the tyres he thought were feet, stabbing the windows he thought were eyes and ripping the metal body of the caravans thinking them to be the monster's bodies.

From his vantage point he watched the monsters spitting out tall and short 'Children' creatures and heard them crying and shouting. He believed the 'Children' creatures' calls and tears were of joy at having been set free. When all the noise quietened down Nix fell asleep and dreamed of his meeting with Merlin and the other Great Wizards and how glad he would be to see them again.

* *

"Have you seen this?" Freddie's father announced at the breakfast table. Freddie and his mother walked round to look at the newspaper.

"Goodness, whatever could have caused so much damage?" Freddie's mother exclaimed.

"Looks like a stampede of wild elephants!" Freddie's father suggested looking at his son.

"Those caravans have been ripped to shreds, it looks like the holiday makers were lucky not to have been hurt. Have the police any idea how it happened, Dad?" Freddie asked.

"All it says here is that some people watched their caravan being torn apart by itself, no sign of wild animals or gangs of hooligans who would have left tracks anyway," his father replied.

Freddie excused himself and went to his bedroom where he sat down at his desk in his special chair and closed his eyes. "Show me the caravan park," he whispered, calling on his magic. The next thing Freddie saw were trees rushing beneath him as he flew towards Amberland County. He hovered over the caravan site and he was truly overwhelmed. "The panels have been ripped away from their frames by someone or something very powerful," he said to himself. "Can you tell who is responsible?" he asked the Merlin ring.

'This is undoubtedly the work of Nix, Freddie,' the Merlin ring answered.

"But why would he do such a thing? People could have been hurt," Freddie said out aloud. He scanned the area but could not see any sign of the Prince of Water Nymphs. The caravan park had been cordoned off and was deserted, so Freddie used his magic to restore the caravans, as this was partly his fault for unintentionally waking Nix.

Freddie opened his eyes and was back in his bedroom. He sighed, "What are you up to, Nix? Why are you doing this and where are you? I need to find you," he said, to no one in particular.

But the Merlin ring replied, 'Freddie, Nix is heading for you. It is your magic that is attracting him. Sooner or later he will find you.'

The school had been closed for a few days while the fire damage was cleared and made safe. Freddie grabbed his rucksack and trundled downstairs, his father having already left for work. "Mum, a problem is looming. A supernatural creature, a water nymph, is heading this way. I watched him leap out of the sea in Amberland County and then he vanished into thin air."

Freddie's mother listened and suddenly had a thought. "Isn't that where all those caravans were damaged?" she replied.

"It is, Mum, and it was most certainly the nymph. I have repaired all the damage, that will cause a commotion, but I had to put things right. The village here is safe, he can't breach the enchantment, only non magic beings can come and go," Freddie said.

"So is this nymph magical too?" his mother asked.

"Yes, Mum, but I have no idea how strong his magic is, but he is nowhere near my strength so I'm only concerned about ordinary people with whom he comes into contact with. I'm going to see Daddly, he may know more about these nymphs," Freddie replied and made for the kitchen door.

"Oh! Are you not imagiporting yourself today?" his mother asked.

Freddie turned and smiled. "It's a nice day for a walk, so I'm off the long way round, I'll be back for lunch, bye now." With that he was out the door and walking down the garden path towards his beloved forest. He was absently humming to himself enjoying the walk along the dusty track, it was something he had not done in quite a while. Now that he could travel instantly anywhere, Freddie rarely came into the forest anymore.

"Hello my Special Christmas tree, you look even more splendid." Freddie stood looking at the magnificent fir tree and holly bush beneath it. Red roses and pine cones decorated the tree from top to bottom and it seemed to sparkle as sunbeams shone on it. Freddie's big smile suddenly vanished.

"Hello, Freddie, long time no see. Where have you been?" The deep voice seemed to come from his Special Christmas tree.

"Huh!" Freddie exclaimed, looking around, but unable to see anyone. "Special Christmas tree, did you just speak to me?" he asked feeling puzzled. He knew the animals could talk to him but not the plants.

"Yes, Freddie, there's no one else around." The voice came from the tree once more.

Freddie was shocked and amazed, thinking he heard a quiet chuckling with his enhanced hearing. "Wiggly, come out now. I'm not falling for your tricks," he called laughing to himself that his friend had caught him yet again. "Come on. Come out, Wiggly!" Freddie encouraged. He heard a definite chuckle and a rustle, then he got another surprise. "Jimmy!" he cried.

"Oh, that was priceless, Freddie. I really had you going there, didn't I?" Jimmy chuckled, peeking out from behind the Special Christmas tree, then running to his friend and wrapping his arm around Freddie's shoulder, laughing.

Freddie had to laugh with Jimmy who let go of his friend and they sat down on the grass together.

"What are you up to in the forest, Jimmy?" Freddie asked.

"Well I got bored at home on my own. Mum and Dad are out at work so I thought I would do something I haven't done in a while. When I heard you coming along the track, I was about to run to you when I heard you talking. I looked around and you were on your own and you seemed to be talking to this tree, so I thought ...."

"..... You thought you'd trick me and you got me good that's for sure," Freddie interrupted.

"Do you often talk to trees then, Freddie?" Jimmy asked, suppressing a snigger.

"Not as much as I used to do. I don't come for walks so much now," he replied.

"You called me Wiggly. What exactly is a Wiggly?" Jimmy asked, catching Freddie by surprise.

This was going to be tricky, especially as Freddie hated to tell lies to anyone, especially his best friend. "Oh, err, um, well to be truthful ...." Freddie could not think straight and in a bizarre moment he replied, "Come with me, Jimmy. I'll show you, but this will come as a shock to you!" he warned his friend. "Firstly, I am a powerful wizard ...."

Jimmy burst out laughing before Freddie could finish. "Ha, ha, ha! Come on, Freddie, pull the other leg. Ha, ha! You can't trick me."

"Come on I'll show you!" Freddie said standing up and grabbing Jimmy's hand to lead him off along the track, deep into the forest.

"Where are you taking me, Freddie, what's the hurry?" Jimmy asked puffing and blowing.

"You'll see, doubting Thomas!" Freddie replied still pulling him through the forest and then coming to a halt and let go of him. "Do you see that big old oak tree over there?" Freddie asked knowing that Jimmy could not see it.

"Huh! Tree? What tree, Freddie? There's no big old oak tree, are you seeing things?" Jimmy replied wrinkling his eyebrows.

Freddie took hold of his friend's wrist and said, "That one!" and chuckled. The moment Freddie took hold of his friend's wrist the big old oak tree suddenly appeared right in front of him.

"Whoah!" Jimmy cried, stepping back and pulling his hand from Freddie's and the tree vanished right in front of his eyes. "What the...?" he cried a little frightened, rubbing his eyes.

Freddie reached out and grabbed Jimmy's hand and the tree reappeared. There was a look of horror and intrigue on Jimmy's face.

"It's okay, Jimmy, this tree has a special magical enchantment on it so you and everyone else cannot normally see it. You'll understand why in a minute," Freddie explained.

Jimmy let go of Freddie's hand and the tree vanished from his sight, then he grabbed Freddie's hand and the tree suddenly reappeared. "This is bonkers, Freddie, how can such a huge tree just vanish? I don't understand. Have I fallen asleep and this is a dream?" Jimmy said, completely confused.

"It's magic, Jimmy. Just try to stay calm and trust me, okay?"

Jimmy nodded.

Freddie placed his hand on the big old oak tree. He no longer had to say the magic words as the tree recognised who he was and created the door that swung open.

"What's happening, Freddie?" Jimmy asked, afraid he was going crazy.

"Just stay calm, Jimmy, you're safe with me," Freddie replied pulling a reluctant friend into the open doorway and down the spiral staircase.

"This is so crazy, Freddie, what's down here?" Jimmy asked.

Freddie could feel Jimmy trembling and when they reached the bottom of the spiral staircase he said, "Look at me, Jimmy." Although it was dark his eyes had adjusted and he could see Freddie's face. "Do you trust me, Jimmy?"

Jimmy nodded. "I always have, Freddie, you're my best friend. You're Freddie Fixit!"

"What you are about to see, I can't let you remember, because it would put the Elfins in danger, so I will take this memory away when we get back in the forest. Okay?"

Jimmy looked hard at Freddie's face and could not see him smiling and playing a joke on him now. "You're serious aren't you? You are a wizard, you weren't joking, were you? Huh!"

"No, Jimmy, I am the most powerful Wizard on the planet, as you will shortly see. There's nothing to be afraid of, just stay close to me."

That did not exactly fill Jimmy with confidence but he did trust his friend.

Freddie placed his hand on the wall at the bottom of the spiral staircase and a door sprung open, flooding the chamber with a bright light.

It took a moment for Jimmy's eyes to adjust, then he gasped at what he could see through the doorway.

"This is Elfin Town and it's underneath the forest," Freddie explained as they walked into the light with Jimmy holding tightly onto Freddie's arm. His brain was struggling to understand what it was he could see. "A town under the forest. An Elfin Town," Jimmy muttered.

"Come on, let's go find Wiggly. You'll like Wiggly and his sister Giggly, she will like you, that's for sure." Freddie chuckled, pulling Jimmy through the street.

"Hello, Freddie!" Someone called out and Jimmy froze, pulling Freddie to a halt.

"Hello, Councillor Bumble," Freddie called back cheerfully as Councillor Bumble in his black and yellow striped jumper came over to talk.

Jimmy was shaking as he watched the strange creature approaching.

"You've brought a friend, Freddie," the Councillor said holding out his hand to Jimmy, who nervously reached out and shook it. "Welcome to our town."

"Councillor Bumble, this is my best Sproggle friend, Jimmy," Freddie said introducing Jimmy.

"I expect this is a bit overwhelming for you, Jimmy. No need to fear though, we're a friendly lot and you will be quite safe down here, especially with our hero, Freddie, with you," Councillor Bumble replied. "I'll let you two get off then, I expect the Tiggly's will be pleased to see you. Bye for now, Jimmy, Freddie." With that Councillor Bumble was off on his rounds.

"What was that?" Jimmy whispered.

"He is an Elfin. Councillor Bumble is over two hundred years old," Freddie replied.

"Two hun...... NO WAY!" Jimmy gasped loudly. "Two hundred years old! Is that even possible?" he gasped again.

"Oh yes! Elfins can live to be four hundred years old or more even. Because I am a Wizard I will age until I'm twenty then stop growing old as I am now eternal," Freddie replied.

"Eternal? What, you won't ever grow old, you will live forever?" Jimmy was doing a lot of gasping. "You're kidding, right?"

Freddie chuckled. "No, that's the truth. Now come on, let's find Wiggly!"

Several more Elfins greeted Freddie and Jimmy as they made their way to the Tiggly's house. Freddie did not stop to chat, just waved and said hello back to them for now.

"You know all these Elfins, you know all their names?" Jimmy asked.

"Yes, I do and they all know who and what I am too," Freddie answered.

"Do they even know you're a Wizard?" Jimmy replied uncertainly.

"Yes," Freddie replied.

"The Councillor called you a hero, what did he mean?" Jimmy was firing questions at his friend.

Freddie chuckled and replied, "Let's go to the Tiggly's and they will tell you all about it, I imagine."

When they reached the house, Freddie knocked on the door and Wiggly opened it. "Freddie!" he cried loudly on seeing his friend and launched himself at him in a bear hug.

"Ooof! Wiggly, can't breathe here!" Freddie chuckled.

"Oh! Sorry Fredd........." Wiggly stopped mid sentence when he spotted Jimmy and stepped back in surprise.

"Wiggly, meet Jimmy, he is my best Sproggle friend. Jimmy this is Wiggly, my best Elfin friend." Freddie introduced his friends to each other.

Wiggly rushed to Jimmy and gave him a bear hug as well. "Any friend of Freddie's is our friend too!" he announced.

Jimmy's eyes nearly popped out of his head in surprise, but his lips eventually found a smile as Wiggly released him. "Hi, Wiggly, Freddie talks about you a lot," Jimmy said taking a deep breath.

"Freddie!" Giggly cried as she came rushing to the door, pushing past Wiggly to hug him. Then she noticed Jimmy. "Oooh, who is this very, very handsome boy?" she cooed, then released Freddie and feigned being shy.

"Hello, Giggly, pretty as ever," Freddie chuckled. "This is my Sproggle friend, Jimmy. This is Giggly, Jimmy, she is Wiggly's sister."

Giggly pushed past everyone and grabbed Jimmy's hand, pulling him into the house and towards a comfy sofa, where she sat them both down and hung on Jimmy's arm smiling up at his face.

"H - h - h- hello, Giggly," Jimmy stuttered. "Th - that's an unusual name."

Giggly was cuddled up to Jimmy and batting her eyelids at him, making him blush bright red.

Wiggly and Freddie walked to the seating area and sat down on another comfy sofa.

"Looks like you've lost Giggly to Jimmy, Freddie!" Wiggly chuckled as they watched her snoodling.

"Giggly! Let the poor boy breathe!" Mummly cried coming to Jimmy's aid. "Hello, Jimmy, I'm Mummly, Wiggly and Giggly's mother, call me Mummly, everyone does."

Giggly reluctantly released her death grip on Jimmy but held his hand in hers.

"Th-thank you Mrs, erm, I mean, Mummly," Jimmy said feeling a bit more at ease and not minding Giggly's attention, she had just surprised him.

"I'll make some tea then you can tell us all about yourself, Jimmy," Mummly said walking across to the kitchen area.

"Not that I'm complaining," Giggly said batting her eyelids at Jimmy again, "but why have you brought Jimmy here, isn't it dangerous?"

Mummly brought tea and snacks while Freddie explained how Jimmy had fooled him by pretending to be a talking tree. Wiggly and Giggly howled with an infectious laughter that made everyone join in.

Jimmy felt much more at ease as he laughed with everyone. He liked Giggly, she was quite a pretty Elfin and it was the first time a girl had been this affectionate with him. He told them about himself and school and how they were in a special group.

Giggly hung on his every word, smiling at him.

Between Wiggly, Giggly and Mummly they told Jimmy all about their mutual friend, Freddie. When they finished Jimmy looked at Freddie in awe, especially hearing about the Mole Goblins and how he had nearly died. His admiration for Freddie just grew and grew as he heard everything he had done to save the Elfins, the village and the world. "Wow, Freddie! Now I understand why Councillor Bumble called you a hero, because you are a super hero. I'm so glad we are friends."

"I have to protect all the Elfins, if Sproggles ...."

".... What are Sproggles?" Jimmy interrupted.

"That's what we Elfin's call you and others like you, Sproggles. We are Elfins, you are Sproggles," Giggly explained.

Freddie continued. "So if Sproggles ever discovered the existence of Elfins they would experiment on them to find out why they lived so long. And if they knew about magic, then there could be wars fought to obtain the secret. Jimmy, I could destroy the whole of Elfington village with the snap of my fingers, so you can imagine what the rest of humanity would do to have that power," he explained.

Jimmy looked shocked. "Are you that powerful, Freddie? That's incredible, I understand why you keep it a secret. Oh, was it you who saved the two school secretaries from the fire?" Jimmy asked.

"Well, yes and no, Jimmy. It was actually him," Freddie said summoning his avatar in fireman form.

Everyone moved with surprise at the sudden appearance of Freddie's avatar.

"Hello everyone. Giggly, you look lovely, Wiggly, you are handsome. Mummly, you also look lovely. Jimmy, you look surprised," the avatar said.

"How do you know our names?" Wiggly asked.

"Well I am Freddie and he is me," the avatar replied and then vanished.

"Wow, oh wow, Freddie, you are amazing!" Jimmy chuckled.

Daddly arrived back from his meeting. "Freddie, nice to see you." Then he noticed Jimmy and had a concerned expression on his face. He walked over to the seating area.

"Daddly, this is my best Sproggle friend, Jimmy. He caught me on the way to see you, so I brought him along. He knows I will be wiping his memory when we return," Freddie replied seeing the concern on Daddly's face.

"Well it's very nice to meet you, Jimmy. Any friend of Freddie's is a friend of all we Elfins," Daddly said. "I see my daughter has taken a shine to you!"

Giggly pouted and clung to Jimmy even more.

"Thank you sir. This is all amazing, you are all amazing and Freddie is amazing," Jimmy replied and looked at Giggly. "Your daughter is very pretty and has made me feel very welcome."

Giggly looked at Jimmy and then her father and gave him a knowing smile.

Daddly sat down and looked at Freddie. "Is this a social call or something to do with the disturbance in your magic?" he asked.

Jimmy was all ears.

"Both really, I was at a loose end, but we do have a problem. My magic has awoken a water nymph and he's causing havoc. He destroyed a caravan park, ripped the caravans to shreds. No one was hurt, thank goodness and I have since restored everything as it was. He is heading this way, drawn in by my magic," Freddie explained.

"I had no idea any supernatural beings escaped the Great Troll Wars..." Daddly began.

"...What were the Great Troll Wars?" Jimmy asked interrupting Daddly.

"Daddly, would you like to explain?" Freddie invited.

Mummly brought more dandelion tea.

"This is really delicious, Mummly," Jimmy complimented.

Daddly got comfortable and began the story. "A very long time ago only supernatural beings like Elfins, Goblins, Pixies, Fairies, Nymphs, Imps and Ogres and so on lived in this land. Over the ocean lived Trolls, who were big lumbering beings and not very smart. The Beastrolls came to the land of the Trolls through an inter-dimensional portal and persuaded the Trolls to invade the land of the supernaturals who were governed by five Great Wizards. When the Trolls invaded there were so many of them that they overwhelmed and extinguished all the supernatural beings. They were protected from the magic of the five Great Wizards by the Beastrolls, who could absorb magic.

The five Great Wizards joined forces and with their combined magic they rained fire down on the Trolls and extinguished them all. The five Wizards were not powerful enough to banish the Beastrolls back to their own dimension or vanquish them. The best they could do was to place them in suspended animation and bury them for eternity.........."

".... But they escaped and Freddie killed them!" Jimmy broke in.

"Quite so, Jimmy, you've heard all about Freddie and Wiggly's adventures. With all the supernaturals gone the five Great Wizards gave up their magic to one wizard, the Greatest ever Wizard, Merlin, then they vanished to roam the cosmos. Soon after the Great Troll Wars, Sproggles appeared and quickly multiplied in numbers making it unsafe for Merlin and we Elfins he had created as his helpers. He built this underground town for us to live safely and then he went into hibernation. It was predicted that a great wizard would one day be born on the 5th day of the 5th month at the 5th minute of the 5th hour where the five lay lines cross. This wizard would be even more powerful than Merlin and would ready the world for his return........"

"....... And that Wizard is Freddie!" Wiggly said proudly hugging his friend.

"Wow, such a lot has happened that we Sproggles don't know anything about!" Jimmy exclaimed.

"Freddie, does this water nymph have a name?" Daddly asked.

"Mmm, yes, Daddly, the Merlin ring told me this water nymph is called Nix."

Daddly was nodding knowingly. "Ah, yes. Nix was the Prince of Nymphs, the most powerful with the most magic," he replied. "Do you have any idea where he is now?"

Freddie shook his head. "Not really, because Nix remains invisible I can only see where he has been so far due to the chaos he's caused. But he is heading in this direction, my magic is attracting him to me, but I can't understand why he's destroying things. I have put an enchantment spell over the village to keep him out, because the villagers have been through too much already, even though they don't remember." Freddie held both his hands in the air and closed his eyes for a moment. "There, I've added an extra layer of protection to the enchantment protecting this town, he will only be able to get in here if I bring him and that's not very likely if he continues his journey of destruction."

Jimmy was wide eyed watching and listening to his friend. "Is your magic strong enough to control him, Freddie?" he asked, not fully realising just how powerful Freddie actually was.

Freddie smiled, clicked his fingers and Wiggly disappeared.

"Oh! Where's Wiggly gone?" Jimmy cried, startled.

"I'm here?" Wiggly's voice said from where he had been sitting.

Freddie clicked his fingers again and Giggly disappeared, making Jimmy jump because he could still feel her holding on to his arm. He clicked his fingers again and both Wiggly and Giggly reappeared.

"Freddie is very powerful, Jimmy, there is no being in this world and probably any world that is more powerful. He can draw magic from the land, the air, the ocean and the cosmos itself if needed," Daddly explained.

Jimmy looked at his friend with an expression of admiration. "How do you stop yourself from using your magic all the time, Freddie? I mean most people with your power would magic up wealth and health and power, but you only use it to help others, like the secretaries at school."

"I've had time to adjust and control my magic. Besides, I have everything I need, like perfect parents and great friends. I like my life as it is, even though it's a bit more complex than most boys of my age," Freddie replied.

"Freddie is very special, that's why it took hundreds of years for magic to choose the right person. Freddie is unlike the majority of Sproggles, Jimmy," Mummly explained.

"Aw, thanks guys, but I don't see myself as special, nor do I feel special, I'm just me, Freddie Fixit, the person you have always known," he replied.

"I've just had a thought about Nix," Mummly said, realising that Freddie might be feeling embarrassed. "Nix must have escaped the Troll Wars before Merlin and the other Wizards destroyed the Trolls. If that is the case, then Nix will not recognise Sproggles, or any of the buildings and vehicles that Sproggles use. He may think that cars and caravans are some kind of monsters and when he saw Sproggles going inside them ....''

".......He would think the monsters were eating the Sproggles!" Giggly said, interrupting her mother.

"And when they all ran out of the caravans as he destroyed them, he might assume the monsters were spitting them out," Freddie concluded.

"He must think he's saving the Sproggles from the monsters!" Wiggly added.

"Wow, you are all so very clever, I'd never have worked that out," Jimmy said, looking amazed.

"If this is the case, then I need to find him before anyone actually gets hurt or even worse," Freddie said.

"But how can you find something that's invisible?" Jimmy asked.

"Do you remember when we found those shiny screws, Jimmy?" Freddie asked.

Jimmy thought for a moment and then piped up, "Oh, yes! Lots of screws went missing and we never did discover how it was happening," he replied.

"But we did!" Wiggly blurted out. "It turned out to be one of us Elfins who had a magic hat that made him invisible, and also anything in his hands."

Jimmy laughed. "Of course, that explains everything. But how did you find out if the culprit was invisible?" Jimmy was beginning to see the similarities and where this conversation was leading.

"Daddly turned an ordinary pair of spectacles into ones that could see magic," Giggly answered proudly. "Then Freddie went on the hunt in your village and caught the culprit red handed."

"So could you use these spectacles to see this Nix boy?" Jimmy asked.

Everyone was nodding and smiling.

"They only work if someone is wearing them though," Daddly explained.

After sipping dandelion tea while sat quietly thinking about the problem, breaking the silence, Freddie said, "Let me show you all something. Can we all link hands in a circle? Daddly, if you come sit between Wiggly and Giggly and hold their hands, that's it. Now whatever happens, don't let go of anyone's hand, it's very important," he emphasized. "Now close your eyes, I'm going to take you on a journey by flying," he explained.

Jimmy opened his eyes and cried, "What!"

"It's safe, Jimmy, your body will stay here, it's just your mind going flying," Freddie reassured his friend. He made sure they were ready, then closed his eyes. "Show me!" he commanded his magic and suddenly they were all high in the air, flying above the trees.

"Wow, this is fantaculous!" Wiggly laughed.

Very quickly they were over the caravan site that Nix had destroyed and Freddie had restored.

"This is Nix's last known location," Freddie explained. "Show us the damage," he commanded his magic and the caravans began tearing themselves apart and people running out screaming.

"He certainly made a mess of those," Mummly gasped. "It does look like my suspicions are right though," she added.

"I believe he is heading for me as it is my magic that awakened him from his hibernation," Freddie said.

"Let's fly in a straight line towards Elfington village then. If Nix is heading for you it would be the logical route for him in a straight line," Daddly suggested.

As they moved away from the caravan sight the vision of Nix destroying it vanished leaving the caravans whole again. Freddie guided them along the course that Daddly had suggested and soon came upon a vast river.

'Freddie, this is the River Umber, it is a tidal river and has dangerous currents. Nix is strong but he is unlikely to choose swimming across the river,' his Merlin ring replied.

"Whose voice was that we heard?" Jimmy asked.

"That's from the special ring Freddie wears. It guides him and is called the Merlin ring, given to him by the great Wizard Merlin." Wiggly answered for Freddie, "but only he can normally hear it, so it must be because our minds are linked with his.

"There is a bridge over there," Jimmy said spotting a huge and beautiful suspension bridge.

"Well done, Jimmy. That's a much easier route for Nix," Freddie replied.

* *

Nix, however, did not use the suspension bridge, he took one look and decided it was far too busy. There were too many monsters speeding back and forth, he thought better than to try and defeat so many of them. Instead he travelled along the riverbank upstream, it was a much quieter option. "This river will eventually become narrow enough to cross without any problems," he said, encouraging himself. His journey was quiet and peaceful, just how he liked it, he already had his fill of battling monsters. But his luck soon ran out when in his path was yet another nest of the monsters.

"What is going on? Why are there so many of these monsters and 'Children' creatures?" he moaned to himself as he stood in front of a big sign. Nix looked at it turning his head one way then the other. His magic allowed him to speak and read the language the 'Children' creatures used, but it was not easy.

"Goo," he began reading, "Wel - co - me t - o Gou - l To - wn! Oh! How do these creatures manage to communicate, no wonder they are overrun with monsters. These 'Children' creatures must be dumb like the Trolls were and look what happened to them!" Nix moaned, feeling frustrated. He had another attempt to read the sign. "Wel - come To Goul Town! Ah, that's it, Welcome to Goul Town," he repeated with satisfaction. "But what exactly is a Goul Town?" he said rubbing his chin. "A Goul must be like a Troll or Ogre maybe," he wondered. Nix looked perplexed and decided to carefully investigate.

It was early in the morning with very few people around, but that changed quite quickly as the rush hour began in the town. There became a steady stream of cars, vans and buses along with more and more people rushing here and there to work or school or shopping.

Still invisible, Nix was walking into the town of Goul when a car sped past him, so close it spun him around, giving him quite a fright. He looked around and said, "Funny, these 'Children' creatures seem not to be fearful of the big monsters, maybe they are these Gouls?"

He could not understand what the tall walls with eyes in them were or why 'Children' creatures seemed to be walking in and out of lots and lots of mouths.

What Nix was seeing were buildings with windows that he thought were eyes, and it was doors he mistook for mouths.

"This Goul Town must be some kind of a maze. Oh, yes, we had lots of fun with mazes, it drove the Pixies potty, hee, hee!" Nix chuckled to himself, remembering the good old days.

"Yes, these wide black tracks turn and go in different directions between the high walls with eyes and these 'Children' creatures are rushing around trying to find their way out. That's it, they are being chased by the monsters, that's why they are in such a hurry!" Nix was so pleased with himself having worked out the unfamiliar things.

To a supernatural being like Nix from the distant past, the road networks with buildings either side did resemble something like a maze and he was not far wrong with that thought. The town of Goul was built on the narrow part of the river and had a short bridge across it.

Nix walked further into the town. It was getting noisy and people bumped into him knocking him about and then looking around confused because they had hit something, but of course Nix was still invisible.

An ambulance sped by with its siren blaring.

The loud noise made Nix jump and cover his ears. "That monster is wailing, it must be in pain. Maybe it has eaten too many 'Children' creatures and has belly ache," he said out aloud, much to the confusion of people around him who could not see who the squeaky voice was coming from.

The noise was becoming unbearable, 'Children' creatures were shouting and monsters were growling and screaming. Nix had now reached the town centre at its busiest time, his head was pounding, his ears hurt and he was getting more and more frustrated and angry looking for a way across the river. He became so annoyed a red aura formed around him and it drew in the magic of the air. It looked as if Nix was about to explode, when he squeezed his eyes closed, dropped his hands from his ears and cried out,

"S-T-O-P!"

His magical aura sent out a massive sound wave that exploded from Nix in all directions with the same effect as a bomb.

The blast sent cars, vans and buses hurtling through the air, rolling over and crashing into each other and the buildings. Houses and shops crumbled and collapsed from the blast and 'Children' creatures were knocked to the ground or were blown along the roads like a piece of paper in the wind. The destruction was everywhere and almost the entire town was destroyed or damaged, with windows and doors blown out on buildings furthest away from Nix when he cried out. Fires broke out all over as gas pipes fractured, jets of water flew up in the air like fountains from cracks and splits in water pipes.

Goul Town fell silent and it was a blessing to Nix's ears, but when he opened his eyes he felt terrified and shocked at the devastation he saw around him. But when he saw all the monsters crushed and broken he laughed. "Ha, ha, ha! That serves those monsters right, there's too many of them and look at those poor 'Children' creatures laid on the ground, the monsters must have spat them out, but they look like they are hurt, just lying around on the ground." Nix scratched his head, he knew his magic was not strong enough to heal the injured creatures and decided to make a run for it while things were quiet.

Water nymphs can run much faster than humans and he sped through the town, over the first bridge he arrived at and scooted across to the other side and into the countryside where he found the peace and quiet he longed for. "Our beautiful land has been destroyed, where are all the lovely forests and lakes and meadows? Now this land is infested with monsters and strange creatures, but how can this be? How long have I slept? These monsters are worse than the Trolls. When I find the Great Wizards and Merlin we will have to use magic to get rid of them all and free the 'Children' creatures," he said to himself, suddenly feeling weary after expending so much energy using magic. Nix searched around and found a nice dry, deep cave to hide away and sleep to recuperate. He made himself visible and settled down on a bed of leaves to sleep and dream of finally meeting Merlin.

**

Freddie flew them all over the Umber suspension bridge.

"We will never see Nix down there, especially if he is invisible," Giggly said a little frustrated.

"All we can do is look for clues. If Nix thinks cars are monsters, he's going to cause problems along his journey, thinking he's killing them," Freddie explained.

The route they followed showed no signs of the water nymph or any destruction and eventually they arrived over Elfington village.

"Hey, that's my house down there!" Jimmy cried. "Oh look, there's yours too, Freddie," he chuckled.

They were all suddenly back in the Tiggly's house and opening their eyes.

"That was amazing, Freddie, I didn't know you could do such a thing," Daddly said as they all let go of each other's hands.

"Elfington village and Elfington forest. They're all named after Elfins!" Jimmy said, pleased with himself for working it out.

"That's right, Jimmy, Elfins once lived above ground alongside Sproggles. We lived in the forest and Sproggles farmed in the open spaces. But Elfins do not grow in number like Sproggles, who soon needed more space and cut down the forests where we lived. The whole of Elfington village was once our forest," Mummly explained

"So how did you get down here then?" Jimmy asked, forgetting he had already been told.

"The Great Wizard Merlin built Elfin Town to keep us safe. He had created his Elfins after the Great Troll Wars to help him," Wiggly explained.

Mummly brought dandelion tea over from the kitchen area and they all sat quietly sipping the hot liquid, deep in thought, for almost half and hour.

"You can't use the magic seeing spectacles from the air, like when we were flying not long ago, because we were not actually up there," Jimmy surmised.

"That's right, it looks like I'll only be able to see Nix when he's almost reached me," Freddie replied.

"But when we were flying we had the same clothes on that we are wearing, so if you wore the spectacles wouldn't you be wearing them when you're flying too?" Giggly announced.

Everyone sat up realising that Giggly was correct and it might actually work.

"That's brilliant, Giggly, you can be so clever sometimes," Wiggly chuckled.

"I'll get the spectacles out right now for you, Freddie, you can give it a try sometime," Daddly offered.

"Time to go now, Jimmy, say goodbye to everyone," Freddie said.

Giggly had Jimmy in a bear hug straight away. "It was really nice meeting you, Jimmy, you're so handsome. Have you got a girlfriend?"

"Giggly, behave yourself!" Mummly called.

Jimmy chuckled and turned bright red. "Looks like I have one now!" he replied.

"Oooh, you look even cuter when you blush, Jimmy. I hope Freddie can bring you to see us again soon," Giggly chuckled, still hanging on to him.

Yes," Mummly agreed, "you've been really helpful and it has been nice to meet you."

"It's nice to know Freddie has good friends around him, he's going to need you in the future," Daddly said and offered his hand to shake.

"Thank you, Daddly and Mummly, it has been my privilege to have met you all," Jimmy smiled.

Wiggly gave Jimmy a slightly gentler hug after prizing his sister off him. "You are really nice, Jimmy, you and I are Freddie's best friends, so look after him, he's special," Wiggly said.

"Thank you, Wiggly, you can be sure that I will look after him, even though I won't remember any of this and I know you all will look after him down here and everything to do with magic," Jimmy replied truthfully.

"Take my hand, Jimmy, we'll go the quicker way," Freddie said holding out his hand, which Jimmy took and suddenly they were no longer in Elfin town but in Freddie's bedroom.

"W - w - what happened?" Jimmy stuttered, confused and feeling just a little bit dizzy.

"My magic gives me the ability to travel anywhere in an instant. Merlin called it imagiporting. I just have to imagine where I want to be and I'm there in an instant," Freddie explained.

"Wow, that's so cool. You're so cool, Freddie. Who'd have thought Freddie Fixit was a real live Wizard? So cool. I can see why you need to keep it secret, what governments wouldn't do to get hold of instant travel!" Jimmy said quite excitedly.

"Let's go downstairs and talk to Mum," Freddie suggested, chuckling at Jimmy.

"Does your Mum know about you?" Jimmy asked.

"Mum and Dad do, but only until it becomes a problem for them to keep it secret," Freddie replied.

"Would you like to stay for dinner, Jimmy? I'm sure Freddie would like that. Actually you could have a sleepover if you wanted?" Freddie's mother suggested.

"Oh, could I? I'd really like that, it's quiet at home. Is that alright with you, Freddie?" Jimmy replied excitedly.

"Yes! That would be great, thanks, Mum." Freddie had a big smile on his face, he liked it when his friends stayed over.

"I'll ring your mother and let her know where you are, otherwise she will worry about you, I'm sure," Freddie's mother suggested.

"Thank you, Mrs Fountain," Jimmy replied.

A little later at teatime, Jimmy was so excited, telling Freddie's parents where he had been with Freddie and that they had flown all over the country. "We even hovered over the village and saw our houses from above, it was such a thrill, Freddie is so clever."

"Giggly took a real shine to Jimmy, she hung on his arm like he might run away!" Freddie chuckled and Jimmy turned bright red in the face.

"Ooh! It looks like someone liked Giggly too!" Freddie's mother teased.

"Well, maybe, just a little bit. She's very sweet, funny and pretty too," Jimmy replied shyly.

"We're very proud of Freddie," his father said distracting attention from an embarrassed Jimmy. "It's a real shame that you and the rest of your close friends cannot know him as a wizard and all the things he has done. But maybe one day in the future that can change. At least for now, you know how special he is, Jimmy."

Later on, while the two friends were sitting on Freddie's bed chatting, there was a knock on the door.

"Come in Mum, we're decent," Freddie called.

His mother opened the door and held out a plump rucksack. "Your mother dropped off some clothes and stuff, Jimmy," she said handing the rucksack to him.

"Thank you, Mrs Fountain, it's kind of you to bring them up here for me."

"You're welcome, Jimmy, you're such a polite boy, it's lovely to have you around. Don't you think so, Freddie?" his mother said.

"Yes, Mum, it is nice and you're right, Jimmy is polite and kind," Freddie replied making his friend blush again.

After Freddie's mother left and closed the door, Jimmy asked, "How did you know it was your mum at the door?"

"I could see her through the door." Freddie smiled.

"No! Really? You have x-ray vision like Superman?" Jimmy could hardly believe it.

"Not quite like Superman, but enough to distinguish who might be there," Freddie replied.

"So, can you see through walls and the like?"

"Mmm!" Freddie nodded.

"That's so cool, Freddie," Jimmy said excitedly. "But you are lucky too, your mum is so nice, she even knocks on your door. My Mum just barges in, I don't know how many times she's caught me with just my boxers on. Once I was completely embarrassed, I had just come out from the shower and the moment Mum burst into my room, my towel decided to fall off. I swear she does in on purpose," Jimmy said scowling.

Freddie could not help but laugh, but he did appreciate Jimmy's predicament. "That must have been quite embarrassing for you. Perhaps you should have a chat with her and suggest she knocks first, you can always say that my Mum knocks and waits for me to say I'm decent. Or, if you like, I could ask my Mum to speak to your mum," he suggested.

"Mmm! I suppose I need to have that conversation with her, she's always done it, so it may not occur to her that I'm all grown up now and would appreciate a little privacy," Jimmy replied. "You know when you do the memory wipe, won't I be confused because we met in the forest and now I'm here?"

"In the morning I will take away all your memories from when we went down to Elfin Town and plant false memories of meeting up in the forest and coming home with me," Freddie replied.

"You can do all that? Will it hurt?" Jimmy asked.

"Yes I can and no it won't hurt. I've actually done it to you before, well the whole village in fact when the Beastrolls attacked and you don't remember any of that do you? One of the Beastrolls was in your house and it had drained you all of your life force, you just about died that day," Freddie explained.

"You're so incredible, Freddie. I'm so lucky to have you as a friend, even if I don't remember all about today, I still value your friendship." Jimmy was close to tears.

"Hey! Want to arm wrestle?" Freddie said to distract his friend.

"No magic tricks then," Jimmy chuckled.

The two friends talked and laughed after both won two arm wrestles each, until it was bedtime. Having showered and cleaned their teeth they pulled on their pyjamas.

"Those pyjamas are 'with it'," Freddie exclaimed, looking at Jimmy in his tee shirt and shorts style pyjamas.

"Mmm, Mum got them for me a little while ago, I felt my Super Hero patterned pyjamas a bit too young for me now," Jimmy replied.

"I like them, I'll ask Mum to get me some," Freddie agreed.

"Why don't you use your magic?" Jimmy asked.

He looked at Jimmy and smiled. "It's strange but I never think about using magic for anything for me. I suppose something in my brain tells me the magic is for me to help others, not to use it for myself," Freddie replied thoughtfully.

"You have a very strong mind then, Freddie, I couldn't trust myself not to use it. I mean, when you need something you could just magic one up, couldn't you? Like all your models, do you still make them?" Jimmy remarked.

"I do, when I have saved enough pocket money I go and buy a new kit and there's quite a lot of excitement saving and going to buy the kit. I could just magic one, but it would not mean the same."

"Wow, Freddie, you're so grown up. Merlin could not have chosen anyone better than you to have magic. I know I'd be hopeless with it. Can you imagine Graham with magic and all his 'Ooops!' moments?" They both laughed. "I think the school would have vanished along with most of the students. He's so clumsy, Mr Thornton made the mistake of asking Graham to hand back the exercise books, he tripped and ended up throwing them up in the air, luckily no one was hurt!"

Freddie and Jimmy lay in bed still talking about things and the events of the day when Jimmy realised that Freddie had dropped off to sleep.

"I guess using all that magic must tire you out," Jimmy whispered and Freddie made a snuffling sound.

* *

Freddie's mother knocked on the door at 8am and when she received no answer went to check if the boys were in the bathroom, which they were not. She opened Freddie's bedroom door and peeked round and chuckled. Jimmy had rolled to the edge of the bed with one leg dangling down from under the duvet. She could only see Freddie's feet, he had somehow turned upside down in the night. "Wakey, wakey boys!" She called loudly and the bottom of the duvet lifted up.

Freddie opened his eyes and asked, "What time is it, Mum?"

"Come on sleepy head it's past 8 o'clock, time for breakfast," his mother replied and the duvet dropped down again.

Jimmy opened his eyes, wide awake. "Oooh, nice feet!" he chuckled and then looked at Freddie's mother, "Morning, Mrs Fountain."

"Morning, Jimmy. Did you sleep well with your foot out of the bed?"

Jimmy giggled and pulled his leg back in. "Yes thank you. I'll get Freddie up," he replied and began tickling the feet sticking out of the duvet. The bed suddenly exploded, the duvet flew up to the ceiling and Jimmy fell out of the bed onto the floor. "Oooof!" he cried as Freddie giggled from having his feet tickled.

Freddie sat up in bed just as the levitating duvet came down and formed a wigwam shape with him as the tent pole.

Freddie's mother laughed but rushed to check that Jimmy was not hurt.

"I'm fine, Mrs Fountain. I must remember not to tickle a wizard's feet in the future," he laughed.

"Elephant stampede!" Mr Fountain called on hearing Freddie and Jimmy galloping down the stairs, laughing loudly.

The kitchen door burst open and the two friends made a dramatic entrance.

"Did you know Freddie has ticklish feet, Mr Fountain?" Jimmy chuckled. Before he got an answer, Jimmy added, "If you tickle his feet it makes the duvet levitate to the ceiling!"

Freddie's mother was chuckling and nodding her head. "Poor Jimmy got thrown out of the bed onto the floor!" she said.

"I'm sorry, Jimmy, I didn't do it on purpose," Freddie apologised.

After breakfast Jimmy looked at Freddie. "I guess it's time to make me forget about yesterday. It's a shame but I would not want to put the Elfins in danger by accident," Jimmy admitted. "How do we do this then?" he asked.

Freddie clicked his finger and thumb.

Jimmy sat upright for a moment then began laughing.

"What's so funny, Jimmy?" Mrs Fountain asked.

"Oh, just waking up this morning and seeing a pair of feet on the pillow," Jimmy laughed.

"Did you enjoy yesterday, Jimmy?" Mr Fountain asked, fishing to see if the memory wipe had worked.

"Oh yes, I had forgotten how much fun playing in the forest can be, I even fooled Freddie into thinking a tree was talking to him. Did you know that the forest and village are named after some mythical creatures called Elfins? We never saw any though, I guess they never really existed," Jimmy replied cheerfully.

* *

Nix had slept the rest of the day and through the night, then woke up just as dawn was breaking. A Blackbird in the mouth of the cave was singing its cheerful song. Nix stretched and yawned then made his way to the entrance of the cave causing the Blackbird to fly off, chattering loudly.

"Ooops!" he chuckled. "Sorry little bird, didn't mean to scare you!" he called. He looked around and smiled, the landscape was much like he remembered, rolling hills, lots of trees, bushes, meadows and the sound of a stream not too far away. "This feels like home, perhaps I'll stay a while."

But he could feel the pull of magic on him once again now that he was wide awake and now it felt even stronger.

"These monsters have nests everywhere, this land is a horrible place now, what can the Great Wizards be doing? Why don't they vanquish these monsters? Why hasn't Merlin done anything either?"

He felt angry that the beautiful, tranquil lands of the supernaturals had been invaded and the Wizards had let them do so. He decided to avoid the monsters in their nests, it was too tiring to fight them all the time and there were just too many. He planned to go around any nests he came across believing it was only a matter of time before one of the monsters caught him, after all, he had rather made his presence known. He much preferred the quiet open countryside and it was not too long on his journey before he came across a lovely big lake. It was a while since he had been in the water and had a swim, so he dived into the lake, morphing into his Merman form. Nix felt relaxed while swimming around, leaping out of the water and diving back, it was so much fun, but he missed his brothers and sisters, they had always had fun together. It was only then he realised that he was completely alone in the water. *'Where are the fish?'* he thought, *'no little ones and definitely no big ones. Surely, wherever there is water it is home to lots of creatures.'*

He swam down to the bottom of the lake and came across a strange layer of the blackest of black. *'What is this? Never before have I seen such a thing,'* he was thinking to himself, both puzzled and curious. Floating just above the blackness that seemed to rise and fall very slowly, mesmerizing him. He reached out with his hand to touch the blackness, his fingers just vanished like they had been chopped off and he screamed a bubbly cry, pulling his hand away and shooting for the surface. He shot out of the lake a couple of metres in the air before descending back into the water where he trembled, fearful to look at his hand.

"Whoopee!" he cried, seeing that his fingers were still there, but the blackness remained on them. He could still feel his fingers and wiggle them but could not see them through the blackness. "What magic is this?" he barked, shaking his hand to remove the blackness, but it remained. Nix swam to shore and morphed into his biped form, then using his magic made the blackness disappear.

"These monsters have some strange magic of their own. Maybe the blackness is a portal through which they had come into our land, maybe it's so well hidden that the Wizards cannot find it. That has to be the reason there are so many of them!" Again, Nix was pleased with himself for working things out. His attention was attracted to a familiar noise on the other side of the lake, it was the sound like the monsters made. He looked and noticed an odd shaped monster arrive right up to the edge of the lake. This particular monster had a big round, shiny belly and Nix watched one of the tall 'Children' creatures pull out a long pipe. The 'Children' creature fastened the pipe to the monster's belly, from which the black darkness gushed into the lake. "These monsters must have enslaved 'Children' creatures to fortify their portal with more blackness!" Nix said to himself.

He decided to swim over and take a closer look. Turning himself invisible, he swam quite close to the noisy monster and watched the tall 'Children' creature, who looked nervous and shifty, like he was afraid.

"That must be a special monster forcing that 'Children' creature to do its bidding," Nix whispered to himself. "It has a tattoo on its shiny belly. That's strange, it's not pictures or symbols, let's see, it says 'Was teC hem icals.' That makes no sense!" he said out aloud then covered his mouth as the 'Children' creature suddenly looked in his direction. He tried again to read the symbols. "Waste Chemicals, whatever that means?" He morphed to his biped form and quietly climbed out of the water close to the monster. This was his chance to ruin the monster's gateway into this land that belonged to the supernaturals. Nix used his magic to create his special dagger again then crept silently up to the noisy monster and stabbed one of its large feet. When he pulled his dagger out the escaping air almost blew him off his feet, then quick as lightening he whizzed around the monster stabbing all its feet. "Ha, ha, that'll teach you!" he cried out. Then he stabbed the monster's shiny belly, it took several blows to pierce the hard shell and from the holes he made, the liquid blackness poured out and seemed to make the ground disappear.

The tall 'Children' creature rushed round the side of the monster, saw holes just appearing by themselves and the black chemical gushing out.

Suddenly Nix's dagger caused a spark and the black stuff burst into flames and the tall 'Children' creature cried out and ran away, as did Nix. "That's good, the tall 'Children' creature is free now," he said with satisfaction as the monster suddenly exploded, shooting flames high in the air.

Nix had actually come across a tanker, illegally discharging dangerous and highly flammable chemical waste into the lake. What he thought to be a portal was a deep layer of heavy chemical waste that had polluted the lake water and killed all the fish and other life. He had inadvertently stopped something that was dangerous and unfriendly to the environment.

"These monsters are really evil, that portal liquid was quite stinky too, no wonder there are no fish in the lake," Nix concluded. He ran away as fast as his legs could carry him, fearful of more monsters appearing to see what had happened, he had no intention of being caught.

After an hour or so he stopped for a rest against a strange grass covered mound, which was very long and flat on the top. Water nymphs are curious creatures and Nix was no different, so he climbed up the mound, it was only two or three metres tall. When he reached the top, he looked both ways and it seemed to go on forever one way and curve off to the right the other way. He rubbed his chin thoughtfully. On top of this long mound were two long, thin, smooth and shiny poles. "Funny! What use are ladders laid down on the ground?" he mumbled to himself scratching his head. When he bent down and touched the shiny bits they felt cold and hard, not like wood at all.

Nix had come across a railway embankment and was looking at the railway tracks fixed to wooden sleepers, which looked like ladders to him. This was something completely strange to him and he had no idea what it was. In his world ladders were used to climb into the trees and he could not understand why they would be laid on the ground and be so long.

When he put his hand on the rails, they were indeed cold but he could also feel a strange vibration. "Are these things alive and trembling?" he said scratching his head again. Then he noticed some puffs of smoke in the distance and heard a terrible screeching sound.

Nix had no idea that a steam locomotive with open carriages carrying holidaymakers was heading his way. He stood on the wooden sleepers between the metal rails and watched, fascinated, wondering what it all could mean. The steam train quickly got closer to him and now he could see the outline of it on the curved stretch of the track. "It's a monster snake of some kind. I can see lots of 'Children' creatures and they're flinging their arms about and shouting. Oh, goodness! It must be another kind of monster taking 'Children' creatures to its nest! I have to stop it!" Nix declared. He was much closer to Freddie now and as a result his magic was even stronger as he fed off Freddie's power. He put both hands in front of him and cried,

"STOP!"

The tracks and sleepers in front of him lifted up in the air and curled over on themselves, twisting out of shape. Then he ran down the embankment and well out of the way.

The steam train driver did not see the twisted tracks until it was too late and even though he pulled on the brakes, the train careered into the screwed up tracks and veered off down the embankment pulling the coaches with it. The train and coaches rolled down the embankment, plunging into the soft ground at the bottom and came to a stop. The train engine blew steam from cracks appearing in the round body, the passengers were screaming and scrambling out of the carriages, crawling and falling over each other. The train engine puffed and wheezed, then suddenly exploded with blasts of steam and flames shooting into the air. The sight was scary but the horrendous noise frightened Nix who ran to hide behind a large oak tree.

Passengers were screaming, some had been thrown out of the carriages as they rolled down the embankment. The rest were running away from the train wreck as fast as they could. By some miracle everyone survived, a few had minor cuts and bruises, no one was seriously hurt, even the train crew had managed to jump to safety, but everywhere there was pandemonium.

Nix looked on clapping his hands. "Oooo, goodie! All those 'Children' creatures are free and running off home. Look! Look! They're so happy, jumping up and down and shouting." He was seeing what he wanted to see. "Clever Nix," he said to himself, "that's another monster dealt with, they won't be taking any prisoners to their nest like that for a long while!"

Believing he had done a good deed saving lots and lots of 'Children' creatures, he ran off in the direction the magic was pulling him, which felt even stronger now.

**

Jimmy and Freddie spent the day together and Jimmy was none the wiser about meeting the Elfins, so Freddie did not have to worry about their secret slipping out by accident. They spent the morning in the park just sitting on the swings and chatting. Strictly speaking, both Freddie and Jimmy were now too old to use the equipment, but then there was no one else wanting to use it and they had no desire to climb up the climbing frame or use the slide.

Freddie reached into his rucksack and pulled out a bright yellow Frisbee for them to amuse themselves with on the nicely cut lawns away from the swings.

"I'm sure that's a magic rucksack, Freddie, you seem to have everything everyone needs just at the right time!" Jimmy chuckled, not quite realising how close to the truth he actually was.

They both ran far enough away from the swings to play with the Frisbee.

"You throw first!" Freddie shouted, running off and distracting Jimmy from thinking about his rucksack and magic.

Jimmy's first attempt landed a few metres from Freddie, who ran and picked up the Frisbee then flung it in the air. A gust of wind caught it and took the Frisbee, curling around behind Jimmy, sweeping back to land almost at his feet.

"Aww, you're showing off, Freddie!" Jimmy shouted and laughed, then launched the yellow disc low to the ground towards Freddie. It hovered just above the grass until it was half way then suddenly lifted into the air, performed a somersault and sailed straight to Freddie, who caught it in his hands.

"Oh, that was epic, Jimmy!" Freddie cried, amazed at the acrobatics.

The two friends played with the Frisbee for almost an hour before packing up and going back to Freddie's home. They had lunch together with Freddie's mother. Jimmy really liked her, she always made him feel at home and she was kind and thoughtful. He liked his own mum as well of course, but Mr and Mrs Fountain always made him feel special, he did not know why, but Freddie's parents knew exactly how special and important Jimmy was. The afternoon was spent studying, the school had given all the students plenty of work to do, but Freddie and Jimmy sailed through it all during the afternoon.

"This is so much more interesting and fun too, than studying on my own," Jimmy said as they had a break to polish off the snacks Freddie's mother had brought for them.

"You're right, Jimmy, maybe we should do this more often. I have enjoyed spending time with you and studying together."

Jimmy returned home after enjoying tea with Freddie and his parents.

The school had informed the students it was safe to return tomorrow.

"You seem happier when Jimmy is here, Freddie," his mother said to him in the evening.

"Mmm, it would be nice to have a brother around, it does get lonely sometimes," he replied.

"You can invite any of your friends for tea or sleepover at any time, son. Your mother and I are more than happy and they're all nice kids. We haven't seen Billy in a while, perhaps you could invite him over some time," Freddie's father suggested.

Freddie hugged his father and mother. "You know my friends all love you, they tell me quite often they wished you were their parents, so you must be doing a good job," he replied.

The next morning Freddie met up with all his friends from the village on the school bus.

"Did you hear about that train crash on the preserved scenic railway?" William asked Freddie and Jimmy.

"Oh! Where was that? Anywhere close?" Jimmy asked.

"About a hundred miles away, so not that far really," William replied.

"Was anyone hurt?" Freddie asked, having a bad feeling about this.

"That's the amazing thing, a lot of people had scratches and bruises, but no one was seriously hurt. Where have you two been, it's all over the news?" William replied.

"We were studying together in Freddie's bedroom so we didn't watch the TV," Jimmy replied looking at Freddie with a smile.

"Did it say on the news what had happened?" Freddie asked.

"They did and showed lots of pictures and the very strange thing is that the railway tracks were all twisted and rolled up, like Superman might have done." William giggled at the thought.

Alarm bells were ringing in Freddie's mind. *'Could this be Nix?'* he was thinking.

The Merlin ring spoke to Freddie as if answering his thought. *'Magic was certainly used, Freddie, this most likely is Nix.'*

During his lunch break Freddie imagiported to visit the Tiggly's and on a map that Freddie pulled out of his rucksack they plotted the possible events linked to Nix. From the caravan site, to the town of Goul and then the train derailment. A pattern was emerging.

"Looks like he did not travel over the Umber Bridge, but went upstream for an easier route," Daddly surmised.

"Well I think we can safely say the destruction in Goul town was Nix, but his magic seems to be getting stronger," Wiggly said.

"There's a chance that your magic is drawing him to you, Freddie, but also feeding his magic making it stronger, hence all the damage," Daddly replied. "It may have been unintentional if Nix did not realise his magic was becoming more powerful."

"If we ignore Goul town and draw a straight line from the caravan park, through the train accident, look where it ends," Mummly said.

"Here!" Giggly exclaimed, suddenly looking fearful. "He's definitely coming here!"

"You have no need to worry, Giggly, he cannot pass through the strengthened enchantment around the town and he can't get into the village, so he will just have to find me. It doesn't look like he is too far away. I just hope no one gets hurt on the way!" Freddie explained.

The news channels and papers were still full of the train crash the following morning. It was Friday, the end of the school week and

537

first lesson of the day was double maths. Freddie liked all his subjects, but maths was his favourite. During the morning break he was sitting at one of the picnic tables with some of his friends chatting when there was a commotion at the front of the school. Children being children, most of them ran to investigate what all the noise and shouting was about.

The staff car park was located at the front of the school and was out of bounds to pupils, but as it bordered on the edge of the playing fields hundreds of students had gathered to stand and watch.

Suddenly, one of the staff cars leapt into the air and crashed down on top of another car making a terrible din. Some of the students screamed and ran off, while teachers began pouring out of the school's main entrance. Another car flew into the air and crashed down on two other cars with a metal tearing and glass-breaking din, then burst into flames. One teacher rushed to the students and told them to run off to safety with many running for their lives.

"Come on, Freddie, you can't Fixit this time. Let's get out of here!" Billy implored.

"Look!" Jimmy cried.

"That's ridiculous. It can't be can it?" William said.

Freddie stood his ground, he knew it had to be Nix and fished out the magic seeing spectacles. "You guys go! Go! Get safe! I'll be okay!" Freddie used his magical, commanding voice and everyone had to obey and ran off without arguing. Now Freddie could get to work and he sent a mental message to the teachers to go back inside, again they all obeyed. Next he created an avatar of Merlin who began to walk into the car park.

"NIX! Stop this now!" Merlin's voice was deep and powerful, all supernatural beings had to obey.

Nix was no exception and he immediately stopped and turned towards Freddie's avatar of Merlin. He called out to the Wizard. "Merlin, I have answered your call, but our land is overrun by monsters consuming these 'Children' creatures," he replied.

"Nix! Come!" Merlin commanded and Nix ran to him and knelt before him.

"Show yourself, Nix!" Merlin commanded and Nix made himself visible.

Freddie stood alone on the edge of the car park, controlling his avatar.

"Rise up, Nix, and take my hand!" Merlin commanded.

Freddie imagiported himself, his Merlin avatar and Nix to the Tiggly's seating area in their home.

"Daddly, Mummly, Wiggly and Giggly were sitting at the big table in the middle of the house, playing a game of 'Snap Dragon,' when three figures suddenly appeared.

"Merlin!" Giggly and Wiggly cried out in surprise together on seeing the tall figure of the Great Wizard. They were sitting facing Mummly and Daddly at the table and had a clear view.

Mummly and Daddly turned around quickly to see the tall, imposing figure of Merlin with his head touching the ceiling.

"Freddie!" Daddly called out and Freddie, Nix and Merlin looked over to him.

Freddie let go of his Merlin Avatar, who just vanished into thin air.

Nix was startled and suddenly disappeared.

Freddie spoke with Merlin's commanding voice. "Nix, show yourself!"

Nix had no choice but to obey Merlin's command even though he could no longer see his master. An aura appeared around the small figure of Nix, which he had created in an instinctive protective move. "What is this? Where is Merlin? Who are you 'Children' creatures?" Nix spoke with a wobbly voice, looking around his surroundings, spotting the Tiggly's, who were still gawping at Freddie and Nix.

"Do not worry, Nix, you are safe. It is my magic that has awoken you and drawn you to me," Freddie explained in his own voice.

"But you are a 'Children' creature. How can you have magic? Only supernaturals have magic," Nix said timidly.

Freddie waved his hand over Nix's aura and it disappeared.

Nix gasped. "How is that possible?" he cried, turning invisible again. Freddie could still see Nix because he was still wearing the magic detecting spectacles. He took hold of Nix's hand gently.

Nix spoke again, feeling completely confused. "How can you see me? This is not possible. Even Merlin cannot see me when I'm invisible."

Freddie used his magic to turn Nix visible again.

"No, no, this cannot be!" Nix shivered, fearful of this powerful 'Children' creature.

Daddly and Mummly walked over to Nix and Mummly took his other hand.

"You have no need to be afraid, Nix, you are among friends here. Merlin created us, we are Elfins and Freddie here is Merlin's advocate. Come, sit down with us and we will explain everything to you. We know this is a shock, but you are safe," Mummly said comfortingly.

Nix sat down on the comfy sofa with Mummly and Daddly either side of him. Daddly waved to Wiggly and Giggly to come over and sit down, Freddie sat opposite Nix who was far from settled.

"Freddie here is a Sproggle, not a 'Children' creature as you thought. His coming was foretold a millennium ago. He is even greater than Merlin with his magic. Listen to him, Nix," Daddly explained.

Freddie took off the spectacles and gave Nix a smile, radiating waves of magical calm to the frightened Prince of Water Nymphs.

Nix sighed and his muscles relaxed, at long last he felt at ease with himself and gave Freddie a smile.

Giggly sighed. "You are so cute when you smile, Nix."

Wiggly gave her a nudge to be quiet.

But Nix turned his smile on her and she blushed.

"Nix, we believe that you think this land, your land of long ago, is infested with monsters, that's why you have been destroying them," Freddie said.

"Yes, yes! I can feel your magic, Freddie, it is very powerful." He jumped off the sofa and knelt in front of Freddie. "I am your servant, master Freddie," he said calmly.

"Thank you, Nix, please get up off your knees now and sit down on the comfy chair."

Nix looked up and did as Freddie had commanded of him.

"Let me explain, Nix. When the great Wizards defeated the Trolls, they managed to entomb the Beastrolls too, but sadly all the supernaturals had been vanquished. The great Wizards gave up their magic to Merlin, who created the Elfins here to help and serve him. Human Kind like me, Sproggles, as the Elfins call us, soon overran this land and Merlin made this underground town for his Elfins to live in safety. Merlin has gone into hibernation, just like you were, and managed to save a thousand Fairies who are also in hibernation hidden away in the crystal cavern. It is my mission to ready this world for his return, to do that I have been chosen to be the most powerful of all wizards. Nix, you cannot live among the Sproggles, they must not yet know of the existence of magic and supernaturals, it is not yet time and they are not ready. You can stay underground with the Elfins, I know they would make you very welcome, or you can go back into hibernation," Freddie explained as kindly as he could.

"No, please! I cannot go back into hibernation, even though I sleep, I am partly awake and it is so very lonely. But I cannot live under the ground, I am a water nymph, I must have rivers, lakes and oceans to roam in."

Nix posed a problem and it worried Freddie, he had no idea what to do with him.

Daddly walked over to Freddie and whispered in his ear, but Nix, with his enhanced hearing, heard what was said.

"Yes, yes, let us do this thing that Daddly suggests!" he cried.

Freddie looked doubtful. "If we do this you can never go back," he warned Nix.

"Yes, but it is the best option. I cannot live alone again nor live underground, all friends and family are gone, there is nothing left for me in this world. Please, Freddie, let's do this, please!" Nix pleaded.

Daddly sat down and held Nix's hand. "Are you absolutely sure, Nix? Like Freddie said, it's a one way trip, there will be no going back, ever." His words were meant kindly, but as a warning at the same time.

Wiggly, Giggly and Mummly were curious. "What is this solution? What is going to happen to Nix?" Giggly blurted out.

Daddly looked at his children and explained. "Freddie will take away Nix's magic and because he is a morphical supernatural, Freddie can transform him into a Sproggle child, then take away all his water nymph memories and give him new Sproggle memories so that he can live above ground."

"You can do all that?" Wiggly asked, still amazed at how powerful Freddie's magic was.

"Yes, Wiggly, think about it, Merlin was able to create all you Elfins and I am able to call upon magic even greater than his," Freddie explained. "Nix, you can change your mind now, but once you become a Sproggle you will be mortal and live only for a hundred years, maybe less. Are you sure this is what you want?"

Nix smiled at Freddie and nodded enthusiastically.

Freddie stood up and held out his hands. "Come to me, Nix, and take my hands in your hands."

Nix stood up and walked over to Freddie, placing their hands together.

"Now, close your eyes," Freddie said, then gave him a command. "Sleep!" A glowing ruby aura began to form around Freddie and Nix, which cocooned them like they were inside a crimson egg. Freddie closed his eyes and commanded magic to do his bidding. A swirling storm seemed to engulf the two figures inside the crimson egg until they could no longer be seen inside. The magic Nix once commanded drifted from him, the scales that covered his body slid from him leaving his skin pink, smooth and unblemished, his eternal life disappeared leaving him mortal. When all this had been accomplished the swirling mist within the crimson egg slowed and disappeared, then the ruby aura melted away leaving Freddie holding the hands of a ten year old Sproggle boy. Freddie had clothed him in blue shorts and white tee shirt and wearing white sandals. "Open your eyes, Nix," Freddie said.

Nix slowly opened his big, beautiful blue eyes and looked at Freddie. He still had his Prince of Water Nymph memories and he had a puzzled expression. "I am the same, Freddie," he said.

Freddie created a full-length mirror for him to see the changes.

"Oh! Oh! Is that really me?" Nix exclaimed, touching his arms and legs. "My beautiful scales are all gone!" he cried.

His concern caused a little chuckle and Freddie put his hand on Nix's shoulder. "Don't worry, Nix, soon you won't remember ever being a water nymph and I promise you will be happy and have lots of friends, you'll never be lonely again."

Giggly jumped up and put her arm around Nix. "Look at you, Nix, you are totally cute with your curly blond hair and big blue eyes. You're so cute I could eat you all up!" she said excitedly.

"Oh no, please don't eat me, I'll taste horrible. Really I will!" Nix cried, jumping behind Freddie.

"It's alright, Nix, Giggly doesn't actually mean she is going to eat you, it's just an expression to tell you how handsome you are," Freddie explained. "Now it's time for you to say goodbye to everyone, and time to meet your new parents and brother," Freddie said making the mirror vanish.

Nix gave everyone a hug and thanked them.

"Am I really going to have a brother and a mother and father?" Nix asked. The idea pleased him more than anything. Giggly gave Nix a big hug and kissed him on the cheek.

"Eeeek!" he cried, "she's trying to eat me, Freddie!"

Everyone laughed and Freddie explained it was a kiss, which only special people received and it made Nix feel better.

Wiggly gave Nix a hug and said goodbye.

"What, no kiss?" Nix said looking disappointed.

Wiggly chuckled and kissed Nix's cheek. "Boys don't usually kiss boys, but it's not wrong or anything," he explained.

Mummly and Daddly hugged Nix too and Mummly kissed him and Daddly tussled his hair.

"It's time, Nix, take my hand," Freddie said and imagiported them into the kitchen of his parent's house, where his mother and father were sitting at the table chatting.

"Freddie, you're back," his mother said, smiling.

"And who's this handsome young man?" his father asked.

"Mum, Dad, this is Nix. Nix, this is Mr and Mrs Fountain, my father and mother, say hello," Freddie introduced.

Nix held out his arms expecting a cuddle and a kiss.

Freddie's mother instantly understood and walked over to him and took him in her arms. "Welcome, Nix, you're quite adorable," she said and kissed him on the cheek. That made Nix beam and Freddie's mother's heart melted.

Mr Fountain walked around the table to Nix and held out his hand.

Nix understood and reached to take it and they shook gently.

Mr Fountain gave Nix a warm and friendly smile then tussled his hair.

The gesture made Nix feel happy and in return gave Freddie's father a big smile. With his big blue eyes, he looked from Freddie to his mother and then his father. "It's very nice to meet you, I think Freddie is very lucky to have a mother and a father." Nix sounded a little sad. "All my friends and family are long gone now."

Mrs Fountain pulled Nix into a warm cuddle. "We're so sorry, Nix, that can't be nice for you," she said comforting the adorable little boy.

"Shall we go in the sitting room and get comfortable while we sort things out?" Freddie's father suggested.

Nix sat on the sofa close to Freddie, holding onto his hand, while Freddie explained to his parents. "Mum, Dad, with Nix's agreement I have changed him from an immortal water nymph to a mortal ten year old child. Very shortly I will wipe away all his memories and give him new ones."

His parents looked surprised.

"Goodness, Freddie, you have changed him into a little boy, your magic must be incredibly powerful to do something like that," his mother gasped.

"Is there anything you cannot do, son?" his father asked.

"To be honest, Dad, I don't know, the source of magic is limitless and I can call on it all. But I cannot change Nix back to being a water nymph, which was a one way thing. Mum, Dad, I know this is a big ask, but would you be willing ...."

Freddie's mother knew exactly what he was going to ask and interrupted him. "Yes, Freddie, we would be happy to adopt Nix, if that's alright with him?"

Nix looked a little puzzled. "What is adopt?" he asked.

Mr Fountain was also very taken with Nix, the thought of having him as a son made him feel very happy indeed. "It means that Freddie's mother and I will become your parents, if you will have us, that is."

Nix was beaming, he liked that idea. He looked Freddie excitedly. "If your mother and father are mine too..." Nix was working things out in his mind and suddenly burst out, "Hey! That means you will be my brother then, Freddie," he said excitedly.

"That's right, Nix," Freddie chuckled, having happy thoughts of finally having a brother. "Are you ready then, Nix, to become part of the best family in the world?"

Nix nodded excitedly.

"Close your eyes then. When you open them you won't remember being a water nymph."

Freddie's parents watched on in awe of their son's power and his ability at only fourteen years old to remain so level headed.

Freddie turned to face Nix and placed his hands over the blond haired little boy's ears and closed his eyes. In a matter of seconds he took away all Nix's memories of being the Prince of Water Nymphs, of being able to morph from biped to Merman and of having magic. Freddie replaced those memories with those of Mikey Fountain, adopted son who was brought up in an orphanage, never having met his birth parents. Freddie gave him all the knowledge that a ten year old boy would have.

"Wake up, Mikey," Freddie said cheerfully, as if Mikey had just nodded off.

Mikey opened his big, beautiful blue eyes and looked at Freddie, then both Freddie's parents.

"Mikey, meet your new Mum and Dad, Mr and Mrs Fountain, they have agreed to adopt you. Go say hello."

Mikey stood up and walked over to his new mother, who opened her arms and hugged him, kissing his cheek, then Mikey kissed her on the cheek and she was almost in tears. "Welcome, Mikey, call me Mum from now on, okay?"

Mikey looked at his new mother and gave her a heart-melting smile. "Yes, Mum," he said in a creamy voice. He moved towards his new father who also held out his arms and the two hugged.

"We're so happy to have you in our family, Mikey, you can now call me Dad, if that's okay with you?"

Mikey looked up at his father and gave him a big smile and replied, "Thank you, Dad."

Freddie's father turned Mikey around. "Go say hello to Freddie, he's your brother and he will love you just like we do."

Mikey looked at Freddie and something told him that he and Freddie had a special bond and he ran into Freddie's arms.

"We're going to have lots of fun together, Mikey," Freddie said smiling. Now he had a brother like he had always wanted. "You can stay in my room for a while so that you can get used to everything and that will give Mum and Dad time to make your bedroom special for you. Is that okay with you, Mikey?" Freddie asked, tussling his hair, which he liked as it made him feel wanted somehow.

Mikey nodded enthusiastically.

"Come on then, Mikey, let's go upstairs and I will show you around, then we can sort a few clothes out for you until we go shopping to buy you your own clothes."

Mikey took hold of his brother's hand and they galloped up the stairs.

"We certainly do have a herd of elephants in the house now!" Mr Fountain laughed.

Freddie showed Mikey where the bathroom was first of all and explained that their Mum liked them to put the toilet seat down after using it. "It's very important to remember that, Mikey, it's the only thing that seems to upset her, I have no idea why." Next he showed Mikey the airing cupboard where the towels were. "You can have a bath or a shower, I usually have a shower before going to bed, it's quicker when you're feeling a bit tired," Freddie explained. He showed Mikey their parents' bedroom. "It's important to remember to knock on the door and wait for Mum or Dad to tell you to come in, okay?" Freddie explained.

Mikey looked puzzled. "Why is it important and do I knock on all doors to ask if I can come in?"

Freddie chuckled and tussled Mikey's hair. "Our bedrooms are our personal space, so it's polite to knock first. We might be sitting quietly, it would make us jump if someone just rushed in," Freddie tried to explain, being as polite as he could. Next he showed Mikey the room that would be his bedroom.

"Oooh, it's a big room, Freddie. In the orphanage we had to share rooms with three others. So I can really have all this for myself?" Mikey said, enthusiastically.

"That's right, Mikey, Mum and Dad will decorate the walls and change the furniture. I expect they will ask you what sort of things you like, so it's special for you."

Freddie took Mikey into his bedroom.

"Cor! That's a big bed, you could sleep four of us in that!" Mikey exclaimed. "Do I knock on your door to come in, Freddie?"

Again Freddie tussled Mikey's hair and he giggled. "Not while we are sharing this room, but when you have your own room it will be polite to knock, but you can just come in then, no need to wait for me to tell you, but just with my room, okay?"

"Okay, Freddie," Mikey beamed him a smile.

Freddie could see that his brother was going to twist people around his little finger with that smile, especially their grandma. He was cute and funny too, it was going to be great having him around. "Let's see what clothes we can find that fit you," Freddie said walking over to the wardrobe. "I think these pyjamas might fit," he

546

said handing Mikey a pair that he had used his magic to create. "I'll hand you some things and you can put them on the bed."

Mikey was quite excited, he did not have many clothes at the orphanage, at least that was the memory Freddie had given him. Freddie created enough clothes to keep Mikey dressed and tidy for a few days until they went shopping.

Mikey hung on Freddie's every word and already loved his new brother. That night Mikey was allowed to stay up later than normal for a ten year old so that he and Freddie could go to bed at the same time. Freddie wanted to be sure that his brother would have no lingering dreams about him once being a water nymph. When they climbed into Freddie's big bed they talked for a while and giggled until Mikey fell asleep hugging the teddy bear that his brother given to him.

Now Freddie had a brother, he vowed to look after him and protect him.

* *

When Mikey was enrolled at the junior school in Elfington village, his cute looks and charming manner soon made him as popular as Freddie had been at his age. In some mysterious turn of fate Mikey liked helping others, just like his brother and he got a happy feeling from doing so. He had real skill for mending anything broken and soon became known as Mikey Mendit. It gave Freddie a thrill to know that his brother was following on in his footsteps.

CHAPTER TEN

Evil will not Prevail

Billy Bates meets his father again,
but it is not a welcome reunion.

Elfington village and Elfin Town had known peace since Freddie had defeated the Beastrolls. Apart from Freddie's magic awakening Nix, the Prince of Water Nymphs, there had been no further incidents. Freddie and his brother, Mikey, who had once been Nix, had become inseparable. Freddie was proud to show off Mikey to all his friends who were completely won over by his charm, especially the girls, who found his beaming smile irresistible. Mikey attended school in the village and soon became popular, just like Freddie had been when he attended Elfington Junior School.

Freddie and his friends had sailed through Grammar school. Their special class of ten students had attained top grades in their CE 'O' Level exams in the summer of their third year. The merging of Freddie and Merlin to defeat the Beastrolls had left him with a genius level of intelligence. He was still the same caring, helpful person he had always been, helping everyone and anyone where he saw the need. He used his magic sparingly, but wisely, where it did the most good in helping others. True to his selfless nature he did not use his magic to improve his own life, although by helping others it helped him too, making him feel happy and contented. Those he helped who were not already his friends saw him as a good and kind person they wanted to be friends with. Aware that directly helping people was drawing more and more attention to himself, he began using his magic remotely to solve problems that seemed to constantly throw themselves in his direction.

Freddie's genius I.Q. had been the inspiration for the school to create a special class for students to advance their learning. Among the ten were all his school friends from the village and Billy Bates. Somehow the Beastrolls invasion had caused all the children affected to become cleverer. They had all done well in their CE 'O' Level exams, especially Freddie, who had achieved straight A's in twelve subjects including Frensh, Germun and Spinnish. His thirst for knowledge seemed limitless and he had learned to play the piano and passed the top grade within a year. He still liked to play the guitar, but had surpassed his teacher, James, and Freddie could regale one and all in classical music.

Throughout this time he never forgot the place where he felt more at home than anywhere else, Elfin Town. Two or three times a week he would lock himself in a toilet cubicle during his school lunch time and imagiport himself to the Tiggly's home and enjoy lunch with them. Giggly had fallen hopelessly in love with Freddie, he was growing towards being the very handsome twenty year old he had transformed into to defeat the Beastrolls.

"Freddie, you grow more handsome every day," Giggly would tell him, she loved to see him blush. But as a fifteen year old Freddie seemed to have outgrown that embarrassing habit.

"You, too, are growing into a fine young Elfin woman," he would tell her, he meant every word and she would giggle with her own embarrassment.

Mummly and Daddly would kindly remind her of Freddie's mission in life and she should not get too attached to him. A union between her and Freddie would never be possible. She knew it and he knew it.

Mikey was keen to spend as much time with his brother as he could, his love and admiration for Freddie made them both very happy. Mikey enjoyed hearing how Freddie had helped his friends and the villagers in the past and regaled his brother with his own tales of helping others. It made Freddie feel so proud of Mikey, who frequently liked to spend the night with him, they would talk and giggle until Mikey fell asleep.

"Mum, Dad, I was thinking of giving my magic rucksack to Mikey, so he can help others like I used to do. What do you think?" Freddie had taken an opportunity to talk to his parents while Mikey was having a sleepover with one of his school friends.

"It's quite a responsibility for Mikey, but he is the same age as you were when it was gifted to you by Daddly," his mother replied.

"Mikey has shown us in so many ways that he is kind and caring, just like his brother has always been. I think he can be trusted to keep the secret about it being magic, but you might have to be prepared to disclose how it came to be magical and maybe trust him to meet the Elfins and know who you really are," his father explained.

Freddie looked thoughtful. "It would be nice to share who I am with Mikey like I have with you both. I guess he would be really hurt if he discovered I am not who he thought I was. I would hate to hurt him, I have grown to love him so much, just like everyone who meets him."

His mother put her arm around her son. "You've grown up so much, Freddie, you're as tall as me now," she smiled. "If things did not turn out as you hoped by telling Mikey everything, could you use your magic to reverse things back?"

Freddie looked at his mother and gave her a huge smile. "Of course, I didn't think of that. I hope it doesn't come to that, but it would solve a difficult situation. Thank you, Mum, and you too, Dad, I really do have the best parents."

"I'm going to pick Mikey up from his friend's after dinner today, why not take the opportunity this afternoon, I'm sure he will be excited and able to keep your secret safe," his father suggested.

* *

"What's going on, Dad?" Mikey asked as he was ushered into the sitting room where Freddie and their mother were waiting.

"Freddie has something to give you and to explain a few things, come on, rascal," his father chuckled at Mikey's excitement.

The moment Mikey saw Freddie he ran to him and hugged his brother. "What have you got for me, Freddie?" he asked eagerly.

"Come sit with me, I want to show you something," Freddie replied lifting his rucksack from behind the sofa.

"That's your favourite rucksack, Freddie, you never go anywhere without it," Mikey said looking a little puzzled.

"That's right," Freddie replied. "Think of something small that you could hold in your hand," he added.

"Huh, oh, erm, an apple!" Mikey answered, his eyes shining with excitement.

Freddie unzipped his rucksack and reached inside, pulling out a rosy red apple. "Like this one," he said.

Mikey's eyes lit up and a huge smile appeared on his face. "How did you know I was going to say an apple, did you put it in there before I came home? You did, didn't you? Ha, ha, ha, ha."

Their mother and father were chuckling away, something about Mikey's happiness was so infectious, he made everyone laugh with him.

"Watch." Freddie chuckled and put the apple back into his rucksack, then handed it to Mikey. "See if you can find the apple in my rucksack, you saw me put it inside."

Mikey chuckled. "Easy peasy," he replied and put his hand inside the open rucksack and felt around. A puzzled expression appeared on his face and he looked at Freddie.

Their parents could not contain their amusement and were giggling away watching their young son.

Mikey pulled his hand out and looked suspiciously at Freddie. "It's a magic trick like the wonky wand, isn't it? That's so clever, but where did the apple go?"

Freddie put his hand inside the bag and pulled out the apple once more, holding it up for Mikey to see. "It was in there all the time," Freddie said with a smile on his face.

Mikey jumped up and clapped his hands he was so excited. "Show me how you did it, Freddie, that's so clever. I've got a magician for a brother. Yay!"

"Stop teasing him, Freddie, and explain things to Mikey now before he gets too excited," their mother implored.

"Okay, come sit and I'll tell you everything," Freddie replied as his brother sat and hung on his every word. "This rucksack is magical, anything I think of, I can pull out of it. Before you say anything, let me show you. You felt around inside and it was empty, right?"

Mikey nodded his head with a puzzled expression on his face.

Freddie reached inside the rucksack and pulled out a torch, then a wooden ruler followed by a book almost as big as the bag.

Mikey's mouth fell open in surprise.

Freddie put everything back in the rucksack and gave it back to his brother, "Have a look, Mikey and you'll see the rucksack is empty."

Mikey pulled the rucksack wide open and looked inside, then at Freddie. He put both hands inside and fumbled around, then looked at his brother again. "How did you do that, Freddie? Are you a real magician with real magic?"

"Yes, Mikey, I'm a wizard with very powerful magic. Mum and Dad think you are old enough to keep my secret, do you think you can?" Freddie asked hopefully.

"I'll do whatever you want me to do, Freddie. This is all a trick, though, isn't it? It's not real. I mean magic isn't real is it?" Mikey replied looking more than a little baffled.

"Freddie thought you would be hurt and upset if one day you discovered who he really is, that's why he is telling you now, Mikey," his mother explained.

Freddie sent a telepathic message to Wiggly and his family. *'I'm bringing Mum, Dad and Mikey to see you all, I've just explained I'm a wizard and he's finding it hard to understand.'*

"Okay, Mikey, there's more, lots more. I think it's time for you to meet Wiggly. Ready, Mum, Dad? Hold my hand, we'll go on a trip to see my special friends."

In the blink of an eye, Freddie, Mikey and their parents appeared in the Tiggly's home, next to the big table in the middle of the house.

"Freddie!" Wiggly called out and rushed to meet his best friend.

Mikey looked fearful seeing a strange boy running towards them and in a strange place. "Freddie, I'm scared!" he cried and slipped behind his brother, holding tightly around his waist.

"It's alright, Mikey, you're perfectly safe. I used my magic to bring us to meet my best friend and his family, they are a bit different from us, but you have nothing to fear. Come out and say hello," Freddie explained, calming his brother.

Mikey crept around to stand at Freddie's side and his mother moved round to hug him as well.

They all sat down in comfy chairs, with Mikey next to Freddie on a comfy sofa.

"Mikey, I want you to meet Mummly first of all. Mummly, this is my brother, Mikey. Say hello, Mikey." Freddie's voice was soft and soothing.

Mummly stood up and approached Mikey holding out her hand. "It's nice to finally meet you, Freddie talks about you all the time. He's very proud of you," she said.

Mikey automatically reached out to shake hands. "Hello," he said nervously. "He does? He is?" Mikey mumbled with a slight smile appearing on his face. As Mummly sat down again Mikey looked at his brother.

"Mikey, meet Daddly, he is the head of this family like our Dad is of ours, say hello."

Daddly stood and offered his hand. "We are all pleased to meet you, it's time you got to know who your brother really is, a hero," Daddly said.

Mikey shook Daddly's hand and this time a bigger smile appeared on his face. "Yes, he is my hero, he helps lots of people," he replied as Daddly returned to his comfy chair.

"Now, Mikey, I want you to meet my best friend Wiggly and his sister Giggly, say hello." Freddie introduced his friends to Mikey.

Wiggly reached out and shook Mikey's extended hand. "We love Freddie so much, and I know we are going to love you just as much."

Giggly eased her brother out of the way and launched herself at Mikey hugging him while saying, "I'm Giggly, Mikey, and you are so cute. You have lovely eyes, I bet you have lots of friends too?" she chuckled.

Mikey looked at Giggly and they just seemed to bond, she squeezed herself next to him and they held hands. He was feeling all warm and happy now, the sense of fear had left him completely.

Between the Tiggly's, Freddie and Mikey's parents, they explained everything about Freddie, leaving out anything to do with Nix and those adventures.

Mikey looked at Freddie in complete awe and for a few moments just stared at him before giving him a big hug. "So, you really are a wizard, Freddie. I know why everyone likes you so much, you're amazing, I'm so lucky to have you as my brother and I have

Mum and Dad too. This is all so fantastic, it's hard to believe. I'm not dreaming, am I?"

"No, Mikey, it's all real and from now on you can visit this place, called Elfin Town, with me when I come to visit. Would you like that?"

Mikey beamed with excitement. "I would, that will be so amazing, wait till I tell my friends that my brother is a wizard!" he cried.

There was a deathly silence and Mikey looked around a little mystified. "What's wrong?"

"We have to keep all this a big secret, Mikey," his father began to explain. "If humans ever discover the Elfins they would dig their way into the town and take them away to experiment on them. If they discover Freddie has powerful magic, they will want him. That will mean you, me and your mother will not be safe, either. No one must ever find out. If you think it's too big a secret to keep, then Freddie can take away all these memories and you will forget everything about him being a wizard, his magic and Elfin Town."

All eyes were on Mikey, he pulled close to Freddie and looked at his brother with big blue eyes. "I can do it, Freddie, I don't want to forget what an even more amazing brother I have. I can keep your secret, really I can," he implored.

Freddie looked at his brother's cute face and believed that Mikey could keep his secret, after all, he had been Mikey's age when he discovered the Elfins. "I know you can, Mikey, and I don't want to hide anything from you, you are my brother and I trust you to keep everyone safe, just as I did when I was your age."

"That's settled then. I'll make a nice pot of dandelion tea," Mummly announced.

While Freddie and Wiggly were engrossed in conversation, so were Giggly and Mikey. Both sets of parents were also chatting to each other, there were always a lot of things to catch up with when they all got together.

"Can I take Mikey to meet some other Elfins and play in the park for a while?" Giggly asked while Mikey was nodding excitedly.

Mr and Mrs Fountain were also nodding. "I think that would be a lovely idea, Giggly," Mrs Fountain replied.

No sooner agreed than Giggly was leading Mikey, hand in hand, out through the door and off towards the park and more Elfin children.

"Let's pay a visit to Merlin's library, Wiggly, while our parents talk to catch up with all their news," Freddie suggested. Wiggly was more than keen and Freddie imagiported them into Merlin's laboratory and library. "I think it's time we cleaned Merlin's library, don't you, Wiggly?" Freddie said smiling to himself.

"But that would take hours and hours and be so messy, Freddie," Wiggly resisted.

"Not necessarily," Freddie replied. "I could just do this." Freddie snapped his fingers and in an instant everywhere was dust free, equipment stacked neatly, all the books turned with the spines facing outwards again.

"Wow, Freddie, you're amazing, that's the quickest tidy up I've ever seen. Don't tell Mummly though, otherwise she'll have you cleaning the house from top to bottom!" Wiggly chuckled, looking admiringly at his brilliant friend.

They scrambled up the staircase to the gallery library and began looking through the books.

"Look, Wiggly," Freddie cried with a smile. "I understand all of this now, this is an incantation to summon a time vortex!" What was once a foreign language now made sense to Freddie.

Wiggly got very excited, then suddenly froze on the spot.

"What's the matter, Wiggly?"

Freddie's very best friend slowly turned to look at him. "I just remembered how those horrible time thieves attacked me from the time vortex!" Wiggly shuddered.

Freddie wrapped his arm around Wiggly's shoulder comfortingly. "It was horrible at the time and we also lost Grundly," he said with sadness in his voice.

Seeing Freddie's expression, Wiggly chirped, "But we saw the miracle of rebirth and baby Grundly!"

Freddie's eyes lit up as his mood was lifted with that wonderful memory.

"Oh gosh, Freddie, what's happening?" Wiggly exclaimed in a high-pitched voice.

Both he and Freddie were no longer standing on the gallery floor, but hovering ten centimetres above it. Around them books were floating, moving around and slowly colliding.

Freddie laughed and Wiggly did too.

"Your magic is so incredible, Freddie! How do you not use it all the time?"

Freddie snapped his fingers and they settled back down again to the floor. The books whizzed around slotting themselves back on the bookshelves.

"The Merlin ring." Freddie showed Wiggly his finger on which he wore the ring.

"It's no good, Freddie, you know I can't see it!" Wiggly giggled.

Freddie whispered something that his friend could not hear properly.

Then suddenly Wiggly declared, "Oh, I see it now, Freddie, it's so beautiful!"

"It keeps me grounded, Wiggly," Freddie explained. "Sometimes I'm tempted to use magic more often, but this ring speaks to me, warning me of the consequences of exposing magic to a world that is not yet ready. Let's get back before a search party comes looking for us. Take my hand, Wiggly," Freddie said. In an instant they were both back in the Tiggly's house.

"Welcome back boys," Mummly greeted them warmly. "Dandelion tea anyone?"

Freddie still loved Mummly's tea. His mother had attempted to replicate it and to be fair it was not bad, but not as amazing as Mummly's.

"I think it may have something to do with being in the company of Elfins," Freddie's mother had suggested. "It's not a missing ingredient, but a missing atmosphere." She concluded that was why her Dandelion tea and Mummly's tasted different.

Nonetheless the Fountain household was besieged with visitors, all requesting a cup of dandelion tea. One of her close friends had even suggested she made it available to sell, believing it would be a huge success. Susan Fountain had declined out of respect that it was not her recipe to take to market, although that was not the real reason she gave for fear of exposing the Elfins, knowing people would want to know who's recipe it really was.

"Giggly and Mikey are not back yet, Freddie. Could you go find them and bring them back? It's about time we returned to the Sproggle world," Freddie's mother asked.

Freddie vanished and it never failed to make Wiggly chuckle, bringing home to him how powerful his best friend really is.

Freddie appeared in the park and looked around for Mikey and Giggly. The park was deserted apart from a group of children gathered around the statues of himself, Wiggly and Grundly. As he wandered over to them he could hear Giggly's voice. There she was, stood in front of a seated audience regaling them with stories of Wiggly and his adventures. Mikey was sat with the Elfins, completely absorbed in the story that Giggly was telling them.

"Freddie!" Mikey cried as he spotted his brother approaching.

Giggly stopped talking and looked towards Freddie, who disappeared in a puff of smoke, much to the surprise of the children. Then he reappeared next to his statue, dressed in his wizard's outfit including a pointy hat. The children cheered and applauded.

Mikey sat with his mouth wide open in surprise. *'It will take a bit of getting used to having a powerful wizard as a brother,'* he thought.

"Time to go, Mikey and Giggly, say goodbye to the children," Freddie said.

Everyone stood up and gathered around Mikey, hugging him in turn. He had memorized all their names and said goodbye to each one. "Ready now, Freddie," he said as he stood beside his brother.

Freddie snapped his fingers and all the Elfin children vanished.

"Where have they gone, Freddie?" Mikey asked, full of concern.

"I've sent them to their homes. You seem to be getting on well with everyone," Freddie replied.

"Mmm, they're all really nice, they love you, you're their hero. Violet told me how you saved her from the Mole Goblins, you and Wiggly were so brave. I understand why the Elfins think you are a hero and made these statues of you both." Mikey's eyes glistened with the threat of tears he was so proud.

"Come close, Giggly, let's get back," Freddie replied and suddenly all three were back in the seating end of the Tiggly's home.

Mikey was full of excitement as he rushed to his parents. "Mum, Dad, they have a statue of Freddie and Wiggly in the park and I made lots of friends. Violet told me all about Freddie saving her from the Mole Goblins, he and Wiggly are so very brave." He paused to take a breath.

"We're pleased to hear you've made friends, Mikey, I'm sure they'll all love you like they love Freddie. I think he has one more surprise for you," their mother said proudly.

Freddie held up his rucksack. "I think it's time for you to inherit my magic rucksack, so you can continue to help people in the village and maybe down here in Elfin Town too."

Mikey was so excited. "Can I really? That will be amazing, but you said it only works for you," he replied a little disappointed.

"That's right, Mikey, but if you take the rucksack, I will change it so it is only magical for you," Freddie replied as his brother took the rucksack, then Freddie snapped his fingers.

The bag twinkled and sparkled for a moment and made Mikey's fingers tingle. "That tickles!" he chuckled. "Oh look, the rucksack has my name on it!" Mikey cried out.

"See if you can find a nice shiny red apple inside the rucksack, Mikey. Just think about an apple, then unzip the top, put your hand inside, that's it," Freddie encouraged.

Mikey unzipped the rucksack and placed his hand inside, thinking hard about an apple. "Oh, look!" he cried, pulling his hand out and holding up a shiny red apple. "That's for you, Giggly," he said without thinking of keeping it for himself. Then he pulled out another and gave it to Wiggly.

"It looks like Mikey is taking after you, Freddie, he generously gave away what he found," Mummly said joyfully.

* *

During a lunchtime visit to the Tiggly's, Freddie asked Wiggly if he would like to come to school with him.

"Really? I can do that? Really?" Wiggly said surprised. "Well yes, I would love to. But I'm not like all your Sproggle friends, how would it be possible?"

Freddie gave his friend a warm knowing smile. "Like this!" he replied snapping his fingers.

Giggly jumped and screamed.

"What? What is it Giggly?" Wiggly asked as he jumped in his chair from her sudden scream.

"You! You're a Sproggle!" Giggly exclaimed.

Freddie created a mirror for Wiggly to look at himself.

"Oh, wow! This is amazing. Err, I won't stay like this forever, will I?" he asked.

Freddie chuckled. "No, Wiggly, I will change you back when we return. Best call you Wiggy though, it's more like a Sproggle name and less likely to result in lots of questions."

Freddie imagiported them to the boy's toilet cubicle at his school. He checked that the coast was clear and then they set off for Freddie's first lesson, Frensh Oral. Freddie, unbeknown to Wiggly, had magically given him the ability to understand and speak Frensh. Freddie's genius group were quite advanced in speaking the language and naturally everyone, especially Jimmy, wanted to know who Freddie had brought with him. In perfect Frensh, Freddie introduced Wiggly as his pen friend, Wiggy, from Fransh. On hearing this, the rest of the group began firing questions at Wiggly and he answered them with a beautiful Southern Frensh accent. Wiggly understood everyone and replied comfortably, it was only at the close of the lesson when the teacher spoke in Anglish that Wiggly realised what he had been doing.

He found a moment to speak to Freddie alone. "That was so incredible, but how could I understand and speak Frensh? Actually I have no idea where Frensh Sproggles live!"

Freddie spoke one word, "Magic!"

The next lesson was advanced physics. Again Freddie gave Wiggly the ability to understand the lesson, much to the admiration of the other students and teacher. But no one was more surprised than Wiggly himself.

When the school day finished, Freddie took Wiggly home on the bus. This was very exciting for him, he only knew two ways of travelling, walking and imagiporting. Freddie's mother was intrigued who it was her son had brought home.

"Bonjour Madame Fontaine!" Wiggly smiled.

"Oh, how wonderful!" Freddie's mother exclaimed.

Both Freddie and Wiggly laughed.

But Mikey was looking at Wiggly suspiciously and a little jealously.

"Who is he, Freddie?" Mikey said, suddenly clinging to his brother almost pushing Wiggly away.

"Wiggy, this is my favourite little brother, Mikey, they call him 'Mikey Mendit' at school and in the village," Freddie said smiling at Mikey and tussling his hair.

Mikey backed off a bit hearing Freddie calling him his favourite little brother and even gave Wiggy a smile.

Wiggy held out his hand. "It's very nice to meet you, Mikey. I'm glad to hear you're carrying on the Fountain tradition. Freddie is known as Freddie Fixit because he seems to fix everything."

Mikey shook Wiggy's hand, who burst into a fit of giggles, then Freddie snapped his fingers to reveal it was really Wiggly.

"Wiggly!" Mikey cried and rushed to hug him. "You fooled me!"

Freddie's mother had cottoned on to what was happening and smiled when the real Wiggly was revealed. "Wiggly, will you stay for tea, I know you'll be keen to get home, but it would be nice if you could?"

"Thank you, Mrs Fountain, I'd be honoured," Wiggly replied and was promptly dragged upstairs to Mikey's bedroom to be shown the model plane that he was building.

"That was nice of you to give Wiggly a taste of life above ground," Freddie's mother said. "Did he like it and get on with everyone?"

"He did, Mum. I gave him the ability to be on the same level as the others and me, so he fitted in very well. He impressed everyone, including my little brother it seems," Freddie laughed.

"Best go up and rescue him," his mother replied, chuckling.

Freddie galloped upstairs and knocked on Mikey's door then stepped inside to find Wiggly fascinated as Mikey was showing him how to glue the plastic parts of the plane kit together. "I see you've been kidnapped by my monster brother then, Wiggly!" Freddie chuckled and lifted Mikey up off his chair and gave him a hug.

"Aww Freddie!" Mikey protested and hugged his brother back.

"You two get on better than my sister and me," Wiggly said laughing at Mikey's giggling.

"I like your sister, Wiggly," Mikey said with a huge smile.

"Mmmm! Giggly is also very fond of you, Mikey," Wiggly replied.

"You do have funny names though, Wiggly and Giggly," Mikey commented.

"Ah! Well my sister was always giggling so my parents called her Giggly and ...."

"...... I bet you wiggled all over that's why they called you Wiggly!" Mikey interrupted.

"There's no flies on you, Mikey," Wiggly replied.

"Oh! Do people have flies on them then?" Mikey asked screwing his eyebrows up.

Freddie tussled his brother's hair and he giggled again. "It's a saying, it means you are smart," he explained.

During tea Mikey monopolised the conversation asking all sorts of questions, but no one minded, he was such a happy child. When it was time for Wiggly to return home he suggested they all went for a visit and Mikey was very enthusiastic.

"Okay mischief!" Freddie said tussling Mikey's blond curly hair, "let's go visit Elfin Town. Hold hands everyone." Freddie imagiported them to the Tiggly's front door.

When Wiggly opened the door Giggly rushed and pounced on Mikey, dragging him inside.

Mikey was in fits of laughter that quickly infected Giggly, the two of them sat on the comfy sofa chuckling away. Mikey let Giggly cuddle him without fear or objection and he seemed quite happy.

"Freddie, nice to see you again, Susan, Jacob, come inside, we might have to rescue Mikey in a moment," Mummly said with a big smile as she invited them inside and closed the door. She and Daddly were always pleased to see Freddie and his family. Mummly walked into the kitchen end to make them all some dandelion tea.

Daddly walked with Freddie and his parents to the seating end and let everyone sit in comfy chairs.

When Mummly arrived with a tray of hot tea, Freddie's mother announced, "Oh Mummly, I've managed to make dandelion tea at home, it's not as delicious as yours, but all my friends really enjoy it when they come to visit. I'm so glad we are friends and can share such things."

Wiggly regaled his parents, Giggly and Mikey with his afternoon at Freddie's school. Mr and Mrs Fountain had already heard some of his exploits but were just as fascinated as everyone else. Wiggly smiled so much his jaws ached, but he loved being the centre of attention, for a little while at least.

"Say something in a funny way?" Giggly requested of her brother.

Freddie clicked his fingers and gave Wiggly the ability to talk in Frensh.

"Je ne pense pas pouvoir. Oh, I didn't know I could do that!" Wiggly replied shaking his head.

"Oooh, what did you say? What did you say, Wiggly?" Mikey said bouncing on the comfy sofa.

Wiggly looked at Freddie, who smiled knowingly at his friend. "I think I said, 'I don't think I can,' is that right, Freddie?" Wiggly asked.

"That's exactly what you said, now try telling Giggly she is pretty," Freddie replied.

"Vous etes assez, Giggly," Wiggly said, looking at his sister, who appeared a little stunned at his newly acquired skills.

Mikey burst into laughter and said, "It sounds so different. Why don't they speak our words so we can understand them?"

"That's a very good question, Mikey, but the answer is not easy to understand. We live on a continent, surrounded by the ocean. Way back in history people could not travel very far and each region developed their own language. That's as simply as I can explain for you," Mikey's father replied.

"Mikey, we hear you are following in your brother's footsteps....." Mummly did not get a chance to finish before Mikey interrupted.

"...... Oh no, Mummly, his shoes are bigger than mine and he takes longer strides, it would make following his footsteps quite difficult!" Mikey confessed.

Everyone started laughing and Mikey looked around with a puzzled expression.

"Did I say something funny?" he asked.

"Yes, Mikey, I didn't mean that you were actually walking in Freddie's footsteps, it's an expression or saying to explain that someone is doing the same thing. So it seems you are helping people just like Freddie did and still does," Mummly explained.

Oh I see, it would be funny to see me trying to hop into Freddie's footsteps," Mikey said smiling again.

Daddly looked at Mikey and said, "When you help people you can use your magic rucksack to be an even better helper. But you need to use it wisely, otherwise your friends will get suspicious and may ask awkward questions."

"Yes, Daddly, I will be careful. My brother is Freddie Fixit and I'm Mikey Mendit!" Mikey replied proudly.

"I think it's time we headed back home," Freddie and Mikey's mother announced.

Everyone said their goodbyes, Giggly hugged Mikey and kissed his cheek, much to his amusement.

Wiggly hugged Freddie and thanked him again for the amazing afternoon.

Then the Tigglys were on their own again in Elfin town and the Fountain family were back in their home in Elfington village.

** **

Mikey knocked on Freddie's door and walked in to see his brother laid on his bed reading a book.

Freddie looked up and smiled, suspecting Mikey was about to pounce on him judging by the look on his brother's face. Before Mikey had the chance to pounce, Freddie levitated him in the air and floated him over to the bed to sit next to him, all the while Mikey was laughing his head off.

Mikey hugged Freddie. "You're the best brother, Freddie. Who else has a wizard for a brother? I love you, Freddie. Thank you for trusting me, I promise you I will keep our family secret!" he said so sincerely.

Freddie tussled his brother's hair. "I love you too, Mikey, and I would not have shown you everything if I didn't think you could be trusted. When you help people, I used to say, 'I think I might have something in my rucksack to help,' and no one will ever know it's a magic rucksack and if anyone asks you where you get all this stuff, just reply, 'here and there,' it's not telling a lie, but not letting on what you really have."

"You are clever, Freddie, no wonder everyone likes you, the teachers still talk about you at the school you know," Mikey told him.

"I hope that doesn't make you feel embarrassed." He was concerned his brother felt he had to follow in his footsteps.

"Oh, no, I always smile and feel warm inside my chest. I'm proud of you, Freddie, and proud to be your brother. I will try to be just like you were," Mikey replied beaming with admiration.

"Well you'll be coming to my school very soon, I'm sure you'll make lots more friends there too and we can meet up and have lunch together. It will be really great!" Freddie was looking forward to September when Mikey would move up to his senior school.

* *

During the first week of July in the summer of Freddie's fourth year at school, between CE 'O' and 'A' level exam years for his special class, the ten high IQ students were taken on a weeklong camping field trip on the Moors. Two members of staff, Mr Mead and Miss Horsham, accompanied them in the school mini bus. It was a jolly journey with the students singing popular songs along the way. When they finally arrived at the designated area it was mid afternoon and everyone helped to set up camp.

While Mr Mead and Miss Horsham put up their two tents, the boys were busy attempting to put up their own tent and the girls were similarly engaged.

"How come we can do advanced maths yet not work out how to put together this tent?" Billy Bates chuckled, seeing William with guy ropes wrapped around his legs and Jimmy playing ghosts inside the flysheet.

The girls, on the other hand, seemed to have their tent finished and had folding chairs set out for them to sit on and be entertained by the boys' struggle.

Freddie had laughed and resisted using his magic for a while, then secretly gave Billy the knowledge of how to sort things out.

Billy suddenly announced, "Stop! Stop! Everyone stop!"

The other four boys and Freddie did not argue and downed whatever parts of the tent they were holding.

"Right! This is what we're doing," Billy cried. "Freddie, grab the fly sheet and stretch it out over there, Jimmy and William grab the main tent, Brian, you're with me. Take this other tent pole and we will climb inside, then lift the tent on to the tent poles. Come one everyone! Hop to it!"

Like little soldiers the boys soon had their tent put up, much to their relief and applause from the girls. The rest of the afternoon was devoted to establishing ground rules, like no boys in the girls' tent and no girls in the boys' tent.

"Oh! Sir, why would we go in the boys' tent?" Melanie had asked.

The two teachers looked at each other, a little surprised any of them would ask that question, being the age they were.

"We want you all to get on well with each other, like you do at school. But for the sake of privacy, it's the same reason boys are not permitted in the girls' toilets or the girls in the boys' toilets. We all have to learn and respect each other's privacy, at school, at home or wherever you may be. For example, how many of you ask your parents to knock on your bedroom door and wait to be invited inside?" Miss Horsham replied.

They grinned and looked at each other, as one by one they all raised their hands.

"Consider your tents as your bedroom, which they basically are, so exercise polite and good manners towards each other. You must all look out for each other, there are no wild animals out here, but the ground can be unpredictable," Miss Horsham explained. "Should one of you wander off and twist your ankle or break a leg, you must let someone know where you're going or preferably have another person with you, that way Mr Mead and I would know if you were missing."

As they were many miles away from the nearest town, the teachers wanted to make sure that they were all safe. If they needed to go anywhere they had to tell someone and that was a golden rule not to be broken. There were a few more common sense rules that were necessary for it to be a relaxed and safe field trip.

* *

The Moors had been the ideal place to build a high security prison. The location was remote and secluded and the prison did not appear on any ordinance map. Unbeknown to the school group, they had set up camp only four kilometres from the prison, which would normally have been of no consequence. The prison was so secure it would take magic or a Houdini-like person to escape from it.

It just so happened that Billy Bates' father had been transferred to this prison because of two escapes and recaptures from other prisons in which he had been sent to serve his sentence. On top of that he had been involved in more than one serious fight for which his sentence had been extended.

When coincidences happen they do so in the most spectacular way. What were the chances that Billy and his father would ever be within a few kilometres of each other, considering his father had so far been locked away for all of Billy's teenage years?

Robin Bates, Billy's father, was on his best behaviour and had charmed his way into working in the kitchens. It also helped that he was quite a good cook, or at least that is what he claimed.

Short on suitable inmates for the most trustworthy of positions, the Governor had little option but to allow Robin Bates to enjoy the privileged position, despite being warned that he could be charming for sneaky reasons.

For three weeks Robin Bates was a model prisoner, nothing was too much trouble for him and the prison Governor and guards wanted to believe he had finally come to terms with his imprisonment and turned over a new leaf.

"Mr Bates," the Governor said to him at his first assessment meeting, "it has not gone unnoticed that you have become much more willing to toe the line."

"Thank you, Governor, I'm seeking to be released at the earliest opportunity. I haven't seen my wife and son in a long time," Bates replied.

What he actually meant was as soon as he found a weakness in the system, he would avail himself for an early escape.

"Good to hear, Mr Bates. If you continue with your current behaviour and attitude and stay out of trouble you could be up for parole in five years time," the Governor advised.

By the time Robin Bates had left the Governor's office he had established that all staff cars were parked outside the prison, so that avenue offered no opportunity for escape. However, he already knew the only vehicles allowed inside the prison gates were the daily trucks delivering fresh food and the bus bringing new inmates. For the next ten days Bates made sure he was the one assisting with the unloading of the food trucks to the kitchen storeroom, while he formulated his plan.

* *

Freddie and his school friends had settled in on their first day. The camping field trip was designed to give the students a rest from the intense study routines and challenge them in other ways.

"Sir, where are the matches so we can get the camp fire going to cook the meal?" Jimmy had asked Mr Mead. Jimmy was puzzled by the smirk on his teacher's face until he replied.

"No matches, Jimmy, you will have to find a way to make your own fire!"

Jimmy's expression was priceless, his happy smile falling like a lead balloon. "But sir!" he protested.

"Look around you and talk with each other and see what you come up with. Off you go!" Mr Mead smiled sending Jimmy on his way. Of course, Mr Mead did have matches, but only in the event the students failed their first challenge.

Jimmy hurried back and gathered the others together, explaining what he had been told.

Freddie could easily have solved their dilemma, but only at the risk of exposing his magic.

Billy came to everyone's rescue. "When Mr Mead said look around, I think I know what he meant," he said. He picked up two greyish looking stones and held them up. "I think these are flint. I remember from somewhere, if they are struck together they make a spark."

Brian chipped in, "We need something light and dry for the spark to ignite."

Jimmy jumped up and vanished, returning moments later with some dry fluffy wool-like material. "I spotted this stuff while we were putting up the tents," he smiled.

Billy struck the two stones together hard and sure enough a single spark shot out. The rest of the friends cheered, now all they had to do was create fire.

"We should gather a few small dry sticks and twigs to put over the woolly stuff it if catches fire then add thicker and thicker sticks until we have a blaze," William suggested.

"Good idea, Will," Billy replied and they all trotted off in search of suitable material, returning with armfuls of it.

The two teachers watched with interest and pride as their students unwillingly solved their first problem.

"All set," Billy said, now a little uncertain. He began hitting the two flints together at speed and to everyone's delight, produced lots of sparks.

Freddie watched and made sure the woolly stuff caught fire, although he need not have worried, as everything went well.

"Oh, look, we have a flame!" Melanie cried excitedly.

"Put some little twigs on it first," Susan said, doing just that.

The fire soon took hold and turned into a great campfire. The teachers came over and congratulated the students.

"Well done everyone. If you ever get lost and are alone you know how to keep warm at least," Miss Horsham said. "Now who's going to be chef?"

Blank looks were passed around from one to another with plenty of shaking heads and hunched shoulders, until someone volunteered.

"I'll give it a go, Miss," Freddie offered.

"Freddie Fixit!" Nine other voices cried in unison with cheers and back patting.

Freddie laughed. The two teachers laughed. Everyone laughed.

Freddie no longer felt embarrassed being praised or called Freddie Fixit, in fact he loved the sense of fellowship it created with his friends. He knew whatever happened they would all stick together and look out for each other. Freddie had watched and helped his mother prepare and cook meals many times, so he felt capable of preparing simple meals. The teachers brought out sausages, eggs and beans, Freddie looked at the items and smiled. He soon had the beans bubbling away in a saucepan on the fire supported by a couple of small rocks. The big frying pan had sausages sizzling away and he was ready to scoop them out and keep them hot in the pan of beans while he fried the eggs. He appointed two others to find more firewood and Jimmy to butter slices of bread. One of the sausages exploded with such a bang, two of the students jumped with surprise and cried out.

"Sorry everyone!" Freddie called out. "I missed stabbing holes in one!"

Mr Mead and Miss Horsham were laughing their socks off watching their students' antics.

Freddie used tongs to lift and drop the sausages into the pan of bubbling baked beans then set about frying the eggs. He found he could get six eggs in the pan and when they were almost ready he called Jimmy over to act as server. "Two sausages, one egg and a large spoonful of beans, plus two slices of bread for everyone," Freddie instructed.

The first two meals were offered to the teachers who smiled with satisfaction at the way their students had succeeded.

**

Robin Bates had used his privileged position to study how he might escape from the high security prison. He determined that the only vehicles other than the prisoner coach to enter the prison were the food delivery vans and that would be his route to freedom. In preparation he concealed three large black bin bags close to where the food delivery van parked. Tomorrow was to be the execution day of his plan and he arranged to be the only person helping unload the food delivery.

That night he went over his plan in his mind. "With any luck I won't be missed until the van is back at its base in the town!" he muttered to himself quietly. He was so excited that he was about to be the first and probably the last inmate to escape this state of the art high security prison. Bates slept peacefully that night, having dreams of wandering about in open spaces and breathing fresh air in the sunshine.

At 5am, Ken, one of the prison officers, unlocked Bates' cell. "Come along, Bates! Duty calls. Double delivery today, you lucky man!"

Once Bates was dressed he was escorted to the kitchen delivery area where he and the prison officer waited for the van to arrive.

"The Governor is pleased with your new attitude and the other inmates reckon your cooking is the best they've had, Bates. You've made quite an impression, it will help with your review in the near future. You never know, the authorities might even cut your sentence for good behaviour," Ken said chatting with Bates.

But Robin Bates' mind was on his plan and he merely grunted in all the right places.

To ensure there were no possible ways for any prisoner to escape, the delivery vehicles were thoroughly inspected before they left the prison. A heavy-duty roller shutter door made sure the vehicle was locked inside the building before any unloading took place. It was designed to prevent anyone trying to escape from this access and it suited Bates perfectly. Double delivery day meant the vehicle was a truck rather than a transit van and for Bates' plan this was ideal.

The truck arrived at 5.30am exactly, it was still dark outside and would be for a couple of hours or more, again this was perfect for Bates. Once the truck was safely inside the prison building and the roller shutter closed and locked, Ken unlocked the kitchen stores gate to allow Bates into the delivery area. While Bates and the driver unloaded the truck, Ken went off to put his feet up for a while.

Bates had got to know the driver quite well and they chatted away like old mates and this was diversion number one.

By 6.15am everything was off the truck and Bates made the driver a cup of tea and sat with him in the kitchen away from the loading bay. This was diversion number two.

Bates excused himself, "Bit of tummy trouble," he said to the driver. "If I'm not back by the time you leave, I'll see you tomorrow, Charlie, okay!" This was diversion number three.

Bates moved swiftly back to the loading bay, not the bathroom. He grabbed the three black bin bags and climbed on top of the truck. His plan was about to be completed. Once he was on top of the truck he headed for the airfoil above the driver's cab. This had been one of those modifications to an old style truck to make the air flow over the top, so the vehicle used less fuel. It consisted of a moulded plastic shell mounted on a steel frame, leaving a vee shaped space between it and the cab roof. Bates slipped a black bin bag over his legs, then another with a hole in the bottom over his hips and chest. He placed the third bag over his head and arms, then tucked himself tightly into the vee space, making him seemingly disappear into the shadows.

"Where's Bates, Charlie?" prison officer Ken asked when he checked in.

Charlie chuckled. "Ere, he got the squirts! Had to run to the loo, heh heh," he replied.

"Must be all that dodgy stuff you deliver, Charlie!" Ken replied and laughed.

"On yer bike! All top quality, only the best for my best customers!" Charlie chuckled.

"I'd best do the inspection then, Charlie, before you toddle off," Ken replied, then walked inside the truck and saw it was completely empty with nowhere for anyone to stow away. Then he looked underneath with a mirror on a long handle, he could see everywhere and was happy no one was hiding under there. Finally he climbed up into the driver's cab, looking under and around the seats. Satisfied none of the inmates were hiding and trying to escape he turned to the driver, "You're all good to go, Charlie, see you tomorrow then."

Bates could hardly contain his mirth and derision for the so-called escape proof prison. He heard the roller shutter open and felt the truck reverse out, then heard the shutter close again. The truck did a three point turn and headed for the main gate, where a second inspection took place before the truck left the prison. The gate officers looked inside and underneath the truck using long handled mirrors, the driver's cab was also inspected. One officer used his long handled mirror to briefly look on the truck roof, completely missing Bates wrapped in black plastic bags.

"All good to go, Charlie, see you tomorrow, drive carefully." The gate officer waved Charlie and his empty truck through the main gate.

Charlie was whistling along to a snappy tune on the radio as he drove his truck through the main gates and on the road back to the village.

Bates let go a breath he had not realised he had been holding. He had made it out of the prison undetected and was on his way to freedom. He could hardly contain his excitement and knocked his head on the cab roof making a metallic clang. He froze, his mirth turned to fear. *'Did Charlie hear the noise I just made? You stupid idiot!'* Bates berated himself in his mind.

If Charlie stopped now, they were still in sight of the prison and the guards would be out in force wondering what was the matter. Luck was on Bates' side, Charlie was so engrossed in whistling along to the radio he had not heard the clang on his cab roof.

Bates was still free.

About a mile away from the prison and well out of sight of it, Bates carefully began removing the plastic bin bags, making sure not to bang on the cab roof again. Having just pulled the bag off his legs, he again froze as fear flooded his mind on hearing a loud bang like the sound of a gunshot. "Oh, that's torn it, they've noticed me missing already. What to do? What to do?" Bates whispered to himself trying to come up with a plan to help him get out of this situation. When the truck came to a halt his heart was racing believing he had been discovered and he rolled out from his hiding place very quietly to look around. It was still dark and to his surprise he was not faced with gun wielding prison officers with searchlights. Bates then peeked over the edge of the truck and he saw Charlie looking at the front end of the truck and scratching his head.

"Typical!" Charlie moaned. "It had to be today didn't it, couldn't be tomorrow, oh, no! Had to be today I gets a puncture. Blow, blast, and bother!"

While Charlie was on his mobile phone calling for the breakdown truck, Bates seized the chance to slip off the roof of the truck on the opposite side undetected. Then he made a run for it across the moors in the dark. He raced away not knowing in what direction he was running other than it was away from the prison. He tripped and stumbled on rocks and hollows as he ran, having to hold his tongue not to cry out otherwise he would give the game away. Dawn was just breaking when he was well out of site of the delivery truck and he stopped to catch his breath. Realising that his escape may have been detected at the prison by now, he continued his trek across the moors in haste. Bates could not help laughing, once again he had shown the idiots, no prison could hold him for very long.

* *

Freddie was the first to wake the next morning, the same morning Robin Bates had escaped.

'Freddie, there is danger, be vigilant today,' his Merlin ring warned.

'What kind of danger? Are my friends at risk? What should I do?' Freddie responded in his mind to his danger warning.

'Unknown, Freddie, just be extra cautious today,' his Merlin ring replied.

Freddie shuffled out of his sleeping bag and smiled to himself looking at his friends still asleep in all manner of positions in their sleeping bags. William had completely disappeared and Freddie lifted the top of his sleeping bag to make sure he was okay. William was fast asleep and way down in the sleeping bag, he wondered how he could breathe. Leaving his friends to sleep he pulled on his coat and put on his shoes quietly so that he did not disturb the others, then unzipped the tent flap very slowly, stepping out into the cool, fresh air. Zipping the flap back up he looked over at the fire, it had not lasted the night and burned itself out. Looking around to make sure he was alone he put several logs in the stone circle of the fire pit and clicked his fingers. The dry wood burst into flames and made him feel warm and cosy. Freddie did not have to snap his fingers, a single thought would do the trick, but he liked the sense of drama. He filled a big pan with water and set it across two large stones where it began to heat up for hot drinks. Next, he went over to Mr Mead's tent and called for him to wake up, but when he did not respond Freddie sent a magical invisible hand into the tent to shake him until he woke. Then he did the same with Miss Horsham, she was actually snoring and it made Freddie giggle.

Mr Mead stuck his head out of his tent. "What is it, Freddie?" he asked a little sleepily.

"I'm not sure sir, but I feel there is something not right, that we might be in danger," he explained.

"Okay, Freddie, I'll be out in a moment. Can you get everyone awake and assembled? Oh, I see you've got the fire going already. Well done, let's get everyone around the fire then, okay?"

Freddie nodded and headed for the girls' tent and was just about to shout when Melanie popped her head out of the tent flap.

"Oh, Freddie! You're about early," she said in surprise, then spotted the fire and her face lit up.

"Melanie, can you wake the others and get them around the camp fire, ASAP."

While Melanie woke the girls, Freddie crawled back into the boys' tent and began waking the others up.

"What's happening?" Jimmy said wiping the dribble from the corner of his mouth.

"Time to rise and shine. Camp fire, five minutes," Freddie said and shook the rest awake with the same message.

The boys and girls were soon assembled around the camp fire, still a little sleepy and mesmerized by the flickering flames. Freddie chuckled to himself seeing they were all holding out their hands in front of them feeling the warmth of the fire.

"Hey, Freddie, it's only 7.30am!" Billy croaked looking at his watch.

"Okay everyone," Mr Mead interrupted as he approached the group. "Freddie has started the fire so we can get nice and warm, so let's get breakfast cracking. It's scrambled egg on toast, but you have to toast your own bread."

"Oh, I can scramble the eggs, sir, I've helped my Mum many times," Freddie called out.

"Freddie Fixit," someone whispered, to a round of sleepy chuckles.

"Okay Freddie, I'm sure no one is going to fight you over that pedigree!" Miss Horsham giggled.

"Freddie Fixit again!" Jimmy sang out and that made everyone laugh again.

Freddie set to work cracking eggs and beating them while the others paired up and began toasting their bread. He soon had all the beaten eggs in a pan and was merrily stirring away.

Miss Horsham brought him a pack of butter. "I suggest you put half in the eggs and leave the other half for the toast," she said.

'Freddie, there is danger approaching!' his Merlin ring was warning him and he was not sure what to do, he was inexperienced in so many ways.

While everyone was enjoying their breakfast he told Mr Mead he needed to go for 'number two's' and headed off with the folding shovel and toilet roll. He was using this as an excuse to patrol the perimeter.

'What is the danger?' Freddie asked his Merlin ring.

'A dangerous creature approaches the campsite, be ready to use your magic to protect everyone,' his Merlin ring replied.

As confident as he was, having saved his friends and family more than once, this unknown danger had him very concerned. It was not for his own safety, he was immortal and had a charmed life, but for his friends and teachers who did not. He began circling the campsite, out of sight, hoping no one would come looking for him before he completed his search.

* *

Robin Bates had made good progress across the moors, although he had no clue where he would end up other than he was moving away from the prison and that would suffice.

Prisons normally issued the inmates with a standard set of clothes all visibly marked with the prison name. This was a deterrent for anyone thinking of escaping, as it would easily identify them as an escaped prisoner.

The prison from which Bates had escaped was so confident it was impossible to escape from, they allowed the inmates to wear normal street clothes, jeans and tee shirts. This served Bates rather well because his previous escapes were foiled by the attention his clothing had drawn.

The dew damp moors had, however, soaked through his clothes, but that was the least of his worries. He knew a helicopter would soon be launched to look for him.

Bates laughed out aloud. "I bet those idiots haven't yet worked out how I did it though! Ooof! Ow!" he cried, tripping over a moss hidden rock and landing flat on his face. He picked himself up, his bravado a little bruised and his clothing a lot wetter. He continued scrambling across the carpet of heathers, down the dips and up the rises. He was more than aware there was nowhere for him to hide on the open moors, so he began picking strands of heather and tucking them in his clothing thinking it may give him a sporting chance to hide from a helicopter. He spotted a babbling brook and it made him realise that he was very thirsty. The cool fresh water tasted wonderful as he scooped it up in his cupped hands and drank.

His stomach rumbled as it had been a while since he had eaten, it had been the only part of his plan he could not solve. The food at the prison was meticulously counted down to every slice of bread. There was no way he could even take an apple without there being a 'witch hunt' to find the culprit. However, he had assumed he would be skulking around the nearest town by now and able to steal what he needed. Having satisfied his thirst, Bates climbed the rise and praised the Lord for his good luck, he could see a blazing fire in the distance and if he was not mistaken, the faint whiff of something cooking.

* *

While Freddie began his trek around the camp, Mr Mead had brought out some sausages. Jimmy volunteered to cook them, having watched Freddie the day before.

"Don't forget to stab them with a fork, Jimmy. We don't want any more bangers!" Billy laughed sarcastically.

The others sniggered, now fully awake and the sudden waft of sausages frying was making them all feel hungry.

William needed to pee and excused himself, reluctantly. "Don't scoff them all, save some for me!" he cried as he scurried off behind the tents. On finding a suitably large bush, William unzipped and relieved himself with the customary, "Ahh!" and a shiver. He had just pulled up his trouser zip when someone grabbed him from behind. A large hand closed over his mouth and another trapped his arms to his body. Thinking it a prank, most likely from Billy, who he had become really good friends with, William did not struggle.

But it was an unfamiliar voice that whispered in his ear. "If you struggle or shout I'll twist your head off your neck!"

William froze, fear paralysed him temporarily and despite emptying his bladder earlier, a damp patch rapidly increased in size on the front of his trousers.

Bates, being a big bloke, lifted William off his feet and carried him away into the dip. There he threw poor William down onto the damp ground, straddled across him pinning him down and covering his mouth.

A terrified William trembled as he looked at the person who had grabbed him.

"How many adults?" Bates asked lifting his hand from William's mouth long enough for him to answer.

"T.. t ..two," William's voice trembled and his body quaked.

"How many kids?" Bates demanded gruffly.

William looked at Billy's father almost too terrified to speak.

Bates pushed William with his foot, threateningly. "How many kids?" he repeated angrily.

"T.. t.. ten," William replied and began to cry.

Bates looked content and smiled, thinking he could deal with those numbers. "What's your name, boy?" he demanded.

"W.. W.. W.. William," he stammered, sucking in a breath.

"Well, William, this is what we're gonna to do. You and me are gonna crash your cosy camp and if anyone so much as tries to stop me, YOU'RE a GONNER! Got it?"

William nodded, unable to stop his tears as his body trembled with a fear he had never before experienced.

"I'm gonna release your mouth now kid and if you make a sound........." Before Bates could finish his threat, William farted with rather stinky follow through. "Oh! You kids are all disgusting little monsters. Make another sound and you won't see your mommy ever again! GOT IT KID?"

William nodded as tears welled up and dripped, he hitched a breath when Bates released his mouth.

Bates picked William up roughly and carried him towards the camp, where the boys and girls were so invested in the smell of frying sausages, they failed to notice Bates approach carrying William until they were virtually on top of them. Bates grabbed a long tree branch intended to be broken up for the camp fire, but no one could work out how to cut it into smaller lengths.

Mr Mead reeled back in surprise, suddenly spotting Bates, armed with the club and dragging a terrified William along.

"Who are you?" Mr Mead cried. "Put that boy down this minute! What do you want?"

Everyone stopped their chatter and bread toasting hearing Mr Mead shouting, looking at him and then at Bates holding the branch style club threatening a terrified William.

"Dad?" Billy cried out, not wholly sure it was his father, not having seen him for a few years.

"Billy? Is that you, Billy?" Robin Bates cried out looking at his son who had definitely grown up since he last saw him.

"Dad!" Billy repeated rather unhappily, hanging his head in shame.

"You little monster. I got put away in prison because of you and that Freddie Fountain boy. Why can't people mind their own business? You'll get what you deserve, all of you. Just wait and see."

"Mr Bates, what do you want? Please release young William, can't you see he's terrified and he has done no wrong to you," Miss Horsham demanded in an authoritive voice.

"Well aren't you a posh one, teacher. Just shut your cakehole!" Bates roared.

"FREDDIE!" Jimmy cried out on seeing his best friend appear behind Bates, then slapped his hand over his mouth as his brain connected with what Bates had just said about Freddie.

Bates swung round to see his nemesis, almost clubbing William's head in the process.

"Mr Bates, let William go, take me as your hostage," Freddie said calmly and bravely.

"NO!" Jimmy cried out again and slapped his hands over his mouth.

"Well, well, Freddie 'nosey' Fountain. You little, interfering, good for nothing. GET HERE!" Bates roared, dropping William to the ground and holding him down with his foot.

Freddie approached and allowed Bates to grab him roughly, holding his make shift club threateningly over Freddie's head.

"Let William go, I'm your best hope of escape," Freddie demanded, still calm and collected. He could have finished all this with one thought but was trying not to give away his secret.

Bates lifted his foot from William's chest and pushed him away. William scrambled towards his friends, sobbing and hyperventilating.

"Mr Bates, just take the mini bus, here are the keys, leave the boys alone. No need to harm any of them," Mr Mead pleaded.

"I told you to shut your face. This little monster is not going home with you lot. Oh no! I'll give his parents something to be sorry for, a CORPSE! Ha, ha!"

The boys and girls gasped hearing Bates' threat. One of the girls fainted and Jimmy wet himself. This was his fault, all his fault that Bates had hold of Freddie.

Freddie watched his friend, William, reach the other students and magically cleaned up his little accident to make him feel better. He did the same for Jimmy.

William was so upset and still sobbing he did not notice what Freddie had done for him. Now that William was safe, Freddie decided to stop this going any further.

"Mr Mead, can you call the police on your mobile phone please?" Freddie said.

Bates cried, "Do that, teacher, and I'll end this boy in front of you all, then do them all one by one!" His face was red with rage and hate towards Freddie.

"Do it, Mr Mead," Freddie called, "he can't hurt me!"

Freddie sent Mr Mead a telepathic command and the teacher took out his mobile phone, but not of his own choosing, Freddie was mind controlling him.

"You STUPID IDIOT! I warned you!" Bates roared.

Some of the students screamed as they watched Bates club Freddie's head with the branch several times until Freddie fell limp in Bates' arms, blood dripping from his head. Bates let Freddie fall to the ground with a loud thump, roaring with laughter.

Billy cried out, "DAD NO!" But he was too late, Freddie lay in a motionless, crumpled heap.

"I warned you, you stupid idiot. This corpse is your fault, Mead!" Bates growled unremorsefully, glaring at Mr Mead.

William and Melanie collapsed and the others covered their eyes.

Miss Horsham stood rigid and unmoving, but Freddie was far from dead and had both teachers under his control. Mr Mead had dialled 999 and was calling the police, just as if he had not seen Robin Bates club Freddie.

"PUT THAT PHONE DOWN!...... YOU BRAIN DEAD OR SOMETHING?" Bates roared.

Mr Mead totally ignored Bates and continued his phone call. Freddie was in control.

Bates was furious and bright red in the face, looking like he might explode. "What's the matter with you idiots?" he cried, with a sound of surprise in his voice. "What the ...." Bates could not believe his eyes.

Freddie sprang up like a stepped-on rake, his head no longer blood covered. He stood, staring Bates right in the face. "Give me the club, Mr Bates," he said calmly, in his commanding voice.

Bates' eyes were almost popping out of his head. His hand holding the tree branch club extended out towards to Freddie. "How are you doing this?" Bates gasped, feeling a sense of fear run through him.

"You really have no idea who I am, Mr Bates, and what I can do," Freddie replied calmly. "If you did you would run a mile. But it's too late for you now."

Miss Horsham shivered as Freddie released her from his mind control. Mr Mead put away his phone and looked like he had just woken up as Freddie also released his mind. The two teachers looked on the scene with unbelieving eyes. They had seen Bates crush Freddie's skull with the club, yet there the boy was, calmly commanding Bates to hand the club over.

On hearing Freddie's voice, the students who were still conscious looked up and opened their eyes to see Bates giving Freddie the tree branch club.

"You are not a nice man, Mr Bates. Billy deserves so much better than you and so does his mother. Did you know your son is a genius? In fact all these kids here are geniuses. They have more intelligence in their little finger than all of your evil brain," Freddie taunted.

Bates cried out, "YOU LITTLE ...... I'LL SHOW Y........."

Freddie stopped Bates in his tracks and levitated him two metres into the air, upside down. Then he brought the couple of students who had fainted back to consciousness and addressed them all. "What you are seeing and about to see, I'm afraid I cannot allow you to remember. I'm sorry, but my true identity must remain a secret for some time yet," he said to them, then Freddie took away everyone's fear and made them feel calm.

"Freddie, how are you doing this?" Jimmy asked rushing to his best friend's side.

As Freddie was going to wipe all their memories he saw no harm in telling his friends who he really was. He had wanted to share his secret with them for so very long, but knew it would put them, him and the Elfins in danger.

"Freddie put his arm around Jimmy's shoulder and spoke to everyone. "I am a wizard, Jimmy, everyone, in fact I am the most powerful wizard to have ever existed. I can control all the magic of the world and the cosmos. Three times I have saved the world already, but I've had to take those memories from you to protect you," Freddie explained. "Watch and know what danger you have all faced in the past," Freddie said and created a 3D portrayal of the Morphlins and the Beastrolls.

Two teachers, nine pupils and Robin Bates watched in horror at the things they saw, gasping and crying out, then cheering when Freddie vanquished the monsters.

"Freddie, you certainly fixed those horrible things, but why did we not remember all of that?" Jimmy asked somewhat in awe of his best friend.

"I mind wiped everyone, Jimmy. My true identity must be kept a secret, the world is not yet ready to know about the power of magic," Freddie answered.

Freddie turned his attention to Robin Bates, turning him the right way up and lowering him back down to the ground. "Now, Mr Bates, do you realise who you are dealing with? There is no escape for you this time. Look at your son, you should feel proud of him, look what he has achieved, despite your bad influence. Billy is a better person than you will ever be. Watch and shudder with fear, Mr Bates, for this is your undoing." Freddie snapped his fingers and an image of Bates grabbing William and treating him cruelly, then clubbing Freddie, appeared as if projected in a cinema.

"How can you be doing this?" Bates said meekly.

"I have already told you, I am the world's most powerful wizard. I could propel you into space, or transport you onto the moon with a single thought. Now do you understand?" Freddie replied calmly. "Now it is time to dispatch you, Mr Bates, this will be your last chance to see your son and to tell him how sorry you are." Freddie sent a telepathic message to Billy and he walked over to his father. "Is there anything you want to say to your father, Billy?" Freddie asked.

Billy looked at his father, he was no longer afraid of him, on his face was a look of shame. "I am ashamed to be your son, how could you try and hurt Freddie and William like that? I disown you, you can no longer call me your son."

Robin Bates looked at Billy, his face full of shame. "I'm sorry," was all he could say.

"Go sit with the others, Billy, while I deal with Mr Bates here." Freddie twirled his hand and Bates began to spin, then a thick rope appeared out of thin air and wrapped around his arms, body and legs until he looked like a butterfly chrysalis. Once he was secure, a length of tape appeared over his mouth.

"I will allow you to remember all of this, Mr Bates, of course no one will believe you, they will think you have lost your mind. But remember this, if you ever escape from prison again, I will find you." Freddie's staff appeared in his hand and he pointed to the sky. Dark clouds suddenly formed above them and bolts of lightening struck the ground around Bates' body, burning the ground around him. Then the clouds just vanished as quickly as they had appeared.

His friends flocked around Freddie.

The teachers were dumbstruck.

Mr Mead and Miss Horsham recovered from their apparent awe and joined Freddie and the other students, patting Billy on the back.

"So, Freddie, magic really exists then?" Mr Mead remarked calmly.

Freddie smiled and asked everyone to stand back. "Allow me to demonstrate, Mr Mead." Freddie tapped the ground with his staff and he was instantly transformed into a pointy hatted, cloaked wizard, as seen in books. Then he tapped the ground three times and the very ground rumbled. Suddenly, on the other side of the tents something began to grow.

"What is it?" Jimmy asked.

"Watch," Freddie replied.

From the ground rose a fairytale castle with round towers and a drawbridge.

"Oh, wow!" Jimmy exclaimed.

Freddie tapped his staff again and a forest of trees sprang up around them. He tapped his staff again and the ground became a beautiful marble plaza with ornate fountains and statues, their tents and camp fire vanished. He tapped his staff once more and a ship's horn blasted out so loud they all covered their ears.

"Look!" Melanie cried, pointing to the front end of a huge ship sticking up from the trees quite close to them.

"No way!" Billy cried, pointing to the sky where a huge aeroplane appeared, hovering above the castle and forest.

Finally, Freddie tapped his staff and the plaza was filled with gold and precious jewels sparkling in the morning sun.

The two teachers and Freddie's friends looked upon his creations in awe and amazement, then back at Freddie, wide eyed and dropped jaws.

Miss Horsham found her voice and said, "You are correct, Freddie, the world is not ready for such power. Countries would fight each other, eliminate each other just to get their hands on you. We cannot be allowed to remember anything about your magic."

"I know this, Miss Horsham. I could take control of the world right now and force every man, woman and child to live perfect, peaceful lives, but they would not be free. Merlin said there will come a time when mankind lives in peace, only then will magic have a place."

"Aw! Don't tell us Merlin is a real wizard?" Susan chuckled.

"Oh! Indeed he is and he is in suspended animation waiting for a peaceful world for him to return," Freddie replied.

"So do Fairies and Pixies, all those creatures exist?" Billy asked.

"They did, Billy, but there was a great Troll War and all but a few Fairies were killed, they wait with Merlin," Freddie replied.

"Tell me, Freddie, did you use your magic to give you and these students genius level IQ's?" Mr Mead asked.

"No sir, I did not, but when I merged with Merlin to defeat the Beastrolls that came from another dimension, it left me with my high intelligence."

"Are you saying there are other dimensions with monsters like those Beastrolls?" William asked.

"Yes, Will, our universe is like the page in a book. There are untold numbers of universes side by side, sometimes a tear allows creatures to invade our world, but I am here to stop them," Freddie replied.

"I am in awe of you, Freddie," Mr Mead said. "You carry the responsibility of all this power, yet you do not use it for your own desires, for power and riches. You are a most remarkable young man, Freddie Fixit!"

Freddie's friends all chanted 'Freddie Fixit' while Freddie tapped his staff and the fairytale castle vanished along with all his creations, then he changed to his regular Freddie image. "It's time Sir, Miss, everyone, please go to your tents and lay down. I will put you all to sleep and when you wake, you will have no memory of what has happened."

Mr Mead put his hand on Freddie's shoulder and offered him his other hand.

Freddie took his teacher's hand and they shook.

"Thank you, Freddie, for being a guardian angel looking out for us all. What will happen as you grow old, who will carry on your vigil?" Mr Mead asked.

Freddie smiled, still holding onto Mr Mead's hand. "I am eternal Sir, I have been granted a charmed life, I cannot be harmed or killed, as you saw with Mr Bates' attempt. When I reach 20 years old I will stop aging and live on forever."

"Goodness, Freddie," Mr Mead gasped. "You are a very special young man. I don't know how you keep a level head and deal with the power of life and death, like a god."

Again Freddie smiled and let go of Mr Mead's hand. "I have a special ring," Freddie held out his hand and snapped his fingers, the Merlin ring became visible. "This ring speaks to me in my mind, warns me of danger or disturbances in magic, it keeps me grounded. Plus my parents and younger brother also know, I allowed them to remember and I keep level headed for them too. In truth I have everything I need, great parents, brother and friends, I'm happy and contented too." Freddie snapped his fingers and Wiggly appeared.

"Freddie? What's happened?" Wiggly cried out.

Mr Mead jumped back and tripped, falling backwards and about to crack his head on a rock behind him.

Freddie levitated his teacher back to standing upright. "Sorry Sir. Sorry Wiggly, I'm just explaining to my teacher about me, before I mind wipe them and wanted to introduce my best friend to him," he replied.

Wiggly held out his hand to Mr Mead. "Pleased to meet you Sir, my name is Wiggly Tiggly and I live under Elfington Forest in an underground town with all the Elfins, who Merlin created as his helpers."

Mr Mead was again gob struck. "You're an Elf, you're not human?" was as much as he could manage to say.

Freddie chuckled, "Yes Sir, Wiggly is an Elfin, let me show you his home town." Freddie clicked his fingers and an image appeared in the air showing the whole town bustling with Elfins.

"This is just incredible, Freddie, we have no idea what is beneath our feet," Mr Mead replied and shook Wiggly's hand.

"Time to sleep now, Mr Mead," Freddie said and his teacher crawled into his tent, as had all the other students and laid down on their sleeping bags. The moment their heads touched the pillow, Freddie's magic put them to sleep and he took from them the memories to do with Billy Bates' father at the camp.

Then he walked over to Bates. "Mr Bates, if you ever escape from prison again I will know it and I will find you. You now know how powerful I am and I will turn you into a frog and your freedom will not be as you thought it might. You had better be a model prisoner and serve out your sentence. If you do not, if you falter, I will visit you and turn you into a frog, there and then in front of the whole prison. Do you understand me?"

Freddie turned to Wiggly. "Time to send you home, Wiggly, you have another tale to regale your family and friends with." He hugged Wiggly then sent him home again.

Freddie snapped his fingers and wiped Robin Bates' memory of Wiggly and Elfin Town, then levitated a wriggling Bates into the air, imagiporting them both to within a kilometre of the prison. Using his magic, Freddie levitated large rocks into the air and arranged them in the shape of an arrow on the ground, pointing to the completely bound and helpless Robin Bates. Freddie warned Bates once more what fate awaited him if he ever tried to escape again, then imagiported himself back to the camp. He vanished all the food that had been cooked and replaced it with food ready to cook again, so no one would ever suspect a thing. Then he woke his friends and teachers to begin the day anew.

"Okay everyone," Mr Mead interrupted as he approached the group. "Freddie has started the fire so we can get nice and warm, so let's get breakfast cracking. It's scrambled egg on toast, but you have to toast your own bread."

"Oh! I can scramble the eggs, sir, I've helped my Mum many times," Freddie called out.

"Freddie Fixit," someone whispered, to a round of sleepy chuckles.

"Okay, Freddie, I'm sure no one is going to fight you over that pedigree!" Miss Horsham giggled.

"Freddie Fixit again!" Jimmy sang out and that made everyone laugh.

Freddie set to work cracking eggs and beating them, while the others paired up and began toasting their bread. He soon had all the beaten eggs in a pan and was merrily stirring away.

Miss Horsham brought him a pack of butter. "I suggest you put half in the eggs and leave the other half for the toast," she said. "Oh! I've just had one of those 'Deja vu' feelings like we've done all this before, how strange," she chuckled.

* *

The prison was in turmoil, all inmates had been put in lock down, none of them were allowed out of their cells for any reason. Meal preparations had been cancelled and a routine search instigated throughout the prison.

"Bates has to be in the prison somewhere," the prison Governor declared to his assembled team of Officers. "He cannot escape, no one can! I want him found! Search every nook and cranny, he will not make a fool out of me!" he instructed all the officers at an emergency meeting when Ken had failed to find Bates in the toilet after the food delivery truck had left. The Governor was furious that he had let his guard down to a conman like Robin Bates, especially as he had been warned.

An hour later the officers were reporting back to the Governor. None had found any trace of Robin Bates, nor had any of the prisoners admitted to having seen him, although they were not over confident the inmates would say, even if they had.

"It looks like Bates is missing sir," the chief Prison Officer reported to the Governor.

"Bring me the last person to see Bates," the Governor demanded.

Ken Meredith knocked on the Governor's door and walked in to face his boss.

"Sit down, Ken. Talk me through the events nice and slowly, don't miss out any details."

"Well sir," Ken began, recalling what happened, "I woke Bates at 5am and escorted him down to the kitchen area where we waited for the truck to arrive. At 5.15am I opened the loading bay entrance from the kitchen and escorted Bates to the truck........."

"....Was the roller shutter door closed and locked before you escorted Bates?" the Governor interrupted.

Ken became a little flustered. "Oh! Yes sir, I always close the shutter before opening the kitchen gates, as per the regulations......."

".... Where was Bates while the driver unlocked the back of the truck?" the Governor interrupted again.

Poor Ken was becoming nervous, fearing he was going to be blamed. "Well sir, let me think. I unlocked the gate and Bates was behind me, we walked through the gate and he was still behind me. Charlie, the driver, met us at the back of his truck and Bates was beside me then. Charlie lifted the tailgate, then he and Bates began unloading, so I retired to the rest room until they had finished. When I returned, Charlie was just finishing his cuppa and Bates' cuppa was part drunk on the counter in the kitchen....."

"......Was the gate still unlocked when you returned from the rest room?" the Governor interrupted again.

Ken scratched his head and was beginning to sweat. "Yes sir, I didn't lock it until after Charlie left, he said Bates had the squirts and had dashed off to the toilets. I escorted Charlie back to the truck and inspected it inside, outside and underneath. Bates was most certainly not hiding on the truck, so I let Charlie drive away and went in search of Bates in the toilet. Needless to say, sir, he was nowhere to be found. I searched every possible place he could be hiding and found no sign of him. I actually think he has somehow found a way out of the prison."

"I see," the Governor replied, rubbing his chin. "A new procedure from today, the kitchen inmate assisting unloading the truck must have an officer with them at all times, even to the toilet. Thank you, Ken, you may return to your duties." The Governor was deep in thought. "So where are you, Bates? I will find you one way or another." He suddenly gasped with realisation. "Bates you cunning devil, you had to be on that truck, you had to be!" He called for the gate security guards and the three men entered the Governor's office. "Sit down, gentlemen. Now run through with me the events of the truck approaching the gates."

"Well sir," Matthew began, who had been elected as their spokesman. "The truck pulled up in front of the gates as usual and turned off the engine while the three of us checked the truck. I used the mirrors to check underneath and found it clear. John checked inside and Brian checked the roof of the vehicle and found nothing, sir."

"Describe the truck to me please," the Governor asked.

"Well sir, it was the big truck rather than the small Transit van as it was double delivery day. So it is basically a big box on wheels with a driver's cab at the front. There's nowhere for anyone to hide without being spotted," Matthew replied.

"I don't know if it's significant, sir," Brian began, "but the truck is an old vehicle with one of those plastic wind diverters on top of the cab, I did give it a quick glance but it seemed to be clear."

Something was beginning to form in the Governors mind. "It was still dark, was it not?"

"Yes sir," Matthew replied.

"If Bates covered himself in black plastic bags and hid under the deflector, he could have gone unnoticed in the darkness. Did you shine your torch under the deflector, Brian?" the Governor asked.

"N-no sir, I didn't, maybe I should have. Do you think Bates was tucked into that space, sir?" Brian replied.

"Bingo!" the Governor cried, making the three guards jump in their seats. "Got you, Bates, that is the only way he could have got out of this prison. That won't happen again. Dismissed!"

The disbelief that any prisoner could escape from the high security prison, and the delay in taking action, had given Bates a couple of hour's head start. Had the delivery truck not blown a tyre Bates would be skulking around the nearest town by now and well on the way to permanent freedom. Instead he was bound in magical rope, hardly able to move or shout, not that he wanted to draw attention to himself. Struggle as he may the magical rope just tightened even more around him, it was getting hard to breathe and he was wishing he had remained still.

Almost two hours after Bates had gone missing, the Governor finally accepted that he was no longer in the prison and ordered his officers to find the delivery truck and pull it apart if need be to discover how Bates had made a fool out of them.

* *

Freddie woke his friends and teachers, who crept from their tents. Freddie soon had sausages frying and a bubbling pan of chopped tomatoes. The students and teachers had no memory of doing this a little while before and gathered around Freddie as he served everyone.

"Freddie Fixit!" Jimmy cried, laughing away as he helped serve the teachers.

Teachers and students alike were just happy to be tucking into a hot breakfast and mopping the tomato juice with a slice of bread.

When all the plates and cutlery had been washed and stored away, Freddie entertained them all with some classical music on his guitar. They were all sat around a blazing camp fire and went on to sing 'Row Your Boat' in rounds. Freddie started the boys off, followed by the girls and then the teachers, all were in good voice and looking happy with smiling faces.

Their cheerfulness was interrupted by a helicopter flying over, which caused them all to stop singing and look upward. They suddenly ran for cover, the helicopter was flying low and the down draft caused a dust storm, almost putting out the camp fire.

Once it had passed, everyone crept from their tents back around the fire that Freddie was already reviving with more wood and twigs.

"These moors are used for military exercises, I expect the army are out doing something of the sort," Mr Mead explained. The students had no reason to believe otherwise, but Freddie, of course, knew the truth.

* *

The helicopter, which had flown over the campsite, landed close to the fully bound Robin Bates. The officers looked puzzled, wondering who had done this and placed the arrow of stones.

"Well, well, well, Bates. Seems you've met your match somehow!" the chief officer said looking pleased and relieved. He ripped the tape off Bates' mouth, who howled with pain as it took with it bits of his skin.

"What happened here, Bates? How'd you get so tied up?" a second officer said, smirking.

"It was Freddie Fountain. He's a magician," Bates began blabbering. "He made this rope wrap around me all by itself like a magical snake. Then he sent me flying through the air like a balloon! It's the truth, he's got real magic. I bashed his brains out and he died....... Oh! Flip!" Bates moaned, realising what he had just admitted doing.

"Is that so, Bates? Attempted murder and escaping again, I think you'll be with us for a very long time," the chief said after Bates incriminated himself.

"It's all true, that kid is dangerous, he's got magic. He created a castle on the moors, I saw it, and a huge ship and an aeroplane and fountains, I saw it. I did!" Bates prattled on while being carried into the helicopter.

The officers tried to remove the rope but it would not come off, if anything it seemed to be getting tighter and Bates was getting redder in the face.

The helicopter and cargo landed outside the prison and Bates was carried inside. Once the gates were closed and the prison was secure the Governor came to see him.

"Governor, we have been unable to remove these ropes, we may need a saw or something to cut him out," the chief reported.

The Governor was all smiles. "Perhaps we'll leave him cocooned like that, he won't be able to escape again."

The officers stood Bates on his feet and to everyone's amazement the rope uncoiled and fell to the ground. Attached to Bates' shirt was a large envelope addressed to the Governor.

"Well I'll be blessed," the chief declared. "Would you look at that?"

"What is this, Bates, a love letter?" the Governor chuckled, lifting the envelope and opening it. "Ah! There's a letter and a thumb drive here."

"Who's the letter from, Governor?" the Chief asked.

The Governor looked the letter over and it was not signed. "No signature, but it says, '*On this thumb drive is evidence that Robin Bates gate crashed a school campsite, brutally treated one of the boys and murdered another. Please make sure Robin Bates serves a long sentence.*' Well I never."

"Well Bates, you admitted the very same thing earlier, seems we have evidence too," the Chief remarked.

"It's that wizard, he's doing all this!" Bates cried, then fell deathly silent, turning white as a sheet.

Freddie sent a telepathic message to Bates' mind. '*Do not attempt to escape again. I have put a magic spell on you. If you leave the prison without permission you will instantly turn into a frog.*'

Bates screamed, "He's talking to me in my head, he's gonna turn me into a frog. He's crazy!"

The Governor and officers looked at Bates in disbelief, thinking he had lost his mind.

"What are you babbling about, Bates? Is this another of your tricks to get you shipped to a mental hospital?" the Governor asked, determined that Robin Bates would be going nowhere for a very, very long time.

*** The End ***

EPILOGUE

Freddie and his friends went on to Canebridge University and became some of the youngest men and women to pass their degree at just eighteen years old.

Freddie, Jimmy, William, Billy, James and all the girls continued their education and took their Masters Degree, all achieving top marks.

Freddie turned his mind to politics, the Merlin ring guiding him to the path most effective for changing the world. When he reached the age of twenty, becoming the man he had transformed into fighting the Beastrolls, he was elected as the youngest Prime Minister in history. From this position he slowly befriended every country, where he used his magic to bring about the changes needed for world peace and ready for Merlin to emerge from his very long hibernation.

It was not all plain sailing though, Freddie and his friends had many adventures along the way as he used his powerful magic to smooth the path to a united and peaceful world.

But that's another story.

www.ingramcontent.com/pod-product-compliance
Lightning Source LLC
Chambersburg PA
CBHW021833010726
47493CB00005B/1370